I0718725

Cover Design & Interior Format

© KILLION
THE
GROUP INC.

DIANNA LOVE

TREOIR DRAGON CHRONICLES
OF THE BELADOR WORLD
VOL. 1
BOOKS 1-3

BOOK 1

PRONUNCIATION GUIDE

Note: A complete guide of unusual names, places and terminology for the Belador series is located on any Belador book page at www.AuthorDiannaLove.com, but below are from this book.

aiteann – ah chin
Brynhild – burn HILD
Casidhe – CAH sih duh
Cavan – cah VAHN
Connell – kuh NAIL
Dragani – drah GAHN nee
Eógan – OH un
Evalle – EE vahl
Fadil – fah DEEL
Fenella – fuh NELL ah
Garwyli – gar WHY lee
Germanus - jur MAN us
gorse – GOERS (rhymes with course)
Gruffyn – GRUFF in
Imortiks – im MORE ticks
Immortuos Grimoire – im MORH tue ose gruhm WAAR
Jennyver - JENN uh vir
Lann an Cheartais – lahn nah KAIR tus
Luigsech – LOO gi sehk (g is hard like 'egg')
Maistir – MY stir
Medb – MAVE
Noirre – NOIR ay
Ossian – AH see un

Pliny Laelius – PLY nee LIE lee oos
Phoedra – FAY druh
Renata – REY not ah
Ruadh – ROO awn
Scamall – SKAH mull
Scáth Force – SCATH (like bath) Force
Seanóir – SHAWN ore ee
Skarde – SKARD
Timmon – tim MAHN
Tzader – ZAY der

"If you don't fight for what you love, then don't cry for what you lost." ~ Unknown

———◆———

Every major war and crisis can be traced to a specific moment in time.

During the medieval time of chieftains and kingdoms in ancient Ireland, betrayal triggered a dragon war and consequences have rippled through time to today's world. A supernatural being on a path to expose nonhumans is sparking chaos across the world with Atlanta at the epicenter. Powerful preternatural beings have waited patiently for an opportune moment to strike at their enemies and with no regard for human casualties. Now is the time.

The Belador supernatural race living secretly among humans freed a cursed dragon shifter, who now reigns as their king. Daegan takes a stand to fight for his nonhuman followers as well as vulnerable humans. Tortured by what he lost two millennia ago, Daegan has vowed to destroy any who threaten his new family and allies.

Atlanta and the entire human race have one hope of surviving what's coming for them, but only if fear of the unknown does not drive them to kill their greatest protector first.

WHERE IT ALL BEGAN …

22 AD during the time of dragon kings in Ériu, **an island later known as Ireland**

What the hell are ya doin', Fadil? Daegan roared telepathically as he flew hard in dragon form toward the battle his father's men fought.

On the far side a cerulean sky stretched from horizon to horizon. Fadil's brown dragon flapped his wings just as fast, head down and not a sound in reply.

Fadil had heard him.

Fadil! Call off your men! Daegan shouted again mind-to-mind.

The brown dragon lifted his head at that, but the eyes coming into view did not belong to a friend. Wild hate seared those dragon eyes.

Fadil, I do not want to kill ya!

Daegan had to stop this. He didn't want to kill someone who had been the brother he never had since the age of ten, but neither would he allow anyone to harm his father's warriors. His men, who would march into battle on Daegan's word alone.

Protected by Fadil, a new wave of King Anasch's warriors topped the hill to the south. The distinctive earth-dragon standard snapped in the rising wind as they marched toward the village.

Daegan's powerful dragon, Ruadh, made a wide arc then descended, blasting a fiery path to cut off the approaching contingent.

Smoke rose from most of the dwellings, many still on fire, in a village on the outer edge of his father's land. Hundreds of warriors battled below and blood soaked the ground.

A troll fighting for King Anasch flew through the air, knocked off his feet by King Gruffyn's Belador soldiers using their kinetic powers. The Belador Maistir, Seamus, protected a group of villagers as the enemy of human soldiers and supernatural beings, including jackal-headed human forms, surrounded them.

Belador cheers thundered when they realized Ruadh had come to their aid.

Peace had reigned the entire twenty-nine years Daegan had lived. He'd been tasked with holding that peace because of possessing the most powerful dragon known of in this land.

No one wanted war with King Gruffyn's fierce warriors and fire dragon.

Why would Fadil and his king?

Daegan's Beladors had done nothing to incur this attack and deserved to go home to their loved ones. They'd been sent here to secure this small village on his father's land.

But King Anasch had declared war by attacking those under King Gruffyn's protection.

Under *Daegan's* protection.

All these years of peace.

Watch your back, Daegan! Seamus shouted mind-to-mind. He grabbed a village child clinging to his leg and tossed the young one over his shoulder.

Ruadh had already started banking hard to the right, bringing into view the threat closing in from the south.

Daegan spoke to his dragon. *Do not kill Fadil. Give me a chance to stop this.*

He is not your friend to attack you. He should care more for his life, Ruadh replied, then flapped his huge wings hard, catching air to lift toward the heavens.

Daegan and Ruadh fought as one, but his dragon would destroy anyone who attacked them.

Fadil's dragon had not slowed even to help his men.

Go high, Ruadh! Daegan ordered. No better place to battle another dragon than high above the ground to protect those below.

The brown beast with the eyes of an enemy and wings tipped in black did not rise to meet him.

Instead, Fadil's dragon swooped low, flying barely above treetop level, approaching the battle. The ground visibly rocked back and forth in his wake. Massive chunks of stone and earth exploded high into the air as he arrowed toward vulnerable humans as well as Beladors.

Daegan yelled, *Dive, Ruadh.* His dragon flipped and shot down fast as a giant spear. Ruadh spewed a fiery ball at the brown dragon.

Fadil's dragon rolled to the right to escape, but the ball slapped his tail, sending him flipping. His dragon hit the ground, bounced, and shoved off, flying straight up with wings struggling to lift his giant body into the air.

That blast of fire had singed the brown dragon's tail. It also stopped Fadil's dragon from pounding the Beladors, the villagers, and Fadil's own army with boulders and burying all of them under piles of dirt.

Daegan's dragon curved his body up, lurching away from the ground. Ruadh watched for anything unexpected, but the earth dragon continued to ascend with each draft of air caught beneath his wings.

Before Fadil's dragon reached them, Daegan called telepathically, desperate to get through to a man who had been friend until now. *Are ya crazy, Fadil? Why are your men attackin' mine? What has happened to ya?*

A sick thought entered Daegan's mind. Something he could not accept in his heart, but he had to ask. *The truth, Fadil. Are ya the one startin' a Dragani War?*

Still, he received no answer.

Instead, the earth dragon angled around and flew at him with furious speed. Fadil's beast weighed a third more than Daegan's. He couldn't kill Ruadh, but he could crush bones that would take too long to heal with a battle raging.

Ruadh whipped his long body around quickly, twisting at the last moment to rake the earth dragon's back with a blast of fire. Brown scales heated to the color of glowing embers, then cooled, leaving a black scorch behind.

Fury collided with Daegan's desire to not kill this ally. His friend.

Ruadh had fought along with Fadil's dragon to save King Anasch's castle when a high king of the north lands had thought to claim it with twice as large an army as Fadil's forces.

But that army had been no match for one dragon, much less two.

No match for men who fought to protect each other's backs as if they'd been born brothers of the same womb.

Ruadh dodged and rolled until they had no choice but to fight. Daegan's red dragon rammed into Fadil's. The sudden jarring felt as if they'd flown into the side of a castle. The dragons tangled up, spinning as they fell with their wings tucked in. Claws ripped at each other. Daegan's dragon couldn't torch his opponent face to face, not this close.

An earth dragon would suck that fire inside and send it back as a blast of glowing lava rocks.

The earth dragon's jaws clamped around Ruadh's throat, gashing the thick skin. Ruadh's claws ripped into the brown dragon's chest over and over until blood poured from a deep gash.

Ruadh could defeat Fadil's beast at this point, but Daegan could not kill the man who had bled alongside Daegan in one battle after another. He'd as soon gut himself.

But if Daegan did not give the order to finish the earth dragon, Ruadh would wear down from battling the heavier beast and risk crushed bones if they hit the ground. If Ruadh could not fly until healing, Belador lives would be at risk.

Daegan told Ruadh, *We must take away the advantage of being in the air and drive this fight to the ground.*

Ruadh countered, *Earth is his strength.*

Only if we allow him to use it.

Opening his jaws to blast a fierce roar, Ruadh pushed off and broke away from the heavy brown dragon to fly up, up, up, then ...

Daegan shouted, *Seamus! Move everyone out of the way. Our dragons are falling to the ground. Save our Beladors and the villagers. King Anasch's army is Fadil's problem.*

Aye, sir.

When Ruadh broke free of the clouds, he flipped around and dove straight down.

Fadil's dragon had been slowly ascending and could not maneuver fast enough to avoid the unexpected attack.

Crashing into the brown beast, Ruadh roared and his claws dug deep while he kept Fadil's dragon wrapped inside giant red wings.

Not prepared for this kind of attack from above, Fadil's dragon wings collapsed in.

Daegan kept alert as Ruadh tumbled over and over joined as one with the brown dragon, falling as swiftly as a boulder shoved off a cliff.

Fadil's dragon kept swinging his huge jaws around as far as his head would turn, snapping desperately at Ruadh's neck.

Daegan's dragon spewed a small blast of fire to stop the vicious jaws from succeeding. Ruadh struggled to hold as the heavy dragon twisted to break free. Both bodies vibrated with power and strain.

A hundred feet from the ground, Daegan told Ruadh, *Free him now!*

His red dragon's wings flared. Ruadh shoved off hard.

That move sent the earth dragon hurtling faster toward the ground, still out of control.

Ruadh's muscles bulged under the strain of flapping fast enough to avoid following Fadil's beast to the ground and suffering a vicious hit. He arched his long back, rising until he could bank to the right and glide for a moment to breathe.

Fadil's dragon crashed into the ground and bounced. He rolled over and over until stopping in a cloud of dirt and plowed-up grass with wings spread and head down.

Beladors had raced away from the colossal giants falling to earth. Seamus shouted, *Daegan! The Beladors stand to assist you.*

Daegan ordered, *Do not touch the dragon.*

Aye, sir.

In a deep voice rough from spewing fire, his dragon pointed out, *Enemy is weak. Easy to kill.*

Pain lanced Daegan's heart. He argued, *Fadil is not my enemy! I would give even an enemy a chance for last words.*

Ruadh puffed out a cloud of black smoke that ended in an angry snarl.

Daegan's dragon slowed until he lifted his head and lowered his rear legs to land smoothly in spite of the painful injuries Fadil's beast had inflicted. But the red dragon feared by all possessed faster healing powers than Fadil's and would never show a weakness.

Daegan remained in dragon form as Ruadh stood above the downed earth dragon. Slashes and scorch marks crisscrossed the brown body and wings, but Fadil would live.

For now.

After a long moment, the earth dragon rumbled out a furious sound and lifted his head. He pushed his body up until he and Ruadh were almost eye level. That one may weigh more, but Ruadh stood taller, especially with his head held high.

Fadil's dragon arched his neck, drawing his head back as if to hit Ruadh with a blast of lava rocks.

Speaking out loud in Ruadh's booming voice, Daegan warned, "Do not dare, Fadil. I have shown the only mercy you will see this day if you attack my dragon again."

The brown dragon closed his jaws and brought his head forward. Hate seared the reptilian eyes.

Daegan asked, "Why would your army attack a defenseless village and our Beladors? Our men have shown great restraint with their powers. They have fought your men on equal ground, but kill even one of mine and you will have no army."

Fadil's dragon eyes narrowed into black slits. When he spoke, his dragon normally had a much smoother voice than Ruadh's. Not this time. Fadil's dragon bellowed, "*Murderer!* Ya attacked my father's kingdom while I was away. Ya burned my cousin to death in front of his mother. Ya savaged our villages. I do not fear ya, red dragon!"

If Daegan had been in human form, his jaw would have dropped. His dragon boomed, "I did no such thing. I have attacked no one since the last time we fought together against an enemy. What evidence do ya hold to accuse me?"

The merciless eyes of an adversary glared back as Fadil replied, "A red dragon attacked, shooting fire from above. There is no other dragon of such color but yours. There is no other dragon spewing fire but yours. My da watched the massacre from the castle, too far away for his guards to save the innocent servants, livestock, and children. *Innocent* children."

"No. I swear on my honor that was not me," Daegan's dragon shouted. His head and heart could not accept this. Not from Fadil. Not the only friend Daegan had growing up.

"Your king grows feeble and it is said you want to rule all. Ya were my friend once, but no more. Do not ever fly near my land again. If ya do, I will be prepared to kill your dragon next time. Even a demigod can die."

"Let me talk to your father, Fadil, so that we will know what happened."

"You question my father's words? Our people died under your dragon's fire. *That's* what I know."

Daegan struggled to accept any of this. Hurt clogged his throat, but Ruadh had no problem delivering his words. "We can war. We can kill. We can blood each other, but that will not change that I did not attack your people. If you leave now and call your army back, I will allow you to live. If your army continues to attack, my Beladors and I will leave them for you to bury. If you attack my dragon again, he will burn yours and eat the ashes."

"One day, you will not be all powerful, Daegan," Fadil warned in his dragon voice, shaking with anger. "When that day comes, you will know the pain of watching those you love die when you cannot save them." With that, the brown dragon took several steps and pushed off with fast flaps to lift all that weight.

How could he lose Fadil this way? *Why are ya doing this to me, Fadil? Ya know me.*

I thought I knew ya.

White hot rage shook him. *Fadil! Don't do this!*

For a moment, Daegan wished for another dragon like his to drag to Fadil's castle, but his father had made it clear there would be no more dragons, or additional children, from his blood line after Daegan. His two older sisters possessed dragon blood, but would not birth a dragon unless they bound themselves to one.

The ice dragon clan had attempted an arranged marriage between Daegan and Brynhild, a dragon shifter who had been but a child of sixteen years at the time. Many women took a mate at that age.

Daegan had not been ready for a mate, much less with a female whose body had yet to develop past a child's.

Could King Eógan's ice dragons be behind this?

Surely not. Months after refusing to take Brynhild to mate, the oldest male ice dragon, Herrick, had joined Daegan to defeat the highland chieftain who had attacked Daegan's clan.

No dragon family had ever warred over a failed bride pact. Brynhild remained free to choose another, one better suited to her.

Besides, the ice dragons were neither red in color nor at war with King Gruffyn, nor could they spew fire.

What dragon had Fadil's king seen, though?

Seamus came running up. "Sire, King Gruffyn's personal guard called to me. He feared distracting ya while your dragon battled. Your da asks for you immediately."

His father's personal Belador guard had earned that high

position by being a powerful warrior and one of the strongest at relaying communications mind to mind.

Daegan's dragon lowered his head to meet Seamus's gaze and spoke out loud. "Secure the village and care for our wounded, then return to the castle. Fadil's army retreats. But if I find his second contingent pushin' on this way, I will deal with them myself."

"Aye, sire. Are we at war with King Anasch?"

"We are at war with no one. I refuse to subject our people to a war I did not start."

Nodding, his Maistir backed away then turned to issue orders.

Ruadh lifted off and flew hard for the castle in Meath. Ruadh slowed only for Daegan to confirm Fadil's second line of warriors did indeed retreat.

Perhaps Fadil still possessed some sense.

All the death and destruction after so many years of peace ripped Daegan's heart. Of all the ways this conflict could have ended, he never thought to lose someone so dear as Fadil.

As King Gruffyn's castle came into view, Ruadh slowed to drop low, gliding until he opened his wings and landed in a wide patch of ground all knew to avoid crossing. Emerald grass shin-high covered most of the ground inside the curtain wall with ivy growing at a lazy pace. His king had chosen an excellent location high atop a rise in Meath, which sat along the eastern coast in the middle of the island and stretched a hundred leagues from north to south.

In two long Ruadh steps, Daegan called up his power, quickly shifting into his human form. A wool cloak with thick fur at the neck fell open as he strode, allowing cool air to reach him through the linen shirt over wool wrapping his legs. Fur and hardened-leather boots encased his feet. He found the battle helmet adorned with two horns a comforting weight on his head.

He strode with purpose and anger, quickly passing through the arched walkway which led to the chapel if he continued straight. His father would often go there to call out telepathically to Daegan. That he had not done so this time added to Daegan's concern.

Hunting his father's guard, he shouted mind to mind. *Where is my father, Manus?*

He is abed, sire.

What? 'Tis hardly midday. Where are ya? Worry slithered through Daegan. He'd never known his father to take to his bed except when injured in battle.

I am with my king, sire. He fell ill while you were away. I brought the healers immediately. I sent for you when the king's condition became grave.

Without another word, Daegan teleported to his father's bedchamber and rushed to his side. He grimaced at the pungent odor of sickness slithering through the room. It had an odd taint Daegan had not smelled before.

A burnt lime odor.

His father's face had lost the flush of health he'd had only two days ago before Daegan's dragon had flown west to Connaught. A battle had broken out among their Beladors and what Daegan believed to be a rogue pack of soldiers carrying no standard, but whom had once been loyal to the ice dragons.

Another dragon clan he considered allies.

He believed not in coincidence. Concern clawed his neck as more arrows pointed at the ice dragons.

After today, he would have to figure out just what allies he had.

In light of today's fight with Fadil, Daegan sincerely hoped the ice dragons were willing to speak before attacking.

Dropping to his knee next to the king's bed, Daegan grasped his father's over-heated hand. "I'm here, Da. What ails you?"

The king's face normally projected a robust vitality. When he spoke, his voice would boom with a power and authority that all knew to heed. Every child of the king had inherited supernatural energy from his dragon blood, but Daegan had received so much more from his father and the mother he'd never met.

Today, the skin on his da's cheeks held a gray hue.

His da rasped, "The healers do not know what ails me. I recall walking among the gardens this morning when I came upon a lovely red flower new to me. I bent down to sniff it and woke up here."

Daegan tucked that information away for when he had time to do a thorough investigation of all who had come in contact with the king.

His da's once commanding voice carried a weakness Daegan had never before heard as he struggled to speak. "We have greater concerns, my son."

"There is no greater concern for me than your wellbeing."

His da gave him a smile of appreciation, but pushed on. "I asked for your sisters. Macha delivered Jennyver, but Maeve sent word Lesley was unable to make the trip. Maeve's servant described Lesley as suffering an ailment similar to mine."

Daegan felt an emotion he'd never before experienced.

Fear.

He would battle a hundred dragons and armies to keep his family safe, but he had no defense against a silent killer if this sickness turned fatal.

How had his father and Lesley contracted similar illnesses? Lesley resided in the realm of TÅµr Medb, ruled by Queen Maeve, a witch goddess responsible for the wellbeing of his sister.

Pressured for a child of dragon blood by two goddesses, Macha and Queen Maeve, King Gruffyn had feared losing his kingdom to one of them if attacked for he would not hand over a child even if he had one.

Every babe he and his queen conceived over the years had died in the womb.

King Gruffyn finally agreed to a pact only to protect his family and kingdom, which allowed each goddess to be gifted one of his next two children, believing he would never see any born.

To this day, the king believed one, or both, of the goddesses had used majik on him when he had a dream of he and his queen spending a night of passion. Within weeks, his wife grew round with what he had thought would be one babe.

She died giving birth to two daughters of dragon blood.

Macha and Queen Maeve arrived the day of the birthing, neither lifting a finger to save his wife, and both leaving with a promised child.

That had broken the king for many months.

To this day, Daegan knew how deeply his father still mourned losing all three females, the only family he'd had, and regretted his agreement with the goddesses. But King Gruffyn had been wily enough to negotiate as much protection as he could on the chance of producing even one babe.

After that loss, he spent months on his knees, pleading with the dragon god Dewi for a dragon-shifter son who could protect him and his daughters. A son so powerful all other deities would not dare try to harm him.

Dewi finally answered his prayers.

Today, Daegan drew every breath to first perform his duty to his da and sisters, then his people.

Having visited with each sister annually, Daegan had come to believe they were both safe. Now, he had deep suspicions and asked his king, "What would ya have me do, sire?" He looked around and added, "Where be Jennyver?"

His father's breathing sounded painful. "She went to pray in our chapel. She shows no sign of sickness. While she is safely nearby, I wish for you to see Lesley and determine if Maeve is able to heal her. If not, bring her to our healers."

Daegan nodded. "I fear leaving ya before our healers cure what has attacked your body."

"Time is of the essence, son. The healers make headway. Lesley is young, but you and I are strong. Maeve surprised me by taking the smaller of the two females when they were birthed. I have feared Lesley and Jennyver's safety for all these years, but more for Lesley. If she does not show signs of healing, you carry the word of your king and are the most powerful dragon around. Queen Maeve and Macha fear all dragons, as they should. They have more to gain by being allies. You will speak for me and convince Queen Maeve to do the best for Lesley if the child requires more than can be provided in TÅµr Medb."

"I will always do as ya wish, Da." Daegan hated being pulled in two directions, both for family, but he feared leaving without offering the king Ruadh's healing blood. Only one born of dragon blood could take such inside and be healed. "Please drink a sip of my blood before I go."

"No, son. I know ya mean well, but my stomach sends back all that I swallow." Lifting his other hand weakly from the covers to dismiss more discussion, he said, "Now for the greater concern. The ice dragons war with King Anasch and I am told they intend to attack here next."

Had the world gone mad? Daegan grumbled, "I feared such. I hearkened your call just after battlin' Fadil's dragon. He swears Ruadh attacked his father's people. What is happenin' to cause this strife among the dragon clans?" He quickly informed his father of the battle and what Fadil had claimed. When he finished, he asked, "Is there any chance of another red dragon besides Ruadh?"

"No." His king laughed at that, ending in a fit of coughing. He regained his breath. "When I begged the god Dewi for you, I received three conditions. First, you would be the last of the red fire dragons. Second, you and I are forbidden from uttering your mother's name with the exception of you being at the point of death with no way to survive. Trust me when I say you do not want to call that goddess to you even then. Third is for you to take care when visiting a hostile realm. You would not be as safe there as you would here or in your mother's realm, which I hope you never visit."

"I have no desire to create more conflict," Daegan confirmed.

The king added, "You are safe in Treoir as that realm

was created specifically for children of my blood. Jennyver thrives there as do the three babes she birthed from the match I arranged for her. If the need ever arises, you must enter that haven."

Daegan had a moment of guilt over not agreeing to take Brynhild as his bride. Perhaps that would have protected his father's lands and people from one enemy. Still, who would have thought any dragon would willingly become an enemy of the red dragon?

Had overconfidence put his family at risk and cost him a friend he considered family?

Clearing his throat, his da said, "Queen Maeve has always concerned me. The best I got from her prior to birthing Lesley was to agree that no child of mine would die by her hand in TÅµr Medb. That means you and Lesley are safe there, too." Sounding older with each breath, his da said, "One more condition all dragon shifters must pay heed to is when you choose a mate, she must either be dragon-shifter born, as you are, or a direct descendant of a female dragon."

Daegan's heart squeezed at realizing his father's words rung as if this would be their last meeting. He would not allow this man to die.

Trying to sound lighthearted, and failing, Daegan squeezed his father's hand and smiled. "Choosin' a mate is of little interest to me at the moment, Da. As for my enterin' other realms, do not fash over it. I have no reason to enter any realms besides Treoir or TÅµr Medb where each goddess would not dare destroy an alliance that has stood for thirty years."

His father's eyelids fluttered shut.

Daegan did not want to leave him. He could not make himself release the grip he had on the hand that had raised him.

Struggling again to breathe, his da's eyes opened. He turned his head to Daegan. "Once both of your sisters are safe, you must meet with King Eógan. I fear the ice dragons have not found a worthy mate for Brynhild and may hold us responsible."

While Daegan appreciated the difficulty in finding a suitable mate for a female dragon shifter, this warring still made no sense. "Very well, I shall go to Lesley at once and bring her to ya if she shows little healin'. That should not require more than an hour, maybe two, before I go to King Eógan to demand answers. If Lesley's health appears to be improvin' quickly, I will allow Maeve to continue carin' for her and send word to ya as I travel on to the ice dragon clan."

Daegan would like a moment to see Jennyver, whose smile always held sunshine for any around her, but he could waste not one second. He would see his sister when he returned to his father's side.

Standing, Daegan leaned down and kissed his king's forehead, which felt too warm. He squeezed the clammy fingers again, hesitating to step away.

His father lifted a weak smile to him. "Go, my son. You are the only one I trust. I shall be here when you return."

Daegan's heart faltered at the possibility of never seeing his father alive again. He had to trust in their healers, but he stepped to a side table where an empty goblet had been placed next to a jug of wine. Calling up his sword with his power, Daegan sliced his arm and allowed two fingers of his dragon blood to run into the cup. He had never used his blood to heal anyone, but had heard of other dragon shifter families healing with their blood.

Then he smoothed a finger over the cut on his forearm, restoring the skin without a sign of the wound.

Carrying the goblet to his father, he placed it on a heavy wooden stand next to the bed. "If ya do not heal soon, I have left ya a small amount of my blood. Do your best to hold it inside."

"I will try. Please save my daughter. *Bheith sábháilte, mo mhac.*"

Be safe, my son. How many times had his da sent him off with that farewell?

Not enough. Daegan needed to hear those words many

more times in his life.

He shook off the worry planting his feet near the bed.

He had duties. The sooner he saw Lesley and determined the extent of her illness, the sooner he could meet with King Eógan. Daegan's dragon would have no problem fending off more than one dragon, but to battle a family of five ice dragons might not be as simple to survive even for a dragon shifter born a demigod.

He waited for his father's eyes to close again and his breathing to calm as to one asleep. Then he walked out into the hallway as a healer hurried up.

Daegan ordered, "I left blood. Make sure he takes it."

He'd lost Fadil today.

That pain would live in his heart for a long time, but he would not lose his family.

Shifting into his dragon form would only raise Queen Maeve's hackles.

Daegan teleported from the castle to a tall rock mound shooting up from the Irish Sea. Ship captains knew to avoid this area, which held more dangers than jagged rocks.

When he appeared on the rock pile rising as tall as the tower on his father's castle and two strides wide in any direction, wind buffeted his body.

He shoved a foot behind to brace himself.

Raising his voice and pushing power into his words, he called out, "Queen Maeve, I wish to speak with ya."

A disembodied voice belonging to Maeve replied, "Why do you call me, dragon?"

She had never addressed him properly, but he had more concern than her lack of decorum.

"I come at King Gruffyn's request. The king has informed me Lesley is ill. He said she was not healthy enough to visit when he asked for her."

"What trick do you play? I took Lesley to your father while he waited on Macha to deliver Jennyver. He now complains when I paid heed and teleported her immediately?"

What could Daegan say to this?

Had his father been delirious? "Neither the king, nor I, play any trick," Daegan explained. "I just left my father's bedside. Perhaps he was not at his best and failed to recall your visit. Is Lesley sick or not?" Maybe his da had that part wrong as well.

"Your sister was the vision of health until she visited your father. Within minutes, she turned pale. Her knees buckled. To be honest, I do not recall if your father's eyes were open during this as I stood back to allow them time alone. He appeared to be dying. I teleported her back to TÅµr Medb at that moment."

Tightening his fingers into hard fists, Daegan held his anger at being told his father could be dying with the same importance of discussing a meal improperly prepared. "My father will heal. I wish to report the same to him regardin' Lesley, but why would ya not leave her for our healers to attend while they were close by?"

Queen Maeve sounded appalled. "Why would I do such a thing when they appear to be failing your father? Do you not care for your sister to survive this strange illness?"

How dare this irritating goddess question his devotion to his family? He would die for every one of them. Nothing would cut him more than to lose even one family member.

Powering his voice against a wind that continued to grow stronger, Daegan shouted, "Of course, I wish for Lesley to be healed." He didn't trust Queen Maeve to care for Lesley. The goddess had power, but it carried too much darkness for him. He steeled himself to sound polite. "I ask ya to teleport Lesley into my open arms for me to take to the castle. My father will not rest until she is recovered. Our healers are making headway with my father and are ready to care for her." He wished the part about his father had been true, but he would do whatever he could to save Lesley.

"Are you mad, dragon?" Queen Maeve shouted. "She is the only child I have of dragon blood. I will not risk her for your whims. I will not teleport her anywhere when her condition is weak."

That left him only one choice. "Then I ask to see my sister so I may report to the king." Daegan waited for an answer.

Maeve made a hissing sound that carried over the wind.

Waves crashed harder against his rock tower, splashing him. As if getting wet would deter him?

Sounding more resigned than welcoming, she said, "If I agree to allow you to enter TÅµr Medb to see your sister, what do you give me in exchange?"

What a soulless bitch.

But Daegan wanted to insure Lesley would survive so he could return to his father. If he convinced Queen Maeve to allow him entrance and Lesley did not appear to be healin', he would teleport Lesley away and face the consequences later.

Lifting his voice above the roaring sea, he called out, "What would ya have me do in exchange to see my sick sister, Queen Maeve?"

Completely unbothered by his subtle accusation of her keeping a sick sibling from him, the queen replied, "I have not thought on it, but I do need a sword arm. Someone to lead my warlocks to avenge a wrong done to me."

Daegan couldn't believe she expected him to lead a group of vicious warlocks, but asking for details and arguing would take too long. He made up his mind right then he would teleport Lesley to his father's castle and wait there for this dark queen to visit. "Very well, I will do this for you one time only, but I feel 'tis unkind to ask such a favor."

"You may enter," Queen Maeve said, not addressing his complaint. "When you teleport in, do not forget this is *my* realm and think to spout orders. I will not be pushed around or insulted by the king's pet monster."

Daegan thought about all the times he had dealt with Queen Maeve for his father. She had never shown any grace. Just a goddess with a nasty temperament, but that did not make her unique.

After noticing dark shadows under Lesley's eyes last year, he'd asked his sister privately, "Do ya wish to return home?"

Lesley had been startled by his question and whispered with wariness, "Queen Maeve will never allow me to leave."

Keeping his voice just as soft, he had told her, "I do not mean to tout myself, but I am no mere dragon. I have powers Queen Maeve would not dare test."

"I do not wish for her to harm you, brother."

"That will not happen. Ya must know I will do anything required of me to protect ya and Jennyver, should either of ya need me."

Lesley had kissed his cheek then shook her head. "We all have a duty. This is mine, but I thank you for the offer." That had been the last time he had seen her until now.

"What will it be, dragon?" Maeve bellowed over the churning water and wind.

"I accept your generous offer to allow me to teleport into your realm." Those words had struggled to leave his throat. "I have no quarrel with ya, Queen Maeve, and have agreed to stand as your sword arm. Therefore, I will cause no trouble."

"Very well. I will send you a vision as your destination."

That was different.

The one time he'd visited this realm in the past, the queen had teleported him into the tower where he had been provided time to visit with his sister within the realm.

He had found no reason to complain back then.

But never had this queen provided a vision of her inner tower for teleporting on his own. He would hold that vision in his head should he ever need to return without an invitation once he withdrew Lesley from this realm.

Perhaps he should accept this olive branch and not display poor manners wrought by suspicion on his part, even if Queen Maeve had asked much for a visit.

In the next second, a swirling vision formed in front of his eyes of a bedchamber with his sister sleeping.

He called up his power and teleported into the realm.

Unlike the last time when the teleporting had been calm, spinning energy and power buffeted him much worse now than the wind and ocean. As the swirling finally ended,

Ruadh growled in his mind. *Bad smell. Leave.*

Not now, Ruadh. My sister needs me. Daegan moved across the room, admitting silently that his dragon had a point. What was the awful smell? Burned limes?

The same smell as in his father's bedroom?

Perhaps Queen Maeve had grounds for demanding Lesley remain here.

As he approached his sister sleeping beneath a fur in the black-wood bed, he took in her pale skin against hair the color of dark wine. Her sunken cheeks and thin arms had not happened in mere hours. She had lost weight since his last visit when she asked him to once more turn down the king's proposal for a marital match. Was Lesley happy here?

Daegan leaned down to kiss her cheek.

His vision blurred.

He blinked hard and reached out for her hand.

Ruadh shouted in his mind. *Stop!*

But Daegan had already latched onto her hand.

A black fog burst around him in a thick cloud. He froze. His dragon shouted words, but they were muffled.

Everything slowed as if the world had become weary of moving. Daegan watched in horror as his sister's eyelids opened and she turned to him.

White orbs stared back at him.

This was not Lesley.

He called upon his power to teleport out.

Nothing happened. His hands and arms refused to move. He struggled, but no muscle obeyed his order. Even his mouth would not open.

His body suddenly yanked and twisted, sending him teleporting again. He landed on a hard floor in the middle of an area with poor lighting and dried blood splatters. Body parts of some unknown creatures lay along the edge of the round area, stinking. The walls were stone and sizzled with energy. Seventy feet up, a ceiling of smoky fog rolled around.

Only a fool would believe that an escape route.

Daegan tried again to bring the rock tower in the sea

to mind and teleport away from this realm. Still nothing happened.

His gut twisted and churned.

Why would Queen Maeve do this? His jaws worked now. He roared, "I came in peace. Ya risk your pact with the king."

No one answered.

Ruadh's voice returned, now clear. *I smell death everywhere.*

I am sorry, Ruadh, but we will find a way to freedom, Daegan assured him in spite of worry sitting heavy as a cold stone in his chest.

Energy pushed at him when another being teleported in. He wished for it to be Maeve. She would face his fury.

Not a goddess. A large wyvern appeared. The dull-gray beast before him resembled a dragon but with two legs. This miserable creature could not defeat Ruadh.

Daegan had no choice but to call up his dragon. When Ruadh burst forth, he stood tall with bloodred wings outstretched and roared a furious sound that shook the stone floor beneath them.

Had the queen done all this just to watch his dragon fight a wyvern?

She should pay close attention.

It would be a brief battle.

The wyvern dropped down to launch itself at Ruadh.

Daegan's dragon shot his head forward quickly, biting the wyvern's neck to snap off its head.

Black fog boiled from the headless beast engulfing the red dragon in a muddy cloud of putrid smelling energy. *A trap!*

His dragon roared, *Teleport now!*

Daegan called upon all his power to break free, but he still could not. Neither could he speak a word. He'd never tried to teleport in dragon form, never had a reason to do so, but the action should have worked.

Voices filled the fighting ring, circling him and repeating the incantations.

His vision blurred. His body no longer belonged to him,

refusing to task a muscle.

But through the haze, he saw Queen Maeve in a sparkling black gown, floating around his dragon body, chanting nonstop.

He would kill her and take Lesley home. The queen had breached the agreement.

Daegan called up his power, pushing hard to shift back to his human form. He remained in the same spot, still in dragon form.

He fought the urge to panic. He had to stay calm and get out of this any way he could and take his sister with him. A witch could not bind him this way, but he had never been tested by a goddess witch of dark powers.

That sickening burnt lime smell filled his head.

Black majik had to be at work.

Time slowed and sped up as his body warped in and out of shape as if pulled one moment and hammered the next. Pain unlike any he'd ever suffered flooded his muscles, burned his skin, and filled his throat.

If she returned him to human form, he might still teleport out.

He would never forget the words of the incantation she repeated over and over. He would use them to reverse whatever she hoped to gain.

His eyes rolled up into his head.

When he next came awake, he could move no part of his body. He couldn't speak. Everything about him felt wrong. He could barely turn his head.

Not his head.

His dragon's head.

He lowered his gaze. Horror flooded his mind. He couldn't believe what she'd done to him. This could not be real.

Queen Maeve had turned his dragon body into a throne with a seat and square arms, all covered in red scales.

His mind fought the vision, refusing to accept what his eyes saw. He called telepathically to his dragon, *Ruadh, can you hear me?*

A rough moan came through, breaking his heart. What had she done to his dragon?

The queen appeared in the air before him, floating down until her bare feet touched the ground. She laughed and laughed, finding it more amusing every time she looked at him.

He could only imagine the king's ransom she would demand for his return.

She finally gained enough control of herself to speak. She leaned in, placing those wicked fingers on him, so close he could see every black eyelash and the hate glittering in her evil eyes. She whispered, "You, the mighty red dragon, feared by all, dared to think you could kill *me*?"

I never threatened such a thing. The words stayed in his head, unable to be uttered.

She cocked her head and her smile tightened. "You question my words? You rush here at the king's bidding, so sure you could enter my domain and do as you please. I *know* you tried to take Lesley from me upon your last visit. Stupid lizard. No one will ever take her. Dragons wait in line to take over your father's kingdom. He does not have long to live. Not like me. Lesley will now be able to fulfill her destiny and you will never know how all this ends. Your father's pet monster now helpless to save anyone."

Damn you, witch, Daegan shouted in his head. *My father kept his bargain.*

He had never considered calling his mother's name, but he would risk even that to escape this realm. He struggled to open his dragon jaws. They barely moved and only a puff of smoke came out when he tried to speak.

Queen Maeve dropped her head back and howled with laughter then faced him again. "You will not sleep. You will not speak. You will never be able to tell anyone what happened here even if you could speak. You will remain my throne for eternity."

Daegan screamed in his head. *"Noooo!"*

A FEMALE REPORTER WALKED UP WITH her cameraman following ten steps behind. "Excuse me, I'm Lydia Stone with Atlanta New Millennium News. I'd like to ask you about the recent paranormal activity rumored to be going on in Atlanta. Do you believe preternatural beings exist?" She smiled as if to let him know she found the mere idea amusing.

He glanced around at Woodruff Park in downtown Atlanta then touched the tie at his neck, careful to maintain the look of a legitimate businessman before answering. "I don't wish to comment."

She had a tenacious attitude. "So you don't feel threatened walking around Atlanta at night when these scary creatures are supposed to be out?"

"No, I assure you I am safe at night." As a warlock who answered to Queen Maeve, he feared little and continued toward the meet point for local members of his coven.

CHAPTER 1

Present day Atlanta, Georgia

RENATA SANCHEZ PAUSED HER STEP at the odd silence that caught her attention as quickly as someone shouting. A city such as Atlanta had a heartbeat and pulse almost like that of a human. This city was known for many things, quiet not being one, not even in the shadows along the old railroad tracks below street level, the original Underground Atlanta.

Having traveled here from Brazil to aid her Belador counterparts, she'd been assigned a local partner for this patrol in temperatures dropping only to the sixties at night in June. Probably cool due to the scattered showers across the city.

"Do you notice the quiet that just happened?" she asked Devon, who had stopped walking. As a Belador teamed up with her because he knew the city, Devon had proudly stated he was a Cajun from Louisiana. His sexy accent backed up those words. Good thing she loved her Roberto, who had just as wonderful a Latino accent. Devon and Roberto shared similar qualities, both tall with nut-brown skin and deep brown eyes, great smiles and just plain nice.

But Roberto was the only man for her. She hoped to gain the dragon king's permission to mate with a human.

"I did notice the quiet." Devon glanced around. "But I'm not pickin' up any supernatural presence nearby. What about you?"

"No." As she spoke that one word, the sounds of life in

the city returned. She glanced over to find Devon frowning. "That is not normal?"

"Not that I know of, but hey, what's the definition of normal in *our* world?" He scratched his chin. "I'm thinking on calling that into Trey, just don't know what I'd say. Everything got quiet, then noisy again?"

She'd been told that as the most powerful Belador telepathic in the Southeast, and maybe in this entire country, Trey McCree coordinated their teams patrolling the city. "I must admit that does not sound significant without anything else happening."

"Tell you what. Let's see if it happens again. Right now, we just need to keep an eye out for any demons or other supernatural threat showing up, and keep humans from seeing those things."

"You mean like the Medb," she muttered, amazed that VIPER, a coalition of supernatural beings who protected humans from preternatural threats, had allowed Queen Maeve to send witches and warlocks into the human realm recently.

From what Renata had heard, the invasion had been for a short time, but some bad decisions are not easily reversed.

She could understand the friction between local Beladors and VIPER these days. They reached the corner of Turner Drive where they could turn left to walk in front of a large entertainment arena or take a right toward the center of the city. "Which way, Devon?"

He shrugged. "Let's hang a left then take the next right. That'll bring us to the World Congress Center then back to Centennial Olympic Park. We have another team working from that area to Baker Street. We'll check to see if they've noticed anything strange like a sudden silence."

"Good idea. I will follow you." She fell into step with him. "Do you think humans will learn of us even with all the effort Beladors are putting into shielding the presence of supernatural beings?"

Devon ran a hand over his short hair. "I would have said no

at one time, but we think someone, a nonhuman, is behind trying to out us. A few weeks back, one of our females riding a motorcycle through the city was intentionally wrecked along with a witch who's an ally. Nasty wreck. They kidnapped the motorcycle rider. Of course, some humans were around that time of night with phones and filmed it. That started the first signs of our secret identities unraveling. But someone from our community had been there, ready for prime time video."

Standing five-foot-eight, Renata had no trouble keeping up with Devon's long strides. She had hoped the rumors about being outed had been blown out of proportion, but evidently not. "Do you mind if I ask if you're married, Devon?"

"Nope." He laughed. "I'm not. You hittin' on me?"

"No." She realized how that sounded and laughed, then quickly explained, "While you are attractive, I am spoken for."

"Just cuttin' up with you." He gave her a friendly smile. "Congratulations. Is it just dating or more?"

"Maybe."

His smile faltered. "Why do you say maybe?"

She debated on saying anything, but she had yet to meet any married Beladors back home mainly because she lived out in the country where there was little need for those with her powers. "I have been in this relationship for two years and he has asked me to marry him."

"Well, damn." Devon grinned. "That's serious enough."

She killed demons and other strange predators on her own when she did run into them, but having Devon excited about her engagement made her blush.

He eyed her hand. "Where's your ring, woman?"

"I don't want to wear it until I find out if ... it will be approved."

Tossing a serious look her way, Devon nodded. "I get it. Your fiancé is human, right?"

"Yes. I would have traveled here just to help out my Belador family anyhow, but I jumped at the chance to come so I could ask the dragon king for permission. I have told Roberto nothing, because we are to not tell humans about what we are unless they are family or a spouse."

Devon lifted a finger. "The dragon king's name is Daegan, and I can't see him denying you that opportunity. We have quite a few marriages with humans here. The only thing is he will warn you that now is a dangerous time to bring humans into our world."

"I know this. I feel confident I can keep Roberto safe. We live so far from the city. I have only had to face two trolls and a demon in the past three years. Roberto had no idea when I fought them, but he was never in danger." She considered Devon's words and admitted, "I do not know if I can call our dragon king by his given name."

Devon shook his head and chuckled.

She gave him a wry smile. She'd just turned twenty-five and felt a little intimidated at the idea of meeting a dragon shifter even if he was on the side of Beladors. More like ruling the Beladors, but things had improved greatly since he kicked Macha out of Treoir realm. Just the fact that he had done so spoke volumes about his power.

"Don't worry." Devon waved his hand to dismiss her concerns. "He's a good guy, the best. He'll do anything to protect us and he's down to earth."

"I have heard the story of his rescue from TÅμr Medb. It is hard not be a fangirl over our dragon king." She smiled at Devon.

That made Devon laugh even more.

She enjoyed the Cajun. He was the first Belador from Louisiana she'd ever met.

They had just walked across a highway bridge, which ran in front of the gigantic event arena. This walkway and drive spanned the old railroad tracks below.

Silence once more dropped over her like an invisible shroud.

Devon stopped as abruptly as she had. He held up a finger and whispered, "Stay here."

Then he walked over to a set of steps going down to a parking deck perched to the side of the tracks. He stood on the second step, looking all around.

All at once, normal sounds of rats scurrying along the gutters and automobile engines droning returned.

Even the air seemed to move again.

Her skin prickled at the odd sensation.

Devon bent over the stairway rail to look down.

She called out telepathically, *Anything unusual going on, Devon?*

Not sure, came back. He turned his head to look her way then returned to whatever had drawn his attention. He added, *But this is enough for me to contact Trey.*

Hair raised on her arms. Even so, she never ran from anything and said, *Want to go down and take a closer look?*

As soon as she said that, he backed away and turned toward her. He called out, *Get out of ...*

His body was yanked backwards over the rail and out of sight.

Using her Belador power, she rushed over there in seconds, but couldn't hear or see Devon. No humans were around her. She leaped off the steps to drop sixty feet and land next to the tracks.

Devon! she shouted to him mind-to-mind.

Nothing came back.

She opened her mind to call Trey.

Without a sound of warning, a hand grabbed her arm. Claws pierced her skin.

She swung the other arm around to hit whatever it was with her kinetic power. Her hand slapped energy. Not a body.

And she had no kinetics.

The hand on her arm disappeared.

She called out to Trey, *Devon was ...*

A cold sensation covered her as if someone had dumped ice water over her body. She shouted over and over telepathically, calling for anyone who could hear her, but her muffled words bounced around in her head.

No one called back to her.

A male figure two feet taller than her appeared as if it formed from mist in the air and glowed yellow. The face that formed had empty holes for eyes and a black maw full of needle-sharp teeth.

Torn and ragged, a translucent robe hanging on the body.

Renata tried to run. She couldn't move, no matter how much power she called up. She tried shifting into Belador battle form with thicker muscles and a head twice her normal size.

Nothing changed in her body.

She couldn't open her mouth, couldn't push words out, but heard them in her head when she shouted, *What are you?*

He latched translucent fingers around her wrist. Searing pain rushed up her arm. She trembled, her body shaking with shock. Tears sprung from her eyes. She silently pleaded for help. Anything to stop this abomination from whatever he was doing to her.

Then he shoved his other hand straight into her chest.

CHAPTER 2

DAEGAN! NEED YOU IN PIEDMONT Park.

Hearing his second-in-command call out telepathically, Daegan considered the Medb warlock he'd caught skulking around the east side of downtown Atlanta on a rainy night. He tossed the limp body aside.

It landed in a mud puddle near Vladimir Quinn, Maistir over the North American Beladors.

Daegan wiped water from his eyes. "Tristan called for my aid."

"No worries. I've got this, Daegan." Quinn had dressed as one of the businessmen of this era for an earlier meeting before being requested to lend a hand tonight. He hadn't hesitated to come immediately, showing no concern for the drizzle that soaked his suit and flattened his blond hair against his head. Under that civilized exterior beat the heart of a confident Belador warrior capable of battling preternatural beings.

In addition to kinetics and telepathy, Quinn had the unusual gift to mind lock with a supernatural being or human as well, though he avoided using it except in dire situations.

Quinn noted, "I'll interrogate the warlock once he regains consciousness to find out if he's hunting humans for Queen Maeve. Then I'll call Sen to pick him up for VIPER."

Daegan glanced around to insure no humans observed them at close to ten at night where they stood knee-deep in weeds behind a school no longer in use. Trash had been dumped back here, including a couch, and thick vines climbed the crumbling building.

With a short nod at Quinn, Daegan teleported just north of the city.

When he appeared in Piedmont Park, everything came into focus around the copse of trees where he stood within dark shadows. He'd used this access point for teleporting to the park in the past to prevent humans seeing him appear out of thin air.

That would send humans screaming.

Especially those with phones that filmed videos and snapped photos. In today's world, everyone had those damned things.

Tristan had explained they were called devices.

Strange words on Daegan's tongue.

If not for the ability to manipulate the images and, thereby diluting the authenticity of the photograph, humans would have figured out that supernatural beings existed by now.

He and his Beladors were doing their best to shield humans from realizing preternaturals lived among them. Some of the Beladors possessed excellent computer skills to combat the problem at the source, an evil thing called an Internet.

These humans were fortunate Beladors had continued to thrive through the ages while remaining hidden among their population. Some nonhumans were predators, but his Beladors were honorable. They'd lived peacefully, protecting humans for all these centuries while he'd been ... gone.

Rain pelted the trees and fell in a steady drizzle down Daegan's face and the back of his neck.

Looking around, Daegan saw a handful of humans jogging alone and some walking dogs, but no Tristan.

Daegan called telepathically. *Tristan, I am at the south end of the park where we normally enter. What is the problem?*

Tristan's reply came back quickly. *Great. I'm close to ... umph, the foot bridge. North end.* Tristan paused, sounding out of breath. *I could use your...* His voice cut off sharply.

Then a woman screamed, the sound coming from the same direction as Tristan's location.

Using the cover of darkness to hide his speed, Daegan

wove in and out of deep shadows to reach the footbridge in seconds.

Standing in a barely lit area far from the road bordering one side of the park, Tristan held a sobbing woman draped over one arm as he slapped kinetic hits at a troll losing its human-like glamour, plus a demon not trying to hide its horns or the tail dragging behind.

Daegan stormed forward to take on the demon, which would normally be the greater threat.

Trolls were difficult, but as an unusual Alterant Belador able to shift into a gryphon, Tristan had plenty of power.

The demon whipped its dirt-brown head around at Daegan. A wide red mouth opened to expose long fangs. Thick black outlined the rabid yellow eyes. It growled a warning.

Daegan replied with a punch of power. He drove the demon thirty feet back to slam against an old oak tree.

Tristan called over, "Careful, boss. Locals are watching. Whoa!" The troll tried to slide under Tristan's kinetic wall. He got his hand stomped on for that and mud splattered in his face.

Twisting around, Daegan realized five humans stood way over on the opposite side of Tenth Street from the park, maybe a hundred feet away.

All of them had their damned phones out.

Daegan wished for a downpour, but the rain had slowed to a sprinkle.

But Tristan had said the quality of images taken at night would not be recognizable unless those phones were brought closer. The female Tristan held away from the troll no longer screamed as her limp body sagged, clothes and hair soaked.

Daegan tossed him a quick look of question.

Wearing glasses with dark lenses to hide his glowing green eyes, Tristan shrugged. "She passed out. Probably best for now."

Growling at Tristan like a crazed animal, the troll scooted back. "That's mine."

Tristan kept his voice down. "Not helping your case, troll."

Daegan started to reach for the troll when loud footsteps splashed, coming up from behind. He spun around and shoved an arm up, but not before the demonic creature latched razor-sharp teeth on his arm and clawed his chest.

That stung like being hit by a giant wasp.

His dragon grumbled, but they could tolerate demon saliva.

Daegan pounded a fist on the demon's head, busting one horn off. That unlocked its jaws, but then it squealed a high-pitched cry. Shouting started up from the humans across the street. This demon had to go.

Calling mind-to-mind, Daegan told Quinn, *This is Daegan. Do you have a place for a demon?*

If he's contained, yes. Send him.

The demon snarled and leaped at Daegan again. He grabbed the four-toed monstrosity by its throat and shoved a hard blast of energy into its body. The demon went rigid and its back arched. The crazed eyes bulged out and teeth clacked when the mouth shut.

That looked contained to Daegan.

With his back to the street and the human attention on Tristan battling the troll, Daegan laid the demon on the ground then teleported him.

"You're gettin' tired, Hollywood? You'll be dinner, too," the troll shouted.

Daegan swung around, glanced at the insane humans now crossing the road to enter the park. He told Tristan, "I shall handle this nuisance."

"All yours, boss." Tristan dropped the hand he'd been using to flick kinetic hits and backed away.

Before the troll could jump on Tristan, Daegan latched a hand on its shoulder and jerked the troll around.

Fool tried to bite him.

Daegan had lost all patience with being bitten.

He grabbed the troll by the throat, surprised the troll's lower half still appeared human in dirty gray work pants. Must be getting tired trying to hold a glamour. From the chest up, coarse black hair hung six inches long, plastered against the wet leathery green skin. A horn protruded from the back of his boxy head, bright yellow eyes full of murder bulged, and thick pointy ears to go with all that. Slobber dripped from a mouth filled with jagged fangs. Two large ones jutted up from the troll's lower jaw.

Lifting the snarling being to eye level, Daegan said, "Are you a local troll or have you come from afar?"

The idiot raked sharp claws across Daegan's arms, growling the whole time.

"Boss, we got company coming."

Angling away from Tristan so the humans only saw his back, Daegan clenched his fingers tighter, surprising the troll by his ability to even hold the creature's heavy weight one-handed.

Then Daegan called up his dragon just enough to turn his eyes reptilian with a bright silver glow. He ordered in a deep voice, "Look at me."

The troll's gaze lifted and lost its glow. Dull eyes now the color of a rotting banana peel focused on Daegan's face. The troll's mouth dropped open. He made a guttural sound that could be, *"Dragon?"*

Close enough.

Nodding, Daegan kept his voice low. "You have one chance to live. Tell me who sent ya."

Indecision flittered in the troll's gaze.

Disgusted, Daegan tightened his fingers again. The next time he did it, he'd break bones even as thick as these.

He could hear the humans now, chattering excitedly as they crept closer.

They clearly hadn't come running to save a woman, but they'd put their foolish lives at risk to record what Tristan had explained as a video worthy of going viral.

On an invisible Internet.

Rough throat noises dragged Daegan's attention back to the troll with its mouth opened like a fish sucking in air.

Daegan loosened his grip and whispered, "If you lie to me, I will take you to my realm and let my dragon burn you alive."

"No." The troll gulped and swallowed hard. "No one sent me. Came for the gold."

That was new. "Who offered gold?"

"No name. It's on the darknet. Said if we loaded an original film proving preternaturals exist, gold would be delivered."

A darknet? This world might have worse things than trolls.

Tristan stepped close, telling Daegan telepathically, *I'll explain the darknet later, but it's part of the Internet.*

Daegan sighed. Life had been simpler two thousand years ago without phones, Internet, and the need to hide his true identity.

Keeping his voice soft, Tristan asked the troll, "Where was the gold to be delivered?"

Shooting a death glare at Tristan, the troll grouched, "Don't know. Didn't get to find out."

"What's that *thing*?" a human called out from behind.

Daegan looked over his shoulder to find the pack of humans had made it much closer. One male with curly black hair stepped forward ahead of the others.

"Fuck," Tristan muttered then swung around to them with a hand up. "Hey, no filming. We've got this under control."

One of the two girls in the group warned, "Don't get any closer, Lonnie."

"Hush," Lonnie shot back. "This video is gonna have a million hits." Out of the six people approaching, this mid-twenties male in jeans and a rain slicker appeared to be their leader. They must have had little to choose from to pick that one.

Tristan told Daegan silently, *We need to prove he's not a troll.*

Daegan replied the same way, *Can you do that?*

If you keep a grip on the troll and hold the woman, I can handle this.

Daegan held his free arm out.

Tristan slid her body off his arm and onto Daegan's, then he turned to face the humans.

Having paused ten feet from Tristan, Lonnie took another tentative step closer, appearing confident even though his hand trembled. "Is that thing, uh, dangerous?"

"Him? Hell, no." Tristan made a pfft sound at the possibility. "This fool loves to dress up like a troll and scare people. He's off his meds. We're here to take him back to the facility. Please stop filming. His family is embarrassed enough."

Pausing in stride, Lonnie complained, "Aw, shit. I thought he was one of those weird things running around the city."

"What weird things?" Tristan asked, sounding sincerely curious when he knew exactly what the humans hunted.

"You know, supernatural beings."

"You're kidding, right?" Tristan scoffed, making it sound as if Lonnie was an idiot. "Did you really buy into all that crap?"

Daegan admired Tristan's relaxed manner and ability to blend in as a human with his wheat-colored hair cut in a modern short style, plus his usual worn-looking blue jeans and a gray T-shirt, all of which the rain had drenched.

When Lonnie started mumbling, "I can still make this work," Tristan inched toward him.

"If you want weird, you should all be at UnveilCon in Buckhead," Tristan said, still making small deliberate movements hidden by his shifting stance.

Lonnie foolishly continued forward, still holding the camera up. When the human stepped close enough, Tristan snatched the phone from Lonnie's hands and tapped on it quickly. Then he handed the device back in a matter of seconds.

Lonnie whined, "What'd you do?"

Tristan shrugged, "Sorry, man, but I get paid a lot of money to run security for the family. This can't make the news."

The human stared at his phone as if his favorite toy had been broken. "You wiped out my freaking video, you asshole. That would have gone viral even if he isn't a troll."

"Exactly," Tristan agreed. Pushing power into his voice, he added, "Now get out of here before I make you regret owning that phone."

The troll started kicking his feet. Daegan gave his body a shake and his captive settled down again.

Fear finally showed up in Lonnie's eyes.

He backed away. When he turned to the others, they had all left him, running back across Tenth Street.

Daegan had his doubts about that one reaching old age, maybe not even next week.

Once they scattered, Tristan turned back to Daegan with a grin.

Daegan arched an eyebrow and cast a look at the woman on his shoulder.

Smile wiped away, Tristan stepped over to take her. "Sorry, boss. What are we doing with the troll?"

"Hey, you two, stop scaring off the locals," a female voice called.

"Dammit." Tristan wheeled around, ready to face the next problem, which turned out not to be one.

Evalle Kincaid, an Alterant Belador like Tristan, who could also shift into a gryphon, came striding up, laughing with each step. She'd pulled her long black-brown hair into a ponytail and didn't seem to care one bit about water running off the bill of her cap. She never wore makeup, which Daegan found pleasing. He could see no reason for painting her face and preferred that natural look.

Tonight was like any other for her clothing choice. She had on the same black jeans, boots, and a sand-colored, short-sleeved shirt that had been around a long time. She'd explained once that she loved shirts she called vintage BDUs, short for Battle Dress Uniform.

The humans wouldn't understand the dark sunglasses she also wore rain, shine, daytime, or at night, because they protected her sensitive eyes the color of a baby green lizard. Tristan's eyes didn't have that sensitivity, but they were just as bright an Alterant green as Evalle's.

In spite of the irritating issues in Atlanta, Daegan returned Evalle's smile. "'Tis good to see you back. You look well.

Congratulations on completing your bond with Storm."

"Thanks. I am not just well, but ready to kick ass." She took in the troll, then the unconscious woman. "I'm sure there's a good story behind all this. What is it?"

"Hey. Did you forget I'm ... " The troll's words died in his throat when Daegan squeezed out of reflex. Claws swung at his arms again. With a flip of his wrist, Daegan spun the troll in the air and caught it by the neck again. At least now that hideous face and sharp claws were turned away.

Daegan warned in a low voice, "If you say another word, I'm not only handing you over to my dragon, but I shall allow him to keep you as a toy before he eats you. Understood?"

A wobbly nod answered him.

Inside Daegan, Ruadh vibrated with a sarcastic rumble then said, *Too stupid for toy. Too small for food.*

Daegan agreed.

Tristan suggested, "Let's deal with the troll and this woman, then I'll explain everything to Evalle. We've probably gotten as much as we can from the troll. So, what do you want to do, boss?"

"Call Sen. He can pick up the troll plus wipe the woman's memory for the past hour."

Tristan and Evalle groaned at the same time.

Narrowing his eyes, Daegan asked, "Or would you two prefer to deliver the troll to Sen?"

"Hell, no," Tristan said, taking a step back with his hands up.

"Nope, nope, nope." Evalle waved off that idea.

Sen could normally be found at VIPER headquarters located inside a mountain in North Georgia. As the liaison between Beladors and the coalition, Sen tested Daegan's patience at every turn.

Daegan called out telepathically, *Sen, I request your presence at Piedmont Park.*

I'm busy, came right back.

Ignoring Sen's belligerent reply, Daegan made it simple. *Very well, I shall handle this problem myself.*

The Tribunal, composed of a mix of three gods or goddesses at any given time, stood as the supreme power over the coalition. Sen acted as their enforcer, no matter what they ordered. Daegan had proven to be a thorn in all their sides after the Beladors freed him from the TÅµr Medb realm where his dragon had been trapped in the shape of a throne.

No one expected him to leave TÅµr Medb alive, least of all Queen Maeve.

He and his dragon had survived two thousand years of imprisonment and torture.

Never again.

Looking around first to determine no humans were nearby, Daegan told the troll, "I suggest you behave when you arrive at your next destination. I am sending you to someone who is not as understanding as I."

The troll shook his head. "You can't ... "

Daegan teleported him to VIPER headquarters.

Tristan frowned. "I thought you were calling Sen here."

"I did request his presence, but Sen refused to comply. I sent the troll to him instead." Daegan crossed his arms, waiting.

Evalle took a few steps back.

Cocking his head at her, Tristan asked, "What are you doing?"

"Standing where I can watch the apocalypse about to unfold without getting my hair singed."

Daegan snorted at her.

Power flushed hard all around them.

Sen appeared. He stood six feet four and clearly boosted his muscle mass for intimidation, stretching the black material of his T-shirt. His hair never seemed to remain the same in length or color. Today it was a dirty-blond color worn short above a face with Asian influence and odd blue eyes.

As his usual surly self, the VIPER liaison glowered at everyone before turning that hateful gaze on Daegan.

A wasted effort. Daegan had fought and defeated far greater than him.

Daegan locked gazes with the glaring demigod. "You risked exposing teleportation to a human, Sen."

"You're the one who called me, *dragon*." Sen leaned hard on the word dragon as if using it as a slur then slashed a look at Evalle. "You have a *lackey* whose time is not as valuable as mine."

Sen had an unnatural hatred for Evalle no one had figured out from what Daegan's Belador advisors had shared. He could overlook the VIPER liaison's shortcomings as long as Sen crossed no line.

Far from a lackey, Evalle had proven herself time and again. She knew her significance to Daegan and the Beladors.

She crossed her arms and tilted her head, giving Sen an amused look. "We understand. Sen probably had something dirty to wash out in the sink. His mouth. His mind. Lots of laundry possibilities for someone whose resume has one line. VIPER errand boy."

Slicing a death look her way, Sen sneered, "One of these days, Alterant."

She said nothing, merely staring him down.

Sen ordered, "Stop dropping your trash at the front door of VIPER."

"I have an agreement with VIPER," Daegan replied in a deep voice that rumbled with his dragon's power. "My people patrol and clean up the city wherever possible. If we capture a nonhuman being, we send it to you to discipline according to Tribunal rules. We all have a responsibility, Sen. Assisting in cleanup and managing anything we send to VIPER is yours."

"Hey, don't forget about wiping the last hour of this woman's mind," Tristan added.

Daegan nodded in Sen's direction. "He's right."

If Sen could look any more furious, he did right then. He slashed a hand over the limp body hanging on Tristan's arm. Drenched and pale, the woman jerked as if the power had hit her too hard.

Sen said, "Done. Now, let's be clear. I am not at *your* beck and call."

Tristan scoffed, "Just what is your problem besides that corncob up your ass?"

Sen whipped sideways, slapping a hit of energy at Tristan.

Tristan jerked to the left and shoved a kinetic hit at the ground to keep from falling on top of the woman sliding from his arms.

Evalle jerked her hands up to defend Tristan.

Sen spun toward her with a vicious look of glee at the chance he'd been waiting for.

CHAPTER 3

RAGE BURST THROUGH DAEGAN. RUADH roared to be set free.

Moving faster than a thought, Daegan flashed between Sen and Evalle. That this bastard would dare to harm her. His voice dropped into an inhuman level. "I have allowed you time to realize this is not a game to me, Sen. Strike out at another of mine and there will be no mercy."

Sen chuckled. "What're you going to do, dragon? Piss off three Tribunal entities when you have to explain putting a scratch on me?"

Daegan came right back at him, pushing energy out in a blast.

Sen fell back on his ass and snarled, jumping to his feet.

Not giving Sen a chance to speak, Daegan warned in the deep voice of his dragon, "I don't give a bloody damn what anyone thinks when it comes to my people. This *is* your last warning. Touch one of mine again and the Tribunal will be in need of a new liaison."

Some of the cockiness slid away, but not enough for Sen to appear contrite. He would never go that far. Not sounding as confident, Sen still curled up his lip. "The Tribunal doesn't have time to indulge the riffraff you waste my energy on. Consider this *my* last warning. I'm killing everything you send to me that I don't feel is worth bothering the Tribunal over. They'll thank me." Then he vanished.

Tristan shook his head as he shoved his body up to stand and lifted the woman back into his arms. He muttered, "That piece of shit packs a punch."

Daegan stared at the empty spot Sen left. Years spent replaying his father's and sisters' deaths had stolen pieces of his humanity. This world had no idea to what lengths he would go to protect what belonged to him. Ruadh rumbled steadily, still ready to battle, but helping Daegan clear the red haze of fury.

"Did he injure you, Tristan?" Daegan asked.

Running a free hand through his tawny-colored hair, Tristan dismissed it. "No big deal. I've taken worse hits."

Having been rescued from TÅµr Medb only recently, Daegan knew little of Tristan's full history. He'd met the young man for the first time when Tristan joined a Belador team that went rogue to rescue Daegan.

What had Tristan been through to brush off a powerful strike?

"What are you going to do with her?" Evalle nodded in the limp woman's direction.

Tristan held up a hand, indicating he conversed with someone telepathically. When he lowered his hand, he said, "I made a call to one of our Beladors on the police force. He's sending someone who's close by. They'll take her home."

"Well done," Daegan told him.

"Let's walk toward Tenth Street to meet him." Tristan took the lead, heading that way. As he walked, he explained to Evalle how the troll had been intentionally trying to film a video for uploading to the darknet, which was the only reason he hadn't dragged the woman off somewhere for a meal.

Evalle's face twisted into disbelief. "How'd the troll plan to make the video if he was starring in it? I didn't see a tripod."

"Humans were across the street using their phones when I got here. He probably planned to take one of their devices once they moved in for a better shot, which they did. Idiots. I dealt with the only one who had a close-up video." Tristan increased his pace as a police vehicle appeared coming down the street. He met the officer on the sidewalk. They talked a moment, then the officer put the woman in the backseat of his cruiser and left.

That had to be one of their Beladors working secretly with the human law enforcement.

Daegan appreciated Tristan's expertise when it came to managing so many human situations. Just one of the many reasons he'd made Tristan his Rì Dtùs, an ancient title for his second-in-command. His entire council was priceless when it came to navigating both the preternatural world and the human realm.

Jogging back to them, Tristan said, "One problem down, but now for the bigger one I called you about, boss."

That surprised Daegan. "What is it?"

"You know I have a human friend who has her ear to the ground on preternatural activity in the city, right?"

"Would that be your *girlfriend*?" Evalle interjected with an arch of her eyebrow. "The one who works for Jacob Kossman, who hunts for supernaturals?"

Tristan shot Evalle an annoyed glance. "Yes. But that's not the point. Her boss is an ally, or would be if we could tell him we really exist. Anyhow, she said someone is going to prove supernatural beings exist and in a way no one can deny it, which will involve the Beladors."

All humor fled Evalle's face. "What does she think is going to happen?"

"She doesn't *think*, she knows." Tristan looked all around them, and kept his voice low as he explained, "She said a message was delivered anonymously to every major news outlet in the metro area in the past hour. Someone intends to prove supernatural beings are here and specifically used the term Belador. They said Beladors were dangerous supernaturals and this person claimed the humans would get to see how a professional rids the world of them. We don't know which of ours they're targeting, but this person claims that the Belador will suffer before dying if their leader doesn't show his true self first. They are taunting you to show your dragon."

Fury boiled Daegan's blood. "No human can be behind

this. It's one of our kind. Have none of them learned that anyone who harms one of mine will die a painful death?" What would it take to stop his enemies?

Evalle turned deadly serious. "We have to stop this, but you can't show your dragon, Daegan. This could be a trap just to get you out in the open where your dragon would be killed."

Daegan's voice dropped to a deep, gritty sound. "Who dares to think they can kill my red dragon?"

"Uhm, boss," Tristan said in a calming voice. "Chill for a minute, okay?"

Evalle kept quiet, watching both of them.

Daegan pushed his dragon back down from the edge of shifting. He was tired of his people being attacked. A bounty hunter had kidnapped Evalle three weeks ago after crashing her body and motorcycle into a wall. Then he'd imprisoned her in Scamall realm and shoved Noirre majik in her body, preventing her from healing from daily torture in a desperate attempt to gain immortality from the goddess Macha.

Evalle had barely escaped with her life.

That realm no longer existed after Daegan teleported his people home to his Treoir realm just as Scamall imploded. Seeing what had been done to Evalle disturbed him on a deep level.

Every night since then, what Evalle suffered reminded him of losing his sisters and father. At least he'd been able to save her.

He hadn't been present to protect his own family.

Evalle had healed with the help of her Skinwalker mate, Storm.

That reminded Daegan to ask, "Is Storm around tonight?"

"Not unless we need him. He's trying to be good and not hover while I get back to work." She allowed a quick grin. "It's making him nuts. Just say the word and I'll call him if you need him."

"Not yet, but having dealt with the troll reminded me we may have need of Storm's ability to detect lies at some point." Daegan had witnessed Storm's gift first-hand while searching for Evalle. "We have to narrow down where this threat is originating."

Tristan had continued to scan the area. "Let's head for our teleporting spot. I've got a troll friend who lives in a hotel on Peachtree Street. He might have information. I can pop in there and no one will see me."

"Are you our new troll whisperer?" Evalle quipped, waving him ahead to lead the way.

"Very funny. Whoever is behind this probably has a larger goal than just harming, or killing, a Belador." Tristan leaned past Evalle to address Daegan. "We have plenty of preternatural enemies, and most of them want to kill you, boss. No telling what the bounty is on your head from your favorite pair of homicidal goddesses."

Daegan would be surprised to find either Queen Maeve or Macha behind this. They were malicious enough to do worse, but he'd proven once already to be a dangerous opponent.

Evalle jumped in, strategizing. "First thing we need to do is get a head count of all the Beladors in the metro area, especially with the new influx of warriors I heard you brought in from other countries. Hopefully, we can stop this in Atlanta before it spreads to other cities and countries. Nothing worse than copycat criminals. Thankfully, most sane nonhumans prefer anonymity. For now, we need to know where all of our people are at all times."

"She's right." Tristan stared off in the distance with a look off deep thought in his eyes as he kept a quick pace. "You might want to set a rule that no one patrols or goes anywhere alone. We've paired locals with our out-of-town Beladors, but some locals are running solo. It's been an option until now."

Evalle's dark ponytail swung from side to side with her determined steps. "Good idea. Two Beladors are harder to take down than one. That gives one a chance to call for help."

Having considered their suggestions, Daegan replied, "I agree with both of you." He told Tristan, "Call Trey to put

the word out to all Beladors in the metro area to do just that."
As the most powerful telepath in North America, Trey could
reach Daegan or Tristan almost anywhere.

Evalle leaned in. "I can see what you're thinking, Daegan."

Daegan caught his breath. Jennyver had once said that to
him when he had yet to reach manhood, but believed himself
ready to take on a battle with a full-grown dragon who had
insulted her. He swallowed at the memory.

When his gaze turned to Evalle, his lips twitched with a
smile. "Is that a new gift you have acquired?"

She huffed at him. "No, I just know how you men look
when you think you're going to handle something yourself.
Plus, you don't think anyone can harm you or your dragon,
because none of the deities know who your goddess mother
is."

Daegan stepped off the sidewalk to allow a woman pushing
a three-wheeled stroller while she ran behind. A light
mounted to it lit her way. The child inside a clear protective
sheet to block out the rain appeared happy.

Evalle stood with her arms crossed, waiting for an answer.

Her words held truth, but he'd made it clear he had no
intention of calling on his mother. Ever. "You are not correct."
When she opened her mouth to balk, he explained, "I do not
hold the belief that I cannot be killed, only that it would be
an extremely difficult task to accomplish. My dragon and I
have no fear for ourselves, only for the safety of my people."

Tristan grabbed the back of his neck, something Daegan
noticed when his second had something to say Daegan
might not like. "Look, boss, we know you can hold your
own against those from our supernatural world, especially
with all of us backing you up, but the humans have greater
weapons."

Daegan glared at his second. "How can mere humans be a
threat? I have seen their puny excuse for weapons."

"You've seen rifles and handguns, but you haven't been
in our world long enough to have seen the human military,"
Evalle argued. "They have bombs that can destroy this entire

country and jets with rockets that could blow your dragon to pieces. We don't want that to happen."

Destroy an entire country? Rockets?

Daegan tried to imagine such things, but could not. "I must see these things for myself so I will know how to defend against it."

Tristan blew out a rough blast of air. "I doubt that will happen unless they see you in dragon form, which would kick off World War III."

"There were two others?" Daegan asked.

"*Yesss*, and we don't want to repeat any of them," Evalle confirmed.

Tristan stepped off the sidewalk, turning them toward the copse of trees they used for teleporting in and out of this area.

Three young men with a mix of a half-shaved head, bushy curly hair, and a ponytail emerged from the dark shadows Daegan and his people headed toward. Their jackets had odd emblems. One wore a chain from a belt loop to his back pocket. Tattoos covered most of their exposed skin.

The three men slowed, but Tristan, Evalle, and Daegan continued forward.

The one with half his hair flipped open a knife.

Evalle glanced at Daegan.

Tristan stared down the group.

Daegan allowed his energy to flow out quickly, knocking all of them off balance.

Curly-haired one muttered a curse. "Let's get the fuck outta here."

Tristan chuckled as the bunch took off. "You'd be great help for gang control, boss."

"They were more foolish than dangerous."

Glancing around first, Evalle returned to Daegan. "Anyhow, the bottom line is the worst thing that could happen with Atlanta on edge is for your dragon to show up in public, Daegan. If we can find out who is behind the threat and stop them without any bloodshed or exposure, the media will blow off tonight as a stupid prank. Then they won't be so quick to jump at the next anonymous tip. But if you shift and fly through Atlanta, it will be game over. We'll all be outed to the humans. Then we'll be hunted simply because they fear the unknown. As Beladors, we'd have our hands full just staying alive and protecting each other's backs, but the human families of Belador warriors would also be at risk. Having a war with the humans would turn bloody and destroy any semblance for Belador family life."

She had a valid point.

Much as Daegan hated to admit it, he couldn't expose his dragon in this world. Additionally, he couldn't use his powers most of the time either or the humans would see it.

How was he supposed to protect his people with his greatest weapons out of reach and no way to shield them all in one place?

Tristan stopped short. "I just heard from Trey. Devon Fortier hasn't checked in for the last two hours. Trey sent two teams to search his area. No one can find him or Renata. Trey hasn't heard from her or Noah, another out-of-town Belador. I told Trey I was with the two of you so he'll send all of us a message of anything new. I also told him what we'd heard about an expected attack on Beladors tonight."

Daegan's muscles tensed with the need to mount an attack and lead the charge to defend his Beladors.

The tension of holding himself back riled Ruadh. *Kill enemy.*

His dragon only echoed Daegan's deepest desire. He'd hated war, but he had never hesitated to jump into battle. *Soon, Ruadh,* Daegan soothed silently, which eased his mind as well.

Evalle asked, "Who are Renata and Noah?"

"Renata is a badass female Belador from South America," Tristan replied. "We teamed her up with Devon. Noah is skilled as well. He came in from the UK, but said he knew Atlanta well from having lived here for three years during college so we let him patrol alone. Other than that, we've been partnering local warriors with our people coming here from other countries."

"Devon has faulty telepathic ability." Evalle sounded hopeful that this could explain a Belador being unable to communicate with Trey.

Daegan angled his head at Tristan to address her point.

"You haven't been back long enough to know all the details, Evalle, but we've brought in over *fifty* additional Beladors. That means we always have a Belador close enough to help another pair." Tristan slowed his steps and looked down, shaking his head. "Even Devon could contact at least one of our people with so many around. Renata had no problem with telepathic communication. Neither did Noah."

Evalle planted her feet at the edge of the trees and squared her jaw. "We don't have time for any more planning right now with three of ours missing." She snapped her fingers. "We need our allies."

Tristan's eyebrows jumped at that. "Who?"

"Adrianna for one, and Isak for another."

"I thought those two were at war," Tristan said.

"They'll just have to call a damn truce," Evalle snapped.

Daegan brought up, "Isak is a good choice if he has no conflict of choosing sides between us and humans." Isak happened to be one of a small group of humans who knew about the Beladors and other preternaturals.

Evalle shook her head. "I have no doubt he'll step up to help us. He will definitely protect other humans, but he has friends in our community, too. I also think he'll do anything to keep Adrianna safe, regardless of their chilly relationship right now. His electronic surveillance and intelligence rivals that of any government."

Even Tristan admitted, "He did supply key information when we were hunting for you."

That information had gained Isak ally status from Daegan.

A dark thought passed over Evalle's eyes at the mention of her ordeal, but she lifted her chin like the powerful Alterant she was and continued. "We need Adrianna, too. She's key to managing Isak so he doesn't take things into his own hands."

Tristan gave her a look that questioned her sanity. "Are you on crack? Ask Adrianna to manage Isak? You want to piss off a witch who literally holds Witchlock in the palm of her hand?" He referenced an ancient witch power Adrianna possessed through no desire of her own.

Daegan lifted a hand to intervene in what was tipping toward a quarrel. "Evalle makes a sound argument for contacting Isak."

Holding up his hands in defeat, Tristan said, "Okay, got it. We'll hope for the best." He turned, leading them into the copse of trees they'd reached. Tristan possessed the ability to teleport, but not a natural gift. He'd been given what he called a witch highball and some immortal blood while imprisoned by Macha.

Once he stood in the center of the dark spot, Tristan turned to Daegan and Evalle. "Here's my plan. I'll find out the last place Devon and Renata were before they went dark then I'll ..."

Trey's voice boomed in Daegan's head. *Three Beladors have been reported captured and are to be used to prove preternaturals exist. That just broke on every local news station. Media teams are on the way to three locations. One is downtown in the area around the big Ferris wheel. Another one is Sandy Springs on a building under construction near the mall, and another location is around that UnveilCon in Buckhead. What do you want me to do?*

Based on Tristan's and Evalle's deadly quiet posture, they'd received the same message.

Daegan replied to Trey, *Send teams of six to each location. Tell them to wait for me, Tristan, or Evalle. Tell them not to approach anyone until one of us arrives, which will be in less than a minute.*

Got it. Trey's presence in Daegan's mind vanished.

Turning to Tristan, Daegan ordered, "You head to Sandy Springs since the location did not sound specific. You can move around best with your knowledge of the area and being able to teleport. Evalle, do you know about the UnveilCon in Buckhead?"

"Yep. Heard about it when I got home. I have a good place to arrive unnoticed. I'm envisioning the top of a one-story coffee shop in that area." She dropped to stretch her body out, only touching the ground with the toes of her boots and her hands. "Send me."

Daegan pointed at her and she vanished.

Tristan repeated, "Please don't shift, boss. Like Evalle said, this could all be just to get a clear shot at your dragon."

A snarl ripped out of Daegan, but not at Tristan. He could not fight a war with his hands tied. "We will know soon enough who is behind this."

With a grim look on his face, Tristan teleported away.

Daegan recalled a short building close to the large entertainment wheel in the middle of downtown Atlanta, but had no idea if people would be able to see him arrive.

Following Evalle's example, Daegan squatted down to remain on his feet while maintaining as small a shape as possible while teleporting.

He would not expose his people to humans for anything, but neither would he allow even one to die.

A woman's voice with a Latin accent screamed in his head. *Help me, Daegan! They're killing me! I am Renata Sanchez. I am Belador. Please, someone, help me.*

She screamed a blood-curdling sound.

CHAPTER 4

TRISTAN ARRIVED IN SANDY SPRINGS two blocks from the mall often crowded on a Saturday night this time of year with summer shopping. He stood very still, because a cluster of humans were huddled just fifteen feet away with their backs to him.

Sirens whined somewhere nearby but didn't seem to be heading this way. Only ten miles north of Piedmont Park, he'd expected more rain. Water dripped on everything from grass to leaves on trees, but no more drizzle. For now.

Humans in the military were known to have a developed sixth sense, which alerted them to someone watching or approaching. This group of twenty-to-thirty-year-olds were too excited about whatever had their attention to realize they'd left their backs unprotected.

Strolling up calmly, Tristan asked, "What's going on?"

One woman jumped all the way around to face him. She slapped a hand on her chest. "You scared the crap out of me. Where'd you come from?"

Three more turned to glance at him and gave a casual look at their surroundings before resuming their observation. No sixth sense there.

He gave the woman an incredulous look. "You didn't see me walk over here a few minutes ago? I'm just looking for a good place to watch what's going on. Heard the media was headed here."

"I don't know. We haven't seen anything yet." She gave him her back, easily dismissing him.

That easy acceptance made her prey in his world. Good

thing he was here to protect humans, not hunt them. But first, he had to find out who had threatened a Belador's life.

Another female in the clueless group twisted to send him a sexy look and pointed when she spoke. "We're waiting to see what flies off that building."

Tristan's gaze snapped up in the direction she indicated. He stepped around them. In his peripheral vision. he could see the crowd growing and the media trucks setting up at the base of the twelve-story office building under construction. Shiny glass exterior walls had been installed, but two roll-off trash bins were full and miscellaneous materials had been piled around.

No one appeared around the edge of the roof.

He had to get up there and do it fast.

But he couldn't just blink out of sight with all the wide-open area between him and the building. He started running toward the building, not giving a damn that he might look like a human international track star.

Trey shouted in his head. *Just heard from Devon. He's on top of a building in Sandy Springs. A troll with crazy energy has his hands bound and is going to throw him off head-first.*

I'm here, Trey. Tell him I'm coming.

Will do.

Tristan gave Trey the location of the building for the six-man team Daegan had ordered to each of the three areas, and for Trey to remind them to wait for directions from Tristan.

He was still sixty feet from the foundation of the structure when someone powered up a spotlight.

Throngs of people holding their phones tilted up to film someone's death got in his way and pissed him off. Tristan shoved them aside to the sound of curses shouted at him.

He swallowed his own curses for anyone wanting to capture someone's murder for the Internet.

Not someone.

These humans probably thought a supernatural being was some kind of monster, not a person.

Or did they think this was just a media prank?

Someone shouted, *"Look up there!"*

A woman screamed, *"Oh, no!"*

Instead of looking, Tristan ran between two large news vans and teleported away. Tough shit if someone saw him. They'd have to prove it happened.

He appeared on the roof, surprising a troll all the way across to the other side who clutched Devon's body that lay stomach down on the parapet wall.

Tristan shot across the roof.

The troll pushed Devon off.

CHAPTER 5

EVALLE APPEARED ON THE GRAVEL roof of a coffee shop in Buckhead, the upscale wine-and-dine district for the affluent in Atlanta. Roofs were one of the best landing spots she knew of for teleporting to at dark. She only knew her way around this area from having patrolled at night to hunt preternatural predators, not to wine and dine.

Lifting her head to check beyond the dark roof, no one noticed her from the sidewalk. They were dressed in a mix of costumes, many characters she recognized. They laughed and cut up, probably happy not to be in the middle of a downpour. The bloated air still soaked her clothes, but nothing more than a misting rain fell.

Where was Noah? She sent a message to Trey. *Evalle here. Has anyone found Noah?*

Trey replied, *Stand by.*

Quinn's familiar voice with a British accent came into her head. *Evalle! I am in Buckhead.*

Quinn! Evalle probably shouted that too loud telepathically. *Any idea where Noah is?*

Unfortunately, yes. Quinn gave her directions for where he waited a mile away.

I'm on the way. She hurried to the backside of the building, saw no one outside, and leaped to the pavement behind the busy coffee shop, then took off. When she reached Peachtree Street, she struggled to weave her way through bands of people on the sidewalk.

Were all these people here for the first UnveilCon?

Who came up with that idea?

And why was it out here in Buckhead in early summer when the big paranormal con happened every year during the fall in downtown Atlanta?

Who knew?

She only cared to find Noah, a Belador who deserved to go home to his friends and family after helping out, not be targeted by some lunatic supernatural.

She almost fell over one of the many thin scooters dropped on sidewalks around the city when someone had reached their destination. The scooters required an app to activate them, but she didn't have time for that. She grabbed up the one by her feet and started pushing it away.

An alarm beeped loudly. Argh.

Ignoring people glaring at her, she flicked her fingers covertly in the direction of the sound. Something made a pop. She moved the scooter again and no sound screeched. Dropping it off the sidewalk and onto the road, she took off running in that space between the road and sidewalk. She jumped on and used kinetics to spin the front tire fast.

This was not her Suzuki GSXR motorcycle still in pieces in the garage, but she managed to zoom down the street quickly, passing cars.

People turned and pointed. Jaws dropped.

Let them figure out how her scooter went so fast any way they wanted.

In less than a minute, she reached the spot where Quinn had told her to meet him.

He had a dignified profile clothed in one of his pricey suits, but lacking a trench coat to protect it this time. The British clip to his words came from his education in England, but he had a face carved of old world Russian features with a thin nose, narrow jaw, and light blue-gray eyes. Standing next to a bus stop shelter, he watched for her like a lighthouse beacon searching the dark night.

She raced up to the shelter, propped the street scooter against the covered structure, and hurried to him.

Quinn opened his arms and gave her a quick hug. "I've

missed you and want to catch up as soon as we can, but first we save Noah." Releasing her, he got down to business and pointed. "This way."

"Good to see you, too, Quinn. I thought con events tonight were going on in a warehouse a few miles from here."

Without turning away from where he pushed politely through the crowds, he gave a short nod. "That is correct, but the media has swarmed this area in the last few minutes. I got here as soon as Trey put out a call for three locations. I was closest to this one."

"I'm glad." She'd met her two best friends, Quinn and Tzader, when the three of them were captured by Medb warlocks a few years back. Those two had been the extent of her world at that time, but she now had Storm and her adorable two-foot-tall rescue gargoyle, Feenix, plus more friends than she could count on two hands.

Her heart had always held a raucous party whenever she thought of her man, but everything between them had strengthened even more during bonding. She'd never known love, not the kind she shared with him. If anything, it had made her more confident, but she did miss having him at her side.

"*Shit!*" Tired of bogging down in the crowd again, she told Quinn telepathically, *We need these people out of the way.*

I agree, but we can't very well tell them we're looking for a supernatural predator.

True, but she had an idea.

Evalle cupped her mouth and added a bump of power when she shouted, "Be careful where you step. Looking for my boa constrictor. It's out here somewhere. Please don't hurt it, but keep small dogs away."

Women began screaming in panic.

Actually, men too. Everyone was doing their best to get away from Evalle. That worked exactly as she'd hoped, because no one had a specific exit point, which would have meant a stampede. Instead, the fifty to sixty humans right around them dispersed quickly in multiple directions.

Quinn glanced at her. "Mean, but–." His face jerked past her. "*Noah!*"

Some people had moved away, but a crowd of at least eighty still gathered between them and two people staged at the entrance to a building.

Driving his body like a human wedge, Quinn raced into the throng with Evalle right behind him, then he hit his brakes abruptly.

She skidded to a stop, barely avoiding hitting him.

Large television cameras propped on shoulders and phones held up to capture the main event. Personal videos were being shot from everywhere in a semi-circle crowd standing around steps to an elegant office building. The smooth stone finish reminded her of other buildings erected long ago when land cost far less than now in this area.

Six steps up led to a half oval-shaped landing fifty feet across and twenty feet deep, which allowed plenty of room for business visitors to come and go.

The doors appeared locked with a panel for punching in numbers to enter.

Someone close to six foot tall stood in a dark blue robe with a hood, tanned feet in sandals, and what appeared to be stubby male hands holding a young man off the ground without touching his body.

No wonder these people crowding closer had not budged when she shouted.

Don't come here. It's a trap, screamed in Evalle's head in spite of the Belador victim showing a calm face.

Quinn winced, having clearly heard it as well. "We have to be careful or we could kill Noah."

She tried talking to Noah telepathically. *Do you know what being has you in its grip?* Finding that out would help her and Quinn come up with a way to attack the guy in the robe without putting Noah at greater risk.

All she got from Noah was a moan. She asked Quinn softly, "Can you talk to him?"

"I tried. I'm just getting sounds now. No words. The bastard holding Noah might be blocking his telepathy."

The man in the robe lifted his hands and Noah floated up a foot off the ground.

Cheers went up all around.

Humans thought this was a show.

When Robe Guy moved his thick fingers as if playing a keyboard on each side of Noah's neck, Noah howled in Evalle's head.

She started up the steps with Quinn shouting at her.

He zipped up right beside her and ordered, "Stay back."

"No." She could not stand down while one of her Beladors suffered.

Quinn whispered, "Let me try mind lock with his captor."

Good point. Quinn never used his ability to push inside a mind without permission except in a life or death situation.

This qualified. Quinn had the ability to kill with that power, too.

She stopped, chest aching and heart pounding. "Hurry."

Quinn stared straight ahead for five seconds. Then he grabbed his head and fell to his knees. He shouted, *"Shit! Sorcerer ... maybe demon, too."*

Noah's face remained a blank look, but he screamed again in her mind as if someone stabbed his eyes with ice picks.

Poor Noah's calm face turned bloodred.

Quinn struggled to stay upright.

Evalle made a growling sound of fury Storm made when her Skinwalker mate shifted into a jaguar and wanted to kill something. Screw worrying about what the humans saw.

She shoved up both hands and pushed a load of kinetic power at the sorcerer.

His robe whipped back and forth.

The humans made awed sounds, happy to be further entertained.

Robe guy dropped Noah to the ground where his feet touched and he stood rigid. The mystery guy moved an arm covered with a bell sleeve in her direction. Whipping a finger up and down, he shot power at her.

She snapped a kinetic wall in place, struggling to push forward one step at a time.

Noah's eyes bulged and his mouth fell open. He couldn't speak.

That's when a chain wrapped Noah's waist and pinning his arms to his sides began to glow bright gold. The sorcerer pulled a trailing end of the links and the chain tightened.

If Evalle could get Noah and Quinn out of here, the Beladors might later be able to spin this as an elaborate show created just for the con.

She didn't care as long as Noah and Quinn lived.

Dropping her protective field, she slashed a direct hit of kinetics at the sorcerer's hand that clutched the end of the chain.

Energy lit up his hand with a yellow glow. In fact, his hand turned translucent. She looked down. His feet were radiating too.

She'd never seen kinetics cause that before. The whole glow thing had to be generated by him.

Robe Guy growled and stumbled sideways. His blue hood fell and a translucent being stared at her with boiling red eyes. Then he vanished.

The robe pooled on the cement landing.

No cheering this time. The humans had finally realized this was not natural.

Evalle jumped forward, catching Noah before he face-planted.

She lowered him to the ground. Energy buzzed from the chain around him. Noah's body vibrated. She had to break the chain binding him.

Reaching for the loose end of bright yellow links, she yanked hard, breaking the chain and freeing Noah.

Power struck her in the chest and sent her flying backwards off her feet.

Her head slammed a hard surface and bones in her back

cracked when she hit the sharp edge of a step. Energy ran up her arm, burning her.

She screamed.

CHAPTER 6

DAEGAN STOOD UPON THE ROOF of a two-story building under the neon glow of the gigantic wheel structure that rose two hundred feet above the ground. He'd cloaked himself from view the second he appeared to prevent any of those riding the Ferris wheel to see him pop into existence.

Brilliant lights, changing colors continually, lined the spokes and lit up the exterior of the cars holding patrons. Was someone holding Renata hostage inside one of those gondolas?

Media showed up, parking tall trucks and personal vehicles anywhere they could find a spot large enough. Some of the trucks raised tall poles so they could transmit from this location, according to Tristan. Their celebrity people jumped out, fixing hair and straightening clothes, then grabbed microphones. Camera operators followed, finding a suitable place to set up for filming.

They were all headed for Centennial Park, a large open complex created when Atlanta hosted an international sporting event, and pointing cameras at the Ferris wheel.

After a quick walk around the roof, Daegan spotted a place to teleport down behind the building where he could be at road level.

Hiding his abilities in this era tested his patience greatly. Tristan had worked out a series of suitable locations for teleporting without being detected or landing close to a human.

Once Daegan appeared in the dark alley, he hurried around the building to join the crowds moving in singles, pairs, and groups. The only supernatural energy he picked up belonged to his Beladors patrolling throughout the crowd. Some were in uniform as part of Atlanta Police Department or other protective agencies, but more were dressed just like the humans to blend in.

Judging by physical appearance only, Beladors appeared human.

The difference came when it was time to battle a powerful supernatural enemy. If the Beladors knew what they were up against and deemed the action a reasonable risk, they could link their powers and show a more formidable front.

The downside being that if one in the link was killed, they all died.

For that reason, Daegan had ordered them not to link unless they had no other way to survive.

While casting another look at the giant wheel, which had paused at the landing platform to allow people to step out, Daegan bumped into a group of four human men. They smelled of ale and fried food.

One that failed to reach Daegan's shoulder in height jerked around. "Hey, what the fuck?"

Turning to the angry male holding a half-spilled beer in one hand, Daegan said, "My apologies. I did not take care where I stepped."

"Not take care … ?" one guy snickered. "What planet are you from?"

Daegan's dragon rumbled.

The men looked at his face then his chest. Half-empty-drink guy asked, "Did you make that sound?"

Now he had to explain his irritated dragon. He had no time for this.

Sighing, Daegan pulled out a paper bill. This one had a one hundred on it. He handed it to the one who had lost part of his brew. "Will this buy peace?"

"Shit, that's like … " The beer drinker grinned. "We're all good."

Finally.

When they didn't move on, Daegan crossed his arms and allowed his energy to seep out.

In a few seconds, all four smiles were replaced by expressions of deep concern. The only astute one mumbled, "Let's get away from the freak."

This time, they hurried in another direction.

With that handled, Daegan began looking across the landscape again. He sensed more than saw when the large wheel just behind him began to turn.

The speed increased slightly.

Sounds of hands slapping against the glass windows drew his head around. Humans yelled and beat the inside of their compartments as one gondola after another passed the platform without stopping.

He strode over to get a closer look at what might be going on. Two gondolas passed the platform with the people inside quiet, but most of the others were not happy.

Why hadn't the operator stopped the mechanism?

When the wheel had spun halfway, it paused, but no person walked up to open the doors that had likely been locked from the outside.

Daegan started over to free two women banging on the door and making panicked sounds to be let out when he heard a hideous scream from high up.

The wheel began moving again.

He backed up several steps to view gondolas two hundred feet up paused at the top just starting down.

The dazzling lights on the wheel provided enough glow to see beneath each gondola. The flat underneath had smooth surfaces everywhere except one where a woman in a white blouse and jeans appeared to have the back of her body and limbs glued to the metal surface.

Renata.

If the car continued all the way down without stopping, it would crush her as it reached the landing platform with too narrow a space beneath for a body to clear.

Human spectators began murmuring. An elderly woman

gasped. "Is that a body on the bottom of a gondola?"

News crews came running.

Daegan's heart slammed his chest.

This was no time for indecision. He called out telepathically, *I will not allow you to die, Renata. I will teleport you to safety.*

The monster won't let me go, she cried in his mind. *Please save me.*

Her terror-ridden voice would haunt him forever if he failed her.

Who had her? Daegan brushed that question aside, unwilling to lose her to a*ny* predator. Clearing his mind, he first tried to teleport her off the gondola.

Her body and the gondola shook. Those inside screamed and Renata moaned in pain.

He stopped immediately.

Next, he lifted his hands to use kinetics to break the gondola away from the wheel then teleport the entire thing along with her body to another location where he'd land it on the side. That way, he could prevent the car from crushing Renata. Then he'd dash to the dark and teleport to the same place.

Humans would lose their minds, but with that wheel turning, he had few choices. Sen would just have to deal with wiping all the minds of this crowd.

Daegan would worry about fallout later.

His teleportation attempt caused the whole wheel structure to shake and cracked the foundation. Panicked human faces plastered to the clear windows. Their mouths opened, screaming in terror.

The crowd yelled and pointed. "It's falling!"

He didn't dare try to teleport the wheel structure after that. Instead, he pointed power at the base, pushing the wheel gently back into place.

Someone had clearly used a powerful majik to attach Renata to the bottom of the gondola and to insure no teleporting could save her.

Daegan would pay heavily for his next decision, but he could not watch her die.

Standing in the middle of humans, he teleported to the roof of the car just below Renata. He came back into view standing with his feet straddling a motorized box mounted on top of the one he'd landed on.

The crowd sound died sharply, then they began shouting like mad. He ignored the ruckus below and focused on the only thing that mattered.

Keeping Renata alive to free her.

Dragon king! Shouted in his mind. *I am Vincent and with six Beladors below the Ferris wheel. Tell me what you need.*

He told his man, *Try to stop the wheel from turning. If not, just keep the humans back and prevent them from using a weapon on me if they panic.*

Yes, sir.

Daegan doubted even he could stop this wheel at the moment without knowing what majik had been used.

A yellow glow of energy outlined Renata's body. Daegan sidestepped to keep his balance on the moving gondola beneath him. He feared waiting until this roof lined up better with the surface of where Renata stared at him wild-eyed.

She had green eyes, like Jennyver.

Renata would be crushed under the landing platform in eighty feet.

Using his kinetics, he leaped up to grasp a metal bar at the base of her gondola, his body hanging by one hand.

More humans screamed and yelled. Powerful lights turned up, blinding him. He slapped a kinetic hit at the light beam, smashing it.

The crowd roared and panicked, running everywhere.

Renata had sixty feet.

Her voice broke when she called into his mind, *Please don't die dragon king. Ask someone to tell my fiancé I am sorry and I love him. The Belador who called for me to come here to help will know him.*

I will not leave you, Renata. Stay strong.

The monster has me ... her words cut off as if someone choked her. Renata's eyes and mouth froze. Her face turned a dark shade of red.

Muscles in Daegan's arm burned with the strain.

Fifty feet.

Renata's head rolled forward.

Daegan shoved a hand on her shoulder, testing to see if he could break the ward or chain of power holding her. His arm lit up a brilliant yellow color.

Energy attacked his power.

Renata screamed in his head then suddenly quieted. When she turned her face to him this time, a horrible glowing face replaced hers. Needle-sharp teeth smiled.

The monster spoke in Daegan's head. *I have you, dragon.*

Daegan couldn't pull his hand free.

The creature's power bound his energy in place.

Everything around Daegan paused. All sounds died. Not even the wheel moved.

The voice that came out of the monster now sounded thick and gravelly. "She is mine, dragon. If you want her and the others back, you will bring me two volumes of the Immortuos Grimoire."

"What are you talking about?" Daegan shouted. He tried teleporting. Nothing happened. He called his dragon to the surface. Ruadh growled, but the sound came from far away.

Out of Daegan's reach.

The hideous face turned furious. "You have lived thousands of years and claim to not know of this ancient book of majik? You lie."

"*I don't!*" Daegan shouted. "I have no idea what you speak of." He racked his mind for a way to yank himself and Renata away from this monster. She'd named it right.

Hideous black holes stared at him. "Find those volumes or the blood of your people will run everywhere."

"Where do I even start to find these books?" Daegan kept talking to buy time. He called up his power again, but this glowing translucent being had his energy bound.

What was this thing?

The filmy yellow head shook. Black eye sockets now burned with red fire when it screamed, "Your people *stole* one volume twelve hundred years ago and gave it to VIPER. *Start there, dragon!*"

Daegan mentally raced for questions. "Who are you?"

"I am master of the Imortiks," the being bellowed loud enough to rouse the dead.

Imortiks meant nothing to Daegan. Power burned his arm and sent spikes of pain shooting through his chest. He shouted back, "I cannot find anything while bound here. Free me and the woman."

"You have a fortnight to deliver both volumes to the center of Oakland Cemetery or Imortiks waiting to walk this land again will bond with the bodies and powers of your Beladors. Know this, dragon. I make the same offer to other powerful beings. I possess their followers, too. The first leader to bring me both volumes will receive *all* those I capture."

The time frame dawned on Daegan.

He had fourteen days to find some ancient volumes of majik or Belador bodies would be overtaken by these Imortiks. How much more difficult would Imortiks be to kill when they inhabited his Beladors?

The glowing being vanished along with Renata's body.

Power surged through Daegan's arm and more pain blasted through right behind it.

Time spun up again.

Everything moved normally, including the wheel.

His dragon roared inside of him. Fire burst around Daegan's hand. Tall flames crawled up his arm.

Ruadh battered Daegan's insides, demanding to be freed and burn their enemy. His dragon pushed hard to the surface. Daegan's back split as wings began emerging. Locking his muscles, he stopped the move half-formed.

Not now, Ruadh, Daegan ordered. *Pull back!*

His wings stayed as they were.

The worst that could happen would be for his dragon to

become stuck halfway into a shift.

Ruadh roared, fighting to escape.

Daegan shouted telepathically again. *Wait, Ruadh. The enemy is gone. We will kill everyone if we shift now.*

Ruadh growled and rumbled loud as a tornado being held in place.

The wings pulled back inside Daegan's body. Fire would not kill him in human form, but flames engulfed the gondola.

A woman and child inside the gondola above his arm cried and shouted for help.

Wind swept passed his face, feeding the flames as the ride rushed quickly toward the ground.

Daegan called to his Beladors telepathically, *Clear a spot I can see.*

A round open area immediately appeared, surrounded by his Beladors with arms outstretched to block anyone from interfering.

Now free of the Imortik master, Daegan hoped this would work. He teleported the woman and child from inside the gondola to the ground.

Vincent jumped forward to help the dazed woman and child stand, then the team lined up, passing the pair to safety as an ambulance raced up with lights flashing and a siren whining.

More emergency vehicles screeched, rushing toward the Ferris wheel area from two directions.

That's when Daegan realized the wheel had ceased turning. Still clinging to a support bar thirty feet in the air, he swung his body and dropped to the ground, then walked over to his men.

Ambulances spewed medical personnel who began caring for the woman and child. Mouths gaped open, the crowd clearly in shock. Some knelt and held their hands in prayer.

Humans would not forget what had happened.

No explanation would fix this. Even wiping minds would not remove the cameras filming it all live.

Vincent walked up to him with his face tense. "This is all

over the news, sir."

"I know. Good job, Vincent," Daegan said and gave the team a nod of appreciation.

The woman being cared for came out of her stupor, grabbing her daughter protectively to her. She pointed at Daegan and screamed, *"Demons! They're not human!"*

More shrill sirens filled the air. Atlanta Police Department flooded the scene. Some were Beladors, who would place protecting Daegan above themselves.

Daegan sent a blanket telepathic message to those of his in the area. *If your identity as a Belador is still hidden, then continue as you have. I need nothing from you but to remain safe.*

He heard a series of acknowledgements, indicating there had to be another twenty Beladors present.

Daegan had always known when to battle and when to retreat. He told Vincent, "Gather the team and bring them with me."

Clearly receiving telepathic orders, the men rushed to follow Daegan, who walked them toward the dark spot behind the building where he could teleport them out undetected. No point in making this any worse than it was.

They'd made fifteen steps when four police cruisers rushed up the street he'd been heading toward.

A blinding array of lights flashed.

Car doors flipped open and officers spilled out, standing behind the doors with weapons drawn.

Floodlights hit his group from behind.

A man using a mechanical horn called out in a shaky voice, "Stop and put your hands in the air."

Daegan turned to a small army of law enforcement with impressive-looking weapons held ready to shoot. A helicopter flew fast toward the scene on its way from the center of the city with yet another searchlight beaming down.

He forced himself not to smash the lights.

Heavy-duty trucks roared up from the only other escape route on one side.

Vincent explained, "Those big trucks and the helicopter are part of a SWAT team, sir. Specially trained law enforcement with high-powered weapons. They will not allow us to walk away alive if we confront them."

Daegan had not heard of SWAT teams, but he had no problem assessing the danger they were in.

"Tell the men to prepare to teleport," Daegan ordered in a furious voice.

"What about the humans seeing us, sir?"

Daegan's gaze rolled over the crowd that had silenced. Humans stared at them as if Daegan and his men had butchered children in front of them. The curious pushed close to get a look at strange beings.

"What about them, Vincent? Preternaturals are officially exposed to humans."

Daegan had greater problems than exposure right now.

He and his men vanished.

CHAPTER 7

CASIDHE SMILED EVEN THOUGH HER heart pounded with trepidation as she waved goodbye to the guide who could go no farther with her, though he'd offered. He reminded her of a Sherpa she'd once trained with in these same remote mountains of the Caucasus range, which separated Europe from Asia. But where this young man with spiraling brown hair dressed in a red fleece pullover, loose-fitting gray pants, and cap influenced by clothes of international mountaineers, the old Sherpa had worn his traditional bakhu, a robe-like covering over his pants.

As her guide waved and headed home, poking his walking stick with each step, she turned to face the rest of this trek alone.

With daylight running out soon, she tugged her backpack higher and tightened the strap across her chest. Time to complete a trek that started unexpectedly in County Galway, Ireland two long days ago.

She stifled her moment of fear at traveling the last twenty-three miles and stared at the daunting landscape. The rough terrain didn't bother her so much as the obstinate sword hidden inside a scabbard where her backpack rested against her body.

She'd enjoyed a heady moment of power when the sword answered her call, rising up and sliding into the sheath on her back, but the stubborn blade had ignored her otherwise. She had no idea why after all these years of protecting the sword she'd been given by Herrick it had come to life. The fact that it had reinforced her concerns about a powerful pair visiting the archival centre in a small village in County Galway where she spent her days cataloguing ancient history and searching for rare books.

Power hummed steadily in the weapon, but she'd been unable to pull it from the sheath since leaving home.

Regardless, her people had to be informed about the strange visit *and* the sword showing life.

Those people lived in these mountains.

Picking her way forward, she eyed the sun as it dropped below the glowing edge of the crooked ridgeline far above.

Soft shadows formed over the rugged beauty of brown stone dusted with white from a recent snow unwilling to melt. Patches of dull green dotted the jagged mountains stretching up to the sky.

Every inhale cleansed the city pollutants from her lungs and filled her with a fresh scent riding along the cool air.

Current temperature might be in the sixties right now, but by dark her skin would feel the chill of dropping into the twenties.

She hugged the thick wool coat with the fur collar close to her, thankful Herrick had thought ahead to gift her ten years ago in case she made this trek alone. She stayed in top physical condition to be in shape for a moment like this, which inevitably had come with no warning.

He'd begun telling her as a child what her duty would be and how every warrior must train daily to be ready for any threat.

The young guide had suggested several tourist stops she might wish to visit while here.

She'd thanked him, but this was no vacation. The fewer people she met on this trip, the fewer who knew of her presence here.

Her family had enemies. Dangerous enemies.

The sword on her back humming with power knew something Casidhe did not, but Herrick would have answers.

She hoped.

How could she protect her family if she could not identify

the threat?

When she glanced again, the glow across the mountain ridge faded with each step. A black silhouette streaked across the sky with large wings.

She snapped out of her daydreaming.

Herrick would criticize her for losing track of her surroundings. That had been just a bird, right?

But even that far away, the wingspan had appeared wider than she'd expect a natural bird to possess.

Could it have been something preternatural?

No. Not as long as Herrick lived in this area.

Her heartbeat ticked up. She waited to catch another glimpse of the giant bird. After a moment of not seeing it again, she shook off her concern, muttering, "Don't be stupid. Nothin' unusual. Just a big-ass bird."

She faulted those two unknown beings who visited the archival centre for causing her jumpiness.

If she'd had time, she would have sent word to Herrick via their complex messaging system managed by humans, such as the Luigsech family who had helped raise her. They'd been loyal to Herrick and his ancestors over many centuries.

But they were human.

She had no idea how to categorize herself beyond *other*. She'd been born human-looking, but as a child she'd displayed an unusual ability to read languages others could not. More recently, she'd noticed potential new powers manifesting by making her eyes glow when agitated. Herrick had predicted that would happen, but he'd had no answer as to why.

A huge black shadow rolled across her from above, then disappeared again.

Rather than looking up this time, she reached over her shoulders and slid her hand inside the backpack. She curled her fingers around the hilt and asked, "Will you come to me, *Lann an Cheartais?*"

Humming immediately ceased.

The hilt felt cold, much like a normal sword. Was that a good sign? She tried to withdraw it, but she might as well have been attempting to pull Lancelot's sword from stone.

That brat on her back wouldn't budge.

She pulled her hand away and shouldn't have felt rejected. But she did.

Frustrating didn't cover how useless she felt at the moment. Herrick might be angry she'd even brought the sword if she couldn't use it. She'd sparred with Herrick from very small until she departed the Caucasus at nineteen to study at a university in England, all part of performing her ultimate duty. She'd trained additionally in martial arts. Hand her any normal sword and she'd hold her own with a worthy opponent.

The *Lann an Cheartais, or Blade of Justice,* demanded more expertise than that of a human-forged blade, which had been fired and beaten into shape the usual way. This one had been imbued with power for the first female to swing it.

Based on the shadows being thrown around her from a potential predator overhead, she reached for a switchblade in a pocket of her wool pants.

The shadow began to shrink. The bird descended closer to the ground.

Or to its prey.

Casidhe tilted her head back.

A monster vulture circled around her. It looked to have a wingspan of twelve feet.

What natural vulture grew that large?

That eagle-shaped head didn't fit any other vulture she'd ever seen.

She glanced around for something dead that might be drawing it in. A carcass. Anything a scavenger would be interested in besides her very much alive body.

No dead body of any kind in sight for as far as she could see.

On the vulture's next low swoop, hairs lifted on her arms. She would not harm a natural creature who did not threaten her life, but this thing could carry a tur off a mountain, if the goat-like animal wandered to the western side of the

Caucasus.

At five-eight, she was no tiny woman, but she weighed less than a male tur and had a bad feeling about this vulture's fixation with her.

Picking up her pace a bit, she tried to not appear as if she ran since running around most predators only excited them.

The damn sword began humming again.

Really?

Keeping an eye on the vulture as it circled high in the air, she began to think it might have dismissed her.

Rejected again. First the sword and now the vulture.

Her ego could only take so much, but she'd happily accept being dissed by that bird if it continued flying away. Just to be safe, she pocketed the knife, which would require close combat, and dipped down to pick up a rock the size of a tennis ball. She had a strong arm and a decent ability to strike a target.

The giant silhouette began to move away from her. Flipping the rock in the air as she hiked over the rugged land, she caught it, smiling over surviving the vulture.

The thought had no sooner cleared her mind when the vulture having flown far out in front of her now banked left in a wide arc, turning right back at her.

She could hardly make out its shape against the dark mountain backdrop. She'd never feared darkness, but terror gripped her at being ripped to pieces by a bird when she could barely see her hand.

Picking up her pace, she dipped into a gulley, then twisted to look up again.

The silhouette changed from gliding up high to the bird now angling her way and folding its wings to dive.

Jumping from the gulley, she took off running hard. No mystique left at this point.

She was prey.

Casidhe ran, leaping over rocks and searching for any place she could shield herself from attack. Her backpack banged against her body and slowed her down.

A loud screech echoed through the valley.

Was it angry at her for running?

She knew the history of the sword buzzing on her back and of the dragon-shifter female who had died protecting her family with it. She knew of the Dragani War from a spoken history passed down from generation to generation of squire families.

She could rattle off the smallest details.

What she didn't know was how to coax a pig-headed majikal weapon out of its sheath for any hope of saving her butt right now.

No one would know her story. The giant predator would drag her off to pick her bones. A shudder ran through at that vision.

The vulture squawked again.

Would Herrick find the sword once she died?

She'd made it over large boulders and rocks the size of basketballs, but one no bigger than her fist tripped her up. She went sprawling across loose stones and dirt. The rock she'd clutched fell from her fingers and her backpack slid to one side. Torn skin on her palms and face bore the brunt of her misstep.

She looked over her shoulder at the dark sky, scrambling to get back to her feet.

The bird shot toward her like a heat-seeking missile.

CHAPTER 8

DAEGAN TELEPORTED INTO TREOIR REALM with the Beladors who had stood with him in Atlanta during the Ferris wheel incident. Each one appeared near where he stood on the grounds leading up to Treoir Castle.

Belador guards in the realm came running up.

Daegan lifted his hand to halt his guards, then addressed the men standing with him. "As soon as I meet with my Council of Seven, we'll have a plan for how to protect our people in the human realm. I realize you have families, some of whom are human, and worry for their safety. Would you prefer to stay here until I know more or return right away?"

Vincent said, "I speak for myself, but I'm pretty sure many here agree. I wish to return to Atlanta and protect our people, but I would like to move my human family out of there."

The other five nodded in agreement.

"Very well, I shall teleport you back. I'll inform Trey McCree of our plan which will address the human family members first. He'll alert you immediately. You will have to shield your presence from humans who might recognize you after tonight, especially with media filming everything. Work only in pairs. Trey will schedule times for you to check in. Do not miss those."

"Yes, sir," replied all around.

Daegan didn't like sending them back without him to protect his Beladors, but with everything going to hell, they would be targets after tonight. He had no choice but to comply with their wishes and instructed, "Put your hand on the shoulder next to you. Vincent, envision a specific place for me to teleport your team where you can appear safely." Once they all clamped a shoulder and Vincent nodded, Daegan sent them on their way.

He turned to Allyn, the guard in charge of Beladors on Treoir. "I want an accounting of how many visitors we can accommodate to spend an extended time here."

The guards glanced at each other, but Allyn ordered, "You heard him. Get busy. I want all applicable information to me in thirty minutes."

"Thank you," Daegan said, striding away.

Before he made three steps, Allyn called out, "Sir? The dragon in the dungeon is making loud noises."

Daegan had forgotten about that one. "Has he spoken?"

"No, sir. He bangs around and ices all the surfaces in the dungeon. Our warriors fear he will eat them when they deliver food. Tzader took over that task when he learned I had been feeding the dragon. I argued, but Tzader reminded me he was immortal where I am not."

"I shall deal with it," Daegan said, sighing. Turning for the castle, he called telepathically to Tristan, who was still in the human realm. *I had to teleport to Treoir. What is your status?*

Not good, boss. I arrived in Sandy Springs to find a juiced-up troll tossing Devon off a building. I couldn't get to them fast enough to stop him, but I had six Beladors below use their kinetics to prevent Devon from hitting the ground head-first. The humans saw it all. I'm sorry.

Don't apologize, Tristan. I had a similar situation. We have much to discuss. Bring any Belador whose identity was exposed here if you feel they're in danger and they wish to leave. I'm calling an immediate meeting of the council. Tzader and Brina are, of course, here in Treoir. Find the other four council members and teleport them here. Contact me if you require assistance.

Okay, boss.

There had been many possible outcomes for tonight in Daegan's mind, but tonight had been what Tristan would call a clusterfuck.

Bile rushed up his throat at the terror Renata suffered. The longer Imortiks held her captive, the more she would endure. Ruadh had not calmed, still banging at Daegan to free his dragon and destroy their enemies.

If only he could. But with all his power, he'd still left without freeing Renata.

Just as he'd been helpless to protect his family while trapped in TÅµr Medb.

What good was it to be a dragon, the most powerful one to live, and not be able to defend those who looked to him for protection?

Shaking with fury, Daegan teleported to the top of the highest point in Treoir, far from the castle. His fisted hands shook with fury. He dropped his head back to roar. Fire burst from his mouth, shooting high in the air.

Faces of his family flew through his mind. Then Renata's.

He had held the peace for years and years only to lose everything. Blood colored his world, pounding his failures until his knees threatened to buckle under the weight of memories turned into nightmares. They were all dead and gone.

He screamed, *"Noooo!"* Fire joined the words, blasting his anguish and fury.

Ruadh had stilled and now asked telepathically, *Better now?*

"No!" Daegan shouted out loud. "Not until all those who have harmed mine pay with their lives."

Release me, Ruadh snarled. *I will burn them all.*

Daegan lowered his arms and heaved hard breaths. "If only I could do so, old friend. We will have our chance, but I will not win this battle if I allow them to kill you or see any weakness. You have been patient. Shift and return to the castle. I need this time to clear my head."

With that, Daegan's red dragon burst forth and blasted out a stream of fire far greater than Daegan could do in human form. Ruadh lowered his body then leaped from the cliff and flew over valleys between the mountains. He soared over the gryphon village where the Alterants living there waved and called out to him.

As they crossed the great island of Treoir realm, Daegan surveyed his people. His to protect and he would not let them down. Never again.

As Ruadh approached the castle grounds, guards looked up, no doubt catching the sound of his giant wings.

Guards shouted at each other, scattering as they opened a wide landing area.

Ruadh set his wings and landed in two steps.

Daegan thanked his dragon and shifted into his human form, clothing himself in jeans and a long-sleeved pullover as he headed to the castle. Once he climbed the steps, he pushed open the tall double doors with a shove of his hand.

"Garwyli!"

A door opened and closed down one hall off to the left of the main entrance. Loud grumbling approached. The old druid eventually rounded the corner. Snowy hair hung to his waist, almost blending into the robe of the same color. He carried one of the chronicles from Daegan's family library, which Daegan had only recently discovered hidden in the realm of Scamall.

"What is it, dragon?" Garwyli asked in a gruff tone followed by an amused smile. He liked to poke at Daegan by calling him a dragon.

Daegan could not humor the old druid today as he normally would. "'Tis not good, Garwyli."

That's when the druid realized Daegan's serious mood. This time, Garwyli's thick white eyebrows pulled together and he spoke with quiet reservation. "What has happened?"

"I have exposed us to the humans," Daegan admitted.

That admission lifted Garwyli's eyebrows. "How did that happen?"

"By trying to rescue one of ours." Daegan should feel more guilt for his part, but he could not justify keeping his people hidden over saving one life.

"Some may question rescuing one when considering the needs of the many—"

"No." Daegan turned his glare to Garwyli. "The needs of the many do not take precedence over the needs of the few. I will not sacrifice anyone. Even one life matters. The Beladors cannot remain hidden forever. I would have preferred such, but nothing ever stays the same in any life, I have learned. We will get through this."

Garwyli gave Daegan a long look, one of assessment. At the end, the druid nodded. "'Tis the right of it. How can I help ya?"

"Have you ever heard of an Imortik?"

Garwyli's wrinkled eyes widened. "Not in many a century. Long ago, they were locked away in an alternate world. That happened before either of us were children."

Not for the first time, Daegan wondered at Garwyli's age. He'd never known a druid to live so long besides Cathbad, a dark druid who had gone into a deep sleep then reincarnated recently with Queen Maeve in her realm.

Thinking of Cathbad, a powerful being who had lived thousands of years, brought Daegan back to the upcoming meeting with his Council of Seven. "We have to determine who is behind the Imortiks and how to locate two volumes of a grimoire related to them. I need you to locate everything you can on the Imortiks and bring it to the meeting. The rest of the council should be here soon."

"Do ya fear some Imortiks will escape?" Garwyli sounded appalled at the very idea.

Daegan's tone deepened. "Worse. Some have absolutely escaped."

What little color painted that old face leached out. Garwyli whispered, "'Tis not possible."

"I assure you it is. I met one while trying to save Renata. He controlled her body."

Garwyli rubbed his forehead. "I need some time to dig through all the chronicles."

"We cannot waste a minute. At least two of our people

have been attacked by these things." Daegan realized he had not asked Tristan what happened to Devon. With Tristan busy rounding up the council, Daegan would wait for a full report with everyone present.

Sparing Daegan a worried glance, Garwyli said, "I'll return quickly with all I can find."

As the druid tottered away, Daegan turned his mind to the closest he had to blood relations. His great niece from many generations, Brina, and her new mate, Tzader, ruled as king and queen of Treoir with Daegan remaining in a patriarchal role as dragon king.

Belador power originated with a blood Treoir living in this realm, which at the moment was Brina and the twin babes she carried.

He called out telepathically, *Tzader, I have called a council meeting. Tristan is bringing the others. I wish for you and Brina to join us, if she is available.*

Tzader called back, *Brina is resting, but she'll have both of our heads if I fail to wake her. Would you call me when everyone is assembled?*

Yes.

Tzader also asked, *Would you see what you can do about keeping that damn dragon quiet? The whole castle shakes and disturbs her rest.*

Daegan gritted his teeth at the stubborn beast locked away below ground. *I will deal with him.*

He could understand the dragon shifter wanting to be freed, but that one had yet to shift to human form or communicate with Daegan, even though he'd saved the beast from Scamall. No, Daegan empathized more with Tzader at the moment. With Brina so close to birthing, she slept in spurts. Once the babes were born, she'd again enjoy the vitality befitting a Belador warrior queen.

Those two would be the first children of Daegan's bloodline he would see born in thousands of years. He wished to hold them in his arms and know a joy only births can bring a family.

They would be descendants of his sister Jennyver.

His chest ached with the reminder of losing her, Lesley, and his father. He swore to himself he would not fail these innocents the way he'd left his family vulnerable by allowing Queen Maeve to capture him.

He had to find Renata and any others the Imortik master held captive.

The Treoir realm could have shielded all the Beladors and their families centuries ago, but not today. Belador warriors were spread across the human world with their families and—*BOOM!*

The castle floor shook beneath his feet.

Daegan teleported to the dungeon. He'd saved the ice dragon's life when he found him in the realm, living a life under a cruel master who had captured him. Like Daegan, this dragon had spent the past two thousand years hidden from all he'd known.

Daegan tried to keep that in mind as the annoying beast refused to simply shift into human form so they could talk or speak to him telepathically in any form. He would prefer to not house that dragon in the dungeon, but Daegan wanted confirmation of his identity and frame of mind before freeing him around those on Treoir Island.

It had been many centuries since being free and they had not known each other well back then.

He might be wrong, but Daegan believed this dragon to be Skarde, the younger of the two male ice dragons.

No other dragon from Daegan's time could teleport as he could, but all possessed the ability to speak out loud as a dragon or telepathically. The fact that this one had not shown an interest in communicating reinforced Daegan's decision to keep him contained.

He could not risk bringing an enemy inside Treoir. When Daegan last spoke to his father, the ice dragons were mounting an attack.

As soon as Daegan appeared in the Treoir dungeon, he felt the frigid change in temperature. He shook his head at the walls, ceiling, and ground covered in ice. He had taken it upon himself to remake this area so it would be habitable for any dragon. A forty-foot-high ceiling stretched across an area seventy feet wide by one hundred feet deep, with a granite floor and stone walls. He'd informed Skarde how to make the lights come on and go dark. He'd provided a bed, chairs, and food for his human form, none of which had been used.

His dragon had fed on a diet of buffalo. Tristan had teleported a small herd to Treoir for those who had to feed the dragon once every two to three days.

Daegan had also provided a soft earth foundation for the last fifty feet at the rear of the dungeon, which Ruadh had suggested for sleeping in dragon form.

Short of being freed, this ice dragon had been treated well and given a pretty nice lair for an unappreciative visitor.

Deep into the dark area against the back wall, Skarde's dragon's scales and wings had an iridescent color that shifted from blue to violet. His massive body lay curled on the ground as if sleeping. A lie.

Two searing blue eyes with vertical black irises stared at Daegan.

The dragon lifted his massive tail and thumped it hard. The room shook and ice broke away from the ceiling, pounding as it hit all around.

Daegan didn't lift a finger to prevent the chunks from hitting him. When the ice hit his body, it sizzled and melted.

An earth dragon could have caused much more damage, but Daegan would not tolerate this one bothering Brina. "I would have expected ya to be askin' to leave here by now."

The bright blue glare didn't change.

Daegan tried reaching the human inside the dragon again. "My people have treated you well, as have I. All I have asked of you is to speak to me. If you have forgotten how to shift into human form, it will come. But you cannot tell me you are unable to speak either out loud or telepathically."

Lifting his big head and long neck first, Skarde's dragon

continued rising until he sat balanced between his tail and rear legs. Then he dropped forward, standing on all four legs.

He opened his wings as if testing them and flapped, causing sparks to flick from the wings.

Skarde had enough room to move around in here and stretch, but not to fly. Daegan would take this dragon out to fly if Skarde would simply communicate. He had to know if this ice dragon presented a threat to his people.

"What is it going to be ... *Skarde*?" Daegan caught enough surprise in the dragon's eyes to confirm he had been correct. "I will treat you fairly if you can show me that my people will not be harmed."

In reply, Skarde's dragon reared back and blew out a stream of icy air at Daegan.

Ruadh growled as Daegan stood there while layers of ice piled waist-deep in the room. It would have frozen a human, and some nonhumans, to death in seconds.

Daegan soothed Ruadh silently with, *I wish to give this one a chance to meet me halfway.*

Ruadh replied, *Ice dragon no longer ally.*

Perhaps he will be once he realizes the world he now lives in requires allies.

Unconvinced, Ruadh grumbled but settled down. Daegan opened his arms out wide and placed his hands on the cold surface, sending his energy in every direction.

The ice melted quickly until the room flooded, pooling around the ice dragon where the floor dropped off in the back.

Ruadh might be right, but Daegan wanted powerful allies with what he saw coming for supernaturals now exposed to humans.

The last time he'd seen his father, Daegan had planned to meet with the ice dragon clan to find out who had started the Dragani War.

Someone who had been able to emulate Daegan's dragon to attack his allies.

He'd expected the ice dragons to be reasonable back then.

He'd also expected to return from TÅµr Medb with his sister, not to spend eternity cursed into the shape of a dragon throne.

More angry now than when he'd arrived, Daegan said, "Enjoy your pond, Skarde. I will not remove it until ya come to your senses and decide to talk. Continue to bash the ground and create problems with the castle and ya will land somewhere less comfortable."

Daegan teleported out of the dungeon and up to the entrance of the castle again. When he appeared, Tzader, Evalle, and Tristan were in a shouting match. Storm stood next to Evalle observing.

"*Silence!*" Daegan ordered. "What are you yelling about?"

They all turned to him.

Tristan said, "I was trying to explain about how the freaky being that attacked Devon inhabited his body like a demon would, but it didn't really seem to be a demon."

"Tell him about Devon," Evalle urged.

Tristan crossed his arms and gave Daegan a grim expression. "I didn't want to hold you up with all the details when you said you were here and calling a meeting. The troll had Devon's body wrapped up with cables. I told you how the troll was throwing Devon off the roof of a twelve-story building. I missed grabbing his feet by a hair. Also, at the last second before Devon's body dropped, this glowing yellow ghost-like creature jumped from the troll to Devon. The Beladors down below stopped Devon's body from hitting the ground, but the minute they touched his body, that yellow thing interfered with their powers."

"I ran into something similar, but it didn't take Noah's body," Evalle added.

Daegan frowned. "I have more information, but in the interest of time, we need to go through this once with everyone present."

"We have to hurry." Evalle grabbed Storm's hand, turning for the meeting room.

"True, but we have time."

Tristan's expression soured. "No we don't, boss."

Daegan had turned to leave and stopped. "Why not?"

"Once our people used their kinetics to hold Devon in place, I teleported down. Sen appeared. Have no idea who called him. Could have been one of Queen Maeve's warlocks. I saw two in the area. After ranting about dealing with our screwups, Sen said he was putting Devon into an isolation cell below VIPER, because the Tribunal wants to keep peace with you."

Daegan had his doubts of the Tribunal's sincerity about wanting peace. It was more like they feared him bringing in his goddess mother none of them knew.

Huffing out a deep breath of frustration, Daegan nodded. "I doubt they care about peace with me so much as fear of me calling in my mother. They have enough survival sense not to go up against an unknown deity."

Evalle called over her shoulder, "Tell him about the deadline, Tristan."

Daegan crossed his arms. "Whose deadline?"

Tristan explained, "Sen said if Devon did not recover from this possession in three days, the Tribunal had given him authority to kill any out-of-control supernaturals or those who were a threat. The Tribunal believes you would agree to not return Devon to the human realm if he's possessed. We have seventy-two hours before they terminate Devon. That deadline started an hour ago."

Daegan's head throbbed when he'd never suffered headaches. "I will not allow Sen or the Tribunal to kill Devon."

Storm turned Evalle back around. "Can you teleport Devon out of VIPER?"

"A valid question, but not possible," Daegan admitted. "I can teleport myself and anyone with me in or out of Tribunal meetings or the entrance to VIPER. There are many levels I can't access. I have recently discovered that VIPER and the Tribunal were created and warded by multiple deities. My guess is different ones have access to everything, but probably no one can go everywhere. Not a trusting group."

"What deities?" Storm's eyes darkened until they appeared black against his teak-colored skin from his mix of Navajo and Ashaninka blood.

"I am not sure, but Macha claimed she played a role in building the Tribunal realm," Daegan replied.

"We'll find no sympathizers there," Evalle grumbled, anger sparking in her voice. "What about Maeve and Cathbad?"

Daegan confirmed, "No. VIPER had not been created when those two faked their deaths to reincarnate in today's world many centuries later."

Tristan shook his head and started toward Evalle. "We need to get everyone together."

Daegan would love to shift and rain hellfire on Sen, but killing the Tribunal's enforcer would start war on a new front.

CHAPTER 9

DAEGAN'S LONG STRIDES ATE UP distance on his way to their meeting area. Tzader stayed in stride with him with Evalle, Tristan, and Storm close behind, their footsteps echoing off the marble floors.

Built powerfully, Tzader had been a deadly match the first time he and Daegan faced off with swords in a dream walk. His niece had clearly chosen Tzader for more than his striking looks and muscled body. Intelligence blazed from almost-black eyes set in his deep-brown face. His bald head reminded Daegan of a foreign intruder he once fought.

Taking in the group, Daegan asked, "Are Quinn and Adrianna here?"

Tzader cut a quick glance at him. "Quinn's not here. Tristan brought Adrianna, Storm, and Evalle. Adrianna is with Brina. Once Tristan shared what happened to Devon, Quinn stayed behind to visit VIPER and find out anything he can on Devon."

"Is Brina available?"

"Yes," Tzader confirmed, but frowned as he did. "Much as I'd rather spare her all of this, she's furious at Beladors being attacked."

That man had an unenviable job of trying to care for a hardheaded warrior queen with her due date so close. But Tzader had battled a castle warded against him when Macha had stood between him and Brina for four years. The man could handle anything.

Daegan slowed and said, "Give me a moment to speak with Quinn and find out if he has anything yet on Devon."

Always quick to pick up on Daegan's frame of mind, Tristan said, "Let's get everyone to the council meeting room."

Allowing them to continue on, Daegan called out telepathically. *I need your help, Quinn.*

You have it, Daegan. What can I do?

Daegan explained what had happened at the Ferris wheel. He added what Tristan had shared and warned, *Take care to avoid contact with these Imortiks. Devon's body may be host to one.*

In a wry voice, Quinn replied, *I've already found that out by trying to mind lock. I was with Evalle when one of those things had Noah. The mind lock turned into ... a painful lesson. I found out nothing beyond blind hate and screaming. I'm almost to VIPER. What do you want me to do about Devon?*

The idea of jumping into the mind of a vicious being such as the Imortik master gave Daegan cold chills. *Push Sen to confirm that Devon is safe and will remain so. If he refuses, then demand an immediate meeting with the Tribunal. Make it clear to all of them if I do not hear back from you in two hours or less, I will be the next one they face. I am fine with them holding Devon in an isolated location so long as he is not mistreated. I would like to question this Imortik siphoning off Devon's energy.*

Quinn pointed out, *That might not be such a good idea, because the Imortik could jump to you, based on what Tristan described. I could try mind lock again on Devon this time.*

No. Thank you for offering, Quinn, but we need you whole. I will wait to see if we have other options before I meet with Devon.

Understood, Daegan, but whatever you think that creature can do to me he could also do to you, correct?

Not necessarily. I will explain more, but their master wants me to find two volumes of a grimoire and deliver those to him in exchange for freeing our people. I believe he will continue capturing more in the meantime.

Quinn asked, *You believe him?*

Of course not, but that is why one of his followers would be foolish to touch me.

That makes sense, Quinn agreed. *I'll let you know what I find out.*

One more thing, Quinn.

Yes?

While with Sen, ask him about the Immortuos Grimoire volume placed in the VIPER vault twelve hundred years ago. I'd like to know where it was stolen from.

Will do.

When the communication ended, Daegan teleported to his meeting room where his council stood in a wide circle, leaving the center of the room open. They had all been present when he created a round table with majik just for these meetings. Daegan raised a hand and called forth the table. Cyrillic symbols appeared on the polished wood and bronze surface. Each six-inch-tall letter had been inserted near the edge, continuing all the way around until joining the last stroke with the first.

Eight chairs appeared next. Seven had tall backs with a different name carved into each and soft deerskin seats. He'd crafted his chair a bit larger to accommodate his size. The fierce dragon carved into the back of his seat had been for Ruadh, who would always share his place.

The Cyrillic symbols embedded in the surface assured all discussion around this table remained secret while seated here, but he trusted every council member with his life.

They'd held Daegan's life in their hands the day they'd gone rogue to break into TÅµr Medb and steal his dragon from the queen's throne room. Every one of them had taken that risk knowing they would face Macha's wrath.

That had been before Adrianna broke the curse after they delivered the dragon throne to Treoir realm. Macha showed up as his mighty beast roared to life.

Daegan tossed her out of Treoir. That had been a satisfying moment, but not as much as making Queen Maeve pay one day for what she'd cost him.

Once Tzader had Brina eased into her chair that had been pushed back from the table to allow room for her middle, Daegan's flame-haired niece asked, "What is going on in the human world?"

Adrianna spoke up. "I shared with Brina what Evalle told me about Noah. We may be able to shut down the exposure of supernatural beings with some creative public relations effort. Maybe get Tristan's friend to help us out."

Tristan leaned in, ready to talk, but Daegan lifted a hand, asking for a moment. When his second eased back, Daegan said, "'Tis more complicated than you know. Too much has transpired that cannot be quelled at this point."

Adrianna LaFontaine, a Sterling witch and in possession of an ancient power known as Witchlock, sat back with a confused expression.

Tristan had a sour look in his face.

Guilt danced through Evalle's gaze.

Daegan wanted to alleviate their concerns first. "Evalle and Tristan are not to blame for exposing us tonight. I condone every action taken in effort to save our Beladors and do not regret trying to save one as well. Now that no one here carries more blame than me, I would have everyone hear what Tristan and Evalle have to report."

"I told you most of mine," Tristan started.

Tzader glanced at him. "Brina and Adrianna were not present."

"Right." Tristan caught everyone up with what he'd shared at the entrance, ending with, "Quinn is on his way to find out more on Devon."

Evalle cleared her throat and shared what had happened in Buckhead with Noah. She grimaced at that. "When I rushed forward to grab Noah, Quinn stopped me."

Letting out a groan, Storm muttered, "Remind me to thank him."

She arched a chastising eyebrow at her mate, who shrugged, clearly not repentant. He smiled and she rolled her eyes, continuing. "Anyhow, Quinn tried to use mind lock to get inside the hooded guy's head, but he ran into something bad that took Quinn to his knees. Then ... " She paused to glance at Storm as she finished, "I went after the guy with the robe to free Noah."

Storm cupped a hand over his eyes, but said nothing.

Evalle lifted her shoulders in a what-else-could-she-do motion and explained how she'd broken the chain and freed Noah. "Power in that chain knocked me fifteen feet back. When I came to, Quinn was coming out of his own disorientation."

She cut her eyes to the side at Storm who lowered his hand and shook his head a little, but said nothing more. Daegan had been around when Storm witnessed his mate go through far worse and come out stronger.

Brina asked, "What about Noah?"

Evalle explained, "It was mad chaos, but long story short, Quinn called in some of our people on local law enforcement who took Noah to a healer and Adrianna showed up to rescue us." She sent a smile to the witch.

A petite powerhouse with white-blond hair and a beautiful face, Adrianna picked up the thread. "Trey contacted me and caught me up. I was in the area of Buckhead. When I got there, Evalle spoke telepathically to the second Belador law officer. He created a disturbance which allowed me to cloak the three of us to walk away."

Storm sat forward, crossing his arms on the table. "What happened to you, Daegan?"

Drilling his fingers against the polished surface, Daegan had been considering Evalle and Tristan's report. "We were all pulled toward traps. Mine used Renata as bait." He described what happened at the Ferris wheel.

"SWAT showed up?" Tristan groaned. "That's an elite group to handle the most dangerous local law enforcement operations. Yep, we're officially outed, but how did you get away from that glowing yellow being?"

Daegan rubbed his forehead where a throbbing sensation

kept building between his temples. "The one I encountered called himself an Imortik and said he would trade our people for two volumes of some grimoire. He also said he'd made the same offer to other powerful beings whose followers he had as well. The person who shows up with the two volumes receives all the captives."

"What if he deals with someone like Queen Maeve?" Evalle worried aloud.

"That is one concern, but I fear we will have more who can end up with our Beladors if we fail to free them."

Brina asked the question on everyone's face. "Just what is an Imortik, Uncle?"

"I have no more of an answer than what I have described, but ... " Daegan paused in mid-sentence. He called out, "Garwyli, please join me at the council table."

In the next moment, Garwyli walked into the room as if he'd been standing just outside, which wasn't the case. He could teleport anywhere within the Treoir realm, but the old guy preferred to walk.

"What you be needin', dragon?" Garwyli asked as usual, but without the humor often lacing his voice. "I am not even close to finishin' your da's chronicles."

"I understand. Please take Quinn's empty seat and join this discussion. We all need your knowledge."

Garwyli went straight to the chair and seated himself. When he did, his gaze studied the table and air around him. When he looked at Daegan, his eyebrows climbed his forehead. "'Tis a protected area?"

Daegan nodded. "Nothing said here leaves this area unless I allow it."

First pushing his long beard off the table, the druid clasped his hands on the polished surface and waited.

Daegan filled Garwyli in on the parts he'd not been able to provide earlier, including a rundown of Tristan and Evalle's events in Atlanta. He asked the druid, "Have you found out more about the Imortiks? What can you tell all of us about these beings and the two volumes the Imortik master wants?"

A look of sadness passed over Garwyli's face. "I do know more. As I read, I recalled bits and pieces from memory as well. I shall start at the beginning. Three hundred years before Daegan's birth, during a dark period, a sorcerer and a goddess, neither of which I know the names of, joined up to create a super force of wendingos, pishachas, nidhogg, whatever ... " Garwyli waved his hand as if to encompass all such creatures. "These creatures were originally flesh eaters, which the grimoire majik formula turned into power eaters. The most powerful of gods and goddesses were not concerned until one Imortik evolved more than expected and overpowered a Fae."

Shock rode every face around the table. Daegan's included.

Unaffected by the horror he'd just raised, Garwyli went on explaining, "That's when the dragon families called to the god or goddess specifically protecting each of them. As we all know, deities rarely become allies unless they fear something. They agreed to create a *mors murum*." Before anyone could ask, Garwyli supplied the translation. "That's Latin for *death wall*. The deities told the dragon families to locate the Immortuos Grimoire and figure a way to lock up the Imortiks in the *mors murum*, then separate the grimoire into three parts."

Tzader had said little until now. "Let me get this straight. The Imortiks were forced behind the death wall, locked inside a place they could not escape, but some have managed to do so even without all three volumes together, correct?"

Garwyli nodded. "Each volume is capable of causing a rift in the death wall if enough majik in that volume is translated and put into action." He returned to explaining the history. "The original monstrosities created continued changing and morphing into abominations capable of taking over a supernatural's body, including the powers associated with that body. After taking over that Fae victim, that monster turned on its creators, before becoming the master of Imortiks, which spread out across what is today known as

Europe, Russia, and Asia."

Brina held folded fingers to her chin, slowly shaking her head. "The fools who started this deserved what they got."

"True." Garwyli lifted a finger, drawing attention back to him. "It required three powerful dragon houses to prevent the human world from being overrun and destroyed. I will search deeper into your family's chronicles, Daegan, but the earliest volumes from that time were written in a language that preceded even the Treoir language."

Daegan found that hard to believe. "Are ya sayin' *you* cannot translate it?"

"Not yet. I will not give up, but I shall focus on what I am able to translate first and search for any mention of the grimoire volumes in those chronicles."

Adrianna tilted her head toward the druid. "How did the dragon families even figure out where to start looking once they had the support of the deities?"

"Best that I can recall, a follower of the sorcerer partly behind this went to the ice dragons and pleaded for help. That's how the dragon families first learned of the book of ancient majik called the Immortuos Grimoire. The Imortiks were named as such because it was believed these beings could not be killed. The sorcerer master was believed to have been overtaken by the Fae Imortik. A goddess, identity not known, had partnered with the sorcerer and was believed to have escaped to her realm to avoid retribution."

"So this goddess might still be around?" Evalle asked, sounding sick at the possibility. "If so, do we know who she is?"

"Most likely the goddess still exists, but her identity has been kept hidden, which makes me think she only managed to escape because she aided the other deities in containing the Imortiks." Seeming to compose himself, Garwyli ran a hand over his white hair before clasping his hands again. He swallowed hard as if his throat had become dry from speaking.

Daegan whispered a command and drinks appeared

around the table.

The druid smiled his thanks, took a sip of his water, and continued. "The sorcerer and goddess created that original grimoire. The complete Immortuos Grimoire was believed to control the Imortiks. The Imortik master Daegan met up with likely does have some power over those beings he's helping to escape through a rift, but I suspect no one holds all the power without holding all three volumes."

"Why would you think that?" Adrianna asked.

"When the three dragon families joined forces and located the grimoire, they still did not know how to kill the Imortiks. They took the whole grimoire to an oracle and explained their problem. She spent five days and nights in a trance. When she regained consciousness, she read the pages of the grimoire with her blind eyes, warning that some Imortiks could become more dangerous if they were killed and evolved into a different form. She explained how to send them to the alternate world." Garwyli took a deep breath and on the exhale said, "'Tis all I have for now. I have much more to read."

"Wow, that's ... crazy stuff even for our world," Evalle muttered.

Brina offered, "I will help you read the Treoir chronicles, Garwyli."

"Thank you, child. I fear we will have to piece together much as some of what I related was from spoken history."

Daegan frowned. "We cannot kill them?"

"I have thought hard on this. I think the oracle told the dragon families that killing an Imortik, which had taken over a human body or a supernatural of less power, would likely result in true death. But killing one that had completed taking over a supernatural body ... could evolve into something worse or multiply, but I am not sure."

Everyone around the table groaned at that possibility. Daegan's headache thumped even harder. "Can you tell us more about how the dragon families stopped the Imortiks?"

Garwyli waited for silence then said, "Unfortunately,

the history may be lost with the grimoire volumes. Once the dragon leaders had it in hand, the oracle sent them to someone older than her who could translate the medieval scribblings to instruct the dragon families on how to trap and imprison Imortiks forever. She warned once they knew what to do they should gather every powerful being from druids to deities they could find to lock the Imortiks away or they would fail."

Storm had listened intently with solemn quiet. "Would you explain again about the three volumes?"

"Aye. The oracle instructed the three dragon kings present that once the Imortiks were imprisoned, they should split the grimoire into three volumes. Each dragon king would take a volume to hide so the grimoire would never again return to power."

Tristan lifted a hand, politely asking for the floor. "If that's the case, how can one volume of the grimoire be on the loose right now?"

"I wish I had that answer, Tristan," the druid replied. "One of the volumes was found twelve hundred years ago and enough translated to disrupt the majik holding the wall in place. A crack formed, allowing Imortiks to begin escaping as they are currently doing. That volume was located, the escaped Imortiks sent back to their prison, and the wall sealed once more."

Brina grimaced as she rubbed her round middle. "Where be that volume?"

Daegan explained, "When I told the Imortik master I had no idea where to look, he said my people stole a volume and gave it to VIPER. That I should start there. I've asked Quinn to inquire about that volume when he meets with Sen. With one volume in VIPER's vault and the Imortik master possessing a second one, that points to locating only the third volume."

Daegan rubbed his forehead. "What three dragon families were involved, Garwyli?"

"Yours or King Gruffyn's ancestors, King Eógan's ice

dragon ancestors, and those of the Egyptian earth dragons ruled by King Anasch."

Tzader had kept his arm on Brina's shoulder, no doubt remaining on high alert for any change with her. "Which volume was found if the dragon families kept them hidden?"

"Good question, Tzader." Brina patted his hand then returned her hand to gently smoothing over her stomach.

Garwyli leaned forward, lifting both hands. "'Twas all kept secret. I only recall snippets I picked up at different times over the centuries, but I rarely leave this realm, which limits what I can learn firsthand."

Daegan pulled his hand down from his forehead. "Based on the Imortik master's accusation, I assume the volume in the vault might have belonged to our family."

"Logical, but not necessarily correct unless Quinn can confirm that," Garwyli countered.

Tristan slouched in his chair. "So much for hide all three volumes and keep the world safe. One is dangerous all by itself."

"'Tis worse with all three," Garwyli countered. "If you think of what is happening now as a crack in a huge dam holding back an ocean versus bringing all three volumes together and opening that dam all at once."

"Okay, point taken."

"My father told me where everything was, including his personal hoard," Daegan commented, thinking out loud. "Why not the hiding spot of our grimoire volume?"

Garwyli gave him a smile of understanding. "Ah, Daegan,'twas so long ago the king either did not consider it of current importance or forgot about it. Why would he mention something that should not have ever seen the light of day again? No problem existed for over twelve hundred years, not until now."

Quinn's voice came into Daegan's mind. *I have some news, if you're ready.*

Daegan announced to the council, "Quinn calls me. Please wait while I hear what he has to say." When everyone went silent, Daegan replied to his North American Maistir. *Tell me what you have, Quinn.*

While I was at VIPER, I was able to view Devon from outside a warded wall. One minute, he looks and talks like Devon. The next, he's grabbing his head and yelling in pain. I think whatever jumped from the troll to him still has Devon in its grip. The healers won't go near him.

Daegan had hoped for better news, but was not surprised by what he heard. *What about the grimoire volume being held in VIPER's vault?*

Quinn continued, *I asked Sen about it. He told me after he brought Devon there and discovered an Imortik had him, he was called out twice more to pick up Beladors taken by an Imortik. After that, he went to the Tribunal, asking what they knew about this. Loki told him about the Immortuos Grimoire and that one volume was in the vault. The Tribunal ordered him to share nothing about it with anyone. They felt the less shared, the better chance to keep those other two volumes hidden. Sen claims it looks like the Imortiks were focused primarily on Beladors. Said he has not been called out about a troll, warlock, or any other being yet. I went to the Tribunal. Loki was pretty agitated, not his normal happy self. He and the other two forbade any discussion of the Immortuos Grimoire, including the one volume in the vault.*

Who are the additional Beladors brought in? Daegan asked.

Sen would not show me the other two Beladors, but the names he gave me were two more out-of-town Beladors.

Was one of them named Renata?

Quinn answered, *No. I'll deal with contacting Belador families if we do not get them back alive, but I did tell Sen to contact me or you before taking any action. He said he'd take that under consideration.*

Daegan ground his teeth. Sen liked to talk, but he had yet to follow through with all that mouthing off. *Thank you, Quinn. Once we've finished here, I'll send everyone I can back to help in Atlanta. Evalle and Storm will fill you in on what we've discussed.*

That works for me, Quinn confirmed. *I need to remain in the human world right now.*

Once the voice vanished from his mind, Daegan told the group what Quinn had passed along.

Brina lifted a fist. "The Tribunal cannot have our people. What of VIPER's healers?"

"They won't touch Devon."

"Then we should have a chance with our healers," she persisted.

Garwyli stepped in before Daegan could say another word. "I do not recommend that, though I do share your concern for them."

"Why not?" Brina only needed a sword in hand to go with her fierce determination.

"We would put healers we need at risk. From what I recall, Imortiks would overtake a body then begin syphoning energy from it for the next week or so until the Imortik completely joined with the body's power and took solid form."

Daegan interjected, "The Imortik master said we had a fortnight to deliver both volumes for any hope of saving those taken today."

"Wait," Adrianna interrupted. "What is a fortnight?"

Garwyli, Brina, and Tzader replied, "Fourteen days."

"Clearly I'm not up on medieval terminology," she mumbled. "Thank you."

Smiling his sympathy at Adrianna, Garwyli finished, "That would mean every day after those two weeks, any new Beladors or other living beings captured in the meantime would be forever gone as well." Pausing for another drink of water, the druid said, "One more thing. If an Imortik went up against a powerful body too difficult to take, it would hold onto the body long enough to push its venomous energy inside."

Daegan sat forward. "What happens then? Would that person be a threat to others?"

"The venom remains in the body, which draws in other Imortiks. If enough of them overwhelm the poisoned one, they can kill the powerful being if they cannot overtake the body individually. Once they overtake a body, then yes, that person would be a threat to others."

Tristan's gaze lit with realization and shot to Daegan, who sent him a telepathic message. *Do not speak further about the venom at this moment.*

Frowning hard, Tristan replied with a silent, *Okay, boss.*

Garwyli had caught the exchange of looks between them, but added, "The Tribunal will have to work with you at some point if all three volumes combined are required to send the escaped Imortiks back behind the death wall."

Storm asked, "How is that going to be possible when we don't know who is behind the rift or where to find the missing volume?"

Garwyli offered encouraging words. "I do not know, Storm, but I trust in the intelligence and ability of this council. I will help you all I can and you will help Daegan find a way through this."

Rumblings of agreement circled the table.

Daegan wished to believe they could find a volume hidden thousands of years ago in one of three places, but they had so little going in their favor. For one thing, he had no idea if the grimoire had been created in book form, scroll, or some other form.

Still, no war had ever been won by starting from the point of doubt.

Adrianna's smooth forehead wrinkled with thought. "Who were the three deities who came together to stop the first Imortiks?"

Sighing loudly, Garwyli said, "I know of only one. Macha. I know about her only because I have been in this realm so long and recall her speaking of it at one time. She had been in conversation with other deities about who should manage supernaturals in the human world. That's when she and two others created the Tribunal realm where court is held."

Evalle fidgeted, not one to be still long. "Is there any chance Macha or Maeve is behind this even if Macha did help put Imortiks away? She probably cooperated back then for her own benefit. Now that she's been kicked off Treoir Island, she might have a different mindset to get back at Daegan and the Beladors."

"Good point Evalle," Daegan said. "But we must be careful in accusing any deity if we end up needing their help to stop the Imortiks."

Evalle groused, "I can see that. It's just that I keep waiting for Macha or Maeve to do something big."

Tristan asked, "Would the Tribunal stand back and let Macha or Maeve have their way if, as Evalle pointed out, they saw this as a chance to take us all down?"

"No." Garwyli shook his head. "Unless a deity joined up with one of those two, most would be livid about anyone creating a rift in the *mors murum* and would make even a deity's life extremely difficult. But on the chance a deity *is* behind this, you should look for the lesser beings who support them. 'Tis much easier to have a follower do their dirty work in the human realm than for one of them to risk being caught."

Looking disgusted, Tristan ran a hand through his hair. "Can you only imagine if crazy Maeve did get her hands on those volumes?"

More groaning around the table.

Tzader offered, "That's all good and fine, but we have a mess in the human world. I would hope you three know I'm not blaming anyone, just wanting to get ahead of the fallout."

Tilting his head toward Tzader, Daegan agreed, "You are correct. What do you suggest?"

Tzader calmly explained, "We have people inside many governments in the human world. I need to visit our Belador high up in the US government, who is involved with national security operations and make sure no one is mobilizing armed forces to kill anything that looks strange."

Brina grasped his arm. "Would ya be safe?"

He patted her hand. "Yes. I have a spot where Daegan can teleport me inside the building and not be seen. As soon as I call out telepathically to our contact, I expect to be brought in immediately. I'll probably be back here in less than an hour." Turning back to Daegan, Tzader said, "That doesn't address our Belador families, though."

Giving it a moment, Daegan made a decision he'd been chewing on, but he wanted to allow Brina to weigh in. "How many Belador family members do you estimate are in the southeastern part of the country around VIPER? Because this appears to be centralized near Atlanta for the moment."

Looking up and moving her lips in a silent calculation, Brina glanced at him. "I'm thinkin' it to be three hundred to three fifty. I've not taken count in a while. Could be over four hundred."

"How do you feel about housing the families in Treoir?"

"You don't have to ask, Uncle. These are our people. Of course we'll bring them here. Will that include the Belador warriors?"

"I will make it voluntary to come here with their families or remain in Atlanta."

"That is what we will do then," she declared.

Tzader stood. "I'm sure the national security group are working on this issue even as we speak, no matter how late it is. I need to get moving before this gets out of hand."

Daegan instructed, "Picture where you wish to arrive."

"Got it." Tzader vanished as soon as the words were out of his mouth.

Garwyli had been tapping his thumbs against each other, as if deep in thought. He turned to Daegan. "How soon will ya be leavin' to hunt the grimoire volumes?"

"Not until Tzader returns," Brina replied before Daegan did. "I do not mean to be oversteppin', Uncle, but I would rather you wait to hear from him. If he runs into a problem, you may be the only one to handle it and bring him back."

Daegan understood the worry in her voice. He had the same concern for every person here, who he considered family as much as Brina, Tzader, their babes, and all his people. If an hour or two would have solved this issue, he would not have returned to Treoir.

"You did not overstep, Niece. We are of the same mind," he assured her. She gave him a smile of thanks. "There's no point in me going to VIPER to ask for any more than Quinn has on that volume. I just have to find the third one, but no idea where to begin my search."

The druid said, "You may have ta do what ya been puttin' off."

"Explain," Daegan ordered, unsure what the old guy referenced.

"Ya been sayin' you're gonna track down yar history. Now would be the time to find the squire family. That person might have carried the stories from much farther back than what you were told."

Was he serious? Everyone stared at the druid as if he'd suggested this would be a great time for a vacation.

Garwyli scowled at them. "Doona question me when I know what I speak of." Swinging that sharp gaze at Daegan, the old guy said, "The original grimoire was created before your time. I will not stop until I find all I can in your family chronicles, but ya need more from the other dragon families."

Adrianna sat up as if she didn't already hold perfect posture. "Are you saying the volumes could have been hidden in places like the ice dragon castle and King Gruffyn's castle?"

Daegan doubted it would be so simple. "That would have made it too easy for enemies to find while ransacking the castles once kings fell from power."

Garwyli gave Daegan a shake of his head. "Ya think every dragon king's enemy hoped to find the king's hoard? I never heard of King Gruffyn's hoard being found until you saw your father's treasures in the Scamall realm, Daegan. Ya keep assumin' about how things happened during the centuries when you were captured. 'Tis hard to allow new ideas in a closed off place. 'Tis why I keep sayin' to find the person who carried the history."

"I just can't imagine ... "

"That yar family's history would have survived after all this time?" Garwyli finished. "What 'tis the harm of hunting the Luigsech family yar father told you he'd trusted?"

Evalle watched the two of them with a surprised expression. "Who's Luigsech?"

Garwyli suddenly lost his cockiness. "Er, I may have spoken a bit too much."

Daegan waved him off. "Anyone at this table is welcome to everything in the chronicles. Garwyli speaks of the last squire family loyal to my father. He feels if I locate the descendants of that human family today, they may be able to shed some light on gaps in my family history after I was captured."

"What all was in the chronicle about the Luigsech squire?" Adrianna asked Daegan.

"My father suspected a traitor among his inner circle and warned me against trusting the squire family we'd had for a long time."

"That traitor was Germanus, the guy who held me in Scamall, right?" Evalle asked in an even voice, but her hand fisted.

Storm reached over and covered that hand, murmuring something.

She relaxed her fingers and smiled at him. "I'm good."

"Yes," Daegan confirmed. "But I have a feeling there was more than one, because my father wrote that he had chosen a new squire family named Luigsech, which I should trust. Squires kept dragon family history by spoken word. My family chronicles are our intimate writings. Female squires were most important. Though many kingdoms educated only the men, dragon families held women in high regard for their sharp minds and intuitive abilities."

Adrianna spoke up. "If you'll give me anything you have on the Luigsech family from back in your day, like specific names and the location of your father's castle, I'll ask Isak to trace the lineage to current day."

Daegan gave Adrianna a smile of appreciation since she was not on the best of terms with Isak. "Thank you, Adrianna. The times have changed so much I have my doubts about the spoken history being preserved at all, but I will not turn down any potential information. I will contact you immediately if I locate those names." He said that only to appease Garwyli. Daegan had to get his hands on that third volume, not look for someone with obscure knowledge.

"Excuse me, Garwyli," Storm interrupted. "Why didn't everyone just destroy the grimoire?"

"'Tis often believed to be a greater danger in destroying an item with that much majikal influence." The old druid pushed a look at Daegan. "Do ya think the ice dragon in the dungeon can help?"

"Doubtful." Daegan shook his head. "I have yet to get him to say a word."

"Are you *sure* he can talk?" Storm asked.

"Yes, his dragon can speak and he can communicate with me telepathically. I am also sure he can shift, but is staying in dragon form where he feels most powerful if attacked."

"But you saved him from Scamall and gave him your blood when he was dying," Adrianna argued, clearly disgruntled with anyone who lacked appreciation for being saved by Daegan. She had been with all of them when they went to retrieve Evalle.

Daegan agreed. "With Imortiks threatening our people and the entire human world, I am out of patience, but that ice dragon sees me as an enemy. To force him to do anything would only deepen that belief." Standing up, Daegan announced, "I'll teleport anyone who is ready to return to Atlanta."

"I am," echoed around the room with the exception of Garwyli, Brina, and Tristan.

Tristan crossed his arms, waiting to hear what his duty would be.

Daegan instructed, "Everyone should continue working in pairs. Tristan will go with me to hunt for the grimoire."

Giving a decisive grunt of approval, Tristan let Daegan know he had guessed correctly. Considering what Daegan had fought in Atlanta, he would not go without backup again and risk this mission.

Not after that Imortik master had blocked his dragon powers and ability to teleport.

Once he teleported Evalle, Storm, and Adrianna to Atlanta, Daegan told Brina, "I know you can walk and teleport yourself, but I would prefer to teleport you to your room to wait on Tzader. I'm going back to the dungeon. Call me when Tzader returns."

Brina waved him off. "No need to fuss, Uncle. Garwyli and I go to the library. I will wait there." She smiled as Garwyli rose to his feet and gave her a hand getting out of the chair.

Brilliant, beautiful, and stubborn. She was definitely a female of his bloodline. Daegan glowered at her and she laughed as she left. "Find that book, Daegan. I want my people safe."

He shook his head and told Tristan, "I wish to get moving. I think we should—" He stopped short when he had a telepathic call from Tzader to return.

Tzader came into view and headed for Daegan with a furious expression. "We've got a major problem."

"Worse than Imortiks?" Tristan asked in a sarcastic tone.

"Possibly," Tzader snapped at him. He turned to Daegan. "Rumors are running through governments that a red dragon lives and is a danger to all of the world. There's probably a bounty on your head large enough to give someone their own hoard."

"They cannot prove I exist," Daegan argued.

"Yes, they can. There are hundreds of videos taken, plus eyewitness accounts of a red dragon burning a strip of forest in northern Ukraine just before daylight. I saw the films. It's unbelievably real."

This couldn't be happening again. Daegan roared, "I am the last of the red dragons and all others before me are gone."

Tzader held his hands up. "That may be, but every country

knows what happened in Atlanta and is up in arms. Their people are panicking. We have to keep you hidden. Whoever is behind this is fingering you."

Tristan jumped in. "We need to think about keeping you out of sight, boss."

"He's right. You can't leave Treoir, Daegan," Tzader said. "If someone identifies you to a hostile group, or worse, pushes you to shift, you could die before you teleported. Right now, a red dragon is on the top of every country's hit list."

Daegan knew only one way to lead and that was from the front. "Stay here and protect Brina. I am headed to Galway."

Tzader grabbed his bald head. "They'll be looking for you all over Europe. It will take nothing to get fighter jets to Ireland. With what happened in Atlanta, every country will send military, specifically air support, to take down a dragon."

"Thank you for going to find out what you could, Tzader, but I must find the grimoire volume. I will shield my identity. Keep our people as safe as you can and watch over my niece. You are the only one I would entrust with so great a treasure."

Sounding as blown as a horse run to ground, Tzader gave in. "Fine. Stay in touch and please don't fucking shift."

Daegan nodded, then walked out before any new conversation started.

Tristan followed him. "If that red dragon was not yours, which we know it wasn't, then it has to be a bait to draw you out."

"Agreed."

"Also, since that was not you and we have another dragon down below, who could the dragon in Ukraine be?"

Daegan slammed to a stop. His brain felt overloaded and ready to explode. "I have no idea, but I intend to find out for sure."

"Okay, boss, but if you shift, then I'm shifting into my gryphon to fly with you."

As Daegan prepared to teleport them to a spot he hoped

was still as secluded today as long ago, he heard a shout in his mind. *Save me.*

Stark pain, not physical, but of the heart, cried out.

Who had said that?

CHAPTER 10

CASIDHE JUMPED TO HER FEET after regaining her wits from sliding across the rough ground. She had no idea how to escape the giant vulture flying toward her from the twilight sky.

She needed to mentally prepare for what would happen next, but her mind went blank.

No help there.

While that could be construed as a positive to not think about dying, one more rejection from the universe and she'd snap.

The massive vulture opened its wings, slowing its descent to land perfectly, then hopped two steps and stopped. It stood there, majestic eagle-shaped head lifted to the wind. Then black pits for eyes glowered down at her as if she'd dared to enter the bird's kingdom.

What now?

Would it wait for her to die or help the process along?

She'd be damned if she would make killing her easy. Her irritating sword still hummed, content to remain in the sheath. Regaining her calm, in spite of her hands trembling and her breathing coming in gasps, she dusted herself off casually.

Only twenty feet away, the vulture took a step toward her.

Lifting her chin in defiance, she threatened, "I warn you there is a somethin' greater than you in these mountains. I am family. You do not want to piss *him* off."

The eagle head dropped down in a show of intimidation. Taking another step forward, the vulture indicated how little her words mattered.

She took a step back and glanced over her shoulder.

Well, hell. She stood near a drop-off with no idea how deep the black hole might be.

Had the bird been herding her in this direction?

Clenching her hands, she stood firm, ready to fight.

A sharp whistle streaked through the air.

The bird canted its head and turned in the direction of the sound. Then it took a hop and lifted off, flying so close to her as it passed that the wind blew her hair.

Was that vulture answering to a whistle?

She considered taking off running again, but she'd need to use her flashlight this time. That beacon would make tracking her very easy.

No, she'd stay right here for a few moments and hope the vulture had taken that whistle to mean something better than her for dinner.

Who would whistle for a ginormous vulture though?

A movement above her head drew her gaze up to where giant wings far larger than the vulture's carried a massive black silhouette, which dropped slowly to the ground and landed in almost the same spot the vulture had.

She had to bend her head back to take in the silver-gray dragon head and brilliant blue eyes glowing with black vertical slits.

In the next moment, power flushed around her.

She grinned and drew a breath of relief, rushing forward.

Herrick appeared in human form, wearing his usual leather clothing and fur vest. He opened his arms and caught her to him, his thick beard tickling her face. All her fears fled in the protection of the person she called father even though she wasn't his child. She had been no one's child, but he raised her and the Luigsechs had taught her all they knew of the dragon families.

His deep voice normally soothed her, but not the words he spoke this time. "You should not have come."

Her heart hit her feet. How could Herrick not be happy to

see her after ten years apart? Written messages had kept her close, but it was nothing like visiting in person.

She pulled out of his arms, exhausted from traveling nonstop to get here as fast as she could. "I don't understand."

Eyes still a bright blue even in human form, he said, "You risk bringin' the enemy to our door."

How could he think that? "I have not even told you why I'm here yet. What makes you think an enemy knows where I am?"

"They do not yet, but the seer told me you were comin' and Shannon's sword is active. The seer believes an enemy came to you, but she could not see the enemy once you struck out to travel here."

Casidhe thanked the dark for shielding any sign of disappointment washing over her from being chastised. She had only the family's best interest at heart and had never been careless. That seer had never liked Casidhe. Herrick needed to hear her out first.

Glancing around, she could see little in the moonless night besides the white beak tip of the vulture that had returned to stand near Herrick.

Keeping her tone even to hide the hurt, she spoke the words she'd been taught to use to indicate they should talk privately. "We should be speakin' in a quiet place."

Herrick's eyebrows lifted at that.

Really? Hadn't he just acted as if she'd brought the grim reaper with her? She rubbed the scratched skin and wiped grit from her face, anxious to hike to the castle and end this day. At least she wouldn't have to fight off any other attacks with a dragon shifter and overgrown vulture nearby.

Herrick seemed to just now take in her condition. "Did you fall?"

That sounded as if she were a klutz.

Sending a glare to the vulture, she mumbled sarcastically, "Your *pet* found chasin' after me entertainin'."

"Stian? No, he meant only to determine if you were an interloper."

"Stian?" she pushed out between clenched teeth.

Nodding at the vulture, Herrick said, "He is a griffon vulture from the Himalayas. I befriended him."

Sounded as if the vulture had taken her spot. "Well, it sure felt like he hunted me for dinner."

Herrick spoke to the bird in Gaelic and the vulture lifted its head, making a chortle sound.

Smiling like a proud father, Herrick's gaze returned to Casidhe. "Stian's favorite meal is carrion."

"So he would not attack a live bein'?"

"Oh, he would. I have trained him for eight years. He is unlike other griffon vultures. In fact, he is the alpha among those he convinced to follow him here."

No wonder the bird had a cocky attitude. She studied the tall profile. "Is he entirely natural?"

Herrick reminded her, "Did you not say you'd like a quiet place to speak?"

In other words, he didn't want to discuss the bird being natural, or not, out here. "That I did."

Staring off for a moment as if sorting through his thoughts, Herrick turned to her. "You have traveled far. Your trip to the castle shall be short."

All the sting and hurt she'd suffered fled under what she hoped he was saying. She smiled in anticipation. "Does that mean what I'm thinkin' it means?"

"It does." Herrick stepped back ten steps and called up his dragon. He could speak in this form as well and said, "Hold your arms out in front of you so I may grasp you easily."

"I remember." She'd rather ride on his back, but held her arms out.

Any dragon ride beat walking.

His dragon lifted off with Stian right behind him like a fighter pilot behind a larger aircraft. She didn't turn to watch as Herrick's dragon flew high then around, because remaining still was crucial to not being nicked or gouged by his dragon's sharp claws.

The sound of wings beating as he completed a wide arc

and now on approach from behind to grab Casidhe kicked her pulse into high gear.

One moment she stood on the ground and the next she was yanked up, backpack and all. His dragon climbed quickly to soar over the mountains. Wind buffeted her face and hands.

She laughed wildly for the first time in too long.

Her partner at the County Galway Families Centre, Fenella, always warned Casidhe she was missing out on her life by putting off living it.

Casidhe would always place duty ahead of fun.

But this, flying with a dragon, counted as living her life.

She wrapped her fingers around thick toes, marveling at how tough and hard they were to be holding her so gently. For this one moment in time, she soaked up peace and happiness.

But Herrick's words indicated that would not last long.

Too soon, the flight ended as his dragon circled a black pit below she held no fear of dropping into.

She'd seen this from the air before.

He descended slowly for her benefit. He'd always cautioned her not to assume, even with her gifts, that her body could sustain the abuse his immortal body could accept. When they passed through the ward he'd placed over this area thousands of years ago, the energy tingled across her skin and lights came into view below.

Herrick's dragon made a slow pass close to the ground.

Ready for him when he released her, she jumped down. Momentum carried her backwards several feet until she had her footing.

The village he'd built two thousand years ago was home to around fifty to sixty people at any given time, the majority from Fenella's family. All human except Herrick and whatever the seer considered herself.

Herrick had provided for every generation, sending their young to universities just as he had with Casidhe. That replenished the secret group of humans in this part of the world who provided outside support when needed.

Many went on to live along the route Casidhe had used for the last two days to reach the northern Caucasus. Some of the same people shuttled cryptic messages to Herrick sent by Fenella.

He sent few messages back. Casidhe treasured every one of them.

Some of the castle villagers paused while cooking over fires to wave a hand and smile.

The fresh mountain air held aromas of foods she'd missed.

People of different ages visited in groups of three or more. Five children ranging from two to eight in age chased a pair of auburn Mastiff pups while the mother watched from where she stretched out near a hut. Casidhe didn't think Herrick had found the Mastiffs locally either, but he could travel a long distance at night in his dragon form.

Not everyone smiled when Stian landed, but the bird appeared to suffer no bruised feelings.

Anyone loyal to Herrick would be welcome here.

Right behind Stian, Herrick's beautiful dragon set down, taking two steps. He shifted to his human form, clothed again and grinning at everyone. He shouted, "Casidhe is back."

They cheered and the sound of being missed smoothed away dents in her ego. These were her people as much as those in County Galway where she'd built a reputation at the archival research centre of being able to find and translate any historical information.

Her first duty would always be to protect Herrick and every member of his extended family, which included the Luigsech squire family and Fenella of the Connell squire family.

She doubted she'd have to include that scary vulture in her protection.

Herrick waved her over as he turned for the castle.

She hurried to fall into step with him.

Lights from torches, campfires, and candles allowed for moving around at ease since darkness fell here just as it did outside the ward. While some villagers lived inside the castle built by his father's ancestors, others happily resided in structures they'd constructed or moved into when empty.

Herrick had the castle as his residence. In truth, he slept behind the castle in a cave deep into the mountain the castle had been built against. She'd never been in that area. He'd told her long ago that dragons needed a lair of some sort, somewhere private. All dragons might not have required a mountain lair, but a place to rest without fear of attack.

She stared in awe at the shimmering blue-silver iridescent structure that rose a hundred feet in the air.

An ice castle for an ice dragon.

The fires and torches were only for the villagers, to give them a sense of home and comfort in this remote spot. His dragon was at home in the dark as he was with light.

Herrick had made this home even though he'd lived in ancient Ireland long ago.

He'd lost his family and lands, barely surviving himself to reach this destination.

For every day she'd known him, he had one goal. To find his brother again. He believed out of his five dragon siblings, Skarde had been the only one to survive. His father's castle in Ireland had fallen during the Dragani War. His three sisters died brutal deaths.

He would not let go of the belief his brother lived.

Casidhe tried to be encouraging every time she came up with any piece of history not given to her in verbal form, but she had serious doubts.

Why hadn't Skarde contacted Herrick in thousands of years? Searching for Skarde topped all her duties, but she had no idea where to hunt for a dragon.

Still, she remained alert to any possible lead. She would dearly love to hand Herrick what he wished for most.

He walked her through the central yard leading to the castle steps. Fenella said her grandmother had loved growing flowers, herbs, and trees here. Someone clearly continued that hobby as her grandmother had passed in her sleep right after Casidhe had left ten years back.

At the tall pair of stone and glass doors carved with an image of a fierce dragon in each side, Herrick pulled one open for her to enter. Inside the castle, a woman serving food called out, "Casidhe! 'Tis good to see ya."

Casidhe waved and would remember the woman's name, but it escaped her at the moment.

"You're back," shouted at her from another direction.

She flicked her gaze around and smiled at the elderly man tending a fire at the hearth. "Hello, Mick. How's your daughter?"

"Quite fine. Kind of you to be askin'."

She cherished every single person here.

To lose an arm would be less painful than losing anyone of these people, starting with Herrick.

That's why his first words upon seeing her had hurt.

She reminded herself that he could be surly at times and let it go.

He walked her over to a seat on his right at the long table in the great hall. The dining table had been created for when his parents had a large family.

He still had a good sized family, just not of his blood.

She unlatched the backpack she had customized for carrying the sword long before she had any idea this day would come.

Herrick had taught her so much from childhood on. She'd missed him while waiting to return.

She could forgive his gruff attitude when she considered how long Herrick had spent without even his brother. Her heart ached at all he'd lost because of one greedy dragon.

Immortality could be a curse if you were forced to outlive everyone you loved. She doubted she could spend eternity without her family.

She had no idea how long she would live or where her strange gifts originated. He told her he'd taken her in as he had others along the way when he found her with no family, but wouldn't speculate on her powers.

To be honest, she'd only been able to read some very old passages as a child that no one else could at first. As the years passed, she'd begun to realize she could run her fingers over ancient script and see the words come to life completely translated.

She'd like to claim a new power with the sword coming to her, but not when she couldn't remove that blade from the sheath.

It had been like carrying a stranger on her back.

The woman who first called to her inside the castle now walked up to place steaming plates in front of them. Lobio soup made from beans in one bowl. Her mouth watered over fresh-made khinkali in another bowl. She loved the twisted dumplings filled with meat and seasoned with spices that always brought her home mentally.

"Smells wonderful, Shauna." Casidhe smiled when the succulent smell brought the woman's name to mind. "I have missed this dish."

"Take the recipe back with ya."

Casidhe waved her off. "I don't have time to cook anythin' but basics."

"You will when ya take a mate."

"That is not in my immediate future." Not any future she could imagine. Not until she could give Herrick absolute proof of his brother's existence, or passing.

Herrick had his heart set that Skarde still lived.

How could that be after all this time even if he was an immortal dragon? They could speak telepathically from long distances and he'd never heard a word from Skarde. For years, Herrick flew away for a day at a time, calling to his brother. It had broken her heart as she'd grown up seeing his downcast face upon return.

After chowing down until she'd had her fill, Casidhe thanked Shauna again. So nice of the woman to wait on her as if she were royalty when Casidhe was far from it. At nineteen, she'd told Herrick she couldn't wait to go to the archival centre and see if she could track down the name of the woman who birthed her.

He'd immediately shut that down, warning she could open a door to exposing the family. She'd let it go.

Easing back in a broad chair built for an ancestor his size, Herrick asked, "Now talk to me, child."

She had turned twenty-nine this past year, but he would always call her child. She didn't mind. In reply, Casidhe got up and pulled her backpack over so she could unzip the hidden pocket that laid against her body.

She lifted out the sheath and placed it on the table where dishes had been cleared away.

Herrick became very still. His fingers closed and opened where he gripped the chair arms. He stood and reached over with a hand hovering above the hilt.

Humming from the weapon increased.

Casidhe felt the stillness in the room and turned to find everyone present watching in awe.

Lifting his hand to his mouth, Herrick's gaze moved to her.

She explained, "Two beings, a man and woman, visited the ancestral research centre while I was out of sight, but close enough to hear them. I have a spot for observin' when Fenella speaks to anyone so that I may know she is safe. The man asked Fenella to research a family. His power felt ... old. Like yours. He called himself Cavan, but I believe he lied. The woman did not give her name, but I felt her energy, too."

Lowering his hand, Herrick asked, "What research did he request?"

"On the Treoir family. He did not bring an artifact of any sort and claimed he came in place of a family member. That could also be a lie."

"Treoir?"

"Yes. That's why I had to come to you. I was not sure until I went to my secret location for this sword and ... " She paused to draw in a breath. "I called *Lann an Cheartais* to me and it came, but now it refuses to leave the sheath."

"*Lann an Cheartais* will bond with you when it believes in your cause and in you."

She stared openmouthed in disbelief. What greater cause was there than to take up the weapon to protect her family? She fought to beat down yet another wave of frustration.

What had she gotten wrong? He'd said to let him know immediately if the sword came to life or if someone powerful visited the archival centre.

Both had happened.

Herrick sat with his hands flat on the table and a look of decision in his gaze. "We must speak with the seer."

Casidhe's anxiety shot out of sight.

The only time the seer, an older woman with strange hazel eyes, had spoken to Casidhe, she'd just turned nineteen.

The seer had told her to leave and never come back.

CHAPTER 11

CASIDHE CUPPED HER HANDS ON the table, trying to calm her nerves. This had not been the comforting family reunion she'd envisioned.

Herrick motioned to one of the servants who came quickly. "Yes, sire."

"Bring the seer."

Five minutes passed in stilted silence before a statuesque woman an inch taller than Casidhe with black hair so dark it shimmered blue, walked in wearing a gray robe that moved sluggishly as if sewn of wool. The searing lavender eyes stood out against the nut-brown color skin on her smooth face, which showed no sign of aging for a woman in her fifties.

She wore three strands of silver chains in different lengths. A charoite stone with swirls of deep purple that seemed to move hung from the shortest chain close to her neck.

She went straight to Herrick, never wasting a look at Casidhe. "What do you require of me?"

Herrick said, "You know Casidhe."

The seer nodded. "I heard she had returned." Now turning to Casidhe with a forced smile, she said, "'Tis good to see you again." Then her gaze roamed to the sword and sheath. She stepped back, her body tense where she'd been relaxed a moment ago.

Casidhe asked, "What's wrong?

"You have brought *Lann an Cheartais* with you. That disturbs me."

Ready for yet another blow to her battered ego, Casidhe's

question came out with an edge. "Why?"

Herrick intervened. "She does not criticize you, Casidhe."

Sure as hell sounded like criticism to her. Casidhe waited for more. She'd done her duty and would not apologize when no one was providing more information.

Herrick stated to the seer, "I need your sight so we can understand what is goin' on. An unknown bein' came to the archival centre. Neither Casidhe nor Fenella know who it was, though he did ask about the Treoirs. I must know if this has anythin' to do with the red dragon."

Casidhe silently thought, *Here we go again.* The red dragon Herrick had told her about had been captured and locked away in TÅµr Medb during the Dragani War. Still there, supposedly. She'd feel some sympathy for anyone trapped in a realm, but not the dragon who started the war that ended peace among the dragons and cost Herrick his family.

The seer gave him a pensive look. "Allow me access to the blade."

Before she was ordered to do so, Casidhe stood and stepped aside so the seer would be able to move as close as she wished.

The woman stepped up until her body bumped the edge of the table. She extended her arm with a wide sleeve covering it and held her hand reverently above the blade. Then she moved her palm facedown above the sheath back and forth horizontally.

On the third swipe across, the blade slid out of the sheath and rested on the table.

Unbelievable. Casidhe narrowed her eyes at the sword. It wouldn't come out to help her protect herself, but it showed off for the seer?

After standing in that position and not moving for a minute, the seer lowered her fingers to touch the blade. Her reaction was immediate.

Her body straightened with her hands away from her body. Her eyes rolled up in her head. She stayed that way for the longest time, so stiff looking Casidhe wondered if she might break.

Casidhe tossed a look of question to Herrick, who shook his head in warning to not touch her or speak.

After at least two minutes of watching the seer while she appeared to be straining with her hands trembling and muscles tight in her neck, her arms dropped loose at her sides. Her shoulders relaxed and she blinked, her eyes returning to normal again. She took several deep breaths and clasped her hands in front of her.

Drawing one last calming breath, she turned to Herrick. "Something important has changed. The red dragon appeared to me in his dragon form, no longer locked inside of a throne in TÅµr Medb. I do not know what that means."

"You think he lives free *today*?" Casidhe questioned.

The seer turned a flat gaze to her. "I speak only of what I know. He lives."

That changed everything. She started thinking of how to research him. "What of his family? Would his sisters still be alive?"

Herrick pushed that aside. "I do not care about *his* family, only mine. Besides, his sisters were not immortal like him." He returned to the seer. "If Daegan managed to escape Queen Maeve, he is a threat to all of us. It's too coincidental that he is free and my sister's sword comes to life at the same time. Daegan would not want any dragon to live besides him."

Casidhe lifted a fist. "He will never touch our family."

Sadness burrowed into the seer's face for a moment then she blinked it away.

Did that woman doubt all that Casidhe had done since going to the university so she could easily explain her ability to read ancient text? Did the woman not see how hard Casidhe worked or what she sacrificed?

Just as Fenella had pointed out, Casidhe had no one to share her life with and no other activity besides training her body and pouring through tomes for a sliver of information on Skarde.

"There is more," the seer announced. Without waiting for

an invitation to speak, she continued. "I saw Skarde for a fleeting moment."

Herrick's demeanor underwent a striking change from relaxed to tense, as if waiting for something that might crush him. He whispered, "Does he ... does he live?"

"I will need to focus on this longer, but I saw a glimpse of him traveling between two great clouds. He was being moved by a force, not his wings. He ... " She shook her head, unwilling to say more.

"Tell me," Herrick demanded. Power in his voice rattled every piece of furniture in the room.

"Keep in mind that I only say what I see, which does not mean it is definitive. My visions are fluid. Anything can change once I have seen them."

Herrick crossed his arms and spoke quietly this time. "Tell me all."

Nodding, she said, "Skarde appeared to be close to death so I could tell nothing about the place he left or where he was headed."

Herrick sucked in a breath. "No."

"I do not say he has died. I have not seen such. I only tell you he was very weak as he moved from one place to another."

Casidhe's pulse kicked up. Could she really find Skarde after all the years of hunting? She asked the seer, "What do you think the two clouds represented?"

The woman surprised her by angling her head in thought and not snapping at her. "I do not know, but I sense that it was not of this human world."

"Maybe he was in a realm all this time like the red dragon," Casidhe murmured. Then she asked Herrick, "Do you think Queen Maeve captured Skarde, too?"

Herrick lost his ferocious look and studied on her question. "I do not think so. The queen loved announcin' that she had the red dragon. She had no ally among dragons and would have shoved it in our face if she had captured Skarde."

Dead end on that line of thought, but Casidhe had a fire in

her gut. She would find Skarde then Herrick would celebrate having her in the family. He would see her value beyond being someone to watch for visitors at the archival centre.

Now, if only she and Shannon's sword could get along. She told Herrick, "If you can show me how to bond with this sword, I will find this red dragon and Skarde."

"No," Herrick boomed. "You are not to ever go near Daegan. You are not to invite any opportunity to meet him. All I want you to do is find out what you can about him. He will not stay hidden if he is free. Watch for any sign of him that comes through all of your technology and communication devices. I only want to know how to find Daegan then I will find Skarde."

That splashed cold water on her fire. She argued, "What if findin' the red dragon leads me to Skarde? You just criticized me for comin' without notice and possibly bringin' an enemy to the village. I cannot be doin' this with my hands tied behind my back."

Lifting a large hand to his forehead, Herrick muttered something to himself. When he lowered the hand, he looked tired. "You cannot go up against any dragon, but especially the red dragon. I know you work hard and want to do more, but I only have ever asked you to use your gift to find anythin' you can for me. If that Cavan person returns to the archival centre, take on his work and find out all you can about him. Make sure to keep your energy hidden. I can tell you grow stronger. If I can, someone else can."

Again, she'd like to know her roots, but if looking into her own past would bring unwanted attention to him and the village, she couldn't do it.

Tension from the seer drew Casidhe's gaze. The woman stared down with her mouth in a hard line and her hands clasped in a white-knuckle grip.

What had made her so angry?

Could she not be happy that Casidhe came for a visit?

Everyone here enjoyed kinship day after day. All Casidhe wanted was a slice of that for herself.

Herrick said, "You should sleep some, Casidhe."

Give up this time with him? No. She smiled, "I'm refreshed from the meal."

"'Tis good, but you will need to head back in a few hours."

So much for her slice of time.

The seer cast a dark look her way, then turned and left.

CHAPTER 12

CATHBAD THE DRUID TELEPORTED TO a familiar wide ledge high atop a snow-swept mountain range in the Himalayas.

He clothed himself in a heavy coat, boots, and thick pants even though he could take pretty much any temperature. No matter the era, he enjoyed fine clothing.

After allowing another few minutes of peace before facing an antagonistic woman with a one-track mind, he turned to the hidden entrance. He called up his power and moved a massive stone to the side. That obstacle would only hold back natural beings, but it prevented Brynhild from looking out, or anyone seeing into her lair.

With the stone out of the way, he walked through the ward shielding access to anyone but himself, and preventing her from leaving without his knowledge. While she could not teleport, she'd shown off her ability to turn invisible in dragon form. He had not known she possessed that ability when he brought her here unconscious during the Dragani War. He'd put her in a frozen pool sealed by a powerful spell. She stayed there until he woke her weeks ago.

She had failed to see the value in his efforts and tried to kill him.

He kept alert as he strolled deep into the cavern lit by torches positioned in the far left area where the wall dipped deep. Brynhild's hoard remained piled to the ceiling and stretched out toward the center of a cavern large enough for her to fly around in dragon form. This cave had belonged to another dragon who lived and passed on long before she'd been born.

Continuing slowly, he watched for her as he moved around the edge of the deep pond created just for holding her all these centuries.

She had to be here. What was Brynhild up to right now? He and Queen Maeve had created a clever plan not long after the Dragani War where they would go into a deep sleep and reincarnate centuries later when they would have an advantage.

Neither of them expected the way this world had changed.

He'd expected dragons to have died off, yet some lived besides Brynhild.

That red dragon for one.

The water exploded straight up, driven by a massive dragon with diaphanous-blue and pearl-white scales over the silvery skin. Her dragon arched before slamming the ceiling and banked hard to land between him and her hoard.

"What do ya protect from me, Brynhild? I be the one who saved that treasure for ya."

Fierce blue eyes flashed hatred.

He'd dealt with worse and calmly waited for her to come to her senses.

She opened her wings and lifted her huge dragon head, roaring so loud the ice on the ceiling ruptured and flew around the cavern in a sparkling cloud.

If she hit him with even one piece after he warned her last time, he would lock her underwater again.

But the ice slowed and floated gently as a child's mobile spinning.

"'Tis time for ya to shift so we can talk, Brynhild."

She lowered her dragon's head the size of a car and opened her jaws. "That is all you do, druid. Talk, talk, talk." The dragon had a smooth, but full voice. "Then you dare to teleport me here and seal me in this cage again?"

"'Tis a nice cave, not a cage."

She shifted, power flooding the area as she made a quick change. He'd begun to notice how fast she shifted and wondered if that was her natural way or something she worked on recently.

Now standing tall, dressed in her black battle armor with her family's dragon crest in silver on her chest and impressive metallic boots, she lifted her head. Vivid eyes, outlined in kohl, stared down her nose to insult him. Her blond hair remained in a mass of braids twisted around her head, all but a thick one that fell over her shoulder.

Cathbad sighed. "I have come to tell ya what to work on next so that we can try takin' ya into the human world again dressed as a contemporary woman."

She raised her arms and stomped around, growling, then swung back to him. "I have been in the human world with you. I executed everything you needed excellently. I tire of you tutoring me as a child on stupid things. I am a warrior and I have yet to kill Daegan as you promised. You put me off and threaten to break your oath."

He bristled. To break an oath in their world came with severe repercussions. "I do no such thing. Ya never remember our agreement, constantly tryin' ta twist words. Do not accuse me of that again," he warned. "Unless ya wish to spend another couple millennia in that pond."

She shoved her hands on her hips. "What do you want, druid? For me to perform as a pet monkey yet once more? I have done my part, twice in fact. Do you actually think I will jump every time you order me?"

"A pet would be a more willin' partner," he countered. "We have made a good start. I need ya out with me as much as ya wish to leave this cave. To do that, ya must learn all ya need ta move fluidly among humans and I must be able to trust ya to keep your word outside this cavern. Ya push the limits every time we leave."

"You are such a—"

"Do *not* call me a nag again. That will not gain yar freedom, Brynhild." He had given her space to accept her life and become the woman he needed to reach his goal of gaining Treoir Castle and all within that realm. If she could do her part, she would see Daegan die and rule alongside Cathbad, but only if he could risk turning his back on her.

She shrugged. "Nag is not the word I reached for. I have kept my part of the agreement. I told you I would join you to gain Daegan's death, but I weary of waiting. Have I not done as you have asked?"

He could answer that question two ways. She sounded so contrite, but she didn't possess that emotion. She had done what he'd required of her, but not without conflict each time.

Gifting her with a smile, he said, "Yes, ya have been impressive." Women needed stroking, even medieval dragon shifters.

Her lips hinted at smiling. That was as close as she'd get to preening under his compliment.

"Did I not give ya the ability to breathe fire?" he pointed out.

She grumbled. "That is not true fire. Nor do I like that you cast some spell on me."

Unappreciative female. "Ya will never breathe it as Daegan does, but ya will have that weapon on occasion."

"Not often enough."

He would not continue that argument. They were finally talking, but it always seemed to take so much effort to get to this point. Getting back to his reason for this visit, he said, "I have somethin' for ya ta read. It's in Latin, the language you were taught, but I also brought books in today's English."

"You *what?*" she asked as if she had not heard correctly.

"Books and women magazines. I need ya ta be able ta read text on things from signs ta news material."

Her mulish expression turned darker. "Tell me when we will go back to that archival research centre to see if they have anything on the Treoirs. Someone hid from us in the back of that building."

Shaking his head, he commented, "Ya almost exposed yar power there. Everything I do is for a reason and my plan is not ta be taken lightly." He'd only gone to the ancestral research centre in County Galway to see if the dark druids he'd consulted had been correct about a woman named Luigsech who could read text from before the time of dragons. If so, she would know of the Dragani War. He'd expected to find a descendant of the Luigsech squire family of King Gruffyn.

Not a mysterious woman hiding from him.

"What plan?" Brynhild shouted. "We left empty-handed."

He would not tell Brynhild everything. His plan had been simple. Confirm who Luigsech was, then come back to kidnap her and hold her prisoner until the time came to use the woman to lure Daegan into the perfect trap.

To push this cranky ice dragon shifter off track, he said, "The one hidin' from us surprised me. I suspect the one who did not show her face while we spoke to the Fenella woman was either the Luigsech female or she knows how we can find her. Would ya have me demand ta see her that first time and scare her off?" The hidden woman had run, but she would be back.

He was sure of it.

If she'd feared a threat at her door, she would not have left Fenella there. He'd discovered the two had been close for many years.

So Luigsech went to see someone. Who?

He could not wait to return and confirm if that missing person was indeed the Luigsech he hunted. He couldn't take this unmanageable dragon shifter with him until she pulled her act together, because Brynhild had come close to blowing that moment when she became demanding with Fenella.

The bookish woman had remained calm, but she had a wily look about her.

He tried again to calm Brynhild. "I need ta find out if the person whose power I felt is that Luigsech woman. The best way to meet her in person would be by me takin' her text that is impossible to translate."

"Where will you find such a book?"

"I have many, but they are in TÅµr Medb. I will go choose one and drop it off at the archival research centre, which will give me a valid reason to visit again." That wasn't exactly what he had in mind, but it might mollify Brynhild.

"I will go with you."

Here came her mule-headed attitude again.

"Not if ya wish ta live. Queen Maeve is not so easily fooled as human women." He could only imagine putting Maeve and Brynhild in the same space.

Cocking her chin as if she loaded a weapon, Brynhild said, "Queen Maeve is no threat to me." The quiet ice mobile that had been floating around them began to turn faster.

Cathbad rubbed his head. "This is why I must go alone. Ya have no sense of the danger ya cause with your arrogant attitude. That's why I have brought the books and magazines for ya ta study." He pointed at an open spot and a comfortable recliner appeared first then a tall bookcase filled with reading material on every shelf. "Half of that material is in Latin, as I mentioned, which makes English easy to learn so—"

Brynhild's face boiled red. She screamed like a harpy. The floating ice shot around them in a circle, moving as fast as a buzz saw then shattered all at once.

Cathbad covered his ears and shouted, "I hate yar voice."

"I hate you! I am not a child to sit and read all day!"

Standing still, Cathbad spun up his power, preparing to deal with her.

She shifted into her dragon.

Oh, no. He would not tolerate that. "Shift back now."

The dragon blew out a blast of sleet, flicking it across him. As she flapped around in a circle, her dragon spoke. "I grow stronger. You will not shove me back in that water again."

Cathbad's muscles bulged from fury. "I hadn't intended to, Brynhild, but an ice bath might take the starch out of yar attitude."

Brynhild's dragon landed, giving Cathbad a moment of relief to not have to battle her again.

But her dragon roared and blasted him with ice from ten feet away, turning his body into a frozen block. He couldn't move his fingers. His head was stuck in one position.

The dragon walked around with humor in her glowing blue eyes. Her voice rolled with power. "You will not treat me as a child or a pet again. I have killed men for less."

In a flush of power, she shifted back to her human form, once again dressed for battle and continued lecturing him. "Now that you know I am not weak we can work as true partners. You will listen to my ideas, too. I may allow you to ... chill out, as you say, in that block of ice for a day, or maybe two, until *you* come to your senses. Is that not what you toss at me all the time? I tire of your ordering me to do this and that, then you criticize me for not thinking like you. I am *not* you. I. Am. ME." She lowered her voice to one of warning. "I am an ice dragon."

A frown marred her smooth forehead as she paused to observe him in the frigid blob. She stared and moved closer, murmuring, "Did you blink?"

The ice exploded out in all directions.

She went flying backward and landed hard, skidding across the cave floor.

Her face suffered cuts and bruises. She could heal them if she wished, but he would not help. She yelled, "You stupid druid. How dare you hurt me?"

"Stand up, Brynhild."

She had a look that said she considered refusing him, but that dragon shifter would never allow anyone to stand above her. She stood and rubbed her arms where ice had slashed her perfect skin.

"How many times do I have ta teach ya that crossin' me is dangerous?" he whispered with cold anger.

She glanced up fast. "If you retaliate, then I will, too. This will go on and on."

Cathbad pointed at the pool of water, which began swirling into a whirlpool with huge ice boulders banging the edge.

She healed her cuts and crossed her arms. "If you put me back in there, you will regret it."

Cathbad bellowed an order in Gaelic.

She screamed as her body shot up in the air and dove

headfirst into the pool.

He strode to the edge.

He waved his hands over the top and the surface iced over solid enough to be skated on. Her furious face appeared out of the darkness. She slapped the ice from below, pounding it over and over, eyes sizzling with hatred.

Then she stopped all motion and stared at him as if he was a dead druid walking. Then she sank deep into the black void.

She would survive. He'd kept her down there in stasis after pulling her out of King Eógan's castle during the Dragani War.

She hated Daegan for refusing to accept the marriage agreement proposed by her king.

Cathbad had thought keeping her alive and giving her a chance to exact revenge on Daegan would make her a worthy partner. A better choice than Queen Maeve, who danced closer to insanity every day.

How had he managed to team up with the two craziest supernatural females of all time?

Brynhild could be managed. She may not like being treated as a child, but eventually she'd fall into line. While she had a chance to cool herself off, he'd retrieve a book from TÅµr Medb for the Luigsech woman to translate.

He hadn't been back to that realm for ... too long.

There was no guessing at his reception.

CHAPTER 13

HERRICK WATCHED THROUGH HIS DRAGON'S eyes as they neared Tegernsee, Germany, a town southeast of Munich. Casidhe had always been a good traveler, rarely needing to stop while they flew. Her gloved hands clutched dragon's scales at his shoulders where she rode on his back.

Daylight crept up from the edges of the eastern horizon. He'd taken a convoluted route to avoid being seen by aircraft at night. The eleven-hour trip one way had cost him close to eighteen hours, but his dragon would fly a different path home. Even if he had to wait in a hidden area for night to resume, he would return home in plenty of time.

He could never be gone more than two days.

Landing gently, his dragon dropped a wing to the ground, allowing Casidhe to dismount.

Thank you, Nuall, Herrick silently told his dragon. *I am sorry to push you so hard.*

I am strong when we fly. See more land.

Guilt punched him at how limited their life in the air had been for so long.

Herrick managed for his dragon to fly at least once a week, but the same route over and over became boring. His dragon had clearly enjoyed this flight.

With Casidhe walking around yawning and stretching, Herrick shifted to his human form, glad for the pleasant weather. He clothed himself in a dark-blue Henley top and jeans over his boots. One of his squires had introduced him to contemporary clothing. He found he enjoyed the easy attire some days more than his furs and leather.

"Casidhe," he called quietly to her, though he'd seen no sign of life on this ridge as Nuall had approached.

She turned with a bright smile in place and wild strands of dark reddish-gold hair flying all around. Her silver-blue eyes sparkled. A blush rose in her cheeks.

His gut clenched at the path he had put her on, but every squire had taken chances from one generation to the next. Those had all been human, lacking her gifts. When he found Skarde and brought him to the castle, Casidhe and Fenella could choose how to spend the rest of their days.

He could not find Skarde without Casidhe's help and her gifts.

She walked back to him. "I loved that ride. I love your dragon, but you know that."

"Ya tell me every time ya see me."

"Which isn't often enough," she grumbled, then heaved a deep sigh. "We all have duties. I will find the information you need. Then we can finally be together as a family. I can tell how excited you are about the seer having a vision of Skarde and it energizes me to get busy. To be honest, I'd begun to question if we'd find Skarde after all the years you've waited while I've hunted for him, but you have always believed he lived."

"I had nothing else to do but keep the faith," he joked. He would not tell her how difficult it was to face another day alive as those he cared for around him aged and passed on. More than once, he'd envied them, but in his heart he knew Skarde had not died.

There'd been no confirmation of his death in all these years, only that he'd disappeared from King Gruffyn's castle.

Someone powerful had taken him.

That person would pay with his, or her, life.

When Herrick learned Queen Maeve had captured the red dragon, he'd roared with laughter. That dragon had insulted his sister and thought to steal all they had. As time went on, Herrick lost his joy of Daegan suffering in TÅµr Medb.

For just one day, Herrick wished to have his hands on that

bloody dragon to gain answers on Skarde.

He'd given Casidhe his sister's sword because only one thing would bring Shannon's beloved blade to life—to protect Shannon or Skarde, her twin brother. And it had to be in Casidhe's possession for that to happen. Another bout of guilt hit him over what he kept from Casidhe, but she had all the information she needed for now to do her duty.

Herrick had seen Shannon's headless body with his own eyes. She and Skarde had both been powerful dragon shifters and warriors, but she had been the more fierce of the two. She'd carried secrets to her grave he'd discovered after she'd died.

She should have come to him with one while she lived.

Casidhe pulled a handful of hair off her face and held it against the wind. "It took me so much longer to cross the land you just flew over in less than a day. Thanks for that, but I don't like you bein' at risk away from the castle."

"Do not worry for me. I would carry you farther, but there are too many human aircraft in the sky after this location even at night." His gut churned with admitting silently that had not been the real reason he flew no farther. He had a deadline whenever he left the castle. "You are sure you can return easily from here?" He had not been this way in a long time to check on the families loyal to him. Fenella maintained a route via squire families for sending messages at any time.

"Absolutely. Fenella and I stay in touch with squire families to insure I will have help to travel this secret route when need be. See that house halfway down to the valley?" She pointed to a small house with smoke rising from a chimney.

"Aye."

"That's a Luigsech family. I know them. They will get me to the cargo hanger at the airport. Once their son packs me up in a box to be shipped as freight, I'll be on the next flight in probably less than three hours. I'll be back in County Galway by early afternoon." She moved in and hugged him. "You need to get out of here. I already miss you."

Holding her close, he wished for her to have the family she had never had and the same for himself. One day, he would have to tell her more, but not until he could leave the castle for longer than two days should she need him. One as curious as Casidhe would act on that information and bring trouble to her door.

He had to fly nonstop to get back in time as it was.

Just knowing the red dragon and Skarde still lived meant there could be others.

It seemed impossible, but no more than him being alive.

Casidhe had only to do what he asked and not put herself in danger. He grasped her shoulders. "Promise me you will take no chances. Just do what you do best and research. When you have it all, ask Fenella to send it to me. I will deal with the red dragon."

She squeezed him tighter and whispered, "I will, but I can't lose you."

He didn't deserve her love.

Pulling her back so she would face him, he said, "I have lived for two thousand years. I am not easy to kill. All I want is Skarde, not to go to war with the red dragon. If the seer is correct, and she has always been, then the red dragon is free and he may be our only key to findin' Skarde. If not, then I will give him reason to find Skarde for me."

Her pretty face squeezed with a frown. "How would you convince him to help us?"

"Every dragon wants somethin'."

"Oh!" Her eyebrows lifted in understanding. "He'll want to add to his hoard. Of course. We can make this work. It may be difficult to find him, but I'll bet those two people who came into the archival research centre know somethin'. No one walks in and asks about the Treoir family out of the blue."

"This is true." He chewed on another worry. "Keep the ring I gave you hidden. It's very valuable and could be used in a trade."

"I have kept it well hidden."

"Good lass." Releasing her, he stepped back. "Off with you. I will watch until you reach the house."

"That's going to take me fifteen or twenty minutes." She glanced east. "The sun will be up soon."

"'Tis worth waitin' a little longer to be sure you arrive safely."

Pulling her coat together and buttoning it closed, she lifted up to give him a quick kiss on his cheek. Then she took off jogging toward the woods that blanketed the incline from this high point to the home.

It took her less than fifteen minutes.

That lass would forever excel at any task.

Turning at the last moment, she lifted her hand in a quick wave, even though she could not possibly see him with darkness still hanging close.

Then she knocked on the door and a woman welcomed her inside.

He quickly shifted into his dragon. Nuall took a step and leaped into the air, staying just above trees with a dusty light brightening the horizon. By the time the sun rose, his dragon had swept along far above the clouds over parts of Russia with little air traffic. Added to that, stormy weather boiled south of him. Staying above that allowed him to cut some distance while remaining out of sight the rest of the day instead of hunkering down until dark.

You should stop soon to eat, Herrick suggested to his dragon.

You are anxious to be home. I can wait.

He had the best of dragons. *You are an excellent companion, Nuall.*

When he realized he would have plenty of time to return home and the storms kept so many aircraft from flying, he gave Nuall freedom to cruise around above the storm and over land with few inhabitants. When the time came, his dragon took a direct route, entering what Herrick considered his territory with two hours to spare. On the way to the castle, Nuall spotted a wild tur grazing in a valley.

Herrick directed his dragon to eat.

Nuall descended to make quick work of killing and eating the animal. The meal took longer than usual, but his poor beast was exhausted.

With his belly full, Nuall sprung into the air and flapped calmly until landing in the castle yard. Herrick shifted, feeling just as worn out in human form, but he thanked his dragon and told him to sleep.

He took long strides to the castle amidst shouts of welcome from those of his people not already headed home for the evening meal.

On his way up the castle steps, his squire, Ryann, who was Fenella's cousin, rushed up to him. "What do you need after your long trip, sire?"

"Nothing. Nuall fed on the way in. We are both tired and require only rest. Send everyone home for the evenin'."

"Yes, sire."

A few servers shuffled around the great room, cleaning up for the night.

He nodded at them. They smiled and continued working. He had never wanted to be a king and no one treated him as such. They showed him respect as their overlord, which placed the responsibility of their wellbeing on his back.

A good relationship for both sides.

He climbed the stairs to his room on the second floor and washed up. Feeling a bit refreshed and with a change of clothes, he had forty-five minutes left. Plenty of time.

Herrick stepped out of his room and felt a disturbance in the air.

Swinging away from his intended path back to the stairs, he found the seer standing as an angry statue at the end of the hall.

"What is it, seer?"

She walked forward, her glower flawing the attractive face. "You sent her back."

His irritation spiked at the condemnation in her statement. He wouldn't tolerate her boldness from anyone else, but she had been his eyes and ears for many years. He'd searched for thirty-eight years to find her after the last seer passed, and another five years to convince this one to live at the castle.

She'd exacted a cost that he would pay one day, when the time came, but finding one with her powers in this current day presented a difficult task.

"Yes, I sent her home," Herrick replied. "'Tis the only place she can perform her work. I flew her half the way to ease her travel."

The seer curled her lips in disgust. "Such a considerate king."

"I am *not* king."

"You should be. Only a king would send an innocent into battle. You should tell Casidhe the truth about who she is and why that sword has come to life now."

Herrick regretted sharing so much with this seer, but he'd had no choice. She would not come here without knowing everything he could tell her. She did not know all, though.

Some secrets could be shared with no one.

Holding his patience and keeping time at the front of his mind, he brushed off her concern. "Casidhe knows what she needs to know. I see no reason to complicate her life."

"Complicate? The girl is in danger."

"She is safe," Herrick argued.

"If you wanted her safe, you would treat her the same as Fenella, who you gave a last name that meant nothing to others in our world. You would not have pinned a name on Casidhe that would be a bright target to your enemies. You use her as a staked rabbit for an eagle."

He carried plenty of guilt for decisions he'd made and did not need the seer shoveling more on him. "I do no such thing!" he shouted, then calmed himself before others heard this conversation. "Casidhe will be fine. She has no background tied to Luigsech for anyone to hunt for her. She thinks makin' her last name Luigsech was brilliant so that the squire families of the same name in any country who know of us will aid her."

"What of the two beings who visited the archival centre? Is that not a threat?"

"No. The red dragon was the only of our kind who possessed teleportation. Had those two been connected to him, he would have teleported to Casidhe immediately. They were treasure hunters, like others before them. You say the red dragon is now free. If he hunts the Luigsech line from those who served his father, all but one died out and that line is the one I brought with me to the castle and protect to this day. No one can find them. The other Luigsechs of the world today are descended from a separate branch of the tree. Do not forget our agreement, seer."

She lifted a hand sharply. "Never insult me. If I intended to break faith with you, it would not be to inform Casidhe. I am not the one lying to her." The seer tapped her lip with a long cobalt blue fingernail. "Casidhe is strong and her gifts are just now coming to the surface. Only time will show if she can manage those gifts, but the day will come when you regret having used her this way."

He stilled. "What day? Have you seen somethin'?"

Slowly shaking her head, the seer said, "I need no vision for this. She will learn the truth in a way not of your choosing."

Herrick struggled under the weight of trying to find his brother and protect his people. All warriors knew the risk of duty. Casidhe would finally have a chance to embrace her destiny. How could the seer not realize this? "You act as if I have not done well by the girl. I raised her and, when the time came, I sent her to the university."

"You did that to shield her ability to see words and translations in a way no one else does."

"Exactly," he snapped. "How can you condemn me for givin' her a chance to use that gift? She enjoys what she does. She has never *had* to earn a penny. I provide for her and Fenella. I pay all the costs for the archival centre and give them more than fair wages."

Angry all over again, the seer dropped her hands and leaned toward him, speaking in a low voice. "Do not dress up what you have put in motion as noble or kind. Every decision you have made has been for your and Skarde's benefit. At least one powerful supernatural has already found her. It may be no threat, but if one finds her, others will as well."

Herrick began to seriously worry about time sliding away. He could not allow the seer to follow him when he left this hallway. This had to end soon.

He argued, "Casidhe did not even meet the Cavan couple. They don't know she exists. Fenella would probably have figured out if it had been an enemy of mine."

"You may have more enemies than you know. If the red dragon finds Casidhe and sees that sword she carries, he may realize she is his enemy. That will lead him here." The seer held his gaze for a second as if debating on her next words then shook it off. "That dragon will want what you hide in your lair."

He'd been so shocked, he failed to hide his reaction. "What are you talkin' about?"

"I have seen flashes of your underground room in my dreams for years, but not what you have placed there. Last night, when I touched the sword and saw the red dragon fly free, I knew then what you have stolen belongs to the red dragon."

Recovered, Herrick drew himself up and gave her a flat look. "What do you *think* you saw?"

"It is not what I saw, but what I did not see."

He was out of time. "I am finished with this topic. Casidhe is my responsibility."

The seer snapped right back, "I will remind you of those words when we bury her."

Herrick breathed a sigh of relief when the shrew spun on her heel and strode off. He wound his way through the castle toward the back wall where the structure had been built against a mountain.

His dragon-shifter ancestor, who raised this castle, had enjoyed resting in his lair inside the mountain. No one was ever allowed in the area, except Herrick. His people realized he asked for few things, privacy being one. They had always respected his rule to never enter his lair.

When he reached the area where an arched walkway had been carved into the stone, oil lamps on poles lit the tunnel. Each one had been stabbed into the rocky wall every fifty feet of the way.

He'd passed three flaming torches when he came to stone steps descending into a deeper part. The cool air smelling of dampness had always been a welcome change to him, when others would have missed the fresh air outside the castle. He felt safe here, which had taken a long time to soothe his soul after losing his family.

His feet knew these steps well, having visited this area every two days since completing this area of his lair after the Dragani War. Nothing had changed in the dun-colored surfaces.

As he passed through the tall stone tunnel and turned to a narrow opening, energy shimmered around him from the ward he'd placed to prevent anyone else passing this way.

Another turn to his left sent him down forty-three steps, where he entered a much colder chamber dark as a bottomless pit.

Four torches always glowed here, but he could find his way with his eyes shut.

The oblong cavern spread out a hundred feet ahead and sixty feet wide with a forty-foot-high ceiling. He strolled forward, enjoying the simple quiet every time he entered this hidden chamber.

The seer's words burned in his gut.

She knew nothing or she would have said more.

At the end of his walk, he paused in front of what appeared to be a solid stone wall just in case anyone managed to breach his ward at the top of the stairs. He wished for his sister's gift of invisibility to allow him to visit any time unnoticed. Brynhild had inherited that gift to use in dragon form from their jinn mother. His sister should have shifted and turned invisible when the castle came under attack in the Dragani

War.

He'd seen her headless body with his other two sisters.

The protective shield he stared at now *had* come from a spell his beautiful and powerful mother had taught him for when he had needed to cloak something for a long time. The only downside was the item had to be stationary or he'd have used it on himself when traveling.

He missed his mother's wisdom and sweet smile.

Lifting his hands with fifteen minutes to spare, he murmured words he'd uttered over and over for two thousand years to protect this treasure. He'd written them down the first year, but those words were carved into the inside of his skull.

He'd actually hoped the red dragon would defy Queen Maeve and escape her realm. Now that Daegan had done so, he was the one person who could find Skarde.

This treasure would force him to do Herrick's bidding.

An iridescent cloud of moving energy appeared, replacing the stone wall, but not even he could pass through that sparkling fog. This majikal enclosure had been created by a mage and a druid he'd brought here during his first months in the castle.

He'd given them specific instructions then left them for five days to figure out how to do what they claimed to be impossible.

To motivate them, he'd warned that his dragon would go after their families if they failed.

In truth, he would not have done so, because the mage and druid had not wronged him.

But a dragon warning had always been effective.

At the end of five days, Herrick returned to find them flat on their backs, gasping for air. Neither were past their forties in age, but their hair had turned white and some had fallen out. Skin on their faces, arms, and legs had wrinkled. Once they stirred to life and managed to hold down water and food he'd brought, Herrick had questions.

The mage and druid explained there was one way to open this energy field and that key could be used only one time.

Once they'd answered all of his questions, he'd lifted a stone humming with majik, which he'd acquired for a single use. Murmuring the words he'd been taught, he removed their memories of the castle and what they'd done. When they fell into a deep sleep, he carried them out then his dragon flew them home.

Gazing now upon the iridescent energy field, he realized the field had begun to lose illumination. He pulled back his sleeve and extended his arm where the druid had tattooed the Berkana runic design on his forearm with spelled ink. He opened his palm out flat and pushed his hand and forearm into the swirling fog.

The mist galvanized around his arm and spiked sharp needles into his skin, all shooting toward the symbol.

He gritted his teeth and fought against the shout of pain working up his throat. Sweat beaded on his face and streamed down into his beard. Tears pooled in his eyes, but a warrior never succumbed to pain.

It seemed to last for hours, when in truth the time to reinforce the power of this wall required a mere minute. When the stabbing needle sensation vanished, he sucked in several deep breaths and withdrew his arm. The tattoo glowed for a second then returned to its natural inked state.

Using the hem of his shirt to wipe his face dry, he stepped back to watch the iridescent fog as it smoked and swirled faster again.

After a few moments, the fog calmed and became filmy until an opening appeared for him to view the protected contents of this cocoon.

Nothing had changed with the skin as smooth and perfect as it had been two millennia ago, just as he'd been assured by the mage and druid.

Fiery red hair flowed around her face as if a fairy wind played with the strands. The emerald gown had not faded a bit since the day he'd captured her.

The same day Skarde had gone missing at King Gruffyn's castle.

The red dragon either knew where Skarde was or could find him. Herrick had the one thing to bring that dragon to his knees.

Daegan's sister, Jennyver.

CHAPTER 14

DAEGAN TELEPORTED INTO THE COOL air of a dark passageway inside his father's castle in Meath. The first inhale brought a flood of memories.

Empty, murmured through his mind.

Daegan whispered, "No." Faces of his father and sisters flooded his mind. The haunting laughter of his sisters, older by a year, running around on their rare visits echoed in the hollow space. His father calling out to him to watch over them time and again. Reminding him he was their guardian. Their eyes stared at him unmoving in death.

Daegan grabbed his head. His mind screamed with anguish and pain of all he'd left behind. He'd failed them.

A sudden flush of power knocked him to his knees.

Ruadh's deep voice pushed inside his head. *Empty.*

His dragon had been trying to get through to him.

Struggling to his feet, Daegan caught his breath and said, "Yes. Empty." He had forgotten Tristan.

Tristan appeared next to him. "You okay, boss? What took so long to teleport me?"

Daegan cleared his throat, glad Ruadh had shocked him back to the present. "I was not sure this passage would be clear."

"It's still better than jet lag," Tristan joked, which meant he would not question Daegan more. Opening his palm, Daegan called up a spark of energy that turned into a flame.

The light glowed enough for him to make out the walls, floor, and ceiling not far from his head. This had seemed so much larger when he'd hidden in here once as a child. He took three steps to find a candle half burned. It might not have been lit since he lived here. He brought the flame to life and extinguished the one on his palm.

Tristan put his hand on the stone wall in the space not wide enough to stretch out both arms. He spoke softly. "Did you miss your landing spot, boss?"

"No." Daegan scowled. "This is a hidden escape route from my father's bed chamber."

"Where does it go?"

"There are two paths. One leads to an underground tunnel where his people could escape the castle if being attacked, but that was before I came along. The other direction takes you up to the battlements."

"What are battlements?" Tristan asked, still not appearing too sure about their location.

"It's the area at the top of the castle structure where warriors defended against an attack."

Tristan said, "Ah. The roof."

"Your architectural history could use some work." Daegan's lips lifted in a reluctant smile. "Follow me." He led the way. He inhaled the dank air and his mind wandered to a time when he'd believed he lived at the top of the world, and the food chain.

The deadliest dragon of his time.

His red dragon had squashed uprisings and flown nonstop to maintain peace in the region. Not just for his family, but for the vulnerable friends, nearby villages, castle folk, and allies he'd been born to also protect.

That had been the only reason for his birth.

To protect the weak and those in need.

He'd failed.

Castle empty! Ruadh growled, snapping Daegan back to the moment.

He growled back, but his dragon had the right of it. He could not fix yesterday, only today.

At one point, the passage continued until he had to choose to take the steps on his left descending or ascend a circular stairway on his right. He turned to go up, stepping into the open space inside of a turret where a gentle breeze ruffled his hair.

"Great lookout post," Tristan noted, coming up right behind him.

"True. 'Tis called a turret. Take care not to show your face." Daegan stared out over the lush hillsides covered in a rich shade of green he believed only existed on this island. The forest far below the castle still grew thick and full. He recalled the days of clearing new tree growth from the hill leading up to the castle, which prevented the enemy from approaching unnoticed.

No one who resembled the villagers of his time walked the path to the castle today. No sheep or cattle grazed in the open land tended to by a young shepherd.

No families lived here anymore.

Tristan took it all in, too. "So this was home? Did your dragon land in the yard down there?"

"'Tis the bailey." Daegan glanced at the area Tristan indicated. "That stone wall around the land next to the castle is called a curtain wall."

Tristan grinned at him. "Feels good to be the one who knows the lay of the land here, doesn't it?"

Daegan returned his grin. "Yes. I admit 'tis often annoying in this new world. So many terms, gadgets, vehicles, and airplanes, none of which I had ever heard of."

"Yeah, I would have been totally lost if I were sent back in time," Tristan murmured, drawing Daegan's attention to the camaraderie he had only enjoyed once in his life with Fadil.

That *friend* had attacked him on the last day they spoke.

Tristan would lay his life down for Daegan. Of all the pain this trip brought him, Daegan would prefer no one else along with him than his second-in-command.

Tristan was a true friend.

White tents covered the area of the bailey once kept clear for his dragon to land. Tables had been set up with a variety of offerings on each one. Throngs of people went from one spot to the next with large paper bags hanging from their arms. Children waited in line at one table as a woman painted on a boy's face.

The smell of food he recognized from Atlanta reached him, but not aromas from a time when Daegan had lived here. "What is all that going on below?"

Leaning to where he could see through one of the slots in the parapet wall, Tristan said, "Your dad's castle is now a tourist destination. Just checked my phone. It's a little after nine. A nice Sunday for tourists to be out. Looks like a fair of some sort in the ... bailey."

Seeing the desecration of his father's home punched him in the gut.

Ruadh's voice smoked through Daegan's mind. *Wish to return to our time.*

Daegan paused at his dragon's words. Would he go back two thousand years if he had the choice?

Part of him longed to see the family he'd lost once more, while the other part gave thanks for what he had today. After the Beladors, who became his council, rescued him from TÅµr Medb, they'd accepted him as their dragon king.

His anger seeped away. He could not return to the past any more than he could bring his father and two sisters back to life.

Backing away from the wall, Tristan pondered, "Garwyli made a strong case for finding a Luigsech. What's the chance one works here?"

"To be honest, Tristan, I thought on it a bit then realized with the millions of humans living today, we may find a Luigsech, but I seriously doubt we find one who still carries the dragon history. Think about it. With your Internet, you can find pretty much anything. Tzader contacted Quinn, asking him to relay any news. With all the resources of today's Beladors, we would have heard immediately if someone had stumbled on significant information."

"True. Plus someone with any knowledge of a dragon would be anxious to be interviewed. Everyone wants their fifteen minutes of fame."

Returning to the reason he'd teleported here, Daegan laid out his plan. "We will go through my father's bedroom, then the steward's quarters to begin our search, if those areas have not been changed drastically. If we find nothing, we shall head to what had been set aside for the squire's family quarters, but I doubt we find anything written there. In fact, I'll be surprised to find anything of value written in the past, still in this castle."

"Germanus was a steward, right?"

"Yes. He held my father's trust, and mine. He had a good life with all he needed. But it hadn't been enough. He wanted to be king." That miserable speck of humanity had made a deal with the god Abandinu to live forever after King Gruffyn forbid worshipping that particular god. Abandinu created a realm where he put Germanus and flying creatures to reside in forever. Not what Germanus had expected. The former steward jumped on a chance to escape from being eternally exiled by making a deal to aid in Evalle's capture.

Daegan had no remorse over the steward's death at her hands.

"Man, you had a bunch of enemies back then, Daegan."

Turning to head down the stairs, Daegan said, "I did. It appears I have even more today." After navigating the tunnels, he reached the secret doorway into his father's bedroom and waited with his ear at the door where voices indicated that someone was in the room. Once silence fell for a minute, he opened the four-foot-tall door created as part of the wall, and stood.

The sight of his father's bed still in this room took his breath. His eyes stung, but he blinked away the tears.

Daegan's gaze had wandered to the spot where his da had carved a notch in the wall for every year Daegan grew until manhood. The last day his da had marked his height at seventeen years, he'd told Daegan, "One day, you will watch your son grow to this height and I will be here to make his marks next to yours."

"What's wrong?" Tristan asked as he climbed through the opening and closed it behind him.

Unwilling to admit the memory, Daegan glared at the bed with a modern cloth covering, not furs. "The bed clothing is not correct."

"You want to tell them?" Tristan asked, smiling.

It was enough to ease Daegan out of the sadness. Casting a hard glance at Tristan, Daegan replied, "Definitely not."

Stepping toward the heavy doorway where a gold rope had been hooked between two stands, Tristan glanced out in each direction. "I'll watch for the next tour while you search."

Another tour group came up the hallway before Daegan had finished his search. He teleported the two of them to the hidden passageway again. Once the tour had moved on, he teleported them back to the room now that he believed they would not surprise a human.

Daegan left with only painful memories from the empty room as he and Tristan stepped into the silent hallway. He led the way to the wide wooden stairs, which would take them down to the great room, but bypassed the stairway and continued to take a second set of steps to the kitchen.

Servants had used this stairway to run between the kitchen and private chambers of the family.

Daegan had to turn his large body sideways. "If I had taken these stairs in my time, I would have torn them down and built the space wider."

"To make it more comfortable for someone of your size?"

"No. I could teleport anywhere, which I did often. I realize now the servants would have benefitted by a wider stairwell for carrying things."

At the last step, he entered the undercroft where supplies had once been stored. Now, stacks of printed materials and a store of bottled water had been placed here. He paused, listening. Voices sounded nearby.

Keeping his head bent to pass through the low-ceiling room with a musty odor, he and Tristan entered what had been the cook's domain in Daegan's time and encountered a human couple. They were admiring cooking tongs and other utensils forged by the blacksmith.

Both of them jumped at Daegan and Tristan walking in. Always on his toes, Tristan said, "Thank goodness. I thought we'd never find our way out of here. We've lost our tour guide. Which way should we go?"

The middle-aged woman with fluffed-up hair and plump cheeks pointed to a doorway. "Go back to the main hall where you started. You should be able to jump into a tour there."

"Thank you."

Daegan took the lead again to exit the kitchen and entered the large room for meals. He had to move around clumps of tourists talking excitedly about the castle to reach the central area that had once been the great hall.

Waving a hand at Tristan, Daegan said, "This way." He headed to where a guide spouted her practiced mantra at the far end of the room.

Daegan had taken several steps and stopped short to read a brass plate on the stone wall. The plaque described his family's history, as if one small plaque could tell everything. And not a mention of a dragon.

Tristan remained silent at his side.

Daegan mentally thumped himself for being sidetracked again. He continued on until he'd exited into a long hallway. As they walked, he could not prevent himself from slowing to glance inside each room. One cozy area held a tall flat loom leaned against a wall. Not the one he'd brought from another land just to gift his sisters when they visited, but similar.

He could almost smell the fresh wool threads and his sisters' flowery soap scent, which had once filled this room.

Up ahead, the tour group had paused at the doorway of what had been the steward's room. They snapped photos with their phones and asked questions, then their guide moved them along.

When Daegan reached the room, he waited until Tristan

said, "All clear."

That was his signal to enter the room while Tristan remained in the hallway to keep watch.

Daegan took in the array of display tables supporting sturdy boxes with thick glass tops. He lifted one most humans would be unable to pick up due to the heavy structure and found a wire attached to it that ran to a small black box mounted on the wall.

A red light blinked on and off.

Security.

Tristan had pointed out similar devices to Daegan.

Lowering the case back in place, Daegan began studying the contents in each one. Some had newer dates from the 1500s, but he finally stepped up to one table where two display cases were labeled with dates from the turn of the century.

Or rather, the turn of the century when he lived here.

The cases had been bolted down and held thick journals of parchment paper. He recognized the perfect script Germanus had used to record all accounting for his king. Once Daegan determined which journal had been the older of the two, he pointed his finger and flicked it left to right, kinetically turning the pages.

A brass plate indicated the documents in this room had been placed on display for the general public, but also indicated additional records were being kept at some historical conservatory.

Those would do Daegan little good. Only this one. It appeared to have been one of the last journals of King Gruffyn's time. He found nothing that hinted at where a grimoire might be hidden, but he had expected no such clue. Still, he held out hope that reading this would jog something from his memory for where to look.

Due to his ability to read the pages quickly, he finished that one and moved to the journal which had a plaque stating it was the last one kept during King Gruffyn's life.

More kinetic flipping and scanning, until he sadly came

closer to the last page. It felt as if he lived through losing his father once again.

A thick knot formed in his throat.

With a handful of pages left, he flipped to one with a different handwriting than the scribbling by Germanus. These delicate swirls seemed to be a more feminine writing to Daegan.

While Daegan had great respect for the intelligence of women in today's world, his father had lived in a time when women were not educated to read and write, except for females of dragon blood. This clearly appeared to have been written by a woman, though.

He scanned the page, reading how Germanus had disappeared and was feared dead. He snorted at that, wanting to update this journal with the truth.

At the end of the first page of newly penned notes, the person signed it Noirín Luigsech, the king's squire.

His heart pumped hard as a fist pummeling an enemy.

He pointed a trembling finger to swipe the page and read more. She went on to declare the king had requested she remain as his squire. As was normal, he moved her entire family into the castle, which included her parents and two sisters. Finding a squire with multiple sisters had been considered most desirable. Female squires were valued for their long memory, which in hindsight made him realize how wrong men of his era had been not to teach them to read and write.

Females had shown a better ability to retain details and carry a family's history forward.

Bards were similar in that they wrote songs to the history, but they focused more on entertainment than mundane details.

This woman had been an exceptional addition to his father's staff.

Daegan chastised himself for not taking Garwyli's words to heart and hunting the Luigsech descendants. What would it hurt to at least look?

Holding his breath, Daegan flipped to the last page with text.

That one ended with erratic scrawling as if penned in a hurry. Her words tore his heart apart.

The king passed this day. The dragons come for which we have no defense. I fear we face our last day on earth.

Dropping his hands to each side of the case, Daegan leaned in, breathing hard. His shoulders shook with anger, hurt, and bone-deep anguish.

Damn Queen Maeve.

Ruadh rumbled. *No enemy to kill.*

I cannot stand this helpless feeling, he told his dragon.

We will find enemy.

Still facing away from the room, Tristan whispered, "You okay, boss? Your energy is shaking the floor."

Daegan exhaled and straightened. He calmed his power and swallowed hard. "'Tis all good."

"I hear voices at the end of the hall. Did you find anything?"

Waiting until he stepped over and ducked under the golden rope, he told Tristan, "Not on the grimoire, but I did find names related to the Luigsech female my father brought in to be his squire. There is a very thin possibility this woman would have been shown where our volume of the grimoire had been hidden since my father did not inform me of its existence. Still, with nothing else to go on, we should try to find a link to these Luigsechs. 'Tis time to contact Adrianna."

Tristan turned surprised eyes to him. "No, shit? That's ... that's pretty freaking amazing."

In spite of the tangled emotions Daegan had suffered since arriving at the castle, he smiled. His right-hand man had a way of lifting his spirits regardless of what they faced.

Daegan clamped a hand on Tristan's shoulder. "Very amazing. What say you we take a quick look at the squire's rooms then eat while we wait to hear from Adrianna? She indicated it would not take Isak long to locate someone if he had specific names."

After a quick review of the squire family rooms, Daegan

came out. "Just as I thought. No written records there. I need a place to contact Adrianna uninterrupted. Let's go to—"

Tristan interrupted., "Do you hear that, boss?"

Daegan had been ignoring the roar of too many voices with his ability to hear everything. Now, he tuned in.

"That can't be a dragon," someone argued loudly.

"Oh, shit," Tristan muttered.

CHAPTER 15

DAEGAN HURRIED TOWARD THE CASTLE great hall where guides had been grouping their tour guests.

The closer he and Tristan came, the more voices lifted excitedly with the word "dragon" being spoken constantly.

He paused to take in the crowd, but Tristan pushed into the room and joined a group as if he'd been part of their pack. He asked in an upbeat tone, "Hey, what's all the excitement?"

"There's a video of that dragon again. The one they saw in Ukraine," a young woman in jeans and a frilly blouse replied breathlessly. "I can't believe this."

Daegan couldn't decide if she sounded afraid or anxious to meet a dragon.

Someone next to her scoffed, "I'll bet it's just CGI, all a bunch of hype for some new movie with dragons."

Another man nearby called out, "No way. Look at this. It's being filmed live on social networks. You can't fake that."

Daegan caught up to Tristan who had moved next to a twenty-something man in shorts and a button-down shirt, staring at his phone.

Tristan asked, "You sure it's not some high-tech mechanical dragon?"

The guy flipped his phone around. "You tell me."

Daegan leaned around Tristan. A red dragon flying beneath an airplane was being filmed from above. It's muscular movements appeared natural. The wing movement, everything about that dragon seemed genuine.

All but the red coloration, which could not be mistaken for his.

Good luck explaining that to terrified humans.

Daegan's jaw tightened to keep from cursing.

Who the hell was out there imitating Ruadh? Daegan could tell more of the dragon if it did not wear a glamour, which it clearly used.

"Oh, no," a young woman cried. "They're going to blow it up."

Angling his head away from the crowd, Tristan led Daegan to the side of the room and pulled out the phone he'd brought when they teleported.

He slid his finger across quickly then stopped and angled the phone to Daegan. "Look, boss."

The video on his phone had the word "LIVE" flashing. The image showed a pair of fierce-looking aircraft taking off as if they'd been shot out of a giant catapult.

"Those are smaller than the airplanes in Atlanta," Daegan commented.

Speaking low in spite of the crowd noise shielding their words, Tristan explained, "That's because these are the fighter jets Evalle and I were warning you about. If they get to the dragon before it vanishes again, they'll shoot it. I have no doubt. They're loaded with weapons that can disintegrate a dragon."

"Why? I can understand the fear of a giant beast torching the land, but I have not heard the dragon has killed anyone."

"True, but humans are in panic mode. Although, some will not be happy, because our books and movies have romanticized dragons as a mythological wonder. As long as a dragon is on the big screen, humans fall in love with them, but now that they're finding out supernaturals live among them and, oh, dragons exist? It's going to be dangerous for our kind."

"Dragons should be feared, but ... "

"What, boss?"

With a heavy heart, he admitted, "I understand humans fearing a monster they believe can burn them to ashes or eat them, but ... that one is another of my kind. I am furious the dragon causing destruction is pretending to be my Ruadh, but I do not wish to kill it. I would save it just as I did the stubborn one in my dungeon."

"Ruadh? That's your dragon's name?" Tristan's eyebrows shot up. "You've never mentioned it."

"And I need you to not. I never speak his name to prevent some powerful being from using it to cast a spell or worse. But yes, that is his name."

"No one will learn that name from me."

Daegan would never doubt Tristan. His second-in-command would go to his death before he would betray Daegan.

Tristan spoke softly as he glanced around. "First, we have to keep you alive for you to save another dragon. That means we need our Beladors everywhere to be safe so they can support us."

"True. Before any of that, we must free the ones the Imortiks hold captive before they drain our people. That is my top priority," Daegan made clear.

Tristan frowned and turned the phone display back to look at then showed it to Daegan again. "You sure that red dragon is not another one like yours?"

Daegan watched the dragon burn a strip of land, then fly high again. He shook his head. "That is no fire dragon."

Tristan lifted a shoulder. "Seems like fire to me, boss."

"Yes, fire is burning the trees, but it does not come from inside the dragon."

"How can you tell?"

"Because the flame shoots straight down as if sent in a pipe. If you recall the times you've seen my fire, mine spreads as it flows out, allowing for the most damage."

"Ah. So what do you think is making the fake dragon's fire?"

"I have no idea, but I intend to find out. Someone emulated my dragon in the same way right before Queen Maeve captured me and the Dragani War ignited, bringing death to my father's door." Daegan fisted his hands, angry that once again his people were under attack.

"No kidding, boss? Do you think this is the same person? Maybe Queen Maeve?"

"I do not know, but I will find out. I cannot expect warriors to fight for me unless they know I will fight for them." But how could he save his people today when he couldn't even shift into his powerful dragon?

Ruadh's deep voice spoke to him telepathically. *We cannot hide and win a war.*

I agree, my friend. But we must take care to not leave our people at an enemy's mercy again. I miscalculated the danger once when I arrogantly entered TÅμr Medb to check on Lesley, thinking no one would dare attack me. I will not make that mistake twice and force you to endure a lifetime of being imprisoned again either.

With a huff of discontent, Ruadh silenced, willing to wait for Daegan to call him up.

That conversation made Daegan whisper, "We could be talking telepathically."

Tristan explained, "Yeah, but speaking like this is more natural and allows us to blend in with humans. This will help us wherever we go to search for that book or ... the Luigsechs."

"Good point, Tristan. With so much going on among the humans out here, I suggest we bypass the meal for the moment and find a quiet place we can talk to Adrianna."

"Copy that, boss. You got a place in mind?"

"Yes." Daegan wove his way through the still-excited humans then back to the hallway. While the humans were distracted, he should be able to use the chapel if Tristan's phone would function there. The closer he came to that location, the fewer people meandered the halls. When any lingered, Tristan informed them everyone in the large hall were looking at a real-life dragon.

That sent them running.

Daegan slowed at the doorway to the chapel and stood to sweep a look over the room. "This is where my father told me Jennyver had come to pray for his recovery the last day I saw him. I had expected to see her at his bed when I returned from checking on my other sister, Lesley, who lived with Queen Maeve."

"Whoa. What?" Tristan asked.

Looking over his shoulder, Daegan said, "I have much to tell you and the others about my family."

"But the one with Maeve was not the sister whose body you were hunting for on Treoir?"

"No. Jennyver lived with Macha." Daegan had not been happy when Tristan figured out that he'd been flying his red dragon across Treoir hunting Jennyver's body the same day Adrianna had broken the curse over his dragon. That had been before he'd given Tristan his full trust. "I was actually hoping to find Jennyver's dragon ring. But if she had been buried with it, I would have actually had to be walking close to her grave to have sensed the power in her ring."

When Daegan tasted his first moment of freedom, his thoughts had gone to locating any remnant of his family.

Tristan kept pace with Daegan as he led them deeper into a fifty-by-thirty-foot room with ceilings that arched high to a point.

"The chapel." Daegan smelled candle wax, but it had been burned too recently to have lingered for centuries. His fingers began tingling. He fisted that hand then stretched it out and the tingling remained.

Tristan followed, continuing the conversation. "But you're not sure Jennyver's dead, are you?"

"A part of me wants to believe she lives, because I have no one from those times and Garwyli badgers me about not opening my mind to the possibility that others could also exist today as I do. That's all well and good, but my sisters were not immortal. Even if Jennyver had returned to Macha before my father died, which I would doubt, she would have had to request my father perform a ritual in Treoir, using the river of immortality that flows beneath Treoir Castle to grant her that request. It was assumed that my sisters would do so since that had been one reason for creating the Treoir realm. But Queen Maeve would not trust Macha to allow Lesley to visit, and Jennyver once told me she would not be happy immortal."

"Why not?"

Stopping next to a series of beautiful wood structures holding more display boxes at an angle for viewing, Daegan tried to shake the tingling from his hand.

Both hands now.

He no longer had the headache he'd suffered for a bit, which had raised his concerns about the venom in his body. Had that Imortik done something to him?

"Boss?"

"What?" He turned to Tristan.

"Why didn't Jennyver want to be immortal?"

"She said she couldn't face outliving her children and all of her family."

Tristan grimaced. "That would suck."

"It does," Daegan murmured then shook off the sad thought. "Let's get the information to Adrianna while the humans are busy."

Lifting his phone, Tristan tapped. "I've opened a text to type in the names unless you want to talk to her?"

"No. I don't care for speaking into a tiny box."

"Okay, boss. Give me the spellings for each name."

Once Daegan did that and Tristan sent the text, Daegan strolled over to observe the display boxes. A few of the crumbling artifacts were familiar.

Something irritated his energy.

He swung around to find Tristan walking across the room toward the altar. "What are you looking for?"

"Nothing. Just walking around looking at stuff," Tristan murmured.

Daegan joined him in front of the altar, curious if Tristan noticed anything. "Do you feel an unusual sensation?"

Sighing hard, Tristan said, "Actually, yes. But it seems to be all over the room. Was this used for something other than a chapel? Could it be Nightstalkers like we have in Atlanta trying to get our attention?"

Daegan had met some of the ghoul informants who exchanged a handshake with a powerful being for ten minutes of corporeal form. "No, this is not like that and the chapel was used for worship. Our family had loads of energy just by being born of dragon blood. My sisters both came here often as they grew up." The closer Daegan got to Tristan, the more he felt energy buzzing over his skin.

He went on high alert and whispered, "This could be a trap."

Tristan became very still then started searching the walls and behind them. "What should I look for?"

"I don't know. Just watch my back as I search. The energy pulling at me is stronger by the altar."

"Should we leave?"

Daegan considered it. "Not yet. The energy does not feel hostile." The energy poked and brushed at him as if trying to touch him, but not in an aggressive way. No, it felt … familiar. His heart pounded at realizing the energy seemed to recognize his.

Tristan took a step back. "I've got your back. Since you seem to be the divining rod, so to say, I'll stay out of the way."

That sounded like a good idea, especially if Daegan was wrong and this energy came from a trap. Someone from the supernatural world could have placed it once word of Daegan's escape trickled out.

He closed his eyes and opened his senses.

The energy tugged at his left hand.

He dropped to his knees to look more closely at the heavy stone altar where the candles burned slowly. Not those from his da's time, but a nice representation.

As he knelt on the right side of the altar, his left hand jerked hard to the left.

He caught his balance before he tumbled over.

"Boss?"

"Stay put." Daegan shuffled over and allowed his left hand to move more freely. His fingers stopped at the center of the stacked-stone altar a foot tall and ten feet wide.

What now?

Lowering his head, he peered more closely at an empty spot between two stones. He recalled being ten and watching a mouse push its head out of that hole during a service. Mortar had continued to crumble, leaving room for a fat mouse. He pushed his index finger into the hole and made it only to his first knuckle. The end of his finger moved across a smooth and narrow surface.

Pulling his finger out, he concentrated using kinetics with his finger and thumb to draw whatever he'd touched out.

It didn't budge at first. Was it wedged tightly?

He dug out additional mortar and tried again.

Tristan's phone dinged. He said, "Isak is bad to the bone when it comes to searching human files. He has a lead for us on a Luigsech woman."

Daegan struggled to leave this and get back on track, but he couldn't walk away. The energy continued to beat at him as hard as he tried to find the source.

"Boss? You want to stick around or head out?"

Driving all the kinetic power he could into that small opening, Daegan said, "Give me a ... "

Fissures in the surrounding stones cracked.

A ring rolled out.

He stared at the circle of twisted silver in the shape of a dragon's head with emerald eyes, unable to breathe. Then he lifted the ring in his trembling fingers.

Tristan squatted down. "That's not the ring you've been looking for, is it?"

"Yes and no. This is half of a ring created with da's power poured into it for Jennyver. Lesley had one as well, but hers had cobalt eyes on the dragon. The ring was created in two halves to be worn as one."

"Well, damn. I know you were hoping your sister would still be alive. Sorry, boss."

Daegan struggled not to shout and bring in the humans. His emotions tangled with logic. Jennyver was not immortal, but she left this half of the ring for a reason.

Could she have survived?

Daegan needed time to think and maybe, just maybe, consider what Garwyli had been trying to beat into him. That Daegan had no idea what had happened while he'd been imprisoned.

Not ready to declare Jennyver alive, or dead, Daegan explained to Tristan, "This ring does not confirm her death or that she lives."

"Why not?"

"My sisters were given the Gruffyn dragon rings to protect them, but if they died, each ring would insure their trip to a holy afterlife. They had only one reason to separate the ring into two parts—to send the dragon's head half with someone to inform the king they had been taken by an enemy." Daegan squeezed the ring in his fist, careful not to damage it. "I have not made it through all of my father's chronicles to discover what my father believes happened to her nor did the Luigsech woman mention Jennyver or Lesley in her last writing."

Tristan scratched his head. "If Jennyver did not go back to Treoir, Macha should have been hunting for her, right?"

"True." Daegan paused at Tristan's words. "Macha has dodged answering my questions about Jennyver." He wanted answers badly, but he could not start a conflict with Macha when he had to still save his people. Much as he hated the idea, the supernatural world might require her help. Rising to stand next to Tristan, Daegan carefully slipped the ring now peacefully buzzing with energy into his pocket. "What did Isak have for us?"

Flipping his phone open, Tristan replied, "He traced that Luigsech squire family through each generation for all three sisters. Two of the lines died out completely before 1600. The one noted as the king's squire had no future generations after your father's time."

"Nothing?" Daegan asked, surprised. "She had no children?"

"There is no history of her after what was considered a battle of the high kings. I guess that was sort of like wars between countries, huh?"

Daegan sighed at how the history of dragons had been turned into myths. "I suspect history has renamed powerful dragon kings to high kings. The Dragani War evidently destroyed the dragon houses, scattering them. That dragon in my dungeon was an ice dragon. They were the most powerful house with a clan of five dragons."

"Five? Holy cow." Tristan scratched his head. "Wait, but your red one was the most feared dragon, right?"

"Yes. I am not sure I could have defeated all five alone, which was one reason to hold them as allies. Someone destroyed that alliance by pretending to be my red dragon."

Tristan lowered his hand and had a look of disbelief. "Sounds like the same thing that's happening now."

Daegan assumed nothing, but … could the same person be after him again?

He would not be so easy to take out of action this time. He would not allow history to repeat itself. "When I find the one imitating my dragon, they will pay." Anxious to move ahead with their search, he snapped, "Back to Luigsech. We have no lead then?"

"Here's what we have." Tristan lifted his phone to read as he gave Daegan what he'd received. "According to Adrianna, Isak searched all current-day Luigsechs, the majority of which trace back to people related to the squire family parents, but not to that specific family."

"Still nothing," Daegan mused irritably.

"Stay with me, boss. Not done." Tristan swiped his thumb across his phone. "Isak found a Luigsech woman who he would call suspicious."

"Why?"

"She has a vague history prior to being accepted into a prestigious university in England." Tristan glanced up. "Says she was an orphan. There's no DNA sample for them to use to trace her background. That's the blood test they use today that can tell a person who their ancestors were."

Today's science amazed Daegan. "Why does he think it's suspicious?"

"Isak said she had an anonymous benefactor who paid for her education, probably because he gave the institution a bunch of money. She now works at an archival research centre in County Galway. She has a reputation among historians for being able to locate rare books and read dead languages, regardless of the time period. Isak did more digging on her and says the probability of that skill is so tiny it isn't believable."

Daegan's pulse stirred at the first hint of a connection to his past. "All squires were human for the simple reason they were no threat to a dragon family and would be loyal to the family who offered them protection. This person Isak speaks of has quite a gift to be human."

"Probably why Isak considered this Luigsech descendant suspicious. Not to mention she's working in an ancestral research centre. That's a bit coincidental."

Daegan stated, "I never believed in coincidences in my time, nor do I now."

Tristan shoved his phone in his jeans pocket. "Me neither. Want to take a look at her?"

"What's the woman's name?"

"Casidhe Luigsech."

Daegan had his doubts that she could be a squire carrying the Treoir history today, but he had nowhere else to look. Then something Tristan had said hit him. "Did you say she is known for *locating* rare books?"

Tristan's eyes sharpened at understanding the direction of Daegan's thinking. "Yeah, rare books, as in maybe ... a *grimoire*?"

"Possibly. We have no other place to search and need every minute to save Devon and Renata. We go to Galway to find out who this Luigsech female is and what she knows."

CHAPTER 16

CATHBAD TELEPORTED INTO THE REALM of TÅµr Medb, hoping to avoid a battle with yet another powerful female.

He hadn't been back since taking off under the guise of needing time to get over the death of his polymorph. Cathbad had spent days pouring power into Ossian, one of the elite Scáth Force warlock warriors loyal to the queen.

But she had squandered that asset by sending Ossian on a deadly and foolish errand behind Cathbad's back, forcing Cathbad to make a deal with Daegan and the Tribunal to head off a war among deities and the queen.

If not for that potential fallout screwing plans he had in mind, he'd have let them have the queen.

Now to find out what she had been up to in his absence.

He walked through the wide and towering hallways, taking his time to assess the warriors before reaching her. The warlocks and witches in this realm were a barometer of Queen Maeve's frame of mind.

Along the way, he began noting the lack of warlocks and witches normally passing through the halls, hurrying to do her bidding.

Had she mentally deteriorated even more since he'd left and killed her followers?

Cathbad had made a blood pact with her thousands of years ago when they put a plan in motion to fake their deaths and sleep for two millennia.

She'd peered ahead in time and claimed those with majik would die off as the world changed. She declared they could rule everything and she'd gain the realm of Treoir Island as well.

He hadn't believed her, but she proved her ability to see glimpses into the future by opening a portal for him to travel hundreds of years ahead.

That little escapade almost killed him.

He refused to even try that again and destroyed the access point after gaining pure Noirre, the blackest of majik, to bring back.

But he'd seen enough to believe what she claimed. That realization had put in motion everything for them to reincarnate in this era when they'd expected to hold all power in the human world.

That hadn't turned out the way either of them hoped and now he'd been forced to make new plans.

Walking more briskly, the entrance to her personal chamber came into view. He strode toward the tall golden doors with erotic figures swirling on the surfaces. Guards positioned on each side cast him a quick look.

Those two would not risk their lives by trying to stop him.

He'd been entering her chamber since they both woke up in this era and could easily teleport in had he not chosen to walk. The guards had come to learn if the queen did not want Cathbad, or anyone else, in her private quarters, she would deal with it.

They spoke at the same time. "Greetings, Cathbad the Druid."

He lifted a hand halfway up in reply.

The giant doors opened with little more than a thought from him.

As soon as he entered, he searched the room, which was easier to do now that a dragon throne no longer sat in the center.

Queen Maeve floated in front of a far wall once used as a scrying surface.

The two of them had arranged for multiple queens to live in TÅµr Medb for six hundred and sixty six years at a time.

A female child born of each queen would take over as a new queen immediately when the current one died.

The very moment Queen Maeve reincarnated, the final stand-in queen vanished, but that female had gained the last laugh on Queen Maeve by leaving a gaudy wall of rare gemstones for scrying. The wall had been corrupted and failed to show the history of all that had happened while Queen Maeve had been absent.

Those large exquisite gemstones were now stacked in a pile to the side.

He shook his head at her ignoring him. She knew he stood waiting. "Ya still tryin' ta make that scryin' wall work, Maeve?"

"No." She turned to him, face as gorgeous as ever with a deadly look in her eyes. Her hair seemed at times sentient, moving around and changing color according to her mood. Today the long locks were woven into tight black and yellow braids, pulled back severely, showing off her high cheekbones. Her gown was a dazzling weave of thick black, gold, and silver threads, all of which crackled as she moved.

Hands still in the air, she said, "I'm creating a new scrying wall. We'll never retrieve what was recorded in the first one after those damned Beladors destroyed parts of it."

"Had ya not kept that dragon here as a throne for all these centuries, the Beladors would have had no reason to invade TÅµr Medb," he reminded her. How many times had he warned her to kill Daegan while she'd had him in a vulnerable position? He added, "Had ya not allowed Daegan ta sleep when ya returned, he would not have been able to contact the Beladors."

"What are you saying?" Surprise registered in her face. She floated ten feet off the floor in place. Her long braids uncurled from being wrapped around the crown of her head and snapped from her agitation.

He'd gained her attention with that comment and pushed on. "I've thought on how Daegan communicated with anyone outside of here for a while. That dragon must have dream-walked. 'Tis the only way he could have reached someone outside of TÅµr Medb. Bein' that those of his bloodline livin' in Treoir could do so as well, was not so hard ta figure out."

"That stupid dragon," she snarled with loathing. "He could have been killed dream-walking."

Shrugging, Cathbad pointed out, "I would think he preferred the risk of death over remainin' trapped another couple thousand years."

She floated lower from the wall, then around the room as if the throne still stood in the center, before she descended the last distance and took two steps on the marble floor. "I don't want to talk about that overgrown lizard. I *will* have him back here where I can enjoy the next thousand years of watching him suffer."

Foolish woman.

He let that go. The red dragon had observed everything in this room for the entire time he'd been imprisoned, his silver reptilian eyes always staring.

Cathbad didn't care what this queen did as long as her crazy actions didn't affect his plans with Brynhild.

Queen Maeve turned in a circle pointing at candles of all sizes sitting on ledges cut into the wall he now realized had been changed from plain stones to rough-cut black granite.

She'd been decorating. Her hair calmed down and unbraided, flowing softly around her now in long curls as she moved. Same as Macha, this goddess changed her hair color and style as often as she took a breath some days. He'd enjoyed the woman inside the queen long ago before the reincarnation had destroyed her mind.

A deadly problem.

Gorgeous and malevolent.

He had loved both those parts at one time.

Finished with her candles, she returned to face him. "Where have you been, druid, and what do you want?"

Her terse words surprised him when he'd expected her to be a tiny bit contrite over getting Ossian killed. "Not a pleasant welcomin', Maeve. Ya know where I have been."

"You seriously want me to believe you've needed this much time to get over losing your polymorph?"

He never thought she'd entirely buy that, but it had sounded good when he'd ranted at her then left. In truth, he'd been furious over losing Ossian. With no reply that would play in his favor, he shrugged.

She lifted her hands to her hair, poking at it. "I remember the Cathbad of before when you tossed people aside like day-old garbage. Have you changed so much since waking from our slumber? More importantly, are you still committed to our partnership or have you changed your mind?"

There was the woman he'd once known.

She'd finally spent some time thinking through all that had happened and knew him well enough to question the real reason for his absence.

"I'll be honest, Maeve. I had my doubts about ya after ya kept losin' control of yar power and yar body. I needed the time ta think to ask myself if I wanted ta continue what we started if ya could not carry yar part."

She rolled her eyes. "Oh, please. That little glitch only happened a couple times."

"One time being in a Tribunal," he reminded her. Plus, she'd lost control here more than once, which probably explained so few of her followers in the hallways. He'd let her enjoy her moment of feeling in charge.

Gifting her with a smile, which had often distracted her in the past, he said, "As for tossin' people who get in my way aside, I am still that person. I got over my polymorph. Ya knew I would."

She lifted into the air, abruptly floating to her wall as she spoke. "To be honest, in return, I have thought long and hard on our partnership, too."

Had he not covered his rear with a second plan before dropping into the deep slumber with her, he would have been concerned about her comment instead of mildly amused at the attempt to push him away. "Is that so, Maeve? What have ya decided?"

She whipped around so fast her gown whined in complaint. "You tell me where you stand first, druid."

"Right here where I have always been, ready ta support your campaign to gain the castle and island in Treoir realm."

A quick flash of power sizzled around her.

He'd surprised her with that reply? Good. She clearly thought he'd returned to break up their relationship, which had often included being lovers.

Flames on candles around the room sparked and changed to red, the color she preferred when they had sex.

She moved back and forth in the air, humming to herself as her way of pacing. Maybe she had learned to calm down and no longer lose control. After a moment of her air pacing, she descended and returned to stand before him again.

But she did not rush him to bed.

That was new.

She accused, "You left me alone to deal with Daegan and the Tribunal."

"What? When did that happen?" he asked, sincerely surprised.

"That miserable dragon called me to a Tribunal. One of his gryphons had been stolen. He tried to blame it on me first, then Macha."

"Which gryphon?"

"Evalle."

"Who took her?"

"I don't know. I did hear later that Daegan and those miserable Beladors rescued Evalle from one of Abandinu's realms. Might have been Scamall. Once I made it clear I was not involved and couldn't care less about losing one of his gryphon herd, I left. That should be *my* gryphon herd. Had we not put everything in place long ago to push those Alterants to evolve into their final form, there would be no gryphons. I will not overlook being put on trial in a Tribunal. Everyone, starting with Daegan, will pay."

The fact that someone had kidnapped Evalle impressed him. He asked again, "Who kidnapped Evalle?"

"Some bounty hunter humping Macha. Foolish of her to take someone so lowbrow to her bed, but she's not as confident and secure as me." Some sinister thought glittered in the queen's eyes.

What point was she dancing around?

He wished to know more about this brazen attack on Evalle. "How did they prove the bounty hunter had taken Evalle?"

"It was simple and Macha, the stupid bitch, didn't realize she'd been tricked into delivering the bounty hunter to a Tribunal where he tried to lie."

Cathbad cringed at that stupidity.

Smiling with a homicidal grin, the queen said, "I left before the fun part. I heard Loki torched him."

Her actions could upend Cathbad's plans after all. "So are ya at war with the dragon now?"

She sneered, "I never stopped being at war with that bastard. Daegan will pay dearly for all he's cost me." Lifting her chin, she continued speaking happily as a child talking about a party. "I've been busy. I have new resources in place in the human world. My Scáth Force warriors are on a mission as we speak."

Queen Maeve also wanted Treoir realm. At one time, this woman had been a brilliant strategist. Now she acted on impulse. He would have to return more often now to keep tabs on her.

He wanted that and more. So much more.

Playing to her insanity, he spoke enthusiastically. "Tell me all. I have missed brainstormin' together."

She gave him a coy look, then backed up slowly.

What was she doing?

He crossed his arms and stood there. "'Tis difficult ta have a conversation when ya will not remain still for a moment."

Her smile disappeared as her happy voice dropped low and deadly. "Don't criticize me."

Cathbad rubbed an eye, begging for patience with another crazy female. "'Tis a simple statement."

She whipped her hands back and forth before Cathbad

realized what she dared to do.

Clear walls surrounded him from the ground to her towering ceiling. How could this happen twice in one day? He was sorely tired of dealing with these two women.

"What the hell, Maeve?"

Now she rose just off the ground to eye level and floated back and forth, staring at him from the other side of the clear wall. "You need to realize this is *my* realm. I am the power here. You have criticized me constantly since we woke up even though I've worked hard to maintain our partnership." She crossed her arms. Her hair spun away from her face and twisted into a mass of curls, which now stood out from her head, reminding him of Medusa.

"If ya care for our partnership to continue, 'tis a poor way to show it." All the while he spoke, Cathbad stood with his hands behind him. Unlike Brynhild, Maeve possessed power as old as his as well as Noirre majik. She could hold him here even longer than she'd kept Daegan if he found no way out of this.

He used a finger to test his majik against the walls. No weak spot yet.

"I want the *truth* about where you've been, Cathbad!" she demanded

"Then treat me with respect and release me from this."

Sending him a look of superiority, she shook her head. "I am not inclined to at the moment. I have no throne to enjoy. This room feels empty. I like the idea of you here *all* the time."

She had to be truly suicidal to do this. He wiggled a finger and pressed his majik harder.

Still nothing.

"Very well, ya have me here," he admitted, doing his best to sound resigned. "What do ya wish ta discuss?"

Her entire mood changed to pure pleasure. "My witches and warlocks are currently infiltrating the human world, particularly the Atlanta area."

"'Tis not news," he deadpanned. "We were sendin' them

in before I left."

"Yes, your little time-out sabbatical. You have yet to explain where you spent the last few weeks."

"I went far away where no people or cities existed. Only a quiet place. I needed that. This whole reincarnation has turned into a stressful time."

Her expression gave nothing away so he returned to the topic. "You've sent more of yours into the human world. 'Tis fine until VIPER rounds them up and kills them."

"You know nothing," she slapped back at him with smug confidence. "When I am done this time, Daegan will have no power and VIPER will beg me to help them."

Just as he'd worried.

He'd left her alone, thinking she wouldn't be so quick to stir up trouble with VIPER after they'd forbidden her from entering the human realm. Foolish of him to expect her to move forward carefully. The woman stood before him, claiming she had proven him wrong.

He would not allow her crazy machinations to interfere with what he'd put into motion. His majik pulsed out and back from his finger, tapping at the wall for even a tiny weakness. She'd proven she made mistakes when she acted impulsively.

He only needed one blemish.

Cathbad warned, "If ya bring VIPER and those Tribunal entities down on yar head again, I will not stand by ya this time. I stuck my neck out ta keep ya safe and ya show me no respect for all I've done."

"You have barely been around lately." She stared at him as if he'd turned into a beetle and no longer amused her. "You're becoming less useful to me by the day."

It rubbed for her to act as if he had not done far more than his share in this partnership. "Careful, Maeve. Ya have no allies except me and ya are wearin' on my patience."

Maeve cocked her head. "So you're saying you do still want to continue with me?"

He clenched his jaw to keep from voicing the truth. Instead, he gave her a wide-eyed look of disbelief. "I have been at your side, supporting ya from day one, and will continue ta do so unless ya put me in a position of havin' to dissolve our alliance."

She burst into laughter. "Where would you go? You have no realm except this one. Who would protect you?"

Seething, he merely said, "I would manage."

Laughing even harder at that, she spun around and around. Sparks shot from her gown, shooting to the candles, driving the flames higher.

That gave him the moment he needed to open up three fingers and try his majik. "What do ya find so amusing, Maeve?"

Slowing her spin, she drifted around the room as she spoke. "You would die without me. Outside of this realm, VIPER would hunt you out of association with me. You should thank me for keeping you here where you'll be safe every minute." She hummed to herself for a bit until the silence must have stopped her.

Turning to him, she chastised, "You're not pouting are you? It's unbecoming."

She kept digging her hole deeper with every word.

One day, he would bury her.

He spoke quietly. "Ya should remember whose power created so much for us before we slept. Ya are extremely powerful, but could not have done all this alone."

Resting her hands on her hips, she angled her head, staring hard at him. "You could not do this alone either."

He tired of this tit for tat. "Release me now, Maeve, or ya will regret this move."

"No." She shook her head like a petulant child and smiled. "Not until you convince me you understand who is in charge."

"Just remember those were your words."

Her smile fell.

Her eyes opened wide, clearly confused about what he meant.

Time to show her.

He poked a finger hard behind him and heard a satisfying chip. Cathbad lifted his hands quickly, shouted an ancient series of words, and slapped his palms against the translucent wall.

It exploded out.

Reminded him of a block of ice being smashed.

When would these women stop testing him?

The power blasted her backwards. She hit the granite wall in a pile of arms and legs. Candles burst into explosions and flames crawled up the walls, leaving a strip of black goo behind.

She spun away from the wall and dropped to the ground, landing on her feet.

Once he'd figured out the formula to crack the glass, he could have simply shattered the enclosure and dropped the shards in a pile at his feet.

Exploding the glass had been intended as a lesson.

Never, ever, go up against any power you were not positive you could defeat.

She began to rouse and shook her head.

That had to have hurt.

He'd intended it to be painful.

When she regained her senses, she straightened her back. Her hair styled itself as she brushed at her gown.

Striding to him this time instead of floating, she stopped two feet away. "Had you not gone that far, I was prepared to share my plans with you. Not now. There is a power greater than you or me out there and I intend to be on the right side of it when the time comes."

What was she talking about now? "I do not wish ta war with ya, Maeve. I only want you ta not push me again. If ya treat me with respect, I will give the same to ya. If ya attack me, I will not be so kind next time."

"Go away, Cathbad. I'm the one who needs a break this time."

"Very well." That worked for him. He teleported out of her

chambers, but instead of leaving the realm, he reappeared in the soldiers' quarters.

This would be his only chance to find out what she was up to before she realized she had to compel her warlocks not to talk to him.

The two men in this area were not just any warlocks, but of the Scáth Force team. They wore clothes and short haircuts similar to average human men, which allowed them to fit in while operating covertly. One had yet to pull his shirt over a body inked in black. He finished while holding Cathbad's gaze.

Smiling as if this visit were natural, Cathbad said, "I understand from Queen Maeve ya have been quite busy. 'Tis good to know we're making progress."

Erath, who now led the small, but highly skilled, pack of warlocks told the other soldier, "Go ahead and I'll join all of you at our meet point in Atlanta."

"Yes, sir."

When the soldier turned to leave, Cathbad realized he had to ask Maeve to teleport him to the human world and offered, "Maeve was restin' when I left her. I'll send ya to Atlanta unless ya prefer ta wake her."

The warlock seemed torn until Erath said, "Thank you, Cathbad."

Wise one there to not question Cathbad and make an enemy of a dangerous druid. Once the soldier had a lock on his Atlanta destination mentally, Cathbad teleported him, then turned to the Scáth Force leader. "How is the mission goin'?"

As the warlock looked around, trying to figure what to do, Cathbad whispered a compelling chant and stepped up close to the man. "Now ya will tell me all."

Erath stood straight and his eyes glassed over. "We are following the queen's orders."

"Which are?" Cathbad prodded.

"To find two volumes of an ancient grimoire. A being who calls himself a master has offered her Belador prisoners, and our warlocks he's captured, in exchange for two missing volumes needed to make the grimoire whole. That master possesses the third."

Cathbad had made as big a mistake by underestimating Maeve. "What is this book called?"

"Immortuos Grimoire."

A master of Imortiks? No, that couldn't be. Cathbad struggled to imagine anyone opening the wall holding back those abominations. Far worse than anything he'd ever created and he had made some nasty beings. "What else does this Imortik master offer?"

Erath's words held no emotion. "He offers freedom to those who work with him."

"What will three volumes brought together do?" Cathbad recalled some memory of the Imortiks being locked away in an alternate world before he came along.

"I do not know."

"What is happenin' in the human realm? Is Daegan not containin' this Imortik master?"

"The master forced Daegan of Treoir to expose Beladors to humans. Humans and beings of power are succumbing to Imortiks who have escaped through a rift in the death wall."

Cathbad stood there dumbfounded.

All this had happened since he went to raise Brynhild from the frozen pond? Still, he didn't see how Queen Maeve considered this to be phenomenal. "Why would any of our kind fear these Imortiks? They sound like demons."

Standing so rigid with only his mouth moving, Erath continued speaking similar to one of the human robotic voices. "Imortik energy blocks that of powerful beings. Our warlocks observed Daegan fighting an Imortik and failing to stop the Imortik from taking a Belador. The Imortik master claims he allowed Daegan to live to find the two volumes for the same chance to trade for all prisoners."

"Is there a time limit for finding these volumes?"

"Yes. Two weeks. The queen believes they will become the deadliest force in the human world. She wants the two volumes before the Imortik master and Daegan join forces."

Scoffing at that thought, Cathbad muttered, "Daegan will not join with an Imortik."

"The queen agrees. She fears the Imortik master will turn Daegan then possess an Imortik red dragon to use against deities."

That could not be possible.

Could it?

If that Imortik being were so powerful, could it turn a deity as well? Was Queen Maeve so stupid to think a being that dangerous would not turn *her* into his puppet?

Not stupid. Insane.

Cathbad lifted his hand, clearing the compelling spell and teleporting Erath away as he did.

He teleported to his library in the realm, glad to find it not in shambles. But now that he knew what held her mind captive, he could not see the queen wasting energy on wrecking his library. Still, he needed these books to be safe and sent them to a tomb created during the stone age. He'd warded the tomb from discovery long before meeting Queen Maeve.

She had always been a potential enemy at some point. The only way he could take her down would be to catch her outside this realm.

Unlike her, he had the patience to succeed at anything.

Taking a slow look around his library, he lifted a one-of-a-kind ancient tome he'd taken from a hundred-and-twenty-eight-year-old sorcerer he'd spent over twenty years befriending.

The sorcerer had not passed the book to him as inheritance.

Cathbad had killed the old crone when he discovered the sorcerer had been misleading him about dying for ten years. He took the majik writings as was his due, but could not read all of the ink marks.

No one had been able to translate those parts of the text. He'd leave this book with the Luigsech woman, who would eventually return to the archival centre. Now he had a greater task for her than merely bringing the dragon of Treoir to him.

Luigsech would find the grimoire.

She would hand Cathbad the way to control the Imortik master.

He could remain gone from TÅμr Medb forever if not for needing to know what Queen Maeve was up to, which meant he'd have to be prepared for a future attack when he returned.

In hindsight, he realized she had only been testing him earlier.

The next time, she'd be better prepared.

So would he.

CHAPTER 17

CASIDHE STRETCHED, WAKING UP FROM her afternoon nap and could have slept longer. The bed in her home had been here much longer than she'd been alive and she slept like a babe in it every time. She'd enjoyed the flight on Herrick's dragon, but the entire trip, which included traveling boxed up as freight, had wiped her out.

No time to waste. She had to find Skarde.

She rushed through a shower, because the water never heated above lukewarm. The downside of living in a three-hundred-year-old cottage. She shouldn't blame the age.

Her salary provided money to live comfortably and to keep all the appliances running. She could ask Herrick for funds, but she preferred to earn every penny she received. For that reason, she would only spend money she earned, even if clinging to the noble notion of independence did freeze her tits on occasions.

She dried her hair and wove the dark gold-and-auburn mass into one thick braid that fell to her lower back. Pulling on a pair of gray wool pants, a soft shirt of white cotton with a pale-blue sweater tossed over that, she stepped into her boots and snapped the closures.

She took in her appearance before the tall mirror, leaned against a wall, and smiled a moment before turning serious.

There stood a woman determined to make her people proud. To do that, she had to use her gift and her brain to accomplish what she'd felt born to do.

Smiling again, which had been a personal rule to start each day, she wrapped up a tin of Fenella's favorite scones she'd cooked before her nap, which were now cooled enough to pack.

When she stepped outside, the temperature had begun dropping to the fifties with the sun about to fall from the sky.

She checked the wildflowers and yellow gorse budding out next to her walkway. The scent of coconut wafted off the gorse sometimes called *aiteann*. Then she moved her old bicycle away from the wall where she propped it each day, placed the scones in her basket hooked to the handlebars, and climbed on, pushing off to roll down the drive.

Breathing in the fresh smell of grass and the woods lining one side of her drive wiped away the stress she'd carried home from visiting Herrick.

She could do what he asked.

She'd had a few concerns after finding out about a red dragon flying around while she'd been in the Caucasus mountain range.

Had that truly been *the* red dragon burning a forest first in Ukraine, then later on in Finland earlier today? What did that dragon have against those countries?

Herrick claimed the only red dragon had come from his time, a child of King Gruffyn. The king had mated with a goddess for one night and that resulted in a red fire dragon who had ruled over all others back then.

More like he'd murdered at will and tried to steal hoards from other dragons. She'd had the history given to her by the last Luigsech to live with Herrick's people in the mountains.

Generation after generation, a Luigsech female had carried that history from back when her ancestor had been saved from King Gruffyn and his evil son Daegan. Similarly, Fenella's Connell squire family passed down the ice dragon clan history.

Her skin chilled at the idea of meeting up with Daegan of Treoir, but Herrick had been firm about her not engaging with that one. She had only to perform research and that was in her wheelhouse.

Fenella joked often, accusing Casidhe she had an insatiable

curiosity, then reminding her of the old saying *curiosity killed the cat.*

Not so long as Casidhe had the Blade of Justice.

That irritating voice in the back of her mind, the one that spoke up only when she made a mistake, reminded her she had no sword on her back at the moment.

"Give me a break. It's hidden in the cottage," she complained to the wind. She kept the ring Herrick had given her in a different spot, hidden even better. What was the point of wearing a ring even on a chain if she had no idea what to do with it? Herrick had only said to keep it close for when he called to give her instructions.

At the end of a beautiful ride along the countryside, she pedaled into a village on the outskirts of County Galway. She waved at store owners and local residents she passed. When the day came for her to move home to Herrick's castle, she'd miss these people who had taken their time welcoming her until she'd become one of the community.

Slowing down, she braked, then parked her bike outside the ancestral research centre. Some visitors showed up here when they were actually looking for the Connemara Heritage and History Centre asking about the tours. Fenella would give them directions with a smile since those were not their customers.

Casidhe's reputation with the old languages brought in plenty of business.

She'd just settled her bike in a stand that could support four when she felt the sensation of being watched. Similar warnings often started in the same spot, between her shoulder blades and crawling down her spine.

Lifting the sweet smelling package wrapped in a worn, but clean, cloth from the basket, she pretended to study it for a moment as she angled her head to peer through fine hairs falling along her face.

No one stood on the walkway across the street, but Sundays could be slow. Two women came out of the bakery Casidhe patronized when she didn't cook. They laughed at a private conversation and continued on past the wide space between buildings filled with trees. She sometimes took her lunch and a book there.

Sending a look down the stretch of street in both directions, she shook off her concern. Nothing unusual in this quiet little village.

Still, had she made a mistake by leaving the sword at home?

Of course not.

For now, the stubborn blade would only draw attention, not blood.

She opened the door, jangling a bell at the top, and carried the tin in. The soothing aroma of old leather and pages of assorted materials, all aged to perfection, filled her nose.

This was her happy place.

"There's my Cas. I've missed ya, girl." Fenella lifted her plump body from a leather desk chair that had molded to fit her shape over the years. "Tell me that's blueberry scones I'm a smellin'."

"It is." Smiling at her friend, Casidhe handed off the treat and Fenella immediately tasted one. She took her time as if she'd been given a rare royal dish.

Casidhe made those for her at least twice a month. "Anythin' goin' on?"

Swallowing a bite, Fenella said, "Aye. Our friend Cavan stopped by this mornin'."

Working to keep the trepidation out of her voice, Casidhe asked, "What did he come askin' for this time?"

"He started in about the Treoirs again. I reminded him that if he be representin' a descendant, that person should ha' sent a family artifact. If his client truly be of the Treoir family, he or she would know such. We had a moment of starin' before he smiled and shook his head. Handsome devil, that one. Told me his client knows not what I spoke of, but Cavan would impress upon him that perhaps he should be visitin' himself next time."

Glad not to be eating anything at the moment, Casidhe's

throat tightened. Had Cavan meant it when he made that suggestion? Did he know the red dragon? She breathed in and out, trying to calm her heart. "Is that all he wanted?"

"No. Wanted to speak with ya."

"Why?" Casidhe stood up quickly. "He doesn't know me."

"Sit down. Don't fash yerself, girl. He heard a woman name Luigsech could translate old books that many others could not. He left one for ya. Appears old enough to have been created at the start of time."

That didn't sound very sinister, right? "Where is it?"

"'Tis on the table at yer right."

Casidhe jumped around as if Fenella had said a snake sat on the table.

"What has ya so angsty, Cas?"

"Just tired," she murmured. Lifting her gaze from the book, she thought about why she was angsty, as Fenella put it. She'd need a scroll as long as the street outside to explain her many reasons .

"How be the clan?" Fenella asked softly.

"Good, though I had little time to speak with anyone before I was sent back."

Fenella winced as if Casidhe had said someone insulted her. Too tired to explain, Casidhe moved to another subject. "I heard about humans finding out nonhumans lived among them in North America. Is it crazy there?"

"Aye. 'Tis enough to give ya chills. Humans have always panicked at every word of anythin' strange, but today they have the Internet. Instead of a handful, thousands jump up in arms." Fenella pecked at her baked good, chewing until she could speak again. "Nothin' like that goin' on here. For now, the locals laugh at those in the states losin' their minds."

"What about that dragon burnin' the forest in Ukraine?"

Fenella sat back with a piece of scone in hand. "I just heard of it when I spoke to old Peadar. Ya know I'm no' much for electronics, but I visited the grocer after lunch and saw the videos on their television. I admit the pictures were convincin' though I been hopin' not, but ya must think so."

"Yes, I do. They appear authentic."

"Do ... *they* know, Cas?" Fenella referenced Herrick and the clan.

Keeping her voice soft as if someone could hear through the walls, Casidhe said, "The seer spoke of the red dragon. I had no way to use my mobile phone while there, but I wasn't about to dispute her claim. I saw the film for a moment before I had to be packed in my box for the cargo flight. I just wonder. Is that *the* red dragon?"

"Well, the video of the dragon in Finland had been poor quality, but aye, it seemed a red dragon to me. Has to be *the* one if there be no other, I suppose. Just canna believe he still lives." Fenella's face tightened with fear she tried not to show by smiling. "Do they think he will come here?"

Still wondering if Cavan was connected to the Treoir family, Casidhe couldn't in good conscience say yes or no that a Treoir would show up here. She tried to brush it off. "Just like Cavan's visit, if someone from Treoir actually comes here, all we have to do is say we'll research and tell them we'll be in touch. If they are human treasure seekers pretendin' to be a Treoir, we stay put."

"If not?"

Casidhe had thought about this a bit while squished up in that box. "I felt Cavan's power the first time he visited, but he may only be treasure huntin' too. If a powerful Treoir presents himself or herself, I will keep my energy hidden from them and assure them I can deliver what they want. A smart person will watch as we leave to see where we go. We would instead use our secret exit route from this buildin' for that reason." The day Cavan and his female partner first presented themselves to Fenella, Casidhe had taken the tunnel exit from this building, which had more than one final route.

She'd traveled underground to the giant hollow tree large enough to move around in, which had stood since the time before the Dragani War. The *Lann an Cheartais* had rested there since she moved here, shielded by a spell preventing anyone from discovering it.

"We will be fine," Casidhe assured her dear friend she considered family. She would allow no one to harm this woman. "I've been given the duty of locatin' the red dragon, but told not to contact him. Just to send any information to the castle as soon as I have it."

Fenella set aside the ledgers she'd been working on when Casidhe arrived and placed her hands in front of her. "That was before ya knew the red dragon was truly alive, Cas."

"I knew. I believed the seer when she spoke of the red dragon."

"Thought ya did no like that one?"

"She's okay," Casidhe muttered then moved off that topic. "In the meantime, I wish to go through Cavan's book, which might indicate if he is a threat or not. Then I'll focus all my energy on figurin' out who could possibly be in contact with the Treoir dragon if he does live. Once I have that, I will give you notes for sendin' a message to the clan."

"Happy to do anythin' to help."

Turning back to the three-inch-thick book with a tooled leather cover the color of wet leaves in autumn, she ran her fingers over a strange emblem and raised letters, which her mind translated into *Before Ainvar.*

What was Cavan up to? Herrick had said the man may have only been a very old mage snooping around for King Gruffyn's hoard, which had never been found.

She knew all about that from the spoken history of King Gruffyn's dragon family.

"What be that book he left, Cas?"

Snapping out of her moment, Casidhe said, "I'm not certain. The title is odd, sounds to be about a person I've not heard of before."

"That surprises me." Fenella smiled.

Casidhe took the ribbing with a smile. "This could be a fictional story or a historical recountin'. By the bindin' alone, I would venture to say it is a historical accountin' of a time before Herrick's based on the strange language I have yet to identify. I'll know more once I sit down with it." She had a feeling she would not be using gloves as she normally did for the rare books brought to her by humans.

Cavan might be nothing more than a gold-hunting mage, but he had power, which meant she'd see more in this text if she used her uncovered fingers.

Standing up and gathering her purse, Fenella announced, "I be headin' out early today, Cas. I am off to see Peadar about the goats he promised me."

Smiling, she turned to Fenella. "That's why you were talkin' to him? Will you be bringin' home kids?"

"Of course I will, and I will be expectin' ya to help feed 'em."

"Deal." Casidhe loved visiting Fenella's farm, even if it was a long bike ride, but worth it to play with the baby goats.

Before leaving, Fenella pulled her sweater on slowly. She spoke low again as if the walls could hear. "So yer trip was good, aye?"

In a weak and lonely moment, Casidhe had shared her sense of feeling on the outside of the clan one night with Fenella and had feared the woman would tell Herrick. Instead, her friend had understood and shielded her qualms.

She couldn't keep the disappointment out of her voice. "Yes, but he would rather I had sent a message in my place."

Fenella quickly tried to soothe her. "He means well and 'tis probably more worried about ya travelin' alone."

That could be it, but Casidhe's heart argued something had been off. She'd like to tell Fenella how the sword had come to her, but Herrick cautioned her from sharing that with anyone.

Casidhe had wondered if he'd included Fenella in that warning, but decided that couldn't be so. In the ten years they'd spent together working in this ancestral research centre, Fenella had become more family than friend.

That woman was as loyal and devoted as they came, but Casidhe would carry her burden alone rather than put this sweet woman in danger by sharing too much.

Standing, she walked over and gave Fenella another hug, whispering, "All is fine. He needs me to find out more on that blasted dragon and we need to know more about this Cavan guy. I will read the dusty old book. His coin is as good as anyone's and he may just be huntin' fool's gold."

Because anyone trying to find and take a dragon's hoard was indeed a fool.

Fenella hugged her hard and let her go. "I shall see ya on the morrow. Doona stay too late and travel at dark."

"I won't," Casidhe promised.

Shaking her head with a sigh, Fenella fretted, "Ya will, because ya have no mind of time when ya open a book. Set yer alarm and go home when 'tis still light out."

Laughing at her, Casidhe opened the door and watched Fenella head to her pickup truck that had traveled a lot of roads in twenty years.

That feeling of being watched sizzled along Casidhe's skin, snapping her attention up to search quickly.

Nothing there again.

She closed the door and walked over to the comfy chair she preferred for reading. If she sat at a desk, it hurt her neck and back. This way, she could also see if anyone walked up to the door.

Turning pages of Cavan's book carefully, she scanned the title page and notes on the next page written as a preface.

Then she reached a page of strange text, which she could not interpret upon first glance. That was odd. She could always pull out bits and pieces just by looking.

Reaching over to grab a soft cloth, she wiped her hands clean of any oil or dirt and tossed the cloth.

Then she extended her index and middle finger together, curling her other fingers out of the way. She moved the tips of those two fingers across the text, barely touching the surface.

Words rose off the page in glowing gold shapes, which would have been difficult for anyone unfamiliar with the odd script to translate.

Not for her eyes and brain.

She started reading quickly. The symbols rose up and fell away with each swipe, returning the page to its natural state as her fingers passed by. She'd been correct about the time period after determining at least some of it had been penned in BCE.

She'd read three pages when she snatched her fingers back.

The last words had been a warning to the person reading to never cross any of the dark druids, especially not the Seanóir. The Elder.

Elder was such a simple word for the deadliest of dark druids.

She'd gleaned snippets of information about this order of druids over years of reading ancient text. There were no more than seven in existence at any time, and one ruled over all the dark druids. The Elder.

The seven names were not spoken or written, which had protected them through centuries.

Many, many centuries ago, and definitely before Herrick's time.

Just who was Cavan?

Herrick wanted all her attention on finding anything she could about the red dragon, but it wasn't as if that information would be easily located. She'd have to find threads that would lead to that dragon shifter, starting with the Beladors.

Humans didn't know they existed.

Correction. They *hadn't* known.

She'd seen the word Belador typed on screen and how reporters frantically tried to find information to determine if they had been invaded by nonhumans.

Scanning on her mobile phone, she'd seen the term misspelled as Beladore or Beladora.

Humans were freaking out in the city of Atlanta and surrounding areas. Fear would spread from there.

Who wouldn't be afraid after that arrogant red dragon had torched forests in two countries? Had that been a clear warning?

If so, who had the red dragon been warning?

She put Cavan's book aside to think on before she read deeper and opened a door she shouldn't. She'd like to ask Cavan who he was and maybe even what he might know of the red dragon. Would she surprise him with those questions?

It shouldn't for someone who came here inquiring about the Treoirs. She'd watch his reaction when she asked him about the dragon the next time he returned to discuss his book.

By the time she'd caught up all the correspondence that had piled on her desk while she'd been gone, she looked around to find the sun had almost dropped from sight.

Fenella would have her head for not setting a clock.

Casidhe packed up fast. She had to grab groceries on the way home and needed to get pedaling.

She locked the door and, for the third time, she could not shake the feeling of being watched.

Either that or the trip to visit Herrick had made her jumpy and suspicious of everything that moved. Probably the latter. She needed to get outside and train to clear her mind. She also had to find a way to work with Shannon's sword, but what she'd learned of how to swing a sword while studying at the university might not be enough to handle the Blade of Justice.

On the other hand, unless a powerful supernatural leaped out of the bushes, she could put a hurting on any human. Laughing at herself for momentarily acting afraid of her shadow, she climbed on the bike and headed for the grocery.

She'd flown on the back of a dragon this morning.

Short of the red dragon coming to her door, she could handle anything else.

She hurried to shop for the few staples she needed but took a moment to speak to the owner who had saved a peck of her favorite apples for her. She'd helped him with some rare vintage books. Being part of the community, she'd refused any payment, but she took the gift of shiny apples grown on a small farm now with a smile.

Her stomach grumbled as she walked out of the grocer with a cloth tote bag filled. She'd parked her bike at the side of the building since the multi-bike stand had been full. The tote bag fit in the wide basket on her handlebars. She paused to fold the excess material at the top down so the wind wouldn't drag it open.

A hand latched onto her arm. "Do not make a sound."

She jolted at the level of power that buzzed against her skin and considered screaming until she stared into the chilling eyes of Cavan.

Everything about him and the energy pulsing under his fingers warned she'd underestimated his casual visits.

Herrick would be yelling at her right now for being distracted and not keeping her power concealed. The calculating look in Cavan's gaze said he'd already assessed it.

She hadn't expected this to happen coming out of a grocery store.

Note to self: Don't make this mistake again.

That would only help if she survived this meeting.

"What do you want, Cavan?" she hissed under her breath.

He said nothing for a moment, lifting his free hand for a second, then lowering it. "I've shielded our conversation. First, I will not hurt ya if ya behave. If ya do not, anyone who comes to interfere will die first, Miss Luigsech."

Her heart slammed her chest and her lungs seized. If she didn't breathe soon, she'd hyperventilate. She swallowed down bile and calmed herself as much as she could.

"Now that I have your attention, we can have a conversation," Cavan said as if they chatted about the cost of peanut butter. She could see what Fenella had meant when she'd called this man attractive. Had he walked up and said hello with a smile, Casidhe would have been dazzled by his dark whiskey-colored eyes, dark brown hair, and smart gray suit.

Instead, she saw a devil staring out of those dark eyes.

She tried tugging her hand away.

He increased his grip.

"What do you want with me?" Casidhe demanded. "I've started readin' your damn book."

His eyes flickered with something she'd almost call surprise, but it happened so quickly she couldn't be sure.

"So ya can actually translate the old languages? I had not believed that part," he mused. "Why have ya been avoidin' me?"

"I've been busy. You're not that important to me," she bluffed. "I thought you were lookin' for information on that Treoir family."

"Aye, and ya have that so do not pretend otherwise."

"I do *not* have anythin' on them, but with a little time to research I might be willin' to track it down if you start actin' like a gentleman."

His fingers didn't tighten this time, but energy pushed out from them, burning her skin.

She ordered, "Stop it." But her voice had come out more frightened than demanding.

"I'm only lettin' ya know it would not take much for me to gain the truth." The burning ended as abruptly as his words.

Damn if she didn't feel herself being watched again. What had happened to her sanctuary in this village? She'd never suffered a moment of fear while living here, but she did now.

She would have assigned the earlier sensation of being stalked to this man if not for it happening while he stood here. "Who are you, Cavan?"

"For now, ya should use that name and not be stirrin' up any more trouble."

"More? What have I done to you?" Her fingers were feeling numb from the bind he put on her arm.

"You ran after I came by yar centre. Fenella does a fair job of coverin' for ya, but I could not feel yar presence earlier today the way I had the first time."

She had gotten slack and stopped working so hard to shield her energy five years ago. To worry about the fact she'd failed to do so yet again at this moment would do no more good than closing the gate after horses have escaped. She said nothing, leaving him to continue the conversation.

"Had ya not run, I might have dismissed ya as unimportant, but the fact that ya did told me ya had noticed my power. So now that we have revealed ourselves, 'tis time to get down to business."

Herrick had been right.

She should not have gone to see him.

Her head throbbed at the mistakes she'd made. Could Cavan track her route? As of now, she would not make that trip again. Fenella could send messages through their secret mail route.

She'd been in this little village for so long, she'd lost all sense of threat. To be honest, she'd begun to enjoy life in spite of being alone with no hope of settling down any time soon.

Good thing or performing her duty would put others in danger.

A duty she was currently failing. Forcing strength into her voice, she asked, "Tell me what you want. If I can help you, I will. Then we don't have to ever see each other again."

"Oh, but we are goin' to be great friends for a bit."

Her stomach dropped at those words.

"Now that we have met, ya know better than to run again," he said, making it clear that had been an order. "If ya do, I will find ya and make ya regret inconveniencin' me."

She refused to appear weak to him even if her knees knocked. "I'm not runnin'. For the third time, what do you freakin' want?"

He arranged his attractive face into an amused expression. "I do wish to have the book I left for ya translated for there is a passage in it I have trouble readin'." He told her where to find that page.

"Okay, is that all?" She should be so lucky.

"No. Ya will wait to open the book to that page until I am there in the mornin' and read it to me as I watch. Unless ya wish to go there now."

"No. I'm tired and hungry. I do not do my best translatin'

when exhausted or bein' threatened."

Would he be able to see what her fingers revealed if he watched over her shoulder? She shrugged. "Meet me at ten and I'll read what I can to you."

But she'd get in very early to get a jump on the text.

As if he'd read her mind, he warned, "If ya touch the page before I arrive, I will know. The book and I have been close for many centuries."

That confirmed her sense of his power being very old. Could he be a druid? *The* Elder? Probably yes on druid, but no on the Elder. She had to keep her imagination from making this worse. Why would someone that powerful come to her?

"Will there be anythin' else?" She tried her best to sound as if he imposed on her time.

His lips shaped into an indulgent smirk. "Tomorrow, ya and I are goin' to search for a grimoire."

"What?" This guy kept blowing her mind.

"'Tis an ancient book of majik," he explained, sounding disgruntled that he'd had to explain it to someone with her background.

She bit out, "I *know* what a grimoire is, but I can't just go off with you." Not if she wanted to be found alive again.

"You should prepare to be gone however long it takes." He completely ignored her words.

Her heartbeat sped up like mad. "What specific grimoire? I might be able to find somethin' on it so *you* can hunt it down."

"'Tis called the Immortuos Grimoire. We shall find it together."

She frowned, thinking back through all the books she'd reviewed and had catalogued into her personal collection. "I've never heard of that. I'll need time to figure out where to start lookin'."

"Ya shall have the time ya need. With me at your side." He released her.

Casidhe rubbed her sore wrist where red marks appeared

as an imprint of his fingers and scowled at him.

"'Twill go away soon." Taking a step back, he reminded her, "Do not think to not be there when I show up tomorrow mornin'."

"Give me a break. I'm not goin' anywhere," she gritted out.

"Wise lass. If ya fail to be there when I arrive or think to run, yar friend will not enjoy waitin' with me for yar return." He turned and casually strode toward the trees.

Her stomach roiled. He'd threatened Fenella.

Nothing would prevent Casidhe from being at the ancestral centre ahead of Fenella. That bastard would not touch her friend.

In fact, Casidhe had to get in touch with Fenella right away. Herrick might not like it, but Fenella had to go somewhere safe immediately and his castle topped anything Casidhe could provide.

She could not deal with Cavan if it meant putting someone dear to her at risk.

Fenella would normally come in early tomorrow so she and Casidhe could go over the schedule before the centre opened since Fenella contracted the work.

She called Casidhe the talent.

Not feeling talented right now.

Cavan had never told her his true name or what he was, but the power radiating from him meant he didn't have to either. Druid fit.

She'd just met someone who only Herrick could go toe-to-toe with and win. She climbed onto her bike and gripped the handles hard to stop the shaking in her hands.

Contacting Herrick took a week sometimes due to the convoluted route a cryptic message had to flow through. Fenella handled it every time. She knew the people along the way for passing along the missives where Casidhe knew only the few families she'd needed for making the trek to the castle.

She would not go to Fenella's farm and risk Cavan following her. If she didn't get in touch with Fenella before they met at the centre in the morning, she'd send the woman out the escape route before Cavan appeared.

Deep in her mind, Casidhe had a feeling Cavan would know the minute she arrived tomorrow morning. She really needed to get in touch with Fenella tonight.

That would be the only way to keep her safe for sure.

Then Casidhe and *Lann an Cheartais* were going to have a heart-to-heart. Now would be a good time for that sword to show it was on her side.

CHAPTER 18

DAEGAN LEANED CLOSE TO THE end of a small stone building across the parking lot from a grocery store. He'd cloaked Tristan and himself so they could move to stand next to the front of the closed business and observed the Luigsech woman as she went in and out of the grocery.

He opened up his senses to hear the conversation going on, then glanced over his shoulder at Tristan, who watched with a tense gaze. Tristan's grim look echoed Daegan's frame of mind.

They'd come to this small village in what was now known as County Galway, thinking to find a woman called Casidhe Luigsech. Daegan had never been one to accept coincidences when it came to the enemy.

He'd watched the ancestral research centre for hours until the man now speaking to Casidhe Luigsech showed up with something wrapped in a cloth.

When he left the centre earlier, his hands were empty.

This Luigsech woman arrived an hour later. An older woman who must have been inside all along left after that by truck.

Now Luigsech spoke to this man who continued to glamour his identity and cloak their words, but not before Daegan heard her call him Cavan.

More questions than answers about this woman.

She had the same last name as the squire family King Gruffyn had written about in Daegan's family chronicles.

The Luigsech family his da had said to trust.

That might have been the case thousands of years ago, but

Daegan had a serious sense of mistrust right now. He hadn't at first thought much about the young woman with her dark reddish-blond hair, eyes the color of polished sapphire, and a shapely body as she pedaled away from the centre. She'd appeared common enough, attractive actually, to be fair, but Daegan had changed his initial assessment.

No common human would be conversing with a being capable of that glamour and shielding their words.

Tristan suggested she looked to be in her late twenties.

Daegan had considered walking into the archival centre upon arriving here to ask questions. His sixth sense had made him wait.

Now he was glad for it.

Tristan spoke to him telepathically. *Looks like Isak's suspicions about this Luigsech woman were justified. Can you figure out who she's talking to or with?*

Daegan replied, *I only caught her callin' him Cavan. He hides his appearance with a glamour for a reason. I wonder why he did not go to her when she sat alone in the building readin'?* Daegan had watched her profile in the chair.

Tristan mused, *We don't think she's human, so he must also think that and decided to err on the side of caution by not walking in while she was there. He may think she has more power inside the building.*

'Tis a valid point about his caution, Tristan. I suspect he's been watchin' for her to leave the buildin' and he likely took a book in there for translatin'. Or perhaps for another reason to do with majik.

Cavan released the woman's arm and took a step back.

Tristan asked, *What now, boss?*

Daegan did not want to lose sight of that woman or Cavan. Following the woman would likely require cloaking, which only Daegan could do. Also, he believed Tristan could track Cavan with little trouble since Tristan could teleport away when need be. *You follow Cavan, but stay far enough back he does not see you. If he cloaks himself and vanishes or does somethin' else where you no longer have a way to follow him, stay there and call your location to me. If you do not hear right back, teleport to the same spot where we arrived earlier. I'm goin' to follow that woman and see what else I can learn.*

Sounds like a plan, boss.

His second-in-command's irreverent speech implied Tristan's confidence to carry out his task. Tristan would have made a great warrior back in the time of kingdoms and dragons.

While waiting for the woman and Cavan to separate, Daegan drew in a deep breath. Every country had its own unique smell. He seemed to notice more here with his dragon senses.

He had lost so much when Queen Maeve cursed him for eternity. Lost time with those he'd loved. The world had flown by and nothing would ever be the same again.

Ruadh grumbled low. *Queen and druid must die for curse.*

His dragon had been patient. He deserved to rip Queen Maeve and Cathbad the Druid to pieces for what they'd done to Daegan and his dragon, but everything in its time. *You are right, Ruadh, and that day will likely come as neither of them can be content with what they have. They will make a mistake and we shall be there to see that they pay for the transgressions against us. Until then, we must take care of how we move forward and locate the grimoire volumes.*

The Luigsech woman seemed angry with this Cavan, but that did not absolve her from being in league with a supernatural being.

Just what was going on with those two?

The woman gripped the bike's handlebar with a strangle hold. Tristan's quiet words floated through Daegan's mind. *Looks like Cavan is ready to leave.*

Daegan warned Tristan again, *Teleport away immediately if you suspect this Cavan realizes you follow him.*

Tristan replied, *I'm on it.*

As Cavan strolled away from the woman, Tristan melted into the scenery, headed in the same direction while remaining fifty feet back from the main thoroughfare.

The Luigsech woman rolled away, but not pedaling so casually this time. Her face muscles tightened and she glanced all around, looking more suspicious by the moment. As she drew close to where Daegan had stepped next to a scrawny tree but still cloaked from view, his gaze went to her hand that trembled when she reached to adjust the bag in her basket.

Her bike hit a pothole and wobbled.

Out of instinct, he leaned forward to grab her before she fell, but pulled back.

What was he going to do?

Jump out and expose his presence to someone he had yet to rule out as an enemy?

She righted herself without falling. That's when he got a good look at the fierce determination in her gaze. He didn't think it had anything to do with her bicycling skills so much as figuring out something that Cavan had said to upset her.

The moment she passed by, Daegan kept his cloaking up and stepped out to follow her. He had no trouble jogging to within twenty feet behind. In fact, he enjoyed the chance to run at an easy gait, which allowed him to take in the countryside before the horizon swallowed the sun.

Another sunset his captured people were missing.

His mind lurched to Devon, Renata, and the others, keeping his focus tight.

The longer Luigsech pedaled, the more her shoulders relaxed until she spun the wheels smoothly. The road she took was unpaved, but covered in grit and dirt beaten down by years of travelers, sheep, and cattle roaming. A dusty truck rumbled toward her. It dropped two wheels off the road out of consideration.

She waved at the man driving and continued on.

Old wooden fence posts of rough cut logs had been sunken along the left side of the road long ago and still managed to contain cattle grazing in fields where the lavender heather blanketed the land. On his right, the hills began to rise.

Locals still farmed the uneven land and raised their herds on the slanted ground as they had in Daegan's time.

Either Luigsech had slowed or he'd picked up his pace, but the sound of her voice startled him into realizing he was within ten feet of her. He eased back.

Long shadows spread across the gentle hills. Night would shroud this area soon with no streetlights as in a city like Atlanta.

She began singing a song he didn't recognize, but the tune had a lilt worthy of an Irish heart. Her sweet voice needed no instruments. The lass must be in good shape to ride her bike up and down these hills on a far simpler version compared to elaborate bicycles he'd seen in Atlanta.

His chest slowly eased. He'd been angry for so long with his people being attacked, he'd forgotten what a moment of peace felt like. Running along behind a pretty young woman singing a love ballad went a long way to calming his soul, if only for a few minutes.

When she took a right turn, she stood up to pedal hard, pushing her bike up a narrow incline that curved around and eventually opened into a setting that belonged in a painting.

The white stone cottage that probably held no more than two or three rooms had a high-pitched roof with a chimney stack on each end. A shorter roofed entrance jutted out from the center of the building with a bright yellow wooden door. Frames around the windows had been trimmed in a deep gold paint. A large barrel sat at the corner capturing rainwater from a spout.

Wildflowers had been planted on each side of the walkway. Ivy crawled up this side of the entrance. He recalled the yellow flowers with the odd scent of coconut, but not the name.

She stepped off the bike and leaned it beside the house then grabbed her bag of groceries. As she took a step, she paused and turned slowly.

Daegan had a moment of debating if he should hide, but she could not see through his cloaking.

She took in everything, then stared right at him.

His breath caught at being pinned by those searing blue eyes. Could she see him?

Shrugging to herself, she entered the building and closed the door.

So she hadn't seen him, but had clearly sensed someone close.

He walked to the house and placed his head next to the door, listening, but heard nothing. Cloaking could dull sounds at times. He needed to find a window.

Moving around the house, he put his back to the wall and eased over to the window on the left side of the entrance. He peeked through sheer curtains. Candlelight inside the room chased away the dark. He heard her voice again, but not singing.

Who could she be talking to? Was someone else inside?

His mind went to Cavan. Daegan's instinct warned the glamoured being who had met with Luigsech today could not be dismissed.

She specialized in locating old books.

Could Cavan have been hunting the grimoire?

Daegan dropped his cloaking then leaned his ear close to the window.

"What do you expect me to do when I need you? I have a duty. We all do. Yours is to support me if I have to battle."

He could see her moving around, but no other person inside.

She kept up her demands. "As soon as I finish eating, we're goin' to find Fenella and get her out of here."

She made a banging noise, which he figured out were sounds from a kitchen.

Cooking? Probably.

Distracted? Definitely

No better time than now to get his answers.

CHAPTER 19

HAVING LIVED ON THE STREETS much of his early life after escaping a witch, Tristan knew how to be silent and invisible.

Following Cavan presented little problem.

Tristan had picked up even more stealth skills while imprisoned by majik in a South American jungle through no fault of his own.

That bitch goddess Macha had stuck him there because he'd been born an Alterant, half Belador and half Medb blood. It did warm his soul to know she'd feared Alterants even before they evolved into gryphons.

Carrying the blood of his enemy was fucked up enough, but Macha had penalized him and other Alterants for something none of them could have changed. Then Queen Maeve and Cathbad the Druid thought to possess all of his gryphon pack, since those two had been behind the crossbreeding. They'd planned to compel gryphons to do their wet work.

Not now.

The day Tristan and his Belador friends rescued Daegan from TÅμr Medb then broke the curse holding him, Daegan threw Macha out of Treoir.

Being of King Gruffyn's immediate family, he could do that sort of thing.

Best day ever.

Tristan bet Macha never saw that coming. Bonus.

If Tristan had a calendar, he'd mark the date to celebrate each year since he could count the best days of his life on one hand. The other four had been spent with Mac.

She'd love this place.

He should bring her here sometime when he wasn't hunting a preternatural. In fact, he should do a better job of spending time with Mac when this all settled down and he could insure her safety.

At what point would his life ever settle down?

Maybe never. That was okay.

Tristan would do whatever Daegan needed, be his right-hand man for as long as Daegan wanted him. No one had ever looked at him and seen anything but an Alterant beast even after he'd evolved into a gryphon. He'd been at the butt end of life for so long and Daegan opened up a whole new world for him.

For the first time ever, he felt respected.

Cavan slowed the steady stride he'd been at for the last twenty minutes and turned off the main thoroughfare. He headed into a wooded area thicker than before, but stayed on a hard-packed path. He seemed to be in no rush.

Was Cavan meeting someone else or heading home?

Tristan had a difficult time believing that being lived anywhere around here because of the glamour. How was Daegan doing following that unknown Luigsech woman? Tristan had a moment of concern about Daegan going without backup, but that dragon shifter could handle himself in any situation.

Tristan had been present when Daegan backed down three deities, while the two of them stood in the Tribunal realm. Few things could harm Daegan, but being attacked in an unfriendly realm upped the chances of him being killed.

His boss should be fine in his homeland.

Daegan's knowledge of the players from so many centuries ago and their lack of knowledge about the identity of his goddess mother kept everyone from risking a power play.

But that didn't mean they weren't all strategizing how to take out the Treoir dragon shifter.

Tristan executed a quick zigzag to avoid making noises as he paralleled Cavan's route. He picked his way carefully over dried leaves and branches that had fallen.

Cavan paused and lifted his head, turning it from side to side, as if looking for something.

Or someone.

The guy stepped off the path as if he'd found what he'd been searching for.

Tristan hurried his steps, grumbling silently at the unexpected shift in direction.

He stopped short and squatted down to watch through an opening in underbrush as Cavan circled back to his right, pausing again every few steps. Then he'd stare up at the trees overhead from time to time.

What was he doing now?

Suddenly, Cavan flipped around and started walking the other way this time.

After making that pass, he stood still for a moment then shook his head and heaved a deep breath. Then he struck out deeper into the woods.

Tristan hurried to follow the circular path Cavan had taken to figure out what he'd been looking for above his head. He kept an eye on Cavan as the strange guy moved slowly through an area of thicker vegetation.

Once Tristan determined if there was anything of note here, he'd teleport to catch up to the druid. He quickly finished tracing Cavan's steps then did an about-face and walked back the other way. Nothing up in the trees.

Nothing weird stood out.

When next he checked on Cavan, the guy had continued on a straight path until he'd had to sidestep around two fallen trees.

Losing patience with this meandering that seemed to go nowhere, Tristan hurried to finish the half circle path, then did his best to track the straight line to Cavan.

He started to teleport to catch up, but he reconsidered. Too risky to make a disturbance when he landed again if he did not know exactly where his feet would hit. Tristan had fifty feet until he reached the two trees Cavan had circumvented.

Deep in the woods with the sun having set, twilight made it harder to keep an eye on the squirrely guy until Tristan realized this weirdo had a pale glow about him.

Was Cavan creating the glow for a way to see?

None of this made sense because—

Tristan plowed into an invisible energy field at full force.

The power reached for him.

That bastard had probably set an obstacle to keep anyone from tracking him. Tristan remained calm. He'd worked his way out of other situations. Cavan continued walking without turning around, which he wouldn't be doing if this was a trap, right?

Tristan tried to pull backward from the invisible net, but the energy felt like a sticky web. Next he tried to teleport and got nowhere. So the invisible web interfered with his teleporting, huh?

He called up his gryphon close to the surface for more power. His head altered shape. His jaw dropped, enlarging for huge fangs, and he snarled.

He batted his fists at the energy, pushing deep into it. His legs dragged against what felt like a rubbery gel.

Fuck it. He called up his gryphon to shift.

Daegan would back him doing this in the human realm, but his boss couldn't help him if Tristan didn't survive. His gryphon pushed hard to be freed, cracking his bones and stretching muscles, painfully slow.

Tristan would break free of this or call Daegan.

His body stopped halfway through the shift.

Oh, shit.

CHAPTER 20

"HOW AM I GOIN' TO escape?" Casidhe muttered, still ranting at the world as she warmed a pot of stew she'd pulled from her freezer this morning to thaw. Cooking for one meant leftovers, but she liked having food she'd cooked again.

She snatched up her mobile phone to call Fenella for the fifth time. No answer. Fenella complained she only got a tower at work, but she tended to show up at work without her phone some days. Had she walked out with her phone today? Casidhe couldn't recall. It might have been in Fenella's purse.

Was she even carrying a phone on her trip to the goat farm? Probably not.

Why couldn't that woman keep the blasted phone with her just in case she got a tower connection?

When the call went to voicemail, Casidhe said, "It's me. Important." She never said much on electronics. Herrick had been right to not trust them, but if he'd had a satellite phone this past week, she wouldn't have taken off on that trek.

Stirring the stew brought the wonderful smell of home to her. Could she do anything else while she waited to talk to Fenella? She had the sword hidden safely from sight even though no one knocked on her door at night.

But what if Cavan showed up?

She had no idea exactly what he was other than powerful.

If he came here, could he find the sword just by sensing its power? He had no reason to visit her tonight. What did he really want other than expecting her to just drop what she was doing and leave to hunt a freaking book with him?

What was so important about the Immortuos Grimoire? In Latin, *immortuos* translated as dead.

Her stomach grumbled at being empty for so long, but her earlier terror had dampened her appetite.

Should I try to coax the sword from the sheath and work with it? she ruminated silently, tired of talking to an empty room. *How am I goin' to deal with someone like Cavan if I'm unarmed?*

Of course, having a sword that refused to leave the sheath left her just as defenseless.

Cavan would likely be at the archival centre no later than ten in the morning, but he might arrive early. If he did, he'd know when Fenella showed up and would notice her missing when he walked in.

She really had to find Fenella tonight.

She had no idea if she could even find the grimoire and he expected her to regardless of what she said.

He also believed she'd go willingly with him.

The minute Fenella was out of danger, Casidhe would have freedom to make any decision in dealing with Cavan. If she knew what kind of majik wielder he was, she might consider escaping, but he'd sounded too confident he could find her.

Scooping the stew into a bowl and breaking off a chunk of stale bread she should have tossed this morning, she moved to the table next to one of the front windows. Her home might seem small to others, but she needed no more than this large room that provided enough space for a kitchen, a two-seat dining table, and a well-used sofa she tossed a throw over to cover a few tears. She had a nice size bedroom with a small bathroom. No problem, since she'd always kept her personal belongings neat.

She'd never brought a man here.

It would have felt weird, because the home had belonged to Fenella's squire family for many generations.

The only time she'd been interested in someone sexually had been back during her days at the university in England. That had lasted three months.

Two and a half months longer than it should have, but she'd been lonely, so sue her.

The long winter months here were just as lonely, but at least she loved this cottage and had felt at home from the moment she moved in.

One day, she'd live with her clan at the castle and find a nice young man who understood her life. All she'd find here would be clueless humans.

Lifting a spoon of stew, she blew on the hot broth.

A chill rushed over her skin as once more she had a feeling of being watched. What the hell? She immediately called up her protective energy to shield her powers.

The sensation of being stalked heightened, as if whoever watched her was closer than before.

Her heart pounded like crazy. Her fight or flight reaction kicked in, but she had no idea what she would fight or where to run.

She put her spoon down slowly, placed her palms on the table and looked up toward the entrance. No one there. She started to tell herself what an idiot she was when a movement drew her gaze farther to the right.

An imposing figure emerged from the dark hallway leading to her bedroom.

A scream climbed up her throat and stuck there. Screaming would do no good.

Who would hear her?

Besides, she couldn't draw enough breath to speak.

He kept coming, very slowly, until all of him came into view.

It wasn't Cavan.

This man filled the room just by standing there. His gray-eyed gaze seemed to swirl. He had muscles that grew muscles if the stretch of that T-shirt indicated anything. Long legs pushed him to tower over her. Power radiated from him, but something told her he held back so much more.

Swallowing hard, she pushed out a sentence. "Who are you and what do you want?"

"I wish to speak with you." His deep brogue reminded her of a famous actor from Scotland.

Was he serious? Did every powerful being think she was here just for them?

Something snapped inside her.

Maybe she'd been terrified one time too many today, but this man sneaking into her cottage had just pissed her off. "You want to talk to me? Really? It is customary to knock on someone's door first then ask to have a conversation." Her voice rose as she got to her feet. "Not break into my house."

"I did not wish to be seen enterin' and put you in danger."

Did he really think she was going to give him points for that? "Who would see you when I live on top of a rise with no neighbors?"

He shrugged. "'Tis best to be careful."

Anger pushed her to throw caution to the wind, or it could be due to the fact that he had yet to threaten her. Whatever the reason, she'd hit the limit of taking everything as it came and ordered again, "Get out of my house."

"I will leave once you answer my questions."

"No. Get out."

"No." He crossed his arms.

Well, hell. What could she do now? Threaten him with bodily harm? Hardly.

She'd hidden the sword nearby, behind a bookcase between her and the front door. How much good would that weapon do her anyhow?

It would probably just humiliate her if she tried, and failed, to withdraw the blade from its hiding place.

She finally realized something. "*How* did you get in here? You're too big to fit through any of my windows and no one has come through the door tonight except me."

"I will answer your questions once you answer mine. I may have entered without permission, but I have not threatened you and I am being reasonable." His voice held a hint of humor, as if he found it ridiculous that she'd even argue with him.

"Reasonable?" she muttered. What had happened to her life?

Until Cavan walked into the ancestral research centre a week ago, she'd had a great life. Now Cavan intended to drag her away to hunt some ancient book of majik and this guy appeared inside her home with no possible way of normal entry.

Annnd he expected her to answer his questions.

She crossed her arms. "I'm tired. People are seriously gettin' on my nerves today, you included. So I'll give you one minute to ask your blasted questions. I *might* answer them."

"We could sit down," he suggested.

Was he nuts? "No, we can't. This is not a social visit. Talk."

"I saw ya speakin' with a nonhuman earlier. Did he ask ya to hunt for a book?"

"Cavan?" His name tumbled out before she could stop herself. "Why should I tell you anythin'?"

"Because hidin' anythin' about that bein' could be a deadly mistake."

Fear chilled her blood for the first time since this guy had shown up. If she gave this man anything, she'd surely bring Cavan's wrath down on her.

If she refused to share what Cavan hunted, she risked not surviving tonight. Cavan would go after Fenella and torture her to find a grimoire that sweet woman had no skills to locate.

CHAPTER 21

DAEGAN SIZED UP THIS LUIGSECH woman, trying to pinpoint why his senses were yelling at him that she hid something important. He could feel an energy in the room, but not coming from her. Could she be a witch with something majikal close by to use against him?

She might be shielding more than what she'd discussed with Cavan.

"Threatenin' to kill me is not the best way to be gainin' information." She spoke through clenched teeth.

"I never said I would kill you," he argued in a calm voice.

"You said hidin' anythin' would be a deadly mistake. That's a threat." She frowned so hard fine lines cut into her forehead.

"'Tis not."

"Liar."

He signed heavily. "For someone who works with history, I would expect ya to be better at listenin'. I said if ya hide anythin' about that bein' ya spoke to at the grocery it could be deadly. Think about it. That means you could be at risk from this Cavan. He hides his identity with a glamour. That should concern ya."

She seemed surprised then recovered. "He didn't break into my home uninvited."

"I have already explained I intend ya no harm. I would not have come here if it were not of the utmost importance."

She tossed her hands up and dropped them back to her sides. "I can't even believe I'm havin' this conversation. Bottom line is that confidentiality is part of my business. If I were huntin' somethin' for *you*, would you want me to share your business with a stranger?"

"Ya would be foolish to do so." He stared her down, determined to intimidate her into giving him what he wanted without terrifying her. Sure, he'd teleported in without her permission, but she would never have allowed him inside otherwise.

The longer his presence remained hidden, the better for both of them.

"Oh, I see. I should protect *your* interests, if you were my client, which you will never be, by the way. But I would not be foolish to share what another client asks me to hunt. I get it."

Tart wench. Daegan pressed on. "So Cavan does have ya huntin' somethin'?"

She grabbed hair on each side of her head, pulling strands loose from the twisted up bob on top of her head. "Stop it. No more talkin' about his project. What the hell do you want? Just tell me and get movin'."

At that moment, Tristan's tight voice came into Daegan's mind. *Cavan is ...*

Daegan's pulse pounded in his ears.

He tried to lock onto where Tristan had been when he called to him and ... nothing came through. Daegan couldn't find the pathway for teleporting. He called back, *Tristan! Tell me where ya are!*

Still nothing.

The woman had moved from the table toward the entrance. She stopped and took a step back from him, bumping into a waist-high bookcase. True fear surfaced in her face. "What's wrong? Why do you look like you're thinkin' to murder someone?"

Daegan no longer cared who he frightened. He pinned her with a furious glare. "Not only will I be stayin' as long as I choose, but ya will start answerin' questions and stop dancin' around."

Whatever she saw in his face had her nodding. "Okay, just

calm down."

"I do *not* need to calm down. I have people in danger and every second you waste they pay a higher price. Now what did Cavan want?"

"To, uh, find an old book."

Daegan's anger built. "What book?"

She looked physically sick about answering, but finally said, "A grimoire. It's called the Immortuos Grimoire."

This was no longer a series of coincidences, but connections. "As I understand, ya have a reputation for findin' rare books and translatin' the ancient languages. Ya will find the volumes for me and translate the text."

"Who are you people to come into my life and make all these demands?" she shouted at him, fear sliding through her angry words.

"Do not confuse us. I have good reason to find this grimoire. Can you claim Cavan does?"

She lifted her shoulders with a lost expression. "I have no idea. I haven't even looked for that stupid grimoire yet. I have no idea if it even exists."

"It does, in three separate volumes. I want them." She might have to hunt all three to find the one he needed. Now that he had her talking, he asked, "What else did Cavan want? Who was he?"

She nibbled on her lip, clearly debating how much to share.

Fear for Tristan pushed power into Daegan's voice. *"Tell me!"*

She flinched, then swiped a hand over her head and sounded resigned. "I have no idea who he is. Cavan originally came in days back askin' about a family known as Treoirs. We gave him nothin', because I had to leave town for a few days and just returned today. I haven't had time to look into that."

For the first time, Daegan looked at this woman and wondered if she could actually be related to the Luigsech squires. "What do ya know of the Treoirs?"

"Nothin'. I told you I haven't had time to research it."

"Lie." He might not have Storm's gifted lie-detecting

ability, but Daegan knew when someone tried to sidestep the truth.

She stared openmouthed at him. Her eyes shot daggers at him. "Do *not* call me a liar. You have yet to even tell me who the hell you are."

Ignoring her outburst, he warned, "Tell me what you know about the Treoirs or I will take ya somewhere and keep you there until ya do."

Color washed from her face.

He felt bad about that, but the longer his Beladors remained captured and now with Tristan silent, the less Daegan's conscience dwelled on minor things.

He hadn't sensed any power from her and took a chance to share something he normally would not. "A Luigsech family was once squires to the Treoirs."

The minute he spoke, the truth showed in her eyes.

She knew.

Her gaze shot past him, not touching his face. "I've heard bits and pieces of the Treoir history. It's hard to miss in my line of work." When she did meet his eyes, she stood straighter and claimed, "In fact, that's the family responsible for the red dragon torchin' forests in innocent countries."

"That dragon is an imposter."

She arched an eyebrow challenging his words. "How do you know this?"

He couldn't believe the backbone of this one. "I did not come here to debate your lack of Treoir history knowledge. How much did you tell Cavan about the Treoirs?"

"Nothin'. Nothin'. Nothin'. Don't you dare call me a liar," she snarled at him. "Cavan expected to meet with me to discuss the book he left at our centre. I tried to tell him I needed time to research the grimoire, but that didn't fly. He has the patience of a gnat, just like you."

Daegan had to find Tristan. "My friend was followin' Cavan and now he is missin'. Ya will help me find him."

"Oh, hell no. I didn't cause any of your troubles, buster. You and Cavan need to leave me alone and work out your differences." Her hands shook when she reached back to grip the bookcase for support.

That was the moment her energy pushed through the room, banging against Daegan.

She was definitely not human.

CHAPTER 22

CASIDHE'S HEART HAMMERED WILDLY. SOMETHING had changed severely with this intruder. What did he mean about Cavan capturing his friend? The quick change in her intruder's demeanor from pushy to furious had happened out of nowhere.

That made no sense.

He hadn't produced a mobile phone.

How could he know something about his friend's situation right now?

"You have lied yet again, Casidhe Luigsech," her uninvited guest said in a quiet voice that sent chills racing up her spine.

She had feared little since leaving the castle to live here and didn't know how to handle that emotion. One minute the fear chewed at her confidence, and in the next, fury flashed through her at feeling panicked. "I'm getting' damned tired of you and your scare tactics. How can you be callin' me a liar yet again when I said nothin' this time?"

Instead of answering her question, he warned, "Ya should take heed of my words and start spoutin' the truth. If anythin' happens to my friend, I will hold ya, Cavan, and everyone who gets in my way at fault." He'd been so relaxed before he brought up that his friend was in jeopardy.

What had she done to make him think she had any part in that?

He took a threatening step forward. "And I dare much when the lives of my people and others depend upon it. First ya will tell me how to locate Cavan. Then once I find my friend, ya will hold the grimoire volumes for me if ya find them in the meantime."

"I don't even know who *you* are." Her brain threatened to explode at this impossible situation. This guy's brogue thickened as he became agitated. She had to get rid of him. "Cavan is at least payin' me. You break into my house, threaten my life, and now want to force me to hunt a book for you without offerin' a penny. Oh, and you think I do missin' persons searches. Just because you say all that about Cavan doesn't mean anythin'. You could be escaped from a mental institution for all I know. You haven't even given me a name."

"My name does not matter. Locatin' Cavan does. Tell me how to find him," he repeated, pushing more fury into his words.

"I don't know. Both times, he just showed up at the centre, then he found me today. He'll be at the centre in the mornin'. There. Now you know. Show up just before ten and you two have a talk. Keep me out of it."

Her tall, dark, and intimidating intruder vibrated with anger. His power pushed out across the room, pinning her back against the bookcase.

Then his face took a turn from furious to decisive. "Very well. I will leave for now, but ya will never be out of my sight. Perhaps seein' me leave will bring Cavan to your door."

"Oh crap, thanks so much. Not."

"Ya have no worry as long as ya do not cross me and give aid to Cavan. I will be close by."

His words hit her square in the chest. "Wait a damn minute. You're usin' me for bait?" Blood rushed from her head.

He stepped up quickly and cupped her arms, shaking her. "Are ya sick?"

She was so much worse than sick. She could not run from Cavan or this man, if this stranger told the truth, and he seemed to understand more than she did.

Her energy swirled and raced through her. The sensation buzzed just under her skin then surfaced where his hands touched her. She shoved him away.

He cursed. "Ya are no Luigsech."

"I am." She straightened away from the bookcase.

"No. They were human. Ya are not. Who are ya?"

Gripping her fingers tight enough to be white, she'd done it again. She'd allowed her shield to drop.

With nothing else at her fingertips for defense, she shouted at him. "You have no right to come here and accuse me of anythin'. I don't even know you. I have no reason to believe what you say about Cavan and you sure as hell don't know what you're sayin' about me. Get. Out."

Muscles bulged in his jaw. His eyes narrowed with fury. He took a step toward her. "Here is my deal. First I find my friend, then ya will find the grimoire volumes. *That* is when ya will no longer see me."

With the edge of the bookcase digging into her butt, she made a decision that might get her killed. She'd hidden the sword in the wide slot between the back of the case and the wall. Taking a last breath, she pleaded silently to not be denied, and reached back to grip the sword handle.

This time, *Lann an Cheartais* slid smoothly from the sheath.

Casidhe whispered her thanks. Power zinged through it as she raised the deadly blade quickly in front of her.

His eyes widened with surprise. He inhaled deeply and stared at the sword in disbelief. "Where did ya get *that*?"

"What made you think we were still chatting?" she gritted out, holding the sword with both hands. "I would not harm someone unarmed, but I have no doubt that you possess deadly supernatural weapons."

"You will explain that sword or—" He cocked his head quickly toward the door. "Are ya expectin' someone?"

What a poor attempt at trying to get her to look away. She muttered, "Unbelievable. Are you dense on top of everythin' else?"

"If Cavan approaches, ya will tell him nothin' about the grimoire volumes or the Treoirs."

She waved the sword back and forth. "I do not take orders

from you."

His voice deepened. "Some bein' approaches. Are ya expectin' Cavan tonight or not?"

"Cavan, whoever. Right now, I'd welcome the grim reaper. He'd be better company."

His frustration erupted. "If ya do not know who comes, ya are in danger."

"Says the man who broke into my home and *threatened* me," she yelled at him.

"Warnin' ya 'tis not a threat," he argued through a clenched jaw.

"Breakin' and enterin' *is*," she countered and walked across the room. She gripped her sword in one hand and grabbed the door latch with her other. She didn't hear anyone outside.

What if Fenella had decided to bring the baby goats by to show her? She hoped so. She had to get Fenella out of this area immediately. Send her to the castle.

Herrick would have to trust Casidhe's decision.

If Casidhe did not show up to meet Cavan in the morning, he'd hurt Fenella.

Lifting the sword, she warned her intruder, "Do not speak to anyone comin' to see me and do not scare them or you will find out just what I'm capable of." That sounded so much better than the truth.

He shook his head and muttered something dark that even she couldn't translate. He shifted his thick legs apart and ordered, "Open the door."

She pushed down on the handle release and yanked the door to her, glaring at him the entire time.

He shouted, "*Move!*"

She'd had it with this guy. "You know what—"

A glowing creature rushed inside, howling and with claws out to kill.

CHAPTER 23

DAEGAN CALLED UP THE TREOIR sword he'd used to fight wars when he'd lived in this land free to fly as a dragon. He hacked at the glowing Imortik with sickle-shaped claws reaching for him. This thing would be impossible to kill unless it had taken over a human body or a being of less power than him.

Daegan slashed across, intending to cut off the head, but the damn creature dove and gouged his leg.

He knew better than to try to teleport this time.

Daegan booted the center of its body, knocking the snarling thing away. The burn of venom streaked up his leg.

The Imortik body struck the stunned Luigsech woman, knocking her off her feet. She fell backwards, crashing into a rocking chair. All of that hit the ground hard, but she held onto her sword still sizzling with energy.

Pointing a finger at the Imortik as it tried to get up, Daegan roared as his telekinetic power would not work. He stepped over and ripped the Imortik off her and dropped it on the floor.

She scrambled to her feet.

With a wild look in her eyes, she slashed down, cutting off a head that bounced away.

Her weapon didn't just smell of majik, it stunk of ancient power.

Another glowing creature raced through the door, catching Daegan distracted. This one looked more troll than human. Could he kill a troll taken over by an Imortik? It slammed into him, knocking Daegan down and clawing at his chest.

Daegan beat the pummel of his sword against the creature's head.

The Imortik jerked hard and tried to reach for its back.

That's when Daegan realized Luigsech had stabbed her sword through the troll's back, barely missing Daegan's privates. That woman would kill *him* if he didn't get her to calm down.

"Don't stab anythin' I'm fightin'."

"You ungrateful bastard! I just saved your miserable life."

His gaze yanked to the doorway. *"Close the damn door!"*

"Stop yellin' at me. You brought these things to my house." Her blue eyes glowed and bulged with wild-eyed panic. She gasped air.

He shoved the Imortik-troll body off his lower half and pushed up with his sword in hand.

Two demons the size of bulls standing upright crashed into each other at the entrance, fighting to get inside.

What had called up demons?

Daegan lunged forward, slashing and driving his sword as he did. One demon barely glowed, but the other one shined yellow bright as the sun. That one lost a hand and spun away screeching. Daegan shoved a boot straight into the chest of the second one, knocking it out of the doorway.

He fought the demon with the sword, unsure if he could use his powers after being stabbed by that Imortik. This demon dodged back and forth, then came at him.

Daegan glanced at the second one holding his wrist, dismissed it then braced for the other demon attacking. He waited until the last second, close enough to smell the demon's disgusting sulfur odor, but Luigsech's sword slashed into view. She swung horizontal, cutting the demon in half. She lifted the blade high, looking like a wild Valkyrie holding off an army, then brought it down fast, slashing off the demon's head.

No one's head would be safe around her.

The demon turned to orange dust and blew away.

What the hell?

He'd never seen one turn to orange dust.

A snarl alerted him just before the injured demon dove at him. Daegan twisted around, bringing his blade with him.

Tristan yelled in his head in that moment. *Caught ... trap ... Cavan is ...* Tristan howled painfully.

The demon leaped, landing half on Daegan's shoulder and clawing his back.

Daegan flipped forward, falling away from the door. He rolled, throwing the demon off as he did. Not stopping, he jumped up, spun around, and brought his blade down across the demon's neck as it crawled to him.

Luigsech had the right idea with decapitation.

With the head gone, that body also turned into orange dust. Another glowing demon shot out of the dark, claws reaching for his chest. Daegan swung and missed. The creature clawed his shoulder. His energy waned. He had to kill this thing fast. Calling up his dragon, Daegan roared an inhuman sound and battered the demon to the ground, then flipped his sword to strike straight down. Another burst of orange dust and everything finally fell silent.

Heaving breaths, Daegan wiped sweat off his brow.

He drew on his dragon's healing power. Maybe it would push out new venom the Imortiks had stabbed into him.

Ruadh rumbled and banged inside him, but energy flooded his body.

Garwyli had warned him the rift would open in different parts of the world and the venom inside him would draw in Imortiks.

His leg felt better, but throbbed. Pain burned in his shoulder.

If he didn't find a way to clean out that venom, it could deplete his powers even more and interfere with getting Tristan back.

Luigsech would help him. To possess such a sword she'd pulled from hiding and draw on its power meant she knew far more than she'd admitted.

She probably knew how to find the grimoire as well and had done an experienced job of lying.

Maybe he had needed Storm's lie-detecting ability after all.

Pain throbbed with every movement he made, but better that he'd been injured than Luigsech. He could not allow anything to happen to her. She was no human and that sword had come from the time of his father, but she could lose to an Imortik.

Aye, she had to live to help Daegan find Cavan.

He cursed himself for being played. Not again.

If he failed to make her tell him who Cavan was and deliver the grimoire volumes to him, he risked Tristan's life plus that of the ones back home.

He'd saved her life. Maybe now they could work together once she accepted that she might need him to protect her from dangerous beings.

Aye, this would work.

Turning to the cottage, he started walking then paused. He could not sense her power. "Luigsech?"

No one answered. He rushed forward. The troll body lay still on the floor.

He roared, *"Casidhe Luigsech!"*

She was gone.

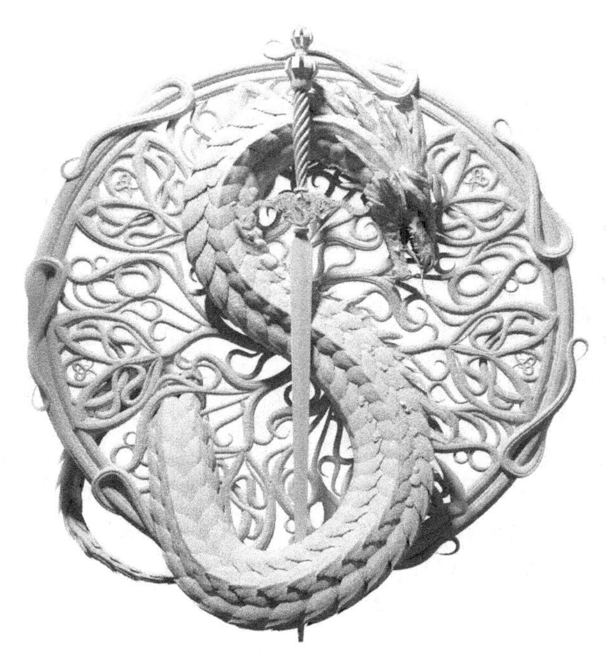

BOOK 2

CHAPTER 1

Galway, Ireland

HOSTILE ENERGY SWARMED CASIDHE'S COTTAGE and buzzed her skin.

Her adrenaline rush crashed, slamming into the shock chilling her. She couldn't stop the ringing in her ears.

She'd killed a live being.

Two, in fact. Neither had been human, but still.

She clutched *Lann an Cheartais* with a death grip. The sword had come to her aid.

The blade trembled in her shaking hands.

What were those two dead yellow things at her feet? One headless body. She'd stabbed the second monster and ... *wait!* Had a hand on that one just twitched? Panicked, she whipped her sword up and chopped off another head.

Her beloved cottage, her sanctuary, would never be the same. *She* would never be the same. She fought for a deep breath.

The air stunk of rotten eggs, a sulfuric odor from the horrid corpses.

Her stomach twisted and tried to dump the stew she'd barely eaten. She swallowed hard at what she'd done, but she'd had no choice. Those glowing yellow beings had clawed her clothes and tried to kill her.

A wailing howl broke through her foggy mind and snapped her back into real time.

Her crazy intruder still battled demons outside. She'd lopped the head off of one that had tried to get in. Unlike the bodies stinking up her home, the demon she'd decapitated had burst into orange dust.

Move, move, move! Screamed through her mind. Stop wasting time on dead monsters.

This was her chance to escape.

Her conscience smacked her brain aside. What about the guy fighting those demons?

Leaning forward, she took a quick look out the open doorway at the stranger who had broken into her home. With shoulders wider than the door and long, powerful legs, he battled like a Spartan warrior. One massive booted foot plowed through her gorse and delphinium flower beds now splattered with blood. He swung a monster sword he'd conjured up as if he'd been born with the hilt in his hands.

That stranger clearly had everything under control. He'd survive.

She could stay here and watch or get the hell out while he was busy. First, she had to reach Fenella and warn her of two threats. Cavan plus tonight's intruder.

Both men wanted stupid grimoire volumes.

Neither one of them were human.

Casidhe had to grab what she needed and escape. *Hurry!* She had seconds to make a decision and act. In her mind, she dashed around the room, but in truth she moved like a wobbly toy top.

Of all the things she'd like to take with her, she really only needed one item.

Her mobile phone.

She dodged headless bodies and searched the destruction at a manic pace. Her phone wasn't on the side table near the door where she normally dropped it along with a small ring of keys.

That table had been shattered.

She jumped around, looking everywhere, but no phone. *Damn!*

A mournful howl outside yanked her head up. She stared out the window as the last demon fell and burst into orange ash.

Nothing left for the intruder to fight.

Her time had run out!

Another glowing demon emerged from the night and raced toward the cottage. Her intruder yanked his sword up again.

Casidhe cursed silently and spun to leave.

Leaping carefully over the bodies, she raced to her bedroom and laid her sword on the bed. Gripping the oak footboard, she pushed the bed toward the door. Old, but smooth, oak flooring slid apart to reveal a hidden trapdoor someone would have to know was there to find.

Grabbing her sword, she climbed down in the hole, set the blade aside, and reached for a thick rope running through pulleys. Fear gifted her with a boost of strength. She dragged the bed frame and flooring back in place. The boards made a click as they snapped together, leaving her in the dark.

She sat on the step listening to the muffled sounds of the battle. Farther away, but the darkness ramped up her fear. Felt like the battle was right above her.

Keep moving or there'd be hell to pay if a demon caught her in this pitch-black tunnel. She knew this passage well, but had no light. That meant moving slowly or catching her toe and falling on uneven ground.

She could do this. Gipping her sword, she swung the blade up to point ahead of her.

The sword began glowing.

Okay, then.

Her heart thumped wildly. Every breath hurt. She had to stop sucking in air so hard and calm down or she'd hyperventilate.

Easier said than done with what she'd just gone through. She rushed ahead, bent over so she could clear the low ceiling. Her ears roared with blood rushing hard through her body. Halfway, she stopped short, expecting to hear the trapdoor open and something dangerous come chasing after her.

The stranger. Demons. Glowing yellow beings.

Any and all made her crab walk faster.

What had caused those hideous yellow beings to attack? One looked like a troll, but she doubted trolls normally lit up as bright as caution lights.

With every step, she chastised her inability to think clearer under stress. She should have grabbed her backpack, clothes, food ... so many things.

There had been no time.

Her intruder must have finished off the last demon by now.

In fact, he was probably searching everywhere for her.

Her heart thudded at pissing him off. There would be a price to pay for that, but he had to catch her first.

Cool air did little to stop sweat from streaming down her face. She clamped the sword hilt tighter in her damp hands, glad for the blade's glow or a slug would outrun her. This weapon had been made for Herrick's sister, Shannon, another dragon shifter who had died in the Dragani War.

Would she be pleased or angry an adopted nobody now held her sword?

During Casidhe's time with Herrick and even in college, she'd been trained to swing an average sword one-handed.

Not this one. *Lann an Cheartais* required all her strength to wield the blade with any accuracy.

She'd like to ask Herrick if Shannon had used two hands.

She'd like to ask Herrick a thousand questions right now.

As she reached the end of the tunnel she'd traversed many times over the years, she slowed and turned to her left. Three steps in, she swung the sword down and changed her grip so she could carry it with one hand as she climbed.

At the top step, she unlatched the metal covering and waited, listening.

The tunnel had been created centuries ago and ran a hundred meters away from the cottage. Rocks stacked along the walls had been there so long they were settled and tight. Low ceilings allowed women and children to escape as husbands fought off an attack. If a large male enemy followed, he'd be crawling.

That would allow even more time for the vulnerable to flee.

Much as she appreciated the forethought of an escape route, she hated to feel vulnerable.

A demon would crawl that length fast as a rat after cheese.

She pushed the cover up slowly and peeked through the opening. No boots, feet, or unnatural sounds. Lifting the lid out of the way, she climbed out beneath the cover of darkness and stretched her sore back.

Pain zinged in muscles strained from remaining in one position for so long. She clamped her lips tight to trap the groan climbing her throat.

No time to complain. The physical challenge would only get more difficult from here.

Quieting her breathing, she searched the dark forest for any sound of threat.

Nothing but a soothing cricket symphony.

Black shadows surrounded her in every direction, even with the sliver of a moon trying to spear light through the trees. The sweet scent of heather blooming rode on a pleasant summer breeze.

She sucked in a deeper breath and exhaled to wash away the stench from those dead beings.

Hair flicked her face. Propping the sword next to her leg to free her hands, she pulled her hair back into a snug ponytail. Better.

She felt more in control.

Time for a plan, now that she could think for a moment. She'd heard no one tracking her through the tunnel, but that didn't mean her late night intruder couldn't find her.

Deep in her gut, she had a feeling that stranger had abilities beyond the majik he'd used to produce a sword.

And how had he entered her cottage without making a sound?

After dropping the trapdoor back in place and rearranging the weeds until the area appeared undisturbed, she took stock of her situation.

No money. No clothes. No phone.

She had *Lann an Cheartais,* which had stopped glowing.

Did that mean the blade had gone dark to shield her position in the woods or that the cranky weapon had returned to slumber mode?

Shaking off worry over things she couldn't change, Casidhe started walking in the only direction that made sense.

To Fenella's farm.

Getting the woman she considered a sister as much as a best friend to safety was her one priority at the moment. With no bicycle, she'd have to walk fast to reach Fenella's farm twenty-seven kilometers away. She did a quick calculation and estimated it would take her almost four hours, less if she could make up time jogging the flat ground.

What if that stranger who broke into her cottage got to Fenella first?

He'd mentioned seeing Casidhe's friend leave the ancestral research centre yesterday. What if a demon or yellow thing had followed this stranger ... then Fenella?

Terror had her moving faster. She took off jogging with determination.

After two short rest breaks and sweating a bucket of water, she had one last hill to cross before reaching the quaint farm she loved to visit. She gave herself an attagirl for running most of the way. That should be the current time between one and two in the morning.

Sparing a moment to catch her breath, she pushed again to make it up the last incline. In fairness to her aching legs, she hadn't stretched before running this distance. The limited lighting allowed her to find her footing and reach the crest of the hill quickly where she paused to enjoy the moment.

Her tight chest muscles eased.

She'd reached Fenella's home in time.

Her friend's white farmhouse and barn stood out against the dark night.

Casidhe had always wanted to find someone to paint a picture of this wonderful place. It would make a great gift.

How many times had she visited here in ten years? Fenella would greet her with a smile and make her sit for a piece of pie and milk, then they'd visit all the farm critters.

New energy pushed her to rush down the slope, smiling the whole way. She'd been switching hands while carrying the sword as she jogged and her arms were turning into rubber, but she'd get a break soon. She'd suffer any discomfort to keep her friend safe.

As Casidhe neared the house, she looked up, blinked, and looked again. The relief she'd enjoyed spun away as fast as the last water swirling down a drain.

Something was wrong, very wrong.

CHAPTER 2

DAEGAN KILLED THE LAST DEMON. He watched it turn into orange dust as he took a breath. His heart pounded his chest, but he'd survived and the lass was safe. What must she think after being attacked by Imortiks? In fact, where was she after being in his way earlier?

The silence tipped him off.

He took off running to the open door on the cottage and rushed inside. *"Casidhe Luigsech!"*

Gone.

Dropping his head back, he roared with fury.

The walls shook.

How had she escaped without him seeing her? She'd admitted the only door to the house had been the front entrance. That door had never been out of his sight.

Standing inside the cottage, which had been tidy and smelled of coconut when he'd first teleported in secretly, now looked like a bloody battleground. He wiped Imortik and demon blood from his sword on one of the bodies no longer glowing yellow, but the place stank of sulfur.

He raced around searching the cottage, opening every cabinet and closet door, hoping to find Luigsech hidden somewhere in the small structure. Nothing.

He shouldn't be surprised she'd escaped.

The woman who had pulled an ancient sword from a hiding place behind a bookcase and wielded it in panic might have been terrified at first, but she'd also decapitated Imortiks. She hadn't broken down into tears or run away screaming.

She'd swung that sword with the fury of female warriors

from his time.

The minute he'd been distracted killing the demons, she'd slipped away.

Why?

He hadn't threatened her.

Ruadh made a sound he took as a snort. *You scared woman.*

Maybe he had.

Regret washed through Daegan, because he *had* intimidated her about Cavan. She'd met with the mysterious being in the village not far from the ancestral research centre where she worked.

Who the devil could that Cavan be?

Why had he captured Tristan?

Without Luigsech, Daegan had no way to find Cavan.

He needed Cavan to get Tristan back. First, he had to track down the Luigsech woman.

What a mess. He'd come here to find a grimoire to protect all of his people the glowing-yellow Imortiks threatened. More pressing even than that? He had just two days left to save one of his Beladors back in Atlanta from execution by Sen and a Tribunal. Both would face Daegan's red dragon if they killed Devon.

But retribution would not bring Devon back.

He had no time for regret. His honor drove him to take care with any woman, but he'd be damned if he'd lose even one follower. When in battle, succeeding to protect his people came first. When Daegan found the Luigsech woman this time, he wouldn't allow her to escape so easily again.

No dancing around when it came to answering his questions either.

She *would* give him the information he needed and tell him how to find Cavan.

After one more thorough search of the cottage, Daegan limped back to the main room, favoring the leg an Imortik had clawed. His leg ached and his head throbbed just like he'd experienced after the first Imortik attack in Atlanta.

Those bastards shoved venom into him.

How long before he ended up with two much venom to overcome?

Having been a druid in the Treoir realm for many centuries, Garwyli had warned Daegan the rift in the hidden death wall imprisoning Imortiks would crack in other areas of the world. When new cracks occurred, Imortiks that escaped would be drawn to the venom still inside his body.

Daegan tested his power. He teleported the two bodies, along with the disembodied heads, heartened to see them reappear on the ground outside when he stepped from the cottage.

Pointing his finger at the bodies, he called up his dragon fire. Flames burst across the cadavers. Their nasty odor of sulfur and burned skin rose with the smoke as the corpses sizzled in the fire.

To clear his head of that smell and try to find Luigsech at the same time, he teleported around the area surrounding the cottage. He made a wider circle each time until he'd reached a mile out in all directions.

Every time he teleported, it took him longer to reappear.

More frustrated than before with no result, he returned to the cottage.

Tristan's last telepathic words to Daegan haunted him. His second-in-command seemed to have only an instant to shout that Cavan had him. But recalling the sound of Tristan's agony gripped his heart and twisted his insides into a mangled mess.

Daegan's dragon rumbled, angry and ready to break free to hunt Tristan. His dragon had accepted Tristan's gryphon flying with them and recognized the young man's loyalty.

He had to calm his dragon. *I want to find our friend, too, Ruadh. When we do, the one who kidnapped him will pay. Until then, we must focus on huntin' the Luigsech woman.*

The silence that answered burned his chest.

There had been a time when Daegan would have known who had captured his people. A time when he would have shifted into his dragon form and flown to the enemy's hold.

Just the sight of the feared red dragon of Treoir bearing down on a castle would have been enough to hand over any captives.

Daegan ran his hand over his hair, gripping his head.

One day, his enemies today would know the penalty of touching his people. One day, the red dragon would be enough to hold peace again.

He could do nothing about finding the grimoire volumes or locating Cavan without that woman. Night had dragged into early morning with his circular search around the cottage. Daegan had no choice but to teleport to the ancestral research centre and watch for Cavan, who was to meet Luigsech there this morning, according to her.

With a last look at the house, Daegan flicked a finger to shut the door. Then he teleported to the village in County Galway, a small place on the outskirts of the larger city. He returned to the very spot he and Tristan had teleported to less than a day ago.

With daylight approaching, no one stirred as yet in the quaint community. Daegan cloaked himself and settled in where he could observe the ancestral centre.

Swinging his gaze down the narrow street bordered by attractive buildings, Daegan recalled Tristan's first question upon arrival and smiled.

"Are these buildings really old, boss? Like 1500s?"

Daegan had chuckled at him. "1500s 'tis not old."

Where was his friend?

By the time daylight broke, Daegan noted how the villagers smiled and chatted with one another. It reminded him of the people who had lived on his father's land. He longed to see their faces again, to remember a happier time.

The sound of someone knocking on the door of the ancestral centre pulled Daegan from his musings. Sunshine slowly burned away the early-morning mist and shadows began to lighten.

A boy of thirteen or fourteen stood there. He carried an armful of newspapers and knocked again. "Miss Fenella?

Hello, Miss Fenella?"

Appearing confused, he stood there another minute then left a rolled-up paper beside the door and continued down the street. His next stop was the grocery building where Daegan had observed Cavan talking to Luigsech yesterday.

That boy had expected a woman named Fenella to be at the ancestral research centre this morning. That must be the woman Daegan and Tristan observed yesterday, too, who left not long after Luigsech showed up.

Daegan called telepathically to Tristan again. *Tristan, say anythin', any sound, to let me know ya live.* Once again, his words met with the same disappointing result.

Silence.

At separate times, two shopkeepers from nearby stores knocked on the door of the ancestral centre. Both also called out to Fenella. The female shopkeeper walked away, muttering, "Don't be blamin' me when ya don't get yer hot turnover this mornin'."

She must be the one baking up heavenly smells nearby.

Unease crawled up Daegan's neck.

Had Luigsech met with Cavan somewhere else?

If so, why wasn't Fenella here?

Daegan stood from where he'd leaned against a tree, still cloaked to prevent from being seen. He called telepathically to his Belador Maistir over North America. *I need your help, Quinn.*

Yes, Daegan. Where are you?

County Galway in Ireland.

What do you need me to do?

Daegan explained, *'Tis close to daylight here. Tristan and I arrived yesterday. We observed a bein' who calls himself Cavan, but he wore a glamour. Tristan and I split up. He followed Cavan and I followed the Luigsech woman we had been watchin' who works at an ancestral research centre. Cavan captured Tristan. When Tristan called to me telepathically, all I heard was that he had been captured and what sounded as if he tried to tell me the identity of Cavan.*

Then we may know this Cavan? Quinn asked.

I feel 'tis a strong possibility.

What else can you tell me about him, Daegan?

Not much. Daegan explained how he and Tristan had followed Luigsech when she left work and her encounter with Cavan, who cloaked their conversation as well as his identity.

Quinn grumbled, *We definitely need more. What can I do right now?*

First, how are things in Atlanta?

Humans are frantic over monsters in the city. Fights have broken out at UnVeilCon, because they mistook someone in costume as one of us. Law enforcement has been handling those situations. Quinn paused and made a sound like a sigh. *Three more Beladors have disappeared, but the Medb have also lost five warlocks and witches. If this is due to Imortiks, which we have to assume as much until finding out differently, it appears they are not just hunting Beladors.*

Every time Daegan lost even one Belador or those who allied with him, it felt as if a piece of his soul had been chewed away. But he had to keep moving forward. He could do no more back in Atlanta than Quinn or the rest of his Beladors.

At the moment, Daegan needed his Maistir here more than there. *First thing, Quinn, I need ya to assign someone to take your place as Maistir until ya return, and for that person to coordinate the teams with Trey.*

Quinn sounded ready with a plan. *I say we put Evalle in that position. She'll have Storm and Adrianna as backup.*

Good thinking, Daegan agreed. He paused as someone walked up to the ancestral centre, but they didn't stop. *Next, I would like for ya to bring Reese here, but only if she comes voluntarily. She might be able to help me by usin' her remote viewin' gift. If askin' her is a problem, say so now. I will not think less of ya for your honesty, Quinn.*

After a short silence, Quinn said, *It's her choice. I would not make that decision for her, nor would she allow me.*

I need an hour or so to locate Reese and my daughter, Phoedra, then make arrangements. I'd like to send Phoedra to Treoir where she'll be safe while we're both gone.

Daegan walked around to loosen his stiff joints. *Of course. Your daughter is welcome to shelter in Treoir as well as any others ya feel are vulnerable.*

Thank you. I would also like to send my cousin, Lanna, to be with Phoedra.

Daegan had no issue with that and agreed with his thinking. Quinn would be more at ease here with the young ladies safe from any supernatural threat. *Brina will be happy for the company of them both.*

Quinn's voice picked up energy. *Excellent. Once I have Evalle and our Beladors set, I'll send Phoedra and Lanna on their way, then I'll let you know when I'm ready to teleport with Reese.*

Daegan suddenly recalled Reese becoming ill last time when she used her gift to track a bounty hunter as they hunted Evalle's kidnappers. Either that had made her sick or some other reason. Guilt pushed at him once he'd remembered the incident. He added, *Please make sure Reese knows I will understand if she does not wish to do this after her physical reaction last time.*

Quinn replied, *She might say no if only I asked her, but I seriously doubt she will refuse a request from you.*

When Quinn's presence disappeared out of Daegan's mind, he felt his first flicker of hope.

Reese had an unusual ability of visual projection, which had allowed them to track someone if Reese could sit in the last spot where that person had sat, stood, or fallen.

The Luigsech woman only thought she'd escaped.

CHAPTER 3

"NO, NO, NO," CASIDHE MOANED, rushing down the last part of the hill to Fenella's farmhouse.

Fenella had to be here.

But every time Casidhe searched the darkness for a light inside, she saw none. The white farmhouse with a red door and red shutters remained dark, the outside lit only by a dusting of moonlight.

Nothing made a sound.

Casidhe kept staring at that front window, trying to will a glow to be there.

Fenella left the fixture over her sink on every night, refusing to go to bed until she changed a bulb if it had burned out.

Squinting, Casidhe could make out cows bedded down in the pasture. Chickens were free to roam during the day, but they normally returned to the roost at night. She couldn't see or hear any goats, baby or otherwise.

Fenella would have still been up feeding the kids.

"Maybe she didn't get the goats tonight," Casidhe told herself in a whisper. Talking made her feel not so alone with her fears. "Maybe she's asleep."

Fenella tended to be an early-to-bed, early-to-rise person, but what about the missing light over the sink?

Stepping on the short path of flat stones leading to the front door, Casidhe knocked firmly.

No answer.

Every new confirmation of Fenella being absent drove her pulse higher. Casidhe rushed around the left side of the house. At the window to the bedroom, she tapped on it, softly calling, "Fenella?"

She slapped the glass hard enough to wake the dead. *"Fenella!"*

No freaking sound inside.

Heading back around the front of the house, her heart kept tumbling with fear. Denial drove her to continue to the right side of the house, checking every window on her way.

No one inside. This path led her to the barn. She skidded to a stop. Where was Fenella's beloved truck?

No truck parked by the barn.

No light in the kitchen.

No Fenella.

Casidhe considered other possibilities. Fenella hated to drive after sunset. What could have happened?

Maybe the truck had broken down.

Fenella would have walked home or to the goat farmer's house for help, depending on the shortest distance. She would not stay at the goat farmer's place. Old man Peadar would have given her a ride home. Or she'd have flagged down someone.

Everything pointed to Fenella having had plenty of time to reach her farm by now.

More than all of that, she would have called Casidhe to come help her.

What now?

Casidhe had a choice between heading for the goat farm to look for Fenella's truck along the way or going in the opposite direction toward the ancestral research centre.

If she reached the farm and did not find Fenella, she would have gambled and lost. She might make it back to the centre in time, depending on how long it took to reach Peadar's farm, a far more demanding route.

Cavan expected Casidhe to be at the centre by ten in the morning.

She didn't have a watch.

Her mobile phone kept better time since she didn't have to wind it. Based on how long it had taken her to run here and that the centre was another nineteen kilometers farther back the way she'd just come, it would probably require the same time to reach the village as Peadar's place.

That was based upon her not being physically spent. Factoring all that in, she might need closer to eight hours to cover that distance.

Even that amount of time could run her too late.

And estimating eight hours tops would be only if she struck out in a straight path to the centre without following the flatter winding roads.

Squatting, she placed the sword on the soft grass and rubbed the heels of her hands over her eyes.

What if she chose the wrong direction and something bad happened to Fenella?

One possibility after another assaulted her. She grabbed her head to quiet her mind and make a decision.

When she managed to focus, Herrick's words came to her from the times they'd trained together. She'd once asked him how to make the best decision on the fly.

He'd given her question serious thought and replied, "If only one action will result in an absolute outcome, choose that one."

She dropped her hands and stared into the darkness.

Choose the action with an absolute outcome.

She knew what to do.

If she failed to arrive in time to meet Cavan, she'd guarantee Fenella being harmed. Getting to the centre early would provide Casidhe a way to call Fenella's phone and Peadar's goat farm.

Standing up, she hoped with all her heart the time right now was closer to one in the morning than two. She turned in the direction of the village and begged her limbs for more endurance tonight.

She told herself, *Just put one foot in front of the other and do it again.* Once her stiff muscles loosened up again, she'd break into a jog.

How had her life blown up in less than a day?

This would be a great time for Herrick to have a satellite phone. No matter how she tried, she'd never be able to drag a dragon shifter as old as Herrick into the new millennium. He had no form of electronic communication where he and a small group lived in the Caucasus mountain range, which ran between Asia and Europe.

Contacting him quickly would not be possible and she couldn't entertain the idea of another trip to visit the family. Not after that last debacle.

More importantly, she would not risk leading the stranger from her cottage, or Cavan, to Herrick.

What if the intruder found her phone amid the destruction in her cottage?

Casidhe slapped a hand against her forehead. He'd have access to Fenella if he knew how to crack into the mobile phone.

After considering that likelihood, she rolled her eyes and kept walking.

Nothing about Tall, Dark, and Demanding had left her with any impression of being a techie.

If he was, she could do nothing about it right now.

He'd had muscles on muscles, and moved fluidly when he fought, but his speech reminded her of talking to people living at Herrick's castle. In retrospect, she could admit she found the stranger attractive, in a primitive and annoying way. His face had sharp planes and a nicely-shaped nose, though a bit crooked. Those gray eyes had hid his emotions until an invisible switch flipped him from conversational to furious upon discovering Cavan had captured his friend.

How had he learned of the capture right then?

Why would Cavan take the intruder's sidekick?

What did all these people have in common?

Her.

No, not her. Maybe the Treoirs.

Cavan had asked about the Treoirs during a first trip to the centre, before he returned to deliver a book on dark druids he'd given to Fenella for Casidhe to read. When Cavan surprised Casidhe at the grocery and grabbed her arm, his power had felt old, very old.

The intruder had argued about the red dragon seen in public being a fake *and* asked what she knew about the Treoirs.

Could he possibly know the red dragon shifter?

Was *he* the red dragon shifter?

She gave that serious consideration for all of two steps then snorted at that thought.

Why would her intruder have stood around asking for information and fighting demons when he could have just shifted and flown away with her clutched in his dragon's claws?

Too many questions and not enough answers.

She shoved Cavan and the intruder aside for the moment to concentrate on how to spirit Fenella out of this area safely.

First she had to find her friend. What if she didn't find her?

Casidhe swallowed a lump of emotion clogging her throat.

Negative thinking would not save Fenella. Only getting busy reaching the centre as fast as she could would help. She'd be able to use the desk phone at the centre.

Ignoring the ache in her legs, she picked up her pace to jog faster this time. She'd pay later for pushing her body so hard tonight, but her gut screamed that Fenella was not at the goat farm.

After an hour, Casidhe stumbled forward and dropped to her knees, heaving breaths. She had a cramp in her side. Her legs were spent and she needed water.

Tears stung her eyes.

Time ticked away with every labored breath.

CHAPTER 4

"WHAT THE HELL ARE YOU doing out here before dark?" Quinn shouted at Evalle.

She finished cleaning her spelled dagger on a dead demon, one that had not disintegrated into flames and ash.

She'd killed it near the old train tracks in a rundown area beneath the surface streets of downtown Atlanta.

Her killing a demon was SOP.

But performing that task just after one in the afternoon could be fatal for her if any of the dark clouds overhead allowed sun to come through.

"Don't panic," Evalle murmured with her head down. "'Sposed to rain all day."

"*Rain?* You think that's going to protect you from turning into a charcoal briquette?" He loved her like a little sister, but unlike other Alterant-gryphons with glowing green eyes, she had a deadly reaction to the sun. "The minute a cloud clears one tiny spot—"

"*Adrianna!*" Evalle called out.

Ten feet away, the deadliest witch Quinn knew of appeared out of nowhere in snug denims, a fitted red shirt with a collar, and her white-blond hair pulled back in an all-business look.

"I was right here," Adrianna complained, shoving a phone she'd been tapping on into her back pocket. "Sorry, Quinn. I had us cloaked for her to get close enough to the Imortik. Then she wanted out to fight it. I was keeping an eye on the weather."

Evalle stood with a smile in place below the special dark glasses she wore to protect her unnaturally bright eyes.

"What's up, Quinn?"

"I need to leave Atlanta for a bit. Daegan and Tristan were following a lead on their hunt for the grimoire. They were in County Galway, Ireland where they split up to follow different people. Tristan was captured. Daegan said the being Tristan followed had glamoured his identity and cloaked a conversation with the woman Daegan followed."

As Quinn spoke, Evalle's smile fell.

She had no poker face. When she worried about someone, her emotions rolled into action. "I'll go, too."

"Daegan knows that, but he needs you more here right now. We both do. I'd like you to take my place as Maistir while I'm gone."

"*Me*?" She looked queasy.

"Yes, you. Why not?"

Adrianna also turned a frown on her. "Yes. Why not you?"

Evalle returned her dagger to its sheath at her hip and shoved scattered strands of hair off her face. She lifted her ball cap from where it had fallen on the ground and shoved it back in place. Her vintage short-sleeved khaki shirt known as BDU, or Battle Dress Uniform, had gone through a tough patrol tonight based on the claw marks. Dried bloody handprints decorated her black jeans and her boots always looked scuffed.

Blowing out a breath, she shrugged. "I guess so if I'm the only one you can find."

Adrianna rolled her eyes.

Quinn gave a little shake of his head. "I can find plenty of Beladors. I suggested for *you* to take over, because you are the best choice as interim Maistir. Daegan agreed immediately with my suggestion. Is there a reason you *can't* do this?"

"Of course not." She narrowed her eyes at his insult.

He smiled. "Glad you agree with us."

Covering her mouth with a delicate hand, Adrianna snorted. Of course, she also used that hand to wield Witchlock, a power that could wipe out a city with little effort. She taunted, "Wait until Storm finds out he's sleeping with the

North American Belador Maistir."

Quinn smiled in spite of wanting to finish here and move on.

"Okay, okay. Very funny, you two." At the sound of a noise, Evalle looked around the run-down area she used to travel through to reach her apartment beneath one of the crumbling buildings.

Just a homeless man digging through a garbage can.

Quinn had offered her nicer accommodations time and again, but it had taken her mating with Storm to abandon the basement home she'd preferred for her pet gargoyle.

Now she and Storm had refurbished a four-story building closer to the center of the city and Feenix had a floor to himself.

Quinn checked his phone. Still no return call from Reese. His gut always defaulted to her being injured. Not a realistic reaction unless the woman you cared deeply for was nonhuman and a living demon magnet, as was his case.

Patience. That was key with her.

She never called just to say hello.

One of her less endearing traits, but he could live with that if she'd just answer the damn phone sometimes. "Now that I've got you set, I need to find Reese."

He'd turned to leave when Evalle blurted out, "Is anything up with her and Phoedra?"

Evalle thought of Quinn as family, which meant in turn, she treated Phoedra and Reese as family. She would step in to protect them with her life if she thought they needed her.

He paused, angling back around to assure her, "No, but thank you for asking. Daegan thinks Reese can help him find Tristan." Tossing a look in Adrianna's direction, Quinn added, "I'm exceptionally pleased you are working with Evalle, Adrianna."

"Happy to do it." Adrianna seemed amused at the interplay between Quinn and Evalle. Someone might confuse her with being relaxed, but her instincts had only gotten sharper with Witchlock.

Then he gave Evalle his no-bullshit voice. "But before I go, Evalle, I want your word you'll have backup every single time you are outside your building from here on."

"Don't *hover*, Quinn." Evalle lifted her eyebrows in a defiant motion. She'd fought hard for her independence and relinquished not an inch without a battle.

"I'm not hovering," he snapped. "I'm telling you what I do as Maistir. If I put myself at risk with no backup, then I put all our people in jeopardy if I am taken down during an unexpected attack."

"Oh." She frowned. "I'm not used to thinking that way."

"You should be," he admonished. "You have Storm, Feenix, and many others who depend upon you. It's sort of like being Maistir of your family."

"I know you're right," Evalle admitted. "I'm just anxious to get Renata and the others back. I'm worried about Devon and that stupid deadline the Tribunal set. Now Daegan has to find Tristan." Her lips flattened in a hard line. She dropped her hand to the hilt of her dagger, gripping the weapon then flexing her fingers with frustration. "What are we going to do if Daegan isn't back by Wednesday's deadline? The Tribunal will kill Devon."

"We will not allow that to happen. The sooner I grab Reese and head out, the sooner I can be back to deal with the Tribunal if Daegan can't."

"Got it." Evalle stepped up and gave Quinn a hug, whispering close to his ear. "Fix the problem between you and Reese while you're together, okay? She looks sad even when she tries to hide it."

Quinn swallowed his own lump of sadness, disappointed with himself for having not figured out what was going on with Reese by now. He missed her and his daughter. He had a loaded plate at the moment, but he would not make this trip to Ireland with Reese and return home without sorting things out between them.

He gave Evalle what he hoped was a look of confidence he didn't feel. "Fixing things with Reese is on my list."

Evalle's phone buzzed. She snatched it from her back pocket. "Why didn't you call me telepathically, Trey?"

She yanked the phone from her ear where Trey snarled at her, "Because I'm talking to others telepathically right now."

She pulled it back. "Sorry. Got it. Just text if that's easier." She listened, nodding as she did. "On the way." Shoving the phone into her pocket, she told Quinn, "Let us know what happens with Tristan."

Rain started falling for which Quinn said a word of thanks. Anything to keep the sun from Evalle. "I'll inform Trey and I'll let you know when I return."

"Okay, thanks." Evalle turned to Adrianna. "Ready to cloak? We're headed to Centennial Park."

"I'm on it." Adrianna waved her fingertips. "Bye, Quinn."

They disappeared from sight.

Quinn turned the opposite way. With no humans in sight except the homeless guy now curled up on the ground facing away, he leaped across weeds and debris to reach a road used by delivery trucks on the opposite side from the tracks.

He tried Reese's phone again, letting it ring until her voice message came on. "Not here." *Click.*

Was she really that undisciplined about listening for phone calls and returning texts?

Or just *his* calls and texts?

He'd left plenty of messages over the last two weeks, asking for a time the two of them could sit down and talk. Reese had worked brilliantly with him to save his daughter when a nonhuman kidnapped her before Quinn had ever met his child. Then with the support of some mysterious guardian Phoedra's mother had put in place before Phoedra's birth, Reese ended up living next door to Phoedra and her foster mother in California. Phoedra became close with Reese when his daughter started dog sitting Reese's massive mutt. The woman caring for Phoedra had belonged to her elusive guardian Quinn had never met.

When the smoke cleared, Reese was the one person Phoedra had bonded with over the past year when she'd had no idea who her parents were.

He understood that Phoedra needed time to adjust to everything. She'd been just as uninformed of having a father as he'd been about having a thirteen-year-old daughter.

Still, it hurt to miss even more time with her. He'd gained and lost his daughter all at the same time.

As long as Phoedra was safe and wanted for nothing, he had to be patient and allow her the time she needed to come to him on her own.

He only wished to get to know her and for his child to enjoy her life after all she'd survived.

Rain continued to sprinkle as he climbed the last stretch of road that ascended to the surface streets of Atlanta. He texted his driver the location to pick him up.

Traffic whizzed by at a steady pace. Humans living normal lives.

He'd always been proud to be a Belador and had no desire to give it up even if he could, but there were days he'd like to be just some Joe coming home from work to his family.

Standing under an overhang to avoid becoming slowly soaked, he sent another call which reached Reese's voicemail yet again. This time he left a message. "Please call me as soon as you get this, Reese. It's extremely important."

While Reese made him crazy on a daily basis, he could not ask for a better protector to watch over his daughter. She had an energy inside of her that drew demons to her like flies to honey.

That same energy killed demons.

What if Reese went up against multiple demons taken over by Imortiks roaming Atlanta? Quinn shuddered at that possibility.

As a black sedan pulled up, he stepped to the curb and opened a door to the backseat. He told his driver, "I'm going to Reese and Phoedra's apartment." His driver knew the way.

Quinn tapped the number for Lanna next. His twenty-year-old cousin from Romania loved her phone and always answered if she had it close by.

"*Cousin!*" Lanna's bubbly voice and accented broken English never failed to brightened his world.

"Hello, Lanna. Are you—"

Her voice abruptly changed to a hush. "You are not good. I can feel problem. What is trouble? I will help."

That young woman would never be accused of lacking courage. If anything, she raced into trouble without hesitation if it meant saving someone in her circle of friends and family, or even an innocent stranger.

He was surrounded by fiercely protective women. Not that he didn't love that quality, but he constantly worried about them diving into danger.

Washing a hand over his tired face, he attempted to calm her down. "I'm fine, Lanna. I'm just looking for Reese."

"You do not tell truth."

"Lanna." Little got by that one, but right now was not the time for her to poke her nose into his business.

"Fine, Cousin. She is with Phoedra."

"I figured that, but I can't get an answer when I call Reese's phone."

Lanna didn't speak at first, which was strange in itself because she *always* had something to say. "Did you tell her about dark power in city?"

"I left a message last night for her and Phoedra to stay inside until I had time to tell them what was going on. I said I'd call today."

"Reese said you call all the time. I fear she ignores phone when she sees your name."

He clamped his lips against the curse ready to launch from his lips. Buildings went by at a slow clip in the busy downtown traffic. When he had time, he'd normally prefer walking, but he hadn't wanted to risk this conversation in public.

"Do not get angry, Cousin," Lanna said in a quiet voice. "Reese is not in happy place."

He lost his focus on anger and keyed into Lanna's words. "What's going on with Reese? Is she having some issue with the demon energy inside her? Did that damned Veronika hurt her when we fought that bloody witch to save Phoedra?"

"Stop, Cousin," Lanna said in a soft voice, but Quinn felt power roll through the request. He'd never experienced a push of power over a phone connection. Like everyone else in his family, he had no idea from whom Lanna inherited her powers. She had far more than anything her mother would have passed down.

No one knew who Lanna's father was, not even her mother, who had been missing for most of a year and returned with no memory of her time away, or how she became pregnant.

"I will call Reese," Lanna offered. "I will explain danger. Evalle told me about Imortiks just today. If I had thought Reese would not know by now, I would have called her. I am sorry."

"This is not your fault, Lanna. It's mine." Maybe he should have left a more specific message, but he hadn't wanted to panic his daughter. "I've been out of step with everyone since Phoedra showed up, but I plan to fix that, too. Right now, I have to help Daegan. To accomplish that, I wish to ask a favor of you." He forced a calm to push off his irritation. No one needed that from him right now.

"What can I do?"

"I'm going to ask Phoedra to go to Treoir realm so that Reese can go with me to help Daegan." He paused. "Do you know any reason I shouldn't ask Reese if she would be willing to use her remote viewing for Daegan?"

Lanna hesitated again. "No. If Reese does not want to do this, she will say so."

He deliberated a moment, then continued, "I'd like you to also go to Treoir realm so Phoedra will feel comfortable. Would you please do that?"

"Of course, Cousin. Garwyli told me to return soon. He teaches me when I am there."

"Excellent. Thank you. Where are you right now?"

"At Evalle and Storm's building, in my apartment. I must pack and tell them where I am going, and let Feenix know. I am ready in five minutes."

One task done. "Terrific. When you want to teleport, have Evalle contact Trey McCree. He'll ask Brina to teleport you to Treoir."

"I will, Cousin, but I have request."

"What is it?"

"You must make peace with Reese on this trip. It will be important for ... everyone."

Hair tingled on Quinn's neck.

Lanna never said anything without reason and could be the most cryptic person when she wanted to be. His gut lurched with worry, but he couldn't put a finger on why. His voice came out harsher than intended. "You know what's going on with Reese, don't you?"

Lanna sighed noisily. "Her business not mine to tell."

Could he get that in writing? When had Lanna ever thought *anyone's* business was not hers to interfere with when she deemed it necessary?

She picked *now* to avoid butting in?

Quinn cupped his head, trying to keep the mounting tension from blowing the top of his head off. The women in his life drove him crazy.

"Thank you for helping me, Lanna. I mean that. I don't often take the time to let you know how much you do for everyone, but I should. You are one of the best people in my life."

He heard a sniffle from Lanna. "You too, Cousin. Go to Reese and Phoedra's apartment. I will make sure they are home in ten minutes, if they are not now."

Quinn sat back and rubbed the tight muscles in his neck.

Where could Reese be if she was not at home? Probably in Piedmont Park walking that bloody mutt.

Lanna had been correct.

The time had come to make peace.

The time had also come for him to let go of his anger. Lanna had called it right. He'd been angry since finding out he had a daughter, then learning that some mysterious and powerful guardian who had watched over his child since birth had handed Reese responsibility for Phoedra's wellbeing.

Not him.

Quinn *had* managed to move them from an apartment the guardian had given them into a high-rise protected by Beladors. Quinn could not sleep at night unless his daughter had equal, or better, accommodations and security.

In retrospect, he might have been heavy-handed.

Another side effect of feeling punched in the gut.

He'd met Phoedra's mother, Kizira, a Medb priestess and enemy of the Belador, when they were both young. She'd kept her true identity hidden from him back then. He learned of his child only recently and that had been as Kizira died in his arms during a battle between the Medb and Beladors.

He'd been a tangle of barbed emotions for too long.

Then Reese showed up and smacked his heart around until it came back to life.

He could sit here and convince himself he was angry about not having his daughter with him, but in truth he wanted both of them. His relationship with Phoedra's mother had been long ago with the exception of a few dysfunctional meetings right before Kizira died.

When Reese came into his world, she challenged and comforted him at the same time. She'd also been the one to gently show him that he owed it to Phoedra to become whole again.

She'd kickstarted that metamorphosis.

Then he bogged down in his own head again.

More like his head had been stuck somewhere he couldn't see daylight.

He would find out what was going on with Reese.

If she didn't tell him by the end of this trip, then he'd break his personal rule not to put his child between them and ask Phoedra. They were going to have a real relationship.

No more secrets.

The car pulled up at the entrance to a tall apartment

building on the north side of downtown. He instructed the driver he wouldn't need him for the rest of the day.

Quinn strode across the canopy-covered walkway to the entrance where a Belador, working secretly as a doorman, nodded at him and pulled the door open.

He paused and softly asked, "Have they been out today?"

"Reese was on her way out a few minutes back when someone called. She, Phoedra, and Gibbons, the dog, turned around and returned to the elevator."

Silently thanking Lanna again, Quinn nodded at his Belador. "They'll be gone for a few days. I'll let you know when they return."

"Yes, Maistir."

Quinn started to inform him that Evalle would take over for a while, but Trey would make that announcement telepathically as soon as Quinn left. He made short time of reaching the apartment and rapped on the door.

Reese yelled, "Check the peephole, Phoedra."

"*Ohhh*-kay." After a fumbling noise, the door opened and his beautiful daughter stood there. Chin-length black hair with aqua-blue highlights framed a face that held Quinn's narrow nose, but more of her mother's exceptional features. This young girl would be striking as a woman one day. The idea of that time passing quickly hurt to think about.

Surprise hit Phoedra's face then she smiled. "Hi."

His vivacious, soon-to-be fourteen-year-old was a vision. Phoedra may have been an accident, but he would never regret her birth. Only the time they hadn't spent together.

Would she ever call him dad or father? He didn't know, but held out hope. "Hello, Phoedra. You look dressed for a run."

"We were headed to the park, but Lanna called and said you had something important to tell us."

She meant Piedmont Park. His blood pressure shot up at the thought of those two being exposed to Imortiks, but he'd made a deal with himself to show patience. Not sound like an overly-protective father.

"I'm glad Lanna caught you. May I come in?" Quinn

asked.

"Oh, sorry about that." Phoedra backed up, opening the door as she did.

Reese was nowhere in sight.

Quinn stepped into the comfortable room, admiring the wonderful job these two had done decorating.

Left to himself, he'd have brought in professionals and the result would not have been as warm.

The air held a light floral scent.

Between Reese and Phoedra, they'd turned this into a place of soft colors, comfy furniture, glass vases with fresh cut snapdragons and ... a definite woman's touch. He'd given Phoedra a credit card with instructions to buy what they'd like for furnishings, because Reese had ignored his offer.

What a hedgehog she could be.

Thinking back, he smiled at her stubborn attitude.

She'd put him in a position of handing the card to Phoedra along with the responsibility to purchase furnishings. Reese had facilitated masterfully. He really had to start looking at her actions differently.

Making a show of taking in the room, he said, "You two have accomplished a great deal more since my last visit. It's quite attractive. I think you both have a talent for decorating. You've created a very inviting atmosphere."

Phoedra beamed a smile. "Thanks."

One win today. "I'd like to speak to Reese, too."

His daughter's smile faltered and that sick feeling hit him hard again. "Is anything wrong?"

That was so much nicer than shouting that he wanted to know what the hell was going on. These were not his men to order around, but damn it was hard to be patient when he wanted answers.

Before Phoedra could say anything, Reese walked into the room. "I'm here. What's the big emergency?"

Brunette curls bounced around her sweet face. Whiskey-gold eyes always so full of life and adept at hiding secrets flashed a look his way. For an average-size female, she jumped into battles with any size threat, especially demons drawn to the energy inside her. The long-sleeved pale brown T-shirt and jeans hugged her body in a way he envied.

Her lips parted and he lost his ability to think.

Her mutt jumped up and ran over to her as if he hadn't seen her in months. "Down, Gibbons."

The beast continued to beg for attention.

Quinn suggested, "There are excellent dog trainers in the city."

Her pretty eyes turned dangerously angry. She snapped her fingers. "Go lay down, Gibbons."

Damn if that mutt didn't trot over to the sofa, leap on it, and slump down. Reese turned that same tone on Quinn. "What's going on?"

As always, off on the wrong foot with her. He got right to the point. "We've had a deadly force enter the city."

"Demons?" Reese asked in a tense voice.

"Possibly, but the beings attacking our people are worse. They're called Imortiks."

Phoedra cut her gaze to Reese who shrugged that she didn't know. His daughter asked, "What are those?"

"I don't have all the answers yet. We've had a long night of trying to figure this out and we're not done. That's why I called to warn you earlier, but you must not have heard the phone." He slashed a look at Reese whose cheeks pinked with embarrassment.

Yes, she'd intentionally avoided answering his call.

Phoedra kept her gaze on Reese, who did not look happy. His daughter turned a glare on him. She evidently assumed Reese unhappy was automatically his fault.

Quinn held his temper. "I am not upset that Reese didn't answer my call, Phoedra. I understand you two are busy."

Now Reese's jaw dropped, but she quickly pulled it back up.

Huh. He'd surprised her by giving her an out? Note to self, do a better job of sounding understanding.

Returning to why he was there, he said, "I've come to ask

both of you for a favor."

After fidgeting with her hands, Phoedra stuck her thumbs inside the top of her jeans waistband. "Whatcha need?"

Reese ran a hand through her wild brown locks, then shoved loose curls off her face. "Uhm, yeah, what do you want, Quinn?"

"Daegan is hunting for something to stop the Imortiks and ran into a problem during his search. He asked if you would be willing to use your gift for remote viewing to help him find someone." He'd wait to explain about Tristan once Phoedra was not around.

Reese's face flipped from suspicious to open. "Oh, well, sure. I can do that."

Quinn debated on asking if she felt physically up for the trip, but she bristled every time he asked if she had recovered from the battles. Maybe whatever bothered her had passed by now. Her demon-killing energy might have wiped out a venom or blood that had affected her.

But if that was so, why couldn't she just tell him what the problem had been?

Don't get off track right now, he reminded himself. "Daegan and I appreciate you doing this, Reese. We'll have to teleport to Ireland to help him."

"Wow, can I go?" Phoedra asked, now excited at the idea of an overseas adventure.

"Unfortunately not, but I'd like for you to take *another* trip," Quinn said quickly, hoping to avoid teen drama.

"Where?" Phoedra's happiness fled, but she hadn't pitched a fit. Yet.

"I would love for you to visit Treoir realm again. Lanna is already there. She'd really enjoy the company."

That created turmoil for Phoedra, based on the confusion on her face.

Reese started to reach for Phoedra then glanced at Quinn. He hadn't said a word or made any expression, but she seemed to realize she should let Phoedra work through this with him.

She pulled her hand back and waited.

Quinn's lips turned up. He mouthed the words, "Thank you."

Her eyes widened with surprise.

Maybe if she'd stop fighting him he'd have a chance to show her he could meet her halfway, more than halfway. He held hope they could finally talk and resolve this friction between them.

A longing for Reese hit him that he couldn't put into words. He woke up at night missing her and wishing to see her beside him, smiling.

"Sure." Phoedra started nodding to herself while looking down as she made a decision. Then she glanced over to where that big hairy mutt slept on the sofa. "Gibbons can go with me, too, right?"

Quinn said, "I am certain that would be acceptable if Reese approves."

"Yes, of course," Reese interjected quickly. "I'll be more relaxed knowing he's with you."

"Great. How soon am I leaving?" Phoedra asked, now back to being happy.

"As soon as you are packed. We have to wait for you to teleport before we leave to meet Daegan," Quinn explained.

"Two minutes." Phoedra ran out of the room.

Reese muttered, "More like ten."

To Quinn's great relief, his daughter sounded enthusiastic. He and Reese had not stood alone in the same space for a long time. He hurried to keep the bridge in place that had started between them.

"I really appreciate you doing this, Reese. It means a lot to all of us."

"Sure, Quinn. Who is Daegan looking for?" Her nervous gaze bounced around, never pausing on him.

He kept his voice down as he explained about Daegan and Tristan traveling to Ireland in search of the grimoire volumes. "Tristan has gone missing. That's what Daegan needs your help for."

"Oh, hell." She finally lifted her gaze to his and nodded with determination. "I'm in. Take me to Daegan. I'll do anything I can to find Tristan. I'll do whatever I can to help stop Imortiks, too."

Did he make her anxious? Maybe this was his chance. "Reese, I'm sorry if I've been difficult."

She held up a hand. "You're fine. I'm sorry I didn't take your call. Phoedra might have needed to know if you had been hurt. I won't avoid answering again. I promise."

Oddly, he didn't feel the usual anger that reply would bring on. Instead, remorse filled the hollow place in his chest. He'd failed yet again to fix whatever had broken between them after sharing one incredible moment in time.

While hunting for his kidnapped daughter, they landed in the infamous InchKeith's realm where Quinn had been desperate to make a deal for the kidnapper's identity. The realm had a hidden entrance in a New Orleans French Quarter hotel. The InchKieth had tossed him and Reese separately into a living video game environment where they'd been forced to battle their way individually to the end of a challenge.

No one escaped the InchKeith without entertaining him.

Quinn had waited in a cabin inside the game, pleading with the gods for Reese to survive a gauntlet he'd barely finished alive.

When she finally showed up, relief had shaken him to his core.

They crashed into each other's arms, exhausted and so glad to have both survived. The InchKeith owed them a name, which would put them back on Phoedra's trail.

A message arrived immediately informing Quinn the InchKeith would send for them, but not before two hours.

Quinn's self-imposed resistance to Reese fell faster than a house of cards.

That moment of intimacy seemed so long ago, but it had only been a few weeks back.

Every minute since had dragged by for Quinn with missing

Reese and Phoedra. They would never have normal lives like humans, but ... he'd once thought whatever form their lives took that they'd spend it together.

He would prefer to keep Reese somewhere safe from demons and any other threat, but he had no say in Reese's decisions about putting herself at risk.

That didn't mean he couldn't be at her side to keep her safe.

She finally looked at him with guilty eyes. "Give me a minute and I'll be ready to go. Do I need to pack clothes?"

Keeping his tone gentle in hopes to put her at ease, he said, "I don't expect this to take more than a few hours, but pack some anyhow just in case."

She started to leave then turned back to him. "I'm glad you sent Phoedra to Treoir so we don't have to worry about her."

"We?" Quinn had no chance to hide the longing in his voice.

She almost replied, then shook it off and disappeared down the hall.

Bloody hell. He had to save Tristan and help Daegan lock down these Imortiks, but as soon as that was done he would tackle the only other goal that mattered.

A future with Reese and Phoedra.

He wanted a family and he had one waiting. All he had to do was convince them to let him earn his place with them.

While Reese was gone, Phoedra returned, eyes bright with excitement. She had a backpack strapped on and reached for a leash she clipped to the mongrel. "Up, boy. Let's go."

Gibbons stepped off the sofa, tail wagging.

Excitement poured off his daughter. "We're ready to teleport. I love doing that, by the way."

Quinn smiled and walked over to kiss her forehead. "I'm glad I can do things to make you happy."

Now she looked a bit shamefaced. "I appreciate *all* you do."

He hadn't wanted that admission. It sounded as if he'd said something to make her feel guilty about tangible items.

He wanted Phoedra to care for him and to know how much

he loved her. Not be beholding to him.

Sorrow swept over him, but he kept it from his voice. "Providing material things for you is easy. I want to get to know you better and for our visits to be comfortable. I hope one day that you'll want to travel somewhere with *me,* but I'm not asking for that today. Just know that while I can't change the past, I do want a real future together."

"I do too," she whispered then lifted an arm and leaned forward. He opened his arms. The hug was awkward, but made him smile with pure joy.

She'd reached for him.

Her eyes glistened. Allergies or ... emotion? She sniffled.

He withdrew a handkerchief from his back pocket and handed it to her.

She gave him a watery smile and quirked an eyebrow. "Who carries these around?"

"Gentlemen do." He had to blink away moisture stinging his eyes and smiled. He'd like to stand here and savor this moment just a few seconds longer, but he wanted her to hold onto that smile and depart on an up note. "Ready to go?"

"Yep!"

He called Trey telepathically and arranged to have Brina teleport Phoedra right away. Smiling as wide as he could to send her off with a happy visual of him, he stepped back. "You should be departing any moment now."

She gave him a small wave.

Then she was gone.

His heart squeezed with that tiny moment he'd shared with her. He wiped his eyes on his sleeve. How was he going to get his mind on business after that?

As if in answer, his stomach growled. He hadn't eaten since ... hell, he couldn't remember. He'd had no time for a meal. Heading for the kitchen, he started opening cabinets until he found a bag of crispy cheese snacks.

He grabbed a handful and crunched them.

A wonderful cheesy smell clouded the air.

He'd eaten half the bag when Reese came down the hall,

saying, "I'm ready to go if you—"

When she stepped into the kitchen, she inhaled sharply. Her eyes went round. She covered her mouth and ran back down the hall.

What the ... ? Quinn dashed out to the hallway in time to see the powder room door slam shut.

That didn't muffle the awful retching.

Reese smelled cheese and threw up?

Oh, shit.

She was pregnant.

CHAPTER 5

DAEGAN! TRISTAN SHOUTED TELEPATHICALLY. The word shot back at him, slamming his head so hard he surfaced from being lost in his hell. Where was Daegan?

Bindings cut his wrists. Warm blood trickled down to his arms stretched above his head.

He tried to teleport. Energy inside him spun up, but nothing happened. Shit. He stopped before he threw up.

Searching inside, he called up his gryphon to boost his power.

His beast rumbled, sounding sluggish. What was wrong? Tristan dug through his memory. Had he been drugged?

Teleporting was a dud. He had no gryphon power. And his telepathic communication boomeranged.

If only he had a paperclip to make a bomb out of like on that old television show.

Voices came to him from a distance, as if two people had climbed inside a barrel to muffle their conversation.

That was just stupid.

Think harder.

He focused on the voices in spite of pain jabbing his head. Not just there. His chest hurt like someone had rammed him with a spiked club.

Fog, dark and sluggish, began to slowly clear from his mind. Beladors had exceptional hearing. He should be able to understand words better.

"*No!*" a high-pitched voice screeched.

Tristan clenched his jaw and groaned. Too fucking loud this time. He swallowed a disgusting taste that his stomach considered returning. A chill ran across his skin. He shuddered.

Could this be the afterlife?

Probably not for him to be freezing like this.

Staying still as he came closer to consciousness, he drew on his senses.

His arm muscles burned, holding the dead weight of his body. Not dead yet. Now that he could sort out what was going on, he hung from manacles clamped on his wrists. The blood trickling down came from where those metal torture devices cut into his skin and scraped bone. Similar straps held his ankles to the wall behind him. Bumpy and rough surface. Could be stone.

Damp smelling, too.

Voices rumbled low this time.

Without making a sudden move, he opened his eyelids, peering through eyelashes. His head hung to his left side, but with a small movement, he could see a wide area.

Why was it so freaking dark in here?

Not entirely dark. He squinted. Flames burned in two spots maybe a hundred feet away. Torches?

Was this a castle dungeon? Had he stepped back in time? Doubtful. But where the hell was he?

A low male voice said something Tristan couldn't make out.

That screechy female voice shouted in some odd accent, "You want to be partners, but you treat me like a slave. Worse than a slave."

Tristan kept peeling his eyelids open a fraction at a time. Once he allowed enough light in to see clearly, he recognized Cathbad the Druid, who had captured him.

But he had no clue about the identity of that woman yelling at Cathbad.

Thinking back to when he realized Cavan was actually Cathbad, Tristan tried to recall if he'd been able to tell Daegan about the druid in his last telepathic message. He couldn't say for sure.

Now he remembered why his chest hurt so badly.

Cathbad had hit him with something that had claws. A baseball bat ... with claws?

He didn't know.

Voices rose and dropped, pulling Tristan's attention back to the nattering pair.

They faced each other with their profiles turned to him. Cathbad had on his usual slick suit and perfect hair.

Mysterious screeching woman had a sexy-as-hell body, beautiful skin, and blond hair ... all that dripping wet. She wore some kind of armor. Sure looked as if it had molded onto her shapely body.

At one time, Tristan would have given that one a second look, but not when he had a woman like Mac at home.

Also, Mac was no shrew.

Cathbad argued, "I do not treat ya as a slave. I treat ya as a child, which is how ya behave. If you do not care for bein' kept in that icy pond, stop pushin' me. I have warned ya and warned ya that tryin' to attack me is unwise."

She slapped her hands on her hips and stuck her face close to his. "I am *not* child. I warn you not to test *me*, but you do. You are just as wrong. How can I be partner with one like you?"

Tristan glanced past them to a big freaking pond with chunks of ice floating in it.

Had Cathbad thrown that woman in there?

What a bastard.

With another visual sweep of what he could see in this place, he determined they were in a massive cavern with a sixty-foot ceiling. Maybe higher.

So he *wasn't* in TÅµr Medb? Not that he wanted to be, but at least that realm would make sense. Cathbad normally hung out there plotting evil plans with Queen Maeve.

Why was Cathbad here and not there?

Cathbad and Hot Chick finished a long stare down during the silence.

Backing away first, Cathbad walked off shaking his head.

When he turned to her, he pinned her with a sharp look. "What will it take for ya to realize 'tis a greater plan at hand? Ya wish to kill one person? Why would ya not want more than that?"

The woman facing Cathbad pulled her shoulders up, flashing more armor. Her obstinate attitude rode the air. Golden hair flowed everywhere when she turned her head. Toned legs a mile long stopped at some badass metallic-looking boots. She held a shield at her side.

What era had she come from?

Blond hair and built like a female Viking. She spoke broken English. Was she Swedish? What kind of being was she? A witch, maybe? How powerful could she be if Cathbad bullied her and stuck her ass in a freezing pond? Had he forced her to stay in there for long periods of time?

If so, she had to be tough to survive that.

Also, she must have some level of power for him to be in any discussion of a partnership with her when he already had a deal with Queen Maeve.

Wait a minute. This might be a *new* partnership, which Tristan would bet Queen Maeve knew nothing about.

Hot Chick still stood there, arms now across her chest, glare in place, and mouth shut in a flat line.

Cathbad must want whatever it was he expected her to deliver bad. Instead of zapping her in some way, he released a long sigh. "Let us try a truce again. I will keep ya involved and consider your ideas if ya will cease attackin' me, Brynhild."

She shrugged. "I will not attack if you give me no reason to do so."

Cathbad had not managed to intimidate this woman, but Tristan doubted that she could outmaneuver the druid. He'd seen Cathbad in action. That druid managed to keep Queen Maeve on her toes and had clearly started a second enterprise without her.

Impressive.

If only Tristan could tell Daegan about this.

Brynhild acted as if she had something to hold over Cathbad.

Did she know about Queen Maeve?

If she did, this Brynhild would be wise to consider how Cathbad currently betrayed Queen Maeve in some way by being here with her.

What a strange name. This woman's manner of speech niggled at the back of Tristan's mind, trying to tell him it mattered.

Cathbad continued walking back and forth, pacing in front of the tall female warrior. "I will accept that weak admission as you agreein' to the truce. Gettin' back to the plan, I delivered a book to that Luigsech woman. She is to read a passage to me when she returns to the ancestral centre. If she can indeed translate that passage, she can very likely read anythin'. And that would lead me to believe she had not gained that skill through study at a human university. She possesses power. I felt it, but 'tis not what makes her special. I've never met someone who could translate all of the ancient languages."

Brynhild waved a hand in the air. "How is that important to me?"

The scathing look Cathbad gave her indicated this tense conversation happened every time those two got together. Then why in the hell would that powerful druid choose this woman as a partner at all?

More than that, what was Cathbad up to with her?

Tristan's arms screamed in agony. He tried to move his foot a tiny bit to find a place to push up and relieve the strain. Not happening.

Speaking as if to a slow student, Cathbad explained, "That woman's ability to translate text even I am unable to decipher will mean a great deal to *both* of us, Brynhild. If Luigsech has that level of skill, or more likely a supernatural gift, she can translate the grimoire volumes. You can't. I might be able to do so, but it would require time. If she can do what I think, she can find the volumes *and* translate each one on the spot."

"What will this grimoire do for ... us?" For the first time since Tristan regained consciousness, Brynhild sounded genuinely interested.

"That is the correct question." Cathbad's tone changed to a complimentary one. "The grimoire was broken into three volumes and given to three families to hide."

She cocked her head as if trying to understand his words. "I never heard of such book."

"'Tis no surprise. Breakin' up the grimoire happened long before ya were born. Once we have all three volumes, we will hold control of the formulas and spells. That shall be the point where we can force Daegan to do anythin' we want."

Well, fuck. Yet another plan to screw with Daegan. Cathbad had pretended to work with VIPER and Daegan to keep peace when Queen Maeve helped a deadly witch escape VIPER. Without Cathbad's intervention and willingness to hand over Phoedra, Daegan and the Tribunal would have unleashed an apocalypse on TÅµr Medb.

"You know what I want." Brynhild spat the words at the druid.

Cathbad flicked his hand as if to brush them away. He clearly did not see her as a threat.

Tristan had to get back to Daegan and tell him what he'd learned here. That wouldn't happen unless he escaped.

Not an outlook he'd bet heavily on right now.

He noticed the silence first and peeked through his lashes again to see what had changed.

Brynhild slowly turned to face Tristan.

Her seductive eyes outlined in black carried a deadly warning with each blink. Man, that woman was as smokin' hot as they came, but everything about her said she would be a deadly mistake for any man, human, or otherwise.

Where did Cathbad find that level of crazy women?

The druid also turned to Tristan.

Since they now knew he was awake, Tristan called out, "You practicing witchcraft now, Cathbad?"

The druid lifted a stick he'd been holding at his side.

Tristan recognized the four-foot-long club Cathbad had used to knock him out. The stick appeared to be dense hardwood, like hickory, and had three claws at one end.

Yellow glowing claws.

Ah, shit. That had Imortik written all over it.

Lifting an eyebrow in amusement, Cathbad started toward him. "Witchcraft? Why would ya think I need a lower form of majik than my own?"

"Because of that stick. What is it?"

Smiling, the druid lifted the claw-stick and gave it an admiring once over. "Ah, yes. I made this after findin' an Imortik runnin' around Atlanta. 'Tis a useful tool for capturin' beins'. A demon. A gryphon. A dragon. Anythin' really. This stick, as ya call it, has more than one use, but capturin' nonhumans is a good one. Worked perfectly for takin' ya down."

Yep, Tristan still recalled the excruciating pain of being struck by something sharp that cut him off midstream while calling telepathically to Daegan. His body had vibrated with incredible pain. He could still feel the aftermath of that attack.

But he would show no weakness to this pair of wackos.

Lifting his gaze to meet Tristan's, Cathbad walked toward the wall where Tristan hung fifteen feet off the ground.

Energy pulsed through the straps, which probably created the barrier preventing him from teleporting or using telepathic communication.

It also muffled his gryphon.

He needed his gryphon's power for healing as much as for strength. Maybe Cathbad would ask him to shift.

He'd love that.

Because the next time Tristan let his beast out, any threat in his gryphon's path wouldn't have a chance to scream before he slaughtered it.

As Cathbad neared, Tristan went for casual conversation. "Why did you capture me?"

"I had not planned to do so actually," Cathbad admitted. "But once I sensed someone followin' me, I set the trap and ya walked into it. I never waste a gift. Ya can be useful."

Tristan didn't pop off in response, but the battle to hold his tongue still was close. He kept pushing for information, anything he could squeeze out of this pair. Going for sarcasm, he pointed out, "I'm thinking you want to use my gryphon to do something, right? I can't be much use if you're gonna keep me tied up, causing my muscles to atrophy." He doubted Cathbad would send him to Queen Maeve since Tristan would bet she knew nothing of the partnership underway in this cave.

"Do ya recall Ossian?" Cathbad asked softly with an underlying tease of threat.

Tristan's skin crawled at remembering the only time he saw that creep. He'd watched Ossian's body lose control as he died, shifting through a mix of different identities, including some Beladors the polymorph had impersonated.

Disgust rolled through him, but he had to keep his emotions locked down. Affecting a bland expression, Tristan tried to shrug. Failed. Hard to manage lifting a shoulder when hanging from his wrists. "Ossian? That little pipsqueak? Sure. What about him?"

Brynhild had stood back listening to the exchange, but now walked over to stand next to Cathbad. "Who is this Ossian?"

Infusing his voice with charm, Cathbad explained, "He was what is known as a polymorph. He could shift into the livin' image of another human form, includin' nonhuman beins'. I created him from a warlock."

Wrinkling her nose, Brynhild said, "Does not sound good."

Cathbad kept his attention on Tristan as he continued filling in his partner. "Oh, but he was special. I poured a tremendous amount of power into him until he could alter into any form at any time. He was one of my greatest works of art in many a century."

Tristan brought reality to the conversation. "I'm not so sure about how powerful Ossian was. Whatever that witch

Veronika did to him caused a major malfunction. I watched when he took his last breath. Looked like a wind-up toy coming apart."

Cathbad's humor soured. "Queen Maeve holds all fault for his demise. She sent him on a mission without my approval." Cutting his gaze to Brynhild, Cathbad said, "I do not mourn the loss of anyone, but I will never forgive what Queen Maeve cost me."

Ah, now Tristan understood what had caused a crack in Cathbad and Queen Maeve's union.

He just did not know how deep that fracture ran.

Under Queen Maeve's direction, Ossian helped Veronika escape a warded prison cell beneath the mountain VIPER used as their headquarters. Cathbad had agreed to work with Daegan and the Tribunal deities to prevent Veronika from destroying everything in her path.

No one had understood how she escaped until seeing Ossian lose his shit when his body freaked out. Like many others, Tristan had thought Cathbad agreed to return Phoedra, who he'd captured, in exchange for the Tribunal powers not going after Queen Maeve for her part in the deadly jailbreak.

Based on what Tristan had learned here, Cathbad had only wanted to appease everyone at the time to prevent anyone from disrupting other plans he had in place.

In fact, Tristan couldn't see a good outcome for Queen Maeve in all this.

Cathbad would not mourn her loss, if he could pull it off, but then neither would Tristan.

"I did at first think to barter with Daegan for your return," Cathbad said, jerking Tristan into the present again.

That sounded as if Cathbad had not sent any word to Daegan, who had no way of knowing Cathbad was Cavan. If Tristan had failed to finish that telepathic call and inform Daegan of Cavan's true identity, no one had a clue where he was.

His stomach twisted the more he realized he held little

value to Cathbad. If that ended up being the case, Cathbad could keep him here forever.

His gaze shot to the frozen pond.

Would his gryphon survive being imprisoned in there?

Cathbad turned his head, looking in the same direction as Tristan, then swung around laughing. "I will not throw ya in the pond unless ya give me trouble."

Tristan had to admit that gave him a small amount of relief, but only for the moment. His middle name was trouble when anyone trapped him.

Brynhild slid a look of disgust at Cathbad, who evidently had no issue with putting her in the pond.

She should have thought twice about getting involved with Cathbad. Tristan had little sympathy for anyone in bed with that druid voluntarily.

He sure as hell had not come here of his own free will.

"No, no, no," Cathbad said, still chuckling as if he found Tristan's worry amusing. The prick.

Cathbad turned serious. "I am seein' the benefit of havin' an Alterant."

"In what way?" Tristan asked dryly. "Not like I can fly around with my arms and legs pinned."

The druid spoke in a hushed voice, rapt with excitement, and moved his hands as he worked to paint a visual for everyone. "Just think of the powerful polymorph I could create. One far greater than Ossian. I see a polymorph that could shift into a dragon form and enter Treoir realm once I compel it." He paused and turned his crazed gaze on Tristan. "Ah, yes, ya have so much more potential. 'Tis a very painful process," he warned then his grin widened. "But that does make it all the better for me."

Tristan's throat tightened. He struggled to breathe. He hadn't felt terror in a long time, but his heart dropped like a silver dollar tossed in a shallow fountain.

If Cathbad turned him into a polymorph, Tristan could be compelled to destroy everything and everyone that mattered to him.

He'd become Daegan's greatest nightmare and would die at the hands of the man who had given him back his life.

CHAPTER 6

CASIDHE WRIGGLED HER WAY THROUGH the dark tunnel leading from a massive hollow tree, which shielded the outdoor entrance to this secret route. Soon, she'd reach the hidden doorway inside the ancestral research centre.

Good thing. Her legs and arms were spent from tonight's cross-country race to find Fenella.

She'd used this path when she had snuck out of the research centre covertly to visit Herrick only days ago. The hunched-over speed-walk seemed twice as long today. Carved and reinforced hundreds of years ago, this location had been shared only with Herrick's squire families.

Fenella had never wanted to take the route, claiming her back couldn't handle it, but she may have to now.

Casidhe's fingers cramped from still clutching *Lann an Cheartais* like a lifeline, but for now this weapon was her sole support team.

She'd love to have her backpack with the sheath for carrying her sword. Under normal circumstances when she didn't have to carry this weapon while jogging for miles, the sword weighed little and had excellent balance.

But even holding a butter knife for hours would eventually become tiresome.

Adrenaline had run out long ago, leaving her to function on anxiety alone.

She stumbled in the tunnel and slapped a hand against the rough-cut stone wall to catch her balance. Her damp shirt clung to her and her jeans sagged from the fog that had soaked the denim. She dragged in one long breath after another, which should have refreshed her.

Instead, she sucked in the damp musty smell of a tunnel that seeped water on occasions.

If she wanted fresh air, she needed to push on to the ancestral building. Her legs ached, but she kept forcing one step after another.

When she finally found the two steps up to the hidden doorway, she took them then flipped a latch on the back of a bookcase. That caused the shelving to roll forward, creating an opening.

Relief rushed through her at reaching the centre before daylight. Blood pounded in her ears as she listened for any sound of another person present.

She'd love to hear Fenella humming, but the woman would not be here yet. Not if the time was around eight in the morning.

If Fenella had not been captured, she should be arriving at nine, like normal, an hour before the centre opened at ten.

Casidhe couldn't wait to reach the desk phone and call Fenella's mobile phone.

Easing through the narrow opening, she closed the bookcase and sidestepped two cases over to tug a latch camouflaged as a bookend back, which locked the doorway again.

Just inside the library area, the door to the small bathroom on her right sat half open and the dim light glowed. She silently thanked Fenella's fear of darkness for having a way to see in this back area without having to turn on overhead lights. The soft glow brushed across the floor, allowing Casidhe enough ambient light to traverse the maze of bookcases in this area, far from the harmful rays of the sun.

She wouldn't flip on any lamps up front either.

No point in advertising her presence.

When she reached the narrow opening between cases forming a wall behind Fenella's desk and Casidhe's side of the room, she hesitated to enter the reception area up front.

Would those yellow things attack her here?

Would Cavan or the stranger be waiting for her?

Her heart had been slammed around too many times tonight. Terror seeped into her chest. Her hands shook. She had her sword but not her confidence. What if Cavan showed up and she couldn't deliver what he wanted? He'd use Fenella to punish her ... if he didn't have her friend already.

What would she say to Herrick?

Casidhe had a duty to him and his entire group. He depended on her. The people he protected depended on her, and Fenella depended on her. She could not let them down.

Sucking up her backbone, she lifted her chin and pushed away her doubts, ready to face whatever came next.

Now was the time to prove Herrick had been right to believe in her.

Determined, she gripped the sword hilt tightly and peeked around the end of the bookcase to find the office intact.

Both desks had their normal amount of clutter.

In all truthfulness, Fenella kept hers neat where Casidhe cared little about organization.

She tended to ignore clutter when she got lost in history.

Cavan's book still sat on the side table next to her comfortable chair where she'd left it after reading a bit. That old chair had become a far better place to read than bent over a desk.

Nothing had disturbed the thick cloth she'd placed over the book to shield it from sunlight as well.

On her next deep inhale, she replaced the musty tunnel smell with the rich aroma of history. That wonderful smell lived here along with the coconut scent from the gorse she'd cut and placed in a jar with water before leaving to see Herrick. Though still pretty, the arrangement could stand to be refreshed.

Being in the middle of books had always been her happy place. Research and the thrill of discovery had kept her going forward for years, ignoring how her life flew by one year after another.

She rarely thought on how quickly time passed unless Fenella fussed at her for believing duty overrode a personal life.

But it did.

Casidhe had been trained and sent here with a mission, which she'd been warned might require a lifetime of dedication. She hadn't been born into the Luigsech family the way Fenella had been born into her squire family.

Casidhe had been someone's bastard.

Why else would she have been abandoned and dropped at one foster home after another?

All that changed when Herrick sent one of Fenella's older relatives to bring Casidhe to Herrick. Casidhe had asked him years later why he'd sent for her.

He said he'd been asked to find her and would not disclose who or why someone had made that request, only that she would be treated as part of the Luigsech squire family from there on.

She'd been incredibly fortunate and asked no more questions. To this day, she counted her blessings to be part of Herrick's world.

For that reason, she never looked at her duty as a burden, but an opportunity to prove her worthiness.

The room shifted. Chills and exhaustion shook her body as adrenaline wore off. She clutched the corner of the bookcase to steady herself.

This was not the time to buckle. She braced herself, allowing a few minutes to recover.

Back to business.

She stood the sword in a narrow corner formed by a bookcase and the opening to the reception area. Dropping to her knees, she crawled forward until she could reach Cavan's book, which she then toted back to place next to the sword.

After a couple more trips on her knees, she had snacks from her desk piled with the book, plus one of the cushions she'd used to prop her arms on when sitting in the chair. She plopped the cushion on the floor and lifted a small keychain with an LED light she'd snagged on her last trip to the desk. Some salesperson had given those to her and Fenella. She'd tossed the trinket in her desk drawer thinking it another piece of junk.

She leaned over to hold her hand under her heavy oak desk to test the light. The beam was a concentrated glow.

Perfect.

While close enough to reach the surface, she eased the desk phone to the floor and dialed Fenella's mobile number.

No answer.

Disappointment threatened to break her, but she had one last hope. She dialed Mr. Peadar.

He answered, "How's about ye?"

Casidhe fell into the local dialect, which had helped her fit in with everyone. "Fine, Mr. Peadar. I wish ta surprise Fenella with somethin' for her new goats. Can you give me an idea?"

"I could, but she did not come for them."

Casidhe struggled to keep from giving away how those words had punched in her chest. She forced her voice to sound at ease. "Ah. I'm sure I'll be hearin' about what delayed her when she shows up this mornin'."

"Tell her to come on today. They be waitin' on her."

Tears burned Casidhe's eyes. "I will. Good day, sir." She hung up the phone and curled on the floor. Everything crashed in on her from the all-night run to the terror of worrying and now knowing for sure Fenella was in trouble. She sobbed, a gut-wrenching snotty sound she would be humiliated to allow in public.

How had this happened? She hadn't gone looking for this trouble, but she had stepped in it up to her chin.

After a while, she sat up and dragged a wad of tissues off her desk. Her chest hurt, but she'd survive. She had to pull herself together and think of how to find Fenella.

Or just wait for Cavan to show up and gloat that he had captured her.

Casidhe sniffled, wiped her nose, and turned away from the desk. She didn't stop at her pillow seat, but made it to the middle of the bookshelves blocked from public view and stood. A quick trip to the bathroom resulted with her face washed and her lopsided ponytail straightened. Her blotchy red face was meh. She could only do so much without a pile of makeup.

She had never been considered vain, but freshening up had kept her going many hours at night in the past. She yanked off the blue sweater she'd put on over her blouse after showering last night and tied it around her waist in case she needed it later. Nothing could be done about her ripped and dirty white cotton shirt. She wouldn't have worn it if she'd expected to run through dirty tunnels, but she just had to get through this morning.

Her wool pants were still decent. With a last look at her swollen eyes, she squared her shoulders and told the mirror. "No crybabies allowed. Get busy findin' a way to hold somethin' over Cavan before he shows up."

Fenella had no one else to come for her but Casidhe.

It might be futile, but Casidhe would continue trying Fenella's phone while she waited to learn if Cavan had her friend. If not, then ... Casidhe would be on her own to outmaneuver Cavan and hunt Fenella.

When she returned to the cushion, she glanced at the street outside the large front window while remaining out of sight. She and Fenella had never wanted blinds to impede their view of the village activity.

Maybe that had been shortsighted.

She'd feel less vulnerable with closed blinds she could peek through.

Nothing stirred out there, as it should be until the bakery across the street opened up.

Casidhe settled back on the cushion. She lifted the book Cavan had left and considered her next move.

Hunt for the grimoire?

To do that, she'd need a starting point.

If, or when, she had to leave here, what books would she take?

Abusing her knees again, she moved deep into the research

centre until she could stand and use the tiny light where the glow would not be seen from the front. She searched for reference books, which might give her some idea of where to begin searching for that stupid book of majik. Since she'd never even heard of Immortuos Grimoire before yesterday, she turned to material from before Herrick's birth, but that selection would be small.

An hour of hunting yielded two possible books, both heavy tomes. She found a cloth tote to carry them in along with Cavan's book if she had to make a run for it.

Why would she run? She had no idea, but neither had that been a consideration last night when she sat at the table to eat her stew.

Her new mantra was be prepared to flee at any moment.

Her stomach grumbled.

She'd kill to eat a full meal and sleep for ten hours.

Good fantasy. Not happening.

Weary to her bones, she wiggled around on the cushion getting comfortable. The desk shielded view of her presence from anyone passing by outside where daylight continued to brighten the village. She opened the packages of crackers, careful to put the trash in the can. This position on the floor also allowed her to keep an eye on anyone walking up to the door next to the window.

With Cavan's heavy book on her lap, she cleaned her hands and placed the rag at her side on the floor. She used two fingers, barely skimming the rich-brown front cover. Symbols rose to meet her fingers again, changing shape as they did to form words she could understand.

Before Ainvar.

A dark druid book about a *time* before Ainvar. Who could Ainvar be?

Closing her eyes, she placed all ten fingers on the book.

The tome hummed with energy.

She wished to look at the page Cavan had told her he wanted translated this morning, but he'd warned her to not review the page before he arrived or he would know.

Blinking, she stared at the old tome. A *sentient* book?

Should she open to that page and read?

How much worse could it be if he did figure out she'd read the words? On second thought, she shouldn't toss a question like that to the universe.

Minutes passed so slowly. She tapped her fingers on the floor. The clock hand touched nine and kept moving, not showing the least concern for Fenella's failure to arrive.

A tap on the door surprised Casidhe, but she didn't jump or move. Mrs. Clark had a turnover for Fenella. Casidhe held her breath until the baker crossed the street to her shop. The woman who ran the yarn shop stopped by, knocked, looked confused, then moved on.

Where was Cavan? She'd expected him to appear by now.

What if he never showed at all?

What would that mean?

What if he did show and didn't have Fenella, but Fenella didn't show? Would that prove he had not captured her?

Casidhe sat there in a dilemma, but kept her hand and eyes away from the passage Cavan had warned her against. If he had Fenella, all bets were off. She'd read anything she wanted.

Life began moving around outside. Some passing by glanced at the shop with a curious look since Fenella could be counted on to be here early.

Casidhe stayed in the shadows, ignoring anyone except Cavan, if he ever showed up. She'd tried Fenella's phone every fifteen minutes, unable to give up on the only link she had to her.

Each failed connection drove another spike of hurt through her.

Had she failed Fenella?

When Casidhe had five minutes left until the shop should officially open, she began sweating.

Would Cavan be here by ten? She kept an eye on the small clock on Fenella's desk, replaying Cavan's words. She couldn't recall him committing to a specific time, only saying he expected her to be here this morning.

She would have pinned him down, but she expected today to start like any other with Fenella walking in laughing about her new goats. Everything had changed.

Ten o'clock arrived.

Her anxiety spiked. She had no idea what to do about finding Fenella. Or Cavan.

If he had her friend, wouldn't he want to show up and use Fenella to force Casidhe to do what he demanded?

A logical expectation unless ...

She looked at the book Cavan had left, the whole reason she had to be here now.

Had he made a big deal about her translating a passage in this book just to insure she would be nowhere around Fenella to protect her?

CHAPTER 7

DAEGAN TWISTED HIS NECK AND stretched his arms within the cloaked area where he stood. He stopped in mid-stretch and blinked to clear his eyes. Had that been a smudge of light inside the centre? After a long moment of staring, he growled. Too much time standing around had him imagining things.

He'd thought he'd seen a wisp of wild red hair from that little termagant, Luigsech, an hour ago. But sunrise reflections had been playing with his eyes.

His insides roiled every time he thought about what Tristan must be enduring.

He tried contacting Tristan continually with no success.

Why had he sent Tristan after that being? Yes, he held Tristan's ability in high regard, but damn. Daegan would trade places if he could.

A voice Daegan had been waiting to hear came into his mind. *This is Quinn. I'm ready to teleport with Reese.*

Daegan wasted no time complying, but Quinn and Reese didn't appear as quickly as they should have. He had a moment of fear for their lives if the venom in his body was corrupting his power, but they finally showed inside the cloaking. Daegan expanded it to protect their presence and any conversation.

"I can carry the damned bag myself," Reese argued, hands flying in front of Quinn's expressionless face. She stopped in midpoint and turned to Daegan. Then she gave Quinn a censoring glare. "Why do you *always* make me look like a harpy in front of *him*?"

Daegan didn't know what was going on, but he wanted Reese at ease. "I do not think ya are a harpy."

Jaw set and eyes flashing anger, Reese sweetened her tone. "That's a lie, but thanks, Daegan."

Quinn looked no happier.

Daegan asked telepathically, *What is wrong, Quinn?*

His Maistir huffed out a breath and answered the same covert way. *Nothing as important as findin' Tristan. I'll explain later.*

Daegan turned to Reese, speaking out loud. "Thank ya for comin' to help, Reese. I promise ya we will keep demons away from ya while we do this."

That jarred her out of her silence. Her gaze darted around in every direction. She smoothed her hands over the front of her long-sleeved button-down beige T-shirt. She'd dressed ready to work in jeans and sneakers. "You're welcome. I can handle demons. I just don't deal well with asshats."

Quinn shook his head to just move on.

Daegan agreed. Whatever conflict those two had would have to be worked out later. "Have ya told Reese what is goin' on yet, Quinn?"

Reese jumped in and replied, "No, he hasn't. Specifics would be expecting too much from him."

Quinn did not take the bait. Instead, he explained, "I only shared what was required to request your help. Had you refused, that would have been acceptable, but I would have had no reason to share additional details you had no need for at that point."

"What in the blue blazes ... ?" Reese shot him a death glare. "All that crap you just said can be summed up in one sentence. Information is on a need-to-know basis." After that criticism, Reese turned a friendly face to Daegan. "I would love to know what's going on, like the details of how Tristan was captured."

Daegan would sympathize with Quinn, but since he had no idea what had caused the friction between those two he didn't take a side. "Tristan came here with me. We were investigatin' a woman who works in that ancestral research centre across the street. She rode her bike from here to a grocery buildin' where she met with someone called Cavan. We followed to watch, but the man hid his identity with glamour and cloakin'. When those two parted ways, Tristan followed Cavan and I followed the woman. Cavan captured Tristan while I was fightin' Imortiks at the woman's cottage."

"Wow. Okay, so what's first?" Reese turned to the side and studied the centre. "Is that place across the street open?"

"Not yet, accordin' to the hours on the glass." Daegan cast a look in the same direction. "It should open in ten minutes. The woman who spoke to Cavan yesterday told me she had to be here this mornin' to meet with him, but neither have shown."

"She just told you all that?" Reese asked with a look of disbelief.

"Reese," Quinn said quietly.

"What? I'm just trying to understand everything going on." She returned to facing Daegan.

"No, she did not just offer that information. We had a conversation where I explained how she has to help me find Cavan so we can save Tristan."

"Ah. Not a friendly talk then."

"Not especially and Imortiks attacked before we could finish that conversation. By the time I killed the last one, the woman had escaped." When Reese lifted her eyebrows in surprise, Daegan added, "I have no idea who Cavan is or where he took Tristan. The only person who can tell me is the woman I spoke to at that cottage last night. Casidhe Luigsech."

Quinn's eyebrows lifted at the mention of the woman's name. Evidently Evalle and Storm had informed Quinn of the council meeting details.

Worry entered Quinn's calm demeanor. "So you've encountered Imortiks since coming here?"

Daegan admitted, "Yes. I fought a couple last night, plus demons, includin' one that glowed, at this woman's cottage.

She lives a fair piece outside the village. As I mentioned, Luigsech disappeared while I was outside fightin' the demons."

"Well, that sucks," Reese groused. "She didn't hang around in case you were hurt or needed help?"

Her reaction drew a smile from Quinn, an expression Daegan would call admiration.

Those two had some kind of strange relationship.

He couldn't believe he was going to defend Luigsech, but he would not allow Reese's assumption to stand. "Actually, the Luigsech woman pulled out a sword that hummed with energy. She panicked a little at first, but instead of screamin' and runnin' in circles, she slashed the heads off Imortiks."

"You're joking," Quinn said, sounding unconvinced.

"I am not. She has trainin' and power, which surprised me as much as possessin' a sword with very old energy. I believe that weapon may have come from my time. It's hard to explain, but energy that old has its own signature. I did not realize she possessed power until her shield slipped while arguin' with me."

Reese observed, "I bet she regrets that about now."

Daegan hadn't considered what Luigsech had been going through since they parted. He'd assumed she ran to inform someone of his presence, such as Cavan.

Or had she been escaping out of fear?

"To hear this Luigsech has power conflicts with what Garwyli said about the family of your father's squires," Quinn mused. "So she is not a *human* Luigsech?"

Reese shifted an impudent gaze to him. "What? Are there different *varieties* of Luigsechs?"

Overlooking her sarcasm, Quinn explained, "The dragon squires of Daegan's era were all human. After Queen Maeve captured Daegan, his father, King Gruffyn, wrote in his last journal that he suspected traitors within his kingdom. For that reason, he brought in a new squire family with the name of Luigsech."

"I didn't think people had last names back then," Reese

replied.

Daegan explained, "They used first names, but were known as being of an area, such as Luigsech. Anyhow, the squires were always humans and trusted families as they carried the history of the dragon clans as well as performin' confidential work."

"Do you think this woman is impersonating someone from the squire family or just happens to have the same last name?" Reese asked, turning to watch the entrance to the centre Daegan also kept in sight.

"I do not believe in coincidences, especially not of this sort." Daegan tensed when an older man in dark blue pants and matching vest over a short-sleeved light blue shirt walked up to the door of the ancestral centre. He carried a stack of mail and knocked.

Reese spoke in a hushed voice. "Is that someone you're looking for, Daegan?"

"I do not think so." Daegan watched the confusion on the old guy's face at no one answering the door. After a moment, the man lifted his shoulders, talking to himself as he shoved letters and a magazine into a slot on the door.

Quinn murmured, "Just a postal delivery."

"Okay, I'm ready to do this." Reese turned to Daegan. "You said you're looking for this guy Cavan and last saw him right before Tristan followed him. Maybe you should take me to that spot where you saw Cavan and let me start there."

"I thought so as well," Daegan admitted. "Now that ya are here, Quinn, ya stay to keep watch on the centre. I shall take Reese to the grocery lot." Daegan described Cavan and Luigsech's features for Reese then considered what to do about leaving Quinn. He could normally cloak Quinn, but Daegan hesitated to depend upon his waning power after the slow teleporting.

Quinn must have realized something being off with Daegan. He suggested, "Allow me to step out of the cloaking. I'll drop behind these trees and call to you if anyone shows up."

Once Quinn exited the cloaking, Daegan and Reese walked down the road where it was more open, stepping out of the way of one slow moving vehicle.

At the grocery location, he pointed out the specific place where Cavan had stood. Reese sat there and closed her eyes, then yanked her head back. She opened her eyes and blinked hard. "That's like ... strange."

"What did ya see?"

"He had so much power around him, it was blinding to look in any direction. He's got a crap load of energy." She shook her head. "I can't see through that. Do you want to hunt another spot after he walked away and try that?"

"No. We would be movin' ya all over the sidewalk and probably still have the same result. This was the only place I could point to for sure."

"Sorry, Daegan."

"Don't apologize. Ya are aidin' me in narrowin' down all directions to search until I find the one to lead me to Cavan or Tristan."

When she stood again, they moved back to where Quinn hid. He emerged and Daegan drew the cloaking around all three of them. Before Quinn asked, Daegan told him what had happened.

Running her hands over her hair in an agitated motion, Reese asked, "Didn't you say the last place you saw Luigsech was at her cottage? Why aren't we there?"

He'd been right to ask Reese to come here. She had as sharp a mind for investigating as she had a gift for remote viewing. "The Luigsech woman said she *had* to meet Cavan here this mornin'. If we do not find her soon, we go to the cottage next. But here is the best hope for meetin' up with Cavan."

"It's fifteen after ten," Reese declared. "Either one or both have missed the meeting, unless they're inside doing it right now where we can't see them. What's the plan?"

Reese had voiced Daegan's thoughts. "I shall teleport in. If someone is in there, I will contain them first then drop your cloakin' and teleport ya in."

"Both of us," Reese clarified.

"Of course."

"I should go with you to watch your back," Quinn offered firmly.

"No, stay here. If I run into somethin' unexpected and require help, I will call ya telepathically." Daegan stepped from the cloaking and teleported into the front area of the ancestral centre.

CHAPTER 8

DAEGAN APPEARED INSIDE THE ANCESTRAL centre next to a desk facing the front window.

He called up a sword and stood still.

A distinctive *"click"* sounded at the rear of the building.

He ran through an opening on the left side of the room into an area full of books with blinding speed. No one there. Nothing but walls and walls of bookcases.

Something had made that sound.

He reached out with his senses to detect another energy. Then he inhaled a mix of scents from the fading flowers to a very recent visitor.

Ruadh rumbled, *The woman.*

Daegan agreed. His nose seemed to search out Luigsech's scent immediately. How long ago had she been here? Was that from yesterday or ... today?

Or was he trying to assign a simple noise to her?

A solid wood exit door to the exterior stood shut with a heavy bolt slid into place. That door would have made more noise than a click.

Disappointment swamped him.

He opened his senses to the building, picking up residual energy. Luigsech's, nothing else he could identify, as someone like Cavan, but the woman was no longer here.

Daegan called to Quinn, alerting him to prepare Reese for teleporting. He rushed back to the front room just as those two reappeared.

Reese grabbed Quinn's arm, weaving where she stood.

Quinn glanced at her hand as if unsure if he should

acknowledge her touch. "Would you like something to drink, Reese?"

She shook her head, "No, thanks. I'm good."

When he patted her hand, her gaze shot to his fingers. She snatched hers back to her chest. They stared at each other for a second then Quinn went into mission mode. "Where do you wish Reese to begin?"

Sounding relieved to move ahead, Reese asked, "You remember how my remote viewing works, right, Daegan?"

"Yes, I do." Daegan shook off his distraction from that first noise to stay on point and find Tristan. He didn't know the extent of Reese's gift, but he understood how it had worked in the past. The best result would be based upon finding a specific place in this building Luigsech had used recently.

"To answer your question, Quinn, I have no idea what spot would work best. I wish to determine if Luigsech has been here since I saw her last night, and if Cavan has been as well, though I have picked up no other recent power signature."

Angling his head at that, Quinn asked, "You picked up Luigsech's?"

"Yes, but I have no idea if 'tis from this mornin' or yesterday. She had not left a strong energy residue here as she did last night after battlin' the Imortiks. If she has been here since then, she may have shielded her power."

"Good to know." Reese sounded as if she'd caught her second wind. "Here are my thoughts. You two should spread out and see what you can find to get me set up faster, but what about people coming past the window and door?"

"I have shielded us inside here." Daegan moved to allow Quinn to step past him to where one of two desks sat in an L positioning. Quinn paused in front of the one closest to the door and studied it.

Reese remained in the middle of the room with her arms crossed. "I'm not Nancy Drew, so I'll just stay out of the way and let you two do whatever you're doing."

"Who is Nancy?" Daegan had never heard of this female.

Quinn snorted. "A storybook female detective. We've got

this, Reese." Turning back to the desk where he carefully moved documents and opened drawers, Quinn suggested, "This appears to be the desk of the person who greets visitors."

"Might be where the Fenella woman sits," Daegan commented.

Luigsech's scent surrounded the other desk he stood nearer. He'd been trying to ignore her scent, but hadn't been able to since leaving her cottage.

His gaze traveled over the room and stopped at cut yellow flowers in a glass vase in the corner. Ah, now he identified the coconut smell of *aiteann*. He'd thought nothing of the yellow flowers as he'd seen a few yesterday, but now the image and smell took him back thousands of years to when he'd grown up running through fields covered in the same flowers.

Luigsech had those planted around her cottage.

But he singled out her unique scent.

He allowed his nose to lead him to the right side of the room as he faced the door. The wall behind the desk where Quinn stood ran from the narrow opening to the massive library in the back.

He stepped through the opening and paused, noting a stronger hint of Luigsech in this spot, but mixed with smells of aged leather and ink.

She spent her time here. Every day or maybe only recently?

The wall behind the central desk Quinn dug through had been created by the backside of a heavy bookcase. This area needed light for anyone wishing to read the many oddly-shaped books that appeared to have been written over many centuries.

These books and the aged smell brought back memories of his da's reading room where he'd learned to read. Good memories from too short a life.

This was not the time to be distracted.

Returning to the front, Daegan checked on Reese who had moved to a chair near the window, evidently tired of standing while they determined a place for her to start.

Quinn looked up. "I believe this desk belongs to a woman named Fenella, just as you suspected. From what I can determine, she handles correspondence and has a stack of potential work for Casidhe Luigsech. That would lead me to believe the desk near you is Miss Luigsech's."

That confirmed what Daegan had surmised simply by her scent clinging to the furniture.

Quinn joined him and stared at the messier side of the room. "Why have that old chair next to the desk? It doesn't match the ones like Reese is sitting on, which appear to be for guests."

Daegan examined the worn leather chair with a small dark-wood table on one side with a standing lamp secured on the backside. Another wider table on the opposite side of the chair allowed more room, probably for books. Clean cloths folded into squares sat on the lamp table with a note pad and pen.

Daegan deferred to Quinn who had lived in this modern world longer than him. "What do ya see?"

Quinn gave the chair a long look. "You said Luigsech is the one who translates very old text. Now that I consider her everyday work, I can see her spending more time reading in a place where she's comfortable for hours. I see her only utilizing the desk for things like correspondence or limited research work. Something requiring shorter periods of time. I say we start there."

This was why Daegan believed in surrounding himself with capable people and allowing them the freedom to work.

Daegan took in Reese's pale skin. Could she do this without harming herself? She tended to bristle whenever Quinn inquired regarding her heath. He'd follow Quinn's lead to respect Reese's ability to make her own decisions about using her remote viewing gift or not. "I believe we have a place for ya to try, if ya are ready, Reese."

"Sure thing." Popping up from one of the chairs near the window, she pointed at the spot Quinn had suggested could be Casidhe's place to read. "You want me there, right?"

Daegan nodded.

With Reese's initial burst of irritation having passed, she sounded calmer. She walked over and paused, giving the chair a once-over before turning to sit. Clutching the thickly padded arms, she murmured, "Man, this thing is broken in and super comfortable. I'd like to find one like it back home."

Daegan held his breath when he would normally be ordering one of his warriors to get busy, but not a woman, especially one helping him.

That didn't stop his mind from screaming to take action, save Tristan and Devon. How many others were in jeopardy while he hunted Cavan? He would not forsake Renata and any others as well. But first he had to take care not to lose Reese or Quinn.

His jaw muscles felt hard as stone from keeping them locked.

It was do that or he'd sound like the madman living in his brain.

Ruadh had never possessed patience, but he spoke in Daegan's mind. *The gryphon is strong. He will survive.*

Even so, Daegan suffered over what Tristan might be having to survive.

Nothing moved fast enough for him.

Quinn asked, "Are you sure you want to do this, Reese?"

She lifted her face to Quinn and had an argument going on behind her eyes, but she shook it off. "I'm fine, really." Then she reached over the left side of the chair to pick up a small cushion from the floor she shoved under her left arm. It matched the one next to her right hip.

She cleared her throat and announced, "Let's give this a try."

Stretching her hands out along the chair arms, she clenched the leather again and leaned back. Closing her eyes, her fingers slowly relaxed. Then her forehead creased with what appeared to be confusion. She stayed that way a moment, then cocked her head as if looking at something only she could see.

Then she shoved the cushion on her left off the chair.

What had that been about?

She had just made a point of picking up that very cushion.

After a few seconds, Reese began speaking softly in a monotone as she had done at another time.

"Luigsech was alone ... sitting cross-legged. She pulled a book from the table to her lap. Then she cleaned her hands on a cloth and ran her fingers over the strange letters, or symbols maybe, on the cover. I think she's wondering about the title. She said something like ... *Before An*, no, *Before Ainvar.*" Reese gave a little headshake as if confused. "Luigsech kept turning pages. The text is full of strange shapes and symbols."

Daegan crossed his arms, struggling to remain still. He needed action and results.

Still mumbling along, Reese said, "This woman went back to the first pages and held two fingers together like when you salute someone. She ran her fingers over the text and ..." Reese gasped.

Daegan jerked, startled. He checked Quinn to see what they should do.

Quinn didn't hide his concern, but shook his head to not disturb her.

Sounding awed, Reese's voice went up. "The letters glow and change as they lift off the page. What the hell? The woman is running her fingers as fast as she can back and forth. I don't understand any of it. I think ... she's translating the text with power."

Quinn spoke to Daegan telepathically. *I believe that answers one question about this Luigsech woman. She must have some significant power to do that sort of translating. She is definitely not human, as you said.*

Daegan nodded, unable to take his eyes off Reese, who went on to describe how Luigsech stopped reading at a point late in the day. She got up, tidied up the office, lifting her mobile phone, which had a photo of yellow flowers covering a field on the phone's display, then her backpack, and a tote bag. She locked up and put the tote in the basket on the handlebars of her bicycle.

Reese had been seeing what happened yesterday right before Daegan began following the Luigsech women.

At this point, Daegan relived what he'd seen as Reese continued describing Luigsech through her remote vision as the woman pedaled through the village and stopped at the grocery.

He leaned forward, listening for any hint to what Cavan might have said or his identity.

Reese's jaw tightened and her words came out angry. "That man grabbed Luigsech's arm. She's pissed. She's talking. 'What do you want, Cavan?' Then she tried to yank away, but he held her like he had a steel grip." Reese paused and cocked her head again as if listening to someone and her frown returned. "The man is threatening her if she does not meet him and ... find a grimoire."

Even after what happened last night and Luigsech vanishing on Daegan, his blood boiled at any woman fearing for her life.

With every word Reese shared, it began to sound as if Luigsech had told the truth when she said she'd done nothing to bring this on her.

Now Daegan felt bad about what little intimidation he'd tried at the cottage, but in truth, the deadly woman had not been overly impressed.

He allowed Reese to repeat the conversation, which clearly sounded as if Cavan would harm Luigsech's friend if the woman failed to do his bidding. Now he understood Luigsech's need to be here on time.

But what had happened?

When Reese spoke the words, "Immortuos Grimoire," Daegan sent a telepathic message to Quinn.

The minute Reese finishes the conversation and the woman rides away on her bicycle, I know everythin' that happened yesterday from that point until Luigsech vanished durin' the battle at her cottage.

Nodding, Quinn waited until it was clear Cavan had departed from the grocery building. He leaned down. "Reese, we have questions."

Her face scrunched up and she scowled.

Trying again, Quinn asked, "Did you recognize the man?"

"No. Can't see his face, but I think Luigsech could."

"Come back to us, Reese," he said a little louder this time.

She grumbled then her eyes snapped open. "What?"

Standing straight again, Quinn turned to Daegan. "Ask your questions."

"Oh." She smiled when she shifted her attention to Daegan and gave him a what-do-you-want look.

"Ya said ya could not see the man's face."

Reese stared off at nothing, then shook her head. "Nope. Everything else I saw was in perfect focus, but not his face. All I can tell you about him was that the woman recognized him, but she didn't like him."

"Are ya sure she recognized him?" Daegan couldn't decide if Luigsech was in league with this Cavan or not.

"Yes. She sounded like she'd be here at ten this morning even if she had to drag herself to make the meeting."

Disappointment weighed on Daegan. Everywhere he turned left him with more questions. "Somethin' must have gone wrong. I fear Cavan and Luigsech did not meet this mornin'. I have no idea what that means."

Reese nibbled on her lip. "One weird thing happened at the beginning."

"Was that why you shoved the cushion away?" Quinn asked.

"Yes. I got two images like a double exposure."

Daegan hated the new terms of this era. "A what?"

Quinn explained how the reference came from two overlapping photographic images, then asked Reese, "What do you think was happening?"

She leaned to the side and picked up the cushion she had knocked away. "I think Luigsech held this or sat on it at some point and I was getting *that* vision, too. Could have been in the past, but I saw her reading that book again. I had the impression she'd just cracked it open in my first vision."

Daegan scratched his head and studied the floor.

Quinn glanced at Daegan and followed his line of sight. "What are we searching for now?"

"I am tryin' to see this from Luigsech's position. She had a hidden exit from her cottage. 'Tis only logical to assume there may be one from this buildin'. In fact, when I teleported in, I heard a click noise as if someone had closed a door, but I found no one in the buildin' and the back door secured from the inside. Still, if she suspected I would come here, she could have arrived unseen. The question then is what would she have done once here?"

Reese stood and started searching the area around her. "This seems to be her area so I'll sit at the desk to see if she sat there this morning."

"Thank you, Reese, though I did have that desk in view as I waited."

"I hear you." Reese took the seat at the desk and tried her remote viewing again. She opened her eyes and shook her head. "The most recent time she sat here, she'd filled out a form from five days ago."

While Quinn gave the other side of the room a second thorough search, Reese sat back in the chair looking around. She stretched her neck, staring at something. "What's on the floor over there, Daegan?"

He turned to where she pointed. "A rag. Luigsech seems to clutter more than the other woman, based upon the condition of this area." He leaned over to pick up the wadded cloth that had been shoved into a spot between the wall and a bookcase.

When he lifted the cloth, a tiny note remained on the floor. He snatched it up.

Quinn stepped up to him. "What did you find?"

"A note with two words. *'Go home.'*" Daegan took in the spot where the note and cloth had been. He squatted low, turning his head to look toward the window. "This position would have given the woman a clear view of the street while protectin' her presence from sight. Reese, would ya try your viewin' once more over here?"

"Happy to."

Quinn stepped aside for Reese to reach the spot on the floor Daegan pointed out. She paused at the reading chair to lift the cushion, which had given her the double image. Placing the cushion right where Daegan pointed, she settled on the soft pillow.

Legs crossed, she leaned back against the end of the bookcase, and closed her eyes. "Oh, wow."

"What?" Daegan asked before stopping himself.

But that had not disturbed her. "Everything is sharper like this is a more recent action." Her hands had rested on her knees, but now she moved them toward her waist, moving her fingers as she looked at something in her mind.

Her eyes began to flutter behind her eyelids.

Quinn's voice came into Daegan's mind. *I've seen her look like this when it was a much deeper viewing than what she just executed. We will find out more if she is not disturbed.*

Daegan gave him a strong nod of agreement. He'd had serious doubts about Reese's remote viewing working when she'd been unable to track Cavan from the grocery. On the other hand, a being that powerful might be able to shield his trail, teleport, or open a bolt hole. Any one of those defense mechanisms would very likely prevent her from seeing much since she could not follow a teleportation or bolt hole escape.

But Daegan's pulse jumped with hope that this might be the vision he'd been hoping for.

Reese's face relaxed. Her lips twitched and her expression turned serious. Speaking again in that soft monotone, she said, "Luigsech is sitting here and checking the window. The street outside is in twilight. When anyone knocks on the door, she freezes, but keeps watching for someone. She made a phone call. No answer. Then she's sitting here with that strange book in her lap. She's spending more time checking the window, clearly worried about something ... or someone."

At twilight? *Damn!* Daegan can't believe he stood so close the whole time that woman had been here and resisted teleporting in. He'd had a sound reason not to, but she'd been here.

Close enough to get his hands on.

"Luigsech crawls over to the desk from time to time and punches numbers on a desk phone she's pulled to the floor. No answer each time. Wait. One time she spoke to ... Peter or Peadar? Some guy with goats her friend didn't pick up." Reese's fingers moved to her knees again and curled into fists as she continued. "She has a wheat-colored tote bag next to her with something in it ... books. Two big books. She put the one she's been reading in the bag, too, then she crawled over to find a pen and scrap of paper. She scribbled *'Go home.'* on the paper and put it under a scrunched-up rag. It's daylight outside. Bright. Like an hour or more has passed. She opened the book, then she seemed to debate reading something and slammed it shut, then shoved it in her bag. She hooked the tote strap over her shoulder then ... picked up a sword that had been leaning behind her back. It's glowing."

Daegan imagined Luigsech had escaped last night with only that sword in hand.

He drove her from her cottage by showing up and drawing in the Imortiks. Power or not, she should not have had to run away panicked.

So many decisions to regret over the past twenty-four hours.

Ruadh's voice smoked through Daegan's mind. *Gryphon is strong, but still needs us. Battle not place for regrets.*

Daegan's dragon did not suffer human emotions when it came to battles and war, only to survive and win. But Daegan had to consider how his actions affected everyone. He would fight to save any of his people without the first regret for those who stood in the way, but he could not so easily dismiss his part in Luigsech's terror.

Not unless he discovered she had intentionally held back information.

Huffing out a long breath and shifting her position on the cushion, Reese continued. "The woman crawled away from the front room until she could stand up in the back area. She moved to the right end of two wide bookcases against the back wall and put her hand between a row of books to ... *pull* something? A switch? Damn. A bookend is the switch."

Daegan had the urge to go look, but without more information it would not help.

Taking a couple shallow breaths, Reese cocked her head with her eyes still shut, but seeing something that seemed important by her expression. "The middle of that big bookcase moved an inch as if it's on hinges. She pulled the bookcase out and stopped. She seemed undecided, standing there with her forehead leaned against the open bookcase. Something happened. Power flushed in the building. She jerked her head and leaped inside the opening, then snapped the door shut. She's in a dark area holding her breath and looking through a peephole at ... Daegan. After a minute, she breathes quietly again, pulls a keychain with a light from her pocket and starts walking fast hunched over. It's a long dark tunnel with a low ceiling."

Just as Daegan had suspected.

Luigsech accessed the ancestral centre from a hidden route. He cursed himself for missing her.

He struggled for patience as Reese continued describing the steps Luigsech made and how the woman reached a spot where she climbed into a massive hollow tree, which opened to the forest.

Sitting quietly for a long moment, Reese said, "Luigsech left the tree and ran for ... I can't tell how long. She stopped in a field near a boulder where flowers and weeds grow. She bent down and lifted a section of earth. No, maybe ... oh, it's a trapdoor."

Rubbing his neck, Daegan sent Quinn a look of lifted

eyebrows.

Quinn spoke silently to Daegan. *I wish we could get her to race ahead, but that just interrupts her.*

Reese suddenly came out of her semi-trance wide-eyed. She spoke quickly. "Things started getting foggy, but the Luigsech woman went through another tunnel and ended up in what I'm guessing is her cottage. Do you want me to keep looking from here?"

Daegan shook his head. "Ya may see more clearly following her from the cottage than to struggle with a foggy image. Or she may just be there right now. Prepare to teleport."

CHAPTER 9

LIGHT FLASHED RAPIDLY AGAINST RENATA'S closed eyelids.

Dark sounds growled and half-words shouted nonstop.

A film, something icky, clung to her face.

She batted her hands wildly, striking out to stop another attack, but it was that beast. That nasty yellow thing. She could feel it reaching into her core. Cold crawled through her body, first turning her fingers numb, then heat scorched her skin.

She bit down to keep from crying out.

Never give the bastards anything to celebrate.

Don't open your eyes, she repeated over and over in her head. Beladors would find her. The dragon promised to save her. He'd tried. That hideous yellow thing hurt the dragon.

What happened to the Treoir dragon?

Howling and screams erupted, raising hairs on her neck.

Crazy words she couldn't understand cluttered the air.

Tears spilled down her face. If only she could have seen Roberto one more time.

Where was Devon? What happened to him? Maybe he escaped.

If he did, Devon would come for her.

She'd seen another Belador in this place the one time she opened her eyes. *Don't open your eyes.*

No. She kept them clinched tight. She didn't know the name of the other Belador, could only see that he was male. He'd been so awful, screaming when they ... she sobbed. Bile raced up her throat. She clenched her teeth.

She squeezed her eyes tight. *Stay strong.*

Don't open your eyes!

Noises slowly subdued until she couldn't even hear breathing.

The sudden quiet tempted her to look.

But the glowing monsters played mean tricks.

She'd been in darkness for so long. She had no concept of time. If only she could see what

was ...

No! Don't open your eyes!

She tried calling out telepathically again. *I'm Renata. A Belador. Help me.*

Laughter howled all around her.

Had she said that out loud?

No. Maybe.

Her throat was too dry to talk. She could barely swallow.

Don't ... open your eyes. Don't ... She slumped, exhausted from another round of hell. She had to stay strong. She could do this if she just napped ...

She dropped off.

"Renata!" screamed in her ear.

She jerked wide-eyed awake and ... screamed.

CHAPTER 10

DAEGAN TELEPORTED ONTO THE YARD outside the prim white cottage with a bright yellow door.

Luigsech had an affinity for that color it seemed.

He'd landed out here to enter alone first to insure Reese's safety as well as Quinn's. As soon as those two appeared, Reese ducked out from under Quinn's arm and stood with her arms crossed.

"Ya watch out for Reese," Daegan told Quinn. "Do not forget demons appeared with the Imortiks last night. I need a moment to check the interior to be sure 'tis safe."

Reese cocked her chin up in a show of bravado, but she also paled at the mention of demons. "I have the power to kill a demon."

Daegan lost patience with the friction going on between her and Quinn, but he managed to keep his voice calm. "I have no doubt ya are capable of defendin' yourself against demons, Reese, but your safety is of utmost importance to me. Ya are the only one I know of among our allies with the ability to track someone usin' your remote vision gift. For that reason, I ask ya to not jump into danger unless ya have no other option."

Quinn said nothing, but a wave of relief passed through his gaze.

She pinched the bridge of her nose. "Got it. Sorry. I'm ... just cranky. I want to get Tristan back as much as anyone. I'll sit tight."

"Good. Thank ya for all ya are doin'." Turning to Quinn, Daegan said, "Call to me if anythin', demon or otherwise, appears."

"Understood."

Daegan stepped over to look inside a window. Everything seemed as wrecked as it had when he'd left earlier this morning under the cover of darkness.

He teleported inside and made a quick check of the rooms then teleported Quinn and Reese inside.

"... feel a presence out here," Reese said, finishing a sentence she'd started outside.

"What?" Daegan asked as he shoved a curtain aside to peer through a window at the front of the cottage.

"Right before you snatched us in here, I sensed something around us," she explained. "Not sure if it was a demon or some other being, but not natural. I could probably figure it out if I had another couple minutes out there."

"No." Daegan appreciated the thought, but he would not put her at any additional risk.

She blew a lock of hair off her face. "I didn't say I *wanted* to go back out, only that I might have been able to identify the source."

"Point taken." But Daegan had no time to waste determining if someone, or some*thing*, hid in the tree line. Venom in his body continued to eat away at his power. How long would it be before he could protect no one? The sands of his hourglass poured out faster with every breath, upping the risk of loss on more than one level.

Pushing ahead, Daegan asked Reese, "Where did ya see Luigsech enter the cottage from her secret tunnel?"

"I'm pretty sure it was in a bedroom."

"'Tis only one bedroom." Daegan tossed Quinn a look. "Stay in this front room and keep an eye out for any activity outside. We shall search the bedroom."

"I'll do that and search this room for anything I can find that might offer information on her as well," Quinn confirmed.

"Good idea."

"What's that stink?" Reese pinched her nose.

"'Tis the residue of dead Imortiks."

She nodded at Daegan, who moved ahead of her leading the way to the bedroom.

"Except for the smell and destruction, this is a cool cottage. Probably been here a few hundred years," Reese mused as she stepped into the bedroom. "A wonderful sanctuary in a beautiful country."

Once again, Daegan paused to take in the location from Reese's perspective. Lacy curtains no longer bright white had aged with time, but the delicate material had been kept clean with care. If Daegan guessed, the oak bed had been hand carved as had the standing chest. Not likely to see multiples of that one or the quilted cover on the bed. Nothing showy, but a place that had been lived in, and loved, a long time.

Had this been Luigsech's safe haven?

He felt another twinge of guilt over pushing the woman from her home. Actually, the Imortiks had sent her running as much as him showing up unannounced.

Tristan's face smoked through Daegan's mind.

He got over his momentary attack of conscience.

Who was Luigsech to be so deeply involved with a preternatural such as Cavan?

"I'll sit on the bed and see if she sat there to pack a bag or something." Reese eased down on the neatly made bed.

After half a minute, she got up, muttering, "Nothing recent there." She went to the bathroom.

Daegan tapped on the walls, listening for a hollow spot to indicate an escape route.

Reese came back into the bedroom and stared at the space. She dropped to the floor next to the bed, sitting in her usual cross-legged style. Every ten or fifteen seconds, she'd scoot to a different position, but with her eyes closed.

She banged into a corner of the bed frame. "Ouch."

"Reese?" Quinn called from the other room.

She sagged with a heavy sigh. "Would you tell him I'm not freaking dying?"

Daegan smothered a smile at her aggravation with Quinn.

He called out, "Reese is safe. Stop irritatin' her so she can work."

Silence answered him.

Reese laughed. "I like you. Okay, let me try this spot then I'll keep moving if nothing pops up."

In the next location, Reese remained in one place for a longer period. Her shoulders relaxed and she leaned back against the bed with her eyes closed. That fluttering motion behind her eyelids from before happened again as she began whispering.

"Luigsech stood where I'm sitting. She was here only a second, then raced out to the other room where she searched for something important. She pushed busted furniture around in a panic, then gave up and came back to this room. I can't tell what she was hunting." Reese squinted her shut eyes, then her face relaxed. "She's now looking for ... a backpack? That's it. She unloaded three books from the cream-colored tote into her backpack, strapped it on then—"

Daegan held his breath, hoping this resulted in something useful.

"Luigsech ... shoved her sword into her backpack? That can't be right. She ... okay, I see. She has some kind of sheath inside her backpack. She pulled the sword out, thanked it for some reason, then put it back in the sheath."

Reese blew out a lungful of air as if just tracking Luigsech's movements tired her. "Well, hell. That's how she opened the trapdoor from inside the cottage."

Daegan had never possessed the measure of patience he had before this moment when he waited as Reese muttered a few more things, but no intelligent sentences.

He started to call Quinn in when his Maistir walked up, standing next to him as he studied Reese.

All at once, she shook her head and came awake or whatever happened when she had seen all she could. Her gaze touched on Quinn, but she addressed Daegan.

"Everything started moving fast so I just sat back and watched to be sure I didn't miss anything. I found how she gets out of here."

Daegan squatted. "What did she do?"

"I'll show you." Reese got up and stepped to the opposite side of the bed where it was closer to the outside wall. "Both of you move back."

Once Daegan and Quinn were out of the way, Reese leaned over and shoved the bed before anyone could help her. She grinned when the wood floor beneath the bed moved with the frame, exposing a three-foot-square trapdoor.

Daegan came around and lifted the trapdoor. Luigsech's scent rose from the hole. He froze, confused by how her scent had him inhaling to pull in more. She must have cleaned up. Her distinctive smell came wrapped in lilac this time.

Ruadh normally remained quiet, but alert, with no threat nearby. His dragon stirred suddenly and made a soft rumble.

What the hell was that about?

Daegan closed the lid and pushed the bed back into place, preventing Luigsech from realizing he'd found her escape point.

He straightened. "That was how she escaped so quickly last night and must have left with only her sword. From what Reese saw at the ancestral research centre, it sounds as if Luigsech returned to the cottage for her backpack with a compartment for her sword."

"That's not the only thing she left," Quinn added. He lifted a mobile phone into view, turning it to show the backside covered in bright flowers.

Daegan crossed the room to where Quinn stood in the doorway. "Where did ya discover that?"

"I almost didn't see it until I moved her sofa."

"Ah!" Reese snapped her fingers. "That must have been what she was hunting for in the other room."

Hope filled Daegan's chest at the single discovery. "Tristan tells me we have people who can gain information from those phones. What about this one?"

Quinn tapped on the buttons more than once. He lifted a disappointed look to Daegan. "I'm not skilled at retrieving information from a mobile phone, but we have Beladors in Atlanta who are exceptional techies."

Raking a wad of hair off her face, Reese said, "Here's what else I saw just now. Your woman escaped through that tunnel and ran for a long stretch. I can't always tell distances when I do remote viewing, but it seemed like it was not terribly far from the cottage."

"Dammit. She's in the wind again," Quinn groaned.

"Not exactly," Reese countered. "When she got out of the tunnel—"

"What did the exit point of the tunnel look like?" Daegan asked, interrupting her.

"Another trapdoor. It was that place I told you about next to a boulder. When I saw the spot this time as she emerged from the tunnel, the boulder hid her from easy view unless someone was standing really close to it in the woods. After she closed the lid, she moved weeds and grass to camouflage it really well. You could walk over that trapdoor and never see anything out of place."

"Quite an operation." Quinn sounded impressed.

Reese agreed, "She's pretty slick with her escape routes. Both of them required her to walk hunched over through long tunnels. You two would have a tough time getting through quickly. This last time, she took off into the woods and eventually the ground turned downhill for a short distance to a riverbank. She stopped about fifteen feet short of the water to pull weeds and branches off of something like a jon boat."

"What is this boat?" Daegan asked Quinn.

"They are flat-bottom boats of different sizes, but most are around eight to twelve feet long and intended for two people out fishing."

"Right," Reese said, moving on. "Luigsech climbed in and headed down river, paddling with the current. Again, I can tell some distances when I have a reference like how far the boat was from the water, but I don't know how far she went downstream. She turned at one point, paddling to a bank on the opposite side where she got out and dragged the boat up an incline and then hid it in the weeds again."

"Was someone waiting for her?" Quinn asked.

"No. She climbed the bank and took a freaking convoluted route through the woods. That's why I sat back and just watched. She went through a cave, then she turned by two trees that had fallen in an X pattern. After that, she went underground a short distance. That woman is half mole."

How could Daegan follow that path?

He could not risk his dragon until after dark and that would only be if he knew for sure no one was around. He asked, "Can ya be more specific on the route Luigsech took through the woods?"

Reese puffed her cheeks and blew out air, staring at the wall with a thoughtful look. "Well, it's not like telling you where to turn on streets in a city."

All Daegan heard in her tone was dead end. "Do ya have a visual of where Luigsech got out of the boat on the other side?"

"Yes and no. I can see that spot, but it looks like so many she passed I don't know what drew her to that specific landing. The one thing that struck me were all the blue flowers growing around a half-submerged tree trunk. They were small with white star-like centers. I'd like to say I could nail the location, but I don't trust what I saw enough to try that. I could make it through the tunnel easier than you two. If I did that, we could find the river entrance." She swung to Quinn. "Don't you dare say one word about it being too dangerous."

"Wouldn't dare," Quinn grumbled and turned to leave the room. "That reminds me, I need to check the outside again."

Daegan decided to join Quinn for another look through the front room.

The glass window shattered behind him on the other side of the bed.

A demon dove through, going for Reese.

CHAPTER 11

CATHBAD TELEPORTED TO A ROOFTOP across the street from Luigsech's ancestral research centre. He cloaked himself as soon as he appeared above the bakery pumping out a delicious aroma. He'd have to visit and try out their sweets on another trip.

He'd arrived at half past ten intentionally, curious to see if Casidhe Luigsech had opened his book to the spot he wanted translated.

If she had, then she put little value on the life of her friend Fenella. That would surprise him, but it wouldn't be the first time someone had placed their own interests first.

He wanted to see Casidhe's true colors right up front.

That allowed him to know how to take what he wanted from her.

While he waited a moment to observe the building, a white-haired woman in a pink dress and matching shoes stopped to tap on the door. She ducked her head, moving it back and forth like a bird searching for seeds inside then walked on.

Probably someone who knew Casidhe and Fenella.

Why had no one answered the door?

Casidhe would not have missed this meeting, would she?

When the woman in pink walked away, Cavan teleported into the reception area he'd visited twice before. Those times, he'd entered at street level through the front door.

The first thing he noticed was his book on dark druids nowhere in sight. Shielding his presence from view, he opened up his senses, calling to the book.

It was not here.

Neither was Casidhe Luigsech.

She had certainly surprised him.

He did not believe she would defy him without cause. She had clearly feared him yesterday and he still believed she cared too much for Fenella to put the older woman at risk.

What had changed for Casidhe since yesterday?

Why would she steal his book? If she'd read as much as he believed she had, she would know the danger of crossing a dark druid of his caliber.

He closed his eyes and opened his senses again to search for preternatural residue.

He picked up a lingering trail of energies.

Casidhe had been here recently.

So had that red dragon and two others, one was a being he'd sensed before but could not immediately identify.

Now he understood why Casidhe might have run with his book. Having the red dragon involved changed everything. Cathbad took his time, searching through the library of impressive volumes. Some books had either been moved around or taken, based on clean areas left with a film of dust disturbed near those spots.

How many books had she taken?

Which ones?

His best guess would be something connected to the grimoire. As he moved through the library full of scents from a time long gone he normally smelled only in his own archives, he considered teleporting to the cottage.

Why would she take the books there when he could so easily find her?

He'd located her cottage after his first visit to the ancestral centre when she took off for five days. Locating that cottage had been simple. It was not as if she tried to hide her life, but he had restrained from entering her home in case she had a way of discerning if she'd had unwelcome company while away.

How had she escaped this building after his first visit without notice?

He and Brynhild had remained close by after their first visit. They'd waited for him to see what action Fenella, or Casidhe, who had hidden from them, would take. He'd felt Casidhe's power as she likely had spied on him and Brynhild when they presented themselves as the Cavans.

But Fenella left the centre that day and no one else.

Only Fenella came in for the next two days as well.

Casidhe didn't show until yesterday, entering through the front door. She had clearly left by a secret exit the first day he visited. He'd placed a majik tripwire by the rear exterior door that first time. No one had opened the door since then.

The Luigsech squire family had been humans, but Casidhe was not, which created a new puzzle.

Just who was Casidhe Luigsech? What powers did she possess besides translating lost languages?

He kept turning in place as he thought, taking in every angle of the room, especially around the floor and back wall.

Where would be the best place to hide a secret exit from this building? He found nothing disturbed on the floor. He turned his attention to the back wall covered entirely with heavy bookcases.

Running his fingers up and down each shelving unit, he searched for a secret latch of some sort. Nothing.

A thought kept digging at him.

Had Casidhe gone to her cottage?

He should leave this place be and teleport there. Shaking his head at this odd development, he started to walk away, but ... he gave that back wall filled with books one last look.

Then he took a couple steps to the center of the room and faced the wall. Lifting his hands, he tapped telekinetic power to pull the bookcases toward him.

All the cases shuddered and creaked with strain, but the right side of one closest to the center trembled more. The middle of the structure bowed out.

Could that one be moveable?

He focused his power on the right side and doubled down.

First a screech of metal, then a pop sounded. The bookcase

broke free, swinging open on hinges.

Smiling, he stepped over and pushed the secret door wider and opened his senses again.

Daegan had not been in this spot, but Casidhe had and not long ago.

Cathbad leaned in. If she'd left this way with his book, he still needed to know where she'd gone.

He'd warned her to be here when he arrived.

She could not outrun him. He would find her, and when he did she would learn the price to be paid for her arrogance.

CHAPTER 12

A GRAY-SKINNED DEMON WITH ONE LONG horn curved over the back of his head and sickle-shaped claws crashed through the window.

Reese had already leaped sideways and rolled up on her knees.

Daegan turned as Quinn flew past him, diving into the room.

All that happened in a micro-second as Reese shoved a blast of energy at the demon. Glowing red eyes bulged. She'd hit the demon with the power of a lightning strike.

The unnatural creature exploded into fire, then orange ashes.

Daegan couldn't get over how she'd moved faster than he could teleport her.

Quinn jumped up, his normally well-groomed hair looking as wild as his eyes. He lunged for Reese and lifted her to his chest, holding her close.

Daegan told Quinn telepathically, *There could be more demons and possibly Imortiks.*

"You're right," Quinn said, raking a shaky hand over his hair.

Reese shoved away from Quinn, hands fisted. "Right about what? Are you two talking in your heads?"

Daegan saved Quinn by explaining, "Time is dwindlin'. Can ya give me a better description of where Luigsech got out of the boat, Reese?"

The expression on her face floored Daegan's hope.

"I told you all I know. I should go with you to help, because even if I could tell you how to find that spot, there's no way I can describe her exact path once she took off on foot again."

"I could enter your mind and view the image," Quinn suggested.

That brought her back to life. She jumped up. "Hell. No."

"Why not?" he pressed. "You know I would not raid your mind and it would be far more expedient. Daegan is not taking you any farther on this hunt."

"Why not?" she demanded. "I'm pretty damn useful. What about you, Quinn? Is he taking you?"

"I shall continue with Daegan while his backup is still captured."

Daegan allowed power to surge in his voice, to eliminate any argument. "Ya can clearly fight off demons, Reese, but I am not so sure about Imortiks. They would definitely want to turn someone with your abilities. Demons and Imortiks showed up all at once last night. I would like to get ya out of here before that happens. Quinn is correct. I would prefer to not take ya along. I cannot be sure we will survive. I need to know ya are safe."

Her face fell when she looked over at Quinn. She twisted her hands together, struggling with a decision. "You can look into my mind, but only images from the point she left the tunnel and went to the river, then where she disembarked. That should get you there."

Quinn gave her a curious glance, but agreed. "I will always respect your wishes."

She closed her eyes. "I'm replaying those images in my mind. Go now."

Evidently, she ordered Quinn around as much as anyone.

Quinn focused on Reese for less than a minute. "I have it. Your recall is quite precise. I feel we can find that location."

She blinked her eyes open. "Fine. I get that I can be a liability. I'll head back if you don't need anything else from me."

Quinn sent a short message to Daegan mind-to-mind. *Please teleport her to Treoir so I know she's safe while I'm gone.*

Daegan acknowledged that by saying, "'Tis all we need for now, Reese. I appreciate everythin' ya did today."

"You're welcome." She gave Quinn a loaded stare. "Be careful."

"I will. Take care of yourself as well and ... get some rest."

"Oh, for crying out loud. I. Am. Fine." She turned to Daegan. "Teleport me now. Please."

She vanished in the next moment.

Daegan had expected her to ask where he was sending her, but she likely assumed she would be returning to Atlanta. "I sent her to Treoir."

"Thank you."

"I doubt she will thank either of us when we see her again."

Quinn gave him a grim nod. "That is my problem. I will explain you only did as I asked."

"Is something wrong with Reese?" Daegan needed to know if Quinn would be distracted.

Washing a hand over his face, Quinn stared off for a minute then shifted a look at Daegan. "I shall explain more later, but Reese is pregnant."

Daegan had no idea what this meant. "Do I congratulate ya?"

"Not yet. She hasn't told me about the baby, but she has too much honor to hide that from me, especially after what happened with Phoedra. In my defense, I used protection, but there's more to the story. She's hiding it for a reason I'm pretty sure has to do with protecting me. When this is behind us, I will find out, but I will also raise this child along with Phoedra."

Daegan hoped they would stop arguing long enough to straighten things out. He hadn't expected the shaft of jealousy that struck him. Though not planned, Quinn would have two children. Daegan had no hope for a mate or children with no female dragons around.

With no idea what else to say, Daegan shook his head. "Ya have a hell of a life, Quinn."

Quinn gave a sad chuckle. "That is one way to put it. Now, what is our next move?"

"Did ya retrieve a visual of the boulder where Luigsech climbed out of the tunnel that ran from her cottage?"

"I did. Reese had concise images."

"Good." Finally, Daegan could take action to find Tristan. "We shall teleport to the tunnel exit point and start from there."

"Precisely. If we can't locate Luigsech quickly, we might have to bring Storm here to track her. There is none better at following natural scents or supernatural essence."

Daegan couldn't fault Quinn's suggestion, but he had reservations they could discuss later. He instructed Quinn, "Focus on that—"

Power flushed into the front room. Imortiks?

Daegan teleported them immediately, hoping Quinn had the visual in place. A boulder would move for Daegan's energy, but not Quinn who stood too far from his side.

CHAPTER 13

TORN SKIN AND DAMAGED MUSCLES in Tristan's abused wrists failed to heal. His dead weight kept a constant drag on his arms, which would be noodles once he got out of these straps.

If he got out of this mess.

The possibility of that happening dwindled by the minute.

He had no idea of his specific location even if he could reach Daegan by calling telepathically.

Tried that again and got the migraine for it.

That damn Cathbad had chosen well for hiding from everyone, including Queen Maeve.

Tristan's heart thumped over and over. For the first time ever, he wished his heart could be silenced. An Alterant gryphon had an unusual evolution, which Cathbad and Queen Maeve had forced on Tristan, Evalle, and the rest of their Alterant pack. When those two crazies had the Alterants captured in TÅµr Medb, they'd shoved each Alterant into a life-and-death battle with another creature capable of killing them.

Tristan would never forget the first time he drew his last breath.

That's when he found out Alterants had to die once to evolve into gryphons with the ability to fly. Then each Alterant had two more lives.

Since then, he'd died again and regenerated.

Sounded simple.

Wasn't. Hurt like shit.

Where he'd been forced to die the first time in TÅµr Medb, he'd chosen death the second time when their team had brought Evalle home from the Scamall realm.

The teleportation killed her.

Noirre majik had been shoved in her body to prevent anyone from teleporting her out of that realm, but Daegan, Storm, and the team wouldn't leave her with the realm collapsing.

Tristan had held her hand and taken his last breath with her, thinking he would pull off a trick Evalle had once done. She'd used her last regeneration to save Tzader after he'd died crashing through the ward on Treoir Castle to protect their warrior queen, Brina.

Tristan had been terrified of killing Evalle himself, but he'd held tight to her. He forced her to use their Belador ability to link with him so she would come back to life as he regenerated a second time.

Looked fucking good on paper.

But he'd been sure he lost her at one point.

Worst moment of his life. He never wanted to hold someone's life in his hands again and made that clear to Daegan. The dragon king said it *would* happen again. That protecting and caring for others sometimes came at a high personal price.

Of course Daegan was right, because Tristan would do it again if given the choice.

That damn powerful heart of his thumped faster with the frightening memory. All that blood coursing through his body caused the pain and agony to kick up another notch. He gritted his teeth to keep from yelling out.

Why had he gone off on that mental rabbit trail?

Ah, yes.

Because he'd been searching for a way to beat Cathbad at his game of turning him into a polymorph. It would be so simple if Tristan died from a heart attack, but his gryphon heart wouldn't fail.

If anything, he'd come back as a more powerful monster with his third, and last, regeneration.

Wouldn't that be a bitch?

A polymorph of unimaginable power and the ability to

shift into a flying beast.

Even to emulate a red dragon.

If agony of being captured and used to destroy Daegan would stop a heart, his would have quit the minute Cathbad announced his sick plans.

Daegan deserved better. That dragon shifter would fight the world for his people.

Somehow, Tristan would find a way to do the same for his boss and his people. He just needed an idea. Might be easier to think with a sip of water. He licked his cracked lips and wondered if he still had a voice.

Across the room, Brynhild made a growling noise and slammed her foot hard against the ground. The cavern shook. Ice cracked along the roof and splattered across the ground.

Some hit Tristan's skin, piercing him like tiny daggers.

But she'd held her hands up over her head. Ice sheets that could slice her in half instead drifted to each side of her like a stream flowing around a rock in the river.

She'd been stomping around the cave since Cathbad left. Tristan had grown accustomed to the incessant bootheel thumping when she crossed an icy surface.

What was the chance he could get information out of *her*?

Worth a try.

Tristan called out in a hoarse voice, "If you're bored, you could talk to me. I'm not going anywhere anytime soon."

She ceased her private grumbling and turned to him.

Across the wide expanse of this semi-lit cavern, her eyes glowed a bright blue.

Studying him like a strange beast, she moved her head from side to side. He'd say she moved in an unnatural way, but neither of them were natural.

Walking slowly in his direction, she asked, "What would we speak of?"

That one might be a hard nut to crack, but with the motivation riding his shoulders, he was up to the task. He'd do pretty much anything if it meant finding a way out of this place and protecting Daegan from these two.

He dragged out a smile as far as his dry lips would allow when he wanted to snarl. "You could tell me what this is all about."

Brynhild stood still for a moment, staring at him with indecision in her face. Then she continued strolling forward.

What kind of nonhuman was she?

Tristan couldn't see Cathbad uniting with a mere witch. Could Brynhild be Fae? No, Tristan was pretty sure a Fae could get out of here.

What about a mage?

Still, not as powerful as Cathbad. He had a deadly goddess for a partner. Tristan could not see that druid taking a step down to a less powerful partner, not when Queen Maeve would annihilate both of them.

Brynhild's arm swung as she walked, revealing the yellow claw-stick Cathbad had whacked Tristan with to knock him out.

Well, shit. Tristan didn't want that thing near him.

This might not go as well as he'd thought.

When she stopped fifteen feet away, he forced a wider grin. That alone should earn him an acting award with the pain banging through his head and muscles screaming in his arms being stretched.

He tried to clear his dry throat. "Hi there."

She cocked her head to the side again and speared him with a surly look. Strange woman. "Who are you?"

Tristan found that interesting. So Cathbad hadn't shared much with her, huh?

He could work with that opening as a starter.

Offering her a confused look, Tristan said, "You mean you're holding me hostage and you don't even know who I am?"

Gorgeous blue eyes brightened even more. Blond hair played across her shoulders and fell to her waist. A braid down one side of her face landed on a perfect mound of breast.

Sexy as hell. Evil as shit.

She argued, "I did not capture you."

Ah, wait a minute. She'd said that as if accusing her of such an act impugned her integrity, if she had any.

"Sorry." Tristan tried for contrite. "Cathbad had me convinced you two were in this together."

She scoffed at that. "We are *not* together. He is gone. I am here."

This had more potential by the minute. Tristan continued to play up to her. "At least you have a nice place for a cave. I'm impressed with that whole setup for reading over there. If you free me, we can sit there and chat." He angled his head, indicating the overstuffed chair next to a tall bookcase and reading lamp.

Clearly all of the latest caves came standard with those amenities.

She followed his gaze to the area he commented on then whipped a furious look back at him.

Well, damn. What had been so wrong about that idea?

Brynhild's eyes blazed with dark thoughts. "No. We can speak now."

Definitely a ballbuster when it came to simple conversation.

Fatigue and pain made every effort monumental, but Tristan had to get through to this female. "Sure, this works. Why didn't Cathbad tell you who I was?"

She took a step closer and the soft shape of her face changed to one of curiosity. "How do you know Cathbad?"

Neutral ground. Finally.

Tristan reached for a foothold in this conversation. "Oh, I've known him since he reincarnated or whatever it was that he and Queen Maeve did to wake up after thousands of years of sleeping. You know her, right?"

From the tight expression on Brynhild's face, he'd say the answer was no. He'd guessed that already.

She lifted a smooth shoulder. "Queen is not important."

This got better all the time.

He'd never been one for cat fights, but he'd kill for a beer to watch this one and Queen Maeve go at it.

Brynhild had zero issues with her ego, so he played to her strength. "You must be some kind of badass to make that statement."

The woman's relaxed face fired up again to a ferocious warrior in the blink of an eye. She called out an order in some language.

A shield flew across the room to her extended hand.

She caught it without looking and flipped it in front of her. "I did not capture you, but I allow no one to live who insults me. Make peace with your god and prepare to die." She didn't change shape, but everything about her became more dangerous and aggressive.

"Whoa, hold it, please," Tristan quickly begged. She looked like the kind of woman who would torture him first, starting with his family jewels. "What did I say wrong?"

She frowned. His sincerity must have thrown her a curve. "You call me name."

Tristan grinned. "No, I complimented you." When her anger dipped a notch, he hurried to explain. "In my world, a badass female is a powerful warrior, someone nobody would dare threaten."

Lo and behold, Brynhild lowered her shield and her attitude. Her shoulders softened along with her facial muscles. She began nodding. "Yes. I try to tell Cathbad this. I am badass."

Hallelujah. He'd found a tiny connection, which might spare his life and body parts. "So why are you stuck in here when he leaves?"

Brynhild's shoulders sagged. She stepped away, walking to the right and continuing in an oval pattern, grumbling to herself in some weird language he'd never heard.

When she stopped and looked up at him, she waved her shield at nothing in particular. "Druid is like old woman. Always nagging. Will not listen. I am warrior, not *student*."

Tristan enjoyed the first push of real hope since regaining consciousness here.

Few things worked better in the supernatural or natural world when fighting an enemy than to divide and conquer.

As in, if she was pissed off at Cathbad, Tristan had a chance to gain her ear by convincing her that he could be someone of value.

He had to become her friend.

He altered his face into sincere confusion. "I don't understand what you mean by student? What is he trying to teach you?"

She pointed to his right at the seating area as if he hadn't already commented on the arrangement.

Standing tall and proud, she said, "Druid wants me to read these things about life today. How women talk and dress." She turned her nose up. "Weak women. I know what I need to know. I dress as warrior. *That* is important."

It finally hit Tristan that she reminded him of someone who had lived a very long time, much like Daegan. Back during a medieval time. Huh.

"Well, Cathbad needs his eyes checked," Tristan claimed.

"Why?"

He'd confounded her. Tristan dropped his voice into the tone a lover used. Quite a feat since just breathing hurt. He had to make this comment stick. "Because if that druid thinks you need lessons on being a woman, he can't see anything at all."

Brynhild didn't fall into a puddle of goo.

Well, Tristan wasn't exactly at his best when trying to gain a woman's cooperation from this position.

She'd been staring at him while debating some unknown decision. Speaking now with the regal power of a queen, she asked, "You think I am some foolish woman to fall for your smile and honeyed words? I am no such female. I carry the blood of the most dangerous clan to ever live ... "

Shit. How had this gone wrong when he'd had her almost eating out of his hand?

While she continued berating him and insulting his lack of intelligence, her eyes changed as they continued to glow.

Her dark irises elongated.

Oh. Hell.

No wonder Cathbad wanted her as a partner.

Tristan had a pretty good idea what kind of being she was with those reptilian eyes.

Power flooded around him and shoved against his chest until he couldn't breathe. She started changing into a dragon right before his eyes.

An iridescent blue dragon roared. The cavern shook like a volcano erupting. The pond erupted, shooting chunks of ice into the air. Her scary eyes burned bright blue as a hot flame.

She opened her dragon jaws wide enough to eat a tiger in one bite.

Tristan would be lying if he said he didn't fear what came next.

He'd pissed off the wrong beast.

Fuck it then.

If he had to die at the hands of a rampaging dragon, he'd get his wish.

Cathbad could not turn him into a polymorph.

CHAPTER 14

CATHBAD TELEPORTED INTO CASIDHE'S COTTAGE, disgusted by the nasty odor. He shielded his power to hide his visit, just as he had at the centre today.

But he quickly sensed Daegan's power again.

So the red dragon shifter had been here, too?

Based on the strength of the energy residue, the visit had been recent.

He stepped over debris from a battle that had left the remnants of Casidhe Luigsech's life here in pieces.

When had that conflict occurred?

What the devil had caused that odious smell?

Were Daegan and Casidhe working together or had that dragon shifter tracked the woman here and kidnapped her?

Cathbad searched more of the room, trying to discern what Daegan may have found here on his own. The mix of scents and destruction left no clear indication of a timeline. He spent another ten minutes studying the smashed glassware, upended planters, and broken furniture.

If there had been anything useful here, someone else had found it. Had that person been Daegan, Casidhe, or someone else?

And just where had Casidhe gone?

He continued into the bedroom, which had a smashed window. The glass had landed inside. What had crashed through the window? He inhaled the nasty stink of demon and sensed an energy trail from Daegan and those other two who had also been at the ancestral centre.

Had Casidhe escaped or had Daegan caught her?

Or had she made a truly fatal mistake and allied with the red dragon?

Cathbad mentally sorted through all he'd seen and figured out.

The Luigsech woman had surprised him by not staying put at the centre until he arrived this morning, but that might not have been by her choice.

He considered how he could find her quickly, discarding each idea until he hit on what might be the most productive one.

It might also be the most dangerous choice.

Everything depended upon Queen Maeve having completed her scrying wall and his ability to get back in her good graces.

That scrying wall could locate Casidhe.

CHAPTER 15

LANNA HURRIED FROM THE CASTLE in Treoir realm, running down the steps and out to the lawn, which stretched hundreds of feet to the forest.

Phoedra ran along beside her, staying in step. She murmured, "Reese does not look happy."

Had Garwyli not sat up during a conversation Lanna had been having with him and announced Reese's arrival into Treoir, Lanna wouldn't have taken off so quickly. She'd called her apology over her shoulder, but felt an obligation to help Quinn.

Her Cousin had made a mess of things, but he was a good man and deserved a happy life.

Just as Phoedra had pointed out, Reese stood a ways out on the lawn with arms crossed and eyes shooting fire.

One of the Treoir guards walked up to Reese. She seemed to speak politely, but Lanna could feel the chill in her voice from here. The guard nodded and continued on.

Slowing as she reached Reese, Lanna called out a breathless, "Hello, Reese. Is nice to see you."

Reese opened her mouth and closed it. She shook her head at something, muttering under her breath, then admitted, "It's nice to see you and Phoedra, but I'm not happy to be here. I was not consulted about this destination." Fingers curled into fists, Reese declared, "I am so gonna kill him."

Phoedra asked, "Who?"

"Quinn."

"That's not nice." Phoedra said it with a tease in her voice, giving Lanna the impression these two used that phrase often, because a smile twitched at Reese's lips.

Then Reese opened her arms to Phoedra who hugged her. Looking over Phoedra's shoulder, Reese sent a weary smile to Lanna. When they broke apart, Reese said, "That man is making me crazy."

"Cousin can be difficult sometimes, but he always cares much about you, Phoedra, me, and all he considers family." Lanna hoped to remind Reese of Quinn's big heart. "Beladors and dragon are family, too. Cousin has much room in heart." Lanna turned toward the castle. "Come inside. We will have tea."

As the other two fell into step beside Lanna, Phoedra fidgeted with her fingers. "I'm sorry he makes you mad, Reese."

"Oh, honey, the truth is this is all me. I can't stand near him without losing my temper." Reese sounded embarrassed.

When Phoedra didn't ask why, Lanna took a stab at what she believed was going on. "Is hard to keep secrets, Reese."

Reese stopped, forcing Lanna and Phoedra to turn to her. "What are you talking about, Lanna?"

Flashing a look at Phoedra, who dropped her eyes, Lanna smiled at Reese. "I think Cousin knows truth."

A group of four guards walked past them. One slowed and asked, "Is everyone okay?"

"Yes," Lanna quickly replied with a smile, sending them along. She turned a knowing look on Reese. "Secret makes you angry all the time."

Phoedra lifted her gaze. "Lanna's right, Reese. We can't keep this hidden any longer. It's not fair to ... him."

Hearing Phoedra call Quinn *him* and not dad or father pained Lanna, but this was not the time to tackle that subject.

Reese's eyes swam with tears she would not let fall. "That's why I'm so mad ... at me. The guilt is killing me and I take it out on him because I don't want to hurt him, but I'm doing just that. I know that sounds crazy. Consider the source right now." Then she gave Lanna a suspicious look. "Wait, you said you think he knows?"

"Yes. Cousin would not be careless, but something must not have worked. I think he knows you carry baby. He will not leave you to do this alone."

"We *were* careful, dammit," Reese muttered. "That freaking InchKeith has to be at fault."

That would explain a lot.

Lanna recalled hearing how Quinn and Reese had been put through a difficult time to gain information on locating Phoedra only the InchKeith could provide back then.

It was up to Lanna to fix this for Quinn. No man could be more honorable than her cousin. First she had to find out why Reese had not told him yet. "Yes, I remember you two went to New Orleans and were inside InchKeith realm. Cousin said it was difficult time."

Walking over to the castle steps, Reese turned and sat on the second one up. Phoedra took the spot next to her.

Lanna stood so she could see both of their faces.

Reese leaned back on her elbows and stared up at her. "That InchKeith jerk played games with us the whole time. Half the time I didn't know what was real and what was illusion." She tipped her chin down. "But I swear Quinn and I both thought the condom was real."

"Eww." Phoedra covered her ears. "I don't want details."

Reese smiled and patted Phoedra's knee. "Uncover your ears. I don't want to go into details either, but I do need you to know I would not put him in this situation again for anything and he would not have put me at risk."

Pulling her hands down, Phoedra looped an arm around Reese. "It's going to be okay, really."

Reese just gave her a sad smile then asked Lanna, "But how do you know what's going on? Did Quinn tell you?"

Phoedra groaned. "I told her. I trust Lanna. I'm sorry. I was worried about you, both of you."

Lanna would not have betrayed that trust by telling Reese that Phoedra had only confirmed what Lanna had figured out. She assured Reese, "I will say nothing about this unless you give me permission. I keep secrets, but I think you need to talk to Cousin. Garwyli tutors me each time I visit Treoir. He said InchKeith is old and has dark sense of humor, but can be busybody friend. Maybe thought he was playing matchmaker. Did InchKeith think you and Cousin were more than friends?"

"No, yes, maybe," Reese grumbled. "Let's say yes."

"InchKeith could have thought he was doing favor." Lanna held up a hand to stop Reese from exploding. "I do not defend him. Does not matter. Phoedra is happy for baby. I am happy for baby. Cousin will be happy for baby."

"No. Quinn is not going to be happy to find out he's been tricked twice. I didn't trick him, but the outcome is the same and he has every right to be angry."

"Cousin will understand and will not blame you for this. I think he will be more worried about you and baby staying safe. That is probably why you end up here. Treoir safest place for you, baby, and Phoedra."

Reese sat up. "Damn. Now everything makes sense. Instead of badgering me about why I got sick at the apartment before we teleported, he put up with my bad mood. He does know. He did ask me if I was okay and I snapped at him ... maybe more than once. He didn't lose his temper." She covered her face. "I suck. This won't do."

"Why not?" Phoedra asked. "I think we can make this work and Lanna is right. He's really nice."

Lanna added, "He will be wonderful father to baby and ... " She turned a warm smile to Phoedra. "To you also."

Phoedra's cheeks pinked with embarrassment. "I know."

Reese asked Phoedra, "Would you mind getting me a glass of water, Snook? I'm really dry."

"I'll get it!" Phoedra jumped up and ran into the castle.

Lanna smiled at Reese using Phoedra's nickname.

The minute she was out of sight, Reese stood and leaned close to Lanna, keeping her voice down. "I would never keep the baby secret from Quinn, but you don't understand. He can't be anywhere around me when it's time to give birth."

Icy chill ran over Lanna's skin. "Why not?"

"I can't carry this baby to term."

"I will—"

"No, Lanna. Listen to me. I know you're powerful and how much you care, but this is not something you can fix. I've been cursed, for real, and already lost one child a long time ago. The only reason I didn't die at the same time was because the person who has been Phoedra's guardian for all these years kept me hidden from demons. He's also Phoedra's guardian because Kizira asked him to protect her baby. He's the one who put me on a path to meet Phoedra. Quinn can't be around me or he won't survive either. The father of my first child didn't want me or the baby, but he survived only because the guardian kept me somewhere no one could touch me. I may have to go back to the guardian. You told me you would protect my secret. You have to help me keep Quinn away and watch over Phoedra when I'm gone."

"I will not leave you or the baby to die." Lanna's heart cried at the possibility. She had power. She could do something.

"The baby doesn't have a chance." Reese struggled with those words, but she caught her breath and pushed on. "The baby will grow to full term then ... " She choked and covered her mouth with her hand. Tears pooled in her eyes. Voice cracking, she said, "I'll lose the child. That will be hell to go through again, but even worse if something happened to Quinn or Phoedra. I want your word you will help me protect them by keeping them away from me when the time comes if I can't get to Phoedra's guardian again."

Lanna had never been handed such a difficult task. She lived to make things better for her family and friends. Tears burned her eyes. "Please let me try to help you, Reese."

"You will help me if you do as I ask. Your word." Reese's voice hardened. That strong woman shoved her emotions deep and stood with the steel backbone she'd shown time and again.

Struggling to get the words out, Lanna whispered, "My word."

"Great. I need to get out of Treoir and vanish. That's the

best way to keep everyone I care about safe." Reese pinned Lanna with a look that caused her to swallow hard. "I'll convince Phoedra to stay here to wait for her dad. Maybe those two can finally live together."

"What will you tell Phoedra?" Lanna twisted her hands, frustrated she couldn't use her powers for the ones she loved.

"I have a plan," Reese said, sounding determined, but not offering more.

"Lanna?" Garwyli called out. He stepped aside as Phoedra rushed past him carrying a glass.

Handing the water to Reese, Phoedra glanced at Lanna with an expectant look. Quinn's daughter wanted encouragement that Lanna would make everything right for Reese and Quinn.

Rather than lie, Lanna smiled and winked at her. She turned to look up at the old druid standing on the top landing and froze.

Energy surged and pulsed around Garwyli. Lanna couldn't pull her eyes from the druid's turquoise aura now charged with a fiery red.

Reese and Phoedra chatted comfortably behind her.

How could they not see or sense the power gathering around Garwyli? His eyes burned with a fury she'd never witnessed.

What was going on?

CHAPTER 16

CASIDHE SHIFTED THE PACKED BACKPACK and stopped to tighten the strap. The three heavy books in it along with a change of clothes and a few toiletries, plus the sword felt as if she carried a person on her back. She would have liked enough time to shower and change out of this soiled white shirt, but every second she'd spent in her cottage she'd feared some deadly being showing up.

Her hand trembled when she released the strap.

She'd barely escaped from the ancestral centre today before an unknown being entered. She had just opened the secret doorway to the tunnel exit and changed her mind, deciding to wait a little longer for Cavan.

A blast of energy that swept through the building sent her scurrying through the opening and pulling the bookcase door shut.

She'd closed it as softly as she could, but it still made a soft snick sound. Holding her breath, she'd watched through a peephole to see if Cavan had been the one to arrive.

No. It had been that damned giant stranger again. He'd barreled into the back room incredibly fast.

Well, that had solved her dilemma.

Cavan had clearly been watching the building when she left yesterday to go home. If he'd arrived and observed the centre this morning, he would have seen her intruder. When she got her hands on Mr. No Name who broke into her cottage, she'd throttle him for screwing up her meeting with Cavan on top of everything else.

What if Cavan entered the centre next and ran into her

late-night intruder?

Cavan had captured the guy's friend. Could he kill her intruder? Worry stabbed her.

Why? Maybe that guy should stop breaking and entering. She didn't have a back door to her cottage. How had he entered her cottage *and* the centre without making a sound?

Logic hit her between the eyes.

Had her intruder teleported?

Probably. What other explanation could it be?

She blew out a loud sigh.

In that case, good thing she hadn't slowed down since leaving the centre again. She made her fastest trek ever through the tunnel.

Her toe caught on a root and she lunged to maintain her balance. She scraped her hands grabbing a tree no thicker than her wrist to keep from faceplanting.

Now would be a good time to pay attention.

She'd hiked about four miles since hiding the boat on this side of the river.

She couldn't risk being seen going to the airport she'd just traveled from recently or she'd take a faster route.

With Cavan searching for her, and now the dark stranger, she had to be careful and not make a mistake that would lead any of these beings to a Luigsech family.

If she managed to reach the one she had in mind without any incident, she'd hide out a day to be sure no one had followed her. Then she'd stay with them a couple more days while she researched that grimoire and tried to track down Fenella.

Miserable majik book.

Had Cavan really intended to meet with her? If so, why hadn't he been at the ancestral centre early this morning?

Had he been around to see what happened at her cottage last night?

Did he have Fenella?

If he didn't, then where had that woman gone?

Casidhe had to stop piling questions on an already difficult situation.

She hoped Fenella would find the tiny paper message Casidhe had left under a wadded-up rag and realize they had a problem. Then Fenella could go to one of her squire families and send word to Herrick. Fenella was no fool and had a crafty streak. She could get out of County Galway without notice, too. She knew far more of the squire family connections than Casidhe.

All those thoughts should have quieted Casidhe's fears, but they didn't. Fenella could just as easily be dead.

She struggled to breathe.

How could she face Herrick again if Fenella was dead? He would blame her, the person he'd trained to be a protector.

No. She shook her head, refusing to accept Fenella's death. Not without indisputable evidence. She swiped a runaway tear from her cheek. No stopping until she found Fenella and had her in a safe place.

Dragging in a raspy breath, Casidhe embraced the surge of determination to push harder.

Weaving her way through the tangled forest snagging her clothes and hair, she searched for the next opportunity she could hide her tracks. She'd wiggled through a tapered opening in a rock wall, which had been a small cave with two entrances years back. Erosion since then had worn the outcropping down until little more than a narrow passage had been left.

If she hadn't known this spot existed, she wouldn't have found it so easily.

After snaking her way through that hollowed-out path, she ran ahead twenty feet and stepped into a drizzling stream of water snaking through the woods. Not enough water to qualify as a creek in her estimation, but she continued downstream for five minutes then stepped out.

If anyone following her had the ability to track like an animal, that trick would do little to slow them down.

But it made her feel better to hide her footsteps.

She had another ten miles to cover by foot before she

would reach someone who could help her travel by vehicle. More important than that, the people she headed for would hopefully be able to find out if Fenella had been in contact with any of the other squire families.

If not, she'd have them get word to Herrick.

She would do all in her power to locate Fenella. To find out if Cavan had captured her. Casidhe wouldn't bring Herrick in to rescue Fenella unless she had no other choice. He would come if called, but doing so would expose him to supernatural threats like that murdering red dragon.

Casidhe had to protect Herrick and their people at the castle just as much as Fenella.

She would do as much as she could with the resources available to her. If Cavan had Fenella, then Casidhe would focus the full force of her energy on finding that book.

What majikal formulas in that grimoire could be so important?

Would Cavan, or the stranger, use it to harm others?

Even if she found the grimoire, there was no guarantee Cavan would leave her and Fenella alone once he got it. That created a whole new set of worries. She kicked a clump of dirt out of her way and stomped on.

Who was this Cavan to upend her life this way?

She'd find that book, but no one was getting it until she knew why they wanted the grimoire. She'd threaten to use it against Cavan if he harmed one hair on Fenella's head.

Little wind threaded through this forest, but it felt as if all movement had died. She took three more steps. Her skin tingled with that creepy sensation of someone watching her again.

Don't panic, she silently told herself.

Pausing to take a breath, she let her gaze roam the area around her.

Her stomach growled. She dug out a meal-replacement bar and ate it quickly. She couldn't run for long on crackers and snack bars. Shoving the wrapper into her pocket, she convinced herself she had energy again.

If only that were true. She watched for glowing yellow monsters.

And demons.

Her fingers itched to pull out *Lann an Cheartais.*

She'd like to think the sword had bonded with her after last night, but she had no idea where she stood with Shannon's sword. The air smelled of damp moss and rich woodland.

No sulfuric stench.

She climbed up on a thick log left from a tree that had fallen long enough ago the upper limbs had dead leaves. With a look around, she jumped down on the other side.

Her knees suffered a jarring hit from the weight on her back.

Every tiny sound snatched her attention. Her heart pounded more from sensing eyes on her than from the exertion. Keep moving. The sooner she made it through this forest and over the next mountain, the better.

Wading through knee-deep undergrowth speckled with white flowers, she plowed ahead.

Her thoughts kept returning to her late-night intruder who battled demons and crazy yellow beings without a second thought.

Who was he and what did he really want with her?

Had he been stalking her for the grimoire?

Or was he trying to find Herrick? If so, she could be walking into a trap by asking Herrick to do anything. Yet another reason she had to keep all this to herself.

But none of it made sense.

Like when hunting for a book or tiny piece of historical detail, she needed more information.

A twig snapped. That wouldn't have seemed significant, but the woods had gone quiet again.

Too quiet.

Adrenaline shoved her fight or flight impulse into gear. Bad idea to give into flight if a predator stalked her. She took a couple calm steps, kept watch of her surroundings, and tried to breathe quietly.

That did nothing to slow her erratic heartbeat.

Sounds picked up and gained strength.

Something large and noisy ran through the woods making too much racket to be a natural predator.

Branches cracked and the ground shuddered.

Casidhe reached over her shoulder and gripped the hilt of her sword. She yanked. The sword did not move. "Damn. Come on, brat!"

She yanked again and dragged the sword out this time.

With a double-handed grip, she moved forward, turning the blade back and forth to warm up her wrists. She continued slowly toward the noise, which continued to grow louder. Better to face the enemy than have it come at her from behind.

Now it sounded like two coming.

But two of what?

Ah shit. She sorted out the sounds of two threats on her left and one off to her right.

That meant getting caught with one threat at her back.

Palms damp and breath coming in sharp inhales, she clamped her jaw tight and prepared for attack. The only way she'd survived last night had been with the stranger having a sword.

She *had* chopped off two heads. Three, actually.

But who was counting?

This would be easier without the backpack, but she couldn't risk taking it off and losing the contents. Her heart hadn't received her earlier confidence pep talk and urged her to panic.

Crashing sounds sounded like elephants coming through.

She had training.

Not for bright yellow monsters or demons, but she could do this.

Far over to her left, a hideous glowing beast running on all fours burst through thick undergrowth. Horns protruded from each side of its bald head, all of it shining bright yellow.

Unholy human eyes stared at her. Black hair grew down its chest. It howled insanely.

What was that thing?

She planted both feet. *I can do this. I can do this.*

Another beast clawed through a stand of small trees on her right, knocking two over. Tall, bony, and with a bush of white hair standing like a mohawk that ran down his back, it raged and screamed. The only similarity between the two was that distinctive yellow.

She couldn't fight on both fronts at once.

She didn't have a choice and the odds were not in her favor.

She hoped Fenella had made it to safety.

The first beast rushed her. She swung back and forth, trying to gash its thick hide. The crazed thing swiped a sharp claw at her. She dodged, slashing and chopping as fast as she could. She made contact.

The beast lost a limb and wailed.

Blaring noises erupted behind her.

She flinched at the idea of being ripped apart from behind, but the now three-legged beast she fought jumped at her again. Swinging her blade on a horizontal arc, she put her shoulder into it.

Her sword slammed the body, jarring her teeth, but the blade buried deep. The beast lurched to the side, yanking her with him. She landed on top of the sprawling body, flinching. She expected the claws to gouge her, but this thing was dead.

Blood gushed from her strike.

Had she hit its heart?

Did it have one?

She leaped up, yanking her blade free and wanting to cheer in victory, but a demon followed this one out of the forest.

Lifting her sword, she swung it shoulder height horizontally. The sharp edge whisked through muscle and bone, lopping off head number four.

She'd have to start putting notches in her sheath at this rate.

Breathing hard, she backed up and bumped into something.

Another yellow being!

She shrieked and brought her sword around in a wide sweep for the kill.

CHAPTER 17

DAEGAN BUMPED INTO LUIGSECH FROM where he'd been protecting her back from an Imortik that looked part wendigo and part demon.

Quinn shouted in his head, *Watch your back!*

Daegan yanked his sword up in defense, turning to meet a sword coming at him fast. The blades collided, his blocking hers from a vicious wound. His sword had been known to break an opponent's weapon, but not the sword she held.

It sizzled with energy.

The clash of metal on metal boomed in a loud clang.

Her sword bounced off his.

She still held on and kept her balance in spite of that heavy pack on her back.

They both held mighty weapons, but he had a hundred pounds of muscle on this little warrior.

She stared at him with glowing violet-blue eyes, heaving every breath. "What the hell? Where'd you come from?"

The only reason she hadn't come close to decapitating him had been due to a mismatch in height.

It had nothing to do with restraint on her part. "Ya show a lack of appreciation when I just saved your life." He glanced at Quinn to confirm his Maistir had finished off another glowing troll sixty feet away. Satisfied Quinn was safe, Daegan took in Luigsech.

Her eyes blazed with fire and fear. An odd mixture for those unusual blue eyes. She kept breathing as if she'd been running for the past five miles that he and Quinn had been tracking her.

After having given Daegan a slice of her attention and quick berating, she leaned to stare past him.

Daegan turned to follow her line of sight.

Her gaze turned down to take in the no-longer-glowing body he'd slashed in half after Quinn had used kinetics to knock the troll-Imortik off its feet.

She hadn't lowered her sword an inch. "Or maybe you're the reason I keep bein' attacked."

He couldn't deny that since she'd struck the truth of it. "Ya clearly expected to defend yourself or ya would not have carried that sword."

"Well, we can't all conjure one out of thin air," she snapped back. "Now what are you doin' stalkin' me again?"

Daegan sent Quinn a silent message. *Stand back and allow me to deal with this woman.*

Quinn nodded, probably thinking that meant Daegan understood her.

Not a bit.

She'd taken off all alone through this forest after Imortiks had attacked her at home last night. She swung that damn sword without looking to see what she attacked and had a penchant for separating heads from bodies.

Daegan didn't understand anything about her.

He just needed Quinn a safe distance away while he attempted to talk to her without having to raise his sword again.

When she continued to stare in silence, Daegan ignored her demand of why he was here. "Ya sure are hell on a head." He hadn't meant to sound impressed, but ... damn, he was.

She lowered her sword, but kept it at ready. "Says the man who just cut off a head," she challenged with an eyebrow cocked at the Imortik behind him.

"I never said decapitation 'twas not good use of a sword, but ya would have cut off mine had ya stood another foot taller."

"I can remove your head just fine from here if I'd wanted to, buster," she countered, too smug for her own good. Her arms trembled, likely from adrenaline overload. "Why are you followin' me, intruder-with-no-name?"

"I made it clear last night ya were to go nowhere without me until I found Cavan."

"And I made it clear I don't take orders from you. Besides, looks like you found your friend." She angled her head in Quinn's direction.

"He is a friend, but not the one captured," Daegan cleared up.

"Does he have a name or is he another *nobody* like you?" she snapped.

Had Quinn coughed to catch his attention?

Daegan turned a glare on his Maistir, who showed no expression as he stood quietly. Except his eyes. Quinn found something amusing.

Sighing, Daegan returned to the woman who had escaped him more times than he wished to count. She was harder to keep in one place than a flea on a dog's back. "His name is Quinn. Ya may call me Drake. We know ya are Casidhe Luigsech. I still must find Cavan. Every second ya waste, our friend is bein' tortured."

Guilt spread across her face. "You can't know that and it's not my fault he got captured. Had you not brought him with you to stalk me, he might be just fine."

Daegan silently admitted her point. "I did not accuse ya of such, but ya are my only connection to Cavan. Did ya meet him this mornin'?"

"No. He never showed."

"Are ya not worried he may harm your friend, Fenella, and make her endure his anger at ya leavin'?"

"How do you know Fenella?" She lifted her sword a little higher while her gaze darted between him and Quinn.

"Put your sword down, woman. I do not *know* Fenella, only that she works at the same place as ya. We are no threat to your friend, but ya must know Cavan is if ya cross him." Daegan stabbed his sword in the ground in a show of peace. He hoped she didn't take advantage of the move to prove she *could* reach his neck with her blade.

She pointed her sword at the Imortik bodies. "First, what are these creatures?"

Quinn stepped forward, speaking as he walked. "They are known as Imortiks. They take over bodies of human and supernatural beings. They can be killed ... *sometimes.*"

"What do you mean by sometimes?" She pinned Quinn with a suspicious look. "Looks as though we killed them last night and today."

Quinn expanded, "It depends on the power level of the bein' whose body the Imortik takes over and if they have completed their immersion into the new body. Once they've had time to fully bond with the power in a supernatural body, or if they manage to take over a very powerful being, killin' the Imortik becomes questionable." He kept his arms slack at his sides in a nonthreatening way, but Quinn had kinetic power as well as mind lock.

"What are you two?" She kept dividing her attention between Quinn and Daegan.

"'Tis a good question for ya," Daegan countered.

She shifted her shoulders in an attempted shrug. "I'm just me. Nothing special."

Daegan snorted at that lie. "I will not waste time pursuin' the truth with someone so loosely associated with it."

It took her a minute to realize he'd insulted her. She bared her teeth. "You're not winnin' any points with that attitude, *Drake.*" She waved her sword at him for emphasis.

He lifted a hand. "Put that bloody sword down or sheath it before ya fall and cut yourself."

She stepped back, mouth open, then snapped it shut. Her face flushed red and she yelled, "Arm yourself."

"What?"

She attacked.

His sword flew to his hand. He moved to block her strike.

"I'm sick to death—" *Clang.* "—of your arrogant attitude." She swung back and forth, attacking with surprising skill.

Quinn crossed his arms. He sent mind-to-mind, *Do you*

want any help?

Of course not, Daegan groused silently. *This woman is a constant battle, but she needs to realize she cannot defeat me.*

Battling to stop her and not kill her, he shouted, "Are ya mad?"

Luigsech never slowed. "Damn right, I'm mad. Who do you ... think you are to insult me?" *Clang, clang, clang.* She spun away, chest heaving and mouth pinched in a tight line. "Why should I give you any help? You're in my way and I have my own—" She attacked again. *Clang.* Dodge. *Clang.* "—issues with Cavan."

She blinked.

Daegan moved so fast she stumbled forward with the momentum of her swing.

Spinning around with her blasted sword up, she seethed, staring at the spot he'd left empty. She didn't ask how he'd moved so quickly.

Neither would Daegan admit he'd teleported just to end the fight. *"Enough!* 'Tis time to talk."

"First you insult my skill with a sword, then you want to *talk?"*

Quinn sent a comment to Daegan only. *She'd make a helluva Belador warrior.*

Daegan shot him a hard glare. Shaking his head, he got down to why he'd tracked her to this point. "Ya waste valuable time. Why did ya leave without meetin' with Cavan?"

When she wouldn't give in, Daegan stabbed his sword in the ground once more and shot her a glare of warning. "I will not lift my sword again. If ya wound me this time, ya will be attackin' an unarmed man." He crossed his arms, waiting.

She lowered her blade to the ground. "I didn't see Cavan, because he never showed up."

"Then where were you going just now?" Quinn asked.

She gave Quinn a long look. "I was not on my way to meet with Cavan, if that's what you're thinkin'."

"Answer the question," Daegan ordered. "You're playin' games with someone's life."

Her jaw dropped. "What is it with you blamin' me for what Cavan did? I told you he was comin' to the centre this mornin'. He didn't. Clearly he lied to me. Am I worried about Fenella? Yes, dammit. So if we're placin' blame, you're puttin' her life in danger until I find her. What gives you the right to keep bustin' into my world all the time?"

Daegan took a step toward her and dropped his voice. "When I saw ya talkin' to Cavan before he captured my friend, 'tis what."

Quinn cleared his throat. "Do you think Cavan has Fenella?"

Daegan shifted to him, realizing Quinn had a point. When he turned back to the woman, her face fell.

"To be honest, I don't know." She squatted to wipe her blade off on the troll body, wrinkled her nose, then stood. She slid the blade into a hidden compartment between her back and the lopsided backpack.

"So now you're bein' honest?" Daegan couldn't help himself. He should have found Tristan last night, and might have, if not for her dancing around his questions.

Using both hands to push wild auburn locks that had escaped her long braid off her face, she glared at him. "I'm *also* pretty damn tired of you callin' me a liar."

Daegan leaned closer to her and growled, "Then stop avoidin' the truth."

She closed the distance to him, nose to chin. *"I am tellin' the truth, buster!"*

Quinn cleared his throat. "Perhaps we should continue moving away from this spot in case we're close to a rift. We all have questions and this may not be the best place to talk." He sent a silent message to Daegan. *Maybe if we get her to another spot away from these bodies and try befriending her, she'll be more willing to talk.*

It would surprise me based on what I have seen of her, but I am willin' to try anythin' to find Cavan.

I agree.

She stepped back. "What rift?" Her gaze jumped everywhere as if searching for a hole releasing Imortiks.

Staring up at the tall trees, Daegan begged for patience. He lowered his head. "Quinn, would ya lead her away from here? Head north while I deal with these bodies, then I'll catch up to ya."

"What are you goin' to do?" She eyed him suspiciously.

Bloody woman! Asking questions when she should be giving answers. "Do not expect me to explain my every action to ya." Dipping his head down he glowered at her. "Get movin'."

After a moment of silent debate and muttering to herself, she snapped, "Let's get somethin' clear. Do not expect me to explain my every action to you either. I'm not movin' because you told me, but because I'd like to talk to your friend, who sounds far more reasonable than you."

She turned to Quinn. "Lead the way."

With a look of surprise at her order, Quinn turned and waited for her to fall into step with him.

As they walked, she asked, "Where are these Imortiks coming from?"

Daegan could still feel the heat of her body from when she stood so close to him. He had an urge to call her back, to keep her within sight where he'd know she was safe.

Why? Quinn could protect her.

The venom had to be muddling his thoughts.

Quinn kept his voice at a level that allowed Daegan to pinpoint their placement as he explained, "Imortiks were created by majik from the original grimoire created thousands of years ago by two beings. That same majik was used to imprison Imortiks behind what is called a death wall, but the grimoire was intact at the time. After the death wall was sealed, the grimoire was split into three volumes to be hidden by three different groups. Someone has evidently gotten their hands on one volume and activated majik from that text to create a rift, allowing Imortiks to escape."

Luigsech's voice went up an octave. "Who has *that* volume?"

Daegan watched as Quinn lifted a drooping branch out of the way for her to pass beneath, replying, "We don't know. We also have no idea where all three were originally hidden. What we do know is that these Imortiks can take over all human bodies and those of supernatural beings."

"Wait. *All* supernatural beins'?"

Quinn's voice faded. "Yes."

Daegan had to listen closely to catch her words. "That's ... crazy. That rift has to be closed before more of those yellow things escape."

Quinn had excellent negotiation skills and might manage to build a bridge with Luigsech.

When the two of them sounded far enough away, Daegan pointed a finger to torch the scattered bodies. Fires erupted on two corpses. A layer of flames three fingers tall sprouted on the others.

What the ... ?

Daegan tried it again and actually extinguished one. He glanced around. Quinn had Luigsech far enough away and Daegan heard no other approaching threats.

He called up his dragon.

Ruadh clawed, trying to break free.

Daegan's body shuddered. A frigid chill filled his chest.

"Come on, Ruadh," he whispered in a pained voice. His body twisted slowly. Much too slowly.

Sweat ran down Daegan's face and back in rivers.

His head warped, trying to change shape.

The Imortik venom burned and clawed his insides along the tendrils snaking through his arms and legs.

His dragon pushed power hard through their half-shifted human form. Daegan clamped his jaws to keep from shouting from the force of the agonizingly slow change. He had not experienced this level of difficulty in shifting since his first time as a young boy.

Even then, it had been more strange than painful.

Ruadh finally broke free into dragon form and trembled from the exhausting action.

Daegan asked, *Please do not roar, Ruadh. I know ya want to and by all that is holy ya deserve to, but it will expose us when I much prefer keepin' ya secret. Can ya burn these bodies?*

In answer, Ruadh pushed short blasts of fire at each body, then stepped on flames trying to spread.

When Ruadh had finished, Daegan allowed his dragon to just sit there and breathe.

That had been hell on both of them.

What would happen if they had to shift and battle something stronger than what Daegan could defeat in human form?

Ruadh's words came into his mind. *We will defeat all enemies.*

Daegan believed his dragon would do so or die trying. He had been gifted with a dragon that did not know the meaning of quit.

Ruadh murmured, *The woman is strong.*

She is, Daegan agreed, but what had his dragon meant by that? Ruadh rarely commented unless it was to offer advice in a battle, but his dragon respected strength almost as much as loyalty.

Quinn's voice came into his mind. *What's taking so long, Daegan? Are you being attacked?*

The venom oozing through his body felt like a physical attack. Daegan replied, *I shall be there soon.*

Then he told Ruadh, *I am sorry for another change, but I need the human body.*

Ruadh murmured, *You will be vulnerable in that form if I fail to shift next time.*

Ya will not fail, Daegan sent back, reminding his dragon he had full faith in Ruadh.

They had always healed more quickly in dragon form. Perhaps the time Daegan allowed Ruadh to sit and rest had helped. Though still slow, his dragon made the change back to human form more quickly.

Recalling how he'd been dressed when they found Luigsech, Daegan covered his legs in jeans, his feet in boots, and his upper body in a long-sleeved burgundy T-shirt.

Striding through the woods, Daegan entered the spot where Quinn had the woman turned with her back to Daegan.

She waved her hands as she talked. "You keep askin' the same thing in different ways. I've told you what I know. What makes you and that other idiot think I have any reason to answer your questions?"

Quinn's irritation dissolved his pleasant tone. "I have no idea how you're mixed up in all of this, Miss Luigsech, but you are. That is not our fault just as Cavan capturing our friend is not yours, but you have a chance to prove your innocence in all of this by giving us aid we desperately need."

"I don't have to prove anythin'," she balked.

Aching from that harsh change, Daegan would not lighten up on her. She was no faint-of-heart female, but a trained warrior. "Yes, ya do. 'Tis time to be straight with us, Luigsech. To do otherwise will not go well for ya."

CHAPTER 18

LUIGSECH JUMPED AROUND, FIRE CHURNING her eyes bright blue. "Stop sneakin' up on me, Drake."

Daegan gritted his teeth at the venom shooting through him. "Only the guilty react with such surprise."

"Says the man who—"

"Entered your home uninvited," Daegan finished, grinding out each word. One minute, pain surged in his leg. The next, muscles in his back felt as if they flexed on their own. "I have allowed ya plenty of time to tell what know. I tire of askin' the same questions only to be put off or givin' half answers. Did ya think I was jokin' when I warned ya not to push me any harder or would go to a place far from here where I can get those answers?"

She spit out a Gaelic curse. "Threatenin' me is not the way to gain my aid. If you kidnap me and leave Fenella in trouble, you have no idea what hell will come to your door."

Just when Daegan thought he had her attention, the feisty woman threatened *him*?

Quinn even arched an eyebrow at their exchange.

Daegan took a breath, trying to calm his words. "That was instructin' ya, not threatenin' ya."

"Where did you get your vocabulary?" she chided him as no one had done since before he became a man. "Because you don't have the same definition for those words the rest of the world does."

Quinn's gaze had moved from her to Daegan, then to survey the area around them. He sent a telepathic message. *If we stay here, we may be attacked. If we keep moving we may be attacked. What do you want to do?*

Exhaustion from the difficult shift and lack of rest decided for Daegan. *I will cloak us, but we must be still for a bit.*

Quinn didn't question why Daegan had to sit even though he'd been with Daegan when a group of them had moved around with the cloaking. In an unquestioned show of support for Daegan, Quinn suggested, "Until we know more about where you were headed, Miss Luigsech, I suggest we stay here a bit."

Luigsech wheeled around to him. "I thought you said we should keep movin'?"

"I did, but I have no idea if moving draws attention to us more so than being still. If we remain in one place, I can use my gifts to search for any unnatural being approaching this area. That would reserve our energies."

"Oh."

Nodding his thanks at Quinn, Daegan sat at the base of a tree he could lean against. Once Luigsech chose a small boulder to use as a seat and Quinn settled on the ground against another tree, Daegan created the cloaking.

Luigsech looked around sharply. "What just changed?"

Quinn said, "We are cloaked for a short period."

Daegan's Maistir had not indicated who had cloaked them, allowing Daegan to keep his ability to do so hidden for now.

Daegan lifted a finger in Luigsech's direction, but did not point it. Many supernaturals would react badly as some wielded majik with a finger. "If ya do not know how to locate Cavan, then tell us everythin' ya do know."

He'd try Quinn's tactic and see if he could befriend the annoying woman.

Luigsech's eyes flashed daggers at him, but she huffed a breath and relented. "Cavan left a book for me to translate. I reviewed a few pages only. He was to show up this mornin' for me to translate a specific passage. He did not show at the centre, nor did Fenella and she's not answerin' her phone."

Once again with a pertinent question, Quinn asked, "Does your friend carry a mobile phone? Is she good about replying to calls?"

"Sometimes and sometimes." Luigsech rubbed her arm where she'd been scratched running through the woods. "But I lost my mobile phone in the cottage when I had to fight those Imortiks last night." She shot a glare at Daegan, silently accusing him of being responsible for that attack. "Without my mobile phone, I have no idea if Fenella has tried to call me."

Daegan sent a message to Quinn. *Do not tell her we have her phone.*

Understood. Just so you know, there was no alert of a prior incoming call when I first found the phone and none have come in since then.

Daegan lifted his chin slightly to let Quinn know he understood.

She watched them intently as if she sensed they were communicating silently. "Don't you two feel guilty terrorizin' an innocent woman?"

Daegan scowled at her. "Ya are not innocent."

He must have hit a nerve with that. She had no reply. He pushed her again. "Where exactly were ya headin' today?"

Her lips drooped in a mulish set. "I was goin' to see friends who would help me find Fenella." She lifted a hand. "Don't even ask me about them. I'm not givin' you their names or addresses, because they have no idea I was on my way to see them. They also don't know who Cavan is or that Fenella is missin'."

"What about Cavan?" Daegan asked.

Her eyes slid away from his face in a guilty manner. "What about him?"

"He threatened ya outside the grocery."

That startled her. "How do you know that? Cavan said he cloaked us while we talked."

Daegan hadn't known for sure, but Luigsech just confirmed his guess. His words had been based upon what Reese thought when she'd observed those two during a remote viewing. Reese had sensed some conflict between Luigsech and Cavan.

"How I know anythin' is not the issue." Daegan bent his leg that wanted to cramp and stretched it back out. "What I do not understand is ya runnin' from Cavan with no idea if he has Fenella."

She had that caught-in-a-lie look all over her face. "Okay, here's the deal. Cavan *did* threaten Fenella if I was not at the centre this mornin' to meet him. I was there ... for a bit."

"When did you leave the centre?" Quinn prodded.

"When I showed up," said Daegan. He would not allow her the chance to lie. He'd just figured out the *"click"* sound he'd heard upon teleporting into the building. "Ya left the ancestral centre through a secret doorway."

She crossed her arms, sending an angry look down her nose at him from her perch. "Yes. How is it you keep enterin' a buildin' without makin' a sound?" Her eyebrows lowered over thick-lashed slits for eyes.

Ruadh stirred, taking note.

A staring match ensued.

She blinked after a minute. "Whatever. I have no idea if Cavan has Fenella or if somethin' happened to Cavan to prevent him from showin' up. Doubtful since his energy feels as powerful as yours." Her light-blue gaze struck Daegan like a dagger thrown at a target. "You screwed up my chance at protectin' Fenella."

Guilt found a place to slide inside and join the pain stabbing Daegan. Had he put Fenella in danger? Not in the best of moods already, he countered, "If ya had not vanished last night from your cottage, that might have been avoided."

"Deny it all you want, Drake, but Cavan may have both of our friends. If so, I've got as much at stake as you do."

"'Tis a good start. Keep goin'."

"Hold it. You're not even goin' to apologize for interferin' this morning?" Her jaw flexed with angry muscles.

"Why would I?" he asked. "If not for a deal you made with Cavan, I would have had no reason to be at the centre. Ya told me to go there to meet him."

"You two are a pair," she grumbled.

"Cavan is nothin' like me," he muttered, not sure how this slip of a woman twisted him around.

She spread her arms out. "How can you know that if you don't know who he is?"

The mouthy tart had a logical question, but Daegan wanted more on what she was about. "What exactly is goin' on with ya and Cavan?"

"Nothin'! Just like *nothin'* is goin' on between you and me. I said you two were a pair because, like you, he's a pain in my backside and wants that stupid grimoire."

Daegan leaned forward and roared, *"Ya will not give him that book!"*

"Stop orderin' me around!" She jumped up and shoved a finger at him, clearly unconcerned about any negative reaction. "Stop actin' like you're the only person with problems."

Tension smoldered under the silence.

"You feel you can find the grimoire?" Quinn asked in a calmer tone with a glance at Daegan that said yelling at her would not help.

Daegan dropped back and thunked his head back against the tree. None of this was helping.

Ruadh rumbled softly. *Strong and stands her ground.*

Do be quiet, Ruadh, Daegan snarled silently. What had gotten into his dragon?

Luigsech lowered her hand, but stood in a ready position, still seething. Looking up into the trees, she replied, "Maybe ... I don't know." She lowered her chin. "I grabbed a couple resource books, but I have no idea if they'll give me any lead or insight on how to find that book or not. I'm used to havin' *all* my resources at my fingertips."

She started pacing back and forth.

Before Daegan could ask her to sit again, Luigsech stopped abruptly in the middle of their area. "This whole situation makes no sense. Why would any supernatural bein' want to open that death wall?"

"Power," Daegan and Quinn said at the same time.

Then Quinn explained, "The Imortiks have a leader, who claims to be willing to work with any powerful being who delivers the missing volumes. That's why Cavan could be a deadly player."

"Neither of you have convinced me you're any better than Cavan," she charged.

Daegan's head pounded and a burning sensation rippled through his arms and shoulders. "We could save a lot of time right now by clearin' up Cavan's true identity."

"I told you I have no idea who he is other than who he claims to be." She had her own short fuse.

Quinn bent his knees to his chest and propped his arms there. "We have a vast knowledge of supernatural beings between the two of us. Let's start with you describing Cavan in as much detail as you can."

Daegan gave his Maistir a nod of acknowledgement. In Tristan's last telepathic call to Daegan, he had started to say who Cavan was as if Tristan expected Daegan to know the face Cavan had hidden with a glamour.

For once, Luigsech didn't snarl a reply. Probably because Quinn had a soothing demeanor when he didn't need to kill something.

She stared off into the dense forest. "Cavan is not as tall as either of you. He could be Irish descent. Fenella found him fine lookin', which I guess he is with wavy black hair and green eyes." She lifted her shoulders. "Can't say as I was impressed, but he pissed me off from the minute he grabbed my arm. That rarely leaves me with a favorable assessment of any man."

"Could Fenella have left with him?" Daegan had a momentary image of the woman falling for Cavan and running away.

Luigsech made a loud derogatory scoffing noise. "No. Not a chance. You would have to know ... Fenella. She only commented on his looks, because she's sly enough to realize when a man is tryin' to play her. I don't care what he has for power, he would not woo Fenella and she would not leave with him. She would not leave me voluntarily."

Quinn tapped his fingers on his arms. "You were to meet with Cavan this morning, then what? Go somewhere with him?"

Daegan had come to know the way Quinn's mind worked. The man had a reason for every word and question he spoke.

Daegan didn't interrupt.

"Sort of," Luigsech replied. "Cavan said he would join me in my search for the grimoire, which sounded like he expected me to leave with him to physically hunt for it and not just provide him with where to search. I mentioned he was to meet with me to translate somethin' in the book he brought by while I was out. Fenella and I believed he used the book as an excuse to meet me, which might be true. I don't know. Outside the grocery, he told me how to find the passage he wanted translated, then warned me not to read it until he arrived."

"Did ya read it or not?" Daegan wanted to see if she had been cautious or not.

"I did not, but only because you showed up right as I made up my mind to read it while I remained a bit longer for Cavan." She made that statement and cocked her chin at him.

Daegan pushed up to his feet, wiping his hands more to gather his thoughts than any concern of dirt. "Do not read that passage."

Quinn slapped his hand over his eyes.

Luigsech shook her fist at him. "What is wrong with you?"

Daegan crossed his arms and said nothing.

"How many times do I have to tell you that You. Are. Not. In. Charge!"

"Yes, I am."

Quinn made a noise that sounded like, "Bad move." Then he stood and announced, "We're not making headway."

Luigsech looked from Daegan to Quinn. "I'm not makin' any headway either." She swung her fiery gaze back to

Daegan. "All you had to do was stay the hell out of my life so I could read one freakin' passage from Cavan's book and Fenella might be safe." She grabbed a fast gulp of air and her next words came out shaky quiet. "Fenella is family to me. She may now be sufferin' because I made a mistake somewhere in all this, but so did you."

Guilt squirmed under Daegan's skin, but he had not created this mess either. "'Tis simple. Help us find Cavan. We may be able to get both of our friends back. Ya must also find the grimoire."

Luigsech shook her head, mouth in a bitter flat line. "Then we are at an impasse. I will not risk Fenella's safety. You huntin' me down and harassin' me has solved nothin'. Here's my suggestion. Why don't you two go away and give me some space? Then Cavan might come to see me."

Her fingers stretched and curled in the same motion Daegan had seen on warriors about to pull a sword out to do battle.

CHAPTER 19

AFTER TELEPORTING FROM IRELAND, CATHBAD appeared in a wide and soaring hallway in TÅμr Medb realm. Tall warlocks, broad with muscle and eyes dark as death, stood guard outside the massive doors to Queen Maeve's private area.

Their faces were placid.

But fear rolled off them in sickening waves.

A hideous yell erupted on the other side of the doors. The realm shuddered hard.

Cathbad walked forward, taking his time to survey the landscape.

The guards stiffened and clamped their swords in white-knuckled grips as he approached.

"*Mor-oooons!*" screamed from within the queen's quarters. The only one who dared to speak at that volume would be her.

Cathbad's hope of a calm meeting sank.

The guards watched him with wary eyes.

He understood their concern. With the queen out of control, would Cathbad's presence make it worse?

Truth be told, the same question crossed his mind.

A guard moved to assist Cathbad when the doors did not open on their own.

Cathbad waved him off. He teleported in, remaining above the ground and immediately cloaked himself where he floated fifteen feet in the air.

The queen had her back to him. She stood in the midst of twenty-four warlocks and witches, twelve of each. They waited in pairs.

Cathbad thought back over specific groups he'd created to insert into the human world the one time VIPER had allowed Medb warlocks and witches in. He'd been the one to encourage pairings to appear as human couples so their people would more easily blend.

Females of two pairs were pregnant.

That plan had been working brilliantly. Even after Queen Maeve lost control in a Tribunal meeting, which was reason for her ejection from the coalition, VIPER did not boot out warlocks and witches *appearing* to integrate into the humans' realm.

Fear inside here tripled what he'd felt from the guards.

Her body had grown to ten feet with a head stretched tall and wide on one side as if her change had stalled lopsided.

A robe of black wraiths wrapped her body and moved with her, demonic red eyes staring out from different spots along the undulating mantle.

Her normally beautiful cascade of hair had bristled wildly a foot thick in some spots, shooting straight out in other places. The color couldn't decide between silver, orange, and a putrid shade of green.

Pale skin on her hands had a rough, leathery appearance with dirt-brown splotches.

Screeching at the top of her lungs, her warped body waved back and forth as if her feet had been glued to the floor.

Along with the alteration of her body, her voice deepened to the sound of a monster from the underworld. "You are too *stupid* to be my servants. Unworthy of the duty I awarded you. How can you come to me whining?"

Content to hold his lofty and invisible position, Cathbad searched the faces for any idea what was going on. He hadn't wasted his time asking the guards at the entrance to this room. Not when the penalty of repeating anything she said in here would be far worse than dying.

Queen Maeve had never cared for the swift punishment of death, as was the case with that red dragon she'd kept in the form of a throne for too many years.

Not this woman. Death would cheat her of a pleasure only torture provided when she executed a penalty.

"Who among you deserves to return to the human world?" she roared, turning to face each one. As she twisted around, her misshapen jaws and jagged teeth came into view. A horn stuck from her forehead.

Cathbad had not seen that before. Nothing about the horn could be good news.

All of her followers in the room lifted their trembling hands, volunteering to return to the human world.

Who wouldn't raise a hand when remaining here would end with the equivalent of their skin being peeled away while alive?

She tossed her head back and laughed a high-pitched cackle that grated on Cathbad's ears.

When she stopped laughing, she swept a furious white-orbed gaze at them. "Four will not return."

The warlocks and witches began looking around at each other, clearly trying to determine who went and who stayed.

Slowly, the queen's body began shrinking back to a normal state. Even her hair smoothed out and shaped itself into a towering pile of curls and jewels. She drew in a deep breath as she returned to her normal shape and a dazzling red gown replaced the smoky black robe.

Her voice also returned to its sultry smoothness. "I do not send you to the human world to waste your time there. I expect results." As they all nodded fervently, she continued,"Which four would prefer to stay with me?"

Not a person moved.

They barely breathed.

She broke out a sexy smile. "Oh, come now, it isn't that hard of a decision." After waiting another minute, she shrugged. "I shall allow you to decide as a group. You have one minute to cull your group back to twenty without my help or I will choose who stays here."

The air sucked out of the room as panic set in for a split

second then battle erupted with screaming and blood flying. Some of those warriors were highly skilled. Some were not.

The pregnant females died first.

Cathbad sighed to himself. What a waste.

In less than thirty seconds, ten were dead.

The others fought on.

Queen Maeve lifted her hand and made a slashing move. Every follower still breathing froze in place. "You have fourteen left to complete your task. You will return now and find the damned grimoire volumes. Do not expect to face me empty-handed again and for me to be so understanding."

With a flick of her hand, those still living disappeared.

Had she considered where she teleported them to at this minute? Probably not. If someone reappeared in the middle of Atlanta traffic or on a train track, they would not survive.

Shoving her hands on her hips, she stared at the carnage with a confused expression.

Did she not realize she had created that bloody mess?

He allowed his energy to flow out slowly.

Lifting her head slowly, she turned to stare straight up at Cathbad.

He dropped his cloaking. "I was not hidin' from ya. Merely stayin' out of yar way, love." With a smile in place, he floated to the ground.

She pursed her lips and shifted her head one way then another, studying him as a cat would a tasty prey. "What do you want, druid?"

At one time, she called him druid as an endearment.

Not now. The word sounded as though it tasted bad in her mouth.

"Would ya like me to make this all go away?" He'd often cleaned up her messes.

Without taking her eyes off him, she extended her arm with her palm down and waved it. All the corpses burst into smoldering flames then expanded and imploded into themselves, drawing the blood spilled with them.

With a small *pop*, it all disappeared.

She brought her hands together in front of her in an elegant show of being composed and lifted an eyebrow in question.

"I understand yar message, Maeve. Ya feel ya do not need me or anyone else." He walked over to her. "Sadly, ya have lost yar desire to rule all of this world, while I still wish ta accomplish what we started."

She did not move a muscle to acknowledge or deny his words.

"I do not know where we stepped off our path, love, but I am willin' ta find our way again if ya are. Ya could use some help with yar people. That has always been one of my strengths. In fact, 'twas a duty ya handed me when we reincarnated." He kept his voice pleasant, but business.

This would only work if she returned to the woman who once met him halfway.

If he pushed her, she would never come back.

"What do you want, druid?" She repeated as if she could see inside his head to know his true reason for being here. He'd come to use her scrying wall. His gaze slid past her to check her progress.

The wall swirled with pale blue and gray smoke.

She'd completed the wall? How long had it been active?

He glanced back at her.

She had a cunning smile in place and crossed her arms, tilting her chin up.

Oh, hell. Had she been observing *him* with that scrying wall?

CHAPTER 20

Daegan almost called up his blade when Luigsech pulled hers free of the sheath.

"You are not takin' me away from here, Drake. Not without blood bein' shed and I warn you it will not all be mine." She'd backed up so she had Quinn in view as well.

Quinn's voice came into Daegan's mind. *We're losing her. Maybe if we agree to find Fenella, she'll work with us.*

'Tis a good suggestion. I am makin' an enemy of this one and 'twas not my goal. I keep tryin' to reach Tristan with no reply and this woman will not aid us. It infuriates me.

"Stop doin' that!" she shouted.

"Doin' what?" Daegan frowned at her.

"It feels like you two are talkin' somehow. Are you telepathic?"

Quinn offered nothing.

Daegan said, "Aye. We speak mind-to-mind."

"Just don't," she grumbled, sounding tired and stressed.

Daegan had made a mistake by frightening her. He seemed to be making lots of mistakes since meeting her. He'd sent Tristan off on his own only to be captured. He'd started on the wrong foot as an adversary of this woman by entering her home uninvited. Now, he'd tried to get the information he needed by threatening her.

He'd never been so heavy-handed with a woman who had not presented herself as a threat to him or his people.

Daegan held his arms out wide in a show of being unarmed.

She stared at him with suspicion. "What are you doin'?"

"I did not come here to battle ya or threaten ya, Luigsech. I came to find the grimoire volumes and my man went missin'. We started on the wrong foot last night. I wish to aid ya in findin' Fenella. If ya put your weapon down, I propose we start over and work together."

"What can you do to find Fenella?" She slashed a warning look at Quinn who put his hands up with palms out.

"If I may?" Quinn interjected.

Daegan lowered his arms to his sides. "Go ahead. See if ya can get her to understand."

His Maistir explained, "We have exceptional resources for tracking people. If you could help us figure out who Cavan is, we can probably find him quickly and determine if he has either of our people."

She gave Quinn her attention, but remained with her guard up while she thought. "With all you've said so far, I have a feelin' you might know who Cavan really is if you had his true identity and just need to narrow it down. Is that so?"

No point in pretending otherwise, especially now that she knew he possessed telepathy. Daegan admitted, "My man called to me while I was at your cottage. He only got out a few words, but he said 'Cavan is' then his words were cut off. I am convinced he recognized Cavan and knows that I would recognize him. Discoverin' Cavan's true identity is the one thing standin' between us and freein' our friends."

She took two slow breaths then lowered her sword, but warned, "If this is a trick to disarm me, you will regret it."

"'Tis no trick. Savin' my man, *and* Fenella, is too important to play tricks. Now that ya know what we know, the wise choice would be to work together, would it not?"

"How can I be trustin' you two?" she put to them both. "What will stop you from takin' off just to save your friend and not Fenella?"

How one small woman could infuriate Daegan so much was beyond his understanding. "I do not care how ya come to that point, Luigsech, but sooner would be better than later for both of us. 'Tis easier to negotiate the end of a war than to gain one inch with ya."

"You should have thought about that before pissin' me off last night, buster." She slid her sword over her shoulder and into the hidden sheath.

The hint of a smile tilted Quinn's lips.

Daegan glared the smile off his face.

Moving around until she settled on her rock again, she said, "What more can I possibly tell you that will help you figure out if this Cavan is someone you know? I've described all I saw. No tattoos. No unusual markin'. Nothing else."

Finally, Daegan felt the blockade between them begin to crumble a little.

Quinn scratched his jaw and gave Luigsech consideration. "I don't usually share this, but I have an unusual gift where I can look into a person's mind and see a memory of a place they've been or someone they've met. Would you allow me to do that?"

Her eyes widened. "Go into my mind? No. Not a chance."

"But if Cavan has your friend and sent no ransom demand, plus you missed his meeting, how long do you think he'll keep her alive?" Quinn's voice drifted off at the end.

Daegan heard the insinuation in Quinn's voice that Fenella could be facing death even at this minute.

Luigsech's eyes turned shiny, but this was no weepy woman. Still, Quinn had touched her heart, the one place Daegan had failed to get near.

She stared off past them with a battle of thoughts playing out on her face. Without addressing either one specifically, she started speaking softly. "Cavan warned me if we did not meet he would harm Fenella. I thought she was safe until that meetin'. I expected to find her before he arrived to get her out of the way, but I couldn't find her last night and she never showed this mornin'."

"So that's where you went when you disappeared from your cottage last night?"

"Yes." She shifted a dark glance Daegan's way when he reminded her of last night. "Fenella left early yesterday from the centre to pick up goats from a farm owned by Mr.

Peadar. She's known him a long time. I had called several times to reach her last night before you showed up. When I couldn't get in contact with her and had no phone, I ran to her farm. She wasn't home. No lights were on. Her truck wasn't there. No goats. She would have called me if she had broken down or had any issue, but she didn't. Her farm is halfway between the centre and the goat farm. I had to be at the centre in time to meet Cavan or I guaranteed puttin' Fenella in danger, so I made that choice, thinkin' I'd reach her by phone at the centre. I called Peadar and he said she never showed up."

Daegan grimaced at the regret in her voice. He understood the agony of choosing wrong, but Luigsech had made the best decision under the circumstances. He gently suggested, "'Tis possible Cavan had your friend in hand already by the time he made that threat."

She nodded slowly and scrubbed her eyes with her hands. "I have had that thought." Standing, she addressed both of them. "I don't know why he took your friend, but the only hope I have of savin' Fenella is to find that grimoire." She held a hand up to Daegan. "Do not tell me what I can and cannot do. I don't want the wrong person to have that book and you haven't convinced me you're the right person."

Daegan had negotiated many cease fires and alliances when his father ruled. He found the best way to start those talks was by offering what the other person wanted. "We are willin' to help ya find Fenella. Does that now show ya we are the right side of all this?"

He'd said something that piqued her curiosity. Her voice held hope. "How would you find her?"

His chest eased with the first sign that he might be able to get what he needed from this woman while helping her at the same time. He wouldn't say he trusted her entirely, but neither did she trust him.

Fair enough.

But she held the most significant piece of information in her head and there was only one way to pull it out.

Keeping his tone as nonthreatening as he could, Daegan explained, "I can understand ya not wantin' someone to be diggin' around in your head, but Quinn is exceptional at this. His offer is not one given lightly and should be taken as the gift it is at this moment."

"Oh, sure." She shoved her hands up in the air then dropped them. "I'm supposed to just open my mind for someone to invade?"

"'Tis not what I'm sayin'," Daegan shot back.

She shouted, "I'm not about to allow some stranger in my head."

"Then ya must not care as much for your friend as we do for ours!"

Her head jerked back as if he'd smacked her.

His words had come out sharper than he would have wished, but his head pounded again and he could not be sure if his powers would return or continue to weaken.

The longer she put him off, the more she lowered his chance to save anyone from this Cavan.

Ruadh growled and banged angrily.

Daegan wanted nothing more than to free his dragon, roar at everything, and unleash the power pummeling his insides.

But he'd only add to his people's troubles if anyone saw the real red dragon.

Tears formed in her eyes. She squeezed them shut, denying the tears to leak out. When she opened her eyes again, the pain in them hurt Daegan.

She challenged, "Would you open *your* mind to save your friend, Drake?"

He couldn't spew out a quick answer.

Even he would not believe a reply rattled off with no thought. He gave her truth and hoped she would believe him.

"I have had to make split-second judgements on people to trust or not when in many a dangerous situations. I trusted ya last night to not stab me with your weapon when I turned my back on ya and ya were a dangerous stranger. If I had been presented with someone like Quinn who had not jumped into my mind when he could have at any second during this time together, yes, I would trust him to do as he offers and no more."

She heaved a deep breath and her clenched fingers uncurled. She had not expected him to admit that, huh?

Quinn stepped in. "I do realize how anyone would fear this, Miss Luigsech, but on my honor, I would never intentionally harm you in any way or search for more than intended. I don't believe in entering someone's mind without permission unless there is no other way to save a person from death."

Daegan admired Quinn's ability to manage such a powerful gift many other supernaturals would destroy everything in their paths to possess. That's why the world needed Beladors to protect humans and nonhumans.

Continuing in that same soothing tone, Quinn said, "If you'll permit me to use my gift and you follow my instructions, I will be able to enter quickly, see Cavan's face, then leave just as quickly. By the way, do you have a photo of Fenella with you?"

"No. Why?"

"It will accelerate our search to have visuals on Cavan and Fenella." Quinn paused as she said nothing, hesitating again. He prodded, "If we do not do this, I have no idea how long it will take to find Cavan's identity and then start to hunt for him, as opposed to searching for him immediately."

Her shoulders drooped with the weight of all her troubles.

Daegan hated that he had put some of that burden on her.

She chewed on her lip, struggling to make a decision. After a little nod to herself, she lifted her chin to Quinn and jerked her head at Daegan. "He's wrong when he said I must not care as much for Fenella as he does for his friend. I'd lay down my life to protect her. You say this mind power isn't overly invasive. What do I have to do?"

Relief flowed off Quinn whose eyes warmed when he spoke to the woman. "That is correct. I will go no deeper into your mind once I have Cavan's face. All you have to do is pull up his face and Fenella's, then focus on each one alternately. I'll tell you right before I enter."

Still she wavered.

Daegan suggested, "If you're not sure, lass, ask yourself if Fenella would do this for ya."

Luigsech flinched, but straightened her spine. "I want your word, Drake, that you and your people will work with me to save Fenella as well as your friend."

"You have my word."

Focusing only on Quinn now, she said, "Fenella's face should be clear, but I have no idea if Cavan allowed me to see his real face when we were together. He said he cloaked us. I want your word to go no deeper if you can't see Cavan's face."

Quinn dipped his head in a quick acknowledgement. "You have my word."

"Okay. Let's do this." Slipping one arm out of the strap, Luigsech lowered the backpack to the ground. She stretched her shoulders and neck, loosening up as if ready to battle someone. All that would appear to show how ready she was, but her breathing seemed to increase and get choppy.

She nodded. "I'm ready."

Quinn's voice came into Daegan's mind. *She doesn't look ready. She appears close to hyperventilating.*

Unfamiliar with the meaning of hyperventilating, Daegan guessed it was similar to panicked victims he'd seen unable to breathe properly then passing out. He told Quinn, *I've watched her fight Imortiks. She's tough and powerful. She can do this.*

Nodding, Quinn moved ahead. "Stay calm and focus on the faces. I will do the rest. Understood?"

She sucked in another shaky breath and closed her eyes. Her body needed to be relaxed to make it easier for him to jump in and out of her mind as quickly as possible, but her shoulder and neck muscles were visibly tight as taut ropes. She clenched her fingers. When she spoke, the word came out as if uttered on her last breath.

"Yes."

Quinn closed his eyes, too. He kept his voice low. "I'm entering now. You have a mash of faces in your mind. Try to relax and single out Fenella, then bring her face into focus." He paused a moment. "Ah, there she is. Bring all of her into focus so I can see her body and how she's dressed." He opened his eyes and continued staring at Luigsech. "Good. I have an image of Fenella. I can tell you're worried, but you're doing great. It's crowded again. Push everyone away except Cavan. Bring him to the front of your mind."

Luigsech's face showed the strain she felt. She breathed faster and sucked in her lower lip.

Daegan remained completely still as Quinn used his mind lock on the woman. He couldn't breathe for waiting to see if this worked.

Quinn whispered, "Cavan is blurry. Push the background and other people away. Focus a little harder on Cavan's face, his mouth, his neck, his eyes, all of it." Quinn's voice changed to surprise. "There you go. Stay with it, stay with his face and ... I've got it." He sounded as if he'd won a difficult battle.

Bringing his voice up, Quinn said, "You can open your eyes now."

Her eyes remained closed and her body trembled.

Quinn sent a worried glance to Daegan. "I was careful with her."

Daegan unfolded his arms and stepped over to her, taking the place Quinn vacated. He gently shook her shoulders. "Wake up, lass. He's done."

Her eyes blinked open mere inches from his.

He saw a world of things in those gorgeous blue eyes lost in the moment. It wasn't the time to notice her beauty, but neither could he stop the thought from flittering through his mind.

She blinked fast and seemed to come out of her daze.

Daegan dropped his hands from her shoulders.

She stepped back quickly and crossed her arms. "Keep your hands off me."

That was more like the little termagant. "I did not harm ya. We're tryin' to tell ya that he got the faces."

She bent over and dropped her hands to her knees, expelling enough air to fill the lungs of a bear. "Really? You got both of them?"

"Yes. I could have done this even faster, but the glamour Cavan used actually blurred his face at first. You seemed to change it midstream and his features sharpened."

Smiling with visible relief, she stood up. "I did. I saw his face on his first trip to the centre when I was hidden in the back at the time. He didn't see me then." Scrubbing her hands over her face, she shook off her tension. "Okay, do you know who he is?"

"Yes."

"Awesome! That's great." She looked ready to jump around celebrating. Then she must have realized no one else was happy. "What's wrong?"

Daegan noted Quinn's lack of joy in learning the identity. "Who is it, Quinn?"

"Cathbad."

Now Daegan understood what Tristan was trying to tell him. Of all people to take Tristan, Cathbad knew exactly what Tristan was and his value.

Finding him would be impossible if the druid did not wish to be found.

Dragging Tristan from Cathbad's grasp would be even more difficult. Every minute spent was another minute Tristan paid the price for any more missteps.

Luigsech's jaw dropped. "*Who?*"

Both men turned to her. Daegan asked, "With all your research, have ya never heard of Cathbad the Druid?"

Her face faded three shades lighter. "Of course, I have, but ... he's dead. Been dead forever."

If only that were true.

Daegan spent two thousand years locked in Queen Maeve's realm, thinking he would never see her or Cathbad again.

Then she and Cathbad showed up.

He filled her in. "'Tis true that he and Queen Maeve were believed dead when they vanished, but they faked their deaths. They came out of a deep sleep recently and are both very much alive."

Her lips moved but she couldn't form a word.

Daegan took pity on her. "I know ya care deeply for your friend Fenella, but do not think to go runnin' off. Ya are no match for this druid."

"And you are?"

At one time he would have said yes, but he had no idea what destruction the Imortik venom was causing in his body.

CHAPTER 21

CASIDHE HAD NEVER SUFFERED A panic attack, but she had the makings of a good one. These two men had just flipped her world upside down.

Cathbad-the-freaking-Druid.

She tried to calculate how old he could be today. She couldn't get past the fact that she was pretty sure Cathbad had been alive before Herrick had been born.

What did that make these two men standing in front of her?

Were they just as old? Or had they only recently found out about Cathbad? "Who are you people to know about Cathbad?"

Her question interrupted the murmured conversation that had been going on between Drake and Quinn. Her voice wobbled, but she couldn't help it. She had stepped neck-deep into a hellhole this time. Everything about these two and Cathbad were way beyond her skill set.

Until now, the only significant supernaturals she'd met over the years besides Herrick, had been a mage and one Fae, neither of which had been a threat.

She ordered, "Somebody answer me!" That sounded better. More like she still possessed a backbone even if her knees shook.

Drake sounded consoling when he told her, "The less ya know about the two of us, the safer ya will be. Discoverin' Cavan is Cathbad changes everythin'."

He'd surprised her when she'd opened her eyes to those silver-gray eyes staring at hers with concern. His huge hands had held her carefully, but he'd thrown her off by standing so close.

But that didn't mean she would now let him go alpha on her again. "Hold on a minute. What do you mean by this changes everythin'?"

"By now, Cathbad will have realized we know each other. He has very likely been everywhere ya have been. He probably saw the disaster at your cottage. If he has not returned for his book or the grimoire, it may mean he has changed his mind. That leaves us with little to go on."

"Stop right there." She had given them Cavan's identity. They owed her. "I thought we did this whole mind thing to get both of our friends back."

"True."

"I'm not hearin' a plan to save Fenella."

Daegan stared at Quinn for a few seconds.

They were doing that damned telepathic talking again. *"Stop doing that!"*

Daegan's gray eyes swirled.

She blinked and his eyes were normal again. What the hell? She didn't care about his damn eyes. "Besides being impolite to talk where I can't hear, it's annoyin'. I did my part. I gave you access to my freaking brain! Do your part."

"We were merely discussin' Quinn's next moves, which do not include ya," Drake replied. "He is headin' back to our people. We have a large network of resources. First, we must determine if Cathbad has Fenella, if someone else has Fenella, or if she is simply somewhere ya aren't aware of and has not told ya."

"She would not—"

"Luigsech, listen—"

She would not allow him to talk his way out of this. "You gave your word!"

"Enough!"

The power behind that one word knocked her back a step. She felt the boom deep inside.

Drake's mouth flattened into a stern line.

She'd pissed him off? Too bad.

Fenella was Casidhe's responsibility. She would not contact Herrick until she knew what Cathbad wanted. Drake had been right about one thing.

Learning of Cathbad changed everything.

She had to be extremely careful not to expose Herrick to anyone who might know the red dragon, such as a druid from back when dragons were a natural sight in the sky.

A druid that old, and a dark one at that, could harm Herrick.

Once Drake's power dissipated, he explained, "Ya have gifts and expertise. So do we and our people. Quinn will know by the end of today if Fenella is in this realm or another realm. We need that information to know where to start searchin' for her *and* how to rescue her. I have not broken my word. Do not make that accusation lightly with our kind."

She took her word, and her honor, seriously. Maybe these two did as well. "What are you goin' to do, Quinn?"

"I have the greatest supernatural network at my fingertips as well as our alliance with a human group who can match and sometimes exceed that of international security agencies. We found you by making one phone call yesterday."

To say that surprised her would be a ridiculous understatement.

Just who were these people? They dodged that question as if they were CIA from America. She could handle a human CIA group, but not this mysterious supernatural bunch. Still, if they had the resources they claimed, she intended to tap that and anything else to find Fenella.

Tilting his head in a bow to her, Quinn said, "It was nice meeting you Ms. Luigsech. I'm sorry for the circumstances, but perhaps you will see the useful side of an alliance with us from this." Angling his head to Daegan, he added, "I'll be in touch."

Air, or energy, around her changed. Sounds immediately became sharper. Had Quinn removed the cloaking?

Quinn headed into the forest in the direction of the river,

carrying himself as a man comfortable in the woods or an urban setting.

She frowned. "Where is he goin' to do all this research to find Fenella?"

""'Tis none of your concern."

"For the love of ... do you really think every time you shut down one of my questions I'm goin' to just be a nice little girl and let it slide?"

"I do not consider ya a little girl."

Why had that sounded sexual in his deep voice?

Because the last twelve hours had fried her brain.

She started to speak, but she had to flex her jaw muscles to loosen the tension. "It's good that you recognize I'm not a child, but that was not my point, which you well know. How about showin' me the respect of answerin' my questions?"

That seemed to take him aback. "I answer the pertinent ones."

Arrogant son of a gun. She lifted a finger. "Rule number one of us workin' together is if you want answers from me then you don't get to dismiss *any* of my questions as unimportant. If I ask one, it means I need an answer."

A sigh escaped his big chest and came out as a growl. "Just as ya protect the secrets of who and what ya are, I have no reason to share everythin' about our people. Quinn and I should be huntin' the grimoire volume to save our people being prey of the Imortiks, but I have sent him home where he will be able to tap every resource we have to first locate Fenella. Ask your questions, but know this. We have more people facin' worse than death in the next day in addition to whatever my friend is sufferin'."

Everything he said made sense even if it sounded as if the words had been dragged over a jagged surface. How could so many of his people be in dire straits? His words sat heavy on her heart. Remorse rolled around her shoulders, but she had not been the one to put everyone in jeopardy. "Fine. Here's an easy question. What's your friend's name?"

"Tristan."

"That wasn't so hard, was it?" she muttered.

"I would have told ya earlier had ya asked." Looking around, he commented, "With Quinn huntin' Cathbad, I suggest ya search for the grimoire volumes."

"I had that part figured out, buster. I can research much faster without you interferin'."

He dropped his gaze to her, pinning her with his intense stare. "Do ya truly think I will allow ya out of my sight *again* after last night? Trust is not a word I choose to describe our relationship."

Casidhe straightened him out. "We don't have a damn relationship. I don't even like you."

"'Tis not necessary to like me to form an alliance."

He had an answer for everything.

She had to make up her mind which way to go, but she normally began all searches for rare books with her extensive library. Wall to wall books, some from before Herrick's time and many of which only she could translate. Some she had only read parts of, intending to read further when she had time. She never had that kind of time it seemed.

Daegan cocked his head in the opposite direction Quinn had taken. "We should move. Now."

Hair stood across her arms. "What did you hear?"

"If I knew for sure, I would tell ya, lass. Could be a natural animal, but could also be a demon or Imortik ... or somethin' else. Would ya prefer to stay and find out?"

"Not unless you need more sword practice." She matched his sarcastic attitude.

Then he lifted her backpack and held it open for her to strap on.

This had better be a short alliance or he'd drive her crazy.

She hooked her arms through the openings and snapped the closures shut. "Thank you." Her appreciation lacked any warmth, but she'd said the words. That counted. "I need to return to the ancestral research centre. I would have stayed there to dig around today if I hadn't been *forced* to leave."

He said nothing, his annoyance loud in the silence.

She stomped away in the direction of her boat.

As she walked, confusion began to settle out in her mind. Now some of this made sense. Cathbad and this man knew each other. In fact, Quinn and Tristan, the captive, knew Cathbad. How many people were part of Quinn and Drake's group? Sounded like a large number to have those resource networks.

Maybe the druid not showing this morning made sense if he'd seen Drake at her cottage, but did Cathbad have Fenella?

Casidhe's chest hurt every time she thought about Fenella being terrified and harmed.

She had no reason to believe in Quinn or Drake, but she'd decided to stake her faith in Quinn coming through. She'd done her part by allowing him into her mind to see Cathbad. He'd been nice when he told her she had too many faces ...

Oh, shit.

Quinn's voice had coached her to pick out one face and focus on it. She'd been worrying about Fenella, then Herrick, then the family. When she tried to bring up Fenella's face, she'd had trouble separating it from all of the innocent faces at Herrick's castle who would suffer if Casidhe failed them.

Quinn's voice had soothed her until she could push past her family to pinpoint Fenella. Once that was done, he coached her on Cavan, whose face had been blurry before she dug deeper into her memories to find the first time she'd seen Cavan.

That would have been fine, but pinpointing Cavan had meant going past her memories of Herrick to find an earlier time when she'd observed Cavan's face. Correction. Cathbad's face.

Had Quinn seen anything else? Like Herrick?

Her heartbeat jumped with that possibility.

"What scared ya?" Drake asked.

She swung around on him, almost throwing herself out of balance. "What are you talkin' about?"

"Your body changed. Your heart beat faster."

He sensed that? Granted that she had not met many

powerful supernaturals until now, but she knew only one who could recognize the change in her heart rate.

Herrick.

She pointed out, "You don't just know of Cathbad, you actually *know* that druid, right?"

He arched his eyebrow at her. "'Tis not a new question, but I do."

"Have you spoken to him in the past? I mean, just how long have you been alive?"

"Ya can shout all ya wish, but I will not answer many questions about myself."

Miserable man was so obstinate. "I just want to know how we have any hope of findin' a druid of his power."

"The plan is simple, lass. He will find us."

Her brain stalled at those words.

Drake had come to County Galway hunting the same grimoire as Cathbad. Could she really trust his motives? If she did find the grimoire volumes, would Drake use it to draw Cathbad out?

Or take the book and run?

She started seeing this all play out differently.

She had no idea if Drake would use the volume to protect people or if he'd find a way to save Fenella.

Now that she had a chance to think, how would Quinn find Fenella when he didn't even have her phone number, last name, or any idea where to look for her?

She'd never met Drake's friend, Tristan.

Did Tristan even exist?

Or had all of this been one big con?

CHAPTER 22

RENATA'S HEAD SPUN AND HER stomach cramped, because she had nothing else to throw up.

She'd been a survivor her entire life. She'd lived on scraps as a child while passed around from one poor family to the next in Amazon villages of barefoot children.

But she'd felt her life turn around when she learned at eighteen she was special. A Belador.

Pain streaked up her legs and into her chest.

Her body wanted to curl in on itself, but ... she couldn't move her limbs. Those hideous yellow things that snatched her from Atlanta had stretched her vertically in four directions.

What about poor Devon? Had they killed him?

A grotesque body she'd seen the first time she'd opened her eyes here had terrified her. She'd been sick at the thought it might be Devon, but the vacant gaze staring back at her had held blue eyes. Not brown like his.

Like Roberto's.

How many more Beladors had these monsters captured?

How could they stand to smell themselves?

Her nose should be accustomed to the disgusting sulfuric odor by now, but no. Every breath pulled in that miserable rotten egg stench. The taste lingered in her dry mouth.

Water. Just a sip.

She'd lick it off the floor if they'd let her.

Her head pounded nonstop.

Pain had become her only companion.

That and constant replays of Devon's body yanked over that railing in downtown Atlanta. One minute, he'd been there. Then the next, his body had flown out of sight. She hoped he'd had a fast death. At least he was not suffering—

Energy charged through her as if she stood in a raging storm and grabbed a live electrical wire.

She arched, every muscle tight, straining against the manacles.

Bright yellow flooded her vision behind closed eyelids.

She hated the color.

Whatever these monsters were doing to her continued to build inside her body every minute. For the first time ever, she wished to not be a strong Belador.

She wished for death.

She wished to say goodbye to Roberto.

She wished ...

Darkness sucked her down a black hole.

Time floated, twisted, reshaped, and grew again. Voices rumbled, threatening noises, then quiet.

Silence stretched until one voice stood out. A man's? Maybe.

"This may not work."

She'd lost the ability to shut down her curiosity once she'd seen so much. Renata barely parted her eyelashes to close quickly if she couldn't handle what she saw.

As her eyes focused, she could see nothing in the darkness. This room or whatever place this was felt big and airy. She moved her head in tiny increments, terrified to draw attention.

Light caught at the edge of her vision.

She squinted.

That master, the one Daegan had fought on the Ferris wheel, came into focus. She hadn't been able to understand much of what he and Daegan discussed. The master, as he'd ordered her to call him, had hurt Daegan.

Had hurt a dragon shifter old as time.

A distorted voice said, "It will work. You will be free soon, Timmon."

Was Timmon another name for the master?

Who spoke to him?

Renata sorted the words and couldn't decide if the second voice belonged to a man or woman. It was as if the being was not present. She peeked more. A blurry image wobbled in front of the master ... Timmon.

"I take all the risk here and now you want me to stick my neck out farther?" Timmon moved around, lifting his arms from his body that glowed less than last time. She could see skin sagging in places.

"Your risk is no greater than mine. I have given you an opportunity to finally be free. To rule alongside me."

Timmon raked his head with nails curved into claws. He shouted, "I hate this body. You tricked me."

"You owed me."

"Not this. How could I owe you this?"

"I saved you from a worse fate. Stop complaining. When this is done, I will return you to your former body. All will be well and we will enjoy the spoils of our victory."

Squatting down and cupping his hands over his bleeding head, Timmon whined, "We have to do it soon. The Imortik trying to take over my body is killing me."

"You are stronger, which is why I made you master. Your discomfort is nothing compared to the Imortiks feasting on Beladors." The distorted voice laughed louder and louder until the sound coated her skin.

That's what she had inside her? An Imortik?

Tears burned her eyes.

She swallowed down a sob. Never cry. Not for these monsters.

"Discomfort? This is hideous." Standing up, Timmon jerked and flinched, then calmed down. "I can't keep waiting. What is the next step?"

"Attack VIPER. Destroy the alliance. Put the Beladors on the run, then we turn to the humans." More booming laughter.

Renata clamped her lips shut to stop the scream.

She could save none of her people. Or Roberto.

CHAPTER 23

AFTER LAUNCHING THE BOAT LUIGSECH had hidden near the bank, Daegan took one of the paddles and powered the small boat back upstream.

He had to give her credit.

She'd fought Imortiks and faced off with him and Quinn without knowing just how dangerous they were. Then she'd allowed Quinn to enter her mind.

If he'd heard that told by someone else when he had not been present, he'd have said Luigsech was a fool.

That would have been unfair. She was no fool.

She was loyal to a fault.

Now that he knew who had Tristan, he could breathe a little easier. They would find Cathbad, but only because of this woman.

Daegan could not deny his admiration. Opening a mind to Quinn would be terrifying for anyone. She'd forced her fear down for those she loved. Dark auburn tresses blew around the smooth skin of her face. Blue eyes he'd seen glow almost a lavender color last night and today took in everything then landed on him again.

He felt her intensity as if it were a living thing.

She'd given up paddling when her efforts worked against his powerful strokes and sent them off course. Since then, she'd crossed her arms and pushed herself toward the bow, as far from him as she could get.

"What exactly are you plannin' to do with the grimoire if I find a volume for you, Drake?"

"If?" He paddled along smoothly.

"If." Her mouth flattened in a grim expression.

"*When* ya find a volume, I must take it quickly to save my people in another land." He scooped another deep stroke down one side then the other, propelling them along quicker than a human could.

"Who would you give it to?" she persisted.

"I never said I would give it to anyone."

She sat forward, elbows on knees. "Then how do you plan to use it to save anyone?"

"I have not worked that out yet, but I will. I must save my people *and* keep the volume safe. I need as many volumes as we can find."

"We might not find any. Then what?" Her fingers clawed at her throat in an unconscious motion.

Daegan didn't like seeing her distressed, especially not to the point of scarring her skin. "Do not do that."

She stopped. "Do what?"

"Scratch your neck that way. Your fingernails leave red marks as if an animal clawed ya."

His words held her momentarily silent, then she rolled her eyes. "And that bothers you why?"

"I do not wish to see any woman harmed." He caught her gaze and would not release it as he kept the boat moving. The way she stared at him with distrust shouldn't matter, but it bothered him. He had always championed the innocent and vulnerable.

She showed no sign of believing anything he said.

He owed nothing to her beyond helping save her friend, but the defensive words still came out. "I am not the monster ya chase."

Another stretch of water passed before she spoke.

"You have no idea what monster I chase and don't ask. That's a question I won't answer." She twisted to her left and pointed. "There's the landin'. You got us here in record time."

He angled the boat to the spot she'd indicated and dug deeper strokes, sending the flat bottom boat up on the bank.

She leaped out and grabbed a rope she'd hooked to a cleat and pulled.

The boat would not move.

Shaking his head, he jumped out, gripped one corner and dragged the boat past her. He pushed it into a flattened area the same size as the boat. With it firmly tucked into the hole, he backed away as she made fast work of covering the boat with old branches. She carefully pulled vines back into place where they would naturally fall into the water.

Pink flowers grew along the vines. His father's cook always had those flowers floating in a bowl of water. Seemed odd to him at the time, but he'd like to thank her for the memory now.

Lifting her arms and stretching her back, she said, "We have to hike back to the centre."

"To the front door or your secret entrance?"

That shut down all conversation again.

He wished to exchange places with Quinn, who had shown an endless supply of patience for this woman. "I know of your secret tunnels."

"How can you know anythin' of the sort?" she replied, dodging his comment.

"We brought a woman here who has remote viewing. She sat in a spot on the floor of the ancestral centre and saw how ya opened a secret door in the bookcase on the back wall. Then ya followed the tunnel for a long stretch until you climbed out of it ... into a tree. 'Tis interestin'. How old is that tree?"

Of all the things he'd said to her, that stole her ability to speak.

She'd gone back to eyeing him as a terror.

Why? "Do not worry about your treehouse. I care nothin' for that or your secret tunnels. I only care what ya can find in your books."

She waved off his comment. "There be nothin' special about any of the tunnels. They were built three hundred years ago for women and children to escape during battle. I take those exits sometimes just to be sure the passages are still in good shape. I had actually intended to send Fenella out that way if she had shown up before Cavan. Cathbad."

Had he finally said the right thing to relax her?

Quite a speech coming from her for something of little significance, but he saw no reason to threaten her escape path. "Sounds too small for one of my size."

Her eyes lit up. "Yes. Much too small. The idea had been for the men to fight off an enemy while his family escaped, but if he fell then the tunnel would slow down someone followin' his wife and kids." She almost smiled in relief.

He'd like to see her smile. A real smile.

Ruadh made that low rumbling again as he would do after a day of flying just to relax.

Daegan smiled at whatever had his dragon content for the moment.

Tristan would like this woman's spirit and would tease her. He enjoyed poking at Adrianna and Evalle.

Daegan missed Tristan's humor.

Luigsech's forehead creased with a new concern. What bothered her now?

She asked, "Can you do the cloakin' Quinn did?"

He thought he could do it again, but he had some doubts about his powers such as teleporting a great distance. He'd spoken to Quinn telepathically once his Maistir had left to hunt Fenella. He had Quinn contact Brina for her help returning to Atlanta.

His niece would be delivering her twins soon. Daegan had to get this venom out of his system and return before her birthing. He would not have her dealing with teleporting others, which could take a toll on her energy once her time came closer.

"Drake? The cloakin'?"

"How long?"

She clamped her hand on her forehead. "Would complete sentences be askin' too much?"

Mouthy wench. "How long would ya be needin' the

cloakin'? Give me a distance."

"Ah, you can only go for a short time, huh?"

He heard the taunt in her words and countered, "Not to tout my ability, but I can go longer than the best."

Her cheeks reddened. "Well then it shouldn't matter how long, should it?"

"'Twas only clarifyin' so my answer would be accurate."

She made a sound that reminded him of a small beasty growling. She admitted, "I don't want to be seen enterin' the buildin'. I can get us close, then you'll have to cloak us for maybe fifty or sixty feet."

"I can do such."

"Good." She grabbed her backpack and walked off. "Let's go."

He would not walk emptyhanded as a woman carried a loaded pack, not even one as annoying as Luigsech. He caught up to her quickly and snatched the backpack away before she could stab her second arm through the strap.

She spun around and lunged for it, but he lifted the pack high above her hands. He started to explain he would carry the load so they could make better time and not because he was trying to touch her sword.

Her momentum sent her flying into his chest.

He caught her to him.

His heart rate tripled and his body reacted to her even faster. Daegan froze, unwilling to move with the bulge pressing his normally comfortable jeans.

Fingers clutched his shirt as her foot slid in the mud.

He wrapped an arm around her waist.

Everything stopped.

Daegan could swear the world slowed and the wind lay down as he stared into her searing blue gaze. Her breathing quickened and her heart thumped wildly against his chest.

Had touching him affected her as much as it did him?

Fire blazed in her gaze as realization of her position became clear. She curled her lips back and shoved away from him. "Give me my damn backpack."

"No."

"You can't take my property."

He pushed out a sigh that sounded as if his dragon grumbled. "Why do ya always think the worst of me?"

"You make it so easy." She crossed her arms. An errant lock of the rich auburn hair fell across her forehead.

Would she attack him if he brushed it away?

Why would he do that? Daegan scowled, more at himself than her. "I merely lifted the pack to lighten your load as we walk. Your possessions do not interest me."

She visibly struggled to accept his explanation. Then she smiled, but it had a mean glint. "Liar. Last night at my cottage, ya asked me about my sword as if it did not belong to me."

Lowering the pack to loop one strap across his shoulder, he admitted, "I was surprised to find that sword in this current day. 'Tis very old. Do ya know who once carried it?"

"Yes." She started walking backwards.

He followed her, tempted to smile at the way she used his one word answer to frustrate him.

But this was no time to smile.

Or to be thinking of this woman in any way other than an opponent. Certainly not a sexual liaison.

Surely, it had been too long since he'd had a woman to have those thoughts at this moment. "Ya will not tell me the original owner?"

"Nope." She stopped and shifted her stance, clearly willing to wait him out.

"Very well. Lead the way and I will cloak us when need be."

She stretched out her hand. "The backpack."

Hardheaded woman. He slid it off his shoulder and held it with the straps open so she could hook each arm.

Once she had everything latched to suit her, she muttered an angry, "Thank you."

She may not care for his company, but her anger would not allow her to overlook her manners. Such a funny woman.

After walking a short distance, they stopped at her cottage, which was on the way.

Luigsech walked in and stared at the destruction. She swallowed hard. "What happened to the Imortik *things* I beheaded?"

"Before leavin' to hunt for ya last night, I moved them outside and burned their bodies." Daegan grimaced at her sadness over the destruction inside her pretty cottage.

She wrinkled her nose. "Still smell them."

"The smell will go away." He had not wanted this to happen to her home, but he bore the guilt for it. Imortiks had come for him, drawn by the venom in his body.

He couldn't use majik to fix this mess for two reasons. One was she did not need to know what he could do, and additionally, he had no idea of the limits to his energy right now. He had to be careful not to tap his power when unnecessary.

"We cannot stay long, lass."

She seemed to catch herself. "Right. I need a quick shower and food."

He took in her soiled shirt and ripped pants, then her exhaustion. "Have your shower and I will find food."

She looked at him as if he'd lost his mind. "What will you cook?"

"Whatever I find. Go on with your cleanup. We only have a few minutes to spend." He waved a hand to brush her away.

Grumbling under her breath, she went to her bedroom. A minute later, he heard water running.

Daegan deemed cleaning up the mess a necessary use of kinetics. Once he had it reasonably clean and the broken furniture stacked in a pile, he searched the kitchen. She had a large bowl of stew in her cooling box. Refrigerator. He mentally thanked Tristan for constantly introducing him to modern elements.

Where was Tristan? His second-in-command had to know Daegan would come for him as soon as he had a location.

Daegan found a pot and dumped the stew in it, then pointed

his finger to light a fire beneath the pot. He found two bowls and spoons. The smell lifting from the stew had his stomach growling.

Would Cathbad take care with Tristan to avoid being turned to ashes by Daegan's dragon? Or would the druid think he'd outwitted Daegan and do as he pleased, believing Daegan would never find out?

Daegan's fist tightened and his hand turned bright red from the heat building. Something dripped on his boot.

He opened his hand.

He'd melted her spoons into a silver blob. Hell.

The list of things he'd have to replace in this cottage kept adding up. Opening his hand, he dumped the misshapen spoons into the garbage and found two new ones. He placed those next to the bowls on the small table that had survived the battle.

"I'm finished," Luigsech said, walking out of the hallway with her hair damp and wearing an aqua-blue pullover with a clean pair of jeans. Boot tips stuck out from beneath the pants.

The lass cleaned up nicely. More than nice.

He had just spooned stew into the bowls and stood at the sink, rinsing the pot. He cast a look over his shoulders.

She took in the cleaned-up living area with debris moved into stacks, the table set up for two people, and the stew cooking. Everything in her face said she did not want to utter those two words she had earlier.

But once again, her manners forced her to grudgingly murmur, "Thank you."

"Ya are welcome." Daegan pulled a chair out for her.

She took the other one.

He chuckled and sat, eating quickly. He didn't mind the brief stop since even soldiers needed to refresh and eat. She might have had nothing since her meal last night, which he had interrupted.

They ate in silence for just a few minutes, finishing at the same moment.

"Why were you at the grocery store when I spoke with Cathbad?" She lifted a paper napkin from a decorative stand on the table and dabbed her lips.

He'd originally traveled to the village to find out who Luigsech was and if she could be one of the squire family possessing Treoir history.

He discarded that for a better answer.

"I have told ya I am huntin' the grimoire volumes. I heard of your reputation. That led me to your centre."

She stood, lifting both bowls, but paused before walking to the sink. "If that was the truth, you would have come inside and asked for me, but you stayed outside hidin' and watchin' me." She stood there a moment then lifted a shoulder. "You have not threatened me, but your mere presence puts everyone I love in danger. I will only do so much with all that at stake. Do not be askin' for more than I am willin' to share when you are not willin' to tell me who you are and the real reason you are here."

He weighed the value of sharing his identity, but he could not when it changed nothing about hunting the grimoire.

Her words finally hit him.

One word in particular.

How could his presence put *everyone* in danger?

Who else did she mean besides Fenella?

CHAPTER 24

CATHBAD HELD HIS POSTURE ERECT as he stood in the queen's private chamber, observing her.

He had never dealt with *this* Queen Maeve. He'd known many versions. The seductress who could lure any man into her bed and keep him there for days without chains.

He'd known the queen that also enjoyed chaining virile men to each side of her throne for months.

He'd admired the woman who managed to capture the most dangerous red dragon of all time. Then he'd been disgusted as she'd allowed Daegan to live and eventually escape.

Now he faced a woman whose mind he had to tread carefully around or a battle of wills would erupt with enough power to ravage TÅµr Medb.

And possibly destroy one of them.

He'd proven his point last time when she'd trapped him in a clear enclosure of majik, but he was no fool to believe he knew for sure he could take down Queen Maeve in her own realm.

He'd lived over two millenniums using a simple rule.

Never, ever, go up against an opponent you are not positive you can defeat.

"You dare to come here asking to use my scrying wall, druid?" She'd recovered from her earlier loss of control. Her hair continued to lift and moved on its own, rearranging from multi-colored waves to a golden twist of curls that crowned her head. Her face aged not at all as was the privilege of immortals and those succulent lips deserved their own place in history.

Ah, yes, this queen possessed a beauty difficult to define. Just as impossible as defining her level of malevolence.

"I merely wish ta see if the wall works, love. Show me somethin' on yar scryin' wall and I will go verify if 'tis accurate."

"Why now?" She began moving slowly from side to side as if listening to music heard only in her head.

"I left here thinkin' about how we parted ways. We are headed toward a split. I do not want that after all we have done ta reach this point." He stepped around her to stand in her line of vision.

When she finally paused and looked down, he continued. "I thought long and hard on how we could rebuild trust with each other. It dawned on me that I might aid ya in developin' the scryin' wall. I could fuel it with my majik and make the wall impossible for anyone to ever break again."

"Such a selfless thought."

He ignored the sarcasm dripping from her lips. "I have never claimed to be a saint, nor would I want ta be. I have always told ya the truth regardless if ya would like what I said or not." He opened his arms out, palms up. "I come to ya with a plan for reunitin' stronger than ever." He lowered his hands and waited on a verdict.

Her body descended until her feet touched the floor. She studied him, taking her time as if to memorize his face. A smile began to lift her lips.

He would not race to a conclusion that she'd accepted his words, so he remained stoic.

Sighing gently, her eyes softened and her lips continued to build a smile that would bring most men to their knees. She moved close to him.

He kept his arms loose at his sides.

Lifting a hand, she brushed it over his hair and hooked her other hand lightly around the back of his neck.

Hairs stood on his skin, but he managed to appear unmoved. Just barely. Allowing someone of her power to put her hands close enough to snap his neck would normally be unwise.

But coming here at all was as unwise as it was necessary. He had to show her he trusted her.

She cupped her fingers more snug around his neck in an intimate way and moved her body as close as she could to his. Her lush breasts brushed his chest.

Damn if he wasn't hard.

He hadn't planned on sex as she'd disgusted him so many times recently, but he could make use of her interest. His lips twitched with a smile.

She noticed. Pulling him to her, she kissed his lips, slowly at first until he lifted his arms to embrace her. She gave a tiny moan, just enough to make his dick jump. If she wanted sex, he had always been a willing bed partner and the one male capable of satisfying her voracious needs.

Her fingers at his neck drove up into his hair.

She kissed him with the passion he hadn't received from her in a long time. His hand slid between them, grasping her breast. She made a sound of pleasure and reached for the front of his pants.

Damn her. He loved the feel of her wicked fingers on him.

She whispered, "Don't *ever* ask to use my scrying wall again unless you wish to lose this part first."

Clenching her fingers hard, she dug her nails into his crotch and twisted.

He shoved her away, roaring in pain and fury. "Ya bitch. What the fuck is wrong with ya?"

She'd fallen to the floor, laughing. "Nothing. I am better than ever. If I need you, I'll call you. Get out, Cathbad."

Cathbad teleported away from TÅµr Medb realm instantly.

He reappeared outside the cave in the Himalayas with a snowstorm blowing through. Dropping to his knees, it took him a moment to heal the pain throbbing in his loins.

He sure as hell had no desire to jerk off.

That miserable bitch.

After that little trick, he might not allow someone else to kill her. He shook off the worst of his fury, tucking this moment in the back of his mind. Plenty of time for vengeance.

For now he would not deviate from the plan.

He clothed himself in furs and wool as he gathered himself for another battle. If Brynhild attacked him today, he would lock her in that damn pond forever.

If she couldn't do her part, she became a liability.

In fact, now that he had Tristan, Cathbad had been rethinking parts of his plan. A polymorph Alterant could be more valuable than a crazy supernatural female.

He'd had all he could take of those.

He put his hand on the cold boulder, allowing the fury to slide away as he rose to his feet. He never made decisions when angry. He wouldn't today either.

Brynhild would do her part. She had a value unlike any others. He could put up with her far easier than Queen Maeve.

Now that he'd shaken off the encounter in TÅµr Medb, Cathbad headed for his future. He moved the boulder covering the opening with his kinetics and passed through the protective ward, noting it was undisturbed.

He stopped short, unable to understand what he saw.

The inside of the cavern looked as if a war had erupted. The chair and bookcase were strewn across the cavern, smashed into pieces. Books and magazines had been shredded, paper lying everywhere. Huge blocks of ice were piled randomly all over the place.

Lifting his hand and moving his fingers from left to right, he cleared the debris and ice chunks between him and the far wall where Brynhild's hoard had been stashed.

Still there.

But the chains Tristan had hung from were empty.

Blood splattered the wall beneath the chains.

Not an ice dragon in sight.

CHAPTER 25

THE AFTERNOON SUN DROPPED CLOSER to the horizon as Casidhe walked the last hundred feet to the rear of the ancestral research centre. They did have a back door entrance, but it remained locked from the inside with a bolt latch that slid through a slot as well.

Drake had quieted as they neared the village. She'd intended to hike here without a word to avoid addressing this feeling of being unfair to him.

She hadn't invited Cathbad or Drake.

Now she had to deal with the mess they were both making.

But Drake had started asking about the land and people during their walk. At first, she'd thought he wanted to become more familiar with her country, but he'd murmured almost to himself, "That has changed."

It gave her the impression he'd visited here a long time ago. If he'd lived here, he should have been somewhat familiar with what she'd told him about County Galway.

The more he asked questions unrelated to her, her sword, or the grimoire, the more she lowered her guard while they walked at a fast pace.

Then he'd ask how far they had left, reminding her he was in a hurry, and that reminder of why they were even together would yank her back to the present.

She had to keep her head straight.

They were not friends.

He was a stranger. An unknown supernatural. One who knew a druid who had lived thousands of years. He'd also argued the red dragon on television was not the true red dragon.

A freaking lightbulb moment hit her.

Could her best source for finding information on that dragon be walking an arm's length away from her?

She kept her face blank when her heart started dancing around at the chance to learn something that could help her find Skarde.

When she reached the backside of the ancestral centre, she leaned forward to peer around the corner of the building. The gray light of late day made it hard to see clearly, but everything appeared to be its normal quiet.

She could feel Drake standing close behind her.

Too close.

The man had no sense of personal space. He believed whatever he wanted took precedence over what anyone else wanted.

"What do ya wait for, lass?" Drake asked.

"To see if we can reach the front unnoticed."

"I told ya I will cloak us when ya are ready."

True, but she was stalling.

She had a bad feeling about entering the centre at all. What if Cathbad waited there?

"I will keep ya safe," Drake whispered next to her ear, as if he'd read her mind. Could he?

"Are you liftin' my thoughts?" she groused.

"No. Why would ya accuse me of such a thing?"

She'd insulted him?

Casidhe angled around and wished she hadn't.

He leaned on a hand propped against the wall above her head. The giant loomed over her, his face just inches from hers.

Drake took up too much airspace.

Far more than a normal person, but then he was not normal, was he?

He took up more space than a supernatural, too.

"Have ya lost your tongue?" he asked, sounding serious, but the glint in his eyes taunted her.

"My tongue is just fine." She straightened up, pushing his chest until he stood upright. "I asked because Quinn read my mind earlier."

"He did not read your mind. He only entered to the point of seeing those faces. Nothin' more."

Why was he angry at her assumption? "You two have telepathic communication," she argued.

"That does not mean I can speak to *anyone* mind-to-mind, only with ... my people."

Just who were those people he kept referencing?

She had to find out.

Every time she had her anger securely in place, he knocked it loose.

Drake had been considerate since last night's battle, even if he had hunted her down again. He'd fought, covering her back when those Imortiks attacked at her cottage and when they met again in the forest.

In fact, if she were honest, she might not have survived had Drake and Quinn not have shown up when they did in the forest.

"I did not read your mind when I said I would keep ya safe, lass. I could see your white knuckles on the edge of the building while ya hesitated on goin' forward or not," he explained.

His deep voice spoken so softly rattled her. And he'd started calling her lass instead of Luigsech. A nice change since he'd used her last name almost like an angry curse at times.

Then he destroyed what few good points he'd gained by grumbling, "We need to keep movin' and find that grimoire."

Turning back to check around the corner once more, she said, "Cloak us."

A second later, he said, "'Tis done. Ya have room to walk eight to ten feet from me."

Not nearly enough.

She hurried ahead until she reached the walkway to the front door of her building.

He stood right next to her when she retrieved a key to the lock she'd hidden outside the building.

She'd have to find a new hiding spot.

Once inside, she asked, "Can you shield the office lights?"

"Would be best if we had a candle to carry around inside the cloakin' instead."

She left the lights off and dug the LED keychain light from her pocket and pressed the button to deliver light.

"Clever lass. You can shine that anywhere and my cloakin' will hide it from sight."

See? There he went again giving her a compliment. "Okay, good."

She moved beyond the front office to the bookcases on the backside of the wall behind Fenella's desk. This place seemed empty without her, much like the hole in Casidhe's chest from worrying about her friend.

Casidhe had been here alone many times, but deep down inside she'd always believed Fenella would return.

Now, she didn't know what to believe. "How long before we hear from Quinn about Fenella?"

"I will tell ya as soon as I hear."

Spinning to him, she asked, "Do you have a phone?"

He shook his head.

"Can Quinn reach you with telepathy from wherever he went?"

He nodded. "Where will ya start lookin' for the book?"

She could only stall so long. What would happen if she found the grimoire and Drake took the information from her to hunt for it on his own?

Cathbad would kill her and Fenella.

She had no doubt. She'd realized it while walking today. He'd given her a book of the dark druids. Duh.

And she wouldn't be surprised if Cathbad was in charge of those druids, the top of the heap. The Seanóir.

She could not keep putting off finding out who Drake was. To show him anything on finding the grimoire would be dangerous without full disclosure of who she had staring over her shoulder. He had the ability to take anything from her and cloak himself to leave.

He had other abilities he had yet to show her.

Stepping back as far as the cloaking would allow, she turned to face him. "I'll be honest with you, Drake. I am not comfortable huntin' that grimoire without knowin' more about you."

All the pleasant time spent with this man melted beneath his flash of anger. "Ya will just have to become comfortable. I must have those volumes and soon. Every minute, every hour, and every single day counts. I have many lives dependin' upon it."

"So you say. You've come here and snooped on me, then expect me to just accept whatever you tell me." The backpack had become heavy over the last two miles, but she would not take it off and sacrifice fast access to her sword. "If I make a mistake and give you even one volume—that's *if* I can find it—and then Cathbad shows up, he may kill Fenella."

Drake shoved a hand through his thick hair. "We established that we both have people in danger and we must work together."

No, he had not established that Tristan was a real person who had been captured. "That all sounds fine except I don't know which side of you and Cathbad to stand on."

He stilled. "Ya say you are a Luigsech. Tell me what ya know of the Treoirs."

"Why?"

"If ya truly know the history, then I will give ya a reason to work with me."

"I'm not sharin' Treoir history."

His face erupted in fury. "'Tis not a game. People will die if we do not find those volumes!"

"So you say."

"Is it money? I will pay whatever ya ask."

That was a hell of an offer, but she slowly shook her head. "Information on some families can't be bought. It must be given freely, but only to those who deserve it. Offerin' me money proves you do *not* know who the Luigsech family were to the Treoirs."

He crossed his arms and calm returned to his face. "Actually I know more than ya realize. A Luigsech squire would carry the history from one generation to the next, ready to freely share it with those from the Treoir family. Ya are not human. Ya are not of the Luigsech family. Ya are an imposter."

She snapped, "I know who the Luigsech squires are and I know who I am. The issue here is not me. It's that I. Don't. Know. You! And I don't *trust* you. And everythin' around me has gone to shit from the minute you showed up in my life. I am not huntin' those volumes to have you take the information away from me then destroy the supernatural world."

He shook his head. "I have told ya enough for ya to realize I do not plan to harm others with the grimoire."

"Really? You also claim that red dragon destroying forests in Ukraine and Finland is an imposter. You have called me a liar and now claim *I'm* an imposter, but who are *you*? I think *you're* the imposter. It's you who should know that you must prove you are of the Treoir family to ask for their history."

"I am family."

"Anyone can claim that. A true Treoir would be able to prove it." She crossed her arms, letting him know this was the moment she took her stand. His man Quinn had been gone for hours. If they had such a great network of intelligence, he should have gotten back by now.

If she helped Drake find the volumes, she'd hand over the only hope she had for saving Fenella if a dark druid had captured her friend. Casidhe had one card to play and it was the grimoire.

Drake took a step foward.

She backed up.

He kept coming until her back hit a wall. Dipping his head close, he held her captive with his steely gaze. She couldn't breathe.

Her body had a mind of its own and cared nothing about

her tenuous situation. She couldn't move or think clearly.

His face slowly lowered until she could see every gray fleck in his eyes. Her heart thumped madly.

Then his eyes turned a molten silver and glowed. His black pupils elongated. When he spoke, his voice dropped inhumanly deep into an unnatural sound.

"I am Daegan of the Treoir family. I. Am. The red dragon. Time to prove ya are truly a Luigsech!"

Power boiled around them.

Her throat locked up tight. She struggled to cry out, *"No! You can't be!"*

BOOK 3

CHAPTER 1

CASIDHE FROZE. SHE COULDN'T SPEAK, couldn't catch her breath. She stood all alone with the most powerful dragon shifter to ever live.

Her family's greatest enemy. Daegan of Treoir, the scare-the-spit-from-her-mouth red dragon. Right here in her ancestral archive centre. Her heart tried to catapult out of her chest and run screaming for help.

Daegan of Treoir had started the Dragani War.

Like trying to avoid watching a train wreck, she couldn't peel her gaze from him. Towering over her, he could be mistaken for a human man in worn jeans, a dark long-sleeved pullover, and boots. But that formidable body and those silver reptilian eyes glowed with the enormous power inside that body.

No one outside the centre in this small village could save her.

Plus, Daegan had cloaked them to reach this point unnoticed. He could keep whatever he did to her hidden.

"Breathe, dammit," Daegan ordered in a deep voice. "Ya wanted the truth, now ya have it." He straightened, giving her space, but the force of that gaze held her locked in place. Growling a curse, he turned away, taking long strides, then paused at the opening to the front reception area.

She sagged, suddenly free from his overwhelming presence.

From *the* freakin' red dragon who claimed he had not burned any forests in Europe reported torched by a dragon. As if two red dragons existed today? A lot of people questioned if the stories of a dragon in today's world were true.

A lot of people had never walked in her shoes.

At least Daegan hadn't killed her.

That didn't mean he wouldn't snuff her out of existence if she lost her usefulness.

Her limbs came back online and started functioning again. She still had her backpack on, pinned between her and the wall from where she'd reversed course to this point.

Nowhere to go. Why try to run? If he wanted to kill her, he could.

Then she realized why he had not killed her. He needed her to find the grimoire.

Her life was being royally screwed because he wanted a damn ancient book of majik? The hell with backing away from this dragon shifter. Her fear dissolved under all of what had happened to her from the minute he broke into her cottage.

Not breaking and entering.

He'd teleported into her cottage in the middle of the night.

Imortiks and demons had attacked her because of Daegan.

Casidhe had missed her meeting with Cathbad because of Daegan. She could go on and on, dammit.

He needed her.

That gave her power, too.

"Have ya calmed down yet?" Daegan stood in the passway to the reception area, staring straight ahead in an angry profile. Powerful arms crossed and jaw muscles flexing.

Did he feel bad for trying to scare her out of a year's growth.

"Don't flatter yourself by thinkin' you rattle me, dragon." Lie, but it made her feel good to sound confident. Her pulse still hammered as fast as a gerbil on crack.

He angled his head in her direction, but made no reply. Dark eyebrows lowered over narrowed eyes now a natural gray.

If she had an open mind about him, she'd say he looked tired and sad. But she couldn't spare him the consideration she would a friend.

They were not friends.

What now?

She leaned away from the wall, planting her two feet, prepared to deal with him. She unsnapped the strap anchoring the backpack around her chest as she walked forward and shrugged off the pack.

His deadly gaze tracked her every step.

When she could go no farther, she ordered, "Move."

No please. No manners for this being.

He stepped aside, allowing her passage.

With every muscle she flexed, she felt her strength renew. As long as finding the grimoire remained at stake, she had a few things to get off her chest.

She dropped the backpack hard next to her desk and turned on Daegan. "*What. The. Hell*? You call me a liar every time you take a breath when you've been lyin' about who you are the entire time."

He swung that deadly gaze at her. "Ah, there's the little termagant who berates me with every breath. 'Tis your turn to explain who ya are, Luigsech. I realize to speak truthfully tasks ya sorely, but attempt it anyhow."

As if she weren't pissed enough already? "Listen, buster. I've been tellin' you a lot more truth than you've yet to tell me."

He gave her a dismissive glance. "'Tis no scoresheet to be kept. Lies are lies. I told *mine* to protect my people. Why did ya tell yours?"

"For the same reason." She cocked up her chin in a righteous pose, daring him to question her honor.

"If such is true, then who are *your* people? Ya know who mine are ... or ya should if ya are truly a Luigsech."

He'd walked her right into that trap.

She was not about to speak a word about Herrick.

That left her only one answer she could give, which had served her well through college then working here for ten years. "The Luigsechs are my people."

Daegan stepped into the front office and sat in her reading

chair. "Ya still step too far from the truth. The Luigsechs were all human. Ya are not. This means ya are not of their blood. Do ya deny this?"

Did he think this was a social visit? She wanted to scream at him for all he'd done to Herrick, but those words couldn't be spoken, dammit. "Get out of my chair."

"I think not. 'Tis quite comfortable. At the speed 'tis takin' ya to form a thought, I require a place to relax as I wait."

Miserable dragon shifter. "Insinuatin' I am slow-witted is a poor way to gain information." She curled her lips at him. "I'm merely considerin' if it's worth the effort when you're not goin' to believe me."

Daegan's fingers draped over the chair arm curled tight, his only sign of anger. "'Tis not a game I play. Ya wish to find your friend, Fenella? I *must* find my friend as well. I promise ya Cathbad has a plan afoot and will remove anyone in his path, even an innocent female. If ya want to know what Quinn learns from our people in Atlanta, 'tis time for ya to be forthcomin'. I am not a man of great patience, particularly when my people are in danger."

She'd had it with him. Storming across the room she slapped one hand on a chair arm and the other on his wide chest, leaning close to make sure he heard every word clearly. "Listen up, dragon. I was orphaned as a child. The Luigsech family raised me. I've a strong educational background, plus knowledge passed down to me by former Luigsechs. Do not *dare* to call me a liar about who I am."

Daegan's nostrils flared and his chest rumbled. The sound reminded her of Herrick's chest when his dragon became agitated.

His energy hummed. Her energy hummed.

She'd just challenged the red dragon. Had she lost her mind?

Don't poke a dragon.

And never poke *the* red dragon.

She started to lift up.

He caught her wrist, the one attached to the hand still

splayed against his chest. Heartbeat ramping up again, she swallowed hard and stared into the molten silver in his eyes.

His heart thundered beneath her fingers. Heat soaked into her skin from his touch and made her lightheaded.

That didn't make sense.

Neither did touching Daegan.

She shoved away from him hard, thinking he'd try to hold her in place. He released her immediately.

Momentum from the push sent her flying backwards to land on her bum.

She might have recovered her dignity if his lips hadn't twitched with fighting a smile.

Damn him! She jumped up to her feet. "We made a deal. Quinn *has* to send word if your people can find Fenella. What about *your* honor?"

Daegan sighed on a long exhale.

She caught a tinge of smoke and outdoors, a distraction when she had to pay attention. She tugged on one of the delicate gold triple-loop earrings Fenella had given her as a birthday gift.

Fenella had pointed out more than once that Casidhe should never play cards for money with that nervous habit.

She dropped her hand.

If Fenella had been captured, she had no one to depend upon but Casidhe. Contacting Herrick would put him in danger the minute he came out to confront Daegan, who had followers called Beladors. Small details such as that kept popping into her mind. Daegan claimed to have many followers. If he spoke of Beladors, he had a force of warriors with telepathic and kinetic powers.

That Quinn guy had to be a Belador, too. While not immortal, they physically appeared to be humans, allowing them to blend in with any population.

Daegan had a supernatural army if he had as many followers as he claimed. Too many for Herrick to fight.

Lose Fenella and Herrick?

Over Casidhe's dead body.

Daegan surged to his feet and stepped close, tension vibrating the air. "'Tis the truth no one has tested me as greatly as ya in a long time. Quite a feat considerin' the Imortiks I have fought."

"Really? I'm annoyin'? Don't flatter me. I'm accustomed to people askin' questions politely and *not* standin' in my face when they do it. You have zero respect for personal space."

He pulled his head back, appearing stunned. "What is wrong now?"

She should be used to someone as old as him not understanding terms like *personal space*, because Herrick had the same problem at times.

With Herrick, she showed patience and explained terminology.

With Daegan, she made it simple with blunt words. "Back the hell up and give me room to breathe. Your power is makin' me claustrophobic." When he frowned, she gritted her teeth and jumped to explain before he asked another question. "Claustrophobic means you're makin' me feel like I'm suffocatin'."

"Have ya always suffered this ailment?"

"For the love of kittens ... *move!* In fact, have a seat, again. Clearly at your age you tire easily."

His intimidating gaze darkened, but he hadn't set his dragon on her yet. She'd consider that a victory if not for reminding herself she held a value to him only until she found the grimoire. If she allowed Daegan to push her around in her own territory, she would never get a handle on this mess.

Daegan put his hands behind his head and walked away, shedding frustration like water falling off a pitched roof. He turned an angry human gaze on her. "Ya continue to dodge my questions, yet ya want my help findin' Fenella, who may or may not be captured. But the druid *does* have my man and I *do* have people sufferin' from Imortiks. They are dependin' upon me to find a grimoire. Ya said I had to prove I was of the Treoir family. I have done so yet ya have failed to prove ya are a Luigsech. Do not ask me for anythin' else, even findin' Fenella, if ya have no real proof of bein' a Luigsech. If not, I have sorely wasted my time. Convince me who ya are or I shall look elsewhere for the grimoire and ya can hunt for Cathbad on your own."

He had her there and he knew it, damn his scary self.

She'd been trained for battle, but had been in few verbal confrontations over the years due to spending her life with her nose stuck in books.

That put her at a disadvantage for arguing with Daegan.

When he settled once again in her reading chair, she gave him a narrow-eyed glare and took the seat behind her desk.

What would she do if Daegan just disappeared? He might be her best hope for finding Fenella.

Regardless, she could not allow him to put her on defense or he would do nothing in exchange for hunting his blasted grimoire.

She spun her chair to face him. "I am *not* an imposter. I was adopted and brought into the Luigsech family. Don't waste your breath askin' for their contact information. I will not bring danger to their door when they have shown me nothin' but kindness."

Daegan sat very still for a moment then stretched out his long legs. "Why would they not choose one of their blood to carry the Treoir history?"

Her erratic pulse slowed a bit at his less abrasive words. Or maybe it was how his speech had devolved into what he may have sounded more like long ago. Had he lost some of his natural language by being away from the world locked inside TÅμr Medb for so many years?

Did she give a flying crap? No.

She drew in a calming breath and chose her words carefully. "I was brought into the Luigsech home at a young age. I studied next to their oldest daughter, the one they'd chosen to carry the spoken history of many things, not just the Treoirs."

He arched a dark eyebrow at her. "The Luigsech squire

family my father brought into his castle were to retain and pass on *only* Treoir history. I am findin' it harder and harder to accept ya know anythin' about my family ... or that ya can locate the grimoire."

"This is why it's hard to talk to you."

"What do ya mean?"

"You expect me to accept anythin' you say when you aren't willin' to hear me out." Her fingers fisted, but she put her hand on the desk and forced her digits to open.

Daegan wanted whatever she knew about him and his Treoir family? She'd love to tell him she knew the stories of how his red dragon had murdered everyone long ago, plus how Herrick stepped in to save the Luigsech squire family.

Not happening.

That would require admitting she knew about the ice dragons and ... oh crap.

She froze at the rest of that thought.

Sitting before her might be the only person who knew where to find Skarde.

CHAPTER 2

QUINN BLINKED AS THE SWIRLING colors and disorientation of teleporting from Ireland back to the United States subsided. Jet lag stressed a human body traveling four thousand miles by airplane from a country five hours ahead in time, but teleporting was no simple leap for a nonhuman either.

His head had to catch up. When his mind cleared, he stood in Piedmont Park just north of downtown Atlanta. Heat that had built up during a normal summer day assaulted him.

Right place.

He'd like to eat and grab a shower, but he needed to take care of business here as quickly as he could and return to Ireland to help Daegan find Tristan.

Plus, Daegan had no one watching his back, certainly not that Luigsech woman.

Glancing around to be sure his arrival had been viewed by no humans, he stepped out of the shadowy copse of trees Daegan used often for teleporting into the city. Threatening clouds offered some relief from the blazing sun for the few willing to brave a visit to the park.

Not surprising with preternaturals being spotted in Atlanta.

Quinn headed for the street bordering the park while sending a text for a driver to meet him immediately. With confirmation one would arrive in less than two minutes, he sent a brief message to Trey, letting him know he'd returned. Trey had been slammed with telepathic communication when Quinn left and would probably appreciate a text instead.

For a Tuesday afternoon, Piedmont Park hosted its usual

diverse groups of people running, sitting on blankets with a bottle of wine and cheese, throwing frisbees for their dogs, and one couple pushed a double stroller with a dog in tow.

As a dark sedan approached, Quinn widened his stride to reach the car quickly. He waited for the window on the passenger side to lower and Quinn tossed Luigsech's mobile phone on the seat. "Have the techs go through that to find everything they can. My first priority is for them to determine the location of a woman named Fenella Connell, who is associated with Casidhe Luigsech. I also want any additional information they can find." Fenella's last name had been on all of the paperwork at the centre.

"Yes, Maistir." The car drove off.

Evalle's voice came into his head. *Quinn. Where are you? We need help.*

Quinn had started to smile at the sound of her voice, but he quickly replied, *Piedmont Park. Where are you and what's happening?*

Need you to get up to VIPER headquarters as soon as you can. This place is being overrun by demons and Imortiks!

I'm on the way, Quinn rushed to assure her.

Trey's voice burst into his mind next. *VIPER is being hit hard. Can you help?*

Absolutely. Have Brina teleport me to the entrance of VIPER in fifteen seconds. That will give me time to find cover from humans here in Piedmont Park.

I'm on it, Maistir.

Quinn spun and headed for dark shadows in the trees. This new development just killed any hope he had for a quick visit to the Treoir realm to smooth over how he and Reese had parted ways in Ireland.

She might not be happy with him, but she was safe from Imortiks and demons. That mattered more at this minute than making her smile.

He'd have time for that and to discuss the baby once they found Tristan. As soon as Reese understood that he knew about her pregnancy *and* he accepted full responsibility, they could finally move forward.

Even more, he wanted her to know he cared deeply for her.

He barely made it out of view with a second to spare when his body got yanked into teleportation.

When he opened his eyes, he stood at the entrance of the mountain shielding the VIPER headquarters.

The entrance should be hidden by a sheer face of rock.

There should *not* be a wide open maw with screaming and yelling going on inside.

Quinn ran in to find Evalle, her mate Storm, four Beladors, and four bounty hunter contractors for VIPER in a battle with ten, maybe twelve, demons of all types and two Imortiks.

One demon also glowed yellow. Hell! *Three* Imortiks.

Quinn had to get his people working in teams. He shouted telepathically, *Beladors, do not link, but team up in pairs. Storm can shift into a black jaguar. Do not attack his animal.*

Evalle didn't even look over her shoulder when she repeated Quinn's order out loud to Storm.

Two sets of Beladors paired up, taking on three demons each.

Evalle hit the Imortik demon with repetitive kinetic blasts, knocking it back into two other demons. She couldn't keep that up long, but her attack allowed Storm to shift into his massive jaguar.

Storm's coal-black jaguar roared and rushed the Imortik Evalle fought. She pulled back her kinetics at the last second. The jaguar ripped into the Imortik that clawed the giant cat.

One of the bounty hunters screamed.

Jerking around, Quinn watched in horror as an Imortik dove into the body of a bounty hunter with a black mohawk. Quinn shouted, *"Bounty hunters, pair up and protect your backs!"*

They sort of followed his orders.

That was all he could do for them. As Maistir, Beladors were Quinn's first concern.

Where was Sen, VIPER's liaison and immortal guard over the headquarters?

Quinn jumped into the fray, slamming kinetics to knock aside a demon, aiding a pair of Beladors who quickly terminated the creature. It turned into gray dust and vanished.

He called telepathically, *Sen, where are you? You're being overrun at VIPER's entrance.*

Sen replied in a hoarse voice. *Like I don't fucking know that? I'm underground fighting my own battles.*

Quinn moved with blinding speed to help his people. With the Beladors' opponents under control and Storm's jaguar backing up Evalle, Quinn turned to give the bounty hunters a hand.

The one that had screamed was now on the ground, writhing in pain. While the other three bounty hunters battled an Imortik and a demon, the one on the ground stopped shuddering, shook his head, and jumped up.

Now the black mohawk guy glowed bright yellow and went after his three human associates, who had their back to him. Quinn slammed that newly turned Imortik with a massive hit of kinetics, adrenaline driving his blast as much as Belador power.

The yellow bounty hunter had a body fit to compete in world wrestling. But when he banged into the rock wall Quinn drove him into, the new Imortik turned eyes wild with insanity on Quinn.

No one home there anymore.

But like Devon, one of their Beladors locked under this mountain who had not been turned long enough to become fully Imortik, this guy might be salvageable.

Quinn considered using mind lock, then tossed aside that idea. He'd already tried that move with an Imortik and the immediate backlash had taken him to his knees.

The mohawk guy came at him with needle-sharp teeth now in his wide mouth. His fingers grew dark claws the size of a grizzly's.

Quinn swung one kinetic blast after another at his head, smacking the glowing bounty hunter back and forth. His plan had been working just fine until the mohawk guy dove preternaturally fast beneath Quinn's blasts and lunged for his leg.

Quinn spun around.

Claws ripped his pants, barely missing his leg.

His heart pounded fast in his chest. Quinn could not allow an Imortik to take him over.

Quinn used his fists to hammer kinetic blasts at the mohawk until the claws withdrew. The Imortik bounty hunter pushed up to jump Quinn.

Sen flashed into sight, took one look at them and pointed at the Imortik bounty hunter. In the next instant, the glowing yellow body flew up in the air and slammed the ground headfirst.

Blood splattered Quinn's chest and face.

The other three bounty hunters had lopped the head off their Imortik.

Quinn sucked in air for three fast breaths. "Did you have to kill the bounty hunter, Sen?"

Two of them turned and stared at the bloody pile Sen had made of the Imortik bounty hunter and shrugged.

Evalle came rushing up to him with her ball cap knocked sideways. "You all right, Quinn?"

"I'm fine."

Storm's jaguar showed up right beside Evalle and cocked his head at Quinn as if wondering why Quinn had just lied.

Hands on hips, Sen stared at Quinn with disgust. "You wanted to keep *that* alive? I won't waste my energy next time until after you lose your body to an Imortik."

Quinn rebuked, "That bounty hunter had been human minutes ago before the Imortik jumping him. If it requires three weeks to completely take over a body, we might have saved him."

"After this fiasco, the Tribunal will likely declare a kill-on-sight order. I'm just getting ahead of the curve by starting with him." Sen issued that in a cold voice that said he wouldn't lose sleep over one dead bounty hunter, but that same voice had come out raw as if he'd been yelling for an hour.

Quinn took a hard look at the VIPER liaison. Sen's skin had been burnt in spots. A chunk of long blond hair was missing from the right side of his head, exposing a raw wound. Blood ran from slashes across his body and his face. The jeans he wore had not been ripped, which meant he'd just conjured them before appearing here. But bloody spots stained the front of his thighs.

Sen should be able to heal himself in seconds.

Why wasn't that happening?

Quinn had never expected himself to feel any sympathy for this obnoxious jerk, but Sen looked as if he'd battled an army of Imortiks.

An Imortik had shoved venom in Daegan. Could those creatures do the same to Sen?

"Fuck!" Sen vanished.

Evalle looked around. "Wonder where he went?"

"If he needed help, he should have said so," Quinn said, more concerned about his own people.

Straightening her ball cap, she looked around at the Beladors. "I think our people need a minute to heal and catch their breath."

"Absolutely. We can't go anywhere until Sen returns. I'd rather not have Brina teleport us to Atlanta after she just teleported me twice. I have a feeling we're asking a lot of her at this point in her pregnancy."

"You're probably right." Evalle looked around when her name was called. "Let me see what our guys need." She and Storm walked off to join her team.

Quinn contacted Trey telepathically to inform him of what happened at VIPER and get an update on the rest of the teams. Based on everything Trey started unloading, Quinn had hours of meetings ahead of him, but he would never complain. Their Belador forces were running hard around the clock to save others.

With a little luck, he could visit Treoir later tonight and talk to Reese.

As Quinn finished up with Trey, Sen popped back into existence.

The last bounty hunter wiped his blade off on a dead Imortik and walked over. "What the hell happened to you, Sen?"

The VIPER liaison pointed at the crushed bounty hunter corpse on the ground. "Five of those did, plus a bunch of demons." He slid a glare full of accusation at Quinn. "They were trying to get to the three Beladors we've been putting up with for you."

"How did these demons and Imortiks get inside VIPER?" Quinn had never known anyone to gain entrance without Sen's authorization.

Was that embarrassment on the liaison's face?

Did Sen think stonewalling would work? Quinn spoke in a quiet voice his people knew meant he wanted answers and he wanted them now. "The more we know about these damn things, the better shot we have of getting rid of them. I find it hard to believe they danced past this opening and made it underground before *anyone* noticed, but I'm willing to ask the Tribunal for clarification."

Sen snarled, "Someone called me to teleport in two demons who were supposedly contained. It wasn't Trey, but I thought it was your people since I'm spending most of my time babysitting your peons. I decided, screw it. I'll teleport the demons in and deal with the call not going through Trey later. I was in the holding area when I teleported the demons in. A small army of very much alive Imortiks and more demons arrived with them."

Damn. Quinn hated the way Sen had treated his people, especially Evalle, for a long time, but no one would want to face that alone.

Wiping a hand over his face and back across the top of his head, Sen warned, "After this mess, the Tribunal might up the termination time for your Imortik-possessed Beladors to immediately."

"*No!*" Evalle shouted. "They can't do that."

"The Tribunal can do anything they want." Sen's flat statement came with a smirk. "If they tell me to get rid of all three prisoners, I'll happily comply."

Quinn lifted a hand to stall Evalle speaking. Storm had moved over in front of her and turned a red demonic gaze on Sen.

Storm was no longer ruled by the demon blood he carried, but he had no off switch when it came to protecting his mate.

With tension bloating the air, one spark could set off the equivalent of a volcanic eruption.

Time to get his people out of this place.

"We're solving nothing standing here," Quinn said, changing the direction of the conversation. "My people need to be back in Atlanta so they can keep others safe from this threat in the city. You should inform the Tribunal that I am available for a discussion on our three Beladors locked up here. Speaking on behalf of our Treoir dragon king, to terminate Devon, or any of those three, prior to the deadline and without a meeting with me would be considered an attack on the Beladors. I strongly suggest we continue working together for the best of everyone and not become adversaries."

Shrugging, Sen said, "What-the-hell-ever. I'll pass along your concerns. I don't make the laws, I just enforce them. If anything happens before Devon's deadline, with or without a meeting, that's between you and the Tribunal."

Blood trickled from cuts on Sen's body. His demigod healing sure was taking its time to slow the bleeding. The VIPER liaison had a kicked-in-the-nuts look Quinn had never witnessed on this being before. If an Imortik took over Sen's body ... Quinn didn't want to even consider that possibility.

Calling his people to him so they could teleport as a group, Quinn turned to Sen, determined to end on a professional note in spite of dealing with a jerk. "Thank you for protecting our imprisoned Beladors."

"Don't confuse my actions with giving a shit about you

or those Beladors. I answer to the Tribunal only. No one was tricking me and getting away with it. Your people just happened to benefit."

Quinn would overlook an antagonistic attitude on anyone else that battered and bleeding, but Sen's viciousness came as part of his standard makeup. He ignored Sen slapping his thank-you back at him in favor of sending his people out of here immediately.

Once everyone had a hand on each other's shoulder, Quinn told Sen, "I have a landing spot pictured in my mind. Teleport all of us and we'll leave you to deliver your report to the Tribunal."

A haunted look entered Sen's eyes.

Did this demigod fear admitting the breach of VIPER security to Tribunal deities?

Sen snapped back to his sunny personality of a rabid demon. "The sooner the better."

Quinn, his team, and Storm teleported to the basement area of a tall building he owned in downtown Atlanta. As they reappeared, someone shouted.

Turning to intercept a potential threat, Quinn paused and lowered his deadly hands.

Evalle waved. "Hi, Clyde."

The balding fifty-two-year-old Belador in top shape and dressed as a security officer had jumped to his feet with hands raised to use his kinetics. Clyde dropped one hand and slapped the other one over his chest. "You about gave me a heart attack."

Quinn walked over to him. "Sorry, Clyde. I had no chance to give you a heads-up before our arrival."

"No problem, Maistir. That's why I keep that spot clear at all times as you instructed." He took in the group. "Looks like you just came from a war." Clyde noticed the black jaguar and stepped back. "Shit."

Evalle brushed her fingers over the jaguar's coat. "You're safe. This is my mate, Storm. We look like hell because we just fought Imortiks and demons at VIPER headquarters."

Clyde gave her an embarrassed glance. "I'll stop griping about being bored here. It's ugly out on the streets."

Quinn nodded. "Yes, it is. I want this team to clean up and get a meal before going back out on patrol. It may be boring here, but what you do is vital. I didn't hesitate to teleport our people in. I fully trusted you to provide a safe landing place."

The praise brought a smile of pride to Clyde's lips. "Thank you, Maistir. I'll alert the kitchen to prepare food for everyone."

"Leave us out," Evalle called over. "We're not far from home. We're leaving once Storm shifts and puts on clothes." Then she turned to Quinn. "Before you bring it up, don't fuss about the sunlight. Storm will cloak us to get home if we don't walk out into a downpour based on that thunder I'm hearing. I need to talk to you before I leave."

Nodding, Quinn ushered the rest of the team up three floors to a level available twenty-four-seven for Beladors in need. Clyde directed the management leader to provide everything necessary for the team.

With that handled and no one around to listen, Quinn told Evalle, "We have not found Tristan yet, but we have leads. I sent a mobile phone to our tech team. They're currently going through it searching for something Daegan needs. He's still in Ireland and I plan to return as quickly as I can. I may ask you to continue as an interim Maistir to free me up."

"Understood. While I'm not as experienced as you, I'm okay to keep doing it."

"You are performing just fine, Evalle."

She scoffed. "You're the one who showed up and broke us into groups. I'll remember that for a future situation, though."

Quinn could see her developing into a strong and strategic leader with just a little guidance. "That's as much catch-up as I can give you at the moment."

"Got it." She put a hand on his shoulder to stop him from

leaving. "While you're here, you may want to talk to Reese."

"I do want to speak with her, but I don't have time to teleport back and forth to Treoir at the moment."

Evalle stretched her neck in a move to delay speaking. "She's at her apartment."

"What?" Quinn ground out.

"Yep. Phoedra and Lanna are still in Treoir, according to Edward." She referenced the Belador working as a doorman at Phoedra and Reese's apartment. "I spoke to him when I passed by her apartment on patrol. Edward said he was surprised to see Reese back when he hadn't heard from you. I told him I'd let you know if I saw you first." Evalle had that I-don't-like-being-the-messenger look.

Bloody hell. What was Reese doing here?

And who teleported her back to Atlanta without telling him?

Storm's jaguar nudged Evalle's leg. She said, "I know. I'm telling him." Taking another breath, she said, "You noticed the number of demons at VIPER, right?"

"Of course. Trey mentioned an influx of them in the city. Where are they all coming from?"

"That's what we're trying to figure out. I've never seen so many in the city and no other areas in the south are reporting anything like this. I hate to say this, Quinn, but they started showing up after Reese returned. Edward told me he widened the protective area around her apartment. We mapped sightings and killings over the past twelve hours. Those spots were in a five-to-six mile radius around her building. More are showing up every hour."

CHAPTER 3

TRISTAN'S BODY DANGLED THOUSANDS OF feet off the ground from claws the size of his head. A dark scarf wrapped around his face blocked his view. Cold air battered his body clothed in medieval furs and leathers, none of it comfortable.

All of it soaked and cold as shit.

Brynhild's dragon would freeze Tristan's nuts off if this flight went on for much longer.

She almost managed to do it once before.

He'd have nightmares for the rest of his life, which might not be very long.

All he did was try to talk to this damn dragon shifter to make friends while they were both stuck inside Cathbad's cavern.

Because friends helped friends escape, right?

Not this lunatic. She took offense at his attempt to flirt and lost her ever-lovin' mind.

One minute Brynhild was listening to him, and the next, she snapped. She started shifting into the massive iridescent-blue dragon now flying him who knew where and roared furiously. Her power had expanded and slammed across the cavern. The pond water boiled into a churning sea and huge chunks of ice shot up into the air.

When the crazy dragon fully formed, she pulled her spiked head back with jaws open to snap his head off. In that split second, Tristan had one last idea to save his ass.

He yelled, *"I can teleport!"*

Her dragon's head whipped forward.

He braced for the attack.

She swung her head to the side instead and unleashed a quick blast of fire.

It burned a hole in the rock wall.

Tristan would have ended up a pile of ashes.

No regenerating from ashes.

When he'd stopped breathing like a horse run to ground and realized he'd dodged a fire bullet, he repeated, "I. Can. Teleport."

He'd wanted to be sure she got that part.

Seeing her spew fire brought back the conversation he'd had with Daegan about a red dragon filmed burning forests in two countries.

Daegan contended that could not be a true red dragon. The fire had been confined as if shot through a tube where Daegan's dragon fire spread out for maximum damage.

Brynhild's fire had blasted out in a narrow stream for seconds, then fizzled.

Right after the fire, she blew a stream of frozen water across the ceiling of the cavern. Had her dragon done that to clear the smoky taste from her mouth?

When that giant dragon head swung around to face Tristan, brilliant blue eyes with elongated black irises stared at him. Her dragon had a smoother voice than Daegan's. "What did you say about teleporting?"

Tristan finally exhaled the air from lungs filled to capacity. "I can teleport. We can get out of here." He hadn't wanted to give up his ace so soon, but it would have done him little good to die with that information.

"I do not believe you."

He jumped at the chance to convince her before he faced Brynhild-the-Terminator part two. "I can prove it if you remove these manacles."

"*You think to trick me?*" her dragon roared.

Damn woman.

Tristan's hearing would never recover from that ear-crushing sound so close. "What would be the point in tricking you when I want out of here as much as you want freedom? It should be worth your time to give me a chance to show you what I can do. Don't you want to live without a tether to Cathbad?"

Yep, he had gone all in on escaping.

Her dragon had eyed him for a bit then walked away, hopped, then took flight around the cavern.

Tristan had to close his eyes to keep flying pieces of ice that broke loose from blinding him. Her wings sent ice of all sizes airborne. He had cuts on his face, arms, upper body. Thankfully, he'd still had jeans on protecting his lower half. The air dropped twenty degrees.

As she flew in her tight little airspace, her dragon blew out long streams of ice. She circled again and again, but the constant turning and flapping clearly burned up energy. When her dragon landed, Brynhild changed back to her human form.

She did it quickly and clothed herself in the same battle armor. Walking toward his hanging body, she had the swagger of a warrior who had known victory more than once. In addition to that black armor with silver emblems, her hair wove itself into tight braids, half of which were pulled back and tied with a leather thong by an invisible hand. The rest fell loose.

Black kohl outlined her sparkling blue eyes. That and the thick lashes created a dramatic effect.

Her perfect skin and sculpted lips belonged on a runway model in New York.

Beneath all that blond hair hid a supernatural homicidal maniac.

But she had been Tristan's only ticket out of that cave before Cathbad could begin turning him into a polymorph, one capable of destroying Treoir before Daegan's dragon would have been forced to kill Tristan. Daegan wouldn't have known who he was until Tristan died. Tristan had been willing to do anything to save his boss and friend from so horrible a fate.

Tristan's body ached from too many ice wounds to count, none of which would heal until he could draw on his gryphon's power.

A rumbling noise shook him back to the present.

Thunder?

Getting struck by lightning would cap his crappy day.

Brynhild's dragon made a soft cawing noise as if she liked something she saw.

What had drawn her beast's attention?

And no one could see Brynhild's dragon while she flew brazenly in public. She had the ability to cloak her dragon, even while in the air.

Did Daegan know that little detail?

If Tristan made it through this flight and whatever she had in mind for him, he had a lot to share with Daegan.

First he had to survive.

Brynhild had broken the spelled chains holding Tristan to the stone wall and let his abused body fall to the floor. His right knee had buckled when he tried to stand. The cold initially numbing the pain in his kneecap no longer helped now that a blanket warmed his legs just enough to feel again. Every time her dragon dipped or banked, his knee suffered a jagged ache.

He'd been so sure he could teleport away from her the minute she freed him, but she'd proven to be more clever than he realized and stayed a jump ahead.

The minute he managed to stand on his bad leg in the cavern, she'd produced a dagger. She shoved his wrist against the stone wall and stabbed the dagger through his forearm, pinning him in place.

That had hurt like a mother.

He was lucky she hadn't killed him right then for the curses he'd shouted at her. She'd smiled instead, evidently more at home with confirmation of her warrior ability than a compliment that almost got him killed.

Rocking the knife to pull it loose from the stone, she'd kept the blade stabbed through his arm as she half-dragged him limping beside her to the mouth of the cave. Every move jarred the sharp blade. He'd come close to passing out. With her lack of patience, she would have probably just killed him on the spot, then regretted the rash decision later.

When she reached the front entrance to the cave, she nodded at the huge boulder blocking their exit and said, "Ledge is on other side of large stone. Teleport there."

With blood running down his arm and shivering from shock, Tristan croaked, "You can't move that rock?"

"Yes, but druid put ward in place," she'd yelled at him.

Having his eardrums blasted again kept him from losing consciousness. "You still have to take the other manacle off for me to teleport."

"I will, but know this." She leaned around to his face, leaving no chance of misunderstanding her words. "I will have my hand on this dagger and your neck the very moment I remove the manacle. Try to teleport without me and I stab you somewhere next time that will hold a man's attention."

His balls shriveled at that warning.

He uttered in a thin voice, "No tricks."

Good to her word, she looped the dangling chain from his manacle around the arm holding the dagger. The second she released the manacle from his wrist, she clamped her fingers on his throat.

Tristan considered all the ways teleporting somewhere unfamiliar could go wrong and kill him. He also had a fleeting thought of trying to teleport somewhere he knew, but feared he might be too drained of energy to teleport the entire way. He was not risking his death when he still had a chance to escape.

He'd asked, "How wide is the ledge outside?"

"Four strides away from boulder. Six strides wide. Do not miss or you will fall to your death where I will shift into my dragon and fly away."

That required teleporting up and over the ward shielding the entrance.

He hoped like hell Cathbad had not warded more than this

opening.

Brynhild wouldn't care that teleporting was not a natural gift, but an ability he'd gained by downing a witch highball out of desperation in the past. That had been back when the goddess Macha had imprisoned him in a spelled jungle location in South America just for being an Alterant.

Screwed by another female and no desire to kiss either one. "Get ready. I'm teleporting us."

Brynhild scoffed, "I have been ready for long time."

He called up his gryphon power, hoping for enough to teleport the short distance and that his arm would not heal around the damn dagger. Then he closed his eyes and hoped he possessed a bit of luck.

When he reappeared, snow and mountains stretched forever. His toes hung over the edge of a cliff with nothing below him for thousands of feet with him teetering forward.

His heart tried to claw its way up his throat at the vision of falling to his death.

She yanked him back on solid ground and clamped the manacle onto his bad wrist.

He shouted, "I'm fuckin' freezin'." She conjured up fur and leather clothing on his body.

He'd considered shifting right then and fighting his way out, but Brynhild being a dragon shifter stifled that idea. Even if they had been equal in power, she had not been tortured for hours or stabbed with a dagger.

She immediately wrapped the chain around his neck, ending all hope of shifting.

Whatever spell Cathbad had placed on the chain and manacles blocked Tristan's gryphon power.

"You will teleport us to my homeland."

Tristan had a pretty good idea where that was, but still asked, "Where did you grow up?"

"Are you daft? You know of dragons but not the home of the ice dragons?"

"Actually, I do know where that is, but if we teleport there you might get attacked." Truth, but Tristan was more concerned with landing in an open area without conflict to give him a chance to find a way to escape.

"Humans are everywhere today," she groused.

Tristan thought about the place he'd gone with Daegan with the team where Vikings had once suffocated innocent women and children in an underground cave hundreds of years ago. That's when Tristan learned that Noirre majik, the worst of all black majik, originated from the cadavers in that cave.

He hoped to convince Brynhild of going there. "You're right about humans being everywhere these days, but I once went to a place called County Kilkenny, which isn't far from where I believe your king's castle to be. It has people mostly during the day. I did a lot of hiking there and think I can land us out of view from the humans."

"Yes, do this." She swung her lethal gaze close to his face. "Take me to wrong place and I will cut out an eye."

Bloodthirsty female. His body couldn't hurt more if someone had pushed him headfirst through a woodchipper. "Got it."

When she removed the chain and manacle, Tristan teleported, but that one trip drained his energy big time. When they landed, rain battered his body and drenched him. This fur and leather outfit she'd dressed him in weighed more than medieval metal armor.

Through the downpour, he saw land, but no idea if he'd hit his mark.

Without pausing to say a word, she wrapped his head with a dark cloth, clamped the manacle on his arm again, and pushed him to the ground. The chain jerked like she'd stomped on the section closest to his arm with her foot. Damn her.

Power had sizzled and burst around him.

Ah, shit. When she shifted into that freaking dragon, he'd shouted, "Humans have big weapons to kill dragons." He wouldn't care, but she had no plans to turn him loose and didn't want to be blown to pieces with her.

"No one sees mine. I will cloak dragon."

In the next minute, the chain attached to the manacle yanked hard, pulling him to his feet by his freaking wounded arm. He'd call her a sadist, but she didn't seem to derive pleasure from hurting him.

That would require human emotion.

It was more that she saw her actions as a means to an end.

None of that softened the agony of her abuse.

He'd stood there in the driving rain, waiting for her next move. Then he heard the loud beating of massive wings.

The sound diminished the farther she flew away from him.

Had she left?

What the hell?

His pulse had raced with a renewed energy. He could escape? He'd gotten her to this point.

She didn't need him anymore, right?

He'd decided to give it a minute to be sure she had been gone long enough then ...

A loud whooshing sound surrounded him, then his body was yanked up in the air, claws pinning his arms tight on both sides.

He couldn't guess how long ago that had been. Shock continued to rack his body with cold chills, causing his teeth to rattle so hard he had to clamp them to keep from biting his tongue.

She'd been flying straight into a strong wind since then, getting his head battered. The ends of the blindfold slapped around.

Claws larger than his gryphon's held him in an unyielding grip. If only he could shift into his gryphon, he could heal.

He couldn't see a damn thing.

No idea where she headed.

Sharp pellets of rain smacked any exposed skin as she flew them straight into a storm. Thunder pounded everywhere.

Time passed at its own whim.

Blood loss had him losing consciousness then the dragon's wild movements would jerk him awake.

His stomach flipped when the dragon dropped suddenly from the sky, a move that required Tristan's gryphon to tuck his wings.

He now had more appreciation for Evalle who often suffered vertigo when teleporting.

Flying *Bitch-hild Airline* sucked.

The dragon's movement slowed. That would be her setting her wings for landing.

Ah shit, was she going to land all that heavy-ass body on top of him?

Nope.

She dropped him what felt like ten feet off the ground. He hit, rolling hard until he flopped to a stop. It knocked the wind out of him. His chest hurt like hell and he sucked hard to get air. His head spun.

Human fingers curled around his arm, right above the wound, and lifted him to his feet. He'd never harmed a woman, but this being was no woman.

Brynhild was a monster in female skin.

She yanked the covering off his eyes.

He blinked to see against the deluge of water striking him in the face. She had his bad arm by the chain, but he lifted his free hand to wipe his face. "Where are we?"

"My favorite place when I started shifting into dragon as a young girl." She actually smiled as she tossed his blindfold away and turned her back on him.

It took him a minute to understand why she didn't worry about leaving him on his own as she walked to the edge of the ground they stood upon.

Tristan squinted, taking in the spectacular cliffs far out to his right and left with an ocean beyond.

Lightning sparked and fingered across the heavens like bony witches fingers.

Not a person or building in any direction.

He had no idea where he was, but he had a plan.

He'd left his gryphon alone when he had no chance of healing or breaking free, but he could feel energy seeping into his uninjured arm. Maybe the spell on the chain and manacle only worked if the chain made a complete wrap around his neck or both wrists were shackled, like an electrical circuit.

Brynhild held her arms out wide, staring at the surging sea rocked by the storm. She laughed loud and wildly. *"I am back!"*

While she ignored him, clearly thinking she had him under control, Tristan called up energy into his not-as-injured left arm.

Power rushed through the same arm and flooded his hand.

Claws broke out of his fingertips.

Hope pounded his skull.

He glanced at Brynhild. Still lost in her moment of freedom, holding her face up to the torrent coming down. Her blond braids slapped her body when the wind whipped her hair around.

It was now or never.

His damaged right arm would be useless until it healed. He couldn't teleport unless he freed that arm.

Screw it. He called up his gryphon as fast as he could and sucked up his backbone. The minute his jaws were wide enough to bite off his right hand, he'd free himself and teleport away.

He'd never tried to teleport in gryphon form, but today was as good a day as any to find out if it would work.

His body began shifting.

Excitement rushed through him. His chest expanded. His head reshaped, but not very fast. He needed jaws powerful enough to snap bone and cut through his wrist the first time. He didn't think he could make a second bite.

His wings began to form.

Brynhild turned around and screeched, *"Stop!"*

She stomped her way toward him with hands fisted and face warped in a fit of rage. *"No shifting or you die!"*

Fuck that. He kept begging his gryphon to break free.

Brynhild slammed to a stop. She started peeling off armor

and shifting as she did.

Tristan clenched his fists and called hard on his power, but his shift would not happen in time.

Even if it did, his gryphon couldn't rip off his hand before the dragon chomped off his beast's head.

CHAPTER 4

QUESTIONS HANGING AT THE EDGE of Casidhe's tongue would have to wait. She couldn't very well ask Daegan anything about Skarde right now.

She had to take her time and get to know him well enough to talk about his family's history.

One misstep and she'd expose her connection to Herrick.

Wouldn't the red dragon love that?

What if she failed to get information on Skarde after being this close to Daegan? Herrick would be furious. Worse, he'd be disappointed. She took a couple breaths, trying to keep her heartbeat under control.

"What has your heart racin', Luigsech?" Daegan asked, his eyes taking in her every movement. Legs stretched out in front of him, Daegan had the casual pose of someone relaxed. But one look in his dark silver gaze smashed that image. Fully alert, Daegan dangled on the edge of action.

Damn his dragon shifter abilities for sensing so much.

He was back to calling her by her last name, too. They had been on better footing when he'd called her lass.

Before he noticed anything else, she shrugged and twisted her office chair back toward the desk. "What you claim about the Luigsech family bein' concerned only with Treoir history may have been true two thousand years ago, but—"

"'Twas true," he affirmed.

"Okay, fine." She shifted around to face him again. "I did not live then, but I can tell you that *today's* Luigsech descendant who becomes an ancestral archivist is expected to keep the general history of *many* things from all time periods." Having sidestepped that topic as best she could, she hurried on. "As for why I was chosen, I studied at the feet of a very old Luigsech aunt alongside the family's oldest blood-daughter named Gale. She had a photographic memory. *She* was expected to be the next family historian. I was to have been her assistant."

"What do ya mean by photographic memory?" Daegan leaned back and crossed his ankles.

"It means that Gale could recall anythin' she ever heard or saw after just one time. She needed no promptin'."

"With such a gift, why would she need your help?"

He hadn't asked that in an insulting way, but the question still stung. "If you consider the information accumulated over more than two thousand years, you would realize that no one can pass along every tiny bit of information. She had a natural gift for memory and I have a natural gift for research. We would have made a great team."

The kind of memory Gale had would have been a nice gift, too, but Casidhe would not trade her power of translating any text.

Still, she'd worked her butt off to keep up with so much information over the years.

"Why is Gale not here now?" Daegan asked.

Casidhe hadn't talked about this in years and wouldn't now if she had another choice. Pushing past the lump in her throat, she explained, "Gale had an insatiable curiosity about everythin'. While huntin' a plant in the mountains, a deadly viper bit her. She panicked and ran. By the time her family found her, she was very sick and died a day later."

"'Tis terrible to lose a child."

She paused, surprised by the honesty in his voice.

He asked, "What about the other daughters?"

"The next one in line was too young to be expected to just step into Gale's shoes, plus she became withdrawn when her sister died. The whole family had a tough time. I was thirteen and Gale was my best friend as much as a foster sister." Casidhe's voice trailed off. She cleared her throat, determined to get this all out. "Their elderly aunt passed away in her sleep six months later. I think her heart never recovered from losin' the niece she'd spent most of her last ten years tutorin'. It was all heartbreakin'."

Emotion flooded her at recalling that horrible time.

Gale had been her lifeline, Casidhe's only shield against the deep loneliness of being an outsider.

She and the Luigsechs had been living in Herrick's castle back then. He'd told Casidhe to continue the Luigsech legacy of being a historian of the dragon history from there on. Fenella's Connell squire family filled in spots of history where Casidhe had not received all the details from the Luigsech aunt.

When Daegan didn't badger her for more, she opened her eyes and lifted her head with pride for the position she'd been given. "Everyone agreed I would become the new family historian. I was honored to be handed the duty."

"What do ya know of the Treoirs?"

Shaking off her melancholy, she went back on alert. "Why? Don't you know your own history?"

He leveled her with a look that warned she tipped his patience in the wrong direction. Large fingers on one hand tapped slowly on the chair arm. "To be honest, no. I was captured before my da died and his castle fell in the Dragani War. He and I were doin' all we could to discover who was pittin' dragon houses against one another."

Slicing a narrowed look at him, she said, "So your red dragon had nothin' to do with startin' the Dragani War?"

Fury darkened his gaze and made her want to squirm.

"No. Is that what ya were told, Luigsech?" Suspicion in his voice warned she was back on bad footing again.

Just great. Now he was going to push her even more on the Treoirs.

But he didn't. Daegan stood quickly and changed the subject. "We waste time. Ya should be huntin' the grimoire."

"Wait a minute, buster. I answered your questions." She made no move to stand and start researching. "That should be enough for you to stop accusin' me of bein' a poser. If *you* know so much, why don't you know where to hunt for the grimoire volumes?"

He inhaled deeply and exhaled slowly, which did nothing to lessen the tension in the air. "The grimoire was created, discovered, broken into three volumes, and hidden many years before my birth. I had never heard of its existence until recently. If I had all that information, I would not be here."

She frowned, surprised the grimoire origins went back that far.

"Ya waste time," Daegan groused again.

"So do you," she tossed back at him. "Now it's your turn to produce information on Fenella. That was the deal. At the moment, you don't seem to be holdin' up your end. Where is Quinn and why hasn't he gotten back to you by now?"

"Quinn had to travel to Atlanta to speak with our people."

Her lips parted. "Atlanta? As in the United States?"

Daegan nodded.

She fought off an attack of longing. Quinn hadn't been gone long enough to fly back. He either teleported or someone else teleported him. She'd love to have that ability and visit other places, the US, maybe even a South Pacific island.

He said, "Ya must allow Quinn a bit of time to gain answers."

She knew a delay tactic when she heard one. "Why should I believe anythin' you say?"

CHAPTER 5

DAEGAN FORCED HIMSELF TO NOT snap at Luigsech. Why should she believe him? Because he'd told her his true identity.

Sharing that had been no small thing.

She lifted that pert chin with her stubborn look, the challenging one he saw more often than not.

Still he had a difficult time holding on to his anger while the lass had shared how she'd ended up taking over as the new squire for the Treoir history. He was not Storm, a living lie detector, but he'd heard truth in her words.

If only a niggling feeling that she hid something important did not continue to peck at him.

When she leaned her elbow on her desk to prop her head, golden-red hair picked up small fragments of light from the late day dancing through the village outside the centre.

She had a young and innocent look about her, but he would not confuse that with being naïve.

More reason to not trust a word out of her mouth he could not verify. Now that she realized Quinn might be a while responding, he had to push her back to the task at hand.

Instead of replying to why she should trust him, he asked, "How do ya plan to find the grimoire?"

Her gaze moved away from him.

Had that been to delay hunting the book or to sift through her thoughts for an explanation?

While he waited, he sent another message out to his second-in-command. *Tristan, if ya hear me call back. Just speak to me.*

Nothing again.

She grudgingly began explaining, "I may have to dig through a lot of books to find a startin' point. Sometimes I may find nothin' more than a tiny speck of information linked to a time period, historical event, or geographical area where the grimoire was believed lost. From there, I keep diggin'."

"Grimoire was not lost."

Eyeing him with a chilly glance, she stood and stretched her back. "Ah, that's right, the book was broken into three parts and each one hidden. But as no one knows where any of those volumes are today, that makes them lost in my way of thinkin'."

He knew the whereabouts of one volume locked away in the VIPER vault, but he wanted information on all of the volumes. "What is next?"

"I have no idea." She gave him a bite of her own impatience with that answer. "One snippet of information might lead me to a major detail or it may only put my foot on the first step of a path that could be a short trip or a long journey."

He would not allow her to run him in circles. "Ya have a week to find the grimoire. 'Tis the length of your journey."

She shoved the desk chair back into place under the desk and turned to him. "Do you think givin' me some arbitrary deadline will be makin' this search happen faster?"

His dragon growled in reaction to Daegan's irritation.

Luigsech's eyes rounded and she took a step back.

That infuriated him even more. "I smell your fear. I have not threatened ya. I merely tell ya time shall mean the difference between life and death for others."

Then he lifted his hand in a silent order to say nothing as Quinn's voice came into Daegan's head. *I have information on Fenella.*

What is it?

We retrieved Fenella's mobile phone number from Casidhe Luigsech's phone. I'll spare you how our technical people can track those phones, but Fenella's phone is moving through Ireland. She may or may not be in possession of the device, so it doesn't mean her body is traveling with her phone through Ireland. But it's a good sign that Cathbad might not have her.

'Tis good to know, Quinn. How are things in Atlanta?

A lot going on, but nothing I can't handle.

Daegan felt pulled in every direction. He wanted to protect his people back home and support his Beladors. He had to find Tristan, but he also needed any part of the grimoire he could get his hands on to save Devon, Renata, and the others.

To save their world from Imortiks.

Daegan ended the conversation with Quinn and lowered his hand to address Luigsech. "Quinn has located information on Fenella."

Relief burst into Luigsech's face. "Where is she?"

"He has no specifics yet, only that our people have located your friend's mobile phone and are on her trail. They believe she is likely not with Cathbad ... yet."

Casidhe reached for her backpack. "Good enough. Tell me what you have and I can probably find her right away on my own."

"No."

"No? You can't hold back information on Fenella. I've been worried sick over her. I can find her." She shoved the pack back on the floor with a heavy thud.

"Quinn shall continue to send me information as our people discover more. I shall tell ya what we have after ya locate one of the grimoire volumes."

"No!" She slapped her hand on her desk. "Do ya think I'm just goin' to go off lookin' for this damned grimoire with Fenella in danger? I have no idea how long it may take to find that stupid book, or volumes, whatever. I need to know about Fenella *now*. She could be in trouble and your people might not even realize it."

Venom still pulsed in Daegan's body and concerns about his ability to tap power when he needed it had him on edge. His snarl came out inhumanly deep. "Tristan *is* in trouble.

I want to find him immediately. My people *are* in trouble. Now we both have a strong desire to find the grimoire sooner rather than later. I suggest ya get busy huntin' it."

"I will *not!* I have no reason to trust you."

He took a step and leaned toward her, staring hard into her hostile eyes. "I do not trust ya either, but I need ya." He let that sink in first then added, "Ya need me too. It does not help Fenella if ya go runnin' into one of Cathbad's traps. My man caught by Cathbad could teleport and he has as yet been unable to escape. Ya have few choices. Help me, and I shall help ya. Trust me ... and I shall trust ya."

He got her mulish look in reply.

Daegan leaned until their noses almost touched. "'Tis simple. Work with me ya hardhead if ya want Fenella back."

Luigsech pressed her lips tight and her eyes shined with unshed tears.

Before he had a chance to calm her down, she scowled at him. "I'll look for your damn book, but if anythin' happens to Fenella, you will wish you had never met me."

He would not undermine her show of a strong backbone by soothing her now. Instead, he said, "I shall take that as an agreement. What would help ya find this book?"

Breathing hard through her nose, she stared him down for a minute then shook her head at some thought she would not share. After a stretch of seconds, she became all business. "You said the grimoire was broken into three volumes. It would help to know who the last people were to possess the volumes. That would narrow the hunt down from a *bazillion* possible hidin' places to maybe only a million," she replied sarcastically.

"Ya have a twisted sense of humor," he pointed out, glad to have her snapping at him and not hurt.

"I have lost *all* ability to find any of this humorous. Considerin' my life since meetin' ya, that should not be surprisin'." She walked around him and through the opening into the rear area of the centre with books piled on every shelf.

He held back a retort. His anger grew from many seeds before he met her. He had no desire to wound the lass, who had gone through so much in her life, but he mentally warred between pushing her to act faster and taking a lighter approach to let her work at her own pace.

The lighter approach won out.

He sighed, now feeling guilty over not demanding more, and attributed his desire to not push her harder as nothing more than a natural desire to protect a female.

Ruadh's voice ghosted through Daegan's mind. *You have never lied to yourself before.*

What was his dragon talking about? Daegan replied silently, but with a sharp edge to his tone, *I tell no lie now. Luigsech is annoying, but still a woman to be shielded from harm.*

I see. You would protect Queen Medb?

Daegan had walked into Ruadh's trap, something that had not happened in a very long time. *Ya know very well that queen does not fall under my protection.*

Ruadh quieted, leaving Daegan to stew with those thoughts. He stalked into the book area in the back.

Darkness swallowed Luigsech, her movements that of a shadow. She tossed an order at him. "I'll be needin' some light unless you want me to turn all of them on back here."

He lifted a hand where he called up a flame to sit upon his palm. With the sun not setting until much later this evening and the cloaking he'd created across the window facing the street, he doubted anyone could see a light in here. Still, the flame in his palm would not expose their presence.

"Are you nuts?" she screeched. "Put out that flame." She looked at his hand in horror as if he held the head of a bloody kitten.

"Why?"

"This library is filled with rare books, one of a kind literature, not to mention all the research material I've accrued over ten years." She sounded close to doing what Tristan called hyperventilating.

"Ya need to calm down and breathe, lass," Daegan instructed her. "I have the flame under control."

Her eyes glowed supernaturally blue and she twisted her hands in front her. She whispered in a tiny voice, "Please. I'm beggin' ya. No fire."

His sigh could have been heard a mile away. He closed his hand, killing the flame. He crossed his arms. "Ya still need light."

She had her hand on her chest, breathing fast. "Give me a minute."

Imortiks and demons had not panicked her, but a small flame terrified her. If she knew him better, she'd know that he would protect all this history with his life. He needed to learn what had happened with his family and the world while he'd sat imprisoned for centuries.

Queen Maeve had stolen everything from him.

Luigsech appeared to have recovered. She strode past him, returning to the sitting area where he heard her pulling out drawers and digging around. She muttered to herself the whole time.

The sound of a drawer being shoved closed snapped loudly in the silence before she entered the back area again shining a tiny light. Speaking to him as though he had trouble understanding simple words, she held up the light. "This is an LED, somethin' we use today for instant light instead of startin' a fire in a freakin' archival library."

"I did not start a fire," he argued.

She turned to him. "That's like claimin' a dog won't bite because it belongs to you and you trust it. If the animal has teeth, it has potential. If you flick open a flame in your hand, that flame could burn this building down before you managed to stop the fire."

Dismissing him, she waved her wee light at the shelves as she walked away mumbling to herself again, pausing to read text, then moving on. Halfway back, she pulled out a thick book and handed it to him without looking his way. "Hold this."

He stepped over and took it.

She did that three more times until he had a tall stack on one hand.

"That should be enough to get me started," she murmured as she turned to him. Her gaze landed on the books. She snapped, "Two hands, dammit. Don't ever risk damagin' a book by holdin' that much weight with one hand."

"'Tis not a strain," he told her dryly.

"I don't care. Two. Hands. Give it to me." She shoved the light into her mouth and took the books from him, cradling them like babes. Then she grumbled something he couldn't figure out due to talking around the light between her teeth.

When he followed her into the front area again, she promptly sat in her reading chair and shot him a look he took as *mine*. She placed the books in her lap, removed the light from her mouth, and placed it on the table beside her.

Luigsech asked in a frosty tone, "Are you goin' to stand over me as I read?"

"I have not decided." What an unusual woman who quivered at the idea of a tiny flame but jumped into fight deadly beings.

She huffed out a sound that could be a sigh or a growl.

He walked across the room, giving her his back, anything that would encourage her to get busy.

Anxious to find Tristan, Daegan sent out another telepathic message. *Tristan, call me. Tell me where ya are.*

Tristan's voice erupted in his head, yelling, *I escaped, but I'm not gonna make it. Cathbad and a dragon are after you. Get out of Ireland now and save everyone before ...*

Then nothing.

CHAPTER 6

"*STAY HERE!*" DAEGAN ORDERED, THEN vanished from where he'd been standing only three feet from her reading chair.

Casidhe stared at the spot, trying to wrap her head around what had happened.

He had teleported.

She knew he could, based upon what she'd been taught about that dragon shifter, but it did not lessen the shock of someone disappearing in a blink.

What should she do now?

Daegan was gone.

She could escape and find Fenella on her own.

She snatched up the desk phone and dialed Fenella, excited at the chance to hear her friend's voice. The phone rang over and over, then went to voice mail.

Casidhe slammed the receiver back onto the base.

Why was Fenella not answering her phone?

Because she was not with the phone. Casidhe dropped her face into her hands. What was she missing? She sat up then dropped back in the chair. This was an opportunity, but she had to make the right choice.

What would happen if she escaped and was not here when Daegan returned? She didn't even know how long that would take.

He'd be furious.

She could live with that. Or could she? He'd presented a case for working together.

Daegan would help her find Fenella and she'd help him

find the grimoire to save his people, but then he refused to tell her the location of Fenella's phone.

In fact, she had zero proof Quinn or any of his people had found anything on Fenella's phone. Daegan could have been staring off at nothing when he supposedly received telepathy then just lied to her.

On the other hand, here she was thinking about abandoning him as he tried to help his people.

What proof did she have he really intended to use that grimoire to save anyone and not use it for his own gain?

She grabbed her hair. How had all this become *her* problem?

Because she wanted to find Fenella.

Casidhe jumped to her feet and shook her fists at herself. "You're so stupid!" She'd been so torn up worrying about Fenella, she'd grasped at the first straw of hope. How could she know for sure what was going on with Fenella?

Her friend might be with Cathbad or hiding somewhere if that druid, or someone else, had frightened her. Casidhe only knew one thing for sure.

If Fenella was in no danger, she'd be calling for Casidhe. If the roles were reversed, Fenella would not take some stranger's word that he knew anything about Casidhe being safe or not.

Daegan wanted to find out who had his friend and Casidhe had handed that to him by allowing Quinn to go into her mind.

Daegan's only motivation for helping Casidhe hunt Fenella was the grimoire. If he got his hands on one or more of the volumes, would he still save Fenella or just teleport away?

That was a duh question if she'd ever had one.

Fenella had no one squarely in her corner with no hidden agenda except Casidhe.

Stomping around the room, Casidhe cursed herself for letting emotions make her decisions.

Screw sitting here.

If she figured out how to find even one volume of the grimoire, she'd get her hands on that volume first and have leverage over Daegan to make his people find Fenella.

That sick feeling of missing something and leaving her friend out on her own lightened a little. Casidhe had a plan, which did not involve taking orders from a dragon shifter who was the enemy.

The minute she left here, she might not get another chance to use her library to track anything. She had no idea how much time was left until Daegan popped back in.

She crossed the room and sat in her chair again.

With him gone, she could use her power to translate the pages at a much faster speed.

She raced through the pages, still careful as she turned them. Once she had her power humming, the pages began moving as she waved a single finger across the top of them.

That was new, but welcome.

Nothing helpful showed up in the first book. She put it aside, heart racing to find anything before Daegan appeared.

Where had he gone?

Who cared? Not her.

Was he in danger?

Who cared? Not her ... well maybe. She didn't really care, but she did need him to find Fenella.

What if Cathbad showed up?

"Argh!" Her shout banged the walls. What if she reached old age worrying about crap she had no control over?

Back to the books, she scanned faster, put book two aside, and had cracked open the third one when she stopped over halfway in. This book had been written by a man thought to have been a bard who became a writer. He claimed to have been in the courts of royalty and other places people would not believe.

He wrote of great warriors and battles.

She'd read about similar accounts by others, but then she found a section where he wrote about how myth and reality were two sides of the same coin.

Backing up a page, she slowly went over the text again.

One knowledgeable in reading ancient languages would

have found these passages and translated the magical parts as mythological musings.

She had a trained eye to watch for the meaning beneath the words, especially in medieval text and older.

As she moved her finger slowly above the text, which then lifted off the page in golden symbols, she paused to read one line.

To hide the words is to hide the truth, but those of us who lived before the time of dragons will not lie.

She read on as the writer told of his ancestor who claimed dragons once roamed the world and owned the skies.

Casidhe sat back and considered this man's words as she stared out the window where a woman from the yarn shop chatted with the baker across the street.

Her gaze tripped back to the book. His writing had a cryptic style. He seemed to have a great story to tell, but wrote as if he could not share every piece. She'd been told dragon history by the best, the families who passed it down from generation to generation. She'd read hundreds of books on the mythology and writers who challenged the reader to think past the normal and open one's mind to the fantastical.

Those would often leave her chuckling.

But this book did not raise a smile.

This man spoke of a great war among the dragons that destroyed the families.

What made this war stand out is that in other books, the writers would always state how a powerful dragon belonging to a supernatural being had been victorious.

This book had danced around the dragon history, saying only that a war had erupted between families who had been allies and ended with no victor.

Dragons had vanished.

Sitting up to search the pages again, she ran over and over the same words, looking for any hint at the writer's true name. He'd opened by saying he would not share his identity, only that of his ancestor, the one who knew the truth.

She'd found this book in an estate sale and had kept it

because of a foolish reason. She'd enjoyed the lyrical way he'd put words to paper.

Her eyes glazed over and her finger slipped down to touch the page.

A flash of golden symbols jumped so high she dropped the book in her lap and lurched back.

When she removed her finger from the book, the symbols disappeared.

Heart thumping in her chest, she sat forward again and put her finger on the previous word, then made tiny movements with it until the leading edge of the bright letters of a name began to slowly rise high again.

Who was that? The ancestor?

Once again, she read every word in this small passage, then moved on, reading quickly to the end. When she cracked open book four, she knew in the first ten pages it would be of no service to her.

She put the three she could not use away and lifted her LED light in two fingers. She shined the light over books in that same section from the time of just before Herrick had been born.

Lost in her thoughts, she continued to the end and turned to face the back wall of the library area.

Tall bookcases shielding her secret escape door hung two inches away from the wall on one side. She moved it open slowly. The clasp had been broken and the frame torn. Who had ripped open her exit door?

Daegan? No, he would have teleported in.

Cathbad.

The druid must not have had access to the special ability one of Daegan's people had. That person had remotely viewed how Casidhe had accessed this escape route from the centre.

That meant Cathbad teleported in here too since the front door had not been damaged.

Seeing this only pushed her to hurry more.

She jumped back into her search, pulling out books and

quickly deciding if they were useful or not.

She'd exhausted her initial search. Any time that happened, she'd go to her next resource level of finding someone who could tell her more about what she had discovered so far or where to look if she had hit a dead end.

Who would be able to enlighten her on this topic?

Staring unfocused, she searched her cluttered brain for where she would go next to research more on the time before Daegan had been born.

Humans would not understand what she hunted. They would have no more than what she had and not anything close to what she'd been taught as a Luigsech.

Asking humans the questions pounding her head would make her sound like a lunatic or she'd end up in the media right in the middle of the supernatural chaos leaking into the human world.

She needed to find someone ... *like her.*

Cathbad would probably be a great resource, if not for him possibly wanting to kill her by now.

"If he kills me, I won't return his book." She snorted at that ridiculous thought, an indication she was losing her mind in all of this.

Hold it.

What was in *the druid's* book?

She hurried to the front room and dug through her backpack, pulling out his book. Holding it in this stillness, she could feel a tiny hum of energy.

Should she open the section he'd warned her about?

Why not? Like it mattered now if she read it against his will?

She paused. The book was titled *Before Ainvar*. Before jumping into an ancient book on majik and dark druids that Cathbad had indicated would tattle on her if she read the text without him present, she needed to determine the identity of Ainvar first. That would take some time.

Wait, what the hell was she doing? The one commodity she couldn't waste right now was time.

Was reading *anything* about druids really important when she had to find a grimoire volume and Fenella? She sat back hard, filled with indecision. She was no closer to finding the grimoire than she'd been the first time Cathbad mentioned it.

She slashed a look at Cathbad's book again. That druid was as old as Daegan and Herrick. Why would he have wanted her to translate text from one of his books?

Could it be because the druid book had been written before *his* time?

If so, had the original format for Cathbad's book been a scroll? The scroll could have been converted to a book later on when codex form came along.

What about the grimoire?

She didn't even have the name of the person who wrote the Immortuos Grimoire, much less a scribe who might have assisted. She knew most of the annals on dragon history by heart, the rest she knew from spoken word.

If the grimoire had been created prior to Daegan and Herrick's birth, according to Daegan, chances were the original text had been written on papyrus or parchment.

She sat up suddenly.

Adrenaline woke every nerve in her body.

What if the grimoire was not in a book-like format right now at all? She would be wasting her time to focus on searching her usual way for an actual *book*.

This grimoire was more than an old book or scroll. A supernatural had developed the majik on those pages to create Imortiks and turn them loose on the world before Daegan and Herrick's time.

But the writing had evidently also possessed the power to force Imortiks behind a death wall when used by other supernaturals.

She'd been tackling this from the wrong direction.

Instead of getting bogged down with every vague detail from the time of dragons, she should search for someone most familiar with the history of grimoires written by supernaturals. Basically, someone who would have credible information on the Immortuos Grimoire, which might be impossible. That would require finding someone with intimate knowledge of supernaturals.

Again, someone like her.

She snapped her fingers, mumbling, "Hold everything. I know who to call ... if he'll talk to me."

Placing the last book on the pile, she moved to her desk and dug through the lower right-hand drawer. Yes, it looked like a rat's nest, but she had her own way of organizing her information. Fenella had tried to help her one time and it had taken Casidhe two days to make sense of what the kind-hearted woman had done.

It had also cost them a client expecting information Casidhe couldn't locate in time.

Fenella never helped again.

Muttering to herself, Casidhe pulled out a chunk of papers, then pushed her fingers around the bottom until she found her business card file, which looked like an oversized wallet.

Not very high-tech, but no one cracked her security code. Not even Fenella.

She sat back and flipped from page to page, scanning cards yellowed from time. No one could read her notes. Only she could translate her scribble.

Turning to the last page of cards, her heart fell as she scanned without seeing ... wait. There it was.

Sliding the card for a local artist out slowly, she turned it over and read her code for his name and contact number.

She protected those who she believed worked toward the best interest of supernaturals.

Redmond Mac Seáin had been considered a foremost expert on Celtic history all the way back to the beginnings. No one questioned his skill and knowledge. Highly-respected institutions had paid him large sums to speak to their students and patrons.

They found the mythology he always included fascinating and enjoyable, but no one believed mythological details on nonhumans could have been real. If they did, they kept those thoughts to themselves.

She'd read his papers and watched films of him speaking. One time, as she'd listened with half an ear, she caught something he said and stopped to replay his words. He'd made a comment in passing, then quickly made it sound as if he'd only joked.

The audience laughed.

She hadn't.

He'd mentioned how dragons once lived until one destroyed them all by allowing himself to be captured.

That history was in no books. She'd know.

While she might disagree on specifics of what destroyed dragons, Redmond Mac Seáin knew things humans did not.

She'd kept this card in case she ever found a lead on Skarde and would have eventually gotten back to that search if not for the last few terrorizing days.

Now she had good reason to talk to this man.

He would still be the sought-after scholar he had not been betrayed. Someone had filmed him secretly while the professor sounded as if he had an encounter with a fairy. Of course, the film showed no one in the room with him during a livid one-sided argument.

He tried to justify his moment, saying as a historian that he considered all details. He suggested others in the academic field should acknowledge the potential credibility of a specific ancient parchment scroll.

That might not have caused much of an uproar if the scroll hadn't included specifics on a conflict among fairies.

Casidhe had seen the secret film. Based on his words and warnings, she believed he'd been communicating with someone nonhuman, and very likely a fairy.

His peers thought him crazy and some friends tried to explain away his actions as becoming senile. The media ran with the story about a professor talking to ghosts and goblins, as per their articles.

After that hit the news, media flocked to the university where he'd been the chair of medieval studies to humiliate him publicly. The media might argue they were doing the public a service, but the end result had been the destruction of his career.

He'd walked away. No one could find him.

One day as Casidhe strolled the streets of Wexford on the eastern coast below Dublin, she caught sight of a man sitting alone with his tea.

While she stood in a doorway across the street watching covertly, or so she'd thought, he lifted his head slowly and turned to her. They stared at each other for long seconds, then he folded his paper, got up, and walked away.

She was drawn to the table where she found this card.

Curiosity had paid off.

She'd spent over a year tracking down a contact number for him, but she never tried to call. She held onto the information for the day she hit a wall and needed help finding Skarde.

Sitting here, she struggled, torn between making the call to request help on finding the grimoire or putting the card aside to use only for hunting Skarde.

She hated indecision.

Herrick had trained her to be decisive if she wanted to survive. Hesitation to act would get a person killed.

That solved her dilemma.

If she found the grimoire, she might be able to use it to force Daegan to share what he knew on Skarde, but only if Casidhe had already found Fenella first.

Dialing the number on the old desk phone, she held the receiver next to her ear.

Redmond answered the phone, "What do you want?"

Knowing his history, Casidhe went hard with honesty up front. "I am looking for help that only someone with your background can provide. I am not the media. I am not a treasure hunter. I preserve the—"

"I am not interested."

"Please don't hang up!" she shouted and cringed at how that must have sounded.

No click. No dial tone returned.

She calmed her voice. "I will not in any way expose your help or your location to the public. We ... " Should she say this or not? No time to go halfway. "We have similar backgrounds. I think you knew that when you left your card for me on a table in Wexford. You are the rare person who would understand ... me."

He didn't hang up, but neither did he speak.

She started twice to talk and stopped. How much was too much with a man who she believed knew about nonhumans?

When he finally spoke, his voice came out in perfectly spaced words. "You ... preserve ... what?"

She drew in a deep breath and let it out, calming her frayed nerves. "I preserve ancestral records for specific families that go back two thousand years and more."

"You are Luigsech," Redmond stated flatly.

CHAPTER 7

DAEGAN HADN'T WASTED A THOUGHT for the venom draining his powers before he teleported out of the centre. He only knew he had to reach Tristan immediately.

Teleporting ended up being slow. Daegan reappeared, stumbling in an onslaught of rain and lightning. He caught his balance and stood on an endless stretch of land ... five strides from Tristan. His second-in-command was in the middle of what appeared to be a slow shift into his gryphon.

Daegan started for him. "Tristan, what is wrong?"

Tristan shouted in Daegan's head, *Watch out for the dragon!*

Whipping around, Daegan took in the miles of cliffs dropping far below to the ocean.

Closer to the edge than he stood, a shifter changed into a sparkling blue and silver dragon.

An ice dragon?

With no time to waste, Daegan called up Ruadh, who had been hammering him to be released. In spite of the sluggish teleportation, his dragon ripped out of his body in a fast, but agonizing change. Muscles stretched, bones lengthened, and his jaw warped with the change to Ruadh's elongated reptilian head.

Rain poured from the heavens as if a dam had been ruptured.

Thunder pounded and shook in a deafening sound.

The iridescent-blue dragon roared and shot a frozen stream of ice and water straight up into the storming skies, then lowered a deadly blue gaze to Daegan's red dragon.

Brynhild.

Her dragon started running and flapping before it shot out another blast of ice and dove at his dragon with jaws open.

Tristan's weak and failing voice warned, *She's with Cathbad. They want to kill you. You gotta go, boss.*

Daegan had no time to reply.

Ruadh dipped down and leaped straight up in the air right before the stream of ice and her dragon reached him. Ruadh launched high enough to kick her dragon in the head and flap hard, leaping away.

She made a crazed screeching sound.

Brynhild might want to annihilate him, but Daegan did not want to kill her if he could help it. He did, however, expect her to pay a price for what she'd done to Tristan.

Ruadh took another step and pushed up, flapping fast to go airborne. His massive dragon body remained thirty feet off the ground as he swooped for the cliff. Gray-blue ocean reached forever until blending with dark clouds releasing a torrent of rain. The ground fell away hundreds of feet beneath Ruadh to where the sea thrashed boulders, which appeared no larger than small skipping stones at this height.

Is she following, Ruadh? Daegan asked, unable to see unless his dragon looked.

Twisting around, Ruadh found the ice dragon hurrying to catch them. That would allow Tristan a chance to finish shifting.

The sea churned waves fifteen feet high and slammed the rocky coastline of Daegan's beloved island. Once Ruadh reached a steady speed flying into the buffeting wind and constant deluge, Daegan directed him to head for the outcroppings farther down the coast.

Brynhild's beast followed, trying to catch Ruadh.

She had never been the most powerful ice dragon. That title had belonged to her brother, Herrick. But she was no easy opponent either.

Ruadh told him, *First we test her.* His dragon banked hard, coming around fast to catch Brynhild's beast by surprise.

The move forced her dragon to cut away hard just before Ruadh sent a short blast of fire.

Daegan told his dragon, *We need that one alive.*

Ruadh replied, *Yes, but she must pay for harming the gryphon first. We must defeat her or she will continue to attack.*

Daegan would not quibble with Ruadh. His dragon had been patient while they waited to find out if Tristan lived. Ruadh valued loyalty above all else and Tristan had proven his time and again.

Ruadh finished his wide bank and continued back along the coastline, intending to push Brynhild's dragon from behind.

But her dragon arced her head straight up, flapping fast, and curled her body over the top of Ruadh's.

Daegan warned, *Ya can't get by her before she lands on top of us. She shall drive us into the rocks below the walls if she comes close enough to blast us with ice.*

She will not.

Ruadh pushed incredibly fast, muscles pumping feverishly to get the most from every flap of his giant wings. The wind knocked him back and forth. Daegan's dragon would expend twice as much energy working against this gale.

Bad idea just before a battle.

Daegan wanted to make Brynhild pay, but not at the risk of crashing into the walls of rock they sped past. Ruadh flew out of reach before her dragon could ice them.

He tried calling out telepathically to Brynhild. *Stop your attack and let us talk.*

Her throaty voice came back sharply. *You. Will. Die.*

Ruadh made a sound that Daegan interpreted as a snort of disdain. He would always support his dragon just as Ruadh supported Daegan no matter what.

He asked Ruadh, *Do ya recall how we trained with Fadil's dragon before I reached adulthood?*

Yes. I forget nothing.

We go there.

His dragon turned into a wind that battered and pushed his large body around, much like the days they had fought Fadil. During those early times with someone Daegan had once called friend, most battles ended in a draw.

Eventually, the red dragon could not be defeated.

As Daegan grew, he studied every warrior in human form, nonhuman form, and dragon form. How else was he to defeat those who wished to war when his duty was to keep the peace?

But while Ruadh would not admit a weakness, Daegan could feel the effort his dragon put out to fly against a strong gale he normally blasted through many times before.

I am the red dragon, Ruadh told him, quieting Daegan's concerns.

Daegan's father had always said, "'Tis only winnin' the next battle that matters, nothin' before, nothin' after. Pay attention to what 'tis right in front of ya."

In the distance, long sections of land jutted away from the coastline reaching toward the horizon. Supportive columns of stone and earth ran from the land to the ocean below. Though solid many thousands of years before Daegan had been born, wind and water had joined forces, carving away the weak parts to suit its purpose.

The result had been tall columns Daegan and Fadil as young boys had used as a training ground for their dragons. They lived for any chance to put themselves through the ultimate test of flying in and out of the narrow passages. They'd shift to their human forms back at home skinned and limping, but recalling every tight turn and bank their dragons had executed.

In the distance, the openings between columns appeared a bit more worn down today, but not much. As Ruadh drew closer to the tall earthen columns interwoven with rocks, Daegan had doubts about his mighty beast weaving through those narrow openings and surviving.

Ruadh twisted his long neck, checking Brynhild's distance from his tail. If she could pull close enough, she would blast ice water and freeze his tail, sending him cartwheeling into the sea and sharp boulders.

She could catch him in those columns.

Daegan would find another way to stop her. He told his dragon, *Go around the columns and find another place to take a stand.*

Ruadh said, *No. We must show her we are strongest. She will not listen to your words if we do not.*

What about the venom that had drained his power for teleporting? Would it affect Ruadh's ability to fly?

Ruadh flew straight at the columns.

Brynhild's dragon screeched a war cry, closing in on Ruadh's tail.

Daegan tried to find the excitement he'd once embraced while flying this course back when he was young, but that had been when no dragon would seriously injure the other. When their community of dragons had an unspoken alliance to protect all of their lands from outsiders.

Entering the hollowed-out vertical openings, Ruadh banked hard left, then back to the right. He wove his way through brilliantly, bursting free over the open sea, then turned in a tight circle.

Ruadh headed straight for the ice dragon emerging from the narrow columns.

Daegan knew his dragon's next move. You didn't share a body for this long without being truly joined.

Brynhild's dragon had only one hope for avoiding the blast of fire coming from Ruadh.

Her beast dove hard, dipping underwater as the blaze boiled water above her. Ruadh eased around in a gentle flight to regain energy. No sign of Brynhild.

Daegan warned, *She sets a trap for ya.*

Ruadh flapped harder heading out to sea through a nonstop deluge of rain, then whipped around quickly and picked up speed, flying to the columns.

Ruadh?

His dragon replied, *This is our battleground. Not hers.*

Daegan said nothing, a solid show of support when they were in the midst of a battle.

Just before Ruadh reached the columns where he had to bank hard right to enter the narrow space sideways, Brynhild's furious dragon exploded out of the sea right behind him. Rivers of water rushed off her dragon's head and wings. With the next flap, she cruised through rain hammering every surface.

Daegan held his thoughts. To remind Ruadh that flying this course backwards had almost crashed them once would only distract his dragon.

Ruadh had the lead and remembered their time here.

Brynhild's dragon had rolled in the air and shot in so fast, Daegan caught sight of that shimmering blue beast as Ruadh made the next hard cut to the left.

His wing tip banged the tower. Bone cracked.

Ruadh kept flying, though that tip flapped loose.

Ice blasted across his tail. Damn.

His dragon dipped to one side.

They would slam into the next column.

Ruadh strained every muscle and made a tight turn, rolling onto his side. Daegan readied himself to take the body before his dragon crashed into jagged rocks below.

But his wily beast slammed his tail against the stone structure, breaking the ice.

Daegan felt the excruciating pain.

Ruadh only rumbled, always focused to win any battle.

Escaping the columns, Ruadh struggled to bank this time with his injured tail. He fought the wind, angling around to face the columns as Brynhild's dragon shot free.

When her dragon screeched this time, it was a victory cry.

Ruadh roared.

Both dragons flew at each other.

As victory gleamed in the glowing blue eyes of Brynhild's dragon, Ruadh dove at the last moment, flying fast, ignoring the pain burning through him. She tried to turn out to sea, but Ruadh had anticipated the move and lurched up, blowing out a fiery blast at the ice dragon's vulnerable underside.

Ruadh kept pushing up. He knocked her dragon sideways into the open sea.

Brynhild's dragon hit the ocean, bouncing and thrashing, until she stilled. The huge blue and silver body half under the surface.

She started changing back to her human form.

Daegan felt every bit of the agony Ruadh suffered as his dragon circled above her.

Pick her up, Ruadh. I need to talk to her.

Ruadh blew out a smoky growl then slowed to catch her naked body in his claws and lift up into the air. They flew back to the place where Tristan now waited in human form much farther back from the edge.

Daegan called to him telepathically. *Are ya hurt, Tristan?*

I'll live.

Stay there while I deal with this one first then I shall come to ya.

Not going anywhere, boss.

Ruadh dropped Brynhild on a pass over the land.

Daegan pointed out, *Ya could have gotten closer to the ground.*

She is dragon. Not fragile.

She'd also caused Ruadh to break bones in his wing and tail. Daegan could accept a little rough treatment of an ice dragon in return as justified.

Brynhild had grown up training with four dragon siblings.

She fought as powerfully as any male shifter in dragon or human form.

Ruadh landed and gently lowered his tail. Head turned into the wind, he took time to repair the damage inflicted. Brynhild remained facedown on the ground, not moving, but not dead. The venom had to be slowing Ruadh's healing, but the tail healed enough to function properly, though painful still.

Daegan told Ruadh, *Ya fought well and showed mercy. Thank ya. Ya reminded me of who we are and our ability.*

You try to save all, even those who would kill you. I fight for us. We spared her dragon this time, but we may not spare it next time.

I understand and agree, Ruadh. Daegan would never expect his dragon to give an inch when their survival hung in the balance.

His dragon gave Daegan back his human body.

Daegan pulled leathers and fur to him, choosing clothing he'd worn when he and Brynhild had first lived on this island. He wanted to appear familiar to her. He strode to where she lay on the ground. Pain shot through his back and right wrist.

If Ruadh could battle with broken bones, Daegan would not wince as he faced Brynhild.

He drew in the smell of singed hair and skin.

Pulling both of her arms back slowly, she shoved her palms down and pushed up, then gave her head a shake. A tangled mass of soaked blond hair stuck out across her head and drooped unevenly down her back. Some of it had been burned off.

She spit out something, cursed, and got to her knees, then to her feet.

As she stood, she clothed herself in black armor and boots of her family's crest, but she did no more. Skin puckered on her face, arms, and legs as the flesh healed.

She should be able to fix her hair and skin by now with her power. Had the battle exhausted her so much?

Grabbing what she could of the thick mass in both hands, she twisted it into an ugly knot.

Daegan asked, "Why would ya attack me, Brynhild? I offered to talk. My dragon could have killed yours, and would have had I not asked to spare ya."

She gave him an incredulous look. "Do not act as if you show mercy to anyone."

"When have I not?" he demanded. "I once fought beside your family, just as I fought beside the other dragon families."

She raised her fists. "*Liar!* You brought death to my family."

That echoed Fadil's words from thousands of years back. Daegan shook his head. "I did not. Whoever told ya such was the liar."

Her gorgeous eyes teemed with fury. "You burned our crops then your allies attacked us."

Daegan yelled back at her, "Did ya see this with your own eyes? Did your dragon fight my red dragon?"

When she didn't answer, he said, "I thought not. If so, ya would have known 'twas not my dragon."

She crossed her arms and stared out at the sea. "Your words are only words. Everyone knows you started the Dragani War."

"I did not." Daegan had suffered much over the thousands of years since being captured, but he would allow no one to hold him responsible for a war he did not start. "I tried to find out who wanted us warrin' each other." He walked slowly toward her. "I am glad ya live. I would like to know how ya survived and to make peace. I would ask ya to help protect our future."

The scorn she turned on him should have singed his skin. "I have no future."

"Ya could. Ya could have that and build a family again." Daegan had not wanted her back then any more than he did now, but ... he had to consider his limited options. There stood a woman he could mate with to protect all dragons and his people. He would accept a marriage of alliance and treat her well to secure the future of everyone.

Her blue eyes fired up. "A future with *you*? I would not have you if you were the last dragon in this world."

Daegan opened his arms. "See any others?"

Her face screwed up and she yelled, "I hate you!" With that, she shifted quickly into her dragon, took a hop, and flew away.

He called to her telepathically. *Do not go, Brynhild.*

I do not need you or anyone.

Daegan cursed and sent back, *Do not fly around humans. They have giant flying machines called jets that can explode your dragon.*

She didn't reply, but her dragon vanished.

Cloaked.

Daegan's jaw slipped open.

Tristan walked up with hair plastered to his head, the shadow of a beard, and naked after what appeared to be a partial shift. He held his arm against his chest. "I take it you did not know she could cloak her dragon."

"No."

"Wait until I tell you everything I found out."

Daegan wanted to learn all his second had to share, but he would first attend to Tristan's injuries. "Is your arm broken?"

Tristan moved his arm to reveal a bloody stump at his wrist. "No. Cathbad made a manacle that prevented me from shifting, teleporting, anything. I was trying to escape when we landed here. I shifted into my gryphon as far as I could, but not that arm. I couldn't teleport, so I ... "

"Ya bit off your hand to free yourself."

"Yep."

"Are ya healin'?"

"A little."

Ruadh growled and snarled inside him.

Daegan could appreciate his dragon's disgust over breaking bones in his tail and seeing their gryphon friend without a hand while Brynhild flew away. "Let me have your hand."

Tristan grimaced and held out his arm. Daegan clasped his hands around the cold stump. Ruadh pushed energy into his fingers.

Heat built under Daegan's hands.

Tristan had been pale, but now turned white and looked close to passing out.

When Daegan pulled his hand away, the bleeding had stopped and muscle began repairing. "'Tis still storming enough to hide ya. Try shiftin' into your gryphon."

Blowing out a series of fast breaths as he stalled, Tristan's face showed the strain of calling up his gryphon. He shifted, slowly, but he made it all the way. Wings opened wide from his lion-shaped body. Dark-gray translucent scales covered the gryphon's body, which would blend with the storm clouds. Tristan lifted an eagle-shaped head and opened a wide beak to release a loud scream of agony. His gryphon stood on a single front leg and two hind legs, flapping wings just enough to remain stable, tail flicking in the wind.

The damaged limb without a paw started to heal slowly.

Daegan had hoped to stay here an hour or longer, but the rain began to subside.

Humans in aircraft would see them at some point.

Tristan realized it, too, shifting back to his human form. He looked at the end of his forearm, which no longer bled. Just skin over the stump with five bumps where fingers would regrow. He said, "Not so bad. I think the base of my hand is trying to grow."

Giving him a light slap on the back, Daegan said, "I am glad ya survived."

"Me too, but … " Tristan lifted an embarrassed face to Daegan. "I didn't want to at first."

"Why?"

"Cathbad planned to turn me into a polymorph like that weird warlock who changed shapes the night we got Quinn's daughter back."

Disgust burned in Daegan's gut.

Tristan nodded. "Yep. I would have been the worst nightmare for you and our people, because he could have made me *look* like your dragon and compelled me to enter Treoir to attack everyone."

Daegan pushed water off his face and shoved wet hair out of his eyes. He searched the sky and ocean for any human contraptions coming toward them. None yet. "I am very, very glad to have ya back. Do ya know if Cathbad has another flyin' creature he's made to resemble my red dragon?"

"I don't know for sure, but I think he tweaked Brynhild. I saw her dragon shoot a short blast of fire."

That brought Daegan's head around to Tristan. "What do ya say?"

"Crazy bastard. Cathbad had us in a cave with a big frozen pond. I pieced together what I *think* happened. If I'm right, that druid glamoured Brynhild to look like a red dragon and he gave her the ability to shoot some fire. My gryphon can produce a little, but nothing like yours. Hers is way more than mine. She didn't sound happy about him doing that to her and hates Cathbad. Evidently, the druid saved her from your time and somehow kept her alive in that frozen pond the entire two thousand years. Might be why she's batshit crazy."

Daegan smiled for the first time in days. "She is that. Do ya want clothes?"

"Yes. Jeans and a long-sleeved shirt would be nice."

In the next few seconds, Tristan wore jeans, a dark-blue pullover, and boots. Daegan had used little power to do such. He could not trust his full powers in a battle, but he would test them constantly to see what capabilities he had.

What a shame about Brynhild.

Daegan had felt a tinge of hope at the chance to have a mate and family even if he cared no more for Brynhild than she did for him.

But he did not hate her where she wanted him dead.

Not a match worth any sacrifice.

Part of him longed to believe other dragons lived besides him and Brynhild, but he had doubts about another female.

Hell!

He hadn't told her about Skarde. On second thought, that may not be something to share yet.

Tristan's teeth chattered and it had nothing to do with being wet or cold.

Daegan said, "Teleportin' has been slow, but I shall give it a try."

Tristan could only nod with his arms folded across his chest.

Just as Daegan predicted, teleporting took a while before they appeared inside the front room of the ancestral centre. They both dripped puddles.

He told Tristan, "The Luigsech woman is here. She should have some food around and a towel for dryin' off."

Daegan called out, "I have returned."

No answer.

Prickly woman did not answer.

He walked into the rear area, thinking she had her nose so deep in a book she paid no attention. "Luigsech."

Stillness answered him.

He remembered what Reese had seen in her remote vision and hurried to the back wall of the room where a bookcase supposedly hid the entrance to a secret exit.

A large section of bookcase hung away from the wall as if torn open.

He pulled the not-so-secret door now all the way open and inhaled deeply.

His lungs filled with a recent scent of *aiteann*, part of Luigsech's unique smell.

Gone. Again.

CHAPTER 8

CATHBAD BEGAN KINETICALLY CLEARING AWAY more debris left in the wake of Brynhild's rage before she'd escaped the cavern. She'd found a way past his ward protecting the entrance he'd thought would prevent her from leaving.

She did not possess the ability to teleport.

He sighed. How had a simple plan gone so astray?

Once he had most of the wreckage moved aside, he surveyed her hoard of gold and other treasures. Her shield had been placed in a prominent spot in front of her massive pile.

Why had she left her coveted shield behind?

Only one answer made sense. She had not been able to move any of this during her escape. It would have required many trips to transport her treasure.

She knew Cathbad could easily uncover her hoard, so the shield had been left as a message.

She warned him to not take one piece.

It certainly appeared that she would return at some point, but would that be in this millennium?

He spotted a distinctive yellow item sitting on the floor between the now-empty chains where manacles had held Tristan captive and Brynhild's pile of gold. Cathbad lifted his Imortik stick with three claws on the end.

Had Brynhild used this on Tristan?

This weapon did not belong to her.

He called the stick to him and caught the handle when it slapped his hand.

Next, he located parts of the leather reading chair he'd brought her that she'd clearly not appreciated. When he had the chair reassembled, he sat and stretched out his legs while he figured out what she'd done.

He would have placed a ward over more than the mouth of the cavern to prevent Brynhild from leaving had he thought she could teleport. To ward this entire cavern would have required a huge amount of energy when he'd seen no reason for it.

She could definitely cloak her dragon while flying. He'd gifted her dragon the ability to shoot out fire in short blasts for temporary periods. She'd shown little appreciation for those efforts, too.

Cathbad's gaze roamed to the bloody wall where Tristan had been chained. That Alterant-gryphon *could* teleport, the only Alterant Cathbad knew of who possessed the ability.

Brynhild would not have freed Tristan unless she had a way to take advantage of his teleportation ability without him escaping her.

Had she offered a trade to help him escape if he led her to Daegan? That would have been a foolish idea.

Tristan had become Daegan's shadow since that dragon broke free of Queen Maeve's curse.

But clearly Tristan had teleported Brynhild out of the cavern. She could have tortured him into agreeing while he still hung from the chains, but to do so would not result in Tristan's compliance once she freed him.

Cathbad had to give her credit for pulling that off. He rose from the chair and stalked the room, needing to be on the move. He'd left Brynhild here so he could meet with Queen Maeve.

This loss hadn't been worth that trip.

Not when Queen Maeve had played with him while he'd tried to access her scrying wall.

He still had no idea if that crazy goddess had been watching him with her wall. He didn't believe she could see inside this cavern or anywhere else he'd warded, but she might have seen him moving about.

Did that ice dragon possess any other power besides cloaking?

He didn't know, just as he had no idea exactly how Brynhild had manipulated Tristan to help her escape. Now she would go after that red dragon to kill Daegan, which would ruin Cathbad's plans. Or she may have managed to make Tristan teleport her out, then killed the gryphon and was currently enjoying her freedom while Daegan came for Cathbad's head.

His pacing finally inspired an idea.

She did not have her freedom entirely.

Walking over to face the middle of her pile of treasures, he pointed a finger, using kinetics to search her stack. Deep inside, he found a solid-gold platter with black embellishments in the shape of her family crest.

She would not leave behind anything specific to her family.

Taking his time and using his own blood, he placed a spell on the platter, which would allow him to locate the treasure in this world at any time.

It wasn't as if she had another realm to hide her hoard in.

He returned each treasure to its original location without disturbing the pile or her shield.

With that done, he had no reason to spend more time here.

He teleported outside again to stand where the magnificent Himalayas filled the world from horizon to horizon. Snowcapped mountains painted a stunning image, more spectacular than those in travel magazines for humans. Frost began to form on his eyelashes and beard.

He'd loved this area for many centuries, returning when he needed time to rest or ... plan his next move, as he did now.

When would Brynhild return?

If he left the ward in place, she would not move any of her hoard.

Stepping around, he walked up to the entrance of the cavern. He shoved his hand into the ward, calling out the words to destroy it.

A huge boom echoed over and over. Snow on nearby peaks shook loose, barreling down in clouds of white powder.

Now she would have access whenever she wanted.

He would as well.

Cathbad! Your presence is requested at the Tribunal.

At the sound of Loki's voice, Cathbad regretted his decision to step outside the warded cavern, which had prevented anyone from using telepathic communication.

Loki did not make requests. That god made demands.

Cathbad had to seriously consider the risk of replying.

Daegan or one of his minions, such as Quinn, could be standing in a Tribunal demanding Cathbad return the Belador Alterant-gryphon. To attend that meeting might require him to tell the truth about what happened to Tristan. Liars suffered severe consequences, which often resulted in death even for an immortal.

That was not the place to admit he'd hidden a dragon for two thousand years when dragons had been known as god killers.

If he failed to respond, Loki would send his lapdog, Sen.

Cathbad could handle the arrogant demigod, but doing so would put him at war with a Tribunal of powerful deities.

Or ... what if Queen Maeve had found one volume of the grimoire and made a deal with the Imortik master?

The Tribunal might believe Cathbad had been involved with Queen Maeve's pursuit of the majik book. At the very least, they would ask him if he was currently searching for the grimoire.

Replying affirmatively to that question would be just as dangerous as lying.

CHAPTER 9

"THAT BLASTED WOMAN HAS RUN off again," Daegan shouted and strode out of the rear library area into the front of the centre.

"We can find her, boss." Tristan's injured hand remained tucked protectively against his body. Worse than injured. He'd been forced to bite off his own hand in gryphon form.

Cathbad would pay dearly for all the pain he'd inflicted.

Daegan stopped short.

"What, boss?"

"A subtle scent near the hidden door to her escape tunnel had been Cathbad's, but I took it to be from a past visit. What if the druid came for Luigsech?" Worry pushed in so hard it shoved his fury away. He could see Cathbad torturing a woman just as he'd harmed Tristan.

Tristan focused, searching the room. "I'm picking up a hint of a past visit from Cathbad. Do you sense his power signature here now?"

Daegan opened his senses wide now and identified the faint power signature belonging to Cathbad. Daegan had been correct in thinking it older than Luigsech's more recent scent. "The druid was here before, but in the past. I do not think he has returned today."

"That fits. I'm not sure Cathbad would be available right now," Tristan mused aloud. "I think he has his hands full dealing with Brynhild leaving his secret cave. Seems to me, Cathbad would take a step back now that you're involved and leave Casidhe free to hunt the grimoire. Then he could pop in at the last minute to steal it."

Too many possibilities. Daegan had to find Casidhe and he had to heal Tristan, but he could not expend too much energy or he could help no one. "Ya need to let me do more with your hand."

"Nope. I will heal. That venom must be draining your power. That was a really slow teleport."

Tristan had a point.

Daegan couldn't help Casidhe until he could find her and should not draw on his power right now short of a life or death situation. His gaze went to Tristan's hand. He could not tolerate his second in so much pain. Besides the ravaged stump for a hand, black and blue bruising covered half Tristan's skin. He slumped when he normally stood tall.

Daegan produced a towel and handed it to his second. "Shed those clothes and dry off."

"Gladly." Once Tristan had dried his skin, Daegan replaced the jeans, a long-sleeved dark-green pullover, and boots. He cringed at how slowly each piece appeared on Tristan's body.

Tristan cocked his eyebrow. "I appreciate the effort, but I can wear wet clothes and save your energy."

"'Tis not a waste of power for ya." Daegan brushed it off as a simple decision, but appreciation glowed in Tristan's bright green eyes. One day, his second-in-command would understand the great value Daegan placed on him for so many reasons, friend topping that list.

Still disturbed by the hand Tristan ripped off to free himself of Cathbad's majik, Daegan asked, "Let me see your hand."

Tristan held out the damaged nub.

Daegan frowned. "Ya must heal before we put you at risk again."

"I'll be fine." Tristan tried to sound unconcerned.

"No, ya won't," Daegan argued. "I need ya fully healed. Ya must go to Garwyli. He shall heal ya."

Tristan smiled at him. "Your brogue or accent, whatever you call it, has shown up more since returning to your homeland."

"Nothin' has changed. Ya are daft from pain."

Mimicking Daegan, Tristan said, "Ya must go to Garwyli. He shall heal ya."

Daegan smiled in spite of everything driving him crazy. "I missed your twisted wit."

Tristan grinned. "I'm back."

"Not until ya heal. Did ya think to distract me from sendin' ya to Garwyli?"

"To be honest, yes. What if we *both* go? Maybe he can draw the venom out of your body." Tristan straightened his shoulders and lifted his chin. His pale brown hair stuck out in every direction from the quick toweling.

Daegan sighed. "To also be honest, I am not sure I can teleport to Treoir right now. I would rather ya preserve your teleportin' power."

Shoving an agitated hand over his wet locks, Tristan said, "Then we need you fixed *before* anyone."

"I have a feelin' the only way to affect the venom is in the grimoire volume that opened the rift," Daegan admitted.

"Let's ask Adrianna, boss. I heard she pulled venom out of Evalle back when Adrianna first came on the VIPER teams. She was just a Sterling witch then, long before any of us had even heard of Witchlock."

Daegan walked over to look out the window, taking time to figure out his next move. Could Adrianna really help him? "How did Evalle get the venom?"

When Tristan didn't respond, Daegan turned to him.

Expelling a long breath of air that ended on a growl, Tristan admitted, "It was back when I'd first escaped from a spelled prison in a jungle Macha had locked me inside. I wasn't happy with Macha, the Beladors, or anyone. I had no idea what an Alterant was, but Evalle was so damned determined to bring me over to the Belador side, she and I tangled up. While we were arguing, a ghoul jacked up on something nasty stabbed a claw in her leg. She ended up with poison attacking her body."

"One day, I should like to hear more of that time in your life over mugs of ale." Walking back across the room, Daegan sorted his thoughts out loud. "I must have my powers for any hope of trackin' down Luigsech and returnin' in time to save Devon and the others. Go to Treoir for Garwyli to heal ya, if he can. Then ask Adrianna if she would come to try removin' the venom. 'Tis a good suggestion."

"I'll do that, but let's see if Isak can figure out where that Luigsech woman went while I'm gone."

Daegan's hope jumped. "He can do this? Quinn has Luigsech's mobile phone."

"Isak's ability to track down information is nothing short of majik for a human." Tristan walked over, studying the desk phone, which had a wire running to the wall. Nothing like Daegan had become accustomed to seeing in the human world.

Nodding as he spoke, Tristan flipped around and sat on the edge of the desk. "Isak's network of resources is scary if you're not on his side. I'll be surprised if he can't get his hands on the call log of this desk phone. You said you left Luigsech hunting the grimoire. If she found something in her library here, she might have called someone who could help her research deeper or she could have made travel plans to go out on her own. Either way, we can start hunting her with the phone history."

"Excellent idea." Though Daegan wanted to rattle the woman if she'd just taken off without waiting for him. "While ya are with Garwyli, I shall teleport to her cottage in case she went there from here, though I would be greatly surprised to find her at home."

"Think you'll make it okay?" Tristan frowned.

"'Tis a short trip, not like goin' to Treoir or Atlanta." A headache pounded and his leg ached, belying his confidence. Still, Daegan would test his powers while Tristan was gone.

Tristan stood, his face in a thoughtful expression. "I need Adrianna's number, because my mobile phone is gone. Hang on. I'll reach out to Trey." Tristan searched the desk belonging to Fenella for a business card and stilled, probably using telepathy. He stared at nothing for a minute, then nodded and glanced at Daegan. "Trey is relaying my message to Adrianna. She should call—"

The desk phone rang a shrill noise.

Tristan snatched it up, sparing their ears. "Hey, Adrianna. Yes, thanks. I'm free and with Daegan again. We need some help." He explained their request for Isak's help, then asked if she could do anything about the venom in Daegan.

When he hung up, Tristan explained, "She'll get Isak's people busy with this phone number, she'll pick up a new mobile phone from Trey for me, then she'll ask Brina to teleport her to Treoir to meet me."

"'Tis valuable to have allies."

"Yes, 'tis," Tristan teased with a grin. "I'll bring Adrianna here when I return."

Good to have Tristan sounding like himself, too. Daegan confirmed, "I shall be gone no longer than the time required to inspect the cottage."

"I'm sending a message to Trey to have Brina teleport me so I can conserve energy. See you in a bit, boss."

When Tristan disappeared, Daegan sat down heavily behind Luigsech's desk. Why would she run? He had promised to help her find Fenella.

Ruadh spoke in his mind. *She does not trust you. You do not trust her. She will not stay unless she needs you.*

His dragon had a point.

Hard to build trust when he had no idea what she was or where she placed her allegiance. Just as she had no reason to put herself in jeopardy for him, but she did need him to find Fenella.

Did she no longer care about her friend's wellbeing?

Or ... had Luigsech found Fenella?

That would destroy any motivation on her part to work with him.

Daegan stood and walked around as he thought then decided to visit the cottage. As soon as he began teleporting, he groaned at the pain shooting through his body from doing this so soon again when it had never been a strain.

Ruadh complained not, but his dragon suffered whatever Daegan suffered in human form just as he felt every injury inflicted on Ruadh's body.

When he reappeared outside her cottage, he leaned over with his hands on his knees to support himself. He'd fought long battles that had not taken so much from him.

Catching his breath, he straightened. Water clung to the flowers from a recent shower, but not even a drizzle fell at the moment. Just fat black clouds hanging close to the ground as a clear warning.

He rushed inside, checking the secret passage beneath the bed first. No recent sign or scent of Luigsech.

Ruadh snarled, *Druid.*

Daegan had noticed Cathbad's scent in every room. The druid had come looking for her at some point.

Tristan had not had a chance to share all the details of his escape with Brynhild, but Cathbad could not have anticipated that happening.

Brynhild. Just seeing her dragon took Daegan back so many years. He first saw her dragon when flying with her siblings. A mighty show of force for all below.

Would life have been different if he'd accepted her father's proposal to mate with her?

Back then, he'd felt too old for a woman so young and had thought to free Brynhild from an arranged mating for a chance at a love match. Clearly she had not seen his action as honorable. Now, her hatred knew no bounds.

Daegan wandered around the cottage, following the robust scent of Luigsech, but not recently. She had gone elsewhere.

Had he frightened her in spite of her show of confidence?

Where was she right now?

You miss the woman? Ruadh asked.

What?

His dragon made a noise Daegan took to be a sigh. *My words are clear.*

I understood your words, Ruadh. I do not know why ya would think I miss the prickly woman.

His dragon withdrew and went to sleep.

What the devil had brought that on?

Angry at himself now, Daegan called up his power to teleport. This trip had taken far longer than he'd expected. He should have returned to the centre by now.

The whirling of colors continued when he expected the teleporting to be over.

Panic pricked at his neck.

He pushed forth more energy, straining muscles. Ruadh rumbled to life, threatening to break free. That could be a very bad idea.

Tristan's voice came from afar. *Boss? Daegan? Where are you?*

Gritting his teeth, Daegan couldn't let up on his power to send back a word. He and Ruadh were in a hideous spin, hurtling somewhere.

Boss? Call me. I'll come get you!

The power snapped loose, sending Daegan tumbling like a feather in a storm.

CHAPTER 10

DIZZINESS STOLE DAEGAN'S ABILITY TO think or speak. Ruadh roared and pounded. *Free me!*

As his teleporting ended, Daegan slammed down on his back and rolled over.

He could barely breathe and had no idea where he was. He laid there, feeling his dragon pound to be released, but the sensation dulled and slowed.

Daegan whispered telepathically, *The venom is gaining strength. I would find a place to free ya if I could, but ... breathing is difficult.*

Ruadh rumbled over and over.

Daegan rolled onto his stomach, took a breath, and forced himself to push his chest and head off the ground. He'd landed in the middle of a field, but had no idea if he remained in Ireland or had gone somewhere else. With his ability, he could have teleported wildly into another realm.

In all his years, he'd never had this happen.

Boss! Tristan's voice barreled into his mind.

Daegan sent back, *I am fine. I need a moment to determine where I teleported.*

I might be able to find you, Tristan offered. Daegan's second-in-command did not possess the same level of teleporting to an unknown point, because of how he'd gained that ability. Tristan needed to know a specific location to find Daegan.

Wait, Daegan replied and struggled to his feet. He took a couple more breaths and searched the rolling land. As he turned to look farther down the hill from where he stood, a forest ran around a pasture with sheep grazing. He turned back and walked up the hill to a high point.

In the next valley sat the small town where the ancestral centre was located.

He wiped sweat off his brow, glad to have remained not only in the same country, but also in the area he'd been trying to reach.

Opening his mind, he called to Tristan. *I am not far. I can see Luigsech's building from here. I shall walk.*

Actually, I've got Adrianna with me at the ancestral research centre. She said she'd rather be outside than risk working on you in a building.

That sounded ominous. *Very well, Tristan. Teleport a hundred feet behind the buildin' ya stand in. 'Tis all open and I shall see ya.*

Tristan and Adrianna appeared close enough for Daegan to gain their attention by waving. They disappeared and showed up closer to Daegan.

Adrianna had a constant put-together look in Atlanta, but wisps of hair flew loose from where she'd woven her blond locks into one thick braid. She had a cut across her cheek and blood on her pale blue blouse. Her arms were hooked through straps to a small backpack. Now that he took all of her in, her boots were splattered with blood and her jeans ripped.

Not stylish clothing tears as he'd seen in Atlanta, but earned in a battle.

Smoky blue eyes took him in. "Yep. You don't look much better than us." She angled a head at Tristan to include him in her comment.

"Thank ya for comin', Adrianna." Daegan cast a look at Tristan who had shoved his damaged hand in a pocket. "Was Garwyli able to help ya?"

Withdrawing the hand, Tristan now had an index finger fully formed and a thumb close to full size, plus three more nubs. "It's coming back faster than anything I could have done on my own. He said maybe a day or two to have it fully regrown."

Adrianna admired his hand. "Not bad." She paused to look around. "Any chance of us finding a less-exposed place?"

"Yes. Follow me." Daegan led the way down the backside of the hill. He walked past sheep who took a few steps away, but were unconcerned, then into a thick stand of trees. He'd rather not use power to clear a spot, plus he didn't want to disturb trees that had been here a long time.

Every piece of this land mattered to him.

After walking for a bit, he saw sunlight pouring into an open spot and hurried forward. He emerged into an area where a stream filled a pond.

"Garwyli sent a message to you, boss."

Daegan finished opening up his senses to insure only natural animals were nearby and turned to Tristan. "What message?"

"He said he believes you are right about the grimoire possibly having a way to remove the venom. It might only be in one volume or it could require using all three." Scratching the back of his neck, Tristan asked, "What do you want me to do while Adrianna does her witchy thing?"

"Witchy thing?" She pfft at him.

Tristan opened his arms. "What would you call it?" He waited a beat and said, "See? You don't have a better answer."

Shaking him off as if a fly had buzzed her head, she told Daegan, "I still don't have full control of Witchlock. I may never have that even with a lifetime of experimenting, but I'm willing to try. I just want you to know I have no idea what my power will do when engaged with yours."

Tristan piped up, "Should be fine because you used Witchlock to end the curse on him when you broke his dragon free from the shape of Queen Maeve's throne. Right?"

"True, in theory. But we had to go to the Treoir realm to break the curse. He was in his most powerful element." She looked down then up at Daegan. "I don't think I can kill you, but I really don't know what Witchlock might do when engaged with another ancient power. I'm only using a quarter of the energy available on days I push it as far as I'm willing."

"Do not worry, Adrianna. I shall not hold ya responsible for anythin'."

She chuckled. "Yeah, but I can't return to the Beladors having turned their dragon king into a charcoal critter."

Now Tristan looked worried.

Daegan shut down all the potential death conversation. "I shall tell ya if ya need to stop. Tristan, would ya keep an eye on our perimeter?"

"Sure thing, boss." Tristan muttered to himself as he walked off.

"He'll be the first one unhappy with me if I screw this up." She released the most delicate sigh Daegan had ever heard.

"Adrianna."

She lifted her gaze to him. "Yes?"

"I trust ya. Do your best. 'Tis all I ask. I endanger everyone if my powers are out of control or if I am unable to depend upon them."

Nodding, she pulled off her backpack and got busy unloading a mix of candles and stones. Once she'd created a pentagram with candles at each tip of the star, she pointed at the center. "Sit there."

He stepped in. "I can stand."

"Maybe now, but you might not if this works. Once I start, don't move, don't speak, don't do anything."

"Understood." Sitting, he pulled his knees up and wrapped his arms around them to remain in the middle area where his boots would not dislodge a stone.

"I wish it was closer to twilight, but it's almost that dark with the clouds. If it rains ... "

"If it rains what?" Daegan asked quickly. Would that set off her majik in a bad way?

"We'll get wet." She smiled, clearly trying to lighten the moment. Then her face changed to serious and she began speaking crisply, uttering an incantation. As she spoke, he felt a surge of power rush past him and head for her.

He wanted to stand and protect her, but her warning had

sounded as if any movement could be disastrous.

Energy swam around him.

She opened her right hand and a glowing orb spun just above her palm. He'd heard about how she had been born into a dark witch family known as the Sterling witches, but had turned her back on them. She'd forged her own path, not exactly dark or light, but had proven her integrity and good heart.

She possessed Witchlock, a power as old as his, maybe older. Though she'd never wanted to hold such a force in her hand, she had accepted the weighty responsibility without complaint. From all he'd heard, she wielded the power with honor.

He'd been mesmerized by the spinning white orb, but now it began to grow from the size of a fist to a ball larger than his head.

Her eyes rolled up in her head.

Hell. Was she in distress?

She pointed her empty hand at his chest and raised her voice, pushing power into her incantation.

His body felt pulled by an invisible rope toward her orb.

She'd told him not to move.

Ruadh had become alert, remaining observant.

Daegan called up his dragon's power enough to have long claws shoot out from his fingertips. He gouged the ground, digging hard and clinging with all his might.

Razor sharp pain tore through his chest.

He bit down to keep from shouting.

A tangle of yellow lines began to stream out of his body as a plant stalk would grow from the dirt. More lines smoked out of his leg where he'd been bitten. The yellow lines thickened. Spikes shot out, now looking like twisted vines with roots dangling down trying to reach him again.

Adrianna's body shook hard. She put a foot forward, using it for support to allow her to lean back, holding her body in place.

She opened the fingers on her free hand and reached for

the leading edge of the yellow tendrils.

More thorns spiked along the long bands.

Daegan's butt slid forward an inch. He shoved his claws deeper, gripping to stay put, and pushed in his heels.

The tip of the first yellow tendril inched closer to her open hand.

No. He couldn't allow that Imortik venom to jump into Adrianna. He tried to call out for her to stop. His voice wouldn't work.

Her fingertip touched the leading tendril. She latched onto it, closing her fingers in a tight grip.

The tendril bulged thicker and glowed. It wrapped her arm from wrist to elbow, thorns stabbing her.

She slapped her spinning orb on top of the nasty yellow tendril.

It screamed and snapped in half. The stench of sulfur filled the air.

She kept the orb pinned to the trailing tendril on her arm, igniting the vicious venom that wailed and burned a brilliant blue color.

That part turned to ash and fell from her arm. The rest of the tendrils sucked back into Daegan's body.

She dropped to her knees, gasping for air, and closed her hand. The orb disappeared.

Released from the tension, Daegan's body shot backwards. He groaned and hurried to sit up, gripping his chest where it felt as if an animal still tried to chew its way out.

"Adrianna?" he rasped. "Are ya hurt?"

"No. I just need a minute." Her normally musical voice had come out hoarse. "I'm sorry, Daegan. I didn't get it all."

"I do not care as long as ya are not harmed. Are ya sure it did not go inside ya?"

Huffing out a tired laugh, she said, "No. Witchlock may be one power not vulnerable to that yellow venom, but I don't want to test it on me. If that thing took over my body ... you might have the equivalent of a nuclear explosion."

Daegan shuddered at that idea, then recalled the flame.

"When it burned this time, the flame was blue."

She frowned. "Isn't sulfur supposed to burn blue?"

He nodded. "But the glowin' creatures I burned a day ago had a yellow flame in spite of the sulfur smell."

"Hmm ... maybe a pure Imortik burns blue and those two had not been entirely taken over," she suggested.

"'Tis a thought. Not sure if I have a use for that information, but 'tis one more thing we may have learned."

"We have to stop that Imortik master, Daegan." She got to her feet, dusting her pants with delicate movements for one so deadly. "I might be able to kill one or maybe even several if I dare power up Witchlock that much, but I have my doubts about an army of those things. If they take you over, the Beladors and many nonhumans will fall along with the humans. If they take over my body ... " She gave a shudder. "The world would have no chance."

She hadn't boasted. Her words were honest and heartfelt.

"I believe ya have the truth of it," he agreed. After a few minutes the ragged pain in his chest dulled. He asked Ruadh, *What do you feel?*

His dragon replied, *Half of the venom is gone. You are better.*

Daegan told Adrianna, "Ya did remove half. That shall definitely help."

"How do you know?" She wiped both hands over her hair, smoothing the windblown strands back from her face.

"My dragon told me. He would know."

"He is quite impressive." She began packing up her items.

Ruadh made a happy rumbling.

Daegan rarely heard that sound. His dragon appreciated the compliment from one so powerful. "Is there an order to picking up the stones and such? Can I help ya?"

"Yes, there is an order, and no thank you. I prefer to handle my possessions." She smiled, letting him see that she meant no insult. When she had everything in hand, he took the backpack from her and held it for her to slip her arms through the loops.

She stopped and dug into her back pocket, pulling out her mobile phone.

Daegan called to Tristan telepathically. *We have finished.*

Tristan appeared next to him, teleporting immediately. "How'd it go?"

"She managed to withdraw half." Daegan tried to make that sound as if she'd cured him.

"Good deal, boss."

Adrianna stared at her phone the way Tristan did when he read a message. Closing her phone, she shifted her backpack and announced, "Isak has information on the phone calls made from the centre. He did more digging than that and thinks he may have an idea where the Luigsech woman went."

CHAPTER 11

QUINN COVERED THE LAST TWO city blocks to Reese's apartment in midtown Atlanta at nonhuman speed, something he cautioned his Beladors from doing around humans. A torrential downpour had citizens racing for any cover and the few humans he'd passed paid him no attention. Hard to tell when the sun had set with everything already dark as night.

Edward, the Belador functioning as a doorman, snapped around as Quinn came racing up to dive under the wide canopy shielding the entrance. With the noise of rain pounding every hard surface, their words would be shielded.

"Reese is not here," Edward announced before Quinn spoke. At almost six feet and with unremarkable features of brown hair and a kind smile, Edward had the ability to blend into any setting. In the doorman uniform, he presented a nonthreatening image. But when it came to guarding family, Quinn had chosen Edward for his keen skill with wielding kinetics and human weapons, plus unmatched protective instincts.

"Where is she?"

"She left half an hour ago, Maistir. I tried to encourage her to stay in a bit and let the storm pass, but she told me she wouldn't melt."

Sounded like Reese. Quinn asked, "Which direction did she take?"

Edward pointed north. "I called in one of ours to follow her. He's to intervene if she has any trouble and report immediately to Trey."

Quinn patted him on the shoulder. "Good man. Phoedra is not here, correct?"

"No, sir. I asked Reese if Phoedra and her dog would need anything while she was out. Reese made a point of saying they would be gone visiting friends for a while longer."

Reese should be in Treoir with her mutt and Quinn's daughter. At least with Phoedra safe, Quinn could put all his attention on Reese.

He sent a telepathic message to the Belador who had been assigned to follow Reese. *Approach Reese and explain you were sent by me. Ask her to call me.*

Yes, Maistir.

A moment later, Quinn heard, *Reese said her phone is not working. She'll get in touch later.*

Quinn muttered a curse. *What's your location?*

We're at Ansley Mall. She seems to be window shopping.

That did not sound like Reese. What was she doing?

Quinn didn't have time to wait for her to return. She wouldn't like it when he showed up, but of all the issues going on between them that would be the least of his worries. He ended the telepathic connection and sent a text to call in one of his drivers.

While he waited, Quinn asked Edward, "How much trouble have you had with demons or Imortiks in this area?"

"I had the patrols in this area beefed up. They were encountering one at a time, but at a steady rate, up until half an hour ago."

"When Reese left," Quinn replied flatly.

"Yes, Maistir."

"Do you think she heard anything about the demons?"

"I think she did. I had two patrols come by in person. When the second one left, she stepped outside with her rain jacket on, but I think she had been hiding just inside the entrance."

Anxiety stirred in his gut. Quinn asked, "How much was discussed?"

Edward's eyebrows drew together as he thought. "We talked about demons showing up from outside the northern perimeter of metro Atlanta to midtown. There was a consensus that the team believes the demons are originating in the Marietta area."

Quinn grimaced. Interstate 285 circled Atlanta, creating a perimeter with Marietta beyond that in the northwest quadrant. He hoped she wasn't intentionally heading out to engage demons.

A dark sedan pulled up to the curb.

"Call me if you need anything, Edward, or if you happen to see Reese before you hear from me." Quinn intended to find her first.

"Will do, sir."

Quinn climbed into the rear area of the sedan where two towels and bottles of water waited for him. "Thank you for thinking ahead, Alekki." He gave his driver directions then dried his face and hair. He ran his hands over his damp locks, unconcerned about style.

The car tires plowed through low spots in the pavement turned into small lakes as his driver headed for Ansley Mall. At least she was not in Marietta.

Quinn drilled his fingers on the console and called to Trey, who coordinated Belador teams. *What's going on with the demons?*

Been crazy how many are entering the city, Quinn. I checked other regions across North America. Something is up here.

Had the problem started *after* Reese returned to Atlanta? Quinn grasped his jaw in a tight grip. He could not allow his personal life to put Beladors in unnecessary danger.

He asked, *Do we have any intel on this situation?*

Trey confirmed, *We're working on it. The demons have been popping up in different places within five miles of midtown. I started pinning a map of the Atlanta area and outlying suburbs to see if I could detect any pattern. We don't have enough information to know for sure if this is a pattern or not, but it appears many of the sightings and attacks have been in the northern half of that circle. Actually, the majority seem to be coming from the northwest section.*

Could this demon invasion have nothing to do with Reese?

More like wishful thinking on his part. He didn't want to point at her just because she was a walking demon magnet.

Damn his soul for this conflict. He couldn't put his interests first, but he wanted her safe.

Quinn thanked Trey and texted Reese.

No reply.

The Belador following her called to Quinn, speaking quickly. *Maistir, she went into a grocery store here in Ansley Mall. I followed her in. She bought something from the feminine product area and went into the ladies room. I stepped outside to not crowd her. Gave her five minutes and went in, asked one of the ladies to check on her. She said the bathroom was empty. When I ran outside, she came racing past me on a blue Honda motorcycle and wearing a silver helmet.*

Quinn slammed his hand down on the seat. *Did you get the tag?*

Yes, Maistir. I called it in first to our people and they've been working with Isak Nyght's intel group. I told them to contact you the minute they located the bike. I'm sorry, sir.

You made no mistake. Fast thinking on your part to submit that information quickly. Return to a local patrol. I'll deal with this myself.

Yes, Maistir.

Evalle's voice interrupted his next thought. *Quinn, we got word from Tristan's troll friend there could be a demon nest near the city. As in someone actively calling them up around here.*

Bloody hell. He asked, *Where are you now?*

I just got to Kennesaw Battlefield. Two were spotted leaving here in the last half hour. I called in patrols for Marietta and the surrounding areas. They found one demon already. We have to shut this down. You haven't been around to see the news, but the humans are forming teams to hunt nonhumans. These demons may look like nasty creatures, but Reese told me about a pair she fought once on the West Coast that could hide their natural look and appear human so they could prey on the vulnerable.

Vulnerable like Reese even if she did possess power to kill *a* demon. She may not be able to kill a swarm of them. He had to stay on point. *Are you alone, Evalle?*

No. Storm is with me and we have two more Beladors. I sent another team to check out a possible sighting in Roswell. But it's not like we can open a can of Belador whoopass out in public.

You're right. Quinn gripped his head. What the hell was he going to do to keep Reese safe and support his people?

Trey's voice broke into his mind, shoving Evalle aside. *Found Reese. We're tracking her motorcycle. She just got off I-285 and is headed north on I-75.*

That would be the route he'd take to Marietta and Kennesaw. Was she headed for the national battlefield park where demons had been spotted or leaving town to draw them away?

Or was she leaving him?

He dismissed that possibility. She wouldn't take his baby and not tell him. He thought back on what Edward had said. Knowing Reese, she had definitely found out about demons attacking the area around her apartment and where they were originating. He'd wager all his assets that she was headed in the direction of Evalle's location.

Instead of solving his problem, her action only compounded his worry. He told Evalle, *Reese may be heading your way.*

Why?

Edward thinks she heard him talking to patrols around the apartment and one commented that demons were streaming in from the northwest.

Ah, hell. That's ... not good, Evalle murmured. *I know. Freaking understatement of the universe. I'll watch for her, Quinn.*

Thank you. He only hoped Reese made it all the way to Evalle. If a nest existed, Reese could be driving into a storm of teeth and claws.

His driver made record time, able to circumvent tangled traffic. Alekki had telepathic communication with Beladors working covertly in local law enforcement, who occasionally cleared the way for an emergency.

This qualified as one.

Once his driver had maneuvered from the interstate and through Marietta, Quinn's car pulled off Dallas Highway onto a drive leading to one of the visitor parking lots for the national park. Two Beladors in uniform manning a law enforcement patrol car waved them on. By then, Quinn's clothes had dried and the heavy downpour had passed. It didn't matter.

Rain or not, the humidity during a Georgia summer would drown a wharf rat.

His driver parked quickly in an area often filled with hikers and runners, which his people were deterring for now. Quinn shoved the door open and leaped out, searching the lot for a blue motorcycle.

"Quinn!"

He jerked around at Evalle's voice. She broke off from her group and jogged over to him asking, "Where's Reese?"

Quinn unleashed a stream of curses.

Evalle's eyes rounded. "I don't think I've ever heard you curse that much in one year."

Grabbing a handful of his hair. "I swear I'm going to put her under lock and key so I can catch my breath."

"I know you don't need my advice, but I don't think that's going to work with her." Evalle crossed her arms and gave him an assessing look. "When did you last sleep or eat? You look run hard and put up wet."

"I'm fine. Or I will be if I could get my hands on Reese." He covered his mouth, stared off into the woods, and tried to come up with what had happened to her. He hadn't passed her on the highway.

Evalle put a hand on his arm, pulling him back to her. She whispered, "Reese will be okay. We have Beladors all over this area."

"She's on a bloody motorcycle. Anything could happen to her." He normally kept his emotions hidden from the world, but he couldn't function and do his job without knowing Reese was safe. He should hand over his position to Evalle permanently.

He should—

"Quinn?"

"What?" He'd said that so sharply at Evalle, Storm spun around from where he stood fifty yards away.

Waving at her mate, Evalle smiled and called out, "All good."

Storm hesitated then nodded and returned to his conversation.

"I'm sorry, Evalle. I just need—"

"Reese?"

"Yes."

"Count to five and I'll make her appear." Evalle smiled with compassion.

Quinn heard a soft puttering noise from a small engine. He swung around.

Reese rode into the parking area on a blue Honda.

Evalle whispered, "The guys at the entrance called to ask me if she should be allowed in. I told them you cleared it."

Reese didn't try to avoid him. She drove right up to where he and Evalle stood, cut off the bike's engine, and dropped the side stand.

Her startling blue eyes watched Quinn defiantly as she pulled off her silver helmet and hung it on the handlebars, then shed her rain jacket.

His world came back into focus with gut-blasting relief. He could not live without her in his world. Somehow, he had to get that across to her without it ending in a bloody argument.

Walking over to her, Evalle said, "Hey! You never told me you rode motorcycles."

Reese lifted her shoulders. "Been a while. I've heard about you and your Gixxer. I'm not at that level."

"Me neither right now. My baby is still in parts in the garage." Evalle glanced at Quinn. "Storm and I were talking with the team about how we should search these woods. When you're ready, come over and we'll catch you up."

Quinn held Reese's defiant gaze as he replied, "Thank you, Evalle."

She trotted back to join her mate and team.

Heaving out a big sigh, Reese got off the motorcycle and used her fingers to shake out her wild curls. He could never decide the color because brunette failed to describe the reddish-brown. At least she'd worn short boots, jeans, and a long-sleeved yellow shirt to ride the bike.

That only meant she'd left her apartment with a specific plan to acquire a motorcycle. He asked, "Did you buy that with your groceries?"

Reese dropped her hands and hooked her thumbs in her jean pockets. "You're so funny. Actually, you're not. You had Daegan teleport me to Treoir without gaining my permission."

"It was for—"

Her eyes flared and she shoved a finger up in his face. "Don't you dare try to justify your action. You don't rule the universe. At least, you don't rule mine."

She stood so close he could smell the warm scent of her from riding in the heat. More than that, he sensed the hurt, anger, and sadness pouring off her.

What the hell had he done to her?

This had to be his fault.

Swallowing down guilt that rolled around in his head, banging back and forth since the minute he'd realized she was pregnant, he said, "I am sorry. You're right to be angry with me. I've been making missteps from the minute we saved Phoedra. I want to make this right, Reese, but I need some help. I need you to talk to me so I can stop running into walls with every frantic move I make when I think you'll be in danger."

She blew out two cheeks of breath and ran her hand over

her mouth, then stepped back. Staring at the ground, she admitted, "No, I'm sorry. The friction between us is my fault."

"No, it isn't." He would not allow her to fall on any sword in this relationship. Not alone.

Lifting shiny eyes to him, her lip trembled. "I haven't been fair with you."

She was finally going to tell him about the baby.

His heart did a backflip, but he held still. He did not want to screw this up. He'd let her tell him everything, then he would wrap her in a big hug and ... tell her how much he loved her.

And the baby. Their baby.

He couldn't talk right now for the lump of emotion clogging his throat anyhow.

Nibbling on her lip, she stared off as if forming her words. When she brought her gaze back to him, her shoulders relaxed and she whispered, "I should have told you all this before now, but I was so confused. I—"

"*Reeese, look out!*" Evalle yelled.

Quinn watched in horror as ten demons emerged from the woods on his left, all racing with claws out for Reese.

CHAPTER 12

HAD IT BEEN THAT EASY to sneak away from Daegan? Casidhe had an unsettled feeling with every mile she covered in her little four-door rental car. She rarely drove, but she'd been taught the skill during college, and maintained the speed limit. Worry over the time kept nudging her to press the accelerator harder, but she had no reason to panic. She could easily reach Redmond's house by eleven tonight.

Besides, she didn't want to draw the eye of law enforcement even with her sword tucked secretly inside her backpack.

A bird flew out of a tree on her left. She flinched, then rolled her eyes. She expected Daegan to appear in front of her car at any minute, but he'd seemed to be in a hurry when he left.

Maybe he would be tied up for a long time.

Long enough for her to evade him and get some answers.

With open roads ahead, she'd had only her mind for company. Not the best place to be stuck alone for hours. Her conscience had been blabbering on and off since walking out of the centre in County Galway.

You should have left Daegan a note.

Why? He was not her friend.

But he would worry. He'll think Cathbad has you.

Casidhe did not want to have this conversation with anyone, especially herself. Daegan was not some good guy. He was *the* red dragon.

People had labeled Redmond, the professor she headed to see, as crazy.

She felt his pain.

In fact, she should be working on what to say to the elusive professor when they met, not focusing on an irritating dragon shifter.

Or her damned conscience who should be on her side.

She glanced at the digital clock in the dashboard every ten minutes and missed her mobile phone. She could have set alarms for each hour she'd spent driving across country to check her progress.

As soon as she returned to County Galway, she'd grab clothes from her cottage and find a hotel to sleep a few hours.

No point in staying in a wrecked cottage where someone could teleport in or attack her at any moment. She'd also be close to a phone store bright and early tomorrow. They would deactivate her original phone and set up a new one with her number.

Maybe there would be messages from Fenella as soon as it went live.

With the information she hoped to receive from Redmond, she'd be able to hunt for the infamous grimoire volumes and Fenella at the same time.

All without having to deal with an overbearing dragon shifter.

After a couple missed turns, she made her way down to M11 motorway heading south along Ireland's eastern coast, south of Dublin.

Before leaving the centre, she'd groomed her hair as best she could on the fly. Her jeans and blouse were clean, thanks to the stop she'd made earlier today at her cottage.

Ten minutes north of Wexford where she'd once seen Redmond, Casidhe took the turn off according to his instructions. He'd been precise with his directions, right down to stating she must destroy any paper she wrote them on.

He'd ordered, "Do not load the information in your mobile phone or into a car mapping program."

No problem. She had no phone.

It would take her longer to figure out the rental car computer system than to just drive based on his notes.

He'd been precise and suspicious. As if she would not comply with everything he'd said after he'd agreed to a meeting?

He'd rattled her when he'd first announced, "You are Luigsech."

She'd quickly admitted he was correct.

He also warned her to come alone. Then he'd uttered one last edict. "If you break your word or fail to show after you initiated this conversation, losing information will be the least of your worries."

Terror had flushed through her.

She had to arrive at eleven sharp or he would not answer the door.

The list of dos and don'ts finally subsided at that point.

The drive had been fairly easy until she ran into roadwork, slowing traffic to a crawl as twilight muted the world into grays. She hadn't expected slow traffic this late in the evening, but it appeared a sinkhole had formed on one side of the road. She drilled her fingers on the steering wheel. Checking her blood pressure right now helped.

When she finally passed that area, she was still on track, but could not lose even five more minutes.

After taking two curvy roads off the main motorway, she found the opening into an unidentifiable wooded area by locating a rotting fence on her right. Tall grass made the path barely visible even with her headlights shining through a long break in the trees. Sprouts coming up in the tire ruts made her think this route hadn't been used in a while.

She should have purchased the insurance on this car.

Creeping off the paved road, she drove slowly over deep dips and small trees pushed over, checking her watch every minute. Before taking this dirt path, she'd picked up a few minutes in her favor and had been feeling okay about her time.

Her palms dampened. She clutched the steering wheel white-knuckle tight.

Finally, her headlights shined on a pile of dirt dumped in the road.

This was where she had to get out and hike.

Yanking the backpack from the passenger seat, she quickly strapped it on and pulled out the keychain with her LED light. Taking a deep breath, she shined the light and started the half-mile trek he'd said would lead to his home.

Did he take this route *every* time he had to go anywhere?

If so, why had there not been a vehicle parked where she left her rental or any sign of a vehicle coming this way recently?

She moved as quickly as she could through the dark woods and kept an eye on her time. She needed her mobile phone now more than ever for accurate and illuminated time, but she'd have to trust an old watch she found in the back of her center desk drawer.

Twelve minutes left.

Had she gone a half mile yet? Was she lost?

She gripped the strap on her backpack with one hand, needing something for a lifeline. Worry sat heavy in her chest. Where had she screwed up?

An old tree in the shape of a Y came into view. One of the landmarks he'd given her.

"*Yes!*" She took off, running past the dead tree and hurried up the next hill where he said she'd be able to see his house through the trees on top of that crest.

Breathing hard from the uphill jog, she stopped at the sight of his house with lights on in every window on the main floor. Yes!

Relief spread across her tight shoulders, relaxing the tense muscles.

She had enough time to reach the doorbell without having to run. Walking slower, she grabbed a cloth from her backpack to wipe sweat from her face and neck on the way.

At the bottom of the hill, she put away the rag and her light. Gaslights on posts illuminated the grounds once she passed through this stand of trees.

Hands grabbed her arms from behind and lifted her off the

ground.

She screeched, *"Let me go!"*

She couldn't free her hands to reach her sword. Her body was tossed up and spun in the air. Her heart slammed around in her chest.

Before she hit the ground, Daegan snatched her to him, eye level with his furious gaze.

CHAPTER 13

WITH TEN DEMONS RACING FOR her, Reese jumped in front of Quinn and balled power in her hands to throw.

She barely got off a flash-bang hit when Quinn snarled and stepped in front of her to shove up a kinetic wall.

One demon had died at her hands. It burst into flames then turned into a wash of ashes.

Nine more slammed the wall.

Evalle, Storm, and two male Beladors ran from across the parking lot and jumped into action.

Storm's body shifted into a massive black jaguar so fast Reese did a double take.

Evalle and her two Belador teammates started hammering kinetic hits at the demons. Four of the demons turned from Quinn's invisible wall and attacked Evalle's team.

Five continued battering Quinn's kinetic barrier. He shouted, "Get in my car, Reese! Alekki will protect you."

"No. Stop ordering me around."

"*Dammit,* woman!"

She glanced at his car, wondering why Alekki was not out here helping Quinn, since that driver had to be a Belador.

But Alekki *had* exited the car. His clothes were half ripped off and he bled from multiple gashes. He stumbled, fighting an eight-foot-tall demon with one giant horn growing over the top of its forehead. That demon must have blindsided the driver to get the jump on a Belador.

Reese stepped toward the driver, spun up her power, and yelled, *"Get down, Alekki!"*

Quinn's driver glanced her way and dove to the ground.

The demon howled and went after him.

Reese hit the demon just before wide-open jaws full of jagged fangs landed on Alekki's neck. The demon burst into a ball of flames, then poofed into another cloud of ashes.

When she swung back to Quinn's invisible wall, he forced his hands from side to side, where demons still shoved back and forth, rocking his wall.

One had enough predatory instinct to realize that wall was not infinite.

That demon rushed to one side, found the end of the kinetic field, and swung around, eyes burning bloodred. That one had sickle claws and slobber falling from its open mouth. Gray and brown hair clung in patches on his chest and legs.

Reese called up her energy, balling power fast to strike him. He ran at her.

She'd drained her energy. It was taking too long.

The demon took another stride then angled to her side as he launched his body in the air.

He was going to kill Quinn first.

She'd never had a demon bypass her energy for anything else.

Quinn must have seen him from his peripheral vision. He turned to defend them but she got there first.

She jammed her fist into the demon's chest as it passed overhead. Her energy shot all around him, lighting up her arm and his body with blue waves of power.

Quinn blasted it sideways with a kinetic backhand.

The demon exploded in flames and ashes rained down on the ground.

But the kinetic wall fell when he pulled a hand away.

Screams of victory and howls of bloodlust charged the air.

She ducked under Quinn's arms. He blasted hit after hit at the four coming hard.

She needed power and had an idea. She slammed one hand over Quinn's heart and fisted her other hand. Energy surged through her body. She pulled her fist close to her chest.

Wait for it.

A demon dove at her.

She blasted her fist as hard as she could at its throat.

Backpedaling, the demon grabbed its throat. Then it stopped and grinned, needle-sharp teeth showing.

It stepped forward.

Oh, shit. She needed a minute to power up again.

The demon took another step and howled in delight.

Then its neck burst into flames destroying its throat. Wild red eyes looked down in shock. Fire engulfed the monster.

She didn't watch for the dust to settle. Hand still on Quinn's chest, she had to neutralize one of the three demons he still fought.

Quinn roared and whipped his fist in an uppercut, but it was the kinetic power that blasted one demon up in the air. It landed behind Storm's jaguar. The super-sized jungle cat whipped around and ripped the demon's head off.

Poof, another one turned to dust.

Evalle, Storm, and her team tackled the last of the demons.

It didn't take long.

Reese had been scrunched down beneath Quinn's arms to give him freedom of movement. She couldn't straighten her legs.

Quinn's warm hand covered the one she'd kept pinned to his chest.

She twisted to look up at him.

He reached for her other hand, pulling her up to him. Without taking his eyes off Reese, Quinn called out, "Alekki? Are you okay?"

"I will be, Maistir. Thank you, Miss O'Rinn."

Reese leaned to the side to see what had kept Alekki on the ground. He had a broken leg. "You're welcome."

Evalle wiped blood off her arm. Storm paused next to her and stared at the wound as it healed in front of him. He smiled. "Your gryphon power is so badass, babe."

"I know, right?" She smiled back at him, then turned to Quinn. "You two good?"

Quinn's grip tightened on Reese's hand. "Yes, but I need a moment. Would you see to Alekki?"

"Absolutely." Evalle turned to her Beladors. "Why don't you two keep an eye out on the far side. Storm will patrol this area while I help Alekki."

"You got it, Maistir," one of the Beladors popped off.

She grumbled, "I'm not the damn Maistir when Quinn is standing a stone's throw away."

The two men smiled and headed out to follow her orders.

Quinn took Reese's hand and walked toward the entrance, then diverted into the trees. He stayed in visual range of his people.

Seconds before the attack, he'd dropped his walls and loosened up his stiff demeanor, taking her breath with his honesty.

She'd sucked up her courage, ready to tell Quinn everything, but he didn't look too receptive right now.

He had that I'm-going-to-hide-you-somewhere-safe look on his face. He whispered, "You could have been killed, Reese. Why did you come here?"

"Because I thought I could lead them to the nest. There must be something going on for that many demons to be showing up in one spot. This isn't normal. Not even for me. These demons are different, based on what I've heard and seen today. Your people need my help."

His jaw muscles flexed in and out. "While every one of them appreciate your help, *I* need you to not go demon hunting."

"I am your best bet at finding a nest."

"Then we'll have to make a different ante. Your life is not to be gambled with."

She pulled away from his hold on her arm. It hurt to withdraw, but the sooner she cut ties, the sooner she'd keep him alive.

He could have died today.

Those demons didn't just happen to show up at this specific location for no reason. Additionally, they craved the energy in her body. If they could get her to the ground, they'd drain her.

But she'd rather face ten more of them right now than that kicked-in-the-nuts look on Quinn's face.

Lob another load of guilt on top of what she'd been toting around since saving Phoedra. She'd known about the pregnancy that long and promised Phoedra she would tell Quinn soon, but not until she made it safely through her first trimester.

That had been nothing but a stall tactic.

Being the sweet child Phoedra was, she'd smiled and agreed to keep her secret.

Reese had worked hard to earn Phoedra's trust since back when they'd been neighbors in California with no idea who Quinn was, but Reese didn't deserve Phoedra's trust now.

She'd lied by omission.

Oh, she'd planned to tell Quinn, but she kept avoiding it. There would be no happy ending to this conversation.

Quinn nudged, "You were in the middle of telling me something important when the demons attacked."

She grabbed her head with both hands and didn't look at him. "I'm gonna do this quick, like pulling off a bandage. I can't stay here." She couldn't stop or look up. The hurt flooding his face would buckle her. "It's not you, Quinn. I think you've figured out why I've been sick on occasion. I never intended to keep the baby from you."

"But you did." Three words spoken softly and filled with pain.

Yep, she'd wounded him badly. She forced her head up. He deserved to see her face when she spoke. "I need to explain. You know some of what I've been through and everyone here knows about my demon energy."

His face softened. "I don't want you to worry, Reese. If you'll just go to Treoir while I'm gone helping Daegan, I'll keep you and the baby safe myself once we can come back here together." His eyes were full of so much emotion. "I want both you and the baby. I ... love you. I do." His eyes were filled with emotion as he struggled and hurried ahead. "I will be the best father ever for this child. We'll raise him or her with Phoedra. We'll—"

"Please stop," she squeezed out from her thick throat. Tears streamed down her face. He was giving her the words and love she'd never gotten from the guy she'd thought she once loved many years ago. The one who turned his back on her the one and only time she'd been pregnant before now.

The price of that mistake had been her child's life.

She'd wanted that baby so much and had been willing to raise it alone. She'd been naïve to not believe the curse.

Quinn stood here, handing her his heart and ready to take on this child to raise. He'd said he loved her.

"What's wrong, Reese?" His raw voice bled hurt.

She would not let him think he had done anything wrong. She put a hand on his chest where that powerful heart banged away. "You are everything I would ever want in a man, Quinn. You are the man Phoedra deserves as a father. You did nothing wrong. I was cursed long ago with this demon energy and to never have a family." She choked on the words, ashamed to admit she'd lost her child.

His face blanched. "What are you saying?"

"You're important to me. So is Phoedra, but you'll both be safer with me far away from you."

"No. You'll be safe in Treoir if you need to be there the entire time of your pregnancy, and even longer. I will *not* lose you." His eyes glistened. "We will find this demon nest and stop the Imortiks. I promise to keep you safe. To keep our family safe."

She hated this. Hated it. "Quinn, I was pregnant once. I went to Phoedra's guardian to keep me safe until the birth. I'd been told as a child I was cursed to not have a family, but I didn't believe it. He kept me safe, just as he watched over your daughter, but the baby ... " She gasped for a breath, unable to get the words out.

He covered her hand. "You lost the baby? What about that bloody medallion you had when I first met you? The one that allowed you to use your powers and even teleport once. Wouldn't it make you stronger this time?" He raged, but his anger was not at her but how others had failed her.

"The medallion was the only way I could access my power at all at that time, but I don't need it with me now." She sniffled. "I didn't lose the baby like you think. I carried him to full term and delivered him ... then—" She burst into tears. It gutted her every time she relived that moment.

He pulled her to him, holding her in his safe embrace. "Why? What happened, Reese?"

"The curse. It's true. That baby died at birth. So our ... " Her face crumbled. She fought to breathe, but she had to get through this and make him understand.

He stroked a hand over her hair. "Tell me, sweetheart."

Clearing her throat, she swallowed. "Our baby will not live a second after birth. There is nothing you or I can do to stop the curse and I need to be far away from you and Phoedra until ... the time comes."

"No, I won't let you do this alone. You don't know that we can't protect you and save this baby." His voice started rising. "The Beladors have healers. We have Garwyli. We have a bloody dragon, dammit." A tear ran down his cheek.

She leaned in and kissed his cheek. "I care deeply for you and Phoedra, too. I care so much I can't handle being near you when this happens. I noticed last time that demons were drawn to my energy even more the longer I was pregnant. I don't think this demon nest is about me, but I can't say it isn't somehow my fault. I don't want deaths on my head. I sure as hell don't want you or Phoedra harmed."

Quinn's hands on her arms trembled. "Please, *please* go to Treoir."

She shook her head and pushed away from him. "Would you risk Phoedra, Lanna, Brina, and her babes or any other lives? I can't and you can't. You and Phoedra are the world to me. I ... don't know what will happen ... after, but I will come back."

Quinn opened his mouth, expression full of argument, but

he paused and stared at nothing. Then he cursed.

"What, Quinn?"

"Trey called me on another demon attack. Look, just please give me tonight."

"Waiting won't change anything, Quinn." She glanced at Evalle and her group who all stared at Quinn, probably waiting to discuss the new demon attack with him since Trey would have informed Evalle as well. "If you want to help me, ask someone to teleport me to my destination."

Quinn got a stubborn look. "If you go anywhere, I'm going with you." He turned and waved a hand at Evalle, then came back to Reese. "I have to go. Please give me at least until tonight. I'll come to you where we can talk without demons or anything else interfering."

She wanted to give him the world or at the very least their child she was growing. But she knew without any doubt what would happen. "Okay, but I can't wait at my apartment. I'm putting Edward and your other people in danger just to keep me safe."

"No problem," he answered quickly with obvious relief. "You can wait inside one of my secure buildings in a comfortable setting where the only people are Belador guards. That puts none of them or humans at risk. I'll come back as soon as I get a break. If you are still determined to leave, I'll take you to a private field where my jet is parked."

"What if I don't want you to go with me?"

He swallowed hard, his throat moving with the effort. "Then, on my word, I'll direct the pilots to take you anywhere you wish and forbid them from sharing that information with anyone, including me."

She couldn't ask for any more than his generous offer. But she had to set a time limit. "I'll wait there until nine tonight."

"I will be there," he vowed.

A large sport utility and sleek sedan drove into the parking area. She gave him a sad smile. "You need to go, Quinn."

"The car is for you."

She lifted up and kissed him with all her heart.

Her rigid Belador Maistir hugged her to him, kissing her with the passion she'd never felt from another man like she had with Quinn. No one would ever take his place.

He finished the kiss and pulled his Maistir image together, running both hands over his disheveled hair as they walked side by side to the new sedan. A woman got out of the passenger side and climbed into the large sport utility the team was loading Alekki into.

She must be a healer.

Quinn opened the rear door on the sedan for Reese.

She climbed in without another word but touched his hand and tried to smile. He tried, too.

Major fail on both their parts.

As the car drove away from the park, she turned to watch the scene. Her eyes latched onto Quinn's sad face. She waited until he was out of sight to face forward again and speak to the driver.

"I need to stop on the way to the building Quinn asked you to take me to."

A worried gaze touched the rearview mirror. "I may have to run that by my Maistir, Miss O'Rinn."

"You can call me Reese. You saw what Quinn is dealing with right now. I'd like to take a quick shower and change clothes at my apartment. I need ten minutes or less. You can ask Edward when you get there. He's a Belador and can vouch for my honesty."

"Oh, I would never question your integrity, Miss ... Reese. I apologize if you thought such a thing."

"I didn't and I would never put you in conflict with your Maistir, but Quinn has a lot on his plate right now. I don't want to add to it with even one more call."

"No problem, Reese. We'll go there first."

"Do you know the address of my building?"

"Yes. All of your guards do."

Good grief. Had Quinn assigned an army to watch over her? That was another reason she had to leave. She took up too much of his defensive resources.

She eased back, glad to get a shower and change of clothes, but that was not the real reason she had to visit the apartment.

CHAPTER 14

"WHAT ARE YOU DOING HERE?" Casidhe whisper-shouted in Daegan's face. He was angry?

Well, she was furious. He had to leave. Now. She had limited minutes to make the front door of Redmond's home.

"I am huntin' for ya," he ground out. "Why did ya leave?"

"Because I don't answer to you. Put me down, dammit."

When he dumped her unceremoniously on her feet, she added, "Now get out of here."

"No." With his muscled-up arms crossed and attitude locked in defiant mode, he didn't budge. "Why are ya here?"

She might as well go with the truth since that could be the only way to get rid of him. "I'm meetin' someone who *might* be able to help me find the grimoire."

His deep frown relaxed. "Good. I arrived just in time."

"Oh, no. You can't go in with me and if you hold me up any longer, I'll miss my only chance to talk to him."

"Why can I not join ya?"

"This man is a reclusive professor. He specified that I come alone or no meetin'," she argued, checking her watch. "I need to go. *Now!*"

"I shall cloak myself."

"No. He might ... sense you."

Daegan unfolded his arms. "'Tis a nonhuman?"

"I'm not sure and you're about to lose our best chance at findin' a lead on this grimoire." She crossed her arms. "Make up your mind."

"Ya want me to trust ya to not run away?"

She fed him irony pudding. "It's up to you, Daegan. Much

like when I had to decide if I would trust Quinn to enter my mind. This should be a simple decision." She kept her voice calm. "I have less than ninety seconds to make it to that door or he won't answer. I've traveled long hours to be here on time. You're about to destroy a lead I can't replace. Do you want that grimoire or not?"

Growling harshly, Daegan waved her past him. "Go. Do not leave here without speakin' to me."

She stepped past, slowing long enough to say, "Do not keep orderin' me around and expectin' good results." Hurrying across the open ground, she took care not to step on flower beds along the beautifully groomed lawn stretching from the house to the road. That's when she saw a freakin' driveway running from a road to the house on the far side of the yard with ankle-high lights illuminating the paved drive.

Damned old coot.

She should have twenty-eight seconds left when she lifted her fist to knock. Could be more time left. She hoped it was not less.

A woman with snowy hair in spite of appearing no older than fifty opened the door. She wore a pale-orange skirt with a blouse a softer shade of peach. Trim and tidy looking. She couldn't be a maid, right?

"Miss Luigsech, I presume?"

Breaking out a smile, Casidhe extended her hand. "Yes. Nice to meet you."

"I am Leelou. Please do not be offended, but I do not touch strangers." Her soft gray eyes, narrow nose, and narrow lips would fit someone with a French name.

"Oh." Casidhe pulled her hand back. "No offense taken."

"Redmond is expecting you. I will take your luggage and show you the way."

Casidhe did not want to part with her sword, but she was in too deep right now to balk. She would not get an audience with Redmond unless she complied with his rules.

Handing off her backpack, which was placed beside the door, Casidhe followed Leelou through a home decorated with layers of history from gently-worn antiques from the early 1900s to framed family portraits painted in oil. One had what appeared to be a younger Redmond with what she guessed were his parents. She walked a long hall decorated with portraits of other men, patriarchs of the family maybe. They all had the same last names.

Glass chandeliers lit the pristine marble floor.

An impressive home, but too much upkeep for Casidhe.

Of course, hers was in shambles at the moment.

Leelou entered a dark-paneled room and stepped aside. "Miss Luigsech."

She'd announced that to an empty room.

Casidhe walked into a breathtaking library thirty feet wide by sixty feet long. Tall narrow windows with dark tinting broke up the ceiling-to-floor bookcases filled with books she itched to get her hands on. Fifteen feet above her, a copper-tiled ceiling stretched from end to end.

On one end of the room sat a massive mahogany desk Casidhe estimated to be from the early nineteenth century with a stately deep-brown leather chair. That had to cost a few coins.

The rest of the room had been arranged spaciously with two matching sofas facing off over a mahogany coffee table supported by lion legs with paws.

"Do you wish to continue admiring my home or talk?"

Casidhe jerked at the sound of Redmond's voice. He sat on a sofa. Where had he come from with her standing just inside the doorway?

She walked over to the seating area and took a place on a sofa opposite his. "Your library is amazin' and your home beautiful, but I did come for information."

"What would you ask of me?" He had a distinctive voice, perfect for speaking and teaching. One that would hold your attention as well as whatever he shared. Hands folded in his lap, he looked much the same as the one time she'd spotted him. Gray beard trimmed into a goatee. The red hair he'd been born with had turned mostly gray. He'd lost some weight since the first time she'd noticed him. Where the wool suit had fit him well before, the similar one he wore today hung on his narrow frame.

Nothing had changed about that steely-blue gaze.

She wished to have a notebook and pen, but that would probably end the conversation. "I'm searchin' for what I was told is a grimoire, but the time period for it does not sound right for it to be in codex form based on when this grimoire would have been written."

He said nothing, so she pushed on. "I believe it was created during BCE," she said, referencing *Before Common Era*. "This leads me to believe the original form could have been scrolls. That's somethin' I will have difficulty trackin' down even with my extensive library."

"What will you do with this grimoire if you find it?"

Heavy question. "I will *not* utilize the formulas in it or give them to someone who will do harm. There is an outbreak of glowing yellow beins' who escaped an imprisonment. They attack humans and ... others." She dropped that and used his term for nonhumans, then paused to watch his face.

Only a flicker of surprise jumped through his gaze, but enough that she believed he did not know about the current Imortik escapees. When he said nothing again, continuing the conversation fell on her shoulders.

"I was attacked by two of these yellow beins' when—"

"How did you escape?"

For a man so proper to interrupt her spoke of an emotional reaction. He'd asked that in the quietest voice. As if he took a risk to discuss the topic.

"I decapitated them, but in all honesty, I had some help." She would not bring up her sword to a stranger, especially one who might be a nonhuman. "So I know these things are a very real danger. I hope to find this grimoire and use it to save humanity as well as those who are nonhuman." Actually, saving humanity would be Daegan's job, but she could claim facilitating it.

"That will never happen."

Interesting that Redmond had not asked what she meant by nonhumans. "What are you sayin', Mr. Mac Seáin? That I can't find the grimoire or that it will not save our world?"

He held his head erect, sitting quietly as he composed his next words. "What you seek can be found. Once those writings are entirely unearthed, there will be someone with power who wants more. You will not keep it from the wrong hands. Therefore, you will not be able to save humanity or ... others."

Good thing her ego didn't need his support. "I understand what you're sayin', but I have a person who I assure you can hide it from the world." The grimoire should be safe with Herrick. He wouldn't want something floating around that might release Imortiks again to kill his dragon.

Redmond sighed. "Those who were once tasked with hiding this deadly book from the world possessed the same confidence and you see how that turned out. Those groups were far more powerful than you."

She had no argument for that, but she'd given her best reassurance. "I have told you the truth and I am desperate to locate this grimoire. I have a duty to protect my family and will do all in my power to see the grimoire does not land in the wrong hands."

"That is quite a vow, Miss Luigsech." He remained still for a long time, breathing slowly.

She hoped Daegan didn't get antsy and pop in here cloaked.

"You should know that locating the three volumes of the Immortuos Grimoire comes with a greater risk than anything you can imagine."

She hadn't said the name of the book, but he clearly knew just what she was talking about. Time to drop all pretense and speak clearly. "Then you know what Imortiks are."

He nodded slowly.

"Is it true one volume can release the Imortiks?" She had to know exactly what she hunted and if Daegan had been telling her the truth.

"Each volume has text capable of creating a rift, which it

sounds as if has happened. All three volumes in the wrong hands will take down the death wall between humans and Imortiks, releasing all of them."

She wiped a clammy hand on her jeans. Maybe hunting this thing was a really bad idea. "Is there any way to get Imortiks back behind the wall or close a rift that's been opened?"

"The three volumes utilized by powerful beings working together imprisoned Imortiks the first time and closed the death wall. I would think it possible to do so again. I believe you will need all three volumes to control anything substantial related to Imortiks."

That sounded better, but too vague for her comfort. "Are these volumes in codex form? Who wrote them?"

Redmond said, "A sorcerer and a Fae created the grimoire when they partnered to become the most powerful beings in the human world. It is believed they brought in a Latin scholar known as Pliny Laelius to write the text, but there is no proof, leaving it unconfirmed. Those two offered the scribe great power but killed him as soon as he finished. The grimoire was originally known as Immortuos Cartis."

"Undead Scrolls. That makes sense," she murmured, mentally translating the Latin. Interesting, but it wasn't helping her find a book, or a scroll.

"The sorcerer and Fae who partnered ran into conflict when one of their more powerful Imortiks dove into another Fae and managed to stay in the body. That wouldn't have been an issue, but the nasty being did so in spite of orders from the sorcerer to touch no Fae. At that point, powerful beings, including deities, got involved." He paused as Leelou delivered tea and poured two cups.

Casidhe accepted hers to be polite. She liked tea, but her nerves did not need any caffeine right now. She took several sips, placed the cup on the saucer, and sat back.

Redmond held his cup as he continued. "When the powerful beings of that time came together to put an end to the Imortiks, they took the scroll and cut it into many pieces. Those were divided into thirds and placed in bronze boxes made for this purpose. That's when the grimoire became known as Immortuos Arca."

She snapped her fingers. "Undead box."

"Yes."

"I knew it had to be something other than a book form." She sat back, enjoying that moment in a search when she uncovered a key piece of the puzzle.

Redmond's lips twitched, almost smiling, as if he could appreciate the tiny victories for researchers. "You are correct. Over so many centuries, the mysterious writings took on different names, eventually evolving into Immortuos Grimoire as those hunting it described the text as a book of majik. That is correct even if it is not in codex form."

Time to gamble. Casidhe wanted to put all the cards on the table and discuss pertinent details. This would either get her thrown out or show Redmond she had come prepared to speak openly. "Are you sayin' an Imortik could harm a deity or ... a dragon? I ask because I am a guardian for my family."

The silence that followed stifled what had been a casual conversation until now.

She held very still. Had she miscalculated?

A noise behind her pulled Casidhe's head around. Shaggy white hair covered a huge four-legged animal she'd call a dog, but had never seen one so tall it stood above her head with her seated. Long tail, square head. Irish Wolfhound? Big enough to have been one from medieval times.

"Come in, Finn," Redmond said quietly.

Finn translated to white in English. Not the most creative name, but it fit.

The beast walked gracefully across the rugs and stepped up on the sofa, turning to lay down with his head on Redmond's lap. The professor stroked the dog's neck.

She waited as Redmond studied her while petting his giant dog. He must have decided to not toss her out when he said, "That is correct. An Imortik can fully bond with a human body or a lesser nonhuman being. To do so takes some time. The only ones they can take over more quickly are demons.

Most powerful beings can destroy an Imortik, but even a deity could be overwhelmed by enough Imortiks attacking at once."

She let out her breath, shocked at his words.

Not only that he'd openly discussed powerful beings, but ... he'd just told her Herrick and his entire family would be at risk. She had to shake herself out of that thought to keep talking. "Uhm, thank you for that information. So all three of these volumes have been hidden for thousands of years, which will make it tough enough, but who hid them?"

He angled his head with a confused expression. "Three dragon families."

"What?" It couldn't be an ice dragon family. Herrick would have told her about this if his family had been involved, right? Wouldn't the Luigsechs have passed along that information if they had known?

"Why are you surprised?" Redmond asked, eyes on her hands.

She stopped twisting her hands. "You knew I was a Luigsech, which means you should know that I carry the history of two dragon families. But I had never heard of this until someone came to me lookin' for the grimoire."

Every time Redmond paused like he did now, she had the feeling he weighed how much more to tell her, if any at all. He took a soft breath and continued. "The three dragon clans involved were the earth dragons, the ice dragons, and the red dragon. The *first* red dragon. They all played a part in shutting down the Imortik dynasty being built. That was the reason for breaking the scroll into individual sheets to be locked inside three heavy bronze boxes. Those boxes were sealed and handed to each dragon family."

The shocks kept coming. The ice dragons *had* played a role in hiding the grimoires.

There had been a red dragon prior to Daegan?

What about Daegan's role in this? Where was the volume *his* family had hidden?

She said, "I don't see how the grimoire can be found if the

dragon families each hid a third. They would have a great investment in keepin' the volumes safe."

"True, but one volume was discovered in the twelfth century. I have few details on what happened, because the incident was kept quiet. The powerful beings of that time found the volume, then dealt with those who had brought the volume to light and tried to use it. All I know is the beings who squashed that Imortik breakout placed the volume somewhere few beings could access."

She asked, "Do you know the country it's in?"

"I know nothing of its location, but someone in today's world does."

Leelou knocked lightly and stuck her head in. "I will be in my study if you need anything more."

"Thank you, Leelou."

Before he dismissed Casidhe just as easily, she hurried to say, "I will share nothin' you have said today with anyone except the person helpin' me hunt for these volumes. He's related to a dragon family and has a vested interest in stoppin' Imortiks." As she made that claim, she realized now Daegan would not use the grimoire to harm others just as Herrick would not. She added, "If you ever need anythin' from me, please do not hesitate to ask."

"That is very kind of you, Miss Luigsech, but to be entirely up front with you, I had no doubt of your integrity or I would not have met with you."

She'd take that as a compliment. She could use an attagirl today. "I greatly appreciate your time and knowledge." But she still needed help in finding the grimoire.

Redmond sat forward, resting his elbows on his knees, the most relaxed he'd appeared since Casidhe had settled on this sofa. He said, "If you are determined to hunt the volumes, I will point you in the right direction. It will then be up to you and the person waiting outside to find the rest of the path."

Not much else to say to that except, "Thank you, Mr. Mac Seáin. I'm listenin'."

CHAPTER 15

DAEGAN STOMPED AROUND IN THE area he'd cloaked within view of the house Luigsech had entered. The house appeared to be nice enough, but that did not mean those inside were to be trusted. He should not have frightened the lass when he teleported in behind her, but he reacted to prevent her from running off.

Was she safe in there with this professor?

She'd all but said the man was a nonhuman.

Guilt piled on top of worry. Had he approached her calmly, he might have convinced her to allow him to go inside with her.

He couldn't protect what he couldn't see, but to enter that home would only hand her more reason to not trust him.

"What's your next step, boss?" Tristan stood with him inside the cloaking.

Staring at the ground, Daegan spoke softly. "I do not know, Tristan. Quinn will be facin' a Tribunal to discuss endin' Devon's life and that of two other Beladors until I can return, but that may not be enough. Renata is still ... sufferin' wherever she is. I have no idea how many more of our people the Imortiks have captured." Frustrated at standing still with time running out, Daegan grabbed the back of his neck, stretching when he'd rather be battling an enemy. Anything to end this insanity. "'Tis my responsibility to protect all of them. Even Luigsech. I am failin' and the venom in my body is drainin' my powers."

"You're not failing, Daegan," Tristan replied. "You're fighting with every breath. We will all fight with you. We all believe in you. You don't know how to fail. You just need to give yourself a break sometimes. Quinn's a silver-tongued devil when it comes to talking circles around anyone. He'll find a compromise."

The use of Daegan's name from Tristan meant his second-in-command meant his words to be heard and accepted. "Thank ya, Tristan. I will take your words to heart and find my strength to do better."

Ruadh's voice rumbled in Daegan's head. *Gryphon speaks truth. Trust him. We are powerful enough. We will get stronger.*

Having Tristan's and his dragon's show of support meant a great deal to Daegan. He shoved his misgivings deep inside, determined to fight even harder for those he loved.

"What's that strange look on your face, boss?"

Daegan smiled. "Ruadh agreed that I did well in choosing ya as my second."

That surprised Tristan into silence.

Before he could come up with a reply, Daegan heard a door open and Luigsech say, "Thank you again."

He turned to observe her leaving the house. Tristan stepped up next to him and noted, "She's smiling. Think she got any information on the grimoire?"

"'Tis difficult to tell with Luigsech. She does not always show her true emotions." Daegan moved Tristan back down the path she'd taken to reach the house so he could remove the cloaking out of view.

She crossed the hill and flipped on her wee light as she started down, backpack jostling as she walked.

When she had a few steps left to reach him, Daegan dropped the cloaking.

She jumped and squawked.

"'Tis only me," he complained at her reaction.

She grabbed her forehead and stomped around for a second then planted her feet. "You keep appearin' out of nowhere. You think that is *normal* for me? I'll answer. No, it's not. And there are two of you now. Stop freakin' doin' that."

Tristan made a coughing noise.

Daegan had heard that in the past. His friend struggled not to laugh.

What could Tristan possibly find humorous in dealing with this woman?

Reaching for patience, Daegan told Luigsech, "This is my second-in-command, Tristan."

She tossed a look at Tristan. "You're the one Cathbad captured, right?"

"Yes, I am."

"How did you get away?"

Daegan interrupted. "There is not time to share all that has happened." Nodding in her direction, he told Tristan, "This is the Luigsech woman."

"Dammit," she bit out.

Daegan held his hands open. "What now?"

"I am *Casidhe* Luigsech. *Not* the Luigsech woman. Not Luigsech. You may call me Miss Luigsech or Casidhe, but cut out addressin' me like some unknown bein'."

Affronted by her anger, Daegan struck back. "But ya are an unknown bein' since ya have yet to share what ya are."

She closed her lips and looked ... *hurt*?

What the hell had he done wrong this time? He glanced at Tristan who twisted his lips as if he also thought Daegan had spoken poorly.

Daegan asked Tristan telepathically, *What is wrong with this woman?*

I think you insulted her about being something unknown.

"*Stop it!*" Luigsech snapped her fingers, back in ordering mode. "You're talkin' to each other. If you have somethin' to say, then say it so I can hear it."

As she wished then. Daegan said, "I was merely askin' Tristan if he could figure out why ya became upset about what I said. He believes I insulted ya. Is that so?"

Her eyes strayed to Tristan again and stayed there. "Thank you. How nice to meet a man so observant."

Daegan's fury boiled fast.

Tristan stepped back, eyes wide. "Boss?"

That one word spoken with an underlying warning that Daegan's power had rushed out brought him back down from a tide of anger. He had no idea what had caused him to react so strongly.

"'Tis fine, Tristan." Working his jaw to loosen it, Daegan told Luigsech, "If I misspoke and insulted ya, it was not intentional. Are ya goin' to blow up every time ya misunderstand somethin' I say?" He used her words this time, thinking she would understand them.

"I did not blow up," she argued. "I am not some strange bein'. I don't even know what I am other than I have the power to translate ancient text. There you go. You figure out what I am."

Daegan had no words.

She did not know what she was? Irritation had caused him to be careless with his words, but why had he lost his temper when she thanked Tristan for being thoughtful?

He would think on that when he had time.

Tristan had done nothing wrong.

They could not stand here debating any of this. Daegan asked, "Did ya find out anythin' on the grimoire?"

She eyed him for a few seconds then nodded. "The professor was very helpful even though he knew someone waited outside for me."

"How could he have known such?" Daegan had opened his senses as Luigsech went to the door, checking for any nonhumans out here. He'd found none.

"I did not ask him, nor did I ask him what kind of bein' *he* was." She pushed that in Daegan's face to make her point.

"I shall not do that to ya again," Daegan assured her, trying to return to better standing. "Do we have somewhere to go next?"

"He told me of an oracle we have to find. She is the only one he knows of who can shed light on the grimoire locations."

Daegan's chest loosened with the first tingle of hope. "Ya did good, lass. How do we find the oracle?"

"We have to go to a specific range of mountains in Morocco."

"How do we find these?"

She reached into her back pocket and pulled out a folded piece of paper. When she opened it, she pointed to the top of an odd-shaped mountain among a line of jagged peaks. "We go there and follow his directions from that point to locate the oracle."

Tristan leaned in, glanced at the picture, then stepped back. "Do you mind if Daegan and I have a private conversation?"

She clutched the photograph, which had come from the professor's files. "Go ahead as long as it does not include me."

"It won't." Tristan spoke in Daegan's mind next. *If you two can get a lock on that location, I can link to your power and teleport. We haven't tried that, but linking works with the Beladors.*

Daegan thought on Tristan's suggestion a moment. *I believe Ruadh would be fine with that. He trusts ya where he trusts no others but me. We shall try.*

Nodding at Tristan, Daegan explained to Luigsech, "We can go there immediately."

"What? Uh, no. I ... " She looked around as if searching for a reason. "I have to return my rental car."

"Tristan will take it back after he teleports with us to the mountain so he will know where we went."

"I can't just take off," she complained.

"Why not?" It seemed a simple decision for Daegan.

"I'm still lookin' for Fenella."

Tristan interjected, "Our people are pretty amazing. They're working nonstop on finding her."

Daegan had heard nothing new, but Tristan's words were truth even though it had sounded like current information. The Belador team would have someone on this task continually.

She gave Tristan what Daegan had once heard him call the stink eye. Funny term, but he understood it now.

"Why should I trust you any more than him?" she asked Tristan, stabbing a thumb in Daegan's direction.

"I haven't given you reason not to," Tristan replied with a charming smile.

"You have a point."

Daegan caught his temper this time, but was his word of less value than Tristan's?

Tristan lifted an eyebrow at Daegan. "Problem?"

"No." Daegan rarely took umbrage with Tristan and could not define why he did at this moment. The venom had to be twisting his reactions.

Luigsech eyed them both. "I want an agreement you will absolutely bring me back to the centre when I ask."

"I will do all within my power to comply," Daegan answered, not wanting to lie, but unsure he could deliver on demand.

She squinted at him as if she doubted his words, then gave a dismissive headshake. "Fine."

If she was still unsure, why would she agree? What else had she learned in that house?

Walking back to her car with Daegan providing light, Luigsech shared what the professor had said about how to locate the oracle. Reaching this oracle would be more challenging than threading a leather strip through the eye of a darning needle.

Tristan took the keys from her and folded his tall body into her wee car. He grumbled, "Couldn't find a smaller one, could you?"

She answered with tart sarcasm. "I tried. There's no turnaround. You'll have to back it out of here."

In answer, the car vanished, then reappeared facing the opposite way.

Her mouth opened and closed much like a fish sucking in water. Daegan wanted to point out to Tristan how he now found the woman's expression humorous as opposed to when she'd been berating him.

He didn't. His words would only irritate her again and

delay their trip.

Once Tristan had all the information on returning the vehicle, he stepped out, locked it, and pocketed the key.

Daegan had been waiting until the last moment to explain the next step to her. "For Tristan to teleport us, we must all be touchin'."

"No touching."

"*Miss Luigsech*," Daegan said, leaning heavily on each word. "We have no time to waste with this discussion. 'Tis the only way we do not lose ya while teleportin'. Otherwise, ya might end up reappearin' in the air and nowhere near a place to stand."

The color washed from her cheeks. "Okay. Where do we have to touch?"

He found her resistance offending, but he would not point that out to her. "Ya would be safest standin' between us with a hand on each of our arms."

"Oh, I see." She stepped over to stand between them.

What had she thought he meant?

She placed a hand on Tristan's arm, then reached for Daegan's. Her touch lit a buzz of energy under his skin.

She yanked her hand back. "What are you doin'?"

Daegan started to say he had not caused that reaction. She had. Instead, he said, "Sometimes energy rises when we teleport."

Tristan sent him a what-are-you-talking-about look, which Daegan ignored and said, "I have the image in my mind. Time to teleport."

Luigsech latched onto his arm, buzzing be damned this time.

Tristan made the leap in a short time, but Daegan would likely need Tristan to get them back. Still, he felt he could teleport short distances if he and Luigsech needed it.

Wind whipped all around them as they reappeared in darkness. Daegan called up more power from his dragon to improve his ability to see in the dark.

Luigsech took a sidestep close to a ledge that dropped

off fifteen feet to the next outcropping. After that the trip would be much longer where a body would end up crushed thousands of feet below.

Daegan grabbed her and hauled her body next to his. She surprised him by not complaining. In fact, she gripped his arms.

"You sure about this, boss?" Tristan yelled. Wind slapped his hair all around.

They stood in a small valley between two taller mountain peaks. Luigsech's professor had described this spot right down to multiple-sized boulders stacked into a three-sided structure ten feet tall Luigsech had called a mini-pyramid.

Sand bit Daegan's skin. It had to be striking Luigsech too. He used his power to swap her short-sleeved shirt with long sleeves and called up a soft scarf to wrap around her head and face, except her eyes. He covered those with clear glasses he'd seen on workers in Atlanta.

All he could see of her now was a shocked gaze.

Daegan called back to Tristan, "Appears to be the place described. I shall call if I need anythin'."

Tristan didn't look convinced about leaving them.

"If I run into trouble, ya shall do me more good bein' somewhere else, but available," Daegan added.

"Okay, boss. I'll be listening for you. Stay in touch."

"I shall."

Tristan vanished.

Daegan returned to Luigsech who had not moved. "Are ya havin' trouble, lass?"

"This was a ... a mistake." Her muffled words were hard to hear in this wind. He lowered his ear near her mouth. She said, "We ... we ... should go back."

Turning his head until they were nose-to-nose, he asked, "What do ya fear, lass?"

"Are you kiddin'? We're on top of a mountain in the middle of nowhere."

He jerked back from her loud voice. "'Tis where ya said to go."

"I know."

Her tiny answer cut into his heart. "I shall not allow any harm to come to ya, lass. But if ya wish to go back, I shall call Tristan to come for ya."

"What would you do?"

"Take your instructions and find the oracle. I cannot turn my back on my people."

She blinked hard as if forcing tears hanging on her lashes to not spill. "Okay, we go together."

"Why?" He had to know what drove her at these times.

"I have people to protect from Imortiks, too."

Of all the times she'd shouted at him and refused to believe what he told her about the Imortiks, what had changed her mind?

That professor. He must have told her something about the grimoire that made this hunt personal.

Daegan would not use her fear against her as he would an enemy. She deserved his support. Maybe now she'd be less difficult.

He said, "We are here to protect many. It shall not be an easy path ya described for us to make around this mountain, but I can see in the dark. If ya take my hand, I shall not let go of ya."

Her soft blue eyes deepened in color. She drew herself up and nodded, then extended her hand.

"Ya should let me carry the backpack," he suggested.

"I'm good with it. I'd rather carry it and be able to grab you if I need to."

Those were her last words before they began the trek.

Daegan executed every instruction Luigsech gave him, not complaining when they had to back up when she felt they'd missed a place to drop down a step or turn. The wind calmed when they slipped between rock outcroppings. After a slow and arduous descent hardly much lower than where they'd begun, he stepped onto a narrow goat path wrapping the outside of the mountain face.

This would test Luigsech more than where they had started.

He'd like to think darkness would ease her worry over heights, but the inability to see into the black void below must have increased her fear. It hurt to feel her terror and have no way to console her.

Wind slapped his face and pinned his hair straight back when he faced into it. He had her grip the waistband of his jeans so he could keep his hands free. She complied, but dread poured from her.

Another thirty steps around the goat trail, Luigsech called out, "I didn't think I had a fear of heights, but I evidently do."

Daegan desperately wanted to teleport her to the next spot they hunted, but the professor had warned the oracle expected someone who wanted her advice to put forth effort. When Luigsech had asked what he meant, he'd said to only use the same abilities a human would once they started the descent.

Turning to walk sideways, which was not as efficient, he pried her hands from his jeans. Gripping her fingers firmly, he said, "Ya shall go nowhere without me and I have no intention of fallin'."

She froze in place.

He shouldn't have stopped.

Wind continued to buffet them.

He spoke softly. "Ya can do this."

Nodding, she swallowed and said, "Keep goin'."

"Good lass."

The ledge dropped a little every ten or twenty feet. She gasped any time he made a sudden move. He had to hug them around a curved and indented part of the mountain face that should be nothing more than a black shadow, but shapes and rock changes held a reddish glow. Nothing shined down on this spot. He'd learned long ago to accept some things in the supernatural world.

When he glanced down, the tip of his boot hung over the end of the goat path.

Beyond that was a long drop.

He searched this carved out part and detected the goat path continued on the other side, but over twelve feet away. Without tapping his power, there was no way to make that leap.

He might, but not without losing her.

"Do you see the crevice and feather?" she called from behind, unable to see past his body.

Daegan searched everywhere for what she'd described, then noticed the shape of a feather carved along a vertical opening in the rocks.

He had no idea how to take Luigsech down to reach that crevice. He scraped his face when he turned his head close to the rock they hugged so he could speak to her. "I found the feather carvin' and crevice. I must go down to be sure the openin' 'tis wide enough for passin' through. Ya wait here until I come for ya."

Her eyes widened. "Are you crazy? I'm not stayin' here."

They were protected from most of the wind, but merely standing with muscles straining would wear them out soon enough.

He had one suggestion. If she didn't agree, he had no idea what to do with her. "Ya can climb on my back and I shall carry ya down, but ya shall have to point out the way. I cannot lean away from the rock and look for my next move."

"You're serious, aren't you?"

He could barely hear her, but nodded. "I am."

Her terror-filled gaze stared at him. She seemed so torn he felt sympathy for her. He'd like to tell her he could shift into his dragon if they fell, but he could not swear for sure he'd catch her in time. Better to remain silent.

Also, using supernatural ability would prevent a meeting with the oracle.

Luigsech nodded. "I'll hold on and be very still."

"Let me get a good grip on the mountain." He ran his fingers until he found cuts and holes to latch onto. He asked his dragon for help. Claws grew from his fingers, sliding deep into the openings.

"Climb on, lass."

She didn't say a word, just patted her hands as if searching for a handhold blind. When he bent his knees, lowering his shoulders, she latched onto him, digging her tiny fingernails in deep. She moved slowly until her arms wrapped around his neck and her legs circled his waist.

He could feel her heart thumping fast and her chest moving with panicked breaths.

After all the fighting between them, her show of trust humbled Daegan. He'd extended his trust, too.

He just did not know if it would be enough to survive this.

CHAPTER 16

CASIDHE HELD ONTO THE ONLY thing between her and falling to her death. Daegan.

The warm glow of shared trust lasted until he shifted to the right, moving a booted foot off the ledge.

Air backed up in her lungs.

She would die a horrible death. Just end up a bloody splat thousands of feet below in the dark.

Daegan stilled. His words came out gentle. "Calm your breathin'. Ya help neither of us if ya panic."

She squeezed her fingers, which were gripped together, and closed her eyes. How long would it take to hit once she fell?

Muscles on his back, arms, and legs bulged as he inched to the right again.

"Have ya ever met an oracle?" he asked loudly.

She turned her head from where she'd smashed her face against his back. "What?"

"'Tis a simple question even for a woman who is easily confused."

He had done it again. "You son of a gun. Stop insultin' my intelligence."

"I did no such thing. I merely made allowance. 'Tis not shameful to be slow to gather your thoughts," he said, sounding amused.

"Here are my thoughts. I bet you have a tough time findin' women."

"I find plenty."

"But do any of them stick around?" she replied tartly.

He did not answer at first.

Had she hit a nerve or was he out of breath?

He finally admitted, "Unfortunately, no. I can only mate with a select few and those women are not so many today."

How did he manage to yank her chain one minute then make her feel guilty about her words the next? She'd lost her desire to bait him at the sadness in his voice.

Did he have to find a female dragon to mate?

Herrick had spent an eternity alone. So had Daegan.

She had never considered the similarities between the two men, only how they stood on opposite sides of a battle line.

Daegan's right shoulder dropped with a missed step.

She clung to him.

He soothed, "Easy, lass. I merely passed a toehold."

When she took in where they were, she noticed two things. Daegan had covered a significant distance since stepping off the ledge and this rock had a reddish appearance as if it held heat.

Like she would question anything weird now?

And he'd managed to calm her terror while doing so.

Daegan said, "'Tis time to tell me where the crevice is. We cannot waste me huntin' it blindly."

"You're right." Her heart still pumped in near-panic mode, but Daegan had moved them pretty far. She felt energized to reach their next landmark.

Tilting her head to the side, she saw it. "We're the length of your body above the top of the opening. Then an arm length and a half left of it."

"Well done, lass." He'd grunted out the words.

She felt a twinge of regret for the grief she'd given him. Here this man risked his life to carry both of them across the face of the mountain and he gave her a nudge of support.

In another ten terror-filled minutes, he had them to the side of the ledge. What was he waiting for?

Sounding exhausted, Daegan's huge muscles were pumped up hard as rock and straining from clinging to the small openings he'd gripped to make this climb. Holding onto his back gave her a personal glimpse into just how powerful a man he was in addition to being a dragon shifter.

"Ya must climb off and step down beside me," he explained.

She squeaked out, "You're kidding, right?"

Speaking in a tense voice, he replied, "What would make ya think anythin' about this is to laugh about? I cannot hold here forever. Ya need to find your backbone and step off me. I cannot reach across the openin' for a hold worthy of keepin' us here."

She worried out loud, "What if I move wrong and make you fall?"

"I shall not let go if ya do this today."

How could he have any sense of humor right now?

He'd literally carried the load up to this point with a backpack on top of her weight.

She had to buck up and grow a pair of lady balls. "Okay, okay, I'm ... I'm doin' this."

"Keep hold of me until ya have a hand grippin' the inside of the crevice."

She eased her legs down. Muscles ached from having her legs locked around his body. She would never try to explain to another person how she managed to make that transition. Nothing about it had been attractive or useful information to a person who knew how to climb.

But she made it and felt a surge of joy she'd never experienced at accomplishing such a feat. "I've got it, Daegan," she whispered.

"Very good. I shall wait until ya go inside before I step on the ledge.

"Okay. I'm on it." She looked into the opening that was a foot taller than her and surprisingly wider than it had appeared from the side. It had a narrow V shape, eighteen inches wide at her feet. She started into the opening, refusing to think about the darkness ahead. Her body stopped short.

Daegan called out, "I can see your foot, lass. Keep goin'."

She couldn't turn and shouted, hoping he'd hear her. "I think my backpack is stuck. I can't move."

"Stay calm," he told her.

She didn't move a muscle except for her heart pumping madly. She held her breath, begging for Daegan to make the transition and not to hear him shout one last time as he fell.

What was taking so long?

His voice came to her quietly. "Ya do not need to grasp the walls, lass. Try to lower your arms. I shall carry the pack."

"How?"

"The openin' above your head is wider," Daegan explained. "Can ya unlatch the straps?"

She scraped her elbows, but managed. "How are you going to fit through if it's this tight for me?"

"I shall pass."

Did that man ever run out of confidence?

The weight on her back vanished and she felt so much lighter.

"Move ahead, lass. Do ya have your wee light?"

She brightened at the idea of having her LED. "Yes. It's in a small pocket on the side of the pack." The sound of the pack being turned and pockets opened continued until his hand snaked over her shoulder.

She grabbed the powerful penlight. "Thank you."

"Ya are welcome. Take care not to hurry ahead. Be sure where ya place your boot."

"I will." She moved tentatively at first, but a few steps in, she began placing more confident steps. What seemed like twenty minutes had passed when she hit a dead end. She shined her light over a solid wall of rock, which was oddly smooth to be in the middle of a mountain.

They couldn't go back and climb up to that tiny goat path ledge again.

Daegan's hand rested on her shoulder in what felt like a touch of support. "What did the man tell ya to do now?"

"He didn't tell me much once we found the crevice in the wall," Casidhe admitted. She didn't have to see Daegan's face to know he was disappointed. "I'm sorry, Daegan. I must have gotten somethin' wrong." She started rambling as she recalled her meeting. "Redmond didn't tell me specifics. He said we had to start from that spot where Tristan teleported with us, then we followed every step after that and found all the landmarks. I can't imagine how this could be wrong when he said the path would run out at an opening in the wall. Of course, he failed to say we'd need wings to reach the opening."

"We used no wings," Daegan said in a light tone she knew he did not feel.

She clamped her forehead with one hand, thinking. Then it hit her. "Wait, wait, I have an idea."

"What did ya remember?"

"The poem. We were discussing this, then his dog got up and trotted out, which pulled us off topic. Right before that he was explainin' how to gain entrance to the oracle's world I would need a poem of time past and time forward."

"Do ya have such a poem?"

Her heart clenched at the longing in his voice. "I had one in mind when he mentioned that, but I thought we'd need it at some entrance. There's no one to recite it to here." She dropped her head against the stone wall blocking their way. "I don't know what I was thinkin'. I just wanted this to work."

Daegan's fingers gently massaged her shoulder. "Say your poem, lass. 'Tis no harm in speakin' it."

His hand comforted her in a way words could not.

She lifted her head and swallowed her anxiety. "He said I must recite a poem of past and present, but only the part that spoke to my heart. A poem that brought harmony would open a door."

"What poem do ya have a mind to be sayin'?"

"One by T. S. Eliot, a famous poet. He died before I was born. I often think of his words when I'm researchin' so many different time periods. I know the whole thing, so what part do I choose?" she whispered, angling her head to look back at him.

He dropped his gaze, seeming to study on her question a moment. When he lifted his bright silver eyes to her again, he asked, "Does it have fifteen parts?"

She mentally envisioned the poem. "Fifteen? It has four parts and way more than fifteen lines. Why?"

"A wise old advisor of my father's once said fifteen represented a source of power, but could also bring harmony. He spoke of many legends of the past, at times soundin' as a prophet."

She allowed what he said to soak in and realized in the few minutes they'd been talkin' her body had relaxed. Her heart no longer raced along at a panicked pace. "Okay, I'll give this a try."

When she turned back to face the wall, she gave the smooth surface a longer look. Would this work?

Placing her hands on the wall, her fingers touched cool stone. As she thought over the poem, she could see no reason to skip around. She would recite from the beginning of T. S. Eliot's beautiful *Burnt Norton* prose.

Dropping her forehead to the wall, she let go of everything else to give her heart to the words.

"Time present and time past
Are both perhaps present in time future
And time future contained in time past.
If all time is eternally present
All time is unredeemable.
What might have been is an abstraction
Remaining a perpetual possibility
Only in a world of speculation.
What might have been and what has been
Point to one end, which is always present.
Footfalls echo in the memory
Down the passage which we did not take
Towards the door we never opened
Into the rose-garden. My words echo
Thus, in your mind."

She waited, breathing slowly, begging for this to work.

Minutes passed. More minutes passed. She had to finally admit the words were not *abracadabra*.

Her heart dropped when nothing happened.

Daegan squeezed her shoulder. "'Twas an interestin' poem, lass. Do ya have another?"

"No. I thought that was the best one to use." She tried to turn so they could start back.

Crack. A tiny sound she barely heard above her breathing froze her. She whispered, "Did you hear that?"

"Yes." He pulled his hand from her shoulder and touched the walls on each side of her head. "I do not feel any vibration."

Crack. Crack. She held her breath. *CRACK!*

She looked around to see fissures rupturing the wall. "I don't think this is what we were hoping for, Daegan."

He snaked an arm around her chest.

Her brain would normally be shouting at her to not allow this stranger to touch her so intimately, but she welcomed his strength and determination to protect her.

With every crack sound in the wall, her faith in surviving this diminished. She fought for air, sucked in the rising dust.

Then the walls on each side shifted.

What the hell?

The shifting changed to moving from side to side faster.

Daegan's grip tightened. He lifted the backpack over her head and shoved it in front of her, shouting, *"Hold the—"*

A loud crack sounded like a gunshot.

The ground fell away.

CHAPTER 17

DAEGAN HELD LUIGSECH AND HER backpack as the world slid out from beneath his feet. He'd shoved the pack in front to protect her, but also for the lass to hold.

That would have freed his hands to use kinetics.

The shearing sound of rocks and sand screamed. A deafening roar of noise rushed around him. Light flashed then darkness, then light again.

Ruadh shouted in Daegan's head. *Shift. Break free. Fly away!*

Daegan doubted if he had the power. Neither would he risk a change only for the mountain to collapse and crush his dragon in mid-shift.

Then everything turned upside down.

Luigsech screamed.

Daegan had her against him in an iron grip and clutched the pack to her front.

He fell through a hellhole with no bottom. Regret over bringing the lass to do this hit him hard. He had promised to keep her safe. If he could not protect one small lass, how could he protect a world full of Beladors, their allies, and those in Treoir?

His world tumbled and flipped.

He bounced against rock and landed hard.

Everything stopped as suddenly as it had started.

Daegan lay on his side with his arms around the lass and her backpack. He spit out dust and grit. He could feel her breathing, but she had not spoken. "Are ya hurt, lass?"

She mumbled something he couldn't figure out.

"What say ya?"

She drew a deep breath. On the exhale, she said, "I want off this ride."

He had no idea what she spoke of, but he smiled because she'd said it in that sarcastic voice of hers. She would be fine.

Pulling a hand free, he wiped dust and pebbles off her hair. "If ya have no broken bones, I shall sit ya up."

"Sounds like a plan," she muttered.

He lifted her as he swung his upper body off the ground. Pulling the backpack away from her chest, he placed it next to his body. Grit irritated his eyes. He blinked, washing them best he could, then squinted.

They were in what appeared to be a tunnel.

Light glowed at the end.

He wished to believe that to be a good sign, but had his reservations.

"Where are we?" She started brushing her hair off her face and spit out a few pieces of grit. "Oh, crap."

"What?"

"I'd like to think there was a light at the end of this tunnel for a good reason, but with the way things are going it could be a train headed for us."

He dropped his forehead to the back of her head, chuckling. "Your wit is welcome, but I am not so sure I would welcome a train."

Her shoulder shook with laughing. "You're screwed up, you know that?"

He took no insult as the words were given with a smile in her voice. "'Tis possible is true."

She twisted around. "You agree?"

"If I were not screwed up, as ya say, would I be sittin' inside a mountain with no way out after havin' followed a lass?"

She rolled her eyes. "You always turn it back on me."

When she began moving to stand, he lifted her to her feet. Then he stood and picked up the backpack to hook over one shoulder.

"I'll take it," she offered.

"Are ya really not goin' to trust me with your pack after what I have dragged it through?"

"Point taken. Thanks." She lowered her hand and turned toward the light. "Let's see where this leads us. I would say it can't get any worse, but I'd end up eating those words in ten feet."

He smiled. His snappy termagant had survived.

She paused when she reached the mouth of the tunnel then stepped out where a soft glow washed over her body. "This is ... not possible."

Daegan followed close on her heels, in a hurry to check for any danger.

They stood at the edge of a round cavern fifty feet across with polished walls rising to a point thirty feet above them. The walls were a mixed painting of cream, beige, black, orange, and cherry as if someone had carved through layers and sanded them to a smooth finish.

Translucent crystals sunken sporadically into the curved wall flickered with light. In the center of the floor, a spring bubbled gently in a pool Daegan could reach across with his arms extended.

"Wow." Luigsech's head tilted back. "I've experienced my share of supernatural events and beings, but this really blows my mind."

"Where is the oracle?" Daegan asked. Hadn't they just opened a door of some sort?

"We have to wait for her to come to us." Luigsech turned to him. "The professor explained what to do if we passed through the door. I'm thinkin' we just did that."

"What is next then?"

"We are to sit quietly and contemplate what we will ask for, because she will only allow us one request."

Just being in this small enclosed space with no way out reminded Daegan of centuries spent locked in the TÅμr Medb realm in the shape of a throne.

He would sit, but he could not promise for how long.

He waited for Luigsech to make a move.

She stepped carefully over to a spot near the gurgling water and sat with her legs crossed. She tossed him a look and patted a space next to her.

Daegan took his place, pulling his knees up to rest his hands on.

She extended her arms in front of her with her palms up. Her thumb and pointing finger on each hand touched. Then she closed her eyes.

Did she expect him to do the same?

He put a forearm across his knees and dropped his chin on his arm. His other hand went to the hard ground where he moved his fingers in a tapping motion over and over.

What was happening in Atlanta?

Had he lost any more people to the Imortiks?

Was Quinn having any luck with the Tribunal?

How was Brina and her babes?

Luigsech's hand covered his fingers, stopping their movement. She squeezed his fingers.

Energy hummed in a pleasant way between them.

He watched her face.

Without opening her eyes, she leaned over and whispered, "Quiet your mind, Daegan. We can't find anythin' unless we pass this test and she allows us to ask our question. We have to do this together or she won't speak to us."

Had the lass heard his loud thoughts or just sensed his nonstop distress to get this done and protect everyone?

She kept her hand on his, waiting on him to do his part.

He let out a long breath and closed his eyes.

Energy continued to whir beneath her fingers. His internal power swarmed to her hand. He focused on their two energies. What was it about her that drew his to the surface as if curious? Who was this woman? In spite of always battling him, he found her attractive. She called to the man in him who longed for a normal life to spend time with a woman who made him feel alive again. Where had that foolish thought come from when in the middle of this mess?

He should not be thinking of her in those terms anyhow.

They would find the grimoire and part ways, her back to her life and him to his.

As his body let go of things he could not affect while here, his thoughts relaxed.

He considered dream walking.

A strong female voice said, "You are here for an answer. Take care with your question."

Daegan opened his eyes slowly, feeling as if he'd rested a full night. The lass came into view first. She smiled politely and slid her hand from his. Reassured that she was fine, he lifted his head, ready to speak.

His first glimpse of the oracle stunned him.

She had no hair on her round head. Fine lines had been drawn on every visible inch of her skin, including her face. Shiny material draped her body held at her shoulders by tiny gold clasps with looped chains of gold.

The cloth was not cloth.

More like a waterfall stolen from a full-moon night. Beneath the draping, her legs appeared to be crossed.

Her lips were a red-brown, wide and full.

Beyond all other features, her eyes stood out against honey-colored skin. The orbs swirled with gold and black at first. Now her eyes became solid dark orange with white irises.

Luigsech's mouth had opened, but she failed to utter a word.

The oracle angled her head at the lass. "I am Zeelindar. You have answers to questions you know not to ask."

What the hell did that mean?

Luigsech closed her mouth, frowning. She said nothing to push this oracle in case she had more to say. Turned out she did.

Those bright eyes moved to Daegan. "You search for more than you know."

That should be understood since he and the lass had made this unimaginable trip to find out what they didn't know. The oracle had a clear voice with no emotion.

She spoke with the assurance of one who expected others to sit up and pay heed.

He cut his eyes to Luigsech.

She nodded, a safe option when in doubt.

Zeelindar's mouth widened in a smile. Her lips parted slightly. Tips of sharp teeth appeared.

He'd thought oracles were human.

As Zeelindar studied Daegan with what seemed to be unseeing eyes, she continued speaking. "Every journey is the beginning of a journey ending. You must take each step to reach the end and the beginning."

Riddles were not Daegan's strength. He kept his face blank of expression, allowing this oracle to set the pace of the meeting.

Zeelindar swept her gaze across both of them. "Ask your question. Be prepared to pay a price."

Casidhe's mouth dropped open. Evidently her professor had failed to share that important detail. Would the oracle require treasure or a sacrifice?

Finally finding her voice, Luigsech asked, "Are you sayin' you want somethin' like a human sacrifice?"

"Have I asked for such?"

"No, I just wanted to find out what we were obligatin' for."

"Is there a price you would not pay to find what you seek?"

Luigsech didn't answer right away.

Daegan did. "There is no price within reason I am unwillin' to pay personally, but I shall not kill another to gain this knowledge."

Nodding slowly, Zeelindar said, "As it should be."

Her words echoed softly off the walls similar to soft chimes ringing.

Shoulders slumping in relief, Luigsech said, "We thank you for this audience, Zeelindar. We seek somethin' hidden long ago that will help us save many people."

"Your reason is your own," the oracle stated bluntly.

Clearing her throat, the lass kept going. "We ask for help locatin' a volume of the Immortuos Grimoire hidden over two thousand years ago by one of the dragon clans, but not the volume locked in a vault a thousand years ago."

Daegan had not realized how much Luigsech had learned during her meeting with the professor. Did she know which grimoire volume was locked in VIPER's vault?

The oracle had not moved or spoken.

Nothing happened.

Casidhe cut her eyes at Daegan.

He shrugged. He had no idea what this oracle wanted next.

Zeelindar cupped her hands and lifted her chin until she stared straight up. He glanced there, but she looked at something only she could see. Her lips began moving, whispering soft sounds.

Daegan recognized nothing she said. Luigsech seemed just as perplexed.

The air moved slowly. Lights sparkled and blurred.

Time had no relevance here. Daegan couldn't say if they'd been sitting here ten minutes, an hour, or more, when the oracle paused in her murmurings.

She lowered her head and placed a hand on each knee, addressing them both. "You will bring me the *Scepter of Dagobert* for the information you require."

Daegan had no knowledge of this scepter. He dove ahead with the most important part of this. "But ya do know where the grimoire volume is?"

Luigsech held a hand up to him. "Hold it a minute. That scepter has been missin' since the late 1700s. No one has any idea where it is."

Daegan turned to her. "What scepter do we discuss?"

The lass quickly explained, "A famous piece that had originally been part of the French Crown Jewels in the seventh century. It was stolen while you were out of pocket at TÅµr Medb."

Out of pocket. A strange way to describe what he had gone through.

Zeelindar sounded pleased. "Your knowledge of this treasure will aid you in locating the scepter."

Luigsech politely argued, "Knowledge is one thing. Do you have any idea how many have searched for that scepter since it disappeared?"

Daegan asked, "Where was it stolen from, lass?"

"The Basilica of Saint Denis." She sounded crushed when she turned back to the oracle. "Why not ask for the Holy Grail?"

Lights flashed brightly through the room.

Luigsech cringed toward Daegan and covered her eyes. He wrapped a protective arm around her shoulders and glared at the oracle. Hair lifted across his arms.

Ruadh made unhappy noises. The growl climbed Daegan's throat and pushed out. He could have stopped it, but he did not care for this oracle frightening Luigsech.

The lights settled back into a soft pulsing, but he would be a fool to think the calming had anything to do with his displeasure.

Zeelindar waited until Luigsech sat up again and Daegan removed his arm before the oracle spoke. "No human will find the scepter."

Daegan asked, "Why?" But he had an idea of the oracle's answer.

"If a human could enter the current resting place of the scepter, that person would not survive."

"That doesn't sound promisin'," Luigsech muttered. "Could take years to find that place."

"Not true." Zeelindar moved her head one way then the other. "You will receive the specific location. You must open a gateway once there."

Daegan realized what she might be explaining. "Are ya sayin' this scepter is inside another world or realm?"

The oracle nodded slowly.

He had new concerns. "Are ya also sayin' ya expect us to find this scepter and deliver it to ya before ya will aid us in gainin' the grimoire? I have no time for treasure huntin' with people dyin'."

Luigsech gasped and grabbed his arm. "Daegan!"

"What? I speak the truth."

Zeelindar's voice dropped to a gravely sound. "Have you not realized I have already aided you?"

Luigsech's eyebrows drew together tight. She flicked her gaze to the oracle. "Is it possible ... a grimoire volume is in the same place as the scepter?"

"Clever child." Zeelindar murmured the compliment as if surprised.

Well, hell. Luigsech had a strong mind for riddles.

"Fail to bring me the scepter and you lose all hope of finding three volumes. When you deliver the scepter, I will answer your next question."

Daegan said, "If we find this volume, ya have aided us plenty. We would not impose on ya again."

"You will wish for another answer," Zeelindar claimed with authority. "Do not think to talk around delivering the scepter. Speak your truth, dragon."

His eyes must have given him away when she raised his ire. "Are ya sendin' us to *steal* from someone?"

Luigsech gave his hand a little squeeze of thanks. She must have had the same worry about this scepter.

"The scepter was stolen from a king. When you hand this treasure to me, I will return it to the rightful owner."

That being the case, the king was long dead if he had been human as it sounded.

Daegan had another hundred questions, such as why the scepter was in the same location as the grimoire. Had she only agreed to help because she had her eye on a treasure? Or would the grimoire not be there and they'd end up delivering the scepter to gain the real answer to their question?

Luigsech spoke up. "Sounds like we have another trip ahead of us. We appreciate you speakin' to us when you had no reason to beyond our request."

The oracle turned to her. "I have been expecting you since the two of you met."

Chill bumps lifted on Luigsech's arm.

Daegan made a note to avoid unnecessary thoughts around

the oracle.

Zeelindar announced, "You must go to the Land of Hadrianna. It is a world within a world. To gain the scepter and grimoire, you must find a way past the satyrs. Upon entry, you will be shown three hallways and must proceed without hesitation. On the way to finding the scepter, you will pass the room of chronicles. Once you take possession of the scepter, you will see the Immortuos Arca in the next second. You will gain what you wish. You will lose what you gain."

What. The. Hell? Daegan hoped they were not being sent on a fool's journey. On second thought, that might describe the trip to this place.

"How do we find this world?" Luigsech asked.

Zeelindar lifted her lips in that creepy smile again. "You will know when your feet rest upon the ground."

The lass asked, "Where are we going? How will we know we're in the right place?"

"I will share the image with you."

Luigsech tensed then shook her head. "How did you do that? Did you enter my mind?"

"I do not enter minds. I share wisdom."

"I have it in my mind, Daegan," the lass said. "I'm worried it will never go away."

The oracle made a noise of disgust. "Do not trouble over small things."

He hated to admit this to the oracle, but he might not be able to teleport to another country or world, not with the venom inside him. He would not try to bring Tristan here either. "Ya should tell us the specific location in case ... we end up astray."

Zeelindar cocked her head in his direction. "Nothing will interfere with *this* trip."

What if it ended up being a one-way trip? Daegan kept his concerns to himself. The oracle wanted no argument. That was clear.

Luigsech asked, "Are we just going to somehow drop in at

the gateway?"

Zeelindar lifted her hands into a prayer position. She closed her eyes, singing softly. Strange tune. Strange words. Strange woman.

Daegan had very little hope this would work.

A piece of parchment floated gently as a feather from out of nowhere. Zeelindar kept her eyes shut and held her hands open. The parchment turned for her and dropped into her hands.

She opened her eyes and handed the parchment that would barely cover one of Daegan's hands to the lass.

He leaned over to view it. Symbols unlike anything he'd ever seen before had been created in ink. Neat, perfect strokes.

Zeelindar. "You hold the map to the gateway."

"How do we let you know we have the scepter?"

"I will know."

Luigsech turned an unsure gaze to Daegan. "We can—"

The air between them shimmered. He immediately felt the odd change he experienced when teleporting.

He reached out and wrapped an arm around Luigsech before he lost sight of her and gripped her backpack with his other hand.

All the rock and lights turned into a spinning mash of yellow, orange, and brown. But this time, the tornado spun around them, leaving Daegan and the lass in a cloud blurring her face and his hands.

Not a hair moved on Luigsech's head. She stared straight ahead then her eyes closed.

What had that oracle done to her?

His eyelids became heavy. He fought sleep, but the whirling colors turned darker and darker until no light remained.

The next thing Daegan knew, he stirred and blinked his eyes. He opened his senses to search for any threat.

Birds chirped and the sound of a light wind rustling leaves drew him fully awake. He sat up in the midst of trees everywhere and still at night.

Squinting, he took in an ocean stretching beyond the high point where he sat among ferns on a mountainside.

Luigsech lay next to him, curled toward his body, probably because he'd pulled her in close instinctively.

They stood at odds with each other so often, but ... he had this deep need to keep her safe. He couldn't explain it away as simply being protective over a female.

Such a conviction had always run strong in his veins.

But what drew him to her and to protect her felt different.

His energy rose to the surface and reached out for her any time she touched him.

What could she be to affect him this way?

He brushed wild curls off her face and ran a knuckle over her smooth skin. She was no striking beauty compared to someone like Brynhild, but this lass a true beauty in her own way. She had a special attractiveness, one that ran deeper than skin. He had a feeling if she smiled, really smiled from happiness, she would be breathtaking.

Brynhild represented the only hope he had for mating and producing a dragon family, but the dragon shifter's heart had become poisoned by hate.

He doubted this lass had the ability to harbor hate. She cared deeply and it showed in her every reaction. She would stand strong for the people she loved.

She would stand strong next to a mate.

Ruadh made a soft growling noise but no comment.

Daegan's dragon had deserved a mate long ago. He'd failed his dragon as much as his family back then.

No, Ruadh stated firmly in Daegan's mind. *We are together in all we do. You have not failed me. Never think such.*

We are together, Daegan agreed, but still felt he had to do more somehow.

Touching the lass's shoulder, he shook her gently. "Wake up."

She mumbled, but her eyes remained closed.

Was something wrong with her? He leaned closer and spoke softly to not startle her. "Time to wake up. We have arrived."

Her eyes opened.

He lifted up.

She stared at him for a second then leaped up, arms wrapping his neck. *"We survived!"*

He hooked an arm around her back. "All is fine. Do not fash." His body welcomed hers next to him. Only a bastard at heart would wish she would not calm soon and break this moment. To prove to himself he could be better, he rubbed his hand up and down her back, soothing her.

It sure as hell did not soothe him. Heat pooled in his groin, igniting a powerful desire from her touch.

CHAPTER 18

CASIDHE REALIZED WHO HELD HER, or who *she* held, since her arms were involved in this embrace. She yanked her arms away and scooted to the side.

Daegan had a surprised expression, then glowered. "Do not give me such a look."

"What look?"

"One that accuses me of handlin' ya improperly," he grumbled. "Ya jumped up at me. I only had soothin' your distress in mind."

Embarrassment heated her cheeks. She had done just that upon waking to discover they were both alive. She'd also recalled him protecting her when everything spun out of shape.

"I didn't accuse you of anythin'," she argued, but without genuine emotion.

"Ya would have."

That he might be right didn't help any. "For the love of turtles, let it go." Guilt soaked her voice.

"Ya have love for a lot of critters," he said, his face without expression, but those silver eyes creased a bit.

He'd done that before. Teased her to dissolve an uncomfortable situation. Who was this man? She had to do a better job of holding on to her anger with Herrick's enemy.

To do that, she had only to remind herself of how many people his dragon had killed long ago even if he might not be on a homicidal tear right now.

She sent him a narrowed-eyed glare. In spite of feeling unfair to Daegan, she had to step up and do her duty as a guardian for Herrick's family.

Consorting with the enemy was not part of that job description.

First thing, stand far enough away from Daegan so her IQ didn't drop with her panties.

Whoa, wait. She was *not* interested in him that way.

She wasn't.

But something seemed to be going on between them and their energies. She'd lowered her guard while searching for the oracle. She could just lift her barricades back up again.

"We must figure out where we go next," Daegan announced, clearly ready to dispense with any conversation related to the two of them tangled up.

Just as willing to move on, she began replaying all the oracle had told them. "Zeelindar spoke in circles so many times I got dizzy. First, we have to figure out where a world inside a world could be."

"She gave ya a map. Did ya lose it?" Now he sounded disappointed.

Good to know some things remained the same, such as him picking at her ability to do something as simple as hold onto a map.

Daegan held his hand above her and pushed light around them. At least he didn't light a flame on his palm again.

She dug the folded parchment from her back pocket, glad she'd thought to shove it there as soon as the spinning started. That reminded her of something. "Did you teleport us or did the oracle?"

Her question caught him by surprise if the time he took to answer was any indication. "I am not sure. I do not think she teleported us, but somehow aided me in doin' so. What is a world inside a world? Ya are the history scholar of supernatural beins'. How would ya open a gateway?"

He'd surprised her by giving respect for her background and skill. She explained, "That world could be what is known as a parallel world or dimension, which is a plane of existence ... " She was losing him. "Think of it like a realm inside of a realm, as if you had found another world coexisting inside TÅµr Medb when you were there."

His eyes turned a deep pewter color at that reminder of his imprisonment.

She held up a hand. "Sorry, probably a bad example. It's like an alternate location existing next to the one we stand in. Actually, I believe we just entered an alternate world where the oracle resides, unless she used majik or some power to take us there and send us back."

That smoothed out his facial features. "I understand. Where do we begin?"

Unfolding the parchment, she said, "I didn't get a chance to look at this and ask her questions before we spun out of the oracle's place."

"If we do not find the scepter first, but locate a grimoire volume, we retrieve that and I shall come back for her scepter."

She rounded on him. "I don't think it works that way. I think we have to leave with both or nothing at all."

He turned a face on her that would rival a volcano about to erupt.

She held up a hand. "Hear me out before you blow up at me."

"I do not blow up."

"Right. You're the epitome of calm at all times," she retorted sarcastically. "I am willin' to help you find this grimoire, but you have yet to give me anythin' on Fenella. You want a show of trust from me? Where's *your* show of trust?"

He appeared to stew, taking his time to answer. "I spoke to Tristan about it. Quinn is sendin' out word to our people in Ireland to hunt for her."

"What will they do when they find her?"

"Do not berate me when I am givin' aid. My people shall not harm Fenella. They only observe to determine where the phone is located and if it moves around. 'Tis unwise to assume anythin' about a situation. They shall alert me when they have more to share."

"You said you think Cathbad does not have her. How can you know for sure?"

"Did ya not see Tristan?" Daegan stormed back at her. "He went through hell to escape. If Fenella is human, Cathbad would not allow her to escape and move about freely. If he captured her, he'd have taken her to a secure place, probably another realm."

Her heart climbed up her throat and threatened to choke her at that possibility. "How secure could it be for Tristan to have escaped?"

"Tristan can teleport, plus he half-shifted into his gryphon and had to bite off his hand to free himself from a spelled manacle preventing him from teleportin' or callin' to me telepathically."

"He ... oh ... that's awful." She swallowed bile that ran up her throat at that vision. She hadn't paid close attention, but recalled Tristan keeping one hand in a pocket. Tristan could shift into a gryphon? He bit his hand off. She still couldn't get past that visual.

"'Tis more than many would do to escape Cathbad, but the druid intended to turn Tristan into a powerful monster capable of killing many. My man would never allow that to happen if he had a chance to protect those he loves." Daegan clearly agonized over what his friend had suffered and been forced to do to survive.

"How would Fenella survive that?" she wondered out loud.

"Cathbad would have to do far less to imprison a human. He had no plan to negotiate a trade for Tristan, but he would with Fenella. The druid would have less negotiatin' room with Fenella's people if he harmed her. I believe she would be safe if he does have her, but Tristan did not see her where he was kept and indicated Cathbad lost another prisoner at the same time. One he would do all to recapture. Fenella may be with her phone."

Casidhe admitted, "I tried callin' her phone after you left. No answer."

Daegan shrugged. "Ya told Quinn your friend was not

good about answerin' her phone. Ya need to give my people in Ireland a chance to do their job."

He had a point.

His people in Ireland? Casidhe's mind slid to a halt. She wanted confirmation about her guess that his people were Beladors. "Who *are* your people in my country?"

"'Tis not somethin' I wish to discuss. We waste time."

She considered yammering on at him to knock his arrogance back down to normal size, but nothing about him was normal.

His people had to be Beladors.

What would Herrick say to all of this?

If he knew she sat talking to the red dragon, Herrick's language would bruise her ears. What about Skarde? Would Daegan tell her if he knew anything?

Daegan stood, stretching his back. "'Tis important to keep movin'. What information is on the parchment the oracle gave ya?"

She'd lost her chance to slip in a leading question about Skarde without drawing Daegan's suspicion. Time for that later. "I don't know what it says yet."

"What good is information if ya cannot read it?" He growled at the end of his words.

"Did you catch when I said the word *yet*?" she snapped at him. She opened her hand, releasing the parchment she'd crumpled while arguing with Daegan. Thankfully, the material withstood creasing more than paper.

He extinguished the light when he put his hands on his hips and gave her a disgruntled look at her lack of action.

Shaking her head in irritation, she ignored him and crossed her legs. Good thing she'd worn jeans with no idea of the escapade she'd end up surviving, but they were ripped and dirty. She still wore the long-sleeved white shirt Daegan must have conjured up. Recalling that reminded her of all he'd done to get them to this point.

She had to let her anger go and work with him as a partner.

She retrieved her LED light then smoothed out the

parchment. As she studied the inked marks, she dug mentally through her vast knowledge of languages. It didn't take long to realize she'd have to use her gift.

To do so now would mean allowing Daegan to see her power in action.

"So ya can read those symbols?" He dropped down beside her, crushing ferns with his weight.

"I think so." She stalled another minute.

"What language is it?"

Crap. She had no way around this. "To be honest, I don't know without more information than what's on this scrap. Callin' it old would be like sayin' you have been alive a long time."

"I *have* been alive a long time."

Casidhe dropped her head to her knees. "I mean it would be an understatement. Are you goin' to argue every comment I make?"

"Not if ya move along and figure out where we go next."

Grumpy dragon.

Lifting her head and stretching her shoulders, she returned to the parchment. "My point is that these symbols remind me of some I've reviewed from 42 AD, but not exactly like those."

Daegan leaned close to her, studying the paper. His warm scent swirled around her, teasing her nose, and waking parts of her body that had no business coming out of hibernation.

Not with this dragon shifter.

But she had no way to stop the undercurrent of energy sizzling and swarming between them like a bee hunting a flower.

She didn't need this strange interaction of their energies going on with so many more important issues to worry about.

Angling her head to catch his attention, she asked, "Are you able to translate it?"

"No." He pulled back and frowned. "I should be though."

"Why? What makes you special?"

"I lived in 42 AD and was taught to read anythin' available then." He shared that in a melancholy voice, full of longing and disappointment.

Through all the years around Herrick, she'd rarely thought about how long he'd lived. He hated talking about the past as much as she thirsted for any details from that long ago era.

But she would not ask and make Herrick sad.

To hear Daegan comment about living back then as she would talk about her college days put a lot of things in perspective.

Seeing him as a man of that time and not the red dragon shifter who she'd been taught had killed everything in his path created havoc in her head. She had to stay on track. Do whatever it took to find the grimoire, save Fenella, then find out if Daegan had Skarde or knew anything about him.

Daegan dropped to his knees and scowled. "Can ya read it or not?"

Typical. When nothing went his way, Daegan became irritable and demanding. "I need a moment to work on this if *you* can't read it. Seems like you should be able to since you're older than dirt."

He snapped back, "I am not. I am in my prime."

She lifted her shoulders "Two thousand and countin'. Just sayin'."

"Foolish conversation," he grumbled.

"I agree. Why don't you walk around a minute and stop hoverin' so I can concentrate?" She tried to think of another tactic to get rid of him.

He surprised her by standing and walking off.

She started to ask how far he was going then changed her mind. He would remain close enough to hear her if she called to him.

Placing the parchment on the top of her knees, she put the small light between her teeth and ran two fingers above the letters. Words began to form in her mind.

A time or place of the mind obeys no rule of such define,
Our hall of all is known, our world is not so known,

To savor the loot of a sleeping king,
For those who lust a Laverna tryst.

She read it slowly, translating Latin words such as *definire* to define and *rex* to king. She read it again and ended up with the same translation.

Clenching the worthless paper in her fist, she pounded the ground.

From behind her, Daegan said, "'Tis not good news?"

She jumped aside and shouted, "Don't sneak up on me! You're lucky I didn't have my sword."

"Not lucky." He held up her backpack. "Wise to keep it from your easy reach. What did ya learn?"

Her shoulders dropped with a heavy sense of failure. This was her expertise. If she couldn't figure it out, no one in close proximity to her could.

She returned to a seated position. "We're screwed. It's a poem or a cryptic message. I won't be able to fully understand it unless I have time to research more. Somethin' I can't do on top of a damn mountain in the middle of nowhere." Tired and frustrated at constantly feeling she was inches from grasping information she needed so often, she turned on Daegan. "Not unless *you* can pull that information out of the air."

"What does it say?" He squatted next to her again.

She repeated the words. "Some of the words are from different time periods. Like the word *definire*. I think it originated in maybe the fourteenth or fifteenth century. It means—"

"Define," he said. "I read Latin as a child and heard the word used in the fourteenth century by warlocks entering TÅμr Medb."

His quiet admission sickened her unexpectedly. He'd been captured and imprisoned to remain in one shape, unmoving, for thousands of years.

Herrick had spent that same time confined to a small area in the Caucasus mountain range, but at least he'd been free to live and fly as he pleased.

Daegan made it difficult for her to harbor the ugly feelings she'd gained from a lifetime of having history imparted to her by the Luigsech squires and the Connell squires.

Who should she care more about? Her family or the dragon that destroyed Herrick's family?

She carried so much on her soul at the moment, she couldn't allocate the time needed to sort through the confusion being this close to Daegan had created.

He stood and walked around a moment, then stilled. He held up a hand, asking for silence as he stared into the forest.

She twisted to look at the same spot and saw nothing except more woods. Did he sense a demon or Imortik? Tossing a second look at him, she realized he was staring at nothing at all, probably communicating by telepathy.

Sweat trickled down the side of her face. She swiped it with her hand, which came back dirty. No telling what her face looked like after climbing a damn mountain then falling through a rock rabbit hole.

After a few minutes, Daegan's unfocused eyes sharpened with a flash of intelligence. He nodded, then turned to her. "I may have more information to help us."

"Whoa. Where'd you get this information?"

"From someone whose knowledge is bottomless on many subjects."

"I don't believe you."

He gave her an incredulous look. "Why would I lie when time to save my people is slippin' through my fingers?"

He had her there, but ... "What did you find out?"

"A short history of Laverna."

She offered in a tired voice, "A Greek goddess, seems like she was of the underworld and catered to pirates, uh ... ?" She lifted her eyebrows at him as in *what else*?

Daegan picked up that thread. "True. She protected pirates and thieves. Among supernaturals, she has been suspected of stealin' a king's treasure to appease a debt she believed owed to her by a Roman ruler."

"Great," she groused. "Now we're huntin' a Greek goddess

and a scepter?"

He gave her a long look. "Ya lack patience for this work."

That just pissed her off. "Me? You're the one complainin' every other word about how I'm not findin' the grimoire fast enough."

"'Tis the truth, but I am now helpin'. This will be much faster."

Was he pulling her leg or serious? She crossed her arms for his benefit. Otherwise, she'd pull out her sword and stab him.

Nope. He had her backpack out of reach.

She'd just have to stab him with words. "Can we get to the part on how to find the scepter or has old age addled your mind?"

Shaking his head at her, he said, "'Tis believed once Laverna found the scepter and stole it, she gave it to her lover, a sorcerer known as Nicabar, as a treat. She bore him a female child, but Nicabar had no use for children, especially females. Rejection of her child angered Laverna, who is believed to have created a home in a special place for Hadrianna. The person I asked did not know what Laverna had stolen from a king. Once I told him about the scepter, he said it was possible Laverna gave Nicabar the scepter until he made her angry about their child. Then she took it back."

Casidhe's mind got back on track. "If that's true, where would it be now?"

"In the Land of Hadrianna, the home Laverna created for her child so that Hadrianna could live in a safe world and visit the human world when she wanted."

Jumping to her feet, Casidhe moved around, too anxious to be still. Could this be the breakthrough they'd been hoping for? "That would be a world in a world. A parallel world or realm."

"Possibly," Daegan allowed.

Casidhe pulled at loose strands of hair, thinking. "Still, it's going to be tough to find a gateway to that world."

"Ya have little faith." He shook his head. "I shall find the gateway, but I wish to return ya to the centre and go forth on my own."

She swung her head slowly from side to side and smiled up at him. "You're the one who said we were goin' to be joined at the hip."

"I said no such thing."

She waved her hand. "It's a sayin'. Basically, you can't do this without me and I'm not lettin' you out of my sight until I get Fenella back."

"I do not need ya, lass," he declared.

"Really? Who is goin' to identify the grimoire? Can you read *any* ancient text?" She crossed her arms. "I'll wait while you answer that one."

A tense muscle jumped in his jaw.

She lifted an eyebrow in challenge.

"You are a most irritatin' lass," he muttered.

"Always nice to have somethin' in common. With that out of the way, what do you propose next since I didn't get to ask your secret resource anythin'?"

"'Tis difficult for one with no telepathy to speak to a bein' in another realm."

Her mouth opened and closed. He spoke to someone in another realm? "Who was it?"

"Someone old and cherished. I will not divulge his name. 'Tis not necessary." Daegan twisted, looking around. "He told me we may not have to hunt this gateway. It may come to us."

"How?"

"By offerin' somethin' Hadrianna's world would welcome."

Casidhe had no response to that. She waited for Daegan to expound.

"When Laverna created the world, she gave the world the power to steal one treasure a year, but it can accept as many gifts as are offered."

That was freaking unbelievable. "What do we give it?"

"That I do not know, but I have words to use to draw the attention of the world Laverna created."

She would say this was the strangest day in her life, but hard to find a suitable comparison after growing up in a hidden castle with a dragon. "I'm game. What have we got to offer as a gift?"

"What do ya have in that backpack?"

Was he insane? "I am *not* givin' up my sword!"

"I did not ask that of ya," he countered, annoyed. "I am merely takin' note of all we have to offer. What of a book?"

"No. I, uh, I can't lose Cathbad's. I have two others that took me years to find and acquire." Her conscience pinched her over not offering something. But dammit, she had so little in life. Her books were everything.

"I understand. I shall search for somethin' I can offer." Daegan became very still again. He held out his hands, palms up. His gaze went to his hands, then he frowned.

"What's wrong, Daegan?"

Lowering his arms, he sounded hollow. "My teleportin' is not workin'. I had intended to bring a chalice that had been in my family for many generations before I was born to offer as a gift. I would have someone in that location teleport it, but my presence is required to expose the treasure."

Now she really felt like crap. Would she give up anything Herrick had given her? No. But Daegan had been willing to hand over a family heirloom, which took on a whole new depth of meaning when passed down in a dragon clan.

Pushing the hurt down this already caused her, Casidhe held her hand out. "Please give me the backpack."

When Daegan handed it over, she dropped to her knees and dug through her pack. She hesitated, trying to choose her least favorite journal. They were only books, but to her, selecting one of these books would be the same as choosing between children.

In the end, she closed her eyes and pulled out one. Opening her eyes, she offered it to Daegan. "See if this will open the door."

Daegan took the tome and held it carefully. "Are ya sure, lass? If I could teleport any of the treasure, I could bring a king's ransom in gold."

Of course he could. He had a damn dragon hoard.

She had a library.

Forcing out the words, she said, "Let's do this before I change my mind, but you had better get the scepter *and* grimoire volume for that."

"I vow to do all in my power to retrieve both."

"Okay, what did your secret source say to do next?"

"He told me to find a safe place, somewhere we will not be disturbed. The darker the better."

"Why?"

"He said we need somewhere no one will see us. Then we must close our eyes and open our minds to Hadrianna's world and offer the gift."

CHAPTER 19

QUINN WASHED THE BLOOD FROM his face and hands. He gave the cracked mirror in the gas station restroom a half-assed glance. He didn't need a mirror to tell him that last battle hadn't gone well.

The troll hadn't been a local. A bruiser from some troll gang two states away.

That being had been stupid to think Atlanta humans would be easy pickings with Beladors battling exposure to humans and demons stalking around the city, many in human form.

The good news? The demons wanted trolls, too.

Oh, they lusted after Reese's demon energy, but she was tucked deep inside one of Quinn's buildings guarded by Beladors.

He dried his face with paper from the towel bin and wiped his hands. If not for outdoor bathrooms still around in old gas stations, he'd have nowhere to clean up before heading to meet with Reese.

He stepped from the small room heavy with the scent of ammonia and urine, welcoming a gulp of fresh air and a dark landscape. He still needed information on Luigsech's phone for Daegan.

Speaking of phones, he checked his. He had a half hour until nine, Reese's deadline for their talk.

That would be his next stop. He had to find some way to convince her to give him a chance to save her and the baby. He opened his phone to call for a car when power flushed around him.

What the hell now?

Sen.

Could there be any being Quinn wanted to see less? "What?"

"The Tribunal has called you in for a meeting." Sen always had a surly attitude, but the raw spot on his scalp had not regrown hair from the Imortik attack earlier. His forearm had a jagged wound.

Had Sen, a demigod, been unable to heal himself yet?

"What's this about?" Normally, Quinn would give more credence to a request from a Tribunal summons, but he was damned tired and had to get to Reese.

"I must not have made myself clear," Sen said, eyebrows dropped low over his hard gaze. "This was not a request open to conversation, but an order."

Pushing his fury down, Quinn stood with arms dangling free. His ready mode for an attack. "For a Tribunal to order the North American Belador Maistir to show up without advance notice, I would expect an explanation first."

Sen lifted one shoulder. "Suit yourself. They told me to bring you or they'd call in Daegan."

Bastard. Sen understood enough about the Beladors to know Quinn would not call in Daegan for something that fell under Quinn's responsibility.

The longer he debated with Sen, the less time Quinn had to meet with Reese. "Let's go."

In the blink of an eye, Quinn stood in the Tribunal realm. Thick grass beneath his feet ran a hundred yards in every direction, forming a circular surface he stood upon. Above him in a dome shape, the night sky sparkled with thousands of stars, reaching from edge to edge of the circular land. It reminded him of a giant snow globe, sans the snow.

Tribunals were a trio of different gods and goddesses from different pantheons, but all in alliance with VIPER. Loki, Justitia, and Hermes stood upon the raised dais in the middle of the realm.

Wearing a simple white robe with a belt, Justitia held the scales of justice in one hand. A gold blindfold wrapped her head. The rest of her face visible above and below the blindfold held the beauty expected of a goddess. A person should never underestimate Justitia or think being blindfolded would mean she missed anything that went on in one of these meetings.

Hermes strummed his tortoiseshell lyre, something resembling a U-shaped ukulele. Shaggy brown curls poked out from beneath his skull helmet, complete with small wings. He had a thousand-yard stare, lost in his own little musical world, though he could be also dangerous.

Quinn expected fairness from Justitia and nothing from Hermes, leaving Loki as his main concern.

Wearing a suit equal to the best in the human world, Loki had probably conjured it up. He could be depended upon to make life as difficult as possible. That god found his enjoyment in other people's misery.

A true sadist at heart since Tribunal meetings generally weren't called to thank someone for a job well done.

Everyone here understood this sometimes trickster god held the ultimate power in a Tribunal. Other deities aligned with VIPER stepped in to take their turn from time to time, but Loki missed few meetings.

"What can I do for the Tribunal?" Quinn asked in as even a tone as he could muster.

For the first time in many meetings, Loki did not play with some toy or smile with glee of anticipation over what he prepared to unload on an unsuspecting soul.

Loki lifted a hand and the music stopped. Hermes tucked his lyre to his chest and stared at Loki.

Unease crawled up Quinn's neck.

"We want the Immortuos Grimoire volume returned," Loki said with the same intensity as demanding a blood sacrifice.

"What volume do you reference as there were supposedly three?"

"The one locked in a VIPER vault for a thousand years."

Cold washed over Quinn's skin. What the hell? "That volume is gone?" Daegan would not be happy with this news.

Loki speared him with a glowing white gaze. *"Do not play with us!"*

Air in the realm pulsed with a turbulent power.

"Wait a damn minute," Quinn shot back. "We don't have it. I'm under the impression no one can breach VIPER's vault. Are you telling me someone broke into the vault?"

Sen spoke to Loki. "I told you they would act clueless."

Quinn wheeled around on Sen. "I fought here earlier today to protect everyone in the headquarters. My people arrived even before I was called. How can you pretend that we know anything about the vault being broken into? How did that even happen on your watch?"

In the past, Sen rarely spoke in a Tribunal. He normally stood by as an enforcer for whatever they pointed him at to handle. But he didn't back down from giving his opinion this time.

"We thought at first the Imortik-possessed Beladors were drawing in more Imortiks. The invasion appeared at first to be an attempt to reach those Beladors in lockdown, but we now believe it was a Trojan horse execution."

"Our people are not fully possessed," Quinn argued.

Sen ignored him. He started to speak then grimaced and pushed ahead. "We believe I was set up to drag Imortiks in when I teleported what I *thought* was a Belador capture to the holding cells. While I was distracted keeping your people alive, someone entered the vault."

Quinn sorted through that information. "Again, do you think *I* did that?"

Loki called out, "We have not accused you of such. Yet."

Turning back to face the greater threat, Quinn asked, "Wouldn't someone have to be able to teleport to access that vault?"

Loki gave a stern nod. "Daegan has that ability."

"He's doing all he can to shut down the Imortiks," Quinn replied, raising his voice.

Justitia turned her blind gaze to him. "Take care with your tone."

She had criticized him? That was another bad sign.

"No insult intended, Justitia, but this *is* an insult to accuse Daegan of stealing that grimoire." Quinn had another thought. "What family had been responsible for hiding that particular volume?"

"Is that not obvious by now?" Loki's lips spread in a sinister smile. "The Treoirs. The volume we had was found in the twelfth century and contained. Then it was locked away in VIPER's vault. As you can see, the Treoirs have either been very careless with their volume or are intentionally trying to use it."

This was incredibly messed up.

Forced to hold his temper and find a way out of this for Daegan, Quinn countered. "Let's look at the timeline. Daegan was imprisoned in TÅµr Medb when that volume was discovered. Macha was in charge. She teleports. Why not go after her instead? The Beladors did not start any of this mess with the Imortiks. Our people are killing themselves trying to protect everyone from demons *and* Imortiks."

"You also exposed supernatural beings to humans." Loki had gathered plenty to throw at Daegan and the Beladors.

Quinn argued, "The Imortiks set traps for our people, including Daegan. It couldn't be avoided."

Justitia stepped in. "If that is so, why did the red dragon burn a power plant in northern Spain until it exploded?"

Quinn couldn't find his voice. Daegan would never do such a thing, but some being had impersonated him. Had there been casualties? A sickening possibility. He had to get out of here and find out more.

He shook off that shock. "That dragon was an imposter."

All three deities turned to him.

Shit. Indicating a second dragon loose in this world probably would not help Daegan, but Quinn had just told the truth. They didn't know about that bloody ice dragon under Treoir castle, which meant there had to be three dragons alive.

Three dragons equaled three dangerous beings capable of

threatening Loki, Justitia, Hermes, and the other deities.

Loki crossed his arms. "You mean to say you learned of a second dragon and said nothing to us about it?"

Hermes returned to playing his lyre, but the tunes he plucked were harsh.

Quinn fought the urge to wipe his forehead or grip his neck to break loose the tension there, but any movement would be seen as a weakness. Tension drove his words to come out hard. "There is a lot going on."

"Where is Daegan?" Loki's blunt words sent a message Quinn would waste his time bluffing.

"The dragon causing damage is *not* Daegan," Quinn countered, losing what patience he'd managed to this point. "Daegan is hunting this other dragon to find out who is pretending to be him, where that dragon came from, and why that dragon is wreaking havoc."

Hermes paused in strumming and asked, "Daegan has the only fire-breathing dragon, correct?"

Everyone turned to the musical god in surprise. He never spoke.

Quinn had to tell the truth in this place or turn bright red. After that, he'd likely burst into flames. Loki would enjoy that show of death. "As far as I know, Daegan has the only fire-breathing dragon, but I have not lived forever. Daegan is searching for the imposter, because he doesn't want a dragon out there causing trouble any more than you do."

"Daegan must come here and answer these questions himself."

Hell, Quinn did not want to say Daegan was hunting the damn grimoire volumes. Quinn believed in his leader and would fight for Daegan with all he had. "I swear to you the dragon causing that damage is not Daegan's."

Nothing happened. Quinn did not turn bright red.

Loki was not sold. "While it is clear that you honestly believe what you say, that does not make it true. Inform Daegan he must return the grimoire or face the end of his people. As for a concern over him calling in his goddess mother, I have already spoken with other deities in alliance with VIPER. We are ready to stand together. If the volume is not returned immediately, the Beladors will be hunted and taken down until it is returned. The first to die will be the ones in the holding cells."

This could not be happening.

Rushing to find a solution, Quinn intended to turn the tables on Sen and have the Tribunal question him. That demigod could teleport. He had access to the damned vault.

Sen made a hissing noise.

Quinn looked over his shoulder to see the liaison grab his leg. "What's wrong with you, Sen?"

Spiking a homicidal look at Quinn, Sen said, "I was struck by two Imortiks. The healers are trying to clean the venom out. It's not all gone yet."

Hell. If Sen had that grimoire volume, he'd have control of the Imortiks, based on what Daegan and Garwyli had said. He wouldn't have allowed venom to be shoved inside him.

Justitia called out, "Please return to the healers, Sen."

"I don't mind waiting until this is done, goddess."

"We will call you back if we need you."

"Thank you." Power pushed away from where Sen had been standing.

Quinn took up the fight again. "Daegan did not take that book. I would know."

Loki lifted his shoulders in a nonchalant dismissal. "Perhaps not, but protection of that volume originally belonged to his ancestors. It is his responsibility to return the grimoire volume, based on the agreement made when a Tribunal at that time took possession of it."

Grasping at any thread, Quinn asked, "Who handed over the volume to put in the vault a thousand years ago?"

Loki and the other two had a muffled discussion. When Loki turned back, he said, "Macha helped close the rift opened when that volume was found once before. As soon as she located the volume this last time, she brought the grimoire to be locked inside the VIPER vault."

Time ticked by with every heartbeat that thumped too loudly in Quinn's ears. What would it take to get this Tribunal off Daegan's back?

How much time did Quinn have left to contact Reese? Twelve minutes? Ten?

Quinn argued, "That doesn't mean Macha didn't take it this time. Why not ask her, Maeve, and Cathbad, who all are capable of teleporting? Queen Maeve has been after Daegan nonstop. She will have learned of the Imortik master's offer to any being who can deliver the grimoire volumes. How can you justify expecting Daegan to bring in the grimoire and not allow us time to hunt it? You are threatening to destroy one of the largest communities of supernatural beings without unequivocal evidence of this crime. We have been here to support VIPER over many generations."

Loki lifted a finger to his chin, tapping a finger. "We called Cathbad earlier and have not heard from him. I will give him what we feel is enough time to appear. I will call Macha and Queen Maeve to testify at this Tribunal as well."

Quinn's chest expanded with relief, then Loki crushed his relief by adding, "But Daegan must be here as well. He is first on our list."

Quinn had no idea where Daegan was, but he'd run into a wall here. He had to call their dragon king to the Tribunal. He announced, "With Sen unavailable, I wish to request a moment out of the Tribunal realm for a better chance of locating Daegan. He's overseas."

Loki sighed. "Very well. We will allow you what we consider enough time to locate Daegan and bring him here. I shall teleport you to just outside the entrance of VIPER. We will uphold the midnight deadline for terminating Devon of the Beladors, but we made no such agreement on the other two Beladors. If you leave or fail to bring Daegan in, we kill those two Beladors by nine o'clock in the human world tonight and close this Tribunal to any additional conversation."

"I will not leave and I will find Daegan." He hoped to hell

he could.

Loki smiled, not a bit of humor involved and warned in an icy tone, "See that you do. I would take great pleasure in dismantling the entire Belador organization ... starting with its Maistir."

CHAPTER 20

DAEGAN LED THE WAY THROUGH the forest that climbed sharply upward. He'd offered to carry the backpack, but the lass had strapped it on, determined to keep her sword close.

The wooded spot they left behind had been too open between trees even at night when animals roamed. They needed a dense area with foliage so difficult to easily pass through a person or animal would walk around to avoid the trouble.

Feminine grunts and struggles filled the otherwise quiet forest air.

As he turned to check on her, she stumbled sideways and tipped downhill.

Lunging, he grabbed the backpack, lifted it, and swung the pack around with her attached. He dropped all of that in front of him.

"What?" she snapped, wrenching the backpack into position again.

"I will not keep the sword from ya. If ya give me the pack, I promise to toss it to ya if we are attacked. I do not wish to run up and down this mountain every time ya go tumblin'. The pack would not be so top-heavy on me."

Blowing a strand of hair out of her eyes, she muttered something to herself and yanked at the strap across her body to unlatch it.

She dropped a shoulder and dumped the backpack off to hand him. "Where exactly are you headed?"

He pointed to his left. "Across this ledge to a darker area of trees which may offer us a place to give this hidden doorway a knock."

She waved her hand. "Move on. I'll follow."

"Ya lead. 'Tis easier to stop ya on the way down."

"For the love of puppies. I am fit for this climb. I just missed my step back there. I would have recovered."

He pulled the backpack strap over one arm and waited.

"Fine. Try to keep up." She pushed forward.

A smile tugged at his lips. He could not help admiring the fight in that one.

When he caught up to her, she angled toward the area he'd indicated. Before dropping down into the small gulley, she paused and looked over her right shoulder.

Her eyes rounded in surprise.

Daegan followed her gaze to an unobstructed view all the way down the mountain to what lay between them and the ocean besides trees growing up the incline.

The lush green forest blanketed the mountain for three thousand feet down, parting around a village built at the edge of a sparkling deep-blue ocean. A cove had been formed by the cupped shape of the coastline along this part of the mountain range. White single story buildings with bright orange roofs stacked uphill from the water. Boats floated in a bay protected by long, sturdy dock-like structures.

"Spain," she whispered.

"Do ya believe that is this land?"

"I think so. I don't recall the name of that settlement or village down there, but I've seen pictures of this cove in magazines. I think we're in the Basque region on the northern coast of Spain."

"'Tis beautiful." Daegan began scouting the surrounding area. "We must watch for villagers."

Casidhe pointed to her left. "If we head over there, I think we're high enough up from the homes we shouldn't run into foot traffic unless someone has a need to burn their calves."

"I shall cloak us while we are in this world." He did not like taking her with him to the hidden world, but until he could teleport her, he had no choice. Plus, she made a valid point about being able to identify a volume of the grimoire.

She had more than skill. She had a gift and power.

He'd watched her translate the parchment.

Just as Reese had said from when she used remote viewing of Luigsech's movements in the centre. When the lass ran her fingers above the text and letters, the symbols changed and rose to the surface. Luigsech had sent him away to leave her alone so she could hide that gift.

He'd allow her the secret for now. No point in starting a conflict when it gained him nothing.

She had taken a couple steps and paused again, staring out to sea this time.

"What is it, lass?"

"Those jets."

Daegan watched two airplanes travel in the distance along the coast. "'Tis a normal sight in your world."

Shaking her head as the airplanes came into view, she said, "Those are F-35s. They're launched from aircraft carriers."

"Aircraft carrier?" This new world had endless mysteries for Daegan.

"Huge ships that can carry an entire squadron of jets." She glanced at him. "I think a squadron is twenty-fourish aircraft, but it could be more. That's not my expertise."

Daegan understood Tristan and Evalle's warnings. Not even a dragon would survive being attacked by a group of those jets with weapons capable of massive damage.

Luigsech picked up speed as the ground leveled out and dropped slowly. The woman seemed to enjoy leading in spite of her earlier protests.

"Why is the sight of *those* jets unusual?" Daegan asked as the aircraft went out of view.

"Just weird. That looked like the American military. If so, why are they patrolling Spain? What's going on?" She grabbed the trunk of a small tree and whipped herself around it.

He couldn't answer her questions, but he called out

telepathically to Tzader. *This is Daegan. Did Tristan arrive?*

Good to hear from you. I wanted to talk to you. Yes, Tristan returned. Garwyli is working on him again and Lanna is helping. That old druid snarled at Tristan for teleporting so much when he hadn't finished healing. With Tristan's healing going slow, Garwyli won't allow Tristan out of his sight for a few more hours. Tristan keeps calling to me to break him out. Hell, I don't want to go up against that old druid when he's pissed off. He's been a bear lately.

That settled Daegan's internal debate on calling Tristan to teleport something from the castle here, which Tzader and Brina would agree to without question. When he had time, he would have to remove the need for his presence to gain any of the Treoir hoard in the future. This trip had taught him the flaw in a plan he created with Tzader and Brina.

Tristan could not teleport Luigsech home at the moment either, even if Daegan did not need her.

He told Tzader, *Tell Tristan I wish for him to heal completely before leavin' again. What were ya wantin' to talk to me about?*

Tzader hesitated a moment, then said, *You have to be careful. Militaries all over the world are sending out patrols looking for any dragon after a new incident. A power plant in Spain was burned.*

What? Daegan almost missed his step. *Is a power plant a living thing, house, or what?*

It's a large facility where they generate power for an area of homes and businesses. Thankfully, no one died. They have reports of sightings in other countries, too, but some or all may be bogus, just people wanting their ten minutes of fame. Still, you can't risk flying.

'Tis not a problem I foresee at the moment, Tzader. This new attack must be Brynhild.

Oh, yes. Tristan told me about her. What a piece of work. We have to prove it's not you.

Daegan wished it were that simple. *I agree, but it does not matter at the moment. A dragon is a dragon to humans.*

Daegan hated to leave Tzader, Quinn, and the others to answer for the phantom dragon attacks, but he could do no more than them. He would return home as soon as he found the grimoire hidden in Hadrianna's world. That reminded him of something Tzader needed to know.

One more thing, Tzader. Do not worry if ya cannot reach me for a short while soon. I may or may not be where I can answer telepathy

Why not, Daegan?

I have a chance to find one volume. It means leavin' this world to enter an alternate one, not exactly a realm.

Damn. I want to be there to back you up. You have no one with Tristan here, but we need him healed. I don't want Brina teleporting anyone else right now. She needs rest.

'Tis fine, Tzader. Ya ease my worry by being in Treoir to watch over Brina and the others. I hope to sneak in and out of this other world without bein' seen. I do have backup, Daegan admitted, not sharing more.

Luigsech might not be one of his warriors, but she had proven her ability with a sword and owned a weapon equal to his.

Should I ask who it is? Tzader prodded.

Tristan knows the person and I spoke with Garwyli about where I am goin'. I shall explain all as soon as I can. Daegan's thoughts jumped to Atlanta. *Tell Quinn to stall VIPER if I run late contactin' them. I intend to do my best to return to VIPER before the Tribunal's deadline for Devon.*

Tzader updated him. *There are three in the holding cells now. I'll get in touch with Quinn. You know he can talk circles around anyone, even powerful beings, when motivated, which he is. Be careful.*

Daegan ended the telepathy and considered his options, which became more limited by the moment. Tristan had to heal fully if Daegan could not teleport out of here with the lass. One problem at a time.

First, he and Luigsech had to find a way into Hadrianna's world.

When the lass entered a heavily shaded location they'd been heading to where a shelter of thick leaves overhead blocked the sun, he searched around them before following. They were very far from any homes. He ducked his head and pushed limbs aside as he stepped down into the pocket of trees and dark shadows. Then he took in every potential spot where they could sink farther out of view just in case someone did wish to burn calves.

The lass seemed to be doing the same thing, no doubt wanting to be a step ahead of him. She had a competitive streak to win every tiny battle. He spied a location that should work, but waited to hear her determination.

Turning to him, she pointed out a different spot than his. "I think we can tuck in there and no one hikin' by would see us without really lookin'."

He joined her and gave the area a serious inspection. "I agree."

She did nothing at first as if she'd expected him to argue, then moved forward, pushing branches aside. He followed, stepping down as the rocky ground dipped even more to create a gulley before the rock jutted up again.

Once she chose a place to sit that suited her, Daegan lowered his body on her left, butting his shoulder up against hers.

She tensed.

He should not be put off, but he'd given her no reason to react frightened to his touch. "Did the oracle not say we must be close for both to enter the world?"

"I'm not arguin'."

Her body appeared to be.

Again, he wished to not take her with him to this unknown world, but he could not make her decisions. Neither of them wanted to forfeit this chance at a grimoire volume after what they'd been through to find it.

The lass had held up her end.

She dug out the book she'd offered earlier. He had stored it in her pack again while they climbed the mountain. The book she chose smelled of old leather and ink, reminding Daegan of his da's library. She lifted it to her lips, gave the cover a gentle kiss, and handed the tome to him.

Daegan's body clenched at watching her lips touch the old book. The desire to feel those lips on his skin swelled inside him. What the devil had gotten into him?

His body had chosen a poor time to take an interest in a woman, especially one he could not be touching.

"Earth to Daegan," Luigsech said in a dry tone. Her strange words yanked him from the foggy moment.

"What earth?" He frowned at her.

"You clearly need some tutoring in pop culture for this era. It's something said in science fiction movies. It means *hey, pay attention.*"

He took the book and placed it on his outstretched legs. "Ya should hold my arm or shoulder so I do not lose ya."

Her small fingers wrapped around his right arm.

Energy inside of him hummed, powering up. So strange.

She tightened her fingers as if she'd felt it too. Clearing her throat, she asked, "You ready?"

"Yes. Close your eyes. Open your mind to another world. I shall do the same and repeat the words suggested by my man." Daegan closed his eyes and forced his mind to quiet. Then he spoke clearly, "World of Laverna, for this gift ..."

When he'd finished making the offer, he waited, listening to Luigsech's quiet breathing. Her grip loosened.

He covered her hand in case she fell asleep. He would not lose her if the world welcomed them.

When nothing happened, he opened his eyes and gave her hand a squeeze.

She lifted her head, blinking, then her fingers slid away. "It didn't work?"

"No."

"Think we need a better gift?" she asked.

"Perhaps." Before he could make a suggestion, she reached up and pulled off her small earrings. "Here. Maybe the world wants gold."

He didn't take them. "Where did those come from?"

"Fenella gave them to me for my birthday."

Her words hurt him. She had been willing to give up one of her cherished books and now offered something she clearly held dear.

Daegan folded her fingers over her palm. "Hold on to your gift. Let me try."

Giving him a strange look, she put the earrings back on. "What are you offering the world?"

He held his hand out and called up his sword, which had been his companion almost as long as Ruadh. He pulled a knife from his boot and rotated the sword hilt to one side where ruby, sapphire, and emerald gems were embedded.

Prying it carefully, he removed the largest emerald, thicker than his thumb.

"Hold it," Luigsech demanded. She placed her hand over the stone. "That's an amazin' emerald. I don't know that I've ever seen one that large." Worried eyes swept up to his. "You may not be able to replace it."

"'Tis the truth it cannot be replaced, but I must try this one first."

"Why not a smaller stone?"

That she cared about his loss eased the guilt he felt for what he had to do. "I fear angerin' the world if we do not offer enough now and continue raisin' the stakes instead of offerin' my best first."

Why did she look guilty?

Sending the sword away so the other world would have no reason to take offense, Daegan said, "We shall try again. This time, I will offer the gift in my left hand."

Her eyebrows dropped low. "And why will that be better?"

"My friend who shared much on Laverna said she would only accept a drink given to her by a left hand. I have no idea why, but 'tis worth a try."

The lass packed her book into her backpack, pulled the shoulder strap around one arm and clamped her hand on his forearm again. "Let's do this."

Confidence powered her words.

Good lass.

He waited until she'd closed her eyes and her breathing had slowed, then he did the same. He found it harder to calm his mind after the first attempt had failed. Eventually, his thoughts quieted.

He held the gem on his left palm and spoke the words again, but in Latin this time. *"Laverna mundi, propter hoc donum ..."*

Luigsech's fingers tightened. She remained awake.

As he finished the words, his palm hummed with an energy that dipped and circled the stone. He held his breath and remained still as a statue.

Cold fingers closed around his hand and pulled him.

His body floated light as a cloud. He kept his eyes shut even as Ruadh rumbled angry noises. His dragon accepted every difficult situation Daegan landed in, never complaining. Not too much anyhow.

The strange sensation pulling him along seemed to go on forever, but he finally felt the weight of his body again. He lifted an eyelash to peek.

White fog rolled around chest high where he sat.

Luigsech! He turned to find her looking over at him with rounded eyes luminous with power.

The gem was gone and they had entered a world unlike the one they'd left behind.

He pushed to his feet and reached back for her while he kept an eye on their surroundings.

Her fingers gripped his hand and his energy stirred with an unusual contentment. When she stood as well, he considered taking the backpack, but she would be safer with her sword at hand if she had to defend herself. He helped her pull the arm straps into place and snapped the front latch for her this time.

With his hands on both straps, he leaned close to her and whispered, "If I tell ya to run, do so. Do not stand around to fight."

Her blue eyes searched his face more than once. "I won't leave you to fight alone."

"Lass, I need to know ya shall be safe. I never intended to put ya in danger. If I could have sent ya home, I would have."

"Then you'd be wastin' all this hard work if I was not here to identify the grimoire."

He wanted to pull her closer and tell her he would protect her against any threat, but he would not give a vow he did not know for certain he could fulfill. His body fought with the venom still inside and he had no idea what his powers would be like in this world.

Tipping his head forward, he gave into the urge he'd been fighting and brushed her lips with his, then smiled to himself at the little termagant's dazed reaction.

He considered it a small victory that she had not clobbered him. "Ready ... Casidhe?"

Her face softened at him using her name. She drew in a fast breath and nodded slowly. "Ready, Daegan."

He turned to search for the halls the oracle indicated would lead to the scepter. Perhaps finding that first would aid them in locating the grimoire volume. The white smoke billowing around his face settled slowly to hover at knee-level.

Three openings a far piece away came into view that could be hallways.

Tugging her hand, he led the way through the hazy smoke, which held no scent. When he reached the decision point of which hallway to take, he said, "Ya choose. Ya have good instincts."

She covered her eyes, then lowered her hand. "I say we take the middle."

Good woman to not whine and debate something they lacked enough information for discussing.

Sounds of nature floated toward them.

Daegan inhaled a flowery smell. Lavender?

As they entered the middle hall, doorways began to appear on each side. The first one opened into a room with violet and white marble surrounding a sunken pool. The only figure to be seen was a golden statue of a young woman wrapped with vines covered in white flowers.

Water trickled from each flower.

Another doorway opened to a garden of mature plants, large blooms of red flowers, and terraces that seemed to have no end. The sky above shined blue with filmy clouds.

The next opening appeared to be a sprawling entrance to a castle. Across the wide expanse of polished floors and rugs, rich wood furniture, and large planters filled with yellow and pink tulips, wide openings on each side of tall beveled glass doors opened to gardens with females dressed in regal gowns and fine clothing on the men. A party?

He pulled the lass quickly past that one.

Opening after opening held different visuals, each one more extraordinary than the last.

Casidhe paused next to a doorway of a library with twenty-foot ceiling to floor shelves filled with books.

She whispered, "This looks like one room the oracle mentioned. It may take a while to find the grimoire if it is even in here. Leave me to search. You look for the scepter."

"No." He feared her being out of his sight.

Sighing heavily, she said, "I will be right here. We can't leave without the scepter and this would be the perfect place to look for the grimoire."

Ruadh warned, *She risks capture.*

Daegan agreed.

She grumbled, "I see that stubborn look in your eyes, Daegan. Don't argue now when we're finally workin' like a team."

He could not overrule her. "Ya are correct. We are in this together and I must trust your decisions." He felt the truth of his words roll over him. They were a damned good team. "I will return after looking into two more rooms to check on ya."

"That'll work." She didn't move, just stared up at him with those shiny-blue eyes, then her cheeks puffed up as she ... smiled. A breathtaking smile. There was the beauty that would stop a man's heart. Before he could say another word, she lifted up, touched her lips to his, then released his hand.

Watching her walk away slammed him in the gut as surely as getting hit with a battering ram.

He lifted his hand to reach for her and pull her back, then closed his fingers and lowered his arm. He had to go.

The sooner he searched the other rooms, the sooner he could return to watch over her. His need to protect the lass overwhelmed his need for the grimoire.

That could spell disaster if he failed to find the grimoire or the scepter.

Moving quickly, he took in the next room filled with exotic statues carved in wood and stone, each one positioned among plants and placed along a winding stream. Birds flew overhead, landing on the statues. Butterflies of brilliant colors flicked around the room, some larger than both of his hands placed side by side.

At the next opening, gold glowed so brightly, he blinked.

Carmine and black rugs placed over a smoky gray granite floor led the way to a throne taller than himself. The heavy structure had been carved of polished black stone with gold inlaid throughout. Tall columns of the same black and gold reached for a starry sky. Dark green bushes with tiny white roses grew around the columns.

The throne sat on a three-tiered dais surrounded by serving dishes, pitchers, mugs ... all in reddish-gold.

But one piece captured his attention.

The scepter had been leaned against the side of the throne, a logical placement. Atop of the staff, an eagle carried a young man. Luigsech had described the scepter as they walked to the shadowed place in the woods.

He paused, listening for any sound from her. Nothing.

Convinced she was fine, he stepped softly on the thick rug toward the throne. When he stood close enough to lift the scepter, he hesitated.

Nothing in the supernatural world was ever easy. Nothing.

Why had this world allowed entry to outsiders?

Could it be as simple as a gift?

Would he and Casidhe be able to leave by using the same words Garwyli had given Daegan to enter with the simple change of requesting they travel back to where they entered? He damn sure hoped so. He reached for the scepter. His fingers trembled.

Not for fear of his safety.

For Casidhe's.

But she had surely handled books in the other room by now. If she had not set off an alarm, why would he do so by lifting the scepter?

Curling his fingers around the short staff no longer than his arm, he lifted the solid weight.

CHAPTER 21

"WILL THERE BE ANYTHING ELSE, seer?" the chambermaid whispered in a trembling voice from the doorway. She gripped her hands in front of where her white cotton blouse tucked into her gray and blue plaid skirt.

Kleio had been nothing but kind to this young woman, yet the chambermaid feared stepping inside the humble chamber of the castle's terrifying seer. "That is all, Holly. Thank you for bringing my food up tonight. I appreciate all you do."

The young woman smiled, her face revealing more relief than happiness, and backed away quickly.

Every resident inside Herrick's castle and in nearby cottages on his land treated Kleio with respect, but many watched her with wariness reserved normally for a black witch.

Yet, let one of them worry over a loved one living in another land and they slipped up close to ask if she could *see* anything.

After all these years, she should be used to the fear and shifting glances, but the sense of being on the outside still rubbed.

Stepping over to close the heavy oak door, Kleio lifted a four-foot-long, three-inch-thick board she dropped into place to bar the door. When she'd agreed to come to this mountain range known as the Caucasus, which separated Asia from Europe, she'd given Herrick a list of her requirements.

One had been an acceptable way to bar her door at night.

Herrick had been insulted that she'd infer any threat to her being. He pointed to the ward he'd placed over this valley, which had protected his people for thousands of years, and reminded her he was a dragon shifter.

She'd calmly explained she would not come at all if her requests were not met. She needed to insure no one would interrupt her when she went into a trance for hours. This provided her with a sanctuary to continually develop her gift and strengthen her mind, preparing her for visions at any time.

Disbelief had been clear in his face, but his need for her services outweighed any hesitation once he'd found her. That had been only one of several stipulations she'd made years ago and he'd agreed to all of them.

With the castle at peace for the evening, no outside noise would disturb her at this time.

She'd spent the first six months here training everyone to respect her space and her time locked away. Holly's mother had been Kleio's original chambermaid. Her fear of an unknown woman who could see things others could not had been passed down from mother to daughter.

For that reason, Kleio did not hold it against Holly, but she had hoped to develop the young woman into a friend.

That effort had failed. Holly jumped away from her own shadow. Time had taught Kleio it would be best to leave them all to their fears even if it made for a lonely existence.

She'd accepted her destiny as a child of five in Greece.

After eating her meal, she washed her plates, stacking the clean dishes and utensils on the tray Holly would retrieve in the morning.

With a glance around, she walked into the next room connected to this one.

No windows. No door to the hallway. No distractions.

She crossed the cozy room and knelt in front of a low altar wider than her shoulders and two hands deep. A yellow candle sat at each corner of the rectangular surface. Three thick purple candles were arranged in a half arc in the center. She made all her own candles, which were infused with specific herbs she gathered on an annual trek through the mountains with Herrick.

Lighting the yellow candles first then the purple ones, she sat back on her knees and placed her hands on her thighs. She closed her eyes and allowed her shoulders to relax, opening her mental pathways to worlds beyond the present one.

The yellow candles deepened her concentration and the purple ones expanded her ability to search beyond herself.

She had no idea how much time passed as she waited to hear a voice.

The voice.

Her mind floated in a sea of autumn leaves, wildflowers, and red berries. She traveled deeper and deeper until ...

"I am here, Kleio."

She smiled at hearing the comforting voice of her mentor, the Greek god Janus. "Thank you for coming, Janus." She gave the same opening words at every meeting since the first one when he'd spoken to her the night she turned five years old. As the god of beginnings and transitions, he had guided her life through all choices and decisions, opening a door when the time came for her to take a new direction.

She had not understood why he wanted her here with this dragon shifter who had lived for two millennium, but Janus had a reason for every word and action.

When she became an adult, Kleio left her family's home, explaining she would be gone many years on a sabbatical. To not look for her or expect to hear from her.

Those words had merely echoed the ones Janus had provided.

"The time nears for the end of this journey, Kleio."

She managed to stay calm, but her heart rhythm changed to a faster pace. Where would she go now? Why would she leave the dragon when he seemed to need her most?

Janus spoke in a smooth baritone full of authority. "Do not distress." His head appeared as a holographic image. The classic profile of a Greek scholar with two faces, each staring in opposite directions. He viewed time of what was and what was to come.

"I apologize, Janus. You have never given me reason to

question you. I may have spent too much time in one place at this castle. I feel I have fallen into a comfortable existence and had a foolish reaction to change."

"Your apology is not necessary. You have caused me no disappointment. I am proud of all you have accomplished over many years. Your ability to share visions regardless of how they would be accepted is superior to many who possess the gift of vision and misinterpret what they see."

Her lips curved in a smile. He had always told her to share a vision as received, good or bad. Janus had been a parental figure as much as mentor. She allowed her appreciation to flow through her words. "Thank you. What do you wish of me?"

"The destiny that has awaited you nears."

Now he confused her, which he had not since she'd learned to fulfill his wishes. She had always accepted that Janus lived by no one's laws but his own. Whatever he asked of her she would do.

No doubts. No hesitation.

He was all to her and his word final.

"I beg your patience for a question, Janus."

"Ask, child."

"Have I failed to fulfill my destiny to this point?" Did he see her lacking in her current duty?

"No. I speak of the next step in this same destiny, which is as if passing through another door. You will face more than one challenge. This time, you will make choices alone."

Her heart thumped harder. What did that mean? Did he never intend to speak to her again? No. She could not continue without him. How could he do this to her?

"Be calm, Kleio," he instructed in a soothing tone.

She swallowed and forced a calm over her body she didn't feel in her heart. "Please help me understand, Janus."

"The human world faces extreme changes with many possible outcomes. You are the one whose visions will influence enemies and allies. Your visions will define the world for dragon shifters moving forward."

Did he speak of Herrick, the red dragon, Skarde, or all of them? "Will my visions bring enemies and allies together or pit them against each other?"

"You will have to figure this out as the visions come to you. The fate of humans will depend upon those considered enemies as well as those considered allies. Your visions will expose a threat, free a life, and cost a bond."

She searched her mind for any hint at what he meant.

Nothing came to her, but visions often had to be cultivated over time.

"Rise up, Kleio, and see the woman you are ready to become."

She rose to her feet, surprised by this move. They normally spoke then she drifted back to her current-day world.

"Open your eyes, wise one," he ordered softly.

When she opened her eyes, she stood in a black void with a ten-foot-tall gilded mirror hanging freely in front of her. She wore a strapless black gown of silk with lace armbands, none of which she'd ever seen before.

Her lavender eyes would not move from the image staring back. That was her face the color of dark honey and her black hair. The chains she normally wore around her neck had molded together to create a silver band across her forehead with a dark purple stone in the center. Ram horns curled off each side of her head. Her eyes darkened to almost black.

She lifted her hands to join them in front of her chest, but her fingers wrapped the hilt of a sword as it appeared. The blade pointed down.

Flames licked all around and sparks flew, but none harmed her. Between the sword and the mirror flamed the crest of a dragon.

Not just any dragon family, but that of the red dragon.

Janus whispered close to her ear. "Your vision will change your path and your path will change the course of the human world. The world will either survive what is coming or burn into eternity. Do not return to speak to me again until you have completed this journey and the future is clear."

CHAPTER 22

QUINN STOOD IN THE DARK outside the mountain hiding VIPER. This time, the entrance appeared sealed as it should be. Nothing more than a solid rock wall.

He called to Trey, their most powerful telepathic communicator. *I need to get word to Daegan. Find him and ask him to call me right away.*

Quinn didn't have to explain to Trey he meant telepathically. Two minutes passed without hearing back. When another minute slid by, Trey said, *I've been reaching out telepathically to Daegan over and over. No answer. I'll reach out to Tzader and Brina to see what they know.*

Quinn had no idea how long Loki would allow him to find Daegan. Sweat trickled down his neck. While he waited on Trey to get back to him, Quinn called Clyde at his building telepathically. *This is Quinn. You know Reese, who arrived earlier at the building.*

Yes, Maistir. She showed up a bit later than I had been informed, but she arrived safe and sound.

Quinn had never had a driver fail to follow through with an order. *Why was she late?*

Told our guy she had to take a shower and change clothes.

Quinn wouldn't fault her for a quick stop at her apartment. He should have thought of it himself, but he hadn't expected to be at VIPER past nine. *I have a message for you to give Reese immediately.*

Uh, Maistir, she's not here. She disappeared at one minute after nine o'clock.

Panic pushed Quinn's heart rate into overdrive. *Send out*

a team to find her. Tell them not to harm her under any circumstances, but to tell her I asked my people to bring her back to the building.

Clyde's words came slowly. *She did not walk out of the building, Maistir. She literally disappeared right in front of me. I was calling to you just as you came into my mind.*

Quinn's heart slammed his chest. He struggled to figure out what the hell had happened.

Then it hit him. She'd vanished once before, but she'd needed help to teleport. Powerful majik help. He asked, *Was Reese wearing any kind of necklace when she showed up?*

Yes, sir. Nothing fancy. Just a medallion on a leather string around her neck.

That bloody medallion.

CHAPTER 23

DAEGAN HELD HIS BREATH AS he pulled the scepter to him.

No sounds of alarm.

Breathing out slowly, he turned and crossed the rug again, keeping his steps quiet.

He hurried down the hallway to the library where he found Casidhe halfway up a ladder. She held a bronze box in her hand, staring at it with a strange look on her face.

What was she doing with a box? He rushed over to the bottom of the ladder. "What do you have, lass?"

Her voice shook. "I think this is one of the volumes."

"'Tis not a book."

"I ... I know. I'll explain later but ... " She squeezed her eyes. "Hurts."

Hell. He lunged up and wrenched the box from her hands.

She stared at the red skin climbing her arm. "Get rid of it, Daegan. It's evil."

"Come down, lass." He could feel the same burning reaching through the skin of his hand. A similar burning to what he'd suffered from the venom.

Was the venom calling to this volume?

She climbed down. Grabbed her backpack and latched it on. "How can you hold that?"

Answering would only scare her more. "Ya believe this is the volume?"

"I read Immortuos Arca on the lid, but there's more."

"You can translate it all later." His arm throbbed. He shoved the scepter at her. "Take this."

Howling and guttural snarls erupted from outside the door.

She held the staff in one hand and clamped a death grip on his arm with the other. Her voice came out strangled. "We have to say the words and get out of here."

"We cannot sit quietly and allow the words to work." Heat built in his arm. He had to find a way out now. Gripping her hand, he yelled, *"Stay with me!"*

He ran from the room and found two additional hallways in each direction. What the hell?

Vicious howls and hideous sounds came from his left. Clutching her hand, he ran to the right. The lass stayed with him. He could hear her heart pounding frantically.

Up ahead, creatures appeared, bursting through the white fog and racing toward them, human upper bodies hunched over goat legs with hooves. Strands of blue, brown, and black fur hung a foot long from their bodies. The heads were of animal bone with gold horns curled forward to sharp black points. Human-shaped eyes glowed white with deep-red irises. Bone plates ran down over the shoulders to human-like arms ending in claws for fingers. Long fangs filled the black hole when they opened their maws to howl.

Were those the satyrs?

Luigsech screamed.

Daegan looked behind.

More creatures coming.

He rushed ahead, dragging her off her feet until she caught up to run faster.

She yelled, "We're heading right for them."

"I see them."

"What are you going to—"

He lunged to the left into the next opening, cutting off her words.

The room stretched on and on.

His feet pounded over short orange and red grass. He slapped long feathery shapes as tall as him colored emerald, gold, and black out of the way. The feathers swept down from puffy clouds fifty feet up in place of a ceiling.

At the far end of the space, he stared at what might be a wall of windows exposing the mountain outside.

Could he trust what he saw?

If so, he could barely make out moonlight filtering through clouds above a black sea.

Could he crash through the glass surface? Or was that merely a spelled image capable of doing any number of things?

Including kill them.

The satyrs burst into the room behind them, hundreds of hooves stampeding.

Daegan shouted the words Garwyli had given him. Nothing happened. Casidhe had gone stone silent, but kept her legs spinning.

He yanked her in front of him, wrapping the arm not affected by the box around her.

Six feet from the glass, she screamed and covered her face with her only free hand.

He leaped, turning in the air to hit the surface with his back.

Everything slowed.

His heart thumped.

He held the lass tight.

A horde of death thundered close behind, slobbering for a kill.

Ruadh roared, ready to change.

Daegan's back slammed a wall. He stayed there for less than a second. Then what sounded like glass exploded out.

The world moved fast again.

He fell backwards, hitting trees, bouncing across limbs. Bones cracked and snapped. Busted branches ripped his skin. He flipped and bounced, then landed on the ground not far from where they'd entered the other world.

Howls followed them.

The satyr herd left the hidden world?

Daegan snatched up Casidhe and raced to the hidden location where they'd hidden in the trees. He shoved her in deep. "Stay here. I'll come back for ya."

She dropped the scepter and lunged to grab his hand not holding the box. "No, don't go. I'll go with you."

His heart broke at the terror in her voice. Terror for him? Yet, she fought that fear, willing to be with him to face monsters. "Ya have to stay, lass. They did not come for us until I touched the box. I shall lead them away and come back for ya." He cupped her head and kissed her hard, a feel and taste he would never forget, then forced himself to back out. "Stay there. Please."

Turning, Daegan rushed out of the black hole and did his best to run downhill at an angle, weaving through the woods on painful legs. When he reached a high point, he spotted the stream of glowing satyrs pouring into this world from an invisible hole.

He roared to catch their attention and waited. He had to be sure Casidhe would be safe.

The horde turned as one with him as their only target.

Daegan streaked downhill, dodging trees and leaping over rocks. He angled away from the cove with homes. That herd might only follow him and the grimoire volume, but he would not risk an innocent stepping in the way.

Clinging to the damn box trying to destroy his arm, he reached open woods and limped-ran toward the sea.

Let him make it far enough to keep them away from Casidhe.

Ruadh rumbled an unholy noise, banging to get out.

Twilight deepened over the land, but a dragon could be seen. Daegan decided to release Ruadh and have more power to fight the satyr.

His dragon strained and roared, but remained trapped inside.

Daegan tried to teleport.

Not happening.

Could the grimoire box be interfering?

His shoulder bled furiously and should have healed by now. Only old majik could do this to him.

The sound of jets cruising the coast approached from way down out of the west.

If this ancient grimoire held even one piece to the puzzle of closing the rift between worlds, it would be worth any bodily harm he'd suffer.

Daegan squeezed the box in one hand.

The lass claimed it was a grimoire volume. He believed her. Even if he could shift, he had to insure this box survived the change. But would *he* survive if he continued to clutch this box? Remaining in human form and unable to teleport severely limited his options.

Wild howling joined with the crashing sounds behind him. Two lead monsters leapt through the trees, hit, and slid, coming close enough he could feel their hot breath.

A huge splash of slimy liquid doused his back from head to toe. What had the satyrs spewed at him?

Daegan stumbled.

The ground shifted downward immediately. His vision blurred. His feet slid out from under him, shooting his body out of the trees, bouncing over a rocky surface.

Grasping with one hand, he tried to slow his descent. Hitting water even from this height might seem like a good idea, but sharp boulders close to the coastline wall would not. If he crushed his body on the rocks, the satyrs would rip him apart before he could heal.

He flipped and bounced, falling forward faster and beating his damaged body even more.

Lights from two jets blinked in and out of his vision. More lights in different spots.

He scrabbled bloody fingers to find a hold, then spun sideways and went over the cliff. His hand banged the rocky cliff, knocking the bronze box from his fingers.

"Nooo!"

Ruadh broke free, but the dragon body didn't form quickly.

Daegan's eyes rolled up in his head at the mind-numbing pain of shifting so fast. He groaned as Ruadh took over, wings beating. His dragon struggled to catch air.

The grimoire volume! Daegan shouted at Ruadh.

His dragon said nothing.

Turn back and look for the box, Daegan yelled again telepathically.

Box killing us, Ruadh argued, the words slurred.

Daegan's vision cleared. His dragon flapped relentlessly to avoid slamming into the jagged boulders below.

His dragon had done his part to save them when their body had been trapped in the shape of a throne for two millennia. How could Daegan not allow his dragon to save them now?

He struggled to not shout again to turn back as Ruadh banked within inches of the sheer rock wall. Ruadh lumbered close enough to the rocks below for water to splash them.

Daegan groaned, *We need that box.*

His dragon began to climb with great effort and caught an air current. They cleared the cliff's edge right in front of jets bearing down on his dragon from both sides.

Growling, Ruadh banked hard as the first bright light from a jet swiped across his massive red body. But Daegan could feel the strain Ruadh suffered from loss of power and broken bones, plus whatever that satyr had coated over him had started drying. Ruadh's scales would not move and shift with his body.

His dragon flew in a series of tight loops, changing the direction constantly. Every difficult move drained their power.

Those jets flew just as tight formations, but at times flew too fast and overshot Ruadh's route.

That they had not fired yet could only be attributed to curiosity. Once that waned, Ruadh would be attacked.

Land, Ruadh. They will kill ya. Maybe not me in human form.

His dragon roared a sound not heard in modern day. A sound of fury and frustration. Ruadh had never flown away from a battle.

Please, Ruadh, Daegan asked softly. *I cannot bear for ya to be attacked by these weapons.*

His dragon arced around hard and flew straight up with jets on his tail.

Then Ruadh folded his wings and dove like a spear shooting down from the heavens. Just before the cliffs, his dragon wings fanned open. Ruadh landed in the pitch dark with a heavy thump, stepping fast until he could stop.

Heaving from the strain, Ruadh gave Daegan control again and shifted.

As Daegan struggled to hold his broken and wounded body upright, he blinked away stars spiraling through his gaze. Dizziness threatened to drop him to his knees.

Coming from out at sea, the sound of a powerful helicopter now headed for him. He'd seen those before in Atlanta.

Swallowing hard, Daegan moistened his lips to talk. "You did well, Ruadh."

Ruadh spoke in his head. *We did not escape.*

"We will," he assured his dragon. Daegan called clothes to his body. Jeans covered his legs. No boots. No shirt. Bloody tears slashed his arms and chest. Skin on his legs felt just as flayed open and bruised.

The noise of multiple human aircraft closed in on him.

Then he realized ... no satyrs. Where had they gone?

Overhead, the loud helicopter approached slowly until it hovered. Wind lashed rocks and sand across his body.

Black human silhouettes began dropping on lines, each one carrying a large weapon.

Daegan had done all he could. Time to ask for help and teleport out of here. He called out telepathically, *This is Daegan. Tristan?*

Men in armor dropped to the ground and swung their fierce weapons at him.

Tzader! Brina! Trey!

Silence.

DEAR READER
This is one big journey. I hope you'll understand that it's not possible to tie up the storylines in these books until the very end, which means there will be cliffhangers along the way. The reason I started writing this series close to two years before the first book released was so that you would not have to wait a year between books. I'm a reader too and I enjoy reading an ongoing story as soon as I can just as you do.

Thank you for reading my books and joining me on my writing journey. You are the reason I step into the cave pretty much seven days a week because I love sharing my stories with you.

Dianna

MORE BOOKS

Thank you for reading my books. If you enjoyed this story, please help other readers find this book by posting a review.

For SIGNED PRINT copies of Dianna's books visit www.DiannaLoveSignedBooks.com where you can also preorder new books.

To be notified of all future releases, please join Dianna's newsletter at https://authordiannalove.com/connect

**The complete 9-book series of
Treoir Dragon Chronicles in ebook and audiobooks**
Treoir Dragon Chronicles of the Belador World: Book 1
Treoir Dragon Chronicles of the Belador World: Book 2
Treoir Dragon Chronicles of the Belador World: Book 3
Treoir Dragon Chronicles of the Belador World: Book 4
Treoir Dragon Chronicles of the Belador World: Book 5
Treoir Dragon Chronicles of the Belador World: Book 6
Treoir Dragon Chronicles of the Belador World: Book 7
Treoir Dragon Chronicles of the Belador World: Book 8
Treoir Dragon Chronicles of the Belador World: Book 9

**The hardback print versions of
Treoir Dragon Chronicles**
Treoir Dragon Chronicles of the Belador World: Volume I, Books 1-3

Treoir Dragon Chronicles of the Belador World:
Volume II, Books 4-6
Treoir Dragon Chronicles of the Belador World:
Volume III, Books 7-9

Note: Hardbacks can be ordered/preordered signed and personalized from www.**DiannaLoveSignedBooks**.com

REVIEWS ON BELADOR BOOKS:

"…non-stop tense action, filled with twists, betrayals, danger, and a beautiful sensual romance. As always with Dianna Love, I was on the edge of my seat, unable to pull myself away."
~~Barb, The Reading Café

"There is so much action in this book I feel like I've burned calories just reading it."~~ Goodreads
"…shocking developments and a whopper of an ending... and I may have exclaimed aloud more than once…Bottom line: I really kind of loved it."
~~Jen, top 500 Reviewer

"DEMON STORM leaves you breathless on countless occasions."
~~Amelia Richard, SingleTitles

"…Its been a very long time since I've felt this passionate about getting the next installment in a series. Even J. K. Rowling's Harry Potter books."
~~Bryonna Nobles, Demons, Dreams and Dragon Wings

"As much as I am impatient for each installment these stories are so worth the wait." ~~ Rosemary, Goodreads
"This adventure win or lose is going to change things for Evalle and her friends. Brava Ms. Love for another fantastic ride." ~~ In My Humble Opinion

**The Belador series is an ongoing urban fantasy
(same characters in the same world), which is best read
in order. Novellas can be read as stand alones.**

Book 1: Blood Trinity
Book 2: Alterant
Book 3: The Curse
Book 4: Rise Of The Gryphon
Book 5: Demon Storm
Book 6: Witchlock
Book 7: Rogue Belador
Book 8: Dragon King Of Treoir
Book 9: Belador Cosaint
Book 10: Treoir Dragon Hoard
Book 11: Evalle and Storm
Tristan's Escape: A Belador Novella

**The League of Gallize Shifters series is stand-alone
paranormal romances written in a larger
urban fantasy style world.**

Book 1: Gray Wolf Mate
Book 2: Mating A Grizzly
Book 3: Stalking His Mate
Book 4: Mating A Grizzly
Book 5: Stalking His Mate

**The Slye Temp romantic thriller series is 'completed'
(great for binging!)**

Prequel: Last Chance To Run
Book 1: Nowhere Safe

Book 2: Honeymoon To Die For
Book 3: Kiss The Enemy
Book 4: Deceptive Treasures
Book 5: Stolen Vengeance
Book 6: Fatal Promise

Dianna Love and Mary Buckham created the sci-fi/ fantasy Red Moon Trilogy, which is appropriate for Hunger Games readers.

Book 1: Time Trap
Book 2: Time Return Book 3: Time Lock

For more on this series, visit www.MicahCaida.com

AUTHOR'S BIO

New York Times **Bestseller Dianna Love** once dangled over a hundred feet in the air to create unusual marketing projects for Fortune 500 companies. She now writes high-octane romantic thrillers, young adult and urban fantasy. Fans of the bestselling Belador™ urban fantasy series will now have the new Treoir Dragon Chronicles of the Belador™ spinoff. Dianna's Slye Temp sexy romantic thriller series wrapped up with Gage and Sabrina's book–Fatal Promise–perfect for bingers! She has new League of Gallize Shifters paranormal romance series. Look for her books in print, e-book and audio. On the rare occasions Dianna is out of her writing cave, she tours the country on her BMW motorcycle searching for new story locations. Dianna lives in the Atlanta, GA area with her husband, who is a motorcycle instructor, and with a tank full of unruly saltwater critters.

Visit her website at **www.AuthorDiannaLove.com** or www.**DiannaLoveSignedBooks.com**

A WORD FROM DIANNA...

Thank you for reading my new *Treoir Dragon Chronicles of the Belador™ World* series. I have been excited to give you this spinoff series for a long time.

As always, I must thank my wonderful husband and partner in this journey, Karl. He is the greatest gift in my life and you readers are another one!

Nothing happens without a good team. High five to Jennifer Cazares and Sherry Arnold, very early super readers who help me hand you the cleanest book possible. You are so valuable.

I am fortunate to have Jodi Henley, who is an amazing content editor. She sees the books first then it goes through a gauntlet of reads before you receive the book. Judy Carney has only gotten better and better over the years. Stacey Krug is a tremendous aid with proofing and always ready to read. Joyce Ann McLaughlin is invaluable when it comes to beta reading as she listens to the audio file. Her ear is far sharper than mine, for sure. I am so happy with my wonderful audio narrator, Stephen R. Thorne, who the fans chose – they were right!

Hugs and a big thank you to Candace Fox, Kimber Mirabella, Leiha Mann and Sharon Livingston Griffiths, who are wonderful about reading whenever I need it and so supportive in other ways.

I can't say enough great things about my awesome early review team - they just keep rocking big time!

The incredible Kim Killion never fails to create terrific covers for me (I love my covers for this series and am so jazzed to reveal them) and Jennifer Litteken has saved me more than once when it comes to formatting (a shout out to DD, too).

I could go on and on, because I appreciate every reader and would love to thank you in person. But ... I keep hearing "write faster," so I'm jumping back into my cave.

Dianna